Rise of the Alliance IV

Nightside of the Sun

Sartorias-Deles Books

Historical Arc
"Lily and Crown"
Inda
The Fox
King's Shield
Treason's Shore
Time of Daughters (two volumes)
Banner of the Damned

Modern Era
The CJ Journals
Senrid
Spy Princess
Sartor
Fleeing Peace
A Stranger to Command
Crown Duel
The Trouble with Kings
Sasharia En Garde

And

The Rise of the Alliance Arc
A Sword Named Truth
The Blood Mage Texts
The Hunters and the Hunted
Nightside of the Sun

Rise of the Alliance IV

Nightside of the Sun

SHERWOOD SMITH

BOOK VIEW CAFE

Published by Book View Café
304 S. Jones Blvd., Suite #2906
Las Vegas, NV 89107
www.bookviewcafe.com

ISBN: 978-1-63632-024-3

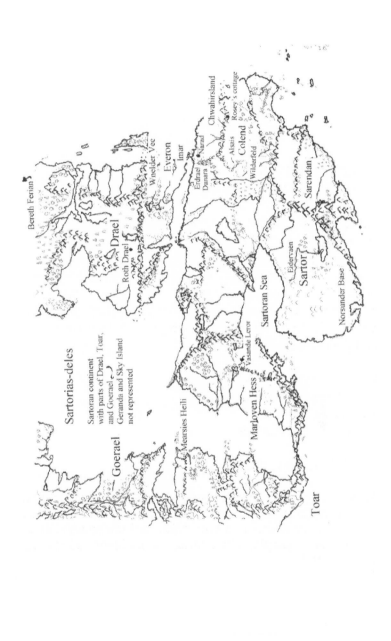

Sartorias-deles

Sartoran continent
with parts of Drael, Toar,
and Goerael~
Gerauda and Sky Island
not represented

Goerael

Bereth Ferian

Drael

Roth Drael

Wnelder Vee

Everon

Imar

Chwahirsland

Rosey's cottage

Colend

Alsais

Naraef

Erdrael

Danara

Wilderfeld

Sarendan

Eiderraen

Sartor

Norsunder Base

Sartoran Sea

Mearsies Heili

Marloven Hess

Vasande Leror

Toar

ELGAR STRAIT
IMAR
The Fangs
BERMUND
DANARA
Narad
CHWAHIRSLAND
TSER MEARSIES
Western Pass
Middle Pass
GASZIN
Eastern
Pass
ALTAN
NASHAN
Alsais
ALARCANSA
Skya Lake
Lassiter
MELIRE
COLEND
Estan
ETH ENDRA
SENTIS
KHANERENTH
Wilderleki
Thora Dei
Locan
Jora
RANFLAR
ISQUA
Northeast
corner
of
GYRN
SARTOR
AR MARDETH
SARENDAN

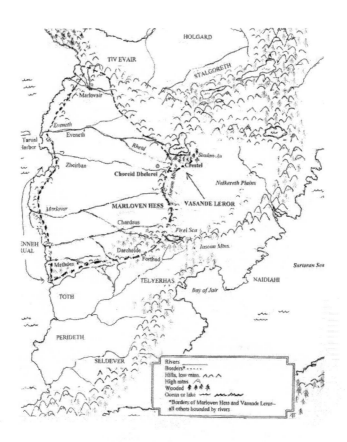

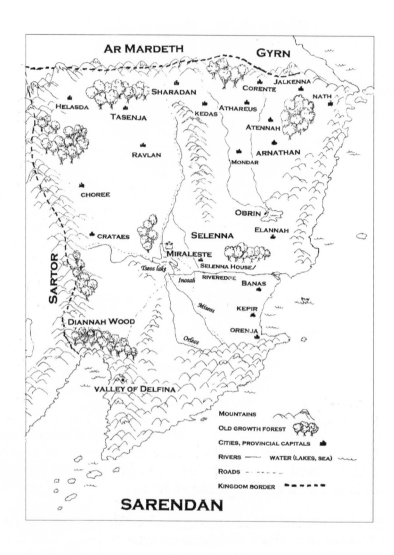

AR MARDETH

GYRN

JALKENNA

CORENTE

NATH

SHARADAN

ATHAREUS

HELASDA

KEDAS

TASENJA

ATENNAH

RAVLAN

ARNATHAN

MONDAR

CHOREE

OBRIN

CRATAES

ELANNAH

SELENNA

SARTOR

MIRALESTE

SELENNA HOUSE

Tseos lake

Inosah

RIVEREDGE

BANAS

Miseos

KEPIR

DIANNAH WOOD

Orleos

ORENJA

VALLEY OF DELFINA

MOUNTAINS

OLD GROWTH FOREST

CITIES, PROVINCIAL CAPITALS

RIVERS ——— WATER (LAKES, SEA) ~~~

ROADS - - - - -

KINGDOM BORDER ▬▬ ▬▬ ▬▬

SARENDAN

Dramatis Personae for Nightside of the Sun

(For more information there is a Sartorias-deles wiki at
http://reqfd.net/s-d/)

NORSUNDER

Benin: Ambitious mage, his specialty the soul-bound (people caught at the point of death, their wills bound to the command of whoever holds the soul-bound magic). Benin tends to not wait until potential soul-bound are dead in order to experiment.

Bostian: Ambitious Norsundrian military captain.

Dejain: Mage specializing in dark magic, one of a succession of Norsunder Base commanders, who tend to be summarily replaced by violence. She has no objections to others dying by violence, but she'd prefer to keep her hands clean.

Detlev: Chief visible mage and sometime military leader, answerable to Norsunder's Host of Lords. Born four thousand years ago, has lived in and outside time ever since. Like his nephew Siamis, has **Dena Yeresbeth**. (A teacher and trainer, his boys are introduced in this volume.)

Efael: Considers himself one of the Host of Lords, the authors of Norsunder. Has a penchant for cruelty. He is the Host of Lords' chief assassin, bloodhound, interrogator; he and his sister **Yeres** consider Detlev their rival for a seat among the Host of Lords.

Henerek: Ambitious low-ranking young Norsunder military captain, originated in Everon. Wanted to be one of the Knights of Dei, but was cashiered due to excess cruelty, drunkenness, and inability to follow orders. Wishes to be a king.

Host of Lords: Authors of Norsunder, existing beyond time, readying for a second try at taking the world. Or worlds. Why, and who they are, will become clearer in the succeeding volumes.

Kessler Sonscarna: Renegade Chwahir prince with considerable military abilities, forced into Norsunder as a result of treachery by the mage **Dejain.** Hates Norsunder. (See **Chwahirsland** below)

Lesca: Apparently lazy steward in charge of Norsunder Base. Overlook her at your peril.

Siamis: Nephew to Detlev, recently emerged (it is believed for the first time) in four thousand years, as a young adult. Formidable mage, and like Detlev, has **Dena Yeresbeth.**

Yeres: She and Efael, her brother, were born off-world, and so thoroughly and spectacularly corrupted that they caught the attention of Svirle of Yssel, one of the authors of Norsunder. Yeres is a powerful mage. She and Efael gladly execute the errands that the Host of Lords, steeped in evil, consider too distasteful.

DETLEV'S BOYS

Adam: Artist, formidable talents in Dena Yeresbeth
Alaki (Ferret): Acutely observant, aware of overlapping worlds, spy
Curtas: Strongly responsive to line and harmony, especially in building
David: Captain of the group, best in most areas
Edde (Noser): Taken from another world, at best a mascot
Laban: Volatile and longing for what he cannot have, a Dei descendant
Leefan: Quiet, strong martial artist, cousin to Rolfin
Mal Venn (MV): Martial artist, studying magic, excellent sailor
Rolfin: Cousin to Leefan, superlative martial artist
Roy: Strong Dena Yeresbeth, mage and scholar
Silvanas: Martial artist and horse master

LIGHT MAGIC MAGES AIDING THE ALLIANCE

Tsauderei: Oldest of the senior mages, independent of the two leading mage schools, living in a historic mage retreat located in the mountains bordering Sarendan and Sartor in the Valley of Delfina.

Erai-Yanya: One of a long line of mages dwelling in the ruined city of Roth Drael. Trained partly by the northern Mage School at Bereth Ferian, and partly by Tsauderei, she works independently, her specialty magical wards. She has one son, 'Arthur', who was adopted by Eveneth and became the titular Prince in Bereth Ferian. Erai-Yanya's student mage is the Marloven exile Hibern Askan.

Evend: One-time colleague of Tsauderei, King of Bereth Ferian (a courtesy title only) and head of the mage school there, he surrendered his life to bind rift magic from being used in Sartorias-deles by Norsunder. His place as titular king was taken by **Arthur**.

Lilith the Guardian: She was a lower ranking mage and what might be called an officer of rites and rituals in Ancient Sartor, which was as close to a government as they got. She had one daughter, Erdrael, who was killed along with most of the rest of the population when Norsunder tried to wrest control of the world, for reasons explored in a volume to come. Her name is a modern adaptation, and she found herself trying to combat Norsunder on this and other worlds around the sun Erhal; she comes out of hiding beyond time whenever she finds evidence that Detlev has been in the world, acting for Norsunder's Host of Lords.

Murial of Mearsies Heili: Recluse mage, living hidden in the western wilds of Mearsies Heili. Born a princess, she supported the transfer of the throne to her niece **Clair** on the death of her sister. Protecting the kingdom from a distance, she has seen to it that Clair gets magical training.

THE YOUNG ALLIES and OTHERS, Listed by Kingdom

BERETH FERIAN

Arthur: Named Yrtur, he adopted the name Arthur after his rescue by young world-gate crossing friends. Son of mage Erai-Yanya, he early showed great ability in learning and magic, but he was unhappy living in isolation. He was adopted as heir by **Evend**, the head mage of the Bereth Ferian Mage School, and presiding King of the loose federation headquartered at Bereth Ferian, a title he shared with Liere Fer Eider in her persona as Sartora, the Girl Who Saved the World.

Evend: (see Light Mages)

Liere Fer Eider: Also known as the Girl Who Saved the World, she was the first of her generation to be born with **Dena Yeresbeth**. At ten years old she left her small town to escape being captured by Siamis, who had extended an enchantment over the world, which Liere later broke. The enchantment is generally known as The Lost Year, as most lived in a dream world while it lasted. She was lauded by all, and given the courtesy title of Queen in Bereth Ferian, a title with no powers or responsibilities whatsoever—but which still chafed her unbearable. Liere is the poster child for Imposter Syndrome.

LAND OF THE CHWAHIR (aka CHWAHIRSLAND)

Jilo: Son of a lowly sergeant, heir to elderly **Prince Kwenz Sonscarna**, he finds himself acting king of Chwahirsland after Norsunder's removal of the previous king, who had ruled for more than a century. What that means is, he is slowly poisoning himself in trying to remove the toxic accretion of dark magic enchantments over Chwahirsland, and especially its capital.

Prince Kessler Sonscarna: The single living descendant of the ruling Sonscarnas, who were systematically killed off by Wan-Edhe, blood relations notwithstanding. Prince Kessler escaped at a young age, made his way to a martial arts group, where he mastered military arts. He allied with a Norsundrian mage, Dejain, and began to assemble followers for his plan to remove all the hereditary rulers of the world, and replace them with his followers, chosen solely on merit. When defeated, he was forced into Norsunder by Dejain, who betrayed him.

Mondros (Rosey), Mage: His origins are a mystery, his intent to battle Wan-Edhe from a distance. He has looked out for some of the Young Allies Wan-Edhe has tried to suborn, and to kill. He lives in a cottage on the border of Chwahirsland; recently repatriated with his son **Rel**. (see **Sartor**)

Wan-Edhe, King of the Chwahir: Descendant of the ruling Sonscarna family, has ruled for close to a century. A powerful dark magic mage, he has managed to create a powerful citadel in the heart of his kingdom, where time itself is distorted.

COLEND

King Carlael Lirendi: Regarded generally as Mad King Carlael. He is as beautiful as he is strange. He seems to exist in a world of dreams, from which he emerges now and then, very alert and very aware. There is a loose council made up of the chief nobles who oversee the kingdom when he is unable to respond to the world around him.

Prince Shontande Lirendi: Son of Carlael, King of Colend, and crown prince.

Karhin Keperi: She is a teenage scribe student in a small town in the west of Colend, who volunteers to function as the center of the young allies' communication network. An indefatigable letter writer, she first met Puddlenose of the Mearsieans, and gradually got drawn into the Alliance.

Thad Keperi: Red-haired brother of Karhin, also a scribe student, but much less passionate about the scribe life. Very social, and friend to all the Alliance.

Little Bee and Lisbet Keperi: Younger sister and brother of Thad and Karhin. Little Bee is blind, has Dena Yeresbeth, though the family is not aware of it.

EVERON

King Berthold and Queen Mersedes Carinna Delieth: King and queen, survivors of rough earlier years. Mersedes, daughter of a con man, became one of the Knights of Dei, dedicated to protecting the kingdom.

Prince Glenn Delieth: Heir to the throne of Everon, and convinced that a strong army solves all questions, especially the threat of Norsunder attacking.

Princess Hatahra Delieth (Tahra): Younger sister of Glenn, passionate about numbers.

Roderic Dei: Commander of the Knights of Dei, once defenders and protectors of the realm. Decimated in the war Henerek brought, and Kessler Sonscarna finished.

MARLOVEN HESS

Senrid Montredaun-An: Young king of Marloven Hess, a mage studying both dark and light magic. First friend to **Liere Fer Eider**, and second to make his unity in **Dena Yeresbeth**.

Retren Forthan: A young man from a farm background, Forthan is the best of the leaders to come out of the military academy. Senrid, the young king, hopes that Forthan will one day lead the Marloven army.

Commander Keriam: Career military man, now head of the Marloven military academy, also titular head of the Palace Guard. Acted as guardian and foster-father to Senrid, protecting him from the regent as much as possible.

Hibern Askan: Light magic student, tutored by Erai-Yanya of Roth Drael, who learned in the northern mage school. Hibern was exiled by her family.

MEARSIES HEILI

Clair of Mearsies Heili: Young queen of Mearsies Heili, a small agrarian polity on the northeast corner of the continent Toar. Niece of the hermit-mage **Murial**, and cousin to the wandering boy known only as **Puddlenose**, she has adopted a group of girls, most of them runaways. Her right-hand and designated 'heir' is **C.J.**

C.J. (Cherenneh Jenet): Found by Clair, who traveled through the World-gate, C.J. is from Earth, adopted into Clair's gang of runaways and rejects. She learns magic fitfully, and is generally regarded as the leader of Clair's gang of girls.

CJ's Gang of Girls: Falinneh and Dhana currently wear human form but are not actually human, Seshe has a mysterious past, Irenne thinks the world is a stage and she is the heroine of the play, Diana is a martial artist and forester, and Sherry and Gwen are followers. Clair adopted all of them.

Mearsieanne: Once Queen of Mearsies Heili after she walked in and took an empty throne and renamed herself. She was taken by Norsunder and existed beyond time for nearly a century, while her son and granddaughter ruled. Now returned, she has stepped in and in the nicest way possible, shouldered aside Clair, her great-granddaughter and the girl queen, in order to show her how ruling ought to be done.

Murial: (see Light Mages)

Puddlenose of Mearsies Heili: Bereft of family at a very young age, and used by The King of the Chwahir in his complicated plots, he was rescued several times by Rosey (Mondros, see Mages). He wanders the world, determined to have fun. His chief companion is a world-gate wanderer from Earth named **Christoph**, but sometimes he's joined by **Rel**.

SARENDAN

Peitar Selenna, King of Sarendan: Reluctant king who would rather study magic, he came to the throne after an especially vicious civil war. He, nephew to the former king, Darian Irad, was one of the leaders of the revolution, but advocated non-violent means. His accession was a compromise between the commoners, who adore him, and the nobles, who recognize that at least he is nominally one of their own.

Lilah Selenna, Princess of Sarendan: Younger Sister to Peitar. She, with friends **Bren** (artist), **Innon** (a noble-born accountant at heart) and **Deon** were deeply involved in the revolution.

Derek Diamagan: Charismatic leader of the revolution, a commoner who wished to overthrow all the nobles, and institute common rule. He was a far better speech maker than he was an organizer; his revolution was a disaster. Close friend of Peitar Selenna.

SARTOR

Queen Yustnesveas Landis V (Atan): New young queen of Sartor, after the oldest kingdom in the world was removed from time by nearly a century. She was found on the border by Tsauderei the mage, and raised by him before the enchantment was broken. She began her queenship as a mage student, with little training in statecraft, but well-read in history.

Mistress Veltos Jhaer: Head of the prestigious Sartoran mage guild, until the enchantment the foremost mage school in the world. Now a century behind. She is further burdened by guilt for having lost the kingdom to enchantment.

Hinder and Sinder: Morvende (cave dwellers), friends of Atan.

Rel: Known as Rel the shepherd's son, and more widely as Rel the Traveler, he was happily raised by a guardian in Tser Mearsies until wanderlust caused him to leave home. Met **Puddlenose** of the Mearsieans, and consequently became tangled in some of the Mearsieans' adventures. Friends with **Atan**, and one of the **Rescuers**. He was the only outsider ever invited to join the **Knights of Dei** in Everon; in the previous volume he discovered his parentage, which he is still trying to process.

Rescuers: The name given to a band of children who had lived in a magic-protected forest during the enchantment. They sheltered Atan before the enchantment was broken. Ostensibly highly regarded as heroes by the Sartorans, there are the aristocratic Rescuers, and the non-aristocratic, Rel among them.

VASANDE LEROR

Leander Tlennen-Hess: Like Senrid, a young king, though of a tiny polity that historically belonged to the Marlovens, then broke away four centuries previous. Leander and Senrid have a lot in common, and would be friends, except for Leander's jealous stepsister:

Kyale Marlonen: Adoptive sister to Leander, relishes being a princess, and is jealous of Leander's attention.

Llhei: Sarendan-trained nanny (sister to Lizana, nurse to the royal children of **Sarendan**), governess to Kyale, remained after evil Queen Mara Jinia defeated.

Alaxandar: Captain of royal guard, quit under evil queen Mara Jinia, protected Leander.

Part One:

PRISONER

One

l-Athann, Aldau-Rayad

BEFORE CONCLUDING THIS PART of the alliance's history (or as a particular Chief Archivist would grandly put it, the *rise*), permit me to reintroduce the four human-inhabited worlds circling the sun Erhal:

The mysterious, cloud-obscured world of Songre Silde.

Sartorias-deles, which most of the Young Allies call home.

Aldau-Rayad, called by Norsunder "Five," arid and lifeless, where Detlev of Norsunder established a stronghold.

Opposite Sartorias-deles, so that the two worlds are invisible to one another, the sister world Geth-deles, known to its inhabitants simply as Geth.

Geth's complicated undersea life is far older than the human civilizations on the island archipelagos, largely uninterested in humans and their airborne gibble-gabble—except as food to certain deep-water species. The human settlers on Geth eventually met other world-gate travelers and refugees—including those fleeing the cataclysm Sartorias-Deles calls The Fall, and so their culture evolved in the usual fits and starts.

There has in recent years been sporadic communication between the four worlds. Not nearly what once had been, of course. At the time I'm writing about here, Norsunder was most frequent in shifting between Five, their single base on Geth-deles, and Sartorias-deles.

They had failed in getting a toehold on Songre Silde . . . so far.

This last chapter in the Rise of the Alliance will begin with a brief jaunt ten years back, which on Sartorias-deles was a couple years after Sartor had emerged from its enchantment beyond time and was struggling to catch up with the rest of the world.

Unknown to any of them, the forgotten world Five hosted not only the Norsundrian stronghold, but hidden deep in one of its mountain ranges, survivors of that long-ago Fall.

We'll begin with those survivors as the last sands slipped from the massive time-measure canister, marking the end of one round and the beginning of a new, "rounds" being the designation for what had once been days, a concept blurred by centuries of cave living. The Elder in charge of swinging the canister upright again and ringing the wake-time bell stood patiently by as five children pattered past him, up the smooth rocky path to the highest cave belonging to the mage Dom Hildi.

Leotay was the first of the ten-year-olds to reach the ledge outside of Dom Hildi's cave. Several other children joined her there, including Leotay's friend Satya. Familiar with one another, they knew that there were no other ten-year-olds due, but still Dom Hildi did not open her tapestry.

"Did you call?" asked the last arrival.

"Yes," Leotay said, for the fifth time.

"We were supposed to be here at Blue," Satya pointed out.

Everybody had come early, before the start of the new round.

Moonbeam, the tallest of the boys, hopped to the edge of the ledge and peered down into the big cavern. "Elder Amau is waiting for the last of the sands to drop," he reported.

His words were unnecessary—no one had heard the Change bell ring —but still the others thanked him with somewhat nervous politeness. When Dom Hildi said that they were to be there at the Blue, that meant precisely when the cannister had been swung around and sand began flowing into the lowest level, marked with a blue stripe. No one wanted to find out what happened to latecomers, so they'd all sidled up during the end of the last sleep-stripe.

They knew that they were to hear The Story this round, but anything more than that (though they'd never tired of speculating) was unknown. Adults, and older cousins and siblings had been disgustingly smirky and teasing, but most repeated tiresome variations on, "We waited until we turned ten, and so will you."

Leotay got up and stared down into the vast bowl of the main cavern, at the familiar glowglobes along the ledge walk-ways outside the smaller, tapestry-covered caves in which families dwelt. She knew that The Story was supposed to be about the Past, but how was the Past different from the present? She couldn't imagine anything different than the family caves along the ledges, the big terrace opposite Dom Hildi's cave with the massive striped double-canister that measured out their awake-times and sleep-times in the continual flow of soft sands, or the people she'd always known.

She turned around, her toes rubbing on the stone smoothed by hundreds of years of ancestors. Hundreds and *hundreds*. She gazed at Dom Hildi's beautiful blue-and-gold embroidered tapestry. As befitted the most respected person in the cavern, she had the best tapestry. Somehow the patterns in the weave seemed to indicate mystery: why were the shapes made this way or that way?

They would find out soon. The thought made her wriggle with impatience.

"Blue!" a boy sang out a heartbeat before Elder Amau hauled the rope that turned the canister, then struck the brass bell down in the cavern to announce the last of sleep-time.

"Ah!" a sigh went through the youngsters on the little ledge.

Don Hildi's tapestry moved aside.

A wrinkled old face peered out, the eyes sharp but the skin around them crinkled in good humor. "Come in, children."

They walked single file past the familiar figure with her white hair tied back into a thin braid. Her outer chamber was plain, much like anyone else's: a few mats, a low table made of silk-tree wood, a patterned weaving on the cave wall. Leotay hoped they wouldn't have to stay there, though this was usually the room where people kept company. Somehow, she expected something different of Dom Hildi.

They weren't disappointed. The old lady pushed aside another even more fantastically embroidered tapestry, one tattered with age, and they filed inside the inner cave. Their gazes passed indifferently over the two low tables with books on them, to the walls where hung several ancient-looking embroidered cloths, these ones not with patterns, but with pictures. The only things recognizable about the pictures were people, though the clothes they wore were as fantastic as the backgrounds. Who were those brown people in their odd clothes? Why did they cover their feet and heads?

Finally, in a jagged corner between two striated slabs, hung . . . the Black Tapestry. Like The Story, it had been whispered about most by those who had not yet seen it.

"Sit down, children," Dom Hildi said, smiling. She pointed to where six guest mats had been set in a half-circle on the floor, and she settled onto her thick one, so much easier on old bones.

"So how much have you heard about The Story?" Dom Hildi said, her brows raised.

The youngsters looked at one another. No one was willing to admit how they'd done their best to get hints.

Dom Hildi's old eyes crinkled with humor. "Thought so. I'll tell you what I've told your older kin—and what we were told when we were small. That is, you don't talk about The Story, because you'll probably get it wrong. Truth is, we may have it wrong. This is all we know about the outer world before our people came inside our caves to live. We don't want to get things even more mixed up."

She paused and studied each face in turn. Leotay met the fierce old eyes squarely, her interest overcoming her awe. She liked the way Dom Hildi's eyelids folded into a cheery wink, as if she were on the verge of a laugh.

"Here's a summary of what we know. The First Age is what we call the time before our ancestors came down into the cavern. The ancestors were part of a great group of people, so numerous that all were not family, cousin-kin, or distant-kin. In fact, everyone couldn't possibly know one another."

Satya sucked in her breath, but she pressed her lips tight against making any noise. Dom Hildi's eyelids crinkled even more.

"They lived up on the surface, all over the world. The surface wasn't barren rock as it is now, it was covered by things called grass and trees and greens and horses and houses, which grew right out of the ground."

She paused as a whisper rustled among them.

"They lived in happiness, until some enemies, called Norss-Dar —" (her voice paused between the two words) " — decided they wanted everything the people had. They did their best to destroy our world, and when our people tried to use their magic to be rid of them, they used stronger magic to be rid of us.

"Everyone disappeared, as far as we know, except for a small village high in the mountains. Magic also nearly disappeared. When our records begin, we had only a hundred twenty-eight families, and one mage, named Hildi. These are our ancestors, the people of Al-Athann Valley. When the troubles came, they withdrew into our mountain to hide, destroying their village behind them so that the enemies would think others of their kind had already been there and would not search farther."

Satya sighed. This story wasn't fun at all.

"Half a year passed before they dared to go outside again. They found thorough destruction. So the first Hildi sealed the cave behind the villagers, and they settled down to life inside the mountains, moving from time to time deeper underground, until they eventually came to where we live now."

Leotay bit back an exclamation of dismay. Was that the end?

Dom Hildi smiled. "It was the job of each Hildi to tell The Story to each new generation so that they would not forget who they were, for they all expected that the time would come when they would go forth from the mountain again and reclaim their world."

"How would they know when?" one of the boys asked.

"When certain signs appeared," Dom Hildi said. "Signs we are receiving in this generation."

All five youngsters cooed in amazement.

"It won't be easy, I expect," Dom Hildi went on when she had quiet again. "You will each have a job. And one of you will be learning mine." She paused to look hard at each face in turn. Leotay held her breath when the old eyes met hers, willing the mage to see how much she wanted to be chosen. "Mage is a fine position, but with the responsibility comes constant learning. I haven't finished yet. My apprentice must face a lifetime of study. You will know who you are, as I did when the Hildi before me, a very old man at the time, chose me."

She clapped her hands briskly. "Enough of that. Let me now explain some of the things that our ancestors thought important. These books on the table have pictures, which we have recopied as the old books fell apart. As you can see, 'books' are bound around squares of silk-paper. In this first, we have 'weather' — water falling right out of a blue sky. And this one is a house. . . "

Leotay stared at the pictures, colored with their silk dyes. She knew she ought to pay attention. But it was hard to do it with the thought of learning magic burning at her like the brightest of glowglobes. Who would Dom Hildi pick? All five thought it should be themselves, and why shouldn't they? She knew she hadn't any more right than the others. It was just that she wanted so badly to learn magic.

"And the last thing is Lady Dulcamara, the picture that talks. She was left behind by someone who had visited the Al-Athann Valley. She is very silly, but still even she serves a purpose: it is she who has kept our language from changing."

"What is a 'Lady'?" Satya asked.

"We think it is a term of respect, like Dom."

"How does that work?" Leotay spoke up. "A picture that talks? Is it a person trapped inside the picture?"

"Oh no," Dom Hildi exclaimed. "It is only a magical spell of great power, a portion of someone's personality, you could say, set within a frame for someone to talk to." She smiled. "She might have been made as a reminder to someone dear. But as one might expect from a portion of a once-living person, there is little of interest in what the picture has to say. She's more a curiosity. Now, before I let you go, any questions?"

One of the boys said, "What kind of glowglobe is the sun?'

"It is a great one, greater even than the world, but at a distance above, which makes it seem smaller." She pointed upward, and the children nodded. They knew how things looked smaller at the heights of the great caves. "It is hotter than our ovens, its light painful to eyes. It cooks the outer world."

Another said, "So does the sun-globe make blue-sky and the rest?"

"Blue-sky is not a globe, it is a ceiling made of air," Dom

Hildi said.

"Then who painted it, and what holds it up?" Satya asked.

"It must have been the job of those who existed outside the world," Dom Hildi said. "Or anyway they knew the answer, because we don't."

The youngsters laughed.

Then one boy sidled a look at the others and said, "When does the chosen one get to start?"

"In three rounds," Dom Hildi said. "Are you all interested?"

All the children murmured assent.

"Then I must hear you sing. Magic requires hearing the proper falls, and not all can, as you well know."

She sang a rhythm quite unlike any of their normal songs, and one by one the others repeated it. Leotay's heart squeezed when she heard her friend Satya's clear, beautiful voice.

"I'm sorry, Ofion," Dom Hilda said to the smallest boy. "You will eventually have work that you like, but it cannot be magic."

Ofion hung his head, though he was not surprised. He'd known from an early age, after patient but fruitless repetition, that he couldn't catch the tone in true.

Dom Hilda said to the remaining four, "If you think you are the one, when you return, have ready an answer to my question: why do you wish to learn magic?"

The youngsters rose, thanked her, and filed silently out. Leotay saw the others exchanging looks.

Sometime during Late Green, Leotay met Satya coming out of Dom Ielem's cave, which was where Lady Dulcamara was kept.

"Hi," she said.

"Is she interesting?"

"Not really," said Satya. "She's ugly, and all she knows is a lot of grownup talk. Do you want to go back?"

Leotay nodded. Her throat was suddenly too dry for speech.

"Me too," Satya said, her face a funny combination of reluctant and eager. "Except what if she thinks my reason to learn magic is stupid? What does she want to hear?"

Leotay shook her head.

Satya sighed. "It has to be more fun than moth-tending or silk-spinning or food-growing, you'd think."

"Harder," Leotay whispered. "A lot harder."

Satya's brows puckered. "You think so?"

"She's old," Leotay pointed out. "And she says she is still learning."

Satya looked thoughtful. She passed on by, and Leotay went inside the plain green tapestry before the cave belonging to the Doms Ielem and Heole.

Dom Heole greeted Leotay with a smile and paused in her silk-weaving. "Go ahead, child," she said.

Leotay whispered her thanks and knelt before the stone table on which the picture sat. The visiting cave around her was neat and plain, much like any other. As Leotay knelt, she wondered why this family had the picture. But of course it would be passed down through family, or cousin-kin in situations where someone didn't have children.

Then she turned her attention to the picture. The 'lady' in the picture was a woman, that much was plain, though she was different from the people in the cave, her eyes a pale, watery color, and her skin brown. She was odd, but Leotay did not think her ugly. Her clothing, what could be seen of it, was pretty—a bright color, and embroidered with shapes that Leotay recognized from tapestries all over the caves. Perhaps it was her hair that the others thought ugly—it was the color of dirty water, and fashioned upward on top of her head, and secured with a lot of decorative things, making her head look too large. Or her skin, with thicker wrinkles than the older folk in the cavern had.

"Good morning, little girl," the woman in the picture said.

"Greetings," Leotay said, wondering what "morning" meant. "I have a question."

Lady Dulcamara smiled.

"What is the difference between weather and water and rain?"

"When the weather changes, it usually means rain," Lady Dulcamara said. "The wet ruins silk."

This was even more confusing than ever, except of course for the word silk, but still Leotay thanked her gravely, and then went outside.

All the next two rounds she eyed her fellow ten-year-olds. One by one the boys made it clear they'd changed their minds; the sleep-time before the third round, Satya whispered to Leotay during Singing that she had also changed her mind. "I hope it's you," she said. "I thought about it, and you are the only one who never gets tired of questions."

Leotay wriggled with the restlessness she could not contain when she thought about magic. "But you sing better than I. That is, I know my tones are true, but not pretty, like yours."

"My father said that the best singer is usually song leader, not a Hildi. I'd rather choose the songs someday," Satya said.

"Whereas I, though it might be the wrong answer to her question, I want to know *everything*," Leotay whispered back. "And I don't care how much work it takes to learn it."

Satya smothered a laugh, and both girls turned their attention back to the song.

The next round at Blue, Dom Hildi was waiting for Leotay, who arrived alone. "Come in, child," she said in a welcoming tone.

Leotay followed her inside, beyond the Black Tapestry. She sat on the indicated mat, her back straight, and waited in painful expectation.

Hildi started to say speak, then her eyes narrowed. "Something wrong, Leotay?"

"The question," Leotay said, her mouth dry. "Aren't you—going to ask?"

Hildi laughed. "That question was for you youngsters to wrestle over. I already know your answer," she said. She pursed her lips. "But first a command."

Leotay sat up even straighter.

"Repeat after me. You, Hildi . . ."

"You, Dom Hildi—"

"No. You, Hildi."

"You. . . Hildi. . ." Leotay faltered at leaving out the honorific.

"Again," the old woman said.

"You, Hildi," Leotay said with slightly more conviction.

". . . are an old bat."

Leotay gasped.

"Go on. We won't get anywhere until you say it—and mean it."

". . . are. . . an . . .old bat." The last two words were barely whispered, and Leotay's face burned.

Hildi laughed. "Child, if we are to work together, you must not be afraid to ask questions, or to argue, if you disagree. Every Hildi taught differently, but this is my way. I know I'm an old bat, what's more, I'm proud of it. I worked hard to attain this fine status! So let's hear it!"

"You, Hildi . . . are an old BAT." Leotay got it out in a rush, but she did it.

Hildi wheezed and rocked. Leotay felt a bubble of laughter behind her ribs. As Dom Hildi whispered "Bat, bat, bat," it grew until at last she laughed too. Then asked, "What is a bat, anyway? We say it, but what is it?"

"They were wrinkly, thin creatures. Still might be, for all I know. We had them in the caves with us at one time, which is why the word lingers, I think. Whatever they ate is no longer with us, so they went away." She touched one of her books. "I have drawings of creatures here, though we know little about them anymore. But they are interesting to look at, and to imagine how they lived in the world."

"I want to look at them *all*," Leotay said fervently.

"And you shall," Hildi said. "But first, the Signs."

Leotay leaped up, joy suffusing her.

"Through here. That's why we magicians have always used this cave," she explained, leading the way through a narrow opening beyond the room. Instead of a sleeping space, there was a single globe set among the rocks in a narrow chamber with a high crack running up into the rocky ceiling.

"We do have certain secrets never told to the other people. Hildis in the past waited, some making their apprentices earn each one, others choosing specific years. I don't have the patience for that," she said, and inwardly, *or the time.*

"Here's one." She pointed to a dagger that hung suspended in the middle of the air. The hilt and guard were made of a black, shiny material. One side of the hilt curved up and one down, just like the daggers with plain stone hilts that Leotay was used to seeing.

She stepped closer and saw that the black material was inlaid with fine hairs of gold in a graceful pattern of interlocked shapes. Unlike their black stone knives, the blade of this was so silver it was almost blue. In the middle of the guard was set a gemstone that reflected light.

"Go ahead. Touch it," Hildi said.

Leotay reached up a tentative hand, but her fingers were stopped by some kind of invisible wall.

"It has magic on it, magic I can't even begin to understand.

It was put there by our ancestors, for us to use when the time was right to fight against those who drove us down into our caves. This is why we really have the knife-practice," Hildi added.

Leotay nodded solemnly. "I thought it was for duels."

"The duels are fun to watch, right?"

Leotay shrugged. She sometimes appreciated contests of skill, but in truth her mind often wandered when people put on exhibitions.

"Duels were not always games," Hildi said. "The touch was actually supposed to be a cut. The sharp edge of the knife was not just a test of skill, it was intended to hurt the opponent."

Leotay flinched.

Dom Hildi glanced away, then back, her tone rough, as if she knew she talked about impolite things, when politeness was so very important. "You will have to read the histories about when some of our people used them against other people. But it's been many generations since those rounds: when our people could not agree, or someone had carried out an act that required it, they were driven from the caves and told never to return lest the knives be used to end their lives."

Leotay shuddered. This was in truth why she had never had the inclination to join the knife-wielders: those sharp edges. Leotay did not like to think about people being lost in the tunnels any more than she did about being able to cut someone open. *But it happened to our ancestors, or we wouldn't be here in the caves.* "This knife has been waiting here for someone to be able to grasp it?" she asked.

"For generation, and generations," Hildi said, from the other side of the knife.

"But will we know —"

Hildi cut in, giving her head a quick shake. "It's already happened. I've also had to test the best of each generation's knife fighters, and just a year ago, Star's son Quicksilver reached up and took hold of this as if he'd put it there. Moss has been training him in private to take over as knife leader ever since, as she is nearly my age, and does not feel she could lead in earnest."

"I didn't know that," Leotay whispered.

"No one does. Yet. There are some among the adults who would expect to be chosen leader in the traditional way, but when the time comes, Quicksilver will have to be the one. It is still a secret. And it's not the only one," she added. "The Thing-That-Does-Not-Burn is in the care of Elder Springblossom's son, Jeory. It too was not touchable—until Jeory came here for his ten-round. Which is why you youngsters weren't even shown it. The ability to touch it is something none of us understand. It is not only what we must use to heal our world, according to the oldest records, it was also a protection one of the early Hildis made, for if the wrong person touched it, it *would* burn them. From the inside out."

Leotay backed away, though there was no such object in the chamber. "Truly?"

"The record is one of the oldest, recopied many times, and errors might have come into those copies, but that is our understanding. And so the test, in my day, was the lightest touch with a finger. It raised a blister on me, and everyone else in my group. Jeory felt nothing, even when he put his hand to it. It seems to be safe enough with him, but he promised not to let anyone else touch it. He took it with him to experiment with. I'll try to remember to have him show it to you."

"What does it do?" Leotay asked.

Hildi nodded. "Its uses are lost, alas. The first Hildi began writing everything down when our ancestors realized how much they had already lost. But some things were lost anyway. Including the use of the Thing-That-Does-Not-Burn."

She led the way out into the work cave and put her hands on her scrawny hips. "It could be that our try will be a dis-aster. Our ancestors might have laid plans for a far different sort of battle than we can envision. We'll never know, to our sorrow. But from these signs, the time has come to try. It could be that we'd soon be discovered anyway, for within my lifetime the enemy has made a structure out on the plain. We can just see them from out-mountain vantage."

Leotay gasped. "You've been out?"

Dom Hildi nodded soberly. "It is something each Hildi has to do. This is how we get the sun-globes for our moth and growing caves. And I cannot claim it is a pleasant duty, esp-ecially as I must leave in secret, and go in the darkness with-out, carrying each precious crystal separately, or at most two. This structure beyond our mountain is a danger," she said. "I've known that much from my dreams. We have to pre-pare."

Leotay rubbed her clammy hands.

Hildi smiled a little. "The third sign—but not the last, which is yet to come—is a personal one. I believe that I am the last Hildi. You will keep your name, because the work of the Hildis is nearly done. And you will begin anew."

Leotay heard that, her skin ruffling along her arms and her middle tightening with pride and fear.

"You have to be a new person, in their eyes as well as your own. No more Leotay, obedient child. But you are not to be a Hildi, for I think your task will be different. I do not believe you will live your life here, seeking crystal for glowglobes, and preserving the old things. I believe you will be discovering new things, and new ways. You must learn to become Dom Leotay."

"Dom Leotay," the girl whispered.

Dom Hildi nodded, and carefully opened one of her old books. "The music of magic is different from our songs, deliberately so. But you have learned to sing, and I know you can sing true. First are the simple note patterns." She laid a finger on a page with curious markings. "So let us begin."

Ten years later — present day

Leotay lay in her bed and used the light of a silk-stiffened glowglobe that she had made to study the walls of the apprentice chamber off Dom Hildi's own private chamber, equally small. Leotay had moved in right after being accepted as Dom Hildi's apprentice, but she never tired of reading the names and messages either painted or etched into the rock walls.

A few of those unknown Hildis had gotten ambitious (or else their apprenticeships had been extra-long) and carved figures. Such comments as *Hildi 17 was here—ha ha!* and *Kill the Enemy, Forward with the Plan!—Hildi XXXIV* characterized most of the carvings, but some of them were personal. *How many Hildis will follow me?* one Hildi wrote. *I am 20, will I ever live under the blue-sky?* another wrote.

Same age as I am, Leotay thought.

During her free time, Leotay had looked up most of these Hildis, trying to discern from their writings what they had been like. She resolved that whatever happened after they left the caves, the Hildis, and their long labors, would never be forgotten.

Her own Hildi seemed to be aging rapidly. She had admitted that she had waited a very long while before the right apprentice had come, and she'd been frightened that she might die before finding that person. So many years, the only children to return to her cave after The Story were two who came for wrong reasons. Now her eyesight was fading, and it took her a long time to get out of bed, but her mind, and teaching, were as clear as ever.

"Leotay!"

The familiar whisper broke into her thoughts.

Dom Leotay got up and threw on her tunic. Batting aside her tapestry, she found Quicksilver and Jeory outside. They had extra clothes rolled up with them; she knew immediately they wanted to make an escape to the Dome.

It was her free round—Dom Hildi had been insistent on her using her free rounds after Leotay nearly made herself sick working too hard—so without a word she went back into her cave, got her extra tunic, and then they left.

"She still asleep?" Quicksilver asked as they ran quickly up the stone path.

"Yes. Council of Elders brangled late. She knows there's one more sign, and they think there isn't, or she'd know what it is by now."

"Scared," Jeory said softly. "Youngsters keep going up the Forbidden Path. Never did in the past."

Leotay bit her lip. She knew that the ringleader of the younger ones was her own sister Horsefeathers. A good girl, but lively and just as full of question as Leotay. She'd never forgiven Leotay for moving away from the family cave when Horsefeathers was six.

"The younger-years are bolder than we or even our parents were. They want the changes to come faster," Leotay said as they started up the long path to the Dome.

"But the elders are afraid of what change will bring," Jeory answered, his black eyes distant-seeing.

Quicksilver grinned. "Little ones won't make it all the way Out. Not without us knowing."

Jeory and Leotay both turned to him. That was his way—he'd tell them something. Always brief, seldom with any discernable judgment. If they wanted to know more, they'd have to ask.

"How?" Leotay said.

"My group split up watching. Each has a trusted younger also watching."

Leotay nodded. "I hadn't thought of that. Much better than making a noise at the Council and bothering with new rules."

Jeory said nothing, but Leotay sensed his agreement.

There was little further talk as they scrambled up the long, treacherous path. Leotay hated this climb. It had been fun when she was smaller, but ever since she grew tall, she had to stoop, like Quicksilver, only it didn't seem to bother him.

She always got a scrape somewhere, and little falls of rubble never failed to sting her on the head unless she saw them first and sang them safely to the side. There were some who went up to the Dome every round, but she only went when the other two wanted to go. Much as she enjoyed swimming, the long trip up — and worse, the dangerous descent after, when she was tired — made her prefer swimming in the cold pool below Dom Sunstream's cave.

She wasn't the only one who got battered by the cold, wind-torn stone. Jeory never failed to stumble or bruise himself, but that was because his mind was usually far away, paying scarce attention to what his body was doing. Yet he never seemed to notice the bumps and scrapes.

Only Quicksilver moved with ease up the narrow path, vaulting over stones and pulling himself up the rock faces without a break in his breathing. He never went too fast, and Leotay had noted with silent approval that more than once it was Quicksilver who prevented Jeory from getting an especially bad cut or fall when Jeory was about to blunder into some hazard. Quicksilver was not only swift and kindly, he was also strong, and graceful, and she liked looking at him when his attention was otherwise.

Dom Hildi had said that the Hildis had always foresworn pairing. Mages must live alone. Leotay had heard that with disinterest when young, but in recent years, she had begun to wonder if this rule, too, might change, like so many others. Because there were times when she'd feel warmth inside and outside, as if new silk slithered over her skin, and she'd turn, and there would be Quicksilver's gleaming black eyes gazing her way, and his smile. What would be so wrong about pairing, especially with someone so responsible? She could understand the rule if one chose someone foolish, or lazy, who might keep the mage from doing their duty. Or who might persuade them to the wrong duty.

Not that there was much time for pursuing this idea. They had so many responsibilities! What if this was the time to leave the caves? What would it be like to say good-bye to this place forever? She shivered at the idea of the unknown. At least this ancient path, lit by stiffened silk glowglobes made by one of the Hildis long ago, was familiar.

When they reached the pool at last, some youngsters were already there, shouting and splashing about, their noise echoing around the stone walls. Quicksilver grinned, dropped his roll, and dove off the highest cliff, cutting the dark water with barely a splash.

"Wish I could do that," Jeory said longingly.

"Try," Leotay suggested.

"Me?" A skinny hand gestured. "I'd probably managed to land on the rocks or drown myself," he said as they picked their way down to a lower level, where youngsters' stuff littered the ancient stone. "Oh well." He turned toward the water, which lapped at the rocky ledge below their feet. "Coming?"

"In a moment."

Jeory pinched his fingers to his nose then jumped in, his arms and legs flapping. Half a breath later he reappeared, flailing his way ungracefully toward a group of youngsters playing a water game.

Leotay watched Quicksilver cut through the water with smooth speed, then dive down after something. They really were different. Jeory so gangling, his mind often so far away, and Quicksilver so strong and so present. As it should be, she thought firmly. If they three were alike, how good would they be on a future Council?

She stared at the hot spring that fountained into the pool. This is us, she thought. Jeory was the hot spring, all splashy and steamy. Quicksilver was the underground water, quiet and there when needed. And she was where they mixed.

She crouched down on the edge of the stone outcropping, her chin grinding against her knees. She hated listening to Council meetings now. They brangled about such unimportant things. Little infractions of rules that the families had followed, for generations, rules whose original reason was long lost, just as the meanings of their names had been lost, except for the fact that they were traditional.

All that would be changed, soon, though no one yet knew how. Her hope was that the three of them would be able to make enough sense of the changes to be better at leading.

She thought back to the business about the Forbidden Path. The idea of going up it and Out into—whatever—mixed a cold fear with the warmth of expectation in her middle, making her shiver. Obviously some of the youngsters felt only the excitement of prospective change, and they scoffed at the idea that they might not like it when it came. Leotay would have tried to cope with Horsefeathers and her friends within the rules. Quicksilver had coped a different way. Their guardianship was completely different, but to the same end.

Jeory splashed, then shouted something to Quicksilver. Jeory did not participate in the guardianship, for he had only one task, to figure out how to wield the Thing-That-Does-Not-Burn to heal the world. But he listened to them all, and when he did come to Council, holding that hollow Thing—as long as a child's forearm, round, with decorative holes down it—between his hands and talking of the images in his dreams, the adults listened to him, even though they rarely understood him when he said things like "blue ice" and "the green of new life." But his low whisper, and ardent gaze that seemed to reach far past the familiar curve of the cave walls convinced everyone that these things were important.

As for Quicksilver, when Dom Moss declared herself an elder, no adult was willing to challenge the person clearly trained by Moss to follow her, and he took over as knife-wielder leader.

Two

THE YEAR ON SARTORIAS-DELES was early 4748 AF when, after months of little communication, Detlev ordered his boys to abandon their lair entirely and fall back to Five.

Which they did, with two prisoners. One according to orders, one not.

The boys' collective mood was grim, even the ones not wounded. Their previous orders, as they knew very well, had been to lie low. It was annoying to retreat when they knew they could have easily defeated the alliance, but no one argued. Instead, they wondered how much trouble they were in.

One of their prisoners was Clair of small, pastoral Mearsies Heili, thirteen years old when she did the Child Spell that kept her from physically aging. She had been queen of Mearsies Heili until her great-grandmother returned from imprisonment beyond time, and resettled herself on the throne.

Once Clair fought down the shakes and nausea of cross-world transfer magic, she knew immediately from the glare-bright yellow-white light and the dusty, dry smell of the air that she was not on Sartorias-deles.

The Destination room she and Laban, one of Detlev's boys, found themselves in was a bare stone antechamber of some kind, with two archways at either end and doors on opposite walls.

Laban's distinctively vivid coloring — black hair, warm brown skin with a dash of color along his cheekbones, dominated by bright, sardonic blue eyes — had bleached to pale, his eyes bloodshot from the combination of pain from a recent wound and the between-worlds transfer.

He indicated a bench against the wall. Clair's head was also still throbbing from the transfer. She plopped down, her head unsettlingly wobbly on her neck.

Light flashed. Cold, wet winter air smashed into the room and another of Detlev's boys appeared, the blond one Clair didn't know. This had to be David, whom she'd been told was their captain, or lieutenant, or chief. Whatever Norsundrian chain of command meant.

He dropped a sheathed sword onto a side table and leaned down, short, wavy blond hair hanging in his eyes as he placed his hands on his knees and gulped air. Then he picked up the sword and walked through a door.

Laban had leaned back with his head against the stone wall, his eyes closed, one hand clutching at his bandaged shoulder.

Clair stared at the door she could see on the other side of the room. It was her duty to escape. She ought to dash for freedom. She ought to get up right now, except her body hurt almost as much as her heart, because of Irenne —

Clair held her breath. She would *not* blub in front of enemies. And when armed guards passed briefly into view through the open door, she let her breath out in an unsteady trickle. At least she hadn't bolted outside and smacked straight into them.

Another transfer, punching the air with the hot-metal singe that warned of too many transfers too close together. This time it was Clair's friend Terry of Erdrael Danara, who fell with a splat. Clair leaped up to help the tall older boy. He groaned, wincing, as Clair tugged his good arm. He held his other arm close to him, the hand with missing fingers curled in from long habit.

Then another flash, and there was MV: tall, lean, yellow flecked light brown eyes that looked fiery in some light, his blade-sharp cheekbones flushed, straight black hair hanging on his forehead.

Rage ignited in Clair. This was Irenne's murderer. For the first time in her life her hands stiffened, fingers curled. The urge to leap on him and exert every muscle and nerve to choke the life out of him was so strong she tasted a bitterness on her tongue.

"This way," Laban said, taking her arm.

She flung him off, as MV ignored her, swayed, forced himself upright, then grabbed Terry by the collar and hauled him through the far door.

"Come on," Laban said, stretching out one hand, the bandaged arm held close to his side.

She stepped away, so angry and upset that her eyes burned, and her throat clogged. She would *not* cry.

"Have to tell Detlev you're here," Laban explained.

Those words shocked Clair, a whiplash to the spirit. As Laban stood by the door, waiting, Clair looked around for any escape. Armed guards outside somewhere, MV through the other door. There was nowhere to run. Escape would have to wait.

She forced herself to follow.

The place was built of a sandy-colored stone, but the lines reminded her more of the way her white palace at home was made, arched windows and corridors aligned with how light fell. They reached another antechamber, glaring light slanting in through high windows. A young man in Norsunder gray, sitting at a desk with papers before him, glanced curiously at them, but said nothing as he pointed with his quill pen toward the far door.

"Here," Laban said in Mearsiean.

Clair stood irresolutely. Impatience drew Laban's expressive brows together and he stepped toward her.

Avoiding his reaching hand, she walked around him and into a room with a wide window looking out on what at first seemed to be a lawn, and huge trees with long, very dark green, glossy fringed leaves, not unlike what she had once seen of Cyclades on Earth. Sunlight glared in from behind thin clouds, lighting a plain desk at which sat Detlev, the worst villain in the entire world.

No, the worst villain in *three* worlds, maybe more, horrid thought. Right there, deep in conversation with a tall black-and-gray clad villain lounging against the windowsill. The man wore a sword over his back, a long knife at his belt, and knife hilts stuck up at the top of his boots, in contrast to Detlev, who wasn't armed.

"But I'm not going to wait. It's gone," the tall one said in accented Sartoran. "Gone, and forgotten, except by you old-time fools. I've got plans of my own—"

Laban shut the door. The quiet snick made Clair jump. Her nerves flared painfully, and she whirled around. Laban jerked his good thumb toward the desk.

Clair wasn't going anywhere near that desk, though she was aware that Detlev was every bit as terrible a threat several paces away. He didn't need weapons. He could kill you with a thought, everyone said. Even the records said so. She backed away, nearly tumbled over a chair, and dropped into it with a defiant thump. Her heart hammered painfully in her chest, and she knew Detlev probably was very aware of her fear, but she kept her face resolutely blank anyway.

The tall man shot her a look of contempt, waved a dismissive hand toward Laban and her, then said something in Norsunder's language, his tone derisive. Back and forth, two, three times, the men talked, and then the tall one uttered a single humorless laugh and made a transfer sign. He vanished, leaving Clair face to face with the worst villain to plague Sartorias-deles during Clair's lifetime.

Detlev listened as Laban made a rapid report in Norsundrian, which was not included in the Universal Language Spell that Clair had put on hers and the girls' medallions a long time ago.

Because he hadn't looked her way yet, Clair darted fast glances as she braced for threats. Or torture chambers. Or being taken out and shot full of arrows. She had never been this close to Detlev before. Considering how many dreadful things she'd heard and read about him, it was unsettling, how ordinary he appeared: above middle height for a grown man, trim build, his brown hair cut above the collar in back, common in the military. Except for the ubiquitous gray tunic-coat over riding trousers and boots, he didn't look like a Norsundrian. He could have been someone's tutor.

He *was* someone's tutor. She stole a glance at Laban, one the boys whom her best friend CJ was trying hard to get everyone to call poopsies. Detsie's poopsies. The nicknames were supposed to diminish their affect of evil. It wasn't working now that Clair was their prisoner, waiting to find out if she would live or die.

Laban began talking in Norsunder's language. Detlev listened to him without interrupting, and though Laban's changeable face registered a variety of expressions, from irony to anger, Detlev's own expression remained bland. Clair's gaze travelled down to his hands; so many times when faces were blank, hands gave a key to a person's thoughts, but Detlev's hands, callused square palms, long fingers neatly manicured, were still.

Without warning the man transferred his gaze to Clair, his hazel eyes, same color as hers, meeting her gaze before she could look away, as words formed in her mind: *Welcome, Clair of the Mearsieans.*

She tried to close him out of her thoughts, but terror made it difficult for her to concentrate on her mind-shield.

Humor laced the next communication: *You are here as an experiment. No one will use means magical, mental, or physical to force you to join us. It is for you to do so of your own free will.*

What?

Had she said that out loud? Detlev did not give her time to be aghast. He uttered a spell, and magic flared. A weird pressure twanged behind her eyeballs, and then Detlev gestured to the boy standing next to her.

Laban grinned, said, "Come on. I'll show you where you'll stay." He spoke in Norsundrian — and she understood it.

She shot to her feet, heart crowding in her throat.

Detlev said, "It's an adaptation of the Universal Language Spell. You will learn to read and write the language yourself."

Clair pressed her lips together, turning her back on him, an action that took all her courage. A crawling sensation tightened along her spine, but she kept her back straight, feeling Detlev's amusement following her out of the room.

Out in the hall she almost collided with tall, gangling, big-eared Roy, who was heading in, carrying that stack of papers she'd glimpsed him reading on the tree platform in the boys' hideaway. Roy, once a friend — until she discovered that he was a Norsundrian spy.

She ducked around wordlessly as Laban led the way into the hall. They left the building, walking across what turned out to be a waxy, stubby sort of greenery somewhere between grass and moss to another long, low building shaded by more of those peculiar large leafy trees. A long hall with doors down both sides bisected the narrow, one-story building.

A little way down the hall, Laban opened a door and waved her in. "This room is yours. You're on your own now, until Detlev says otherwise. Ask if you want to know anything. Meals are in the mess hall, which you'll see through your window. Questions?"

"Are there any other girls?" Not that she wanted to find some other girl in this nasty place, especially as an enemy.

"No. Detlev said he couldn't find any when he found us."

Found? She debated asking, though she didn't want to give him the satisfaction of showing interest in either him or his repulsive companions.

He flicked his fingers up in a casual wave toward the door and walked off. She stood where she was until the ring of his heels had diminished, then she entered the room and slammed the door behind her. The first thing she did was reach inside her shirt for her carefully ensorcelled medallion. She'd made one for each of her friends, with a transfer spell on it as well as the spell to call Hreealdar, the horse-like being made of lightning.

And neither spell worked.

Of course they didn't work—she was really, truly, on another world.

She saw a bed, and threw herself on it, burying her face in her arms and saying all the curse words she'd felt building up inside her, but ran out of words before she ran out of emotions, and flung herself over. Her hot, dry eyes ached, and her head throbbed. The numbness of shock was inexorably, mercilessly wearing off, leaving her raw with agony: over and over she saw Irenne's wide gaze of disbelief, not yet even pain, as her blood pulsed out of that long slice in her neck, then falling, falling, falling, to the snow . . .

Irenne was dead, Clair was a prisoner, and what did the Norsundrians want from her? There wasn't anything to torture her for—she didn't know anything that would be of the least use to them. Maybe they were going to use her for target practice, because surely, they didn't expect her to switch sides.

She was too angry to laugh, too afraid to sleep, too sick at heart to lie still.

She swung her feet over the side of the bed, her head panging, and looked wearily around the room. It was plain, the stone walls the same beige color with faint striations of other colors in the individual stones. The furnishings: a bed, desk, chair and wardrobe. A long, narrow mirror had been fitted into the right-hand door of the wardrobe.

She caught her own reflection, startled to see herself in these surroundings. Her white hair hung tousled every which way over Laban's black cloak, which looked ridiculous, the shoulder seams drooping over her arms and the hem dragging filthy and wet behind her heels. She pulled it off and pitched it into a corner, remembering CJ's de-cootie-izing ritual after touching something belonging to a villain. Thinking of CJ led straight to Irenne, who'd loved ridiculous rituals.

Clair's throat tightened again, and she yanked the wardrobe door open. Behind the mirror side hung hooks, bare. The other side held shelves, on which she found, neatly folded, a couple pairs of riding trousers and tunics, one gray and one green, general kid size. The shelf below that contained plain cotton drawers, singlets, and stockings, and a hairbrush, beside a small sewing kit. A cleaning frame had been worked into the outer edges of the wardrobe doors, which scintillated with greenish traces when the doors stood wide open.

She slammed the doors shut, and gazed out the window. Her stomach was too upset for food. The day stretched before her, full of threat, regret, and the anguish of memory. She needed so badly to be home, with the girls, in the comfort of the underground hideout, the forest above. She longed to take her grief out into the forest air, but the Junky and the woodland of home were somewhere far away, and so was CJ, and Clair would have to tell CJ that Irenne had had her throat cut by that villain MV, and the Junky would have Irenne-shaped holes in the main cavern where Irenne used to sit and laugh and preen in her pretty dresses, and her room would be there with all her things . . .

Irenne.

I couldn't save her.

The grief Clair had been trying to squeeze back inside her erupted, engulfing her lungs, her throat, her head. Sobs ripped through her, impossible to stifle. She flopped down on the bed, pulled the pillow over her head, and cried.

"'Experiment.' What's he on about now?" Husky, dark-haired Leef asked, pointing across the lawn to the visitors' barracks where the Mearsiean girl had been assigned.

David mimed a wide-eyed, innocent look. "Maybe she's here to replace us."

General laughter met this. They all knew Detlev was annoyed. Not that he'd commented. It was his silence. The only one he'd spoken to so far was Laban.

Everyone turned to him. "What did he say to you?" David asked.

"Nothing." Laban lifted his good hand, palm up. "Asked for a report, I gave it, he told me I'd done well in picking Clair. I didn't dare tell him she happened to be walking by, and I couldn't find Senrid. I asked him why he thought Clair a good pick, and he said, 'A change in plans.'"

"Ooo-ooooh." Self-mockery put a spin on the ghostly chorus. When Detlev got this short, he was definitely annoyed.

"I thought I'd better tell him that you'd grabbed Terry Larensar, after putting the stone spell on that other girl whose throat you cut," Laban said to MV.

"What did he say?"

"He just said to stash Clair and leave her alone."

"You're going to eat road," Curtas said, jerking his thumb at MV. "For knifing that girl."

"She twisted." MV shrugged in an attempt at carelessness. "Right into the blade. How was I to know she was that stupid?"

"If you can't block an idiot," Roy said, parodying Siamis's mild voice, "then you're even more of an idiot."

"And why did you finger another prisoner?" David demanded. "You didn't learn anything after grabbing Dtheldevor?"

"That was the Base. This is Five. Why can't I run my own experiment?" MV retorted.

Though everyone laughed, David heard the residual emotions underneath as MV cussed them out, causing them to laugh more. MV was angry, and tense, and the reminder of Siamis reawakened their sense of loss at the news that the lighters had captured him and presumably forced him to his death in one of those deadly Selenseh Redian caves.

MV cursed even more vehemently, then said, "As for Terry, he shouldn't have gone for Ferret. Ferret!"

Curtas said, "He might have mistaken him for Noser."

All eyes turned Noser's way. He ducked his head, his bucked front teeth worrying at his chewed, chapped lips, and he clutched his recently dislocated arm tightly against him.

David glowered at him, then at the others, angry and sickened by the knowledge that he'd lost control of what were supposed to be easy orders. What could be easier than "Lie low?" Who would have guessed that peculiar, number-fixated Tahra of Everon would be so determined to hunt his blood after a fight that her brother had forced on him? Or that . . .

He knew he was self-justifying, an exercise in futility. It was almost a relief when the summons came at last.

He turned his attention back to Noser and said, "Here's a direct order. Which will be the first thing I report to Detlev: you stay away from Terry. If he sees you once, I'll break every bone in your body myself."

"After I'm through with him," Curtas muttered.

"Got it, got it," Noser whined. "It's *not* my fault. I thought when you said deal with that Karhin girl, you meant—"

David walked out. On his way to the command bungalow he saw a small figure emerge, running in toddler fashion on his toes. David leaned down to tousle Sveneric's hair, caught a flash of a smile in response, then the child ran out to rejoin his mates across the way.

So Sveneric had been sharing dinner with Detlev. David knew it was too much to hope for a mellowed mood on the latter's part.

"Why," Detlev said on David's entrance, "is there a girl under a stone spell over at detention?"

"I wasn't there, but MV says she twisted into his blade."

"I thought he had better control. It seems I erred."

Aware of that sick sense intensifying even more, David reported, "He says the girl—Irenne—was two heartbeats from death. He'd worked up a stone spell for Rel. Threw it over her instead. I think he said something about soul-binding . . . you will have to discuss his motivation with him, but first, did you know that Efael took him off-world?" David swallowed, looking down, then forcing his gaze back up. "What he did to him?"

"Efael took care to keep his recruitment effort from my notice," Detlev said. "Anger doesn't excuse clumsiness or stupidity. Though it does motivate both."

David wondered if the slight change in tone—the warning—was not about MV.

Then Detlev's tone changed again. "I've been dividing my time between Songre Silde and here, fending off Yeres's attempt to take this compound for herself. And so Efael seems to have decided it's time to take an interest in your training, since I appear to have failed so spectacularly."

That was definitely a warning. David suppressed an inward shudder at what life would be like with Yeres in command of Five, as Detlev said, "She had a plan, now thwarted. He may show up, his excuse looking for recruits."

David acknowledged that with a flick of his fingers, but felt obliged to add, "Noser was jealous at the news that MV got taken. Since MV didn't say anything about what happened to him, I didn't."

"Noser should be safe from Efael. He's too stunted, too eager to please, and not innocent."

David grimaced, then said, "MV's angry over Siamis's death at the hands of the lighters."

"Siamis is not dead." Detlev's face and voice were devoid of emotion. "He walked out of the Selenseh Redian alive. He wasn't captured. He made a bargain with the mage Tsauderei."

Too much, way too fast. David repeated numbly, "A bargain?"

"In trade for his freedom, Siamis traded all our supply stashes for the coming war." And as David gaped at him in astonishment, Detlev said, "Give me your report, then send Mal Venn to me."

Mal Venn. When Detlev used MV's full name, that meant MV was in for a hot time.

David shrugged that off. MV would survive.

Siamis had *betrayed* them?

Then he saw that Detlev was waiting for his report. He began with his orders to Noser, and summarized the rest as succinctly as possible.

His dismissal felt like an escape.

Three

Al-Athann Cave, Aldau-Rayad

"IT'S SO ... *UGLY.*"

Seshe of the Mearsiean girls found herself standing on a cliff overlooking a dead expanse of land, trying to gather her wits after the weirdest magic transfer of her entire life.

She leaned dizzily against a rock, staring outward. In the distance, maybe an hour or two's ride away, in the middle of the featureless, flat land someone had put some kind of military compound — the buildings too alike, too squared, to be a village, with tiny sentries on a wall surrounding it. Beyond it, flat, dusty land stretched to the rim of the world.

Seshe bent and squinted down at the ground below her cliff, her head pounding even after such a small effort. A dreary color midway between brown and gray, the dirt was so hard packed it was cracked. A cold wind swept across the desolation, fingering her hair. She shivered.

And it was then that the physical reaction eased enough for emotional impact: Irenne, funny and flighty and flouncy in ribbons and lace, dead? Clair, taken by Detlev's boy assassins?

Seshe pressed herself back against the rock, denial so strong it was visceral. But the horrible way her throat tightened, almost choking her: she knew it was true. Further, she'd done something really stupid in reaction. She knew nothing about weapons, or tracking, so what could have possessed her to grab her medallion, utter the words to call Hreealdar, and declare that she would find and rescue Clair?

The strangest thing of all was that Hreealdar — after several years of not appearing when the girls called — had appeared right there in Wnelder Vee, and before she'd even finished her *stupid* declaration.

She shut her eyes and let her breath out.

The cold wind buffeting her hot face carried a faint, strange smell that reminded her of the time she reached into a basket and found a long-spoiled onion. It wasn't the same smell, but that was the closest she could come to: an unwelcome, strange scent.

She buried her nose in the shoulder of her coat, then a soft crunching sound, like a hoof on gravel, startled her. She turned. Hreealdar, now in the white horse form, tossed its head, dark eyes glinting in the glare-bright light. The girls had no idea if Hreealdar was he, she, or even a horse; Hreealdar did not smell like a horse, and its belly and flanks were smooth and flat beneath and below the tail, but a creature so large had always seemed *he* as often as *it* to them. The name, even, was something the girls had given the creature, meaning "lightning branch" in Mearsiean.

Hreealdar had been a part of the mysteries of life in Mearsies Heili when Seshe had joined Clair's gang of strays and runaways. They thought he lived in the jewel cave, coming out now and then to range about in the forest. It was Hreealdar who taught all the girls to ride.

Then, after taking Liere fer Eider around the world to break Siamis's enchantment, Hreealdar had vanished, no longer heeding the magical call Clair had so carefully worked into the girls' protective medallions.

Why had Hreealdar heeded Seshe's call this time? Seshe hadn't even been in Mearsies Heili. She'd been on the other side of the world in Wnelder Vee, where the alliance had joined to chase Detlev's boys out of their warded hideaway. Until people started coming back with wounds, then stories of broken bones, and then Irenne's death and Clair's disappearance.

But Hreealdar *had* come, in the form of white light, and then they both were . . .

Here.

She drew in a slow breath against the knot of grief tightening from her throat to her stomach, then looked up at the horse as the wind brushed her long blond hair against the back of her knees. She shivered in her winter coat.

"You brought me here. Why?" she said. "Will I find Clair and Terry on this mountain?"

Hreealdar's blue-white mane shook like rippling snow. Light sculpted over his pure white coat, fluffy-thick and impossibly soft to the touch, unlike regular horsehair.

Seshe turned around again, sighing. Hreealdar did not talk, but the girls had always been convinced he understood them in some way. Now she wasn't sure of anything, except that she stood on this cliff in freezing wind. She brushed her blowing hair out of her face and squinted at the military compound. It was far away enough to look like toy buildings. She remembered someone saying that Detlev had a base on the fifth world out from the sun Erhal. What if that was a Norsundrian base?

What if it was *Detlev's* base? Detlev's boys had taken Clair and Terry . . . if that was true, then . . .

She shivered again, but from reaction, not from the cold. If that was true, then Hreealdar had brought her all the way to another world, the one Norsundrians possessed. Instinct caused her to duck back behind one of the sandy-colored stone outcroppings so she wouldn't be visible from that distant compound. She pressed her crossed arms tightly against her body, struggling against an overwhelming wash of grief — loss — confusion. What now? What *now?*

The white horse shook its mane then moved through what seemed to be a tall, narrow crack in the stone. Seshe followed, stepping carefully past tumbled boulders and huge, jagged sand-colored stones. Here, she halted in surprise, staring down at rows of crystal glowglobes soaking in the sunlight. They'd been laid out in a pattern too regular to be accidental, sheltered by the rocks encircling them, invisible to anyone below.

The white horse's feet clopped on the sandy-colored stone as it stepped into yet another narrow crack, this one dark: a cave, no, a tunnel.

Hreealdar disappeared in a flash, leaving her alone.

Seshe blinked away the afterimage, peered warily at the

dark hole of the tunnel, then walked out and crouched down, hugging her arms in her woolen sleeves tight against her aching chest as she stared out at the distant camp. The wind off the barren plains was cold and dusty, and stung her eyes. Even the light seemed unfamiliar, a glaring pale yellow that hurt her eyes.

She closed them, but memory brought Irenne before her mind's eye, long brown ponytail swinging, a light sprinkling of freckles over her snub nose, lacy lavender skirts swishing about her feet. This time Seshe did not try to fight the tide of emotions flooding her.

Irenne! So moody, funny, and fun. Irenne, with her costumes and roles and unashamed love of frippery — how could she be gone? Her voice so easy to recall, her memory so alive? Seshe could see her wry grin, the light brown tendrils that always wisped out of those fantastical hair styles she dreamed up. Her love for fancy gowns, and dancy music, and her enthusiastic feuds with villains —

Seshe bit hard on her lower lip. Feuds. That was why she was here, really. Memory threw her back to that snowy woodland in Wnelder Vee, where Detlev's boys had made a hideout — which the alliances had entered in challenge. Images hurt like invisible ice: silver-haired Kyale throwing a gloppy pie in Adam's face, and him grinning as he wiped it off his coat. The memory brought back the unsettling idea that Seshe'd had when she saw the boys' reaction to the Junky: *They are human beings.*

How long did it take Detlev to ruin people, turning them into Norsundrian warriors, their lives constrained to destruction and death?

She shook her head. Worrying about Detlev's boys' futures was an exercise in futility. It was obvious that whatever their thoughts, they were perfectly happy doing Detlev's will; if they'd wanted to escape him, they'd had plenty of opportunities to discuss asylum while they were pretending to be allies. The truth was, she hated seeing her friends acting more and more like them. Was that why she was here, because she'd wanted to act before someone else did something irrevocable?

She got to her feet. She'd done something stupid, something no one had asked her to, but Hreealdar had come, and brought her here, and so she might as well see what "here" entailed.

She walked into the darkness of the inner cave, and began treading cautiously, feeling her way to the tunnel Hreealdar's flash had shown her.

The tunnel was dark, of course. Seshe moved slowly, sliding her feet, and with one hand touching the rough, cold stone at her side. For an uncountable time that seemed forever she walked this way, always down. There were twists and turns, but she did not try to count them, or to guess where she was. She just kept moving, until there was no longer any sense of that cold, weird-smelling breeze on her cheek. The air now was still and smelled only of ancient stone.

She kept moving until her feet were numb and she stumbled frequently. Finally, she sank down with her back to the stone wall, put her head on her knees, and slept.

When she woke, she was achy, thirsty, and disoriented. Putting her hands flat behind her, she remembered sinking down, and that she'd been moving to the left. She shuffled to the left and regained her rhythm.

Deprived of sight and sound, her mind ranged straight back to Irenne, a surge of fresh grief welling up. To fight it, for a time she hummed all Irenne's favorite songs. Hreealdar had brought her, so it couldn't be just to get her lost in old caves. These had to lead somewhere.

She worked steadily downwards in the darkness. After another interminable walk, she stopped humming. Thirst was a motivator, but what heartened her was the sense that the ground was smoother. And within a few steps, she turned a corner and beheld glowglobes giving off soft, constant light.

There were definitely people down there. Her heart raced. She stayed silent. What if this were another Norsundrian lair?

A very short time later, she heard high voices echoing off the stone. Kids!

Seshe felt her way to a place where the tunnel branched. She waited beside a rough stone arch, and saw two small, thin, pale-skinned, black-haired figures come prancing down an adjacent tunnel, talking rapidly in a sibilant language she had never heard before. Seshe waited until they had passed, then stepped out from her hiding place and followed them.

The youngsters ran ahead. Thirsty, hungry, puzzled, she trailed them as best she could. They passed from sight very swiftly, but she toiled after the lingering voices.

The voices disappeared abruptly. She ran a few steps, then stumbled to a stop, catching hold of the stone wall next to her, and gazed with awe at a huge cavern. Carved stone pathways curved down to a floor with a natural stone stage, beyond which a dark pool glittered in the light of huge globes set on stone pillars. In the distance water hissed and splashed. Her tongue felt drier than ever.

Narrow ledges like the companionways on a ship wound all around the walls of the cavern at several levels. Off these at opened archways, most with colorful cloth hangings fit neatly into them, and others opening into tunnels. Here and there along the pathways walked tall, thin, fish-pale, dark-haired people in sleeveless dull-colored silk robes hanging to their knees. Older people wore loose silk trousers under the robes, and youngsters mostly seemed to have bare legs as well as arms.

"It's a city," she breathed. But who were these people?

She ghosted up one of the paths and paused outside a cave-hanging, then, with pounding heart, she lifted it aside and slipped into a small room, lit by large silken glowglobes that looked like moons. The room had two little tunnels leading off it. Someone had painted patterns with pleasing geometric shapes around the upper parts of the walls, and had covered the stone ground with a rag rug, on top of which were piled silken cushions.

It was someone's home! She was embarrassed at her nosiness. But before she could back out, a woman spoke. She jerked around. No one there! Then her gaze dropped, and she beheld a picture frame with an old woman in an elaborate hairdo. She had normal, healthy skin color, though her clothes and elaborate curled hair were not at all like those of the thin, pale people. The woman smiled, spoke, and after a pause, spoke again.

Seshe shook her head helplessly, backing away again. The woman did not seem at all perturbed; when Seshe was nearly out of sight—and quite sure the woman in the picture frame could no longer see her—the woman froze into a smiling pose, her eyes staring into space.

It was a lot like the magical captures of people favored by

the wealthy, but unalike in that this woman seemed to interact with the viewer. The portraits Seshe had seen were moments from someone's life, captured by magic and preserved as long as the spells held.

She backed out of the cave — and almost knocked someone flat. Whirling around, she stared into the huge black eyes of a kid: thin face, glossy-smooth braided hair, skinny body that could have belonged to a boy or girl. She tried to apologize, realized her words meant nothing, so she stopped, and tried a smile.

The child spoke — asking Seshe if she were a stranger, but of course she just stared back uncomprehendingly, and watched as the kid touched thin fingers to mouth, then turned and called, "Dom Leotay!"

Seshe watched, and the locals watched her, as a young woman emerged from one of the caves and approached with careful steps. She smiled tentatively, and Seshe smiled back.

Leotay had no idea what to do. But the intruder did not seem the least dangerous. She reached toward Seshe, her fingers not quite touching the stranger's rough-skinned hand, then turned her palm up in a gesture of entreaty, and backed up as she said, "Come." She gestured to follow.

Seshe did. They walked up a steep pathway to a cave separate from the others. From time-to-time people appeared, staring at Seshe with unblinking interest. The people were thin, with thin, smooth skin, so pale they made Chwahir seem healthily dark. One could see blue veins beneath the surface; Seshe looked away quickly, trying to hide her shudder, and tried to find positive attributes. She did not like thinking of living beings ugly. The people's movements were quick and graceful, their eyes black. They reminded her of lizards, which are lovely, quick, elegant creatures.

When they reached the cave, Seshe stopped short when her gaze caught on a fantastic, embroidered tapestry in interwoven patterns of blue and gold. Then a lean, black-haired young man stepped up. Seshe recoiled, then recognized that he was not MV. The two had only height and build in common, and a lithe, strong way of moving, as well as the black hair. But this young man was maybe a few years older than MV, his pulled-back hair braided, not worn short in a military cut, and he wore rippling silk like the other people Seshe had seen so far.

MV wasn't here, but he was probably in that camp she'd seen. Overwhelmed, and dispirited, she wondered how she could have been stupid enough to think she could rescue Clair and Terry. It was unanswerable, so she turned back to the young woman, who gestured for Seshe to come inside the tent, where waited a very old woman sitting on a cushion.

Dom Hildi said to Leotay, "Here is our last sign. You had better teach her to speak to us, had you not?"

Wonderingly, Leotay turned to Seshe, and touched hand to breast. "I am Leotay."

Seshe heard the distinct words and figured out what they had to mean. "I . . . am . . . Seshe."

Four

"The Den" — Aldau-Rayad

CLAIR WOKE UP, AND immediately regretted it.

Grayish light shone in the windows, too diffuse for shadows, but not diffuse enough to kill glare. Her head throbbed worse than ever, her eyes burned, her throat was raw, her mouth dry as the dusty air.

And she was hungry.

For a time, she was tempted to lie there until she died, but that was surrender. She was far too angry to surrender. That anger was enough to get her out of bed. She changed out of her heavy winter clothes, as already the air coming in the window was warm. She brushed out her hair, then tested her door.

Surprise scraped her nerves when it opened. She was a prisoner, and she expected to be treated as a prisoner. The open door — the pretense of freedom — was as sinister as a dungeon full of torture instruments, but in a different way. It meant that the torture was going to be all in the mind.

Escape. She opened her door and stepped out just as two figures pelted up the hallway. She recognized Noser, the short tow-headed boy with his arm bandaged up. He rammed into her, knocking her into the wall. "Out of the way, ugly!" he yelled.

On his heels sprinted black-haired Silvanas, slim and fast and graceful. They took no further notice of her as they ran past, their laughter echoing down the hall, then banged out the far door.

She brushed herself off where Noser had slammed into her, something CJ had taught the girls. Brushing off villain cooties was little kid behavior, but it felt good to do it.

Then she left the dormitory building and headed across what she decided she'd call grass, though it wasn't like any grass she'd ever seen. She was surprised to see how little the compound resembled her idea of a Norsundrian garrison, except in the plainness of the buildings, without any ornamentation. The single-story blocks were laid out at right angles to one another, divided by those trees with the long glossy fronds.

The aromas of baked bread and braised fish drifted from the left. She hesitated, then decided to test the limits of her "freedom" while planning escape. One thing her cousin Puddlenose had told her time and again: when in trouble, spot at least one avenue of escape. And the second rule was, grab any meal you found, if the enemy wasn't stepping on your heels. Escape always went better after food.

She followed her nose to a building with windows down one side, dark against the glare outside. When she tried to peer in, she made out the shapes of tables and benches.

She opened the door. Her heart sank when she saw that the room wasn't empty. Four men in gray uniforms sat together, and two younger ones in riding clothes sat apart. At another table two women talked in low voices, one young, one old. They glanced at Clair, the younger one smirking with contempt, the older one with flat indifference, then bent toward one another to continue their conversation.

The urge to sit near them vanished. Clair drifted along the perimeter, trying to stay as far away from them as possible, until she reached the long table laden with trays of food. A stack of plates sat at a corner, hefty ceramic mugs next to it. She picked up a plate and moved along to inspect the trays: fried bread with a dish of dark berry compote to put on it; boiled grain with honey; baked eggs; grilled fish; tossed greens. Water, coffee, steep that smelled even more bitter than the coffee, berry juice.

She chose fried bread, berry compote, eggs, and water, and scanned quickly, noting that the tables were mismatched, some with elaborate raptor legs and carving along the edges, others plain, old, and battered. Same with the chairs. They were a wild variety of styles, dominated by great wingback chairs with carved edging. There were also battered benches.

She picked a small table in a corner farthest from anyone else, with her back to the room, though her shoulder blades crawled, and she fought against the impulse to keep looking behind her for poopsies creeping up to attack. But she hoped no one would notice her if her back was to them.

She ate as fast as she could then left, dropping her dishes in a tub on the way out, as she saw others do. The greenish sparkle of magic shimmered round the edges of the tub.

When she got outside she began a circuit of the buildings, keeping close to walls, and stopping at each corner to peer around before progressing. She kept expecting some slavering Norsundrian to jump at her, waving a bloodied sword and shouting threats. Whenever she caught sight of people she headed in another direction, until at last she spotted a stone wall. It was fairly high, but she was a good climber given any hint of toehold and grip.

She saw a couple sentries walking back and forth along the top of the wall, glancing outward. Sometimes they stopped and talked to each other. She watched them pace back and forth five or six times, then slunk along the back of a long building, below some high windows, and spotted the adjacent wall. This was not an enormous compound. She didn't know if that was bad or good. Depended on what was outside of it.

This wall had a gate, above which she made out the tops of jutting mountains in the distance. At home she'd say that was a maybe an easy morning's ride away, but that was at home. A pair of sentries walked along the top of this wall, too.

Further exploration furnished a third wall, with its pair of sentries. None of them ever walked as far as the corners, nor did they seem very alert. Same with the fourth wall.

It couldn't be this easy. But she was going to try. She watched, and when a pair stopped to chat with each other, ran for a corner and scrabbled hard, trembling as she shoved her shoes into the cracks between the stones. With a grunt and a heave, she pulled her way to the top. Then stared out in dismay at a flat, featureless plain. Turning her head into the cold, odd-smelling wind, she saw the same in all directions save that of the gate, with its ridge of blue-gray mountains beyond. Dust obscured the range's features, but they looked rocky, without any greenery.

Her hand slipped — she twisted her head to glance over her shoulder. One of the sentries plainly saw her, but turned away, clearly disinterested in her movements.

She slipped back down again, and wiped her scraped hands on her pants. No wonder those sentries were so lazy! There was nowhere to run. What were they looking for? An invading army? A monster attack?

The cold, weird-smelling wind sprayed dust over her face, and she wondered if it was *weather* they watched for.

She began to retrace her steps, this time not bothering to watch for threats. When she recognized the main square, she crossed toward the building they'd stuck her in, then spied a broad-shouldered boy coming her way. Dark of hair and skin, large of build, he was either the silent one, Rolfin, or Leefan, his brother or cousin. They looked alike to her.

She veered around the side of another building, and continued the long way, eventually finding her room. She stood in the middle of it, hating everything. What to do now?

To kill time she searched the desk and found paper and pens and ink. She scrawled a couple of insults against Norsunder in big letters, and propped the paper up on the desk where it could be seen if anyone came in the door. Anyone nosing would get what they deserve, she thought — and then she frowned ruefully. If they could read Mearsiean, that is.

She walked through the cleaning frame, which took the grime off her hands, but not the raw scrapes. She threw herself on the bed and shut her eyes, but sleep would not come.

She lay restlessly, fighting against memory, and in desperation rose and decided to risk the outside again. She scanned before emerging, and headed for a clump of those odd trees. Halfway there, she was surprised when a group of small children, anywhere from two to five, streamed out of a building, whooping and yodeling. She quickly withdrew under a tree and sat with her back against it as the little ones organized themselves into a game of tag.

The idea of Norsundrian children was nauseating. Hadn't someone said that the Birth Spell couldn't come to Norsundrians? Or was it that anyone who chose Norsunder never wanted children? After all, Wan-Edhe of the Chwahir, the evilest person Clair had ever heard of before the entry of Detlev into their lives, had had children — whom he had killed off eventually. But he'd had them. That prompted the question: where had Detlev's boys come from? Laban had said something about finding. That probably meant stealing.

When a young man opened a door in a low building and whistled, the youngsters ran back inside the building again. Clair sat where she was for a long time, knees hugged tight to her chest. It hurt so bad to think about home, but she didn't fight it. That seemed disloyal somehow, as if she were denying Irenne's memory.

And memory was so clear, painfully so. It had been a spring day when she had finally learned how to do magic transfers, and she'd gone to the Destination on one of the Tornasio Islands, which belonged to Mearsies Heili even though two small countries lay between it and the bay in which the islands were centered.

She was distracted by the sight of a ship luffing into the harbor. She'd sat on a low wall and watched until a group of youngsters ran down the ramp, gear bags bumping on their backs. Most didn't give her a second look — they were teens on the Wander, probably working aboard to earn their keep.

Mincing down the ramp last was a lively girl with a long, light brown ponytail, her buttercup-yellow skirts swinging. At the bottom, she looked around and exclaimed in Sartoran, "Well!"

No one paid her any more attention than they'd paid Clair.

"What?" Clair called.

The girl turned her way, smiled, and said, "White hair! Are you one of the singing cave people? No, I can see you don't have talons instead of fingernails. They all say the morvende have talons, as well as white hair."

"I have just the white hair," Clair had said. "Who are you and where did you come from?"

"Irenne," said she. *Ihr-REN-neh*, three notes, like a bird call. "And today I am a runaway princess. No, a duchas, I think, chased by an evil . . . dragon?"

"What kind of dragon?" Clair asked. "Air, water, or fire?"

She could still picture Irenne as she met her that day, the few freckles on a short nose with a little bump in the middle, her hazel eyes that sometimes looked blue, her ragged gown obviously made for someone shorter and wider, with ribbon lacing up the bodice, ribbon that didn't match the yellow dress.

At the end of their conversation, Clair had said, "Where I live there's a group of girls who really like storytellers. Would you like to spend some time with us?"

"I'd like that right well!"

And so Irenne had ended up staying, just like that. Life then was so much easier, when the worst villain they knew of was Jilo of the Chwahir, his so-malevolent intent to take their underground hideout, because his Chwahir masters wouldn't let him have one for his own.

A sudden wind kicked up in the late afternoon, bringing dust and cold, dry air. With nothing else to do, she went to the mess hall again, to find that most of Detlev's boys were there. She backed toward the door again, then recoiled as someone entered from behind her. She sidestepped to her right, flicking a fast side-eye. Fine, curly unkempt hair floating above his shoulders, brown eyes — it was Adam.

The blond one, David, glanced up, then said, "Hands."

Adam stopped short, and studied his widespread fingers. "It's just paint. I put on a clean shirt. See?"

"You really want to wash every dish in the place if he turns up?"

The slight emphasis on *he* had to mean Detlev. Why would Detlev insist his assassins have good manners? Oh, of course. They were spies. It would be easier to abandon manners to fit into one's company than to assume something one had never been taught.

Adam turned around. Tense, breath held, Clair noted his eyelids flicker to both sides. Surely he saw her, though he didn't react as he walked past her to the door again, sighing the words, "It's *only* paint. And it takes forever to scrub off."

Clair slipped out behind him and marched back across the lawn to her room. The first thing she saw when she got inside was the note she'd written. She let out a bitter laugh. Would it intimidate anyone in this place? Of course not.

She ripped it up and sat down to write out the *Kanis Sel*

Deris—Mearsies Heili's principal laws as recited by new rulers being crowned, and by everyone else each New Year's Firstday. She found those old laws soothing in the quaintness of old Mearsiean, written with the best of human spirit to benefit all.

Five

TWO DAYS PASSED, EACH one exactly like the one before. She decided that Detlev was using boredom against her—but boredom was still preferable to Norsundrian company. She avoided all contact with the denizens of the compound, and sat in her room when the mess hall was full. She only ventured out for meals when it was relatively free of Norsundrians, and never when Detlev's boys were there.

To hurry along the slow drip of time, she wrote long letters to the girls, describing every happy memory of Irenne she could think of. Then she ripped them up when she was done, so that Detlev's gang would not see them and laugh disparagingly.

It was satisfying to watch the bits of paper vanish when she dropped them into the wastebasket. Its magic, like the cleaning frame, whiffed of metal: dark magic.

Finally, driven by unbearable restlessness, she began to venture out to explore the buildings. She stumbled on a small library, but all the books were written in what she guessed was the Norsundrian version of Sartoran. She sat down with one to try to puzzle out the alphabet, and teased out enough (mostly from the diagrams of what seemed to be battle lines) to perceive that the book was unsurprisingly on some military subject, so she put it away.

The morning after her expedition, she'd just sat down with her breakfast—she kept her back to a wall, the better to see danger coming—when she heard a step behind her. Somebody was breaking the invisible wall she'd tried hard to build around her. Alarmed zinged through her nerves as she recognized unkempt brown curls framing wide-set brown eyes, and a wide mouth curved into a smile bracketed at either side by deep dimples. "Adam."

"May I join you?" He indicated his tray.

"Can't stop you." Her shoulders hunched up in an angry shrug.

Adam sat down adjacent to her, his back to the corner, and buttered a roll. She looked at his thin, paint-stained fingers, and the unruly brown curls straggling down over his high forehead. He was the first to have fooled them: even now, after all that had happened, it was difficult to believe he was anything evil. His long-lashed eyes had always seemed dreamy and vague, his mouth curled in habitual good humor. But she'd seen how his eyes flicked to both sides, though his expression didn't change.

He looked so harmless in his paint-splotched, baggy green tunic and dark trousers—though his hands were pink from being freshly scrubbed, except for those stubborn paint stains in the beds of his nails. The poopsies didn't wear the Norsundrian uniform, and for the first time she wondered why not. But she was not going to ask. Showing any interest in them felt too much like giving in.

"I hate to eat alone," he said, looking up. His eyes crinkled as he smiled. "And since you were a friend once . . ."

"Until you betrayed us."

His eyelids lifted. "Betrayed whom?"

"You certainly betrayed Karhin Keperi."

His smile vanished. He shook his head, saying, "I had nothing to do with that."

"Maybe you weren't there," Clair said, "but at least one of your friends was, and you did nothing to stop it. Then there's Irenne. Who *liked* you. All that stuff about loving art when you're nothing but murderers."

"I do love art." Adam looked away, then picked up his fork. "I've never killed anyone."

"You plural, your group. Where do you all come from, anyway? Orphans, or did Detlev murder your families?"

"Most are orphans," Adam said, studying this girl who he knew had traveled all over, looking for girls to rescue, and had made them into a family. "Some have relatives, very much alive."

Her undisguised horror, reinforced by hatred and revulsion on the mental plane, doused any impulse to mention his own family — never met. But he knew where they lived. He'd been there once, in secret, to see what they looked like.

So he changed the subject. "I'm the only one who likes sketching."

She watched as his smile twitched, rueful, mildly mocking. "Though Curtas gets distracted by fine buildings, David plays a reed pipe well enough, and Laban has a taste for fine . . . hmmmm." He hummed the last, his gaze diffuse.

Clair had no interest in Laban's pretensions. "If you don't see the difference between us, then it's not worth discussing."

"Then we won't discuss it," Adam retorted lightly. "Do you have any questions about the Den?"

"Den?"

He shrugged, his fingers opening outward. "What we call this place."

"Just how to get out of here, so I can go home."

He gave a soundless laugh, then returned to his food.

"Why am I here?"

"For that kind of question, you probably ought to ask Detlev."

"And get beaten up? I'm not that stupid."

"He doesn't thrash us," Adam said. "Says we get enough of that already — which we do — and all it does is reinforce an apparent hierarchy. But if we flout orders, or fight among ourselves, he has a nasty habit of inventive exercises that force us together. His favorite is to dump us on the top of some mountain, and go do something else while we find each other and struggle to survive the descent. We had rather a lot of those after, ah, um, we used to fight a lot. The last one was, ah, not that long ago." He laughed silently.

"I wish," she said, "you were still floundering in the snow."

His smile quirked into mockery, but then his gaze unfocused, as if he looked back in memory. Then he twitched a shoulder. "The point is, he never does that for asking questions. If you want something to do, likewise ask."

"Uh huh. I really want to be sent out to spy, betray, and murder."

Adam grinned. "You don't have the training for any of those."

"Nor do I want it." Clair sighed, then went for bluntness. "You lot might get dumped onto mountains, but I'm a prisoner, so I'm waiting for the whips and chains."

"Not here." Adam's expression blanked.

"Well, that's something. I wondered if you were about to deny that you do that as well." She was about to demand Terry's whereabouts, but halted, wondering if mentioning him would somehow endanger them both.

"Do you hold me responsible for what Aldon or Bostian do?" Adam asked, in a voice so devoid of malice she felt unsettled, as much as she had when CJ crashed a porcelain mug over Laban's head while he sat tied up and defenseless.

Clair pressed her lips together, determined not to answer, to provoke him, or to allow herself to be further provoked.

Adam said, "Curious. I don't hold you responsible for what Vandraska Ghandorjien does on Ama Hazanth, or what the Velethi do on the continent just above yours, all in the name of peace, harmony, and order. And yet these are your allies?"

"They aren't *my* allies. I don't know any of them." She was not going to be sidetracked into defending actions of kingdoms she had never heard of, though they might be allies of ones she did know. "I hold you responsible for what Detlev does."

"And I can't stop you." His hand lifted, palm out. "While you're here," he said, "you'll have relative freedom. Ask for something to do if you're bored."

She sat back, trying to find words to express her disgust. As she did her medallion shifted, and Adam's gaze flicked to it. "That necklace, your entire group wears them, don't you?"

Clair shrugged, instantly wary at the subject-change.

"May I see it?"

Clair's heart thudded against her ribs. No one had ever asked about the girls' medallions. She leaned out so the medallion dangled, worked with Mearsies Heili's six star-shaped lilies representing the six provinces.

Adam leaned forward and squinted at the carving with the intent focus of the artist, then nodded and sat back. "It has protective magic on it, doesn't it?" he asked at last.

"Yes," she said, wondering if he'd been ordered to ask about it. And then, because she couldn't resist, "What's happened to Terry? Or is he just target practice?"

Adam sighed. "He's now Curtas's —"

He was interrupted by a call from across the room. "Adam."

Adam's head lifted, and he smiled a welcome. "David!"

"Thought you'd be gone." It was the soft voice Clair had first heard in the tree platform deep in the boys' Wnelder Vee hideaway.

"Tomorrow." Adam beckoned to the tall blond boy.

And I'll starve to death before I'll sit down to eat with the captain of Irenne's murderers, Clair thought, dropping her fork onto her half-eaten meal and rising to her feet.

Adam gave a startled exclamation, but she ignored him. She met David's eyes, which were a lighter brown than Adam's, their expression one of amused awareness. She hoped her own face was as cold and hateful as her heart felt, then she turned her shoulder and walked away.

No one stopped her.

Outside, she ran until she reached her room. There she stood with her back to the door, trying to control her breathing. Ask for something to do! Working for Norsundrians!

She shook her head violently and went out to walk off her bad mood.

This time she struck out in an unfamiliar direction, and before she'd gone long, she saw someone moving slowly between two buildings. The peculiarity of his gait made her step toward a tree to block herself from view, but then she recognized Terry, his limp the worst she'd ever seen it.

He lurched against a wall, rebounded and staggered around a corner.

Dashing after, she called, "Wait — Terry."

He stopped, and she caught up, breathing hard.

Terry peered at her in confusion, his face marked with red patches that were fast forming into bruises, his hair in his eyes and his clothing a mess.

Clair's insides gripped with fear-chill. "What happened?"

Terry heard the words, but their sense took longer to form. His entire body hurt too much for him to say *I was looking for something to eat*. It took all his concentration to raise his good hand and wipe his hair out of his eyes. "Food . . ." Weird, how it looked like someone else's hand, but then it felt like someone had removed his head and put a red-hot ball of pain to wobble on his neck. His fingers collided with his nose, and he winced and dropped his hand. The other hand, with the three missing fingers, stayed tucked in his armpit.

"Come on." She took his arm and pulled him. He was taller and heavier than she, and kept weaving.

After a brief resistance he came willingly enough, though his pace was just as unsteady as before. It seemed to take forever, but no one interfered with them as they made their way slowly to Clair's building, and then to her room.

As soon as she had him inside, he squinted at the bed, seemed to recognize what it was, mumbled something, then flopped headlong on it. His eyes closed. Clair watched for a short time, uncertain whether to try waking him. Finally she dug in the wardrobe, pulled out an extra blanket she'd seen there, and snapped it over him.

Then she left, and started toward the mess hall. Halfway there she hesitated, wondering if seconds were forbidden — if anyone would even notice. Adam and his killer captain were gone. She shrugged, marched to the table, piled a plate high with bread and two chicken-and-vegetable-pies and fruit, and no one stopped her from taking it out.

Back in her room, she put the meal on her desk. Then she sat down in her chair to wait. And dozed off from sheer boredom, snapping awake when she heard a soft groan. She rubbed her stiff neck.

Terry stirred, mumbling something. His eyes opened — or one of them did. The other was purple and swollen. "Where am I?"

"My room," Clair said. "I don't know if this means trouble — if they'll accuse us of conspiracy or something, but — "

"There *might* be trouble? That's a great joke." Terry sat up and winced. "Heyo, what's that?"

"Food. You said 'food' so I figured you might be hungry."

"I was." Terry reached with his good hand, and despite bruised knuckles grabbed the bread and crammed it into his mouth.

Clair waited until he paused for breath, then said, "Why do you look like you went through a sieve the hard way?"

Terry squinted at her wide, innocent gaze. Most of the

alliance were well under the threshold for understanding the agonizing intimacy of being in love, or the even worse anguish when that person — the light, graceful red-haired Colendi girl you adored so much you saw her every night in your dreams — was dead, murdered on a whim.

He blew out his breath. "You seem to be doing all right."

Clair blinked at that answer, but she saw no malice in his face.

"As I should be doing," he went on grimly as he struggled to control himself. He ought never to have gone to Wnelder Vee in the first place. His pretense of helping the alli-ance had been just that. He'd come with one purpose, to kill, with his own hands, the sack of shit who'd murdered Karhin Keperi.

Well, he'd failed in all possible ways, and so, bitter with disgust at himself, he tried to make a joke of it, out of lifelong habit. "But no, I nobly refused to eat. Or to leave the room they'd stuck me in. Then today I was too hungry to stick it out, and tried to sneak to the mess hall. Before I got there up came Curtas, one of the ones who pretended friendship with Karhin. And though he was not the one who . . . killed her," his voice broke on the word *killed*. "He didn't stop it. Maybe he even watched. So I jumped him."

It seemed more like Terry got jumped. But Clair didn't want to say it.

"Or I tried. Mistake." Terry carefully fingered his eye. "When Curtas knocked me off-balance and walked away, I tried to strangle him from behind. MV appeared and handed me my ass. Several times over, in case I might have missed his meaning the first, second, and fifth times."

"Do you have a room to yourself?"

He flashed a brief, pained attempt at a smile. "This place seems to be full of empty rooms. So, yes." He took a few more bites, then said, "This is stupid. No. I'm stupid. Do you know why we're even here?"

"Did you have an interview with Detlev?"

"No." His eyes widened — or one did. "At least I was spared *that*. Why, did you have one? What happened?" He peered more closely. "You're still alive."

It was obvious that Terry was laboring under the effects of a murderous headache. "I think we're an experiment," Clair said. "I'm not sure what for. Maybe they want to turn us into poopsies?"

"Me?" Terry's bruised face shifted as a brief grin flared. "Poopsies. I know most think that's stupid, but I thought it pretty funny. I'm certain MV would love to be known far and wide as MV the Cruel Assassin, or MV the Sinister Archvillain, but never as MV the Poopsie." His expression changed. "As I guess I'll go down in history as Tereneth the Cripple-King who appeared and disappeared in the blink of an eye."

"They'll miss you in Erdrael Danara," Clair said.

"My friend Halad will miss me, and my one good cousin, who incidentally would be a far better king than I. But all the wrong ones will be jostling to fill my place, once they decide I'm really gone."

At least your great-grandmother did not come back to replace you, she thought, then hated herself for disloyalty.

But something of her thought must have shown in her face because Terry stopped eating and frowned at her. "We're quite a pair, aren't we? Maybe that's why they grabbed us. Easily replaced underage monarchs — me underage by a year. I wonder if they think they're going to turn us into them and send us back against our replacements?"

"All I want to think about," Clair said, "is how to escape."

"Did you try?"

"Yes. But there's nothing beyond the wall. I mean nothing but wind and flat land. We're going to have to escape by magic."

"All right, I'm with you. What's your strategy so far?"

"To be boring," she said decisively. "I know fighting them would be useless. Any of them, including that Noser, especially him, can easily be meaner for longer." She saw how anguish tightened Terry's battered face at the mention of the boy who'd killed Karhin, and she said quickly, "I want to bore them so much they ignore me, and maybe I can find some magic books."

"Then what?"

"Find a way to put together world-transfer magic," she said, fingering her medallion.

"Maybe I'll ask for work in the stable. I might overhear something useful," Terry said, feeling his jaw carefully.

Clair remembered something Adam had said. "I hope Curtas isn't the type for feuds."

Terry shrugged. Clair could tell from his expression that he wouldn't really mind a feud all that much.

Six

ROY WAS OUT AT the practice field, relieving pent-up feelings by sending one round of arrows after another into the targets, when a brief contact came, the familiar mental signature of Detlev.

Rolfin had been sitting on the edge of the fence, offering pungent one-word criticisms of hair-breadth misses, infrequent as they were. When Roy unstrung the bow and stashed it, Rolfin sent a look Roy's way, flicking his forefinger to his forehead, the signal for Detlev. "Best hoof it."

Roy did not need the advice.

He assumed that Detlev had finally read the report that Roy had spent half a year writing, comparing the strengths and weaknesses of light magic against dark, after his studies while living under cover in Bereth Ferian, and attending the mage school there.

He arrived at the HQ a short time later, pausing only to straighten out his shirt and finger his hair back into a semblance of neatness. The aide waved him through without looking up from his copy-work.

Detlev was inside, sitting on the edge of his desk staring out through the trees. When Roy entered, he saw his report lying neatly stacked on the table near Detlev's hand.

Roy held his breath. He'd labored hard to avoid the

appearance of partisanship, to attain complete neutrality. But Detlev was a close reader, and had no impatience for inexact thinking or unsupported opinion.

"An admirably thorough job," Detlev said. "As far as you got."

"It would take another five years of study to master mirror wards and lattices, then compare them in any meaningful way," Roy said. "I barely understand the concept now."

"Yes, I am aware." Detlev studied him. Roy braced for that, his mind-shield, habitual from early life, as hard as he could make it. "Do you think you achieved objectivity, then?" There was of course only one answer, if the question even had to be asked, and Detlev cast him an amused glance. "Do you think objectivity is possible?"

Roy was not certain what he should say, so why not say what he believed? "No."

"There are many," Detlev said, "who regard an endeavor at scrupulous objectivity as an effort to hide something."

Roy's body had stilled, except for his thundering heart.

Detlev lifted the papers toward the window. "Roy, I want you to tutor Clair."

"Me?" Roy blinked. "I thought that was Laban's job."

"No, his orders were to select an appropriate candidate. And I was pleased that he was able to look past his regrettable focus on Everon and its environs. He will have other orders presently, once I return from examining the wards along Venn border—which, incidentally, might be a future project for you." Detlev smiled. "Offended?"

Roy shoved his hands in his pockets. "Why me?"

"You are offended. It is meant as a tribute to your patience, Roy."

Roy sorted the words carefully and tightened his fists in his pockets.

"Show her around. Teach her the written language."

"And then?"

"And then anything else you think she ought to learn."

Roy shrugged.

"Any questions?" Detlev asked.

Roy shook his head.

Detlev made a gesture of dismissal and Roy effaced himself.

He cursed under his breath all the way to the mess hall.

Seven

CLAIR DIDN'T SEE TERRY again for a couple of days. She hated not knowing if he was all right, but she was afraid that asking might make things worse for him. She hated pain, and fear, and would loathe being tossed into a dungeon. Yet that kind of behavior would at least let her know what to expect.

This surface-easy life worried her.

She existed, drawing bad pictures with the paper and pens in her desk then shredding them. She wrote letters and shredded those, too, and went to meals not because she was hungry, but because it was something to do.

She'd lingered in the nearly-empty mess hall one afternoon, sipping a berry concoction as slowly as she could. When it was done, she walked out, and turned her mind to getting through the rest of the afternoon.

Then the sense of time lying heavily upon her vanished when she heard footfalls approaching from behind. Instantly wary, she jerked around, and recognized the long, homely face and narrow, observant eyes of Roy.

"Walk with me," he said—no longer with the Geth accent.

"Where?" she asked, her mind flashing back to the dungeons she'd laughably thought she'd prefer. No, she wouldn't.

"Over here, under the trees, will do."

He headed to where the broad, blue-green leaves longer

than she was overlapped enough to blend their shadows and slightly cool the dry air. She sank down on a shady spot, and he dropped down on the ground next to her.

Clair scowled down at the sturdy fabric covering her drawn-up knees. It pained her to remember the liking she'd had for Roy. He'd even saved her life once. That thin scar on his forehead where he'd bashed his head against the hull of Dtheldevor's schooner while holding Clair by the wrist, keeping her from being hurled away by the wind into a typhoon, was a reminder of that.

She'd liked Roy even more than Adam, who was a good listener, but he was an artist, who'd liked talking more about light and color than about history and language. Roy could talk about history and language and magic, subjects Clair loved, and he'd read so much more than she.

"Were you really born on Geth?" she asked. "Or was that story as fake as your accent?"

"Spent some years there. The accent became habit."

"While learning their magic secrets so you could get yourself sent to my world to infiltrate the northern school?" Clair asked, shifting from side to side. She hated being angry, but righteous anger was so much easier—it hurt so much less—than grief. And because her anger *was* righteous, she had to provoke him, to keep flinging accusations until he acted like the villain he was, or went away. "How awful, to think that the first student Geth ever sent was *you*, instead of someone who can help both worlds against evil."

"The next will be Dak," Roy said, as if she'd made a comment, not an accusation. "In fact, I think he's already there."

Clair clenched her fists on her knees, knowing this was one argument she would never win.

"Would you like something to do?" Roy asked.

"What's happened to Terry?" she snapped.

"He asked for work in the stable. So he's there."

She let out her breath slowly.

"I can see that you're angry," Roy began.

"Remembering that one of *your* friends killed Irenne will do that," she flashed, sarcasm twisting the word *friends*. "And she didn't even have a weapon, so save your breath if you plan to claim it was a fair fight, like Glenn's murder." Then, in case her anger would somehow rebound onto Terry, "Terry's really all right? They haven't decided to murder him, too?"

"He's really all right. Except for the lumps he collected after jumping Curtas from behind."

"As Curtas deserved," Clair said stoutly. "He was supposedly Karhin's friend, another who had never touched a weapon in her life. Did he stand by and watch her die?"

"He wasn't there." Roy stared into the distance, tension in his high forehead and around his eyes.

His dark clothes didn't quite hide his bony thinness. Why didn't he eat well? She thought of the food in the mess hall, there all day for anyone when they wanted. Not that he was weak. She remembered his strength and stamina from the sea voyage they'd shared with Arthur.

He blinked and turned a blank gaze her way. "I can fill you in if you have questions. Adam said you were ignorant of how things run here."

"And I'm happy to stay that way," she answered. "Cooperative I can be. Enough to stay alive. Obedient, I won't."

Roy grinned, a wide grin that changed his face. Even his ears seemed to stick out more, making the shaggy tufts of dark hair around them wing out. She returned a stony face, though she couldn't help remembering how much fun he'd been to talk to while they sat on the weather deck, even when he was challenging her ideas. And with the others, even when he beat them at some game requiring skill and strength he'd been — decent. Dtheldevor had liked him a lot as well.

"Eventually they'll want to test you," Roy said, breaking into her thoughts. "Would you rather have one of the others explain things — MV, or David — or me?"

"Don't make me sick," she said, deliberately rude.

"Afraid of them?" The sarcasm was gone now.

She opened her mouth to deny, then thought the better of it. "Of course I am. So?"

"Trying to get enough of an answer to establish some ground. All right, so you want to keep your distance, and when you can't, survive the encounter without collecting your own set of lumps, right?"

She jerked her shoulders up to her ears and down, which was all she could bring herself to do in assent.

"Then here's the setup. We've got relative freedom here, and so have you. There are a few rules, the first of which is, if someone above you in the chain of command gives you an order, you carry it out."

"I'll argue when I feel it's right."

Roy made a negating motion, his face serious. "You don't understand. With Detlev, you can argue all you want to. And with David—most of the time. But any of the others who come through here, argue, or refuse to obey, and you'll be the one to regret it."

Clair considered. "What you're saying is, if I don't want orders from any of the others, I stay out of their notice. Right?"

"If you smell trouble, make the woodwork your home," he said. "The Den is mostly ours, but if any of the Norsundrian captains favored by the Host of Lords show up, anything can happen. And probably will, depending on their whim." His tone flattened.

"I would never want to meet any of them, so I have no problem with this order."

"It's more like practical advice," he said sardonically. "Want a guided tour?"

She shrugged. "I guess."

"Meet me at breakfast tomorrow and I'll take you around. I have things to do right now." He added this last with a squint at the sky.

She rose, squashing the impulse to say something polite, "Okay, see you tomorrow." Politeness seemed too much like giving in.

Roy got to his feet and loped off, disappearing in the gathering gloom.

Clair walked off more slowly and thought about her conversation with Terry. She remembered her discomfort at his unhidden enthusiasm at the thought of a feud with Curtas. She knew the difference between her allies and these Norsundrians, of course, but still the question remained: when did one cross the line into evil—or back? Did good intentions negate evil actions . . . and how should one regard good actions from someone avowedly evil?

Good manners made it possible to live with others. Part of civilization was kindness, and trust. And then, suddenly, she remembered one of those long conversations with Roy while the summer sunlight faded to brilliant color over the western sea. The subject was the polite lie. He'd criticized the Colendi for their diplomatic talk, specifically their hundreds of ways to say no without actually speaking the word.

In less poetic and admiring terms, he'd said, *what they do is make an art of lying to your face.*

But their meaning is clear, and their intention benevolent, she'd said, even though she hadn't been sure, as she'd only met the Keperis, who were kindly and well-meaning. *They do it to avoid conflict. That has to count for good.*

Does a lie ever really achieve good? he'd retorted.

She frowned, trying to remember how they'd resolved it. Memory hazed into a jumble of other thoughts. She shook her head to clear it, and walked back to her room to get her coat.

She went to dinner late, and when she was coming out, her heart nearly stopped when she found herself suddenly face to face with Detlev. He gave her a brief nod, and waited for her to pass before he went into the mess hall.

Good manners. Maybe that made them better spies. But not better people.

She'd been asleep for some time when nightmare struck.

Irenne walked through swirling snow, threads of crimson streaming down her neck as she stumbled on and on, blood-smeared hands outstretched, crying out for the girls, for Clair.

But Clair was frozen as a tree, unable to move, to speak.

The dream changed, and Roy, MV, and the rest ran into view. Then Roy extended his hands like claws and turned into a dragon. His roar whooshed past like a cold wind, and the terror diminished to nothing, leaving her free to wander into the dark, desolate dreamscape filled with dust, heat, weird trees, and gray-uniformed shadows menacing, watching . . .

She woke at last, tangled in the bed sheets, her eyes gritty. She got up and stripped the bed to put the sheets through the cleaning frame in the wardrobe, her limbs heavy. She was more tired than when she'd gone to bed. As she made up the bed again and changed, she tried to rid herself of the dream's aftermath.

Roy was there at breakfast. He regarded her with an air of inquiry.

She knew what it meant: he was inviting her, wordlessly, to sit with him. And at home that would have been enough to turn her steps automatically, whether she wanted to or not. Now she felt a strong urge to turn her face and sit elsewhere.

Why the overwhelming desire to be rude? She had already spoken more rudely here than she ever had in her life. But rudeness was not going to bring Irenne back to life. Or get Clair home again.

"You look determined," Roy commented.

She wouldn't be rude anymore, but she would tell the truth. "Determined to get out of here."

Roy's eyes narrowed in amusement. "Your being here surprised us, too," he responded. "But Detlev wanted someone interesting for his experiment, and Laban picked you."

Clair imagined what CJ would say to that. She could almost hear her voice, high and clear, a steady stream of insults, and a sharp wave of homesickness swamped her right up to her throat. How she wished CJ were here so they could fight this mess together! Which was about as selfish a thought as she'd ever had.

But CJ wasn't here. Clair tried to steady herself with gratitude that CJ and the other girls had been spared.

Except for Irenne.

Grief and anger prompted her to speak. "So Detlev thinks I will turn into a poopsie?"

"Poopsies." Roy's lips parted in a silent laugh. "I love that word," he said. "Who made it up? Has to be CJ."

Actually, it had been Dtheldevor, though CJ had been the first to take it up. But mindful of making anyone a target, Clair shrugged. "Let me ask another way. Is the intent here to turn me against my kingdom or my allies?" A more horrible thought struck her. "Or to take away my ability to think for myself at all?"

Roy's eyes widened. "You don't think we can think for ourselves?" He seemed to be deriving a great deal of inner enjoyment from her reaction.

"Not," she said, "in any way I'd call thinking. But I'm sure you're all very good at making plans for committing various rotten acts and carrying them out."

"Thinking, for you, would be breaking away from Detlev, right?"

Clair hesitated on the verge of saying "Yes." His tone, the extra snap to certain consonants, warned her she was being led into some kind of verbal trap. "What do you expect?" she said instead. "You know how I feel about a lot of important things. We talked about them enough on that trip we took."

"You remember that."

"Of course I do."

"And finding out that I am one of Detlev's 'poopsies' makes everything I said then a lie, and everything we agreed on a mockery?" The edge had now shifted grip to a point.

Clair considered as she finished the last bite of her berry tart, then said honestly, "I keep expecting you to use my words against me somehow. Though I can't say you lied about where you came from—as I remember none of you actually said, except for Geth—but you hid the truth. You were spying on us. And what's the purpose of spying but to get information to use against people?"

Roy's expression shuttered as his hands closed around his coffee mug. Clair realized her eggs-and-potatoes were congealing. She made herself pick up her fork and eat.

Finally, Roy said, "Nothing you told me then, or since, would enable me to conquer Mearsies Heili."

If only she could believe that.

As if Roy heard the thought, he said, "And of course you consider that as suspect as you would my assurance that I don't mean you any harm."

Clair set her fork down. "As if I should believe you?"

"When have I lied to you?"

She shook her head. "We both know you didn't do anything nasty on that trip. But you're part of Norsunder, and they aren't known for their humanitarian plans. I'm the first girl?"

Roy let his breath out in a long sigh. "Right. But don't make assumptions—"

"Already too late. I assume any purpose for forcing me to be here is for terrible reasons. Would you be trusting and obedient if you were grabbed?"

There was that wry smile again. "Depends," he said. "On my own plans."

And while Clair was trying to think of an appropriate answer to that, he finished the last of his coffee and shoved back his chair. "Let's do the tour, shall we?"

Clair nodded. As she followed Roy out, she thought of CJ, and Dtheldevor, and Hibern—all the potential girls who were smart, brave, and skilled—and vowed that Detlev's new plan would not be successful.

Eight

ROY STARTED HIS TOUR at the HQ where Detlev had his office. There was little of interest to be seen, except she noticed on this visit that none of the chairs or tables matched in size or style. Some were crudely made, others embellished with vines, leaves, and one with horse heads in a style that reminded Clair of the frescos on the walls in Senrid's castle.

Two of the offices were empty, the bookshelves bare. These were used by visiting mages—one of whom was now dead, Roy added under his breath in a tone that Clair strongly suspected meant *good riddance*.

They passed another barracks building adjacent to the one she'd been put in. A third small one, almost hidden in a grove of trees, she remembered seeing on her first day. Here, Roy explained, new children were brought for their early conditioning. They were seldom taken over the age of five anymore. "They had two five-year-olds, and one wasn't a success," he said.

"I'd consider turning against Norsunder a success," she said.

Roy gave her a slightly pained look. "He didn't turn against Norsunder. Just against us."

And the difference was? But she didn't ask—she was not sure she wanted to hear the answer, which was sure to be dreary, or worse.

Time for a change of subject. "What's that?" She waved at a low, plain building beyond the library. Hereto she had avoided it; she realized as they drew near that what bothered her about it was the lack of windows down one side.

"That's detention. You can go in but there's little to see, and what you do see you won't like," he said. "That mage I mentioned, he . . . experimented with soul-bound here."

"I suppose this is MV's favorite place." Clair made a face.

"He likes to be outside best," Roy said.

"Are the prisoners here your target practice, too?"

Roy crossed his arms. "Do you really want to know?" When she didn't answer, he added with quiet irony, "Shall we move on or do you want a tour inside?"

"Go on."

They slanted across the grassy central area to the relatively small stables, beyond which was a wide field with obstacles for riding practice, and beyond that, a broad kitchen garden going all the way to the far fence, where she had made her attempt at escape.

"There's an aquifer underground here, feeding the well at the kitchens," Roy explained. "That's why the Den was built here, because that is the closest water to the surface. Even so it took a lot of effort to delve down to it."

As he talked, he led her past the garden to more barren field, obviously not watered from the well. A row of targets sat before the wall. Roy led her across the archery field. "If you want to look over," he invited, waving at the wall, "you'll see why the sentries are mainly here to watch for windstorms."

Though she'd already done that, Clair decided not to admit to it. She took a running start and scrambled up, clinging to the top with both arms. Roy vaulted up easily next to her, swinging a leg over so he sat perched on the wall. She fought to get her leg up, won, and stared out at the rock-barren, blasted land stretching out to the horizon in all directions except the spine of barren-looking mountains, purple and hazy.

"Question," she said.

Roy lifted his brows.

"You mentioned soul-bound. Do you idiots look forward to having your minds and souls subsumed into Norsunder after you are dead?"

Roy laughed, a sudden laugh that rocked him so hard he

was in danger of falling to the ground below.

"I didn't know I was that funny." She scowled.

Roy dashed his bony wrist across his eyes. "Sorry," he said, catching his breath. "It's a legitimate question. Everyone hopes to be the one in command of those miserable wights."

Clair suppressed a snort of derision. Had they any kind of etiquette? If so, she probably had broken a social rule of some sort—not that she cared.

They jumped down to the weird grass inside the compound, Clair sneezing from the dry air.

"I've got to go," Roy said, as one of the intermittent bells clanged. Clair had ignored them until now. "Time for drill. Can you read the Sartoran alphabet?"

"I can, though I prefer translations."

"Well, Norsundrian is the Sartoran alphabet, adapted to the language. You've heard of Dock Talk?"

"That's what Dtheldevor speaks, isn't it?"

"Norsunder is similar in its shortened verb forms, the conditionals altered to degrees of imperatives . . . well, anyway," he said when he saw her blank face, "if you want to learn to read it, I'll write out both alphabets tonight. And I can leave you a basic text to practice reading."

"Is it war?"

"Is what war?"

"This book. If it's about battles and war and how to kill people better, I don't want to read it."

"It's about how to command people better. I am not a prince," he said with mild sarcasm, "but I would think the business of princes would be learning more effective governing, another word for command. This goes into how leaders, of whatever type, need to understand command and communication before they can be effective at control."

Clair had no desire whatsoever to learn from any Norsundrian war manual about how to rule. But maybe she ought to read it to figure out how to work against them.

"All right," she responded. She had decided that she would never utter the words *please* or *thank you*. Those you used when you had a choice. She was not there by choice. Instead, she debated asking if they were drilling for an attack on anyone she knew, then decided she would rather not hear the answer.

Roy left.

She retreated to her room, aware of the never-ending burden of grief that could not be shared, and below that, rage. There she lay on her bed sinking into memory, much as it hurt, until she figured it was time to go to lunch.

She was halfway there when a tall, dark, brawny boy loped toward her. She quickened her pace slightly, grateful at least that it was Rolfin (or Leef), and not one of the worse ones. "Clair," he called. "Detlev wants you."

Shock and fear flashed along her nerves, followed by fury. She almost retorted *Let him want*, when Leef flicked a thumb back over his shoulder.

"Now." And he kept running past.

She stood irresolute, fear and fury churning in her gut. Why should she comply? Because if she didn't he'd come after her. And then what? Torture chambers and execution squads? Why would he bother when he could apparently rip your identity from your brain without coming within touching distance?

Survive, she told herself. She'd comply until she couldn't bear it, if she didn't see a way out first. And definitely, definitely remember her mind-shield.

With reluctant steps, traversed the compound to the HQ, mentally building a thick castle wall.

Detlev was writing when she got there, his pen scratching rapidly across the page in straight lines. He paused long enough to flick the end of his pen toward one of the many different chairs, put the paper in a pile, picked up another paper and resumed writing.

Clair ignored the chair he pointed at and sat down on the edge of a finely carved one with a lyre back and a pattern of laurel leaves running up and around the frame. She dug her nails into the wood of the scrolled arms as she surveyed Detlev's desk with a kind of foreboding curiosity. Piles of papers sat neatly at his left and right, a half-folded map sticking out underneath one pile. Sorting and writing on papers appeared to be such a homely task, though she simply could not see whatever kind of evil was being plotted.

He laid down his pen. "A future plan," he said with a smile. "Perhaps you will be a part of it."

She'd rather be dead.

His smile deepened briefly, and she clenched her fists, terrified her mind-shield was not strong enough, and that he'd heard her. Only how to concentrate on it while he was talking? He went on, "You've had a chance to acclimate somewhat. Have you any observations to make?"

"Why me? Why don't you have girls?"

"Because I found only boys, several on battlefields, one on an abandoned wreck, two more starving in a back alley, one locked in a cage in a stable. Two were offered for sale."

Clair did not believe he'd done any of these abandoned, or sold, boys any favors. She was glad to discover that no girls had been left out for Norsundrians to gather in. And she didn't want to be the first. "I want to go home."

"You will, presently," he said, which surprised her—but only for a moment. "My aim is to send you home with a new perspective on your world."

Horror made her shiver. He *was* going to mindspell her! Or try.

"I need to be away for a time, so I've assigned you a study partner. Here are the alphabets that Roy promised you, and a book to read. Let us determine what else you might be doing, but first a retrospective on your history."

The impulse of curiosity caused her to reach mentally before she was aware of doing so, and he was in her mind, or rather she was in his: suddenly her awareness expanded abruptly, and there was Terry, bloodthirsty and vicious as he talked about attacking Curtas. Had Detlev witnessed—no, this was her own memory. And her own ambivalence about his relish for violence toward Curtas, who had never attacked anyone. Who was the villain here?

Detlev's mental voice, excoriating with mockery, employed the word villain—so self-righteously easy a label.

Next was Tahra, back in Wnelder Vee during winter, hiding her crossbow as she muttered about villains. The word repeated, a flick of salt on raw emotions, as images of adults familiar and unfamiliar appeared—memories not hers—all using the language of justice and righteousness as they demanded death and destruction. And not always against Norsundrians, but neighboring kingdoms, sometimes relatives, and the worst were pretended allies.

In every one, hidden motivations and intentions—if not outright falsehood—belied the surface words and actions. These were the sort of actions she and Roy had argued about that long-ago day on the seas above Hier Alverian: seeming justice that actually serves someone's ends.

Clair refused to believe any of these so-called memories of people unknown to her, but no sooner was she aware of her decision to reject them than here was CJ's jealousy of Rel. *CJ conquered that*, Clair thought.

So you say, Detlev acknowledged, *but it could occur again. Your friend CJ loves to hate.*

True—in a sense. But using CJ as an example of lighter weakness and hypocrisy was a mistake. All the others, from Tahra to Terry, Clair could have private doubts about and still like, but CJ she knew: *It won't happen.* She shot the thought at Detlev, splintering the dismal picture.

He neither agreed nor negated: *Next time we will look at the waste perpetrated by your righteous allies*, he promised: *Magical, material, and human.*

Her insides churned with dread.

He indicated the window, and spoke aloud. "Do you know where the small children are kept?"

Was she going to get away? She forced her chin down, though her neck ached with tension.

"Go there. Help Guem when you're not studying with Roy."

Clair picked up the book and the papers and left, relief at her escape not quite smothering her roiling emotions. She ran all the way back to her room and slammed the door, then stood with her back to it, though she knew that it was only an illusion of safety. For a time she stood there, eyes closed, until her breath calmed.

Detlev was lying, of course. Not outright, but twisting and manipulating the truth to his own ends. That's what Norsundrians did. That reassuring truth was where she ought to begin. Detlev's intent was evil, to cause her to lose trust in her allies. But she wouldn't.

People made mistakes, but all those allies, *their* intent was peace, all good things. Well, maybe that one about CJ and Rel—but CJ had fought the jealousy battle and won. CJ worked hard on her friendship with Rel. All her friends tried to be better people, so even at their worst they were still preferable to a bunch of Norsundrians who chose evil for evil's sake.

Clair dug the heels of her hands into her eye sockets, then dropped her hands and forced herself to leave again. She'd had orders. *They* might be watching. She found herself a few paces from the little ones' house. She'd gotten so used to the orderly blandness of the compound that she was not ready to meet noise and color as soon as she opened the door.

She stepped into a wide, airy room. Blocks and climbing toys occupied the center, and the walls all around at waist level were covered with scrawls and drawings. Beyond this room rose a hubbub of young voices, and next thing she knew a tall young man with a cheerful face and curly light brown hair moved in at an oddly smooth pace—a little as if he skated over ice—while holding two squalling babies.

"Ah! You must be Clair. Here." Guem thrust one of the infants into her arms and then glided out again with the other.

She juggled the yowling baby with awkward movements, making soothing noises. It suddenly noticed that someone new was at hand, and stopped the yells with a hiccough and a blink. She smiled down at the tiny face with the soft fringe of black hair around it. Then she remembered what this child was supposed to grow up to be, and her insides clenched.

"It's not fair," she whispered.

The baby's blue eyes widened, and it waved chubby hands.

But if she had to be there, what could be better? She'd turn this baby—and all the others she could get close to—away from Norsunder!

She grinned, thinking the Norsundrians were idiots.

The baby saw her grin and its mouth opened in a happy smile, gums gleaming.

Then Guem glided back in. "Sorry to do that," he said, expertly taking the baby from her. "But I'm alone in here and it sometimes gets chaotic."

"Alone?"

He laughed. "Mostly. Few of the others can stand the critters for long—"

"Critters?"

"Under fives."

Clair smiled, liking "critters".

"Anyway, few are any good with them."

Clair, thinking of MV, nodded soberly. "I bet."

He laughed again. "Oh, *they're* all right, Detlev's boys. Most of them." He glanced toward one of his critters, a brown-haired toddler bent over a chalk board, absorbed in drawing. Clair watched the dimpled little hand moving carefully as

Guem went on, "I manage the critters until they're old enough to train."

"Will they be all right with me?"

"They'll follow orders," he said cheerfully. "Well, this one is hungry. Why don't you help those two over there with their building blocks?"

And so passed a perfectly normal stretch of time—if you didn't remember that these were all future Norsundrians. The little ones smeared boards with finger-paints, which got wanded off, then Clair played blocks, and puzzles, and led a clapping game that she'd loved when small. The little ones loved it as well.

At last it was time for them to eat and go to sleep. Guem said she could go.

"See you tomorrow," Clair said, aware of a lack of dread— for once. This job, she could bear. As long as she didn't think about the futures of these little ones, she could even enjoy it.

Feeling better than she had ever since she was taken prisoner, she walked straight to the mess hall for dinner. As she was leaving, a bunch of poopsies came in. Roy came her way, the others following.

"Did you get the things I left for you?" Roy asked, giving her a brief but searching gaze.

"I did." And she suppressed the urge to thank him.

"How are you doing?" Adam asked. He seemed absent.

Clair shrugged.

"Good evening to you," Laban said in a goading voice, sketching a courtly bow.

She swept a mock curtsey. "Rotten evening to you," she said.

Laban laughed, and a chorus of good evenings rained around her from them except MV, who merely curled his lip.

Then David stepped in her path, bowing with his hand over his heart. "Welcome to our happy home, Queen Clair."

She pushed on past, her eyes on the horizon.

Howls of laughter rose, and hoots of derision aimed at David. Clair kept walking, feeling David's mocking brown gaze following her.

"Well, that ought to equal any of my poor, hypocritical allies in pettiness," she muttered under her breath. Then she grinned down at her moccasins tromping through the grass. *But oh, Irenne, it felt so good.*

Nine

Al-Athann

SESHE KNEW GENERALLY HOW the Universal Language Spell worked — Clair had carefully explained when she went to the trouble to put it on the medallions she made for the girls.

First of all, it was not a mere spell, that is, doing one thing. It was an enchantment, with a complicated key in spell form. The key bound together, in some way, years — sometimes centuries — of additions of words in most of the world's languages. Each word, or phrase, was worked into the enchantment with its equivalent expression in various languages. When you heard that word or phrase spoken in the unfamiliar language, the spell released the equivalent word in your own language.

Some languages, like Sartoran, had been added to so much over the centuries that the Spell was almost as good as a human translator, and just as fast. Other languages were more difficult to understand because there were not enough words added, or the scribe mages could not, or did not, keep up with the changes that languages are always going through. And even in the most frequently added-to languages, slang and idiom was always going to evolve faster.

Then there were languages never added. Like the one the cave people spoke.

Seshe had never talked about her origins, because she hated remembering most of it, until she ran away and was accepted into Clair's circle of friends. But one of the few good things about her background was having had to learn several languages, including Sartoran. She understood the functions of verb forms and tenses. Same with prepositions and word order.

As time passed — she had no idea how much — she worked feverishly to master Leotay's language, begging everyone she met for more words, and more words, until she fell asleep with new words chasing through her dreams.

It was better than grief and worry. It made her feel she was accomplishing something. She still had no idea how any of what she was doing would help Clair, but she clung to the thought that Hreealdar had brought her all the way from Sartorias-deles to this place. There had to be a reason.

Meanwhile, Leotay and her people caught her anxiety and her desire to learn fast. As soon as Seshe had a rudimentary vocabulary, it was Leotay's idea to have her teach the people about the outside world.

"I'll watch from up here," Dom Hildi said.

Seshe had been brought by Leotay to the elderly mage's cave while they waited for the time change. Seshe saw Leotay flash a worried look at the elderly woman. Dom Hildi shook off her offered hand with an impatient gesture, then said, "I can hear and see everything from the comfort of my own cave. Why not?"

Leotay pressed her lips together.

Seshe reflected on how certain expressions were recognizable no matter where you traveled in the world. Leotay was worried about her teacher, and Dom Hildi did not want to be worried about.

"It's almost Green," came a voice at the outer tapestry.

"Come," Dom Hildi called.

Quicksilver and Jeory entered together, the one tall and controlled, the other as close to gangling and clumsy as these people could ever come.

Seshe had gotten to know Leotay's closest friends as each helped to teach her. Jeory reminded Seshe a little of Adam (before they knew he was an enemy), and more strongly of Morgeh of Wnelder Vee, the prince who wanted to be a bard, though Jeory seemed to know little of music beyond the singing they all did. But his dreamy enthusiasms, the way he uttered words about things he saw — things they didn't have in the caves — made it seem to Seshe that he perceived another world overlying this one. In that sense he reminded her of Adam, when he talked about the meanings and moods of color, and like Morgeh when he was in the grip of composition.

On impulse, Seshe said, "Won't you show me your signs?" It was a risk. She knew that some of the adults still did not trust her, but these three seemed to. Trust might be a conditional thing.

Quicksilver exchanged a quick glance with Dom Hildi, then gestured. "I shall. Come within."

They went past the black tapestry, and he plucked the knife out of the air. When he handled it a certain way it shimmered and grew to sword length.

"I try not to let it do that," he said.

"Why?" Seshe exclaimed. "Swords are a lot more efficient than knives. At least, I've heard some say that. For one thing, it keeps your enemy at a bit more of a distance."

"And it keeps you at a distance from your enemy," Quicksilver countered, eyeing the sword dubiously. Knives, he knew very well. This type of weapon? No.

"Well, but that's what you'll face when you fight Norsundrians," she said.

"Ah." He turned the blade over, squinting down its length, then angled it this way and that. "Thank you for telling me that. It makes a difference. I will have to figure out how to use this. Know you?"

"Only a couple of things," she said apologetically. "I can show you basic blocks and lunges."

"If you'll demonstrate those, perhaps I can figure out the rest."

"Sure."

"Here's mine," Jeory said, holding out a wood-carved musical instrument, a flute, only not made of metal like those she'd heard as a child in court. "We don't know what it does, but when I handle it, it makes me see things." He touched it reverently to his forehead. "I have tried placing various things into the holes, but I do not think I have chosen the right objects. Perhaps these objects were lost with our ancestors."

"That looks like a flute," Seshe said tentatively.

"A what?" the others exclaimed.

"A flute—a woodwind of some kind—a musical instrument," Seshe said, amazed at their total incomprehension. "Look, can I show you?"

"But it can burn if the wrong person touches it, we are told," Leotay said.

"Let me try," Seshe murmured. "If it burns my finger, we'll know."

Jeory watched anxiously, and the others in wary silence as she extended a finger, then delicately touched the instrument on Jeory's palm.

Nothing happened.

She ran her finger along the smooth length of the flute, and when nothing occurred, slowly and carefully picked it up. Leotay held her breath, and Jeory trembled as he watched.

Seshe turned the flute over in her hands, puzzled. Did they really think she would catch on fire? And why didn't he play it? Did they not have musical instruments? Perhaps they had worn away centuries ago, which made sense as they had no wood, except those enormous mulberry trees in the silkworm cavern. Those were centuries old, she'd gathered, regarded as precious, almost sacred. The people certainly did not use their wood. There was no wood in the caves she'd seen, she realized in retrospect.

She stared down at the warm golden wood that might very well be thousands of years old. She wished Clair were here, and could explain how music and magic came together in such objects. Because even though Seshe knew next to nothing about magic, she could feel at a touch that this flute was layered with powerful enchantments.

As the others watched, eyes widening, she raised the breath hole to her lips and blew softly across it, listening in expectation. A soft, humming note, like the vibration of crystal, only purer, sounded sweetly. And her head buzzed as if a thousand bees hummed inside her head.

Leotay gasped, and Jeory fell to his knees, eyes wide and sightless, tears glimmering along his eyelids; colors glowed briefly in the dark striations of rock forming the cave walls.

Seshe swayed, and the bee sensation faded. When four pairs of expectant dark eyes whipped her way, she slid her fingers over the holes, and blew just as softly, this time in expectation of pretty sound as she moved her fingers to cause a cascade of harmonic notes.

Bees hummed on a higher note in her head, so startling she almost missed the effect of those few notes. Color rippled around them, and far off they heard the cries of people.

Dom Hildi gasped. "Stop!" just as Jeory cried hungrily, "Oh, more!"

Seshe lowered the flute, looking from one to the other.

"It is beautiful sound," the old mage rasped, "but it's tearing at our protection magic, like . . . like something wishing to burst forth."

Leotay pressed her fingertips to her lips.

"Sorry," Seshe said, hastily laying the instrument across Jeory's thin palm.

"No," Leotay said earnestly, leaning toward Seshe, the light from the glowglobe reflecting steadily in her dark eyes. "You have done us a great thing. We would never have thought of that—to put air into it, instead of objects." She turned to Jeory. "You will have to experiment, but oh, so careful and soft, no sound."

Dom Hildi nodded. "Sound strengthens its magic reach, that much at least is clear. Leotay, give him a chamber that you can seal with protection magic. Jeory, see that you keep its sound to that one room. It appears to carry magic wherever it can be heard."

Jeory nodded fervently.

"And now it is Green," Dom Hildi said. "The Gathering awaits you."

Seshe sighed as she followed Leotay down the stone pathway to the central gathering place in the vast cave. There, all the people were gathered, each sitting on a rug, and they'd already started their Singing.

Young voices, old, men, women, each had a part, though the melody lines seemed interchangeable. Seshe gave up trying to follow any theme, and shut her eyes to enjoy. Their singing evoked strong images of home, images she gathered carefully in her mind, for when it was finished, she hoped to be able to use those when telling them about the outside worlds.

The singing faded as one by one the voices dropped out, until only a few sang, then they too fell silent.

Dom Leotay stepped out before the expectant people. "Our Visitor is going to show you the Outside, in image. It is not real. Leotay and I have used our magic to reproduce as well as possible these visions."

A susurration of whispers, quick as breeze through grass, sighed through them, and then they stilled in expectation.

Seshe stepped up beside Leotay. "What I will show you," she said, pitching her voice to be heard (for she had been trained in that, too), "is where I come from. And then I'll show you the enemy I think we share."

Leotay sang low and quick, like bird calls, and nodded at Seshe: she'd attributed notes to each image as they'd laboriously worked them out, beginning with Seshe sketching on a chalk slate.

Seshe began with the girls' underground hideout in Mearsies Heili. She knew every detail of the beloved hideout where she had spent so much time. She pointed out their furniture and its uses, and the tree roots making a kind of tapestry in the walls, not unlike the stalactites and stalagmites of the caves.

As she talked, she listened to the quiet voices. They recognized caves, and the emotions Seshe heard in the voices were those of curiosity and interest, not distrust or disgust.

Then she gave them a bright day in the forest outside the cave. The voices whispered in awe at the sunlight filtering through whispering trees, the diamond-bright plash of the stream.

Seshe forgot to worry about making sense, or boring them, and lost herself in sharing all her favorite memory-images with an audience whose interest, delight, and enthusiasm redoubled her appreciation of the beauties of her world.

She shared a sunset, and a night sky, and all kinds of weather. She gave them the splendor of the mysterious jewel cave called a Selenseh Redian, which drew perhaps the loudest response. And she gave them images of all the animals she had ever seen and admired, which captivated them.

But then the time came for her to show them their enemy. "Here's what they're like." A profound silence fell when she gave them images of Kessler's warriors drilling their assassination teams in the desert. Nearby, Quicksilver stirred; she was distracted by his whisper, "We will have to study that again. See how they use those weapons."

The recent troubles in Wnelder Vee came thick and fast, and wavered only when Irenne entered one.

But then Seshe showed them Detlev, the one time Seshe had seen him. He rode on horseback, features distinct, his atmosphere one of menace.

"That's your main enemy," Seshe said. "And ours, too. He might be there in that military camp below the mountains, and if you want to retake your world, you'll have to defeat him. I hope you do," she added, her voice uneven. Too much recent memory brought back fresh grief.

She forced her voice to steady. "But if you do, here are my two friends, the ones I came here to rescue. I believe that they are prisoners of this enemy." And she showed them Clair and Terry, Clair's white hair causing another susurrus of comment on the color of age in one so young.

When Seshe stepped down, the people departed, some murmuring gratitude or thanks as they passed by. Seshe smiled and nodded, her eyes still burning. She wanted to get away, to regain some kind of composure.

Jeory withdrew, his expression distant. But Quicksilver stayed, and knelt beside Leotay's mat. "Those hand-to-hand duels," he said. "I need to see those again."

Leotay turned in silence to Seshe.

"Sure," Seshe said sturdily. "As much as you want. If it'll help to defeat them once and for all. I'll show you what I remember."

Ten

The Den

ANGER, DAVID HAD DECIDED when life turned to shit a couple years back, was the strongest spur to action.

Anger made you faster. It made you stronger. It kept your focus on the target, effortlessly shutting out the distractions you'd otherwise have to exert yourself to ignore. When you were angry, nothing else mattered — pain, thirst, hunger, exhaustion — until you won. And oh, when you did win, the victory was so much sweeter.

Siamis — a few years older than they, and that much more experienced — had usually run the boys when Detlev was gone for protracted periods in Norsunder Beyond. He'd told David that anger was like wildfire: difficult to control, with a high ratio of waste to gain.

"If you want a model for power," he'd said not long before the boys had to leave Geth, "take sunlight. Strongest power there is, and yet look how little effort it takes to use it."

It sounded all right at the time, but look at Siamis now. Betrayed them without a thought, then captured by an old man who could barely walk, and forced into a Selenseh Redian! Detlev said Siamis was alive, but at what cost? So easy to imagine him emerging like the lighter version of the soul-bound, without will or wit, to be used by lighter mages.

He deserved that if he'd really turned against them. And yet right before that betrayal, Siamis contacted David to let him know that MV had been taken by Efael and the Black Knives. And what that meant. The usual instinct, to talk it over with MV, had to be checked. MV still kept his lip buttoned about the details of surviving Efael, but David could feel his unabated fury.

"We need our own run," MV had said earlier that day, catching David at the target field. "Khanerenth winter games."

"We're supposed to be lying low," David reminded him.

"This *is* lying low. We won't be tracking, spying, stealing, or assassinating anyone." He added this last sarcastically. "It's a recruiting competition. No one will know who we are if we give fake names."

"If anyone from Norsunder shows up, they might recognize us."

"Who's going to do that? This isn't the summer game, when everybody is welcome. This is the winter tryouts to gain entry to their academy. Everybody trying is academy age. *We're* academy age. We give false names, false villages, we're all from Khanerenth — we can even use illusion over our faces, if you're scared. No one will know we're there."

David sighed. "I think, given the disaster at Songre Silde, Siamis's brain turning to shit, and our own steaming horse pile in Wnelder Vee, that lying low means playing least-in-sight right here."

"It means least-in-sight away from all of them," MV retorted, hands flexing. "We *need* a run. We need a *successful* run. Siamis — those idiots in Wnelder Vee, none of it was *our* fault. But you want us holed up here like rabbits?"

MV's fury was like standing too close to a fire. David sensed that he was within a hair's-breadth of taking off on his own. So he considered. Really, what would be the harm, as long as they were careful? MV had already competed in Khanerenth once or twice, without repercussions of any kind.

"All right. We do need a run," David said, aware of conceding. See, anger does always win. "Spread the word. My room after dinner."

He used his own irritation to ram his way through his tasks as fast as possible, then he returned to his room to think it all through.

Detlev would have transferred to Sartorias-deles by then, and he'd have to be cautious. The Venn border was enormous. Sniffing out traps and tracers, sorting the destruction of ancient spells and the establishment of new, would take days. Maybe even weeks. If David and the boys kept themselves in covert mode — and he knew they could — they could be gone and back again long before Detlev's return from the northwest of Drael.

"You'll all transfer to different points, and converge at the garrison at Ellir Harbor," David said when they gathered in his room that night. "Half can do the land run, half the sea run the next day. Except you, MV. Go for both. Since this was your idea."

MV gave his wheezing snicker, rarely heard these past weeks.

"Fake names. Draw no attention," David warned. "Bring winter bedrolls. We'll find a spot on the river outside town to camp, avoiding the harbor town, which has to be full of blabbermouths. Roy's making your world-transfer tokens. He'll tell you when and where to go. We'll leave over two days. First ones to go will be those having to travel farthest in."

"We're camping outside? It's still winter in the south," Laban said, grimacing as he rubbed his still-healing shoulder.

A howl of insults about softness and sloth was his answer. Laban rolled his eyes and sighed.

David said, "Laban, you'll do the riding competition. Don't need two arms for that."

Roy said nothing, but listened with an intense sense of relief. It would be good to get away from Five, and to give some purpose to the simmering moods he sensed around him. It wouldn't accomplish anything — even if they won, they would not be able to claim the win — but brainless fun, the physical challenge, might cure their restlessness at least for a while.

It would also get him out of line-of-sight with this weird order about Clair of the Mearsieans.

"*I'm* starting the relay," Noser shrilled. "I can run just fine — and this is almost gone." He smacked his shoulder, where Rel the Traveler had dislocated it. "If I see that soul-sucker again I'm going to gut him with his own sword . . ."

Out of habit everyone ignored Noser's raving threats and dispersed to get ready.

Three days later, Roy leaped down the rocks well ahead of the rest of the scrambling, shouting pack of running competitors, and flung himself into the waiting canoe. Shoving the relay-wand inside his shirt, he used his momentum to launch the craft and grabbed up the double-paddle.

Left, right, left, right, the paddle dipped into the icy rush of river water, sending him scooting ahead. Spray kicked up, a pleasant shock of cold after extreme effort. He laughed, breathing in the chilly air.

Another canoe snaked out, nearly adjacent. Was that a familiar face?

"Yah!"

"Roy!"

"Get *mooo*-ving!"

The shouts came from the river's edge, where Curtas, Rolfin, and Silvanas ran, leaping from rock to rock, Silvanas occasionally turning handsprings and somersaults in the air.

Roy laughed, the freezing wind whipping away his breath as he braced his feet against the canoe ribs and used his entire body to pull the canoe to the right, sending it straight through a narrow passage between two rocks and down a short drop into white foam that propelled him into the middle of the river.

He shot over another more deadly falls to land in the roaring whitewater, and nearly foundered. Jamming the paddle back and using it as a rudder, he fought the current until he broke free and his canoe skimmed out into the stream. Behind, heartbeats after he passed, the next canoe landed. Roy, glancing back, saw the bow shoot skyward and a human figure fly out and land with a mighty splash in the water.

David led the cheers from the sides as the others streamed over the rocks, fallen trees, and icy detritus along the way. A quick glance showed MV leaping down from a huge dead tree and running flat out for the next change point to be ready when Rolfin arrived.

Roy beached the canoe between the planted pennons and handed the relay-wand to Rolfin, who sprinted for the line of waiting horses. Silvanas, who had run ahead with him, had selected the best. He pointed, and Rolfin vaulted onto its bare back.

Roy fell in behind Curtas and their footsteps pounded to-gether as they howled insult-laced encouragements to Rolfin.

Out of all the other competitors, only they ran alongside the dangerous route, sometimes at great risk, to watch each other on the relay. They were all there to cheer as Adam ran the last segment, leaping with seeming effortlessness over the waist-high bars, and flipping over the last three, hands to feet to hands and then onto his feet as the spectators cheered.

Ferret, the most forgettable of them, went to claim the prize, which was invitation into the army under War Commander Randart. Ferret acted suitably humble and impressed, spoke a lot of lies about who his friends were and whence they had come, then triumphantly bore away the token that would permit the boys to eat at the justly famed Ellir Gold. This inn, run by former mariners, was famed up and down Khanerenth's seafaring coast for its brown ale, cornbread slathered with honey-butter, and wine-braised fish.

The boys would have loved the food anyway, but everything tasted better spiced by the exhilaration of triumph. Tired in a good way, Roy enjoyed the camaraderie without the tensions of life on Five.

David's mood was similar to Roy's as he watched Curtas and Ferret and Vana exchanging small bets with locals on the second, sea-based, portion of the competition, their local accents perfect. They really were the best—and it was good to prove it.

"I'm bringing a jug of brown," MV said when they got up to shoulder their gear and go.

"Where to?" David asked Leef.

"Found a spot on the river, up beyond the north end of town. No one around, sheltered from the wind. We can have fires."

David lifted a hand for him to lead on. Even the weather had cooperated, staying clear. And cold, but their winter bedrolls awaited them, and they were warm enough from exertion and an excellent meal.

Falling into single file and following wagon ruts, they stealthed out of the harbor town, Leef on point and Erol at the rear, sweeping behind out of habit, though with no expectation of danger—and seeing nothing to catch the eye.

Night had fallen by the time they crested a hill and descended to walk along the river's edge, to the spot Leef had picked out. The site was everything he'd promised. Because it was winter, they made two fires, and, tired but replete after good food and ale, they gathered around the fires to engage in good-natured critiquing of one another's performance that day, idle speculation about the morrow, leading to some reminiscences about their sea experiences on Geth, a world of islands.

Roy was silent, conscious of enjoying the companionship, the night sky, the cold air redolent of pine and fresh water. Was that true enjoyment, when you took note of it, memorizing every detail, because you knew it must end soon?

He frowned into his mug of brandy-laced coffee, until David struck him on the arm and said, "We won."

Firelight flickered over half of David's face, making his expression difficult to discern. It wasn't a statement, it was a question; Roy knew his somber mood had been detected, and David wanted to know why.

"Not sure, but I think I recognized someone. In the canoe right after mine, before the falls," he said, and then realized that it *had* been bothering him, though beneath consciousness. But he was not about to get into the things within conscious thought.

David's brows twitched together. "From Bereth Ferian? You haven't been anywhere else."

"Here and there. Briefly," Roy said. "That's the problem. I can't peg who, or the setting, except it wasn't anyone from Bereth Ferian. Hate that. Not remembering."

"Too much ale." Laban snorted. "You're skunked."

Roy wasn't drunk because he'd only had a sip or two of the ale served at the Ellir Gold, though he'd raised his glass when the others did.

"Skunked because you're bored," Laban said lazily. "I don't know why Detlev hasn't put us on a major run yet. We just proved—again—that no lighters can beat us, Geth *or* here."

Everyone hailed that with enthusiasm. David seemed to accept that. He certainly agreed, but as a flask was passed hand to hand, he frowned at Roy, who hadn't answered Laban.

David said, "What kind of a run would you propose, if asked?"

Roy shrugged, staring into the beating fire. Then, sensing that David was waiting for an actual answer, he said, "Something worth achieving."

"Here's to fun." Curtas raised the flask before sloshing liquid into his cup.

"Here's to a real kill order," Noser shrilled, looking right and left for approval.

"If you mention Rel again," MV said as he aimed a lazy swat at Noser, "I'll dislocate your other arm, and break it afterward. If there are any orders about Rel, you leave him to me."

"Like?" David said patiently, gaze still on Roy, as Noser hunched up, muttering.

"Something that doesn't break us up any further." Curtas slung the last of his ale into the fire, where it hissed blue, then vanished.

"That's it." Roy pointed his way.

"So you think we're about to be broken up?" David asked. The tone of his soft voice was nearly impossible to make out above the rushing water and the celebrative chatter of the others.

"I think I've run out of coffee," Roy said.

David smiled. "So why," he leaned on one hand, facing Roy squarely, "did Detlev pick you to tutor the Mearsiean girl?"

It was not unlike the opening moves in a sword match: probe, sidestep, beat, retreat.

"You can have the job." Roy threw his arms wide.

"You know her."

And again Roy disengaged: "I know Arthur better." And a counter-thrust, "So?"

Instead of speaking, David sat up and reached one-handed to draw the black sword from its sheath. The ring of steel caused some of the others to look over, and then away again.

David turned the blade, watching the reflection of the campfire on it. Despite its weight his wrist was steady. Roy remembered how long it had taken David to learn to manage that sword with the speed and skill he showed with lighter weapons. Single-minded focus.

"So have fun. But lighten up." David smiled. "Anyone who tries to break us, I will break."

"Us." *Firejive.* They never said it anymore, though once it had been their secret name for themselves, and later an expression of irony, usually before retreating to lick wounds. Somehow the lighters hearing it had spoiled it—or maybe they were just too old for secret codes.

Roy wondered how much of that sense of "us" was real anymore as David shifted his grip and cast the sword javelin style. It struck a tree, vibrating. The others whooped and laughed, almost smothering the shivery ring of steel.

Almost, but not quite.

First the rasp of drawn knives, then shadowy, black-clad figures stepped into the firelight. Two held struggling figures, their hands yanked behind their backs, knives at their necks.

David lunged to his feet, MV a heartbeat after, both daggers out as Efael stepped down from the rocky bank, tall, knife-lean, wearing a heel-length coat of black-dyed man-leather. Leaping firelight emphasized the cruel lines of his face.

"What an inspiration," he drawled, his voice metallic with complacency. "And yet, so ineffective!"

He made a casual gesture, and the two Black Knives holding Curtas and Erol jerked their heads back, knives touching pulsing arteries. "Which one," asked Efael, "might benefit most from a lesson in . . . what was it, breaking?"

Bloody light rippled along the sharpened steel in MV's hands as his grip tightened.

"Come on, my fiery Mal Venn," Efael whispered. "Come to me."

MV stilled, tension making his rigid. Then he forced himself to sheath one knife, then the other. But he didn't move.

"No? You can pick which one is to die."

MV took two slow, unwilling steps toward Efael, who sighed with mendacious disappointment. "Have you truly forgotten your lessons, sweeting? Kneel."

The other boys watched in affront, uneasy surprise, and then astonishment as slowly, unwillingly, MV—who never took lip from anyone—dropped to one knee, then the other. Head bowed.

"Very good, my darling," Efael said, making a casual gesture with a finger. The knives moved away from Curtas's and Erol's necks, but the boys were still held in those excruciating grips.

Efael turned to David, his sharp face highlighted by the leaping flames. "And so, my captain, which one of these shall I take?"

Detlev had warned him. Insight hit David with all the impact of one of those knives. Siamis had shared those memories right before surrendering himself to the Selenseh Redian—that too was warning, the last lesson before he betrayed them.

David glanced from Erol to Curtas—both younger than he—and let out his breath. He knew how this had to go, and saw in Efael's anticipatory smirk that the setup was deliberate. Shit.

"Neither," David said. "If you have to play your games, take me."

"Games, is it?" Efael said and lifted a casual finger.

The Black Knives released their prisoners with a brutal shove. Erol and Curtas stumbled down the bank to fall onto the ground among the others as Efael said, "Let's play."

He moved a lot faster than David thought he would, slapped a transfer token against David's jaw, and the two of them vanished in a stink of greenish burned-steel light.

Without a sound the rest of the Black Knives melted out of the light, and vanished in magic transfer, one by one.

"You *idiots*," Noser rounded on Curtas. "You're supposed to be on watch."

"Didn't hear a sound," Curtas said shakily. "Not a sound."

Erol shook his head.

"You wouldn't," MV said. "The Black Knives' lives depend on not being made. If either of you had heard them, Efael would have flayed them himself."

Everyone's attention turned to MV—who none of them had ever seen back down from a fight—as he sat back in the sandy ground with a thump.

"*Darling?*" Noser scowled, his face scarlet with the intensity of his betrayal. "You rabbited. To *them*."

"You would too, horseapple," MV said without heat. "You would, too."

And then, sparing no detail, he told them why.

Eleven

Al-Athann

GRIEF STILL LEAKED INTO Seshe's thoughts when she was tired or quiet, or something reminded her of home. And friends.

She had no idea how long she'd been in the cavern. Sometimes it felt like a couple of weeks, and others more like a few months. The unrelenting grind of urgency kept her from truly enjoying it, and there was always the grief, kept fresh by little things that would bring Irenne to mind. It seemed disloyal to not want to have them, so she tried to accept the pain along with the memories.

She began to understand that tiredness worsened the urgency. But other times she'd find herself staring down at the food—mostly tubers, mushrooms, and what looked like mosses—or at her hands that seemed to belong to someone else, and she'd wonder what she was doing there. She was no closer to finding Clair.

Seshe's latest crying jag hit suddenly, after one of the sessions in which people gathered to ask more questions about Seshe's world. Her home.

Dom Hildi looked at the shadows under Seshe's odd, light eyes, and said briskly to Leotay, "She is young, and very tired.

Take her to your cave, and let her rest. Whatever is wrong will not be eased by our endless stares. We have covers to our caves for a reason."

Leotay gently coaxed Seshe to her cave, where she sat with her until the river of tears gradually lessened to a trickle, accompanied by the shuddering ribs and broken breath aftermath. Seshe lay back on the cool silken cushions, her aching body melting, melting . . . and she slept.

When she woke again, Leotay was there, with food and water, and kind words.

Seshe tried to think of days as rounds, that is, a full turn of the gigantic ceramic canisters with their ancient painted stripes. She'd discovered that these canisters worked like sandglasses at home, and that people thought of two periods: sleep, and waking. They'd lost the meaning of day and night.

She spent most of her time with Leotay, as she added vocabulary and learned more about the people. It was startling to hear somewhat familiar words now and then, with similar meanings.

Seshe finally began branching out, sharing meals with others. One time she sat with Leotay, Jeory, Quicksilver, and Dom Hildi. As they sat cross-legged around the low table, facing dishes of totally unfamiliar foods, one of the people reached out a thin, attenuated finger and said, "What are these casements upon your feet?"

That plunged her back into talk of her world, but at least it was not of home. Remembering that time was pressing, she floundered into a discussion of shoes, snow, countries, and travel, struggling to find the necessary vocabulary.

As the sand flowed back and forth, measuring waking and sleeping, her comprehension began to widen. She had guessed right. The Al-Athann people had lived in the caves for untold generations, and had never gone out. Only the Hildis, their mages, went out every few years, taking the glow globes to gather sunlight.

Their being hidden for uncounted centuries explained the smooth baby skin they all had, and the soft hair that had never known weather, that they wore at different lengths, usually in complicated braids, some of them long enough to wrap around waists. It explained the bare feet, and the soft voices that managed not to carry, the sinuous grace that had to be inbred from centuries of travelling swiftly over rough, rocky ground that was never even anywhere.

Despite their having been locked up together for at least a millennium, they had obviously learned in some way to deal with troubles between themselves. They were not soft as in weak. Some of them in fact were exceedingly well trained with knife-fighting, well-trained in the way one would get with daily practice over a lifetime.

Seshe gained impressions of long-ago battles from their oldest books, probably over necessities of life, from other cave dwellers. In the shared memory of the cave people, there were two methods of dealing with troublemakers who could not or would not compromise: exile or duel to the death. Being outcast in that barren world seemed a crueler fate that a sudden death, and everyone dreaded it.

Leotay was kind, and sensitive, but more often now she'd also gaze into nothing similar to the way Jeory did, but unlike Jeory, whose face would slacken as he mind winged else- where, her expression remained shuttered. It happened more and more frequently when they came up against new terms from Outside, but also when the talk neared some hidden purpose. At those times Seshe got that neck-grip of warning.

She couldn't explain it. She certainly felt no overt threat, not even from Quicksilver, the one she'd first mistaken for MV. Quicksilver was the leader of the knife-fighters. He was tall and lean and muscular like MV, and he moved like MV, which was perhaps a characteristic shared by many who had that same inborn physical talent honed by ages of single- minded practice, but he was not at all warlike or threatening. He spoke little, listened with patient interest to everything, and he was very popular with adult and youngster alike. Seshe began to sense a special regard between him and Leotay, mostly in the tone of their voices when they spoke to each other, and the way their bodies angled toward the other.

Once, when Seshe was walking a pathway alone and heard the rise and fall of many voices, Quicksilver stepped out from a shadowy access, and she sensed that she was being guarded. No one had said anything, but somehow it was easier to turn around and retrace her steps.

The Al-Athann people didn't just eat moss and root vegetables. They also made a kind of flat bread baked in their stone ovens. On it they spread dollops of different foods before rolling it into a tube. She'd found that their foods were strange, but tasty enough. They grew most of it in a vast cavern behind the waterfall, with light from brilliant glow globes. The soil was fed from scraps and waste much like at home, as they too had the Waste Spell.

They also had a cave of nurtured trees glowing under glow globes, each tree perfectly formed, never disturbed by wind. These monumental, ancient trees fed the moths that made their silk.

The days slipped by uncounted, as Seshe gained fluency.

Then one round early, she had a conversation with Dom Hildi and Leotay. "I know that you are our last sign, because I dreamed long ago that someone would come to us, and again when you reached us, wreathed in white light." Dom Hildi smiled, her face crinkling. "There are some here who think I'm too ancient to have discretion, and they ought to know better. But it is true that our oldest custom warns us that intruders would kill us, as surely as our ancestors were, if they knew of our presence before the right time came."

Seshe said, "Ancestors. I think I know that story. It happened on our world as well, and we call it the Fall. And some of my ancestors went into caves, too."

"Like the one you showed us." Leotay nodded with pleased comprehension.

"Oh, that one we made ourselves," Seshe said. "The morvende caves are very different, I am told. Vast, like yours. With more people. But the thing you have to realize is that we share the same enemy: your Norss Dar is what we call Norsunder."

Dom Hildi folded her hands. "Yes, so you said in my dream."

"Me?" Seshe exclaimed. "I appeared in your dream?"

Dom Hildi nodded again. "I did not see you clearly, but you appeared in my dream a round before you came down the tunnel. And I have come to trust those dreams, just as the past Hildis did. They always come with a sense of kindness, of our being watched over, as if by a mother over a small child."

Seshe wondered if that "dream" could be from Lilith the Guardian. What Dom Hildi said sounded so much like what

Liere had once told the girls about being a child in Imar, the only one in the world who had Dena Yeresbeth, until she met Lilith the Guardian in dreams, and then talked mind to mind.

A sense of inevitability, of a circle closing, gripped her, both unsettling and reassuring. Seshe had not been coerced into summoning Hreealdar. It had been her choice, her wish to do *something* in the face of Irenne's murder and Clair's disappearance, and yet now she had this sense that she was part of an important whole.

"I think that enemy we share is near," she said. "If I'm right, they live in a — place — within sight of your mountain."

Dom Hildi pursed her lips. "I know of this place. Some were afraid you might be from them, so we waited, thinking if you were to betray us, it would be right away. I knew you would not because of the dream. But I was content to wait while the others learned to trust you and you learned our tongue. You showed us your home by magic."

Seshe nodded, comprehending that Quicksilver *had* been guarding her. Probably on orders from their council of elders.

"But since you are here, we know that others could come. It is the time for us to act."

Seshe's mouth rounded. "With Norsundrians nearby? You're going to attack them?"

"We are not without resources," Dom Hildi countered dryly. "But yes. I have seen the lights of that place for some time, where before no lights existed. And other signs are here: we cannot delay. This, too, I have dreamed."

Seshe's anxiety sharpened. If these dreams were from Lilith, she hoped they didn't foretell Lilith's own demise at Detlev's hands. Liere had insisted that Dena Yeresbeth meant communication in the mental realm now — that no one saw the future — but who really knew what Lilith saw, or could do? One thing for certain: someone had certainly guarded the Al-Athann people from the Norsundrians so near.

She let her breath out slowly. If time was running out, for whatever reason, then she'd better get busy. She laid her food back on her plate, finding her appetite quite gone. "All right," she said slowly. "There must be some way I can help."

Twelve

The Den

CLAIR WAS AWARE OF Detlev's departure only by the alteration in atmosphere.

At breakfast, a dark-haired girl a few years older than
Clair came up to her, slid a disdainful scan from her white hair
to the scuffed winter mocs on her feet, and said in pure
Sartoran, "He thinks he'll put *you* in the field?"

"I don't know what 'he' thinks," Clair said. She walked on
by, feeling that scornful gaze burning her back like a spill of
hot oil.

She walked around the corner as fast as she could, then
stood with her back against the stone wall. She was no longer
invisible. No, untrue. Since she'd done nothing differently, it
meant she had never been invisible. She'd assumed she was
beneath notice, and found safety in being ignored, but they
saw her. That meant there had been orders about her.

She looked around for Roy, and Adam, but they were
gone. By nightfall she still hadn't seen any of Detlev's boys.
That should be cause for celebration, except for the
excruciating thought that their being away might mean they
were attacking her allies.

She considered what not being invisible meant. First in

importance, more vigilance. She took to watching the mess hall from a distance, and when it was least crowded, she'd slip in, ears alert for tone of threat as she got her food and carried it out again. Then she'd retreat to her room to eat and, because there was nothing else to do, study.

Time's relentless drag passed a little faster when she studied. It didn't take long to get the alphabet and the vowel markings, then to memorize the half-familiar consonant-clusters. She turned to the book, promising herself at the first sign of something disgusting—lessons in torture or the like—she'd stop reading.

The language was easier to read than she'd thought it would be. Someone had simplified Sartoran, intending the language to be practical, quickly mastered by people from many linguistic backgrounds. All the beauty of metaphorical expression had been stripped from the language, the various ways to express ambiguities. Shades of meaning were possible, but only in the context of variations in the imperative—if these were your orders, but you had these obstacles—or at least so it appeared in this one example of written Norsundrian.

The afternoons brought the only activity she enjoyed, and even that was problematical because she couldn't help worrying about the little ones' futures.

At what point did Detlev take happy "critters" and turn them into monsters? No one to answer that, of course. And she wasn't sure she wanted to hear the answer, because anything was going to hurt too much.

She reported each day to the critter cave to play with them, as Guem didn't play. His job seemed to be seeing to it the really small ones were clean, fed, learning to walk, and guided in very small tasks. He glided here and there, always smoothly.

Clair now had charge of the older ones, the leader of whom was a bright, handsome child named Macadais, nicknamed Mac. The oddly quiet two-year-old she'd noticed on her first day was not there. She gathered that some of them got pulled out for special tutoring. Maybe that was where they got turned into Norsundrians.

Her four and five-year-olds, who happened to be all boys, (a few of the younger ones turned out to be girls) demon-strated some of their games, at which they were adept. It was clear that physical training was held in highest esteem; the five-year-olds had already been drilling before lunch, she learned.

She was hard put to win the games, but she knew instinctively that win she must, or they wouldn't listen to her, and she wanted them to listen. She lay awake at night trying to remember imagination games that depended on cooperation and helping one another.

She also considered all the stories she and her friends had been telling for years, and the history she'd read. She told the critters stories that had a lot of action but still emphasized justice, and fairness, and the value of trust and truth.

The rest of the week trundled by. Then one morning she did her usual stealthy approach to the mess hall. No one seemed to be coming and going in the pre-dawn light, dust limning the buildings enough to soften the edges of the stonework.

She stopped dead in the doorway when she saw the poopsies gathered around a table at the far end, and no one else around. They looked tense. Angry, even. She tiptoed back, though a couple heads turned sharply her way, their furious gazes a psychic blow.

She retreated to her building and watched out her window, which did not take in the mess hall, but a corner of the path leading to it. She waited until she saw the clump of teenage boys emerge . . . was that all? She was sure she'd counted only eleven, and she knew there were twelve of them.

She waited, her stomach growling. She sneaked back to the door and peered in. No one. Good. She put together a plate and scurried back to her room to eat.

When she returned the dirty dishes, she found Roy waiting for her. "Have you made any headway with your studies?" he asked abruptly.

She was just as happy not to have to fumble through social politenesses. "I have learned that intelligencers are not just spies, but locals talking, travelers who don't know that their talk reveals things, deserters, and prisoners."

"You're nearly through the first chapter." He led the way toward the trees where they usually sat. Already the glare-bright light was strong and hot.

"Subheading three," she said. "And when you capture someone's communication system, you must not only find out how things were supposed to be done, but how they were actually done."

Roy didn't miss the lilt of sarcasm in her quiet voice. "Your conclusion?"

"That for all that talk about strict obedience to orders, and chain of command, rules for you people get bent anyway."

"Rules get bent by any people." He opened his hand. "My warning was not so much in praise of Norsunder's interlocked chains of command as a caution."

She sighed. "I know. And I try to be careful about who sees me coming and going. I also try to stay out of everyone's way. As for the language, it seems very limited so far, though that might be this book. Good for giving orders, and categorizing your foes, but that's it. There's even a section ahead, because I looked at what I've got to plow through, and the last part of this chapter is on how to write a report. Wow, I'm so impressed with how smart they are."

"Ah, but there are plenty of things a creative mind can do with language," Roy answered. He rattled off a quick sentence, mixing Norsundrian words and modern Sartoran adjectival endings. The sentence concerned acknowledgement of a superior, but the Sartoran modifiers made a mockery of an otherwise straightforward statement.

Surprised, Clair nearly laughed, but the pulse of humor vanished. She wondered if the poopsies used such tricks to hold themselves apart from the regular run of Norsundrians, who might not have the facility in languages that Detlev had insisted on instilling in his boys. And yet, what was the difference between them all, truly? None.

"Let's talk about reports," he said. "What are you assuming, that anyone reading this text doesn't know how to write?"

"No, it's more like, a section on writing reports seems to assume that no one knows *what* to write. Even I, with no interest in anything military, can guess that if you're forced to be a spy or a scout, you write down what you see and hear. In as much detail as possible."

"That would be true of a certain type of commander, who permits no decision-making below him. But think of the result: this commander is absolutely buried in detailed reports, because if all decision rests on him, then he wants to know everything, right?"

"That," Clair said, "describes the king of the Chwahir."

"Who can serve as an example of the worst possible type of commander, and I'm not talking about him as a human being, though he's right up there in that regard, too."

"Almost," Clair said, "as bad as Detlev."

Roy shrugged, apparently unperturbed, and she scorned him and Detlev both: it was clear that loyalty was a triviality to them.

"The text is going to show you how to shape a report for a better command structure, which is to come to a conclusion first, then list, ranked by relative importance, the observations leading to that conclusion."

Clair had to admit that that made sense. But before she could respond, footsteps approached. She looked up at MV, Irenne's killer. Hatred burned through her. One day there would be justice. The sick fury roiling in her stomach intensified when she recognized that the word "justice" had not brought an image of him making life-restitution to Irenne's family, as he would have to in Mearsies Heili. She'd envisioned him with his throat cut. Like Irenne.

MV ignored Clair. To him she was a complication that he didn't want to exist. So as far as he was concerned, she didn't exist. "Now," he said to Roy, and jerked his thumb over his shoulder.

Roy swung to his feet, saying, "You do remember I had orders here, too?"

MV didn't answer, but loped away. Clair spat where he'd stood.

Roy's head turned at the sound, his expression difficult to read.

"I hope," she enunciated, "he drops dead. Like Irenne. Who was not even armed."

"I don't know if this helps, but he says he didn't intend that to happen."

"Then he shouldn't have had that blade at her throat," Clair said, arms crossed tightly.

Roy dipped his head. "Keep reading." He took off in MV's wake.

The days turned into a week, and two, then three, and then

four, falling into a pattern: she and Roy met after an early breakfast, and they went over her reading in the Norsundrian language.

He tried to translate some of the purely military theory into practical situations. Like, "You rule Mearsies Heili, and you discover that raiders have come over the border. Your people expect the crown to help, so what do you do first?"

Once in a while during those first couple of weeks, she mixed veiled insults into the language lessons, in unspoken challenge. Mearsiean slang usually went past him, but Roy got some of the others, and once he retorted, "Yeah, Adam came up with that one once. Here's a better one. Laban's the expert at word games . . ."

And it was actually funny, which caused another of those unsettling realizations: the poopsies played multi-lingual language games just as CJ did. The girls had always maintained, with smug confidence, that such creativity was strictly confined to *civilized* people. Light magic people.

Clair was always glad when Roy ran off to morning drill.

She woke one day, reflecting that she'd been a prisoner for almost two months. The thought lay like a stone around her heart.

As she levered herself reluctantly out of bed, she glanced at the text lying open on the little desk. What was this tension gripping the back of her neck? Couldn't be the prospect of finishing chapter one. She'd peeked at the second chapter, titled *Strategy*. She tried to shake off the mood as she stepped through the cleaning frame, then headed off to get breakfast.

The tension in the air sharpened. She fell back into slinking along walls, and peering ahead before rounding corners. She only entered the mess hall when she found it empty. Even that rare emptiness seemed somehow threatening.

She ate as fast as she could, but when she emerged, she spotted David crossing from one building to another. He moved stiffly. His head turned sharply, one of his hands coming up in a block before he recognized one of Detlev's office runners coming from the opposite direction.

When his head turned, Clair saw the mottling of bruising on his face. His hand came down and he walked on, but his stance radiated violence. He was the one who'd gone missing. Well, too bad he hadn't stayed wherever he was. If he was looking for someone to beat up, she was not going to be his target.

She worked on moving even more stealthily, always sticking to the perimeters of spaces, peering ahead to spot clear lines of retreat. Moving when gazes were elsewhere. Twice she spotted Terry, both times with Curtas, and both times in the proximity of horses. Though they seemed to be talking with at least surface civility, she backed away hastily, unwilling to draw attention to herself. Terry had not sought her out, so she had to assume he'd found his own manner of surviving.

She hated this kind of behavior. Where she went at home, there she was needed or at least welcome. But in learning this new skill of avoidance, she was now more aware when others used it.

For the most part, the poopsies sauntered about the place as if they owned it, sometimes making the trees ring with sudden, fast games of chase and violent tag that ended up in scraps, after which they'd get up and run away, usually laughing. And once, when no one else was around, she spied them doing handsprings across the grassy stuff, flips in the air, and similar acrobatics — the best of them, surprisingly, was the otherwise nondescript one they called the Ferret. He was almost as good as Dhana.

But then there were the days when they moved quietly, stealthily. On those days, she skipped meals and stuck to her room, except when she had to report to the critter cave.

Thirteen

A WEEK PASSED.

She and Roy had reached the second sub-heading in chapter two (the importance of supply in strategic planning) when she began to be aware that her occasional encounters with David were not accidental. She sensed that he was watching her from a distance.

He never spoke to her. Not as tall as MV, he moved without the martial saunter that characterized MV, and that people like Senrid found so challenging. Also unlike MV, who dressed entirely in black, with at least three knife hilts visible, David still could have passed for an ordinary person in his plain undyed tunic-shirt, usually unbelted, brown riding trousers, and forest mocs, with his fine-featured, thoughtful face.

But her first memory of him she would never forget. She sensed the violence that lay close to the surface of that mild smile and the contemplative gaze, a dichotomy that she disliked as much as she distrusted. She practiced her avoidance skills assiduously when she saw him, or MV. . . though she could not be sure they didn't notice anyway. At least Detlev had not yet returned.

Clair rose one morning, and with an unpleasant inner jolt realized she didn't dread the day as much as she had. The place had become habit.

"Am I switching without realizing it?" she whispered, looking into her mirror.

Her reflection appeared reassuringly the same, but still she resolved to recite the *Kanis Sel Deris* every morning before she left. Standing before the mirror, she watched her expression as she spoke aloud the familiar words. Hearing her own voice run through them without a falter steadied her considerably.

She knew the respite could not last.

The next sub-heading in chapter two caused Roy to take a side-trip into map-making lessons. Clair did not mind this detour. Though she hated thinking of countryside only in terms of lines of attack or retreat, or supply-lines, she knew she was getting a first-rate look into how the Norsundrians approached things. Therefore she ought to regard these lessons as learning ways to defend against them.

Ten days after David's return, Roy finished a study session, then sat back, giving her a considering gaze. "You might have to leave the little ones today," he said. "David runs our training. He says it's time to evaluate you."

She recognized that as a warning.

Roy ran off, and Clair headed toward her room.

She was halfway there when Adam appeared at her side. "Will you come with me, please? We're supposed to do a practice evaluation."

"What will that include?" Clair asked.

Adam gave her his sunny, guileless smile. "Outdoor stuff. Mostly. We already know that you're quick with decision making and leadership."

"So as Test Girl my performance will influence whether or not more girls will be forced to come here?"

Adam shrugged. "Ask Detlev about that. Until he returns, training is our responsibility. You learn fast, and adapt well," Adam went on.

Clair made sure her face and voice were completely neutral. She did not want Adam to notice how every compliment infuriated her the more. "So he's definitely thinking of grabbing other girls from home, is he?" she asked.

Adam gave her a quick look, his eyes narrowed thoughtfully, but he just shrugged again. "You'll have to—"

"Ask Detlev," she finished. *The day I cut off my ears and flap them to fly.*

They did not speak again until they reached the practice

field. No one was about, but she felt very distinctly that she was being watched.

"We can try this first." Adam moved to a rack with battered practice swords.

"I'm terrible at it," Clair said chirpily. She selected a blade too heavy for her hand and moved back, standing with it held at an awkward angle.

Adam sighed as he faced her and flashed his blade in a salute. Surprised by this courtesy, she felt her hand move before she could think: she saluted back, just as Puddlenose had taught her during those long-ago lessons when the Chwahir were a threat. At least her salute was slow and sloppy, as the weapon was far too heavy for her hand.

Adam did not seem to notice how her wrist promptly lost all its flexibility. Their bout lasted the space of a few heartbeats, and Adam repeatedly scored touches against her. Instinct did prompt her to riposte once, but she pulled it an instant later, turning it into a weak, awkward strike that accomplished nothing. Then she reinforced the impression by making three clumsy slashes through the air after his blade had moved away.

"All right," he said. "Looks like you need practice, doesn't it?" He dropped his sword into the rack.

"La," she cooed. "Do you really think I can learn?"

He shot her one of those looks again, then said, "Here next."

Knife throwing was something she was genuinely bad at; she'd preferred the bow. As she picked up the dagger that Adam indicated, she smiled down at it, thinking of the hours of practice a furious CJ had put in years ago, in an effort to prove to big, strong, skilled Rel that anything a boy could do a girl could do better. Even if she happened to be roughly half his size. "But knife throwing doesn't depend on size," CJ had said grittily, throwing knife after knife, then running to pull them out again.

Adam silently demonstrated how to weigh the blade, then reverse it and throw it, all one-handed. She'd never seen him move fast, so was startled when he snapped it with force and precision.

The knife thudded a finger's breadth off the dot in the target center, and Adam shook his head. "Should have warmed up," he said under his breath.

Clair hid her reaction. In her six months of determined grit, CJ had hit the center circle maybe a dozen times. Of course she hadn't practiced all day, or for much longer than those six determined months. There were too many meaningful and fun things to do with one's time.

Clair frowned down at the blade, making no effort to weigh it in her hand. She flung the knife in the direction of the target, knowing that she'd do badly. Still, it was hard not to laugh when it clattered against the target and thumped to the dust below it.

Adam went to retrieve the knives. "Was that an accident?" He dropped them onto the pile. "Or shall we try again?"

"It really was my best." She spread her hands.

He chuckled. "Come on." He picked up a quarterstaff and tossed it to her, then selected one for himself.

She thudded the staff on the ground once or twice, then put her hands on it in a fair imitation of Adam's grip.

Two hits, and she dropped hers. "That stings!" She wrung her fingers. "Ugh."

Adam whipped up the end of his staff and tossed it javelin-style into the holder, where it landed with a rattle. He faced Clair, his hands on his hips. "What would Dtheldevor say if she saw your performance today?"

Clair swallowed a laugh at his severe tone. "She'd say, 'Blast you, Bleachpate, you need some lessons!'"

Adam snorted a laugh. "All right. A couple more things to get out of the way —"

Footsteps crunched behind them. Clair's shoulder blades tightened. She whirled around to see David, MV, and Rolfin walk into the target practice area, other boys behind them. Quick, defensive assessment: MV's strange eyes narrowed to pinpoints of baleful light; Rolfin's hands flexing once, twice; the expression in David's still healing face mild, but tension in his walk. A closer look revealed more bruises under the dust imprinting his visible flesh.

David said, "Can't throw knives? We'll have to teach you."

Laban smiled. "Knifey-whizz?"

MV whirled around and grabbed up practice knives, his hands moving fast. He threw two to each of his friends, who caught them easily by the handles — except David, who snatched his out of the air by the blades and sent them whirling end over end into the sky before catching them again.

Then, laughing, they formed a circle around Clair, throwing knives back and forth within a scarce hand's breadth of her, catching them, sending them spinning close by her again. She knew not to move, and tried not to look at the cold glitter of steel wheeling right by her face and arms.

Raising her gaze to the sky, she waited.

They stopped as abruptly as they'd started, MV catching all the blades and sending them one by one to smack in a straight line down the middle of the target.

Then he flicked his long fingers across the back of her shoulder, shoving her forward. "Go get 'em," he said.

Clair gave him a brief silent look, then she turned and left. Or started to—when the iron fingers caught her arm and yanked her back, she knew she'd made a major tactical error.

"That was an order." David's face was solicitous, his voice a parody of kindness. "Do you have trouble understanding?"

I hate this. No. I hate you.

Clair's gaze went from his hand, with its still-healing bruises, to David's face, and from there to MV's pale brown eyes with the yellowish flecks.

A flash of self-mockery flickered through Clair's brain as she comprehended that this was what being Norsundrian was all about. All the gabble about objectivity, and being trained for every eventuality, and the softness and pettiness of lighters, none of that mattered. It all came down to the fact that the strongest got their way, whether that way was right or not.

She walked to the target, and tugged on the top knife with both hands. It did come free finally, sending her staggering.

Then a hand reached toward the next. Adam was at her side, helping her pull out the rest. He made it look easy, and together they quickly got them all. When they were done she helped Adam carry the practice knives back to the racks. Roy leaned against one of them, his face unreadable.

"I'll take those," he said.

"What's next?" David asked, his eyes wide. Manic. "Shall we see how good you are with your hands?"

Clair ignored him.

"Come on." He stepped in front of her. "Take a swing." Sticking his chin out, he put his hands behind him. "Hit me!"

Clair wanted to paste that grinning face so badly she felt a tingling in her fingers, but she did not make a fist, or otherwise acknowledge him.

"Wooo-hoooo!" the others howled and jeered.

"Please," David implored. "You gotta try. Now, I know you're just so nice and kind and you can't stand the thought of hurting anyone--"

He was drowned out by an even louder chorus of catcalls and moans, amid raucous laughter.

Clair kept her face blank, fighting the first throb of a headache.

"Come on . . . come on-n-n-n-n . . ." David crooned. "You can do it . . ."

Then a big hand thrust her hard between the shoulderblades, forcing her to stumble toward David. Only by wrenching herself aside did she avoid colliding with him.

"Coward," MV said scornfully.

No, I am not, Clair thought, and with a flash of burning anger, she realized she was in trouble no matter what she did. So she whipped her arm up and took a roundhouse swing, right at David's face.

Stars flashed across her vision and the next thing she knew she was flat on the dusty ground, her hair in her eyes. The eternal laughter was almost drowned by the buzzing in her ears.

"She obviously has no contact fighting experience." Roy's voice seemed to come from far away. "What's the point here?"

"Few of the lighters outside of Rel and Senrid are any good with their hands," Adam said patiently, in a You Knew That tone. "Even Dtheldevor's terrible. Though I wouldn't face her blade without a year of practice."

"Why don't you take her on the rest of the test," Roy suggested. "If Detlev's waiting to hear the big results."

David swung his head around and gave Roy a long, considering look—more, Clair thought, than the words had warranted. Roy didn't seem to notice. He lounged against the sword-rack, looking bored.

"What's left?" David asked.

"Archery." Adam extended a hand to Clair, who ignored it.

She got dizzily to her feet. Bending to dust herself off a bit, she breathed deeply, trying to fight the vertigo back. She would not stagger, and she would not let her hands shake. Rage seethed through her.

The archery area lay adjacent. Adam led Clair to the shed where the bows and arrows were kept, and several of the others ran to the targets and began capering in front of them, shouting mendacious encouragements.

She stood very still, aware of ambivalence. Civilized nations had long since agreed to the Covenant, forbidding the use of arrows in conflict. Though that, Clair had learned while traveling, was winked at by ships, as arrows were a defense against pirates. Puddlenose had taught Clair archery as a sport, something he'd learned after his first sailing trip.

The Marlovens had never agreed to the Covenant. Senrid had said shortly during a discussion once that Norsunder would not be so finicky when they did decide to invade.

And here was the evidence.

Well, then.

As Adam eyeballed her and selected a bow the proper length, her rage hardened into a cold determination. She stood by while he strung the bow for her and showed her how to notch the arrow.

Clair watched, making no move to indicate that she was adept at this particular skill already. When Adam put the bow into her hands, she dashed her white hair back from her eyes, and said clearly, "Sorry. I don't shoot at people."

Scorn and catcalls afresh met this pronouncement—as she'd known it would.

She took her time picking from among the arrows that Adam held out, and then, with the strung bow in one hand and an arrow in the other, she stood, looking skyward for a long moment, making sure her wrists were steady.

When she felt centered, she slowly bent to notch the arrow, standing sideways to the targets as she subtly tested the tension in the snapvine string. The catcalls increased.

And suddenly she whirled, aimed and let fly—straight at MV's head.

Trained reflex made him spin sideways and lean back. Everyone stared at the arrow quivering where he'd stood.

"Ooops," Clair's voice was mild, but she knew they heard her. "That was a mistake. Just like Irenne." Despite all her control her voice broke on her friend's name.

MV ripped out a laugh, leaning against the wall for support.

Clair had to leave.

Right now.

She took a few steps, then ran.

Fourteen

THE POOPSIES WERE STILL laughing about Clair's skills test over dinner.

David took their banter with his usual good humor, but Roy could see that something was on his mind. As he had since his return, he ignored the indirect probing about the Black Knives run. MV provided colorful obloquy in his succinct style, which convulsed the listeners.

When everyone had eaten they all got up to go, David moving stiffly.

"Still bad?" Adam asked.

"I'll live," David said, and fell in step beside Roy. "Why haven't you started the Mearsiean with training?"

"Detlev said begin with the language."

David looked sideways at him. "Did you know about the archery?"

"Of course I did. Planned the whole thing out with her. And Adam, who was supposed to do the testing."

David laughed. "See that she starts with the babies. I'll send Noser over to give her someone to work against."

"After tutoring," Roy said. "Mornings, Detlev wants me tutoring."

Bringing in Detlev's name was a shield. It worked, of course.

David and MV took off, Adam soon after.

Roy let out a long, silent breath.

Time to go.

Regret tugged sharply, and dissolved in relief.

That, and the knowledge that there was no turning back.

The next day, after they finished their lesson, Roy said to Clair, "You've got the language well enough, and David says it's time for you to get some physical training. Go to the obstacle course, where you'll start with the five-year-olds."

"Am I supposed to find that insulting?" she asked, annoyed. "If I'm serving as Test Girl preparatory to forcing more of us into this horrible place, I can guarantee that the five-year-olds are going to look like trained warriors next to me."

"Detlev isn't even here. We train because we need to be ready for anything, and a ready mind needs a ready body."

For violence, Clair thought, rolling her eyes. But because she knew what would happen if she disobeyed, she stashed her text in her room and they headed down the hall in the opposite direction, through the door she'd never tried. It opened onto the obstacle course that she'd seen only once, on her tour with Roy.

Here she found a gray-uniformed Norsundrian with a small group of five-year-olds whom she recognized from the critter cave. Her heart jolted when she recognized the blond urchin they called Noser, who appeared to have invited himself along. Close up she could see that the redness of his lips was chapping, and his fingernails were bitten down to the quick. He was not as tall as Clair—came up to her chin—but she did not make the mistake of thinking that he needed rudimentary training.

And so it proved. The leader had them run around in a circle, swinging their arms. He called it slow, but Clair was sprinting hard. As for the five-year-olds, their shorter legs seemed to twinkle with speed. They had obviously been doing this a long time, and Clair found herself put to it to keep up.

When she flagged, a hand thumped into her back, nearly jolting her off her feet. "No slacking off," Noser said with a nasty grin.

Then the leader clapped twice, and the little boys headed off toward the obstacle course. Before they'd completed the vaulting, climbing, hand-over-hand, swinging, and leaping round once, Clair's breath rasped in her throat, and her hair flopping in a sweaty, tangled mass on her back, which was already baking in the hot sun. Any time she flagged, Noser was right behind her, shoving, an insult on his lips.

After the first round, they did it again. And again. Before that last one, she stood with her hands on her knees, spots swimming before her eyes. Noser hit the back of her head flat-handed. "Asleep? How about double-time?"

The hit stung. She turned on him, livid with anger. "Don't. Touch me."

"What're you gonna do, cry?" he retorted. "Or wanna scrap?" He stuck his chin out and danced from toe to toe. He wasn't even breathing hard.

Clair sucked in a breath and forced herself to move, even though she could barely stagger, much less run. At least the five-year-olds were flagging, too, but she caught a few questioning glances, and nerved herself to try harder. She sensed that she would lose any authority she had over them at the critter house if she was worse than them here.

After the obstacle course, they had a moment to catch their breath as they trotted to the archery field. From the smell, the horses had recently been there, and Clair turned her head in time to catch the last of the horses walking toward the stable. She recognized Terry's limping form a heartbeat before he vanished beyond a building.

At least he was all right. Did they make him run obstacle courses? Or did they disdain people who didn't have four sound limbs?

She didn't know — wouldn't ask — and she'd better watch where she was stepping. But it turned out all the horse droppings had been wanded from the dusty ground, no doubt now enriching the soil in the kitchen garden.

Ordinarily she could have held her own at archery, but her arms felt like loose string and her hands throbbed from the ropes she had swung from and climbed. She managed to shoot along with the others, and hit some part of the target each time, but toward the last the effort it took to pull was nearly excruciating.

"See you tomorrow," Noser said, and ran off toward the poopsie barracks.

Clair was too tired to do anything but turn away. The little boys were dismissed to lunch. She was grateful that apparently they were considered too small yet for the knife throwing and quarterstaffs. She hurt too much to be hungry, but made herself get food, and drank three glasses of water.

When she reached the critter cave, Guem welcomed her with a mug of listerblossom steep. "They told me you were there," he said sympathetically.

"Don't you have to do that stuff?" she asked.

"Balance problems," he said with a brief smile. "When I lost my sight and hearing"—as he spoke he tapped his right ear and eye— "I lost the ability to run well. I always feel like I'm on a boat."

So that was why he moved the way he did. "Did you want to become a warrior when you joined Norsunder?" she asked.

He laughed. "I didn't join anything. I was yanked out of my apprenticeship at a brewery when the Guild Council declared war, and the local count needed to fill his quota of bodies. I never did learn how to fight, but we were pushed to the front, I ended up on the ground, and when I woke up, and got my wits back, I was a prisoner of war. When someone came through offering freedom, I chose it. Ended up here." He shrugged. "I like it here. I even brew up some ale, if they bring me my supplies. It never lasts long, though."

No wonder he didn't play with the critters. He continued to move around smoothly and efficiently, but as the day progressed, she noticed for the first time that whenever they spoke, he always had his left side toward her.

So much for her powers of observation.

She'd already decided that this was going to be a story game day, with the boys acting out their story while she watched. She'd put together some of Falinneh's favorites while forcing down her lunch.

When she was done, she skipped dinner, and went straight to bed.

The next day she started out sore and miserable. Noser was there to make certain she was even more miserable. The third day was exactly the same. But the fourth was somewhat easier, and the fifth.

Within a couple of weeks, she found it arduous but bearable, and at least she wasn't lagging behind the five-year-olds. By the end of the month, she could stay ahead of them.

She still hated it, but the morning drill had become routine.

Fifteen

Al-Athann

"I'M WORRIED ABOUT JEORY," Leotay said to Dom Hildi over their first meal of the round.

"Why?" the old woman said, sipping at the spicy hot drink they all loved so much.

Seshe sat quietly, trying not to notice how little the old magician put on her plate, and how long it took her to get through that scant portion.

Leotay sighed. "He never comes down for meals anymore, and he's thinner than ever. Nothing he says makes sense, and he's clumsier than ever. He never seems to see anything real about him; he lives in a world of dream-visions, and he loves it."

"Repeat that last," the old lady said, sipping again, and smacking her lips.

"He loves it," Leotay repeated obediently.

"There's your answer. The Thing selected him, and he it. Whatever the cost of the magic he is learning, he is willing to pay it. Let him be."

"As you wish," Leotay said, with another sigh. "He wants me to give him lessons in the rudiments of our magic, in case it helps him see past the tapestry. I have no idea what tapestry he means. Nor do I understand the things he talks about. Even the visitor doesn't understand many of them."

"Give him whatever he asks for."

"I will."

"And when he's had enough, I think it is time for you to make your visit to the Outside."

Leotay was left with nothing to say. Outside was forbidden to anyone but the Hildis, in charge of the sun-globes.

"Yes, it is time," Dom Hildi said on a firm note.

Change, Leotay thought. At first the prospect was so exciting, but now she felt . . . strange. Unsettled.

"Our Visitor must show you the way once you reach the top."

"And the sun-globes?"

"Leave them. If need be, they can be changed at the regular time. And you gain the benefit of seeing the place, as you explore with the Visitor."

Leotay nodded, and cramming the last of her food into her mouth, scrambled to her feet.

Seshe stayed with Dom Hildi, and they talked of wind and weather and how cracked, flat land might be brought, some-day, to grow things again.

When Leotay returned, it was with Quicksilver. The three of them left, and started up the long, treacherous stone path called the Forbidden Way.

Seshe did not think of herself as sedentary—no one who delighted in roaming forestland for entire days could be—but she still found it difficult. The narrow passage was sometimes mere cracks between stone, requiring them to crawl sideways, bracing hands and knees, and other times, the rubble was dangerous and painful on the feet, and yet Leotay and Quicksilver moved swiftly. She gritted her teeth and toiled grimly behind, reminding herself that old Hildi had made this trip all her life, lugging glowglobes. At last they came to a tiny platform, and Leotay doused her illusory blob of light, and performed an unsealing spell as Seshe watched, wondering how she'd managed to get past that on coming inside.

Hreealdar knows magic? she thought as an illusory rock flickered out of existence. Then she felt stupid. Hreealdar IS magic.

Abruptly the full glare of afternoon hit their faces. Seshe squeezed her eyes shut, and heard Leotay gasp beside her.

When she felt her eyes had adjusted Seshe opened them, to see Leotay kneeling on the stone, both hands pressed over her face. Quicksilver had turned around, leaning his head against the stone, his eyes closed.

"Shades," Seshe said, remembering the darkened spectacles that CJ had once described. "You need shades."

"What's that?" Leotay's voice was muffled by her fingers.

Seshe said quickly, "Never mind. Something from another world." Had their eyes lost their ability to see in the day? No. She remembered the moth cave. It wasn't as bright as noon, but regular days weren't bright as noon all day, either.

"I think we need to come back at sunrise," she said, thinking that she would never get used to being the "expert" for people not just older than she, but in so many ways far more skilled.

"When would that be?" Leotay asked, hands pressed against her eyes. "The Hildis always chose dark time, so they would never be seen. She thought we must be here at light time in order to see."

"When the sun comes up the light comes gradually," Seshe explained. "Maybe Dom Hildi will know when it comes here?" she asked without much hope.

But after the long toil of the return journey, and their disappointing report, Dom Hildi surprised them by exclaiming, "Of course. That has long been a duty of the Hildis, to calculate our dark time visits. Our sands began marking dark from light, though at times of the year our round doesn't quite match the round of day to light Outside. But if you leave at Green, you should be able to achieve what you wish."

Seshe woke abruptly when Leotay came to get her what turned out to be the next morning. Back up that long route — only slightly easier now that she knew what to expect — until they again reached the platform, Leotay dissolved the illusionary rock, and they ventured out.

Starlight blued a sizable cliff, ringed with rock jutting upward like teeth, smoothed by years of wind. Nestled in an area that gained maximum advantage of the sun lay glowglobes, each with a tiny blue star of magic that sucked in sunlight.

They passed those by, walking carefully as the shadows sharpened and the plateau gradually assembled dimension, then color. Seshe marveled at the thin layers of sediment making up the light brown of the stone as the other two stood between two of the rock teeth, staring outward.

The first ray of sun struck gleams into the sediment layers, throwing dramatic shadows westward over the plateau and down onto the plain.

Quicksilver gazed out, then up.

"I feel like I'm going to fall into it," he said, stumbling backward. He landed flat, head upturned, chest heaving under his silken layers, fingers clutching the ground. Leotay cast herself down beside him, and their inner hands laced fingers tightly, outer gripping the ground.

Seshe waited, then got an idea. She walked very slowly around them. She could tell by the minute movements of their heads that they were tracking her. Both their faces tightened, and sweat shone on their foreheads.

But after the third time, Quicksilver was the first to turn his head from side to side. He understood that his body stayed put. There would be no diving upward the way he dove down into the pool that was so small compared to this . . . sky.

He forced himself upright, steadying himself with stiff arms. Leotay followed, then rose to her feet, arms outstretched, fingers spread. "This is enough for today," she said huskily.

Quicksilver looked relieved.

And back they climbed the long, long route to the hidden caves. The tension leaked out of them as soon as they entered the tunnel.

The following day, they chose sunset for their arrival. The sun was westering when they emerged, slowly, carefully, the two with hands out lest they get snatched into the darkening sky.

They bombarded Seshe with questions about distance, shadow, perspective, and the colors of light, until the sun sat on the horizon, an angry red ball, on the other side of the distant Norsundrian compound.

They stared at that compound in grim silence. Seshe divided her attention between it and them. She suspected that Clair and Terry were imprisoned there. But for Leotay's people, that Norsundrian camp represented the wrongness that had happened to their world, and which stood in the way of generations of hope.

Seshe considered how strange it was, that the impulsive decision—almost an accident—in her own life was probably the single most important thing in their lives. What important moments in her life were mere occurrences in others' lives?

That made her think, for some reason, of Morgeh, reluctant prince of Wnelder Vee. "The best music," he'd said once, "is a blend of different melody lines, each a separate voice, with its own story to tell." She teetered on the edge of understanding, then lost the connection. It had to be a question of perception — and oh, how she wished Clair were present to talk it over with!

Leotay turned her head. "You say that those who live there are human, as are you and me. Why is it they can be so different, to want to cause only death and destruction? Can there be misunderstanding, as when we did not know what you meant by 'blue-sky', but thought we did?"

Seshe shook her head. "Their leader has trained them to set aside all their humanity. Well, the good side of it," she amended quickly. "Some people do stupid things, or mean things. But most of us try to see evil in ourselves, and get rid of it. Not Detlev's gang. When we were stuck with them in the forest of Wnelder Vee, it's true that some of my side wanted to make the . . . the dueling games serious. But they didn't know how. It was Detlev's villains," she nodded at the distant compound, "who made it serious by killing my friend." Her voice trembled. "They don't value any of the same things we do. Not friendship, or truth, or loyalty, or beauty. . . " Images flickered in her mind: Adam, at his drawing, long talks about forest life, friends, the past.

But she banished what had to be a pose. How could he value anything that she did, and still live with the rest of them and share their goals? "So they're human," Seshe finished, hardening her voice. "But they're rotten excuses for people. And they'll kill you if they can, and crow afterward about their skills in doing it."

Quicksilver stirred, his fingers touching the hilt of the knife worn at his side. He said nothing as he squinted up, then his face changed. "See? The little lights Dom Hildi spoke of, coming there in the east. Ah, now I can see this sky as a cave ceiling." He waved long, thin fingers toward the sky.

Leotay bit her lip as the last of the sun disappeared. "I think we had better return," she said. "Dom Hildi will be waiting."

Seshe followed, dreading the long journey back.

Sixteen

AT THE END OF Gold, the private signal Dom Hildi had set up with Leotay chimed for attention.

"Do you need anything more?" Leotay asked Jeory.

"I think I have enough now," he said.

Leotay looked about his empty cave, the hairs at the back of her neck lifting. She sensed magic, lots of it, so much that it sang at the back of her mind. As she moved, the air seemed thick with it, and sparkles caught at the edges of her vision.

"Whatever it is you're doing," she said, "I hope . . . "

Jeory waited, smiling, his eyes so wide they reflected the lights of the glowglobes, bright pinpoints that made his eyes seem feverish. When she did not finish, he said, "They are always around, you see. And I am with them, and will always be with them."

"They?" Leotay asked, thinking of Dom Hildi and Quick-silver and the others.

Jeory's thin fingers rippled slightly as his hands rose. His eyes closed. "The light folk," he whispered. "I know not how else to call them, for they do not speak in words. But in music, calling to me, and when I blow into this Thing, just a whisper, I can call back, and there they are, taking aside the tapestry so that I can see them in the green world, rising up and up toward the sky, ever so slow, and full of light, and then they fall down again, slow." He opened his eyes. "The world is full of them, music resounding."

Leotay waited, but he said nothing more, and she realized she didn't even know how to frame the questions in her mind. Music was the key—somehow. She knew that much. Seshe had told her that mages in her world spoke words, or made signs to perform magic. They didn't sing their magic. Jeory seemed to be coming at something important about music, and magic, from . . . where? No one understood him.

She smothered a sigh of uneasiness, and left.

It was a longish walk back down from the abandoned cave that Jeory had chosen for his practice place, but she did it at a run.

As she neared her own platform, her worries shifted from Jeory to Dom Hildi.

She almost didn't see Horsefeathers standing with two friends near the entrance. Her instinct was to brush by, but she forced herself to stop, and smile.

"After sleep, Grapevine, Rilvay, and Ornament are going to the Dome," Horsefeathers said. "Come with us." She added hastily, "The Visitor said she'd like to see it."

Leotay gazed down into her sister's expectant face. The weight of her responsibilities dragged at her, and her head throbbed. But she knew that to deny Horsefeathers before her friends would shame her younger sister, so she said, forcing a smile, "Certainly. It'll be fun."

Her reward was the quick hug from Horsefeathers. Then the girls dashed away, for it was past time for sleep.

Leotay went inside. "You called?" she tried to keep anxiety from thinning her voice.

"A dream," Dom Hildi said huskily, smiling. She did not try to get up from her bed. "A vision in my dream. I believe there is someone in that domicile out on the plain who is with us." She tapped head and heart. "And he comes. Now. You must meet with him, at the place where the Forbidden Path emerges from our mountain. Quickly."

"Me?"

"You. Speak for us, Leotay. This is very important. Things . . ." The old woman pursed her lips, then smiled again. "Things will change now from round to round. But it is for our freedom."

Leotay nodded. "I know."

"And . . ." Dom Hildi reached to clasp Leotay's unresisting hand in her old one, the grip still strong. "And we each attain freedom in our own way. Remember that, too."

"All right."

Dom Hildi pulled her hand away, and made a whisking movement with one gnarled hand. "Now go. And send Quicksilver in, for he and I must talk."

Leotay scrambled to her feet and went out, nearly colliding with Quicksilver at the outer tapestry. "She wants you," Leotay whispered.

He gripped her shoulder, the same gesture they would use to reassure a youngster who woke up with troubling dreams. But the warmth of his touch shimmered through her, and his hand rested there long enough for her to turn her head to meet his eyes. Another shimmer spread warmth through her, and she sensed in the change in his breath that he felt something, too.

They did not speak—too many responsibilities pulled them apart at this moment—but each of them felt a sense of promise. Her hand rose to cup his face, her thumb circling the edge of his chin, then a slight stirring from Dom Hildi's cave caused them both to step away, he to go inside, she to head once again for the long tunnel.

Her feet and hands took her safely along, while her mind lingered on the shape of Quicksilver's lips, the contours of his face. She smiled, wondering how it was that the lineaments of one person's familiar features could ignite the brightest sun-globe within oneself?

Darkness had fallen when she emerged on the mountain into bitter cold. She scarcely had time to rub her hands over her roughening skin when her eyes caught the movement of white to one side.

She backed away, then stilled, recognizing the White Horse of Seshe's story as the horse walked into the tunnel past her, then vanished in a flash of light that caused her to jump back, startled.

Left outside on the cliff stood a human silhouette, someone a little taller than she.

Alarm poised her to run; could Dom Hildi be wrong?

"I'm here to help," the person said, in her own language.

"Then come within," Leotay said, though her heart hammered. "I will not speak with a shadow."

He obliged her by following her into the cave. There, she hummed up a witch light, and in its light, she gazed on a boy somewhat younger than her age. He had wide-set, small eyes like Seshe's, and long ears, and an angular face. His hair and clothing were dark.

"Are you then a friend?" Leotay asked, though she remembered what Dom Hildi had said.

"Yes, sent by another, the one who has hereto helped your Dom Hildi through visions."

Leotay drew her breath in. "You know her name?"

"Lilith has been watching over you, from afar, for many years."

"Lilith. So Seshe said!"

"The Mearsiean is inside?"

"She is one of your own kind," Leotay said, and saw a funny, twisted smile line the boy's face. "She is also a friend," she amplified.

"Yes. I'm here to tell you that you'll have some magic help from Lilith and me, when you decide to come out. But it has to be soon."

"Yes, so we believe as well. The signs are all present, and our people are restless. Can you tell me about yon settlement?"

"Here is a description." He went on to tell her about its gate, protections, and where they would find enemies and where not. He finished with: "Be certain to tell Seshe that Clair and Terry are all right."

"I will carry your message," Leotay said. "Will you come again?"

"If I can. But it's a big risk. I can't be missed." He glanced back over his shoulder, as if he expected watchers to be there. His expression was impossible to interpret.

"Then I thank you, friend," Leotay said. "For me, and for Seshe, and for Dom Hildi, and for our people."

"Right," he said. "Right." He walked out of the cave and vanished from sight.

Leotay thought about what she had heard as she raced back down the tunnel to the cavern that had long been home.

In through Dom Hildi's tapestry, and there was Quicksilver, obviously waiting.

"We have a friend," Leotay said. "And he told me—" But his gaze was no longer warm and tender. Sorrow raised his brows, and made his mouth long and thin. "What?" And her first thought was of Dom Hildi. "No!"

Quicksilver caught her hands before she could burst inside.

"She knew her end was near, and wanted it to be easier for you. But she talked of the plan, and of freedom, right to the end."

"She sent me away on purpose," Leotay said, her eyes filling with tears.

"She's free now," Quicksilver said. "I was to tell you that. Here or outside, her old body was too long a prison. Her books, and spells, and guardianship are yours."

Leotay coughed on a sob.

"I'll call the Gathering," Quicksilver said, and pulled her against him. "We owe her a Singing, maybe our last, and maybe our best."

Leotay swallowed down her grief, though tears dripped down her face. She did what she had longed to: wrapped her arms tightly around Quicksilver, and rested her head on his shoulder. "Let's make it our best," she said, her voice catching on a sob. "Our last song, for freedom."

Seventeen

The Den

FOR CLAIR, FADING INTO the woodwork was now daily habit.

She had no idea how months worked here. Sartorias-deles had a moon, with a cycle of close to thirty-six days—the shortfall made up with New Year's Week. Geth-deles, she'd learned, had at least two moons, and they counted time differently.

Here didn't bother asking how they counted time. Days and nights passed, to be endured while she was a prisoner. She tallied the days in thirty-sixes. When she had counted to six months, she found that fact so appalling that she tried to force herself to stop marking time, because six months again might pass, a year, and then years. A prisoner, away from home, for *years.*

She noticed drearily how the sun slanted differently, and how mornings—still dry and dusty—had become cold. By noon she still avoided the sun, but it was no longer broiling hot.

Clair continued to refine her sneakery, always on the watch, always avoiding any encounter with Detlev's boys if she could possibly help it, while waiting for the inevitable repercussions.

But nothing happened, though she sensed David watching from afar with that shuttered expression and steady gaze that made her nerves flare with warning. There was no friendship in that stare. The way he stood, the angle of his head, made his suspicion — resentment — clear.

Roy continued to tutor her as they sat under the odd trees in what passed for a garden. They did not eat together at meals, and they didn't see one another at any other time, but she knew she was being watched. Evaluated. Found wanting. (Good.)

There were a few not-rotten things: first, Noser stopped coming to her practices, as she was now faster than the little boys. Second, she'd made friends with little Mac, who did not let a day go by without begging for stories. She had begun telling him real history from her world, stories about heroic people and defeats of Norsunder, though she called them "the enemy" in case mentioning Norsunder by name would call attention to what she was doing. And third, there were times when the lessons with Roy were almost enjoyable.

She did like arguing with him, as he never got angry, but always offered interesting examples out of history. He was very, very well read — he reminded her of Arthur in that. And she couldn't help remembering that the two boys had been study and travel friends before it turned out that Roy was an enemy.

Detlev did not send for her, the girl experiment was not cancelled, no one came to get her for weapons training sessions — the poopsies left her alone.

Sometimes she caught sight of them out at the practice field. Noser's laughter rose as he sat on this or that boy's back as they did push-ups or held themselves in plank position just above the ground, elbows bent, pressed tight against their sides. Sometimes they scrapped, with or without knives. And sometimes they rode the horses back and forth, shooting at targets. But they did it by themselves, without the company of any of the others who came and went.

She knew better than to become complacent. The threat was covert rather than overt, but it was still very much there, in David's watchful gaze.

After a time, she became aware that she was reciting the *Kanis Sel Deris* each morning also out of habit, without hearing a word. Her mind had begun wandering while her mouth spoke by rote. The preamble to Mearsiean law was still good, still true, and she still believed every word. But *reciting* it had become a routine without meaning.

Being a lighter meant more than outward forms.

There came a morning when she went as usual to Roy's room for her Norsundrian lessons. These had metamorphosed from map-making into the fundamentals of reconnaissance. She approached Roy's room by a circuitous route, avoiding all wide spaces. Her tension eased a little when she knocked on his door and he answered.

Instead of being told to sit down at the desk as usual, he grabbed up a jacket. "Detlev's gone again."

"So?" Though inside she did feel a cautious sense of relief.

Roy shrugged. "I think you know a little more about what's at stake here," he began.

An ambivalent statement if there ever was one.

"And you can be trusted. Some. So we're going out for a riding lesson." Without waiting for an answer, he added, "It'll be cold. Go get something warm and meet me at the stables."

She crossed her arms and stood firm. "If that means hearing more horrors about Norsunder, I don't want to be trusted."

Roy laughed. "Just the opposite." He gave her a gentle push. "Go."

She considered arguing for form's sake, then decided she was more curious about the ride than she was about how the argument would come out. She snake-in-the-grassed back to her room, grabbed up her cloak, and fled to the stable.

Roy was there waiting, with two saddled horses. They mounted up, and when they reached the gate, he jumped down, performed a spell that flashed over the gate, then he lifted the bar and pushed the gate open as one of the sentries watched idly. Roy left the gate open, remounted, then clucked his horse into a canter.

They rode toward the jagged rock hills jutting on the horizon at a distance difficult to gauge because of the featurelessness of the land around them. They could have been close — or they could have been days away.

Roy rode straight for them, and Clair followed, silent and curious.

After a time he slowed his horse and then stopped. She did as well, and as the horses walked, he said abruptly, "You'll have to save your shock, but I know you won't believe me any other way--"

And without warning he made contact in second, so that she was in his thoughts—and he in hers.

:*I am a lighter.* She heard, clean as air and wind, the pride and conviction in his thought. And from a distance came another mental voice, one she had briefly experienced, but never forgotten: *Roy tells you the truth, Clair. Listen. Time is short.*

:*Lilith the Guardian!* Tears stung Clair's eyes. And though she did not mean it to, still the thought went as clearly: *I thought I was alone.*

:*No.* The thought was warm and tender, followed by seriousness: *But Roy and I do important work here, and that means great risk. Now you are a part of it, if you wish to be.*

Then she was gone. And, swift as water, a vivid series of memories flowed from Roy: Lilith making a deal with a highly placed Norsundrian (who wanted to leave) to swap Roy with another baby. Roy, having been born with Dena Yeresbeth— which Clair heard as *coinherence* in Roy's memory—already had a strong enough connection with Lilith to keep his identity intact.

He was raised with the other boys. At first he started to accelerate past them. When there was talk of making him the leader he had to slow down, until the others his age caught up—and catch up they did, especially when others discovered Dena Yeresbeth talents.

As fast as the memories came, questions flickered faster, like light on water. Who else had *coinhered,* as he called *making their unity*? What was the cost of his having to pretend? How did he feel, having to stand by and watch them do cruel things and be rewarded for it?

There was no answer, no acknowledgement that Roy heard her questions. As quickly as it began, the memory-exchange ended.

"But . . . Detlev assigned you to me," Clair exclaimed, still skeptical.

"That disturbs me, too," Roy said. "Because I think he, and

perhaps David, are beginning to suspect me, ever since my days of study with Arthur."

"Can you get me out of here?" she asked quickly, and when she saw the quick brow-furrow of refusal, she said, "I know you studied light magic as well as dark. A lot. You can make world transfers, right? I could give you this." She yanked her medallion out from under her tunic. "Take it for however long you need to put the world-transfer spell on it."

"Not yet." He shook his head. "That's why we're out here. If it were just a matter of you, me, and Terry, we'd already be gone. But there is something you need to know: there are people in those mountains, the only ones left of the original Aldau-Rayad." He squinted off toward the distant jagged hills. "Right now, Lilith's goal is to see them freed and the world back in their hands. They are nearly ready to make their try, and I hope they can while Detlev is still away."

"Have you told Terry?"

"He just wants out," Roy said. "I don't think he's ready for the extra burden of this secret. When the time comes, I suspect he'd be happy to join any plan going, if it means escape."

Clair nodded slowly. That sounded like Terry.

"He's trying hard to lie low. Be a good stable hand. They won't mess with him if they find him boring. It's you who caught David's interest."

"But I haven't done anything. I've tried to hide, and stay out of sight."

Roy said slowly, "David got marsh-madness on Geth. Never mind what it is. But in certain ways, his cohesion, or coinherence—what you hear called Dena Yeresbeth—far surpasses mine. I suspect you'll make your coinherence before long, and he might be sensing it."

"But what can I do? I'm not in any position to—"

"You can do plenty," he cut in. "Even your hatred of MV might be used as a necessary deflection. Detlev might be gone, but right now David can be considered almost as dangerous. We're going to need to deflect him long enough for those mountain people to arrive and break the wards here. But we'll talk about that later. For now, remember: things are as usual. Including grumping when I ask you for anything extra, and avoiding me as well as the others."

Clair shook her head, remembering those long conversations aboard Dtheldevor's ship. She'd have to reassess them yet again. How lonely he must have been, enacting a double role around all these hateful people —

"Let's race," he said suddenly.

They galloped the horses back again.

Before they reached the gates, he said, "You know how to do mind-shields."

"Yes, Liere taught us."

"Get back into that habit." He looked away. "You should also know that anything you throw into your wastebasket doesn't stay torn up. You can probably figure out the restoration wards. David read the first couple of letters, but then he detailed that duty to me. I haven't read any of them. They went straight into the fire."

She flushed, grimacing down at the reins in her hands. She should have guessed about the letters, and as for the mind-shield, of late she hadn't bothered. Detlev had been the only one to make mental contact, and she couldn't believe anything could keep *him* out. But Roy's words spiked the familiar danger and threat, and she spent the rest of the ride building a wall from the inside of her mind, the way Liere had taught her and the girls.

Roy shut the gate and restored the magic ward, then they trotted the rest of the way to the stables. When Roy threw his reins to the boy waiting for the horses, she caught herself just as she was about to thank him for a good time.

Roy dismounted and walked off. Clair turned away, summoning a scowl as she went in the opposite direction — passing a shadowed alcove, out of which David stepped.

He caught her arm.

She stiffened, the scowl intensifying. She didn't try pulling away — she wouldn't give him the satisfaction. She could feel anger boiling off him like steam from a hot spring.

"Where did you go?"

"Riding out on the plain," she said, short and flat.

"Why?"

"Riding test." The lie came to her lips as if she'd planned it.

He accepted that, let go, and said, "How did you do?"

"I passed." She turned away, her shoulders braced.

But all she heard was a laugh as she retreated as fast as she could.

She thought about Roy all afternoon as she played with the

little ones, re-examining old conversations from this new perspective, and reassessing actions, until Mac, who considered her his own special property, got annoyed with her absentmindedness. "The story," he said impatiently, his voice rising. "You're forgetting the story."

She forced her attention back to her tale about Dtheldevor and her crew defeating a Norsundrian blockade of Wnelder Vee's harbor. But she called the Norsundrians "eleveners," the old pejorative, and Mac didn't question it.

Coming out of the critter cave, she saw David again, this time lounging on the grass beneath a tree, his hands employed carving a piece of wood. MV sat next to him. Cold crawled between her shoulder blades; the way they both stared at her so silently, she knew they had been talking about her. She glanced away.

David's *slash slash slash* of the blade on the wood seemed deliberate.

She walked on, and no one followed.

Eighteen

Next morning she went to Roy's as usual. Though he seemed tense, he acted as if nothing had happened the day before.
Taking her cue from him, she got right to her lesson.

At the end, he said soberly, "Clair, I can't do anything but
prepare you for what's coming next."

She stiffened. "Another test?"

"Not the way you mean. It's your friend. Irenne."

"She's dead," Clair whispered. "I saw her fall. So much
blood . . ."

"Well, yes and no. That is, before she actually expired MV
threw a stone spell on her."

"That's a very difficult spell."

"He had it ready for Rel, never mind why. Didn't happen.
And you need to know the rest. MV used the stone spell in a
desperate attempt to stave what could not be staved. He held
her with a very sharp blade, and she turned her head straight
into the steel. A main artery was cut, which caused her to lose
blood very fast, too fast to remain alive. Detlev told him this is
his responsibility to resolve." Roy heaved a hard breath. "So
he made a bloodknife. The stone spell wore off recently, and
he was there. Made her a soul-bound."

Clair stared in shock and horror, unable to speak.

Hating every word, Roy grimly went on. "But she hasn't

been bound to anyone, or to any, ah, purpose. She's just there, caught between death and a semblance of life."

"And they're going to force me to see her like that?"

"Yes." Another deep breath. "In a way," he said slowly, "MV thinks the situation, ah, um, not right, because there is no right here. But that you ought to see her. Only he won't have anything to do with making it happen. David will, but his motivation is . . ." A sharp, hissing breath. "Let's just say he resents your being here."

"The only thing in the world that we agree on," Clair said flatly, her stomach churning.

"And he resents my being sent to tutor you. He suspects us both. And he won't make it easy." Roy's gaze dropped.

Clair still couldn't bring herself to thank him for the warning. She was too horror-stricken, too unnerved, and too furious. All she could think was that it would happen only if they found her.

She hurried away, avoiding the mess hall. Too open, and she couldn't eat anyway. Not now. Her guts churned with fury, grief, dread. Shock. To hide, she slunk to the library, which was always empty. There she stood, tense and angry, questions each more horrible than the last yowling in her mind. She had no answers. Desperate to distract herself, she prowled the shelves on the map wall, and discovered reports on Sartorias-deles kingdoms.

Of course she hunted for Mearsies Heili—surprised when she found a report with her kingdom's name neatly labeled. It was thin, with few pages, and even in the flat Norsundrian language she could tell that the writer was bored. Written according to the model she'd been taught in Roy's text on writing military reports, it contained a precise description of the geography, borders, main government and trade centers, and finished with a flat statement that the unpopulated western portion of the kingdom was militarily indefensible, but equally there would be little gain but wild land that would have to be occupied and defended.

Last was a description of the white palace as a marble structure whose only defense was its location on top of a hill, and reports stated that there might be a Selenseh Redian nearby, demonstrating the usual volatile attributes.

Volatile attributes. Marble palace.

That palace was not marble. Weird, how everyone

admired the white palace when they were there, and went away thinking it had been made of limestone, marble, anything but whatever it was.

Then followed a list of what they called key personnel. Most of the data was about Clair's Aunt Murial, a hermit mage who had studied at the northern mage school, and was allied with Erai-Yanya. She lived in a heavily warded cottage deep in the eastern wood. The Norsundrian accorded her enough respect (if that was the right word) to state that she would have to be killed outright before any other plan could be put into motion.

The data about Clair was brief. It listed the date of her birth, noted the Child Spell, and said that she left most of the governing to provincial authorities. There was no update about Mearsieanne, and the girls weren't even mentioned.

So little of true importance. And she wouldn't *want* them to know!

She shoved it back on the shelf and killed time until she knew lunch was over, and the poopsies would be doing their drills or whatever it was that took up their afternoons. Then, ignoring her growling stomach, she mooched back to her room.

She'd just dipped a pen to write another letter to CJ that she would then smear out with ink before tearing up when a polite knock on her door made her hand jerk, splattering ink. Every nerve was alive to trouble.

She delayed answering as long as she dared, going to the wardrobe to check her hair, then smoothing the neat spread on the bed. When she sensed that the door was about to open, she sprang to it. Though it was entirely stupid, she would keep David, or any of them, from invading her space if she could.

Sick with fear and fury, she opened the door.

David stood there, his mild expression belied by flat stare of those sleepy brown eyes.

"What?" she snapped.

"We have a dilemma." He smiled. "You've made it plain you are the judge in this matter. We welcome your, mmm, adjudication."

Utterly heartsick, she started, "What if I don't want—" Then she stopped. Would she be putting a summary end to Irenne if she refused? What did soul-bound *mean*?

In any case he grabbed her arm. She flung it off—and

deliberately wiped his touch off her arm, which made his smile flicker, though nothing changed the cold rage in his gaze. When he started moving, he glanced back in a way that made it plain that she was going to follow whether by her own will or his. She forced her feet to move.

He led her past the familiar areas, and straight toward the detention.

:Lilith, where are you now?

No answer.

She followed him inside, keeping her focus on the floor. The air seemed colder inside this building, and she was not certain if that was her imagination. The stone was bare, the doors thick, with locks on them, and she sensed that faint burned-metal smell of dark magic.

They stopped outside a door. "Feel free to solve the problem your way," he said, opening the door, then he thrust her inside.

Irenne slumped on a cot in the bare room; fighting a sickening lightning bolt of shock, anger and grief, Clair recognized Irenne's light brown hair, freckles, and pointed chin, but gone was Irenne's challenging grin, the stylish, extravagant movements, the humor and energy and interest in the world around her. This girl had Irenne's body, night-marishly thin in the same brown-splattered lavender gown she'd been wearing that horrible day, but something essential was missing in that bowed, blank face.

Clair swallowed in a constricted throat and knelt at the chair.

"Irenne." She placed her hand gently on the girl's arm.

Irenne shivered, desolation harrowing her face. Her glassy gaze lifted, and she seemed to recognize Clair, and then her eyes closed, as if she'd suffered the final betrayal.

"They were right." Irenne's voice was barely audible, the words slow, as if each thought came separately, down a long tunnel. "You did turn."

"No. I didn't turn."

Irenne stared at her blankly, and Clair struggled against the violence of anguish and wrath as she fought for clarity. Irenne's body was here, preserved in a sort of half-life, her skin pale as death. Her mind and spirit had been tethered uncertainly to this body by the obscene leash of the blood spell: there on Irenne's neck stretched the snail-track closing of the wound, instantly recognizable. CJ had been slashed with a bloodknife twice. And Senrid, more recently. Clair had seen both wounds.

Irenne spoke slowly, numbly. "Are you . . . really here?"

"No," Clair said, her eyes burning with tears that she refused to let fall. "I'm not real. I'm a magical fake. You are dreaming, Irenne." When Irenne's expression began to slacken, Clair said softly, "Go to sleep. Rest and . . ." Clair's throat choked up on the word *heal*.

Irenne promptly closed her eyes and lay down, and Clair remembered that the soul-bound had to take orders.

She forced her throat to clear. "Dream, Irenne," she whispered. "Dream of the girls. The forest. Our underground hideout, and hot chocolate, and your plays. Dream of fun summer days in Mearsies Heili . . ."

Her throat closed up, choking off any more words as Irenne's face relaxed into a semblance of peace, her chest rising and falling with her shallow breaths. Clair turned away, teeth bared as she fought against sobs. She would *not* break down in front of the enemy, and give him the satisfaction.

The door opened.

Clair turned around. David stood there, smiling. "Well? What's your verdict?"

She pushed past him and went out.

The door clanged shut behind. Two swift strides caught David up beside Clair. "She could be of some use."

Clair gritted her teeth, wishing she could say something to hurt him as much as this hurt her — but she knew she couldn't. He had vastly more experience in the ways and means of viciousness and barbarity, what's more he couldn't have any feelings to hurt or he wouldn't do things like this. And even if she could by some miracle jab back at him with equal cruelty, it would not help Irenne. So she stayed silent, though it took all her will.

David was also silent on that long walk back to her barracks. When they reached it he said, "How about joining the rest of us to talk it over?"

She braced herself, her entire body stiff with her effort to contain her emotions, to turn up a blank face. "Is that an order?"

"An invitation. You are so very clear with your judgments, help us out here. We all have different ideas — MV, Laban,

Roy, Adam—"

She jumped at Roy's name, and hoped he thought it was mention of Adam that got the reaction.

"I'm so sorry," she said. "I have nothing to say to you."

"Think it over. We can wait." He patted her kindly on the shoulder.

She opened her door and shut it in his face. Then she spat on her shoulder, rubbed the spot as hard as she could, and plunged through the cleaning frame.

Another knock sounded on her door. She was going to ignore it, but the door opened quickly, by an impatient hand, and to her surprise Mac popped his head in.

"I get to be a runner," he said proudly. "Here's a note."

He handed her a slip of paper, then shut the door more respectfully behind him, and fled.

She opened the paper, feeling the familiar sense of alarm.

You're asking for trouble if you don't go to your assignment and after to dinner.

She recognized the handwriting: Roy's.

Crushing the bit of paper in one hand, she wished she could so easily diminish her enemies. Was Roy one of them after all—could his journey outside, and all those memories, have been a truly horrendous hoax? What about Lilith's voice?

She was tempted to go to bed and pull the blankets over her head. If Detlev wanted to come and kill her, at least she'd get it over. But she remembered Irenne in that horrible place, in that even more horrible state. It wouldn't BE over.

She tore the note into tiny pieces, and was about to toss it into the trash when she remembered what Roy had told her. Though he had been reading her letters, that might not be true now. Grimacing at the prospect of tasting iron gall ink, she crammed it into her mouth, chewed, and resolutely swallowed it down, where it seemed to swell to the size and heft of a brick.

She ran to the critter cave, where at least she was not asked any questions. But she had no stories in her. In a determinedly bright voice, she said, "Let's go outside. Today is game day!"

She ran them hard, until they were exhausted and she was panting, but she could not run away from grief.

When she was free again, she forced herself to go to

dinner.

David and MV came in just as she was leaving. They greeted her with exaggerated politeness. She matched them gesture for gesture and tone for tone, at the cost of an upwell of that terrible anguish, that helplessness to do anything about it.

The only way she could strike back at them effectively enough would be to become like them, only worse. And then, of course, Irenne would be right.

Her eyes stung again. Fighting it, she forced a few bites down, then gave up and retreated to her room. After sitting at the desk in a bleak funk for a long time, she decided to try to get some sleep. She was just getting up to do so when the third knock of the day jolted her.

Roy opened the door and slipped in.

She crossed her arms and glared.

Roy opened his mouth, saw her face, then frowned. "Set aside your outrage," he said. "And think. How else will you get back there to lift the bloodknife spell. If you believe that's right?"

"I don't know that spell."

"I thought Senrid spread it around."

"He did. And we have it. But I didn't memorize it. It's dark magic, which I hate trying. It always makes me feel as if my skin is withering, too close to a fire." She shook her head. So many questions, and all at once. "Your reason for going along with that was because you felt I ought to see her?"

Roy sighed. "It's always been like this," he said. "A choice between two evils. Detlev says when your choice is between what's going to happen anyway and what you might logically alter, then choose logic, especially if it forwards your plans. That much, I've always agreed with." He hissed his breath out as his hands flexed.

Then he looked up, his face distraught. "But no, my motivation wasn't cruelty. And, strange as it might seem, David's isn't wholly that either. Though he did want to hurt you. But now you have a choice, both inevitable, and you have to decide which is less evil. That's another hurt, I know. Everyone believed you needed to see her first, as she's your friend."

"Friend, adopted sister, and she trusted me as . . ."

Clair couldn't say the word "queen." She wasn't one anymore, and even when she was, her definition of the responsibilities and perquisites of a queen had been different from anyone else's.

And he wasn't waiting for her to define her relationship anyway.

As if in parallel thought (though it wasn't, because she had her mind-shield firmly in place) he said, "Detlev could be back any time. You might want this resolved before he returns." He let out his breath. "And we can't forget the hidden valley people."

She tried to force an interest outside of her horrible situation. "Do you know them?"

"Only met one of them, when Lilith sent me. Lilith says someone among them was born having coinhered without knowing it, and found an artifact saved by the original valley residents that can only be used by someone with cohesion. He's been experimenting, and it has taken all her resources to- - ward those experiments from being discovered by any mage here. As well Detlev has been recalled to Norsunder Beyond. If the Al-Athann people are going to survive, they'll have to act soon."

As he was speaking, Clair was thinking rapidly. If Roy was a light mage in disguise, that meant he had no true friends, no one he could trust. He'd warned her about Irenne, who the last time she saw him screamed insults at him.

He was right. There was no place for outrage here. Only action.

She straightened her shoulders. "For the plan. How can I help?"

His expression changed. "Is that a real offer?"

"Yes." She struggled against fear, because she could imagine what discovery meant in this benighted place. "That's what being in the alliance means, helping each other."

"So I'm in the alliance again?" His smile was twisted.

"Aren't you?" she asked. "I don't mean personal friendships, though I think some do. The alliance helps one another. Intending to hurt anyone in the alliance means one isn't in it. I know you can point to Tahra and talk about how she wants to murder, but David did kill her brother. And one of you— them—killed Karhin, which was in no possible way a fair fight."

Roy's face had tightened on her change of pronouns. He expelled his breath again. "Then I'll be in the alliance. I could use some help with a decoy, a disturbance that draws the sentries to investigate, so I can break the wards on the gate. I'll wager anything Terry would be glad to help, if he thought he could break out of here."

Clair nodded. "A disturbance, you say?"

"Sure," Roy said. "What have you in mind?"

"Setting fire to David's room. With him in it."

Roy laughed, shaking his head. "If you want. But making a lot of noise at one of the buildings is more likely to get the attention of the sentries, who are mainly there to watch for oncoming storms. But no one rides out at night, and the Al-Athann people will have to come at night, in the dark, and I have to break the wards on the gates so they can get in."

"Maybe we can set fire to David's room after. If you point out where it is. And MV's as well."

"Any further questions?"

"No. Yes. When we leave. Could I take Mac with me?"

Roy shook his head, smiling. "I'll see if I can work him in." He opened the door. "Better run now, before someone misses me."

"Sure. Thanks —"

But he shut the door before she could get any farther, so she shrugged and began to get ready for bed, as he walked away quickly.

As soon as he turned the corner from the guest barracks, he found David waiting. Roy didn't change his path or his pace.

David had been leaning against the adjacent building, arms crossed. When Roy drew near, he straightened up. "Your charge," he said, "didn't like knowing you were a part of our plan."

Roy's heart slammed against his ribs. He fought the impulse to deflect, to smooth things. He had to annoy David, and mire the truth in pettiness.

"It was a stupid idea," he muttered. "You know you've put her in an impossible position." Thus striking at David's leadership.

He braced himself for an angry reaction. But David was silent for a long time. Finally he said, "Do you want to plan a run, is that it?"

Detlev, why couldn't you have bound us together with hatred?

David went on musingly, "I forget how good you are at

organizational details. You haven't had a chance, you were stuck so long playing the scholar role in Bereth Ferian. Why not give us a good run?"

Roy forced himself to cut in, his tone snide: "Yeah, you'll let me lead, just to make me look bad. Thanks."

Exponentially more painful to be so petty; he felt David take it as a hit. And drop his shield into place.

David snorted a laugh. "Why, when you do that so well on your own?"

The sarcasm was a relief. It enabled Roy to walk on past. Out of danger—and away from David's dwindling respect.

Nineteen

LATE ONE AFTERNOON, THE critters were playing a wild game of tag under the scarcely adequate shade of the trees. The weather had turned hot again, a breathless heat in which the sunlight stabbed between the frond-like branches straight into Clair's eyes. Her head ached. Her skin was dry and scratchy. The youngsters kept breaking into violent quarrels; her joints twinged when she moved to stop fights, a nasty feeling she hadn't felt since she first began the morning drills.

She kept wishing her shift would be over so she could go lie down and close her eyes, but the afternoon light glared on and on, and the youngsters played with manic energy.

Then the sentry bell began clanging loudly, each sour note a hammer to her head. The boys paid no attention, just yelled louder.

MV appeared at a fast jog. Clair got to her feet, arms braced for self-defense.

"Don't you hear the alarm? Windstorm coming." He smacked her toward the critters. "Get 'em inside. Fast."

He didn't wait to see if she heard, but vanished around the corner in the direction of the archery field. As Clair turned toward the small boys, a hot breeze lifted the clammy hair on her neck. Dust rose, bringing a whiff of hot iron, making some of the youngsters sneeze.

"You heard," she said. "Let's go inside."

The critters obeyed, still arguing in shrill voices. As Clair chivvied them toward the building, a sudden gust of wind buffeted her, hurling a thousand bits of sand into her exposed skin like tiny needles.

The two smallest, both girls, had been knocked flat. "Run!" she screamed at the others as she bent and grasped their wrists, hauling them to their feet.

They protested at being yanked, their high voices lost in the roar and swirl of dust that seemed to rise out of nowhere; Clair could barely see.

She stumbled toward the building as the wind tore past, gaining strength with every heartbeat. She managed to yank the door open, but then the wind ripped it out of her hands and slammed it into the wall. The critters piled inside and she whirled in after, using her entire body to muscle the door shut again. Then she leaned against it, sneezing violently against the metallic reek in the air.

The abrupt cessation of noise hit her ears. The critters ran deeper inside the building without abandoning their game. Clair fumbled alone in the increasing darkness, until glow-globes lit by magic.

A glance at the window—anxiety jolted her at the low, greenish-black sky. The windows snapped to opaque, magic scintillating around the edges. The building shook and vibrated, and she sensed the strong magic that held it in place. For once she trusted in the strength of dark magic: she could smell its hold, a hot singe in her sinuses.

Her knees trembled as she stumbled to a corner and sat on a small chair where she couldn't see the windows. Guem soothed a crying infant in the next room, and the older boys tumbled back and forth in a wild chase game. This storm was an expected thing, then. She breathed easier, but refused to look at the windows.

The storm ended as suddenly as it came, leaving fine gray silt covering everything. But as she exited the critter cave and headed for the mess hall, magic swept through, making the silt disappear, and soon the compound looked the same as ever. The faint, unpleasantly metallic under-taste of strong wind and dark magic lingered, making her feel tired and drained.

When she fell to sleep at last, it was straight into nightmares.

Roy had the briefest warning: he sensed someone's thoughts questing outside his mind-shield, then suddenly there David was: mind-raid.

David could best him in everything else, and now had a reach on the mental plane that Roy did not, but he was still relatively inexperienced, his strength in itself a danger. The mental realm was Roy's citadel. Protection — sanity — had been harbored his entire life behind these walls, and they were strong walls. Strong, supple, and entirely imperceptible.

David's excessive energy was a little like shouting in a well, but Roy encompassed it all, with effortless practice. What David found was mild confusion and question, the jumble of a dreamscape (for Roy had been asleep, and now feigned sleep still) and nothing else whatever.

David's mental signature vanished.

Roy got up and moved to his window to stare out at the starless sky, the same sky he'd looked on all these years, facing the fact that though he'd won this small battle, he'd lost the war. He'd lost *them*.

So he'd better make it worthwhile.

Al-Athann

"You hold a sword like this," Seshe said, demonstrating.

Quicksilver's knife fighters all held out their newly made obsidian swords in a fair imitation of basic guard stance. These swords were lengthy versions of their knives, magic-bound against shattering. The makers had had to traverse tunnels in another direction to find and quarry enough obsidian, and it had then taken them weeks to make these.

They took up the stance, then they broke it, each having to comment — unfavorably — on what they'd just tried.

"This thing is clumsy," said Ofion, Quicksilver's cousin. One of the knife fighters, she looked exactly like Quicksilver, except her braids were longer, and she talked a lot more. "It feels not like a weapon, but like a digging tool for the betterment of the tubers."

"It's too slow," an Elder said, waving his around, as Lyal, Jeory's younger brother, looked from one to the other. "And I think a blow midway will shatter it."

Seshe spoke up. "Here. Let me show you the blocks, and how to thrust, and how to riposte. Then you'll know what I know, and you can do what you want with the knowledge."

Once again they fell silent, but as soon as Seshe showed them a lunge, again each had to comment.

"Graceful!" Ofion exclaimed.

"Awkward," the Elder grumped.

"Much too slow," someone else said.

"And here is a block." Grimly she kept at it.

Quicksilver didn't speak, but stood in the background, and watched. When she was done, he said only, "We move faster than this thing can."

"The Norsundrians are fast," Seshe said.

"But we will be faster with our knives. And we cannot be fast with these swords. Also, Elder Sleet is right. A strike with full strength here," he touched the middle, "might shatter the stone."

He stepped forward, faced his cousin, and they exchanged a light flurry of movements with their knives, too quick for Seshe to follow. The flicker of the blade made it seem as if five or six blades extended from their hands; she had never seen anything quite like it.

"We are better with our own adaptations," Ofion said.

"I want to adapt our fighting to accommodate this stone sword," someone else said.

"We can experiment," Ofion offered.

Seshe left them to it, and went down to the stage area, where she had promised to supervise the making of a house.

Stone they had aplenty. The problem had been the roof. The house was supposed to give the people an idea of life out under the sky, rather than be an actual house, so after a great deal of consultation they had used silk scraps to weave trimmed branches from the mulberries, instead of mulching them as usual. The result was a square one-room cottage with three windows, and a door made of branch-stiffened cloth much like their cloth doors.

The people had been watching with great interest as the workers constructed walls and then the roof. When at last it was done, Seshe demonstrated.

"All right," Seshe said. "First thing. This—is a door." She opened it, and closed it. "Do not barge through, for you'll get hurt. Now, at home, we knock first." And she demonstrated a knock. "This will keep weather out, as well as others."

At once a group of youngsters had to try knocking on the woven slats, then on the stone, but that turned out not to be popular as it hurt until they conceived the idea of scratching, as was done in some countries, or pounding with the flat of the hand.

"And here is a window. There might be glass in it, at least in my part of the world, where glass is easily made. Some places, they have oiled paper, and others, shutters in winter, and open air in summer. If you meet with glass—it is slick, smooth, and you can see through it—you'll need to be careful of it, because it can shatter, and the pieces cut like knives. Like your obsidian."

Again they commented, touched, explored.

"And up there is the roof. It will keep the weather off you."

She stopped, knowing what would come next. Sure enough, the youngsters all swarmed up and leaped out onto the stone. The smack of bare feet on rock made her wince, but they did not seem to notice; however soft their skin was elsewhere, their feet were as tough as the toughest leddas made into boots.

"We shall contrive a plan for getting the enemies to withdraw from these," Quicksilver said, eyes narrowed.

Seshe listened, but she wondered if there was any hope for these people against Norsundrians.

Later on, Seshe had to go up the long tunnel to Outside with yet another small group of people.

Ever since Leotay's return from Outside, they all wished to see the sky and ground for themselves. Six or seven exploratory excursions were conducted up the Forbidden Path. At first by just a hardy few, well-armed and ready for trouble. And when nothing happened to them, more wished to go. This time, Seshe had to go with them, though she dreaded that long, painful climb.

It was the end of the day when they appeared outside. When the sun had set, people perched on rocks, took out little rolls of food, and talked back and forth as they ate.

It was Quicksilver who first saw the thin flash of lightning in the glare-bright light above the rocks.

"Hide!" he called. "Something approaches!"

Hreealdar startled them all by appearing on the cliff, with a rider on his back.

Seshe stared in amazement when she recognized Roy of the poopsies. "You—" she started.

"Clair gave me her medallion to summon this . . ." He looked confused as he gazed at the horse-shaped being under him. "I'm on your side," he added impatiently in Mearsiean. "Why aren't you thinking? You at least ought to know better than to let these people swarm all over here! The sentries all watch for storms, but if one of them happens to scan the mountains with a field glass, you'd be dead within a day."

"You saw us?" Seshe asked, not hiding her wariness and disbelief.

"No. But Lilith, who is guarding the magic made by that flute player, did. And sent me to warn you."

Seshe's demeanor changed. "Lilith?"

And into her mind: *I am here. I did send Roy. He is the one Leotay spoke to who assured you that Clair and Terry are still safe. I must listen on the broader plan, so heed Roy.* Then the warm, kindly presence was gone.

Seshe exclaimed, numb with shock, "The people must get used to being outside."

"Then use the other side of the mountain," Roy snapped. He turned away.

"Wait," she cried.

Roy stopped.

"Clair—"

"She's still fine, and she does not know you are here," he said, his face tense and his voice hard. "But she won't be fine if you don't keep those people out of sight."

Hreealdar flashed into lightning again, taking Roy away.

The Den

Next day, Clair and Roy met under the trees, and he dropped her medallion into her hand. "Thank you," he said.

"Hreealdar really came for you?" Clair asked.

"Lilith thinks that your Hreealdar is a descendant of beings who originated on this world."

"Then how did he end up in Mearsies Heili?" Clair asked—

And both of them said at the same time, "The Selenseh Redian."

Even the senior mages did not understand those weird caves, which somehow moved when necessary, though without any tremors or explosions. It was easy enough to believe that being inside them somehow annihilated space and time to a degree. Maybe more than a degree for indigenous beings.

"Anyway, you should know that your friend Seshe is with the cave people."

"What?"

"She came after you," he said. "That horse, or whatever it is, brought her. And she's fine. She's helping the cave folk adjust to the idea of coming out of their caves. They've been down there hiding for centuries."

Clair had not cried since seeing Irenne, but at the thought of Seshe coming to rescue her, there were the tears again, stinging her eyes and clogging her throat. "Oh, CJ must have been so mad that Seshe got to Hreealdar first," she said, wiping her eyes on her sleeve.

Then she remembered her danger, and fought down the reaction as she lowered her voice. "But Seshe would be perfect for meeting those people."

She drew a deep breath. She also appreciated Roy's not having told her until now. That her friends would try to come after her she had both expected and dreaded. Finding out that one had succeeded, and was safe—and part of the greater plan—could give her pleasure because this nightmare was about to end, one way or another. If she'd known before, it would have compounded the things she worried over, helpless to fix.

She was trying to find a way to word her comment about friends and loyalty but she happened to glance up, and noticed how tired he looked, his face thinner than ever, and his eyes circled with exhaustion.

"You have nightmares too?" she asked instead, sitting back against the bole of the weird tree.

His mouth quirked. "Shall we start with subheading

seven, the math for supply calculations?"

"If we have to," she said. "*Don't* you have nightmares, living in this big nightmare of a pl—oh." She frowned, eyeing the marks under his eyes. "Did you sleep at all last night?"

He shrugged. "Things to do while Detlev is still in Norsunder-Beyond."

Clair whistled softly. "You must be even more glad than I to be escaping soon."

Again that quirky smile, and he pulled over the pad of scratch paper waiting on the desk. Soon they were busy calculating logistics for a week, a month, in winter, in summer.

As she hiked in her usual zigzag pattern across the compound toward the mess hall, she thought back over the conversation, and that odd quirk to Roy's smile. Was it possible he was ambivalent about leaving? Couldn't be. Not if he really rejected Norsundrian and all its works and all its ways.

Al-Athann

Leotay looked down into her sister's face. "Do you want to learn magic?" she asked.

Horsefeathers' mouth dropped open. "Me?"

"You."

"Why me? Why not Ivy? Or," Horsefeathers said with an edge of jealousy-anger in her voice, that hid hurt. "Or Quicksilver or Jeory, since you're with them all the time."

"Because this is the end," Leotay said, no longer trying to control her voice. "Because I might be killed, or Quicksilver, or Jeory. And I want someone who at least knows where to begin learning all the things Dom Hildi taught me, to help our people."

Horsefeathers bit her lip.

"It's no longer a possible thing some time generations hence," Leotay said. "It's now. Us. When we attack that settlement, some of us will be hurt, and some will die."

Horsefeathers was quiet a long time. When she spoke it was in a soft voice. "So why do we go? We could stay here forever."

"Because we must before they discover us. If they do, then

they can arrange the surprise. Not us. So if I am gone, mage would be your job, if you will take it."

Horsefeathers jutted her chin out. "Am I not too old?"

"All I know is, I need help. And the best time to start is now."

"Teach me," Horsefeathers said. "I'll learn as fast as I can."

Twenty

The Den

ANOTHER MONTH PASSED. TWO more storms struck twice in a row, both times when Clair was away from her room, but she knew what to do as soon as the bells clanged. The buildings had been well warded, but the sound of that scouring dry wind harrowed her nerves, giving her a pounding headache while the storm lasted.

Or maybe it was the place, and not the storms.

Clair could never be sure that her own tension was not affecting her perceptions, but it seemed that the atmosphere of the place was changing. It was very subtle—on the surface, things appeared exactly as usual.

She'd become adept at assessing the mess hall in one fast glance: who was there, was anyone prey to someone else's boredom? The adults, mostly men, but sometimes women, all ignored her with obvious contempt. The sight of those women made her feel sick inside, especially when she recollected her smugly complacent conviction that only men would want to belong to Norsunder, before CJ's experiences with the mage Dejain demonstrated that that was not true.

Very few women appeared to belong to the warrior portion of visiting Norsundrians, the ones who fought to be fighting. Clair discovered by listening to scraps of talk that that most of the women who stayed at the compound were mages or spies. The nosiest ones — the ones she saw the poopsies avoiding — were the women who served Yeres, brother of Efael, head of the assassins called the Black Knives.

"Yeres," Adam told her when he met her for breakfast one morning, "wants to take the Den away from us."

While Clair enjoyed the evidence of covert infighting (if the Norsundrians were busy fighting each other, they had less time for attacking innocent victims, right?) she worked hard to stay out of the target area. And being seen could make one a target. So she did a minimum of studying in case Detlev came back to question her, played with critters while trying to tell them stories that showed generosity, trust, truth, and faith in human goodness, and worked on the drills every morning.

At night, when she was supposed to rest, more often than not she wrestled with the question of what to do about Irenne. She had gone past the futility of tears. The ache of grief and impotent anger had dulled to numbness. She was beginning to believe that what must be done would be to remove the bloodknife spell — but that would finish killing Irenne. If she wasn't dead already.

That was it. She didn't *know*.

Once, everything in her life had been so clear: villains and heroes, dark magic practiced by evil people, light magic practiced by good. She still believed in human striving for the good, but oh, there were so many terrible questions about what truly was good, just, and right.

And who.

The poopsies also seemed restless, and they were all there, waiting for Detlev to return and give them some purpose. Clair hated to think what that purpose would be, but she longed for them to be gone. Surely Roy did, too, didn't he? Only what if he got ordered away and couldn't be there when the Al-Athann Valley descendants emerged from the mountains?

Another month crawled by, with Roy talking curtly to her as they worked through assignments on mapping terrain and deciding how to deploy foot troops, cavalry, and supply lines. As soon as they were done he'd leave as abruptly as he came, and she drilled with the five-year-olds, then did critter care.

While running the obstacle course she let her mind wander. She wondered about Roy's distancing himself, but didn't ask. In this place, questions outside of the immediate work could get you into trouble. Every day that dragged by and nothing happened with the mysterious people in the mountains seemed to tighten the tension. Especially now that Clair knew Seshe was among them. She longed to see her.

But then, late one afternoon after her stint with the critters, Clair was killing time by walking around among the trees in the one area not immediately visible from any of the compound windows. She was trying to imagine that there was a real forest around her, instead of this dusty, dry, false environment. As she walked she scanned for threat: never again would she be so absorbed in her own thoughts that she could be taken by surprise. She spied Roy walking across the grass, his head down, hands jammed in his pockets. The set of his bony shoulders was tense. She paused where he could see her — and his steps altered. So he was seeking her, then.

Fear curled inside Clair as Roy neared. Then he sighed and sat down on the grass. "Detlev returned. Now he and David are gone to Norsunder Base." His relief was unmistakable.

"What happened to the side of your face?" Clair asked.

"Fight." Roy squinted up at her. "I had to manufacture an excuse to be sulking, so I can stay out of David's way — "

"If that would work for me — " Clair began.

But Roy cut in with rare rudeness and an absent sort of impatience that said a lot about his own state of tension. "You don't understand. David not only has been waking up his Dena Yeresbeth, he also has that marsh madness from Geth." Roy tapped his forehead. "He can hear me when he wants to. Been doing his best to listen in on our lessons lately. Which is why I've avoided you outside of our assigned time, until now."

Clair swallowed in a suddenly rocky throat. "He suspects, then?"

Roy shook his head, then winced, as if he had a terrific headache. "Don't think so. But he knows something's wrong. Right now he thinks I'm questioning his authority — his right to be leader. So I got into a fight with Leef over it, and now I'm retired to sulk, so they'll leave me alone. I have to prepare the last spells to clear the gate wards."

Clair's heart leaped inside her chest, making her shiver with ferocious joy. It was happening. "I'm ready," she said. "Just tell me when."

Al-Athann

Seshe's throat hurt as she watched the lingering, solemn way
Leotay's people said goodbye to their caves. It had begun with
a last journey of the young ones to the Dome. There, they had
bidden farewell to the dark water, the ancient columns, the
rocky walls, as if each sight was precious to them.

Back at the big cavern, the adults packed up their sparse
belongings, rolling them in the old mats, and carefully and
reverently folding their shimmery silk tapestries. Whatever
happened, they knew, there would be no returning: even if
they lost, the enemy would know of them, and would not let
them retreat to their ancient hideaway. And if they won, they
must live in whatever shelter the enemy made below, until
Leotay and Jeory could find the way to heal their world with
the Thing-That-Does-Not-Burn.

When it was time to go, they gathered below the Forbidden Path, Quicksilver and his fighters foremost, their weapons
to hand. Leotay, her sister, and Jeory followed last, ready with
their magic.

As the people started up the pathway, they sang, softly at
first, then louder and louder, a blending of all their old melodies in a kind of threnody that caught at Seshe's emotions and
blinded her eyes with tears.

No one knew how, or why, but the time had come.

There would be no turning back.

Twenty-one

The Den

CLAIR COULDN'T SLEEP THAT night. Every tiny noise might be Roy coming to say it was happening now. Or it could be betrayal. And what was she going to do about Irenne?

She gave up trying to sleep when her window blued before dawn. She dashed through the cleaning frame and went to breakfast. There she saw Terry, for the first time since that one day. She was tempted to go straight over to him, but she forced herself to sit elsewhere. He noticed her—at least she was fairly certain he had—but he too avoided contact.

When she was done eating, she got up and went to stash her dishes. As she did, she saw David sitting at a table out of her previous line of vision. He raised a hand in a silent salute, smiling gently, and she was very glad she'd stayed away from Terry.

The day passed with excruciating slowness, too tense to be dull.

Clair was asleep.

A hand shook her shoulder. She wrenched her eyes open, sitting up in panic.

"It's time." Roy's voice. "The Al-Athann people came down the mountain last night, and holed up all day behind the rocks at the edge of the plain. As soon as the sun vanished they started coming. It won't be long before they reach us."

"What about Irenne?" she asked. "I can't leave her. But I don't know what to do."

"If we survive whatever happens, I promise I'll see to it that Irenne is our first concern." He looked, and sounded, sincere. Determined.

Clair was too frightened, and too sick at heart, to know how to react to that. She sat up, blinking in the darkness. Her hearing was all the more acute; she heard Roy's breathing, light and quick, and the shift of cloth as he stepped back to the door. "I pulled Terry out of bed first, and told him we're making a break. As I guessed, he's in. He's waiting outside for you."

She felt the air in the room stir as the door opened and closed again, soundlessly.

She changed into her heavy winter clothes from Sartorias-deles, shoved her feet into her mocs, and left. Inky darkness in the hall. Pause. No sounds. Trying to still her hammering heart, she closed her door then tiptoed down the hall to the outer door. Outside, a faint light came from somewhere — there were no stars.

She was just starting to look about her when hands grasped her arms. She drew in a breath —

"Sh!" came a soft hiss, right in her ear. "It's me — Terry. So it's true? You believe Roy, we're making a break?"

So Roy hadn't told Terry everything. To keep it short, Clair said, "I do."

"Okay," Terry said, and Clair grinned to hear CJ's other-world slang again. "Roy told me we need to start a diversion so he can work magic at the gate. Are we running out the gate? I thought it was desert out there."

"There's people coming," Clair said.

"People? What people?"

Clair agonized. "Do you need to know? It'd take time to explain."

"Eh." Terry shrugged. "All I want to know is that we're

really escaping." And on her nod, "To the fun stuff. My suggestion is, we go thrash Detlev's office. All the reports and so forth are there, and the sentries are sure to notice *that*."

Clair grinned. "That'll be fun. And whatever we destroy will probably save someone somewhere."

"Yeah. We're real heroes," Terry said sarcastically.

Clair laughed under her breath as they raced across the lawn, Terry limping on his bad leg as they moved low from tree to tree. Clair did not like how weird and unfriendly the compound looked at night. She would soon be gone. The thought roiled her inside. Gone, either escaped — or dead.

They reached the HQ without seeing anyone, and slipped inside. None of the doors were locked, to Clair's surprise. Ghosting silently down the dark hallways, they made their way to Detlev's office.

When they walked in, a glowglobe flickered to light.

Terry and Clair stared at each other. Terry's eyes were huge, the scar on his face livid.

"Well, this is supposed to be a diversion," Clair said, reached for one of the piles of paper on the desk, and began ripping it to bits.

Terry rubbed his hands. "I want something bigger."

He picked up Detlev's chair and limped toward the window. Clair moved to the desk, yanking open the drawers. They were both startled when the door slammed open. They exchanged a startled glance. This was much faster than they had expected.

MV entered, flexing his right hand. His wrist knife dropped into his fingers. Behind him crowded Rolfin, Erol, and Silvanas.

"What are you idiots doing?" MV asked.

As a diversion, Clair thought, this was not going well. It was not going well in any sense.

"Having some fun." Terry hefted the chair. "I'm bored."

"Not for long," MV said softly, his fiery eyes wide and gleaming with two pinpoints of light from the glow globe.

CRASH!

Terry answered by pitching the chair through the window.

Clair sighed, and closed her hands on a stack of neatly organized papers. Since there was no time to rip them up, she tossed the whole stack into the air, and between the fluttering sheets of white, she saw MV and his companions advance.

Roy was in his room, searching desperately through his wardrobe. He was sure he'd left the coded cheat sheet in the toe of an old sock, which was stuffed inside his old hat. But it wasn't there. He wouldn't have left it in the desk . . . would he? If only he'd been able to sleep . . .

Everything else was in place, or in progress, and he was missing the last—and most important—piece of his plan. He paused, trying to control ragged breathing. Never think of all those hours of sneaking and spying. Could he remember so complicated a spell? He shut his eyes, but he didn't have time to concentrate on memory recovery.

He snapped a spark-light into being, and started searching through the pages of dull reports he'd left in his drawers as cover.

Then he heard the scrape of a shoe on the wooden floor.

"Looking for this?"

David stepped in the now-open door, holding up the cheat sheet.

Roy glanced from the paper to David's mild smile.

"You were supposed to be gone," Roy said, the words escaping before he knew he'd said them.

"You were to think I left with Detlev. He's dancing attendance on Yeres in the Beyond. I transferred to Norsunder Base, and back." David crushed the paper and flung it away. "How long have you been a sellout? Was it Siamis who turned you?"

Roy broke for the door.

David was faster.

When the haze cleared, Roy found himself flat on the floor, his cheek grinding into the stone. Every bone and muscle in his body ached.

David glared down at him, hair in his eyes, his face white with rage. "What is it you're doing? Tell me." David increased the pressure on Roy's arms, which were wrenched behind his back, sending pangs shooting through his eyeballs. "Tell me."

"No."

In shaping the word, Roy became aware of a nauseating metallic taste in his mouth. He spat out a clot of blood, which set him coughing. The spasm sent agony through his ribs.

"Then I'll have to ask your Mearsiean friend."

"She knows nothing."

"We had this lesson together," David whispered, teeth showing in a sudden, savage smile. "It doesn't matter what she knows. It's you who will talk." He emphasized his words by another pressure on Roy's arms, which sent white light zinging through his brain—followed by blessed darkness.

Clair evaded Silvanas a lot longer than he (or she) expected. After all that practice at the obstacle course, she found it easy to vault over the desk, swing over chairs, and dart here and there.

But long legs and arms are tough to outrun forever. After watching the show for a time, MV finally moved, and Clair found herself snagged and yanked off her feet. When she tried to throttle MV, he smacked her hard enough to slam her, arms flailing, into a chair. Her head snapped and she almost fell backward, but managed to lunge upright.

When the winking stars stopped spinning the room around her, she saw MV standing over prone Terry, slapping him awake without a lot of success. The other poopsies were gone. Detlev's office was a spectacular mess; not one piece of furniture stood where it was supposed to, and a lot of it was broken. Glass and papers lay everywhere.

Footsteps crunched glass: a new arrival.

MV's head jerked sideways. He frowned when he saw David, not the usual tidy David but one with hair hanging in his eyes and a torn shirt and anger evident in his enormous black pupils, the thin line of his mouth.

"Roy?"

"I think he's gone over the fence."

MV turned around so fast it startled Clair. "I'll go rip his head off."

David caught at his arm and jerked him back again. "We'll let Detlev handle that when he gets back," he said, flicking a hand impatiently. "We have to stop whatever he's got going here."

Clair blinked, and found David right in front of her. "Shit," he exclaimed. "Why do you have to hit them so hard? How long is it going to take before she gets her wits back?"

Dizzy and miserable, Clair struggled to maintain her mind-shield as David shoved the heel of his palm against Clair's forehead. A weird vertigo intensified the dizziness, bearing a scent of marshland and a sense of fever. Memories flickered by—her ride with Roy, their whispered conversations—horror-stricken, she tried to catch them but she had no hands, no feet. There was the ride to the mountain. Shocked into desperate effort, she withdrew her consciousness behind a solid wall. Slam. The marsh vanished, leaving her staring up into David's angry brown eyes.

"Knows nothing, does she?" he said softly. "This makes everything a lot easier. Clair. We need to know what exactly Roy was planning."

"Get. Lost."

David sighed, and raised a hand—then he froze into stillness.

In concentrating on Clair, David left himself wide open, and Roy slipped through. Clair, braced for attack, peered up, surprised at David frozen in place. Instinctively—she had yet to discover that she had crossed the threshold—she listened on the mental plane, and found her awareness swept into that wide, bright current again, the one she'd experienced when Roy shared his memories. David's mental self arrowed in pursuit, beckoned by Roy. Clair trailed, bewildered. For a time the landscape changed, a rapid progression of half-perceived memories. Clair did not recognize them, and knew them for experiences Roy and David had shared together.

Emotions colored the memories, distorting even familiar moments out of any kind of recognition; at times she saw people and places with a kind of double vision, until she longed to be able to put her hands over her eyes and block the whole thing out. Except she was in a place without eyes, without hands, and she could not be still long enough to rebuild her mental wall.

Anger was the most pervasive emotion, and with it came the threat of darkness, with David's mocking laughter echoing through. If this was a duel, then he was winning, and he beckoned to Roy to try again—to come closer, to stay—

But Roy's perspective shifted, a radical shift that was like fresh air and freedom to Clair: *This is what I want, David. Follow me.* Music with no words: high, clear singing, and Lilith's serene presence, promising harmony and peace.

Clair would have followed gladly, but the other world began to dissolve around her. As it faded she sensed David's cry against betrayal, resonating with pain.

Clair opened her eyes.

David sat on the edge of Detlev's battered desk, his head bowed and supported by one hand. He did not move.

But MV did. He cut a look David's way, pursed his lips, then strolled over and propped a foot on a rung of Clair's chair. Looming over her, he rested one of his hands on his knee. Lightly, as if he intended to use it soon.

"Now," he said, "let's start with Roy's plan. . ."

Clair crossed her arms and scowled, braced for the nastiness that she hadn't escaped after all.

Twenty-two

IT TOOK AN IMMENSE effort for Roy to force his mind back into his aching body, but he did it. Then cursed as he got to his feet. The pressure on what had to be broken ribs nearly sent him out again. He had to hold onto his chair and struggle for control. Then he knelt and felt over the floor for the paper that David had flung away. After that he opened his trunk and pulled two loose buttons from an old shirt, carefully dispelled.

The journey to the gate seemed to take forever. As he walked, he whispered over the buttons, finishing the stone spell he'd set up on each. He reached the gate without encountering anyone—it seemed the distraction, at least had worked—a relief, as he was past being able to defend himself.

No. It hadn't altogether worked: the sentries were still there. Well, he'd prepared for that.

He walked up to the bored gate sentry, winced as he bent and pretended to pick something up from the ground, then said, "Is this yours?"

He tossed the token to the guard, and watched him fall into a stone spell. The second guard peered down, saying, "What's with—"

Roy hurled the second button straight at him, and the man froze where he stood on the wall. Then, fighting the buzzing, metallic burn of powerful dark magic, Roy performed the spell that entirely broke the mirror ward on the gate—one of the most lethal types of ward, which would take any magic done by anyone on the outside and force it back onto them as a weapon.

He pushed the gate open, agony flaring through his ribs. Leaning gratefully against the solid wood, he shut his eyes and waited. Finally he heard a young man's voice, speaking the language of Al-Athann.

"Are you not the helper?" Quicksilver asked.

"I'm Roy," Roy said, forcing the words past the pain in his chest. "Bring them in."

Behind him people crowded, pale-skinned with huge dark eyes, except for the blond Mearsiean girl walking in the middle. The fifth worlders talked among themselves with no vestige of fear—or haste.

Though Lilith had taught Roy the rudiments of their language, Roy turned to Seshe. "Get 'em to hurry. Get the—" A familiar mental flash. "It's too late." He shut his eyes, sick at heart. "Detlev's back."

He slumped against the wall, fighting the darkness seething at the edges of his vision. The plan was a shambles; the Al-Athann people, despite all those centuries of preparation, were not ready to face Norsundrians. They acted like tourists on a picnic, their curiosity seemingly their main preoccupation.

The fellow with the flute thing finally raised it and played music, a sound so bright and clear it sent shivers through Roy right down to the bone. His eyes burned unexpectedly: it was for this, after all, that he had plotted so long.

The fellow's eyes closed, his gaunt face exalted as he poured music into the air with all the assurance of hundreds of years of coalescent magic. No awareness of the world around him; he was alone with the sky, and the ground, and the life beyond the confines of the physical world that Roy, with all his abilities, could just barely sense.

Roy felt Norsunder's protections ripping away like rotten cloth. He knew that Detlev would as well, and it would bring the Norsundrians running. He straightened up to yell a warning, but before he could, someone rang the alarm bell, and the back wall sentries loped into view, followed by Norsundrians from the barracks, the boys among them. When they saw the crowd entering the open gate they charged, drawn steel gleaming in the starlight.

As soon as they saw the weapons, the Al-Athann knife
fighters unsheathed long, thin-bladed obsidian knives and
leaped to meet the defenders, fast and silent and lethal. Seshe
darted out of the crowd, her blond hair streaming as she
looked back and forth. She caught sight of Roy, and ran to
him. "Where's Clair?"

Roy's part was done. "Let's go find her."

They started into the compound, Roy trying to run as he
felt a rising current of air, not one of the terrible dust storms,
but a new kind, clean-smelling and sweet. It's the flute player,
Roy thought, it's all up to him.

For the first time, he felt a little of Jeory's joy seeping into
him. His ribs hurt a little less, and his feet moved a bit faster.
The world was not a losing battleground after all; some things
merely waited to return, life-forces that made Detlev and his
gang dwindle in importance like the dust swirls blowing
across the ordered pathways.

"She was going to. . . be over there," he said, struggling
against the agony in his chest.

They headed for the HQ building, in which all the
windows were lit. Glowglobe light reflected off shards of glass
below a window. Roy led Seshe inside, where they found Clair
in Detlev's office blinking woozily at the ceiling, a rising bump
on the side of her head. Terry lay nearby, out cold. Roy leaned
against the desk as Seshe flung herself on her knees beside
Clair.

"Seshe!" Clair put a hand to the side of her head. "MV
knocked me off the chair. Ow . . . it feels like I cracked my
skull when I fell. Are you really here?"

"I am. What can I do? Want some water?" Seshe asked,
speaking rapidly in Mearsiean. "How are you? I came . . ."

Roy could see that he was unneeded, and there was
nothing he could do for Terry, who was breathing, at least. He
pressed a hand to his side and wandered out again. Lilith was
supposed to be there . . .

Leotay was so transfixed by Jeory's harmonics that she stilled,
forgetting the danger, the ugliness, the terrible people with

their swords and angry, loud voices, and listened with her ears, with her heart, with her soul. Her magic had been focused on maintenance; this was something new, promising glimpses into another world, or the world underneath this world, curtained off by magic, just as Jeory had promised. The unseen tapestry.

Quicksilver yelled something to her before he jumped to defend Jeory, but she did not catch it. Anyway, the music kept sucking her thoughts along with it, promising layers to the world—to the great world beyond worlds. She was so amazed, so exalted, she did not remember the plan to throw an illusion around Jeory.

Reality hit her with the force of a blow only when the music stopped.

One moment Jeory played, his entire body swaying with the swelling harmony, then the music fled and he lay on the ground, his arms outflung, crimson blossoming down his front.

Horsefeathers was the first to move: she grabbed up the Thing. Leotay's mind jolted back to her body.

The enemy who had struck Jeory was in turn struck down by Quicksilver, whose face streaked with tears, though he fought on. Elders closed around Jeory as Jeory struggled to sit, then rocked back and forth, wheezing. Ofion led the knife fighters in defending him.

Horsefeathers waved the flute and cried, "What do I do now?"

"I'll take that thing." Detlev approached, his eyes intent on Horsefeathers. And to his minions nearby, "Secure them."

Sick with the knowledge she had been too late, Leotay chanted her spell and illusion-magic blurred her people with confusing shadows. Quicksilver and the others sprang to deflect the Norsundrians trying to find Horsefeathers. Here and there Leotay's people fell before Norsundrian blades, but Norsundrians fell, too.

Leotay shut them all out and dropped down by to Jeory's side.

"It's not a death wound," the friend—Roy—said, dropping to one knee next to her, a hand clutched to his side.

Jeory smiled briefly. His eyes made clear what Leotay already sensed; perhaps another person would survive it, but Jeory had no spare physical resources at all.

"Here," he whispered, holding out one hand. "Bring . . ."

Horsefeathers silently put the Thing into his slackening fingers, and Roy bent his head and touched Jeory's brow. Then he turned to Leotay. "He wants to give you his knowledge, through me."

Leotay jerked a nod. How was that even possible?

Jeory breathed into the flute as Roy touched Leotay, and vivid images flashed into her mind. Jeory sighed, shut his eyes, and it seemed his flesh gleamed with a soft glow, one not seen in the world but with the mind. No, with the heart, the spirit. The glow brightened through the tears burning her eyes, reminding Leotay of that first glimpse of the sun.

Then Jeory's physical self-stilled, and the light dimmed. Jeory was gone with it, beyond and beyond, where she could not reach.

"The Norsundrians are killing any they find," Roy said sharply. "Use that thing. Find the shadows of their magical bindings, and demolish them."

Leotay raised it to her lips, fitting her fingers over the holes. Knowledge, like a whisper of Jeory's familiar voice, flowed through her, and she made music, at first softly, then stronger. Again, the magic slashed through gray spider webs of Norsundrian tangled over the compound, gaining power with her every breath. Hazily she realized her illusion was fading into nothingness. Then Leotay lost awareness of the world around her, feeling the music twining itself around the beat of her heart. She could see, but made no sense of what she saw. She heard only her music.

And so when she met the gray-green eyes of Detlev, there was no warning, no sense of danger. She knew only that the music silenced as a mental command cut through the music.

He raised his hand in command.

Roy watched in despair as Leotay rose to her feet and held out the instrument. All the Norsundrians saw the young woman fighting against the compulsion, and losing. Some stopped fighting altogether, as there was no purpose in it, and watched with a sense of high entertainment as Detlev used his mind as a weapon against someone who wasn't them.

Others kept fighting because they enjoyed a hard, bloody scrap, though these dead fish-skinned knife fighters turned out to be unexpectedly lethal, and as no one at the Den was among the elite, they, too either fell dead, or decamped altogether.

That was when a burst of sunlight buffeted them all, bringing moist air from a different world. There stood Lilith, gray hair a rat's nest, her robes swaying in the breeze she had created.

"I'm sorry to be late." She lifted her voice as she addressed Detlev. "Your magic here is broken, by your own allies. The Norss of Songre Silde are assembling to transfer here on this mark I am laying now."

She tossed down something and stepped away from it as she spoke. "You will not win singly against them, and Yeres and Efael have abandoned you—again. When will you comprehend that they will *always* betray you? Do you really think these spies can stand against the Norss?" She pointed contemptuously to the staring Norsundrians, many of whom began to drift away. Some with transfer tokens vanished in tiny winks of light and stirrings of air. "Hadn't you better retire?"

Detlev turned his head. "David! You and the boys fall back to Norsunder Base, adjunct transfer," he said. And vanished.

Their old rule at the Den was, at the first sign of trouble, keep a transfer token on your person. They began vanishing one by one. The spies also, some to the borderlands of the Beyond, where gossip was already beginning to spread that while Detlev had been poking his nose around the Venn in an effort to track Siamis, he lost Five.

Roy swayed, one hand going to the ground to support him. Lilith bent and took his arm. Old she was, but sturdily made, and she was still strong: age in someone with Dena Yeresbeth is relative even when they have not spent centuries beyond time. When he took her hand, she pulled him to his feet, though he was half a head taller.

"Excellent work, Roy. This world is Aldau-Rayad again. Well, almost." She looked around at the flat desert.

The Al-Athann Valley people murmured softly, some giving her wondering looks, others solely focused on their wounded and the few dead, especially Jeory.

"But can they hold it?" Roy's voice was nearly gone as she blinked at those thin, silk clad forms, the bare arms and feet.

"For a time, at least, until the world bindings are broken," Lilith said. "And they will need help. But that can wait." She turned her head. "Our young friends are still inside the compound," she said. "Now you may rest."

"No. First Irenne. I promised." Roy forced himself to walk, dizzy, weary, exhilarated. Afraid.

He followed the softly chattering Al-Athann people into the compound. They carried their wounded and dead, Quicksilver and his team with drawn weapons at the front. But the only person they met was Guem, the critter minder. "Where is everybody?" he asked. And, in a worried voice, "Three of my small ones are missing."

"Gone with Detlev, I expect," Lilith said, not without pity. "The new owners are here. You will have to deal with them."

Roy saw Seshe and Clair sitting close together outside the empty HQ, Terry with them, wiping absently at a cut on his wrist. At the sight of Lilith, the two girls started up, Clair wincing, one hand to her head.

Lilith said to Clair, "Your friend Irenne's mind and spirit wander between the dream realm and memory. If you have chosen to release the bloodknife spell, she will slip away from inside the dream-world. I can protect her that far from any Norsundrian spells. But Clair, she is too close to death. Only the magic binds her. She will never waken."

"I don't know what else to do. But I have to be there," Clair said between shut teeth.

"Me too," Seshe whispered—Clair having told her first thing.

"I understand," Lilith said, sorrow deepening the lines in her face.

The silent procession wound to the detention block, where Irenne lay so still. Clair and Seshe each took hold of one of her clammy hands. Lilith's smile was sad as she gazed down at the girl. "She is not afraid," Lilith murmured. "She is drifting in good memories."

Clair's entire body vibrated with fresh grief. She forced herself to speak. "Do it. While she's happy."

The rise and fall of voices singing an ancient threnody in waterfall triplets carried through the open doors, as Lilith whispered. A flash of magic: the binding dissolved, and Irenne's breath stilled at once.

Clair bent over her friend's hand, teeth gritted against the desolation that wanted to tear her apart from toes to skull. Not yet. Not yet. Seshe wept soundlessly, tears tracking down her face. Lilith waited, head bowed, as Roy leaned against the wall, black spots swimming before his eyes.

Lilith touched him, and said, "I will send you somewhere safe."

Before he could speak, the transfer magic seized him.

Back in the compound, Lilith left the two girls with their friend's body, and went to deal with Terry. Then she returned to the detention room, to find that Seshe and Clair had laid Irenne out, smoothing her skirts over her legs so that the ruffled hem reached her toes. They had finger-combed her hair, and retied her ribbons.

At Lilith's appearance, they stepped back.

"Have you decided what to do?" Lilith asked.

Seshe turned to Clair, whose head throbbed. Her eyes burned. She said, "Disappear her. The other girls think her already dead—I think it would be horrible to bring her body back after all this time."

Lilith touched Irenne's body, which vanished. Then she transferred Clair away, where she, too, found herself alone in a room. She dropped onto the waiting bed, and let the sobs rip free.

Seshe found herself alone with Lilith. "Where is she? Did you send her home?"

"I will if she wishes, when she wakes, but I think . . . it might be better for her and Roy both if they have a little time in a neutral place."

Seshe was going to argue, but she looked around, ambivalence making her uncertain. Finally her gaze returned to Lilith's kindly eyes. "In that case, please send me to Mearsies Heili. I can tell the others what happened."

"That," Lilith said, "I shall do. Your preparing the others should make it much easier for Clair when she returns. Thank you for your help. You have done well—all of you."

Transfer magic seized Seshe, and when she emerged, it was to the smells and sounds of home.

Twenty-three

Autumn 4748 AF
Norsunder Base, Sartorias-deles

ANOTHER DAMNED RETREAT FOR Detlev's boys: from Geth-deles to Sartorias-deles, after which they'd made their lair in Wnelder Vee, only to be ordered to retreat to the Den on Five.

And now they'd lost the Den.

And Roy.

Of all the places they had lived, they loathed Norsunder Base the most. But here they were again. Even more annoying, they couldn't transfer directly to the Destination off the command center, as it was still unreliable after Efael's mass transfer in his unsuccessful hunt for Siamis. A whole year had passed before it could be trusted in a limited way. Even non-living supplies sometimes vanished before they could fully materialize, forcing the supply staff to use the outer perimeter sentry outpost as a transfer Destination, from which they had to haul necessities in by wagon.

The warning stench of hot metal pervaded the command center. The more circumspect preferred transfer to and from the sentry outpost, which meant a long, dreary ride either with one of the constant flow of wagons, or (assuming one had enough clout, and there was a horse free) an equally long but somewhat faster horseback ride to the fortress itself. It didn't help that the boys arrived in late autumn under a low sky of clouds tumbled eastward by raw winds, a shock after the endless parched summer of Five.

They transferred in one by one, as they'd been trained to do, some waiting around at the sentry outpost for others to ride with. Here, they caught up on Norsunder Base news: Bostian in charge of the military, Aldon on some mission, Dejain once again head of the mages, though Zhenc, once her ally and now her rival, was lurking around with his own space warded.

When the boys reached Norsunder Base, they slipped upstairs over the stable to find their old rooms empty—not even stable hands wanted those rooms, if they could avoid them—and of course any belongings they'd left behind long gone.

Adam hung back, noticing how red-smeared everyone's aura had become: anger, betrayal. He stood against a wall, concentrating until he shuttered away the auras, which seriously affected his depth perception. Not good in a place like this, where relative safety depended upon seeing danger before it saw you. At least, he thought, auras were not as distracting as seeing ghosts, which Ferret did. Not that he told anyone. But you found out things when you walked in others' dreams.

Adam could see the anger in the others' expressions, in particular David's deceptively sleepy gaze. Even Ferret betrayed anger in the tightness of his skinny shoulders, and the angle of his forgettable face as he lurked in the shadows.

David got to work. It had been Roy's chore to sweep for spy-windows, wards, and tracers, a tedious and exacting task. David began to do the job, and had completed one room when MV arrived.

As soon as MV recovered from the transfer, he heard the mumble of magic, and glanced in at David. "Tracers?"

"Someone has to do it," David said.

MV cursed Roy in three different languages, each of which offered a rich variety of oaths and expletives, then exclaimed, "Why'd he hop the fence? Was it the girl? It can't have been."

David's face tightened. "I think it must have been Siamis."

"But the last person Siamis talked to was you. Not Roy. Who was right there with us in our rat-hole."

"Yes, Roy was there, and yes, Siamis talked to me. Maybe it's because Roy had a steel-hard . . . " He tapped his forehead, indicating mind-shield. ". . . nearly all the time. I don't know. Maybe Detlev will have something to say . . ." They both remembered that they hadn't finished their search, and who knew how many idle ears were listening to them.

They each turned to a room, David aware of his lack of speed compared to Roy's skill. MV was even slower. By the time they finished, everyone had arrived — eleven, not twelve. David obsessively reviewed the last few days before the disaster, wondering what he'd missed. What he could have done differently.

MV considered which bone to break first when they did catch up with Roy.

Sallow, hunch-shouldered Erol looked at no one. Roy had helped him with reading, and found tricks to help him master his stutter. Why wouldn't Roy say anything?

Ferret also wondered what he'd missed. He prided himself on his observation. He'd had to be observant to discern the difference between the living and the dead, and then he used observation as a defense during the rougher days before David took over leadership. Ferret loved being the best tracker and spy. What had he missed?

Rolfin refused to get hot over something that couldn't be helped. He and his cousin Leefan pushed into their old room and shut the door to talk it over.

Rolfin muttered, "Has to be 'cause of Efael. Didn't want to be next. Who does?" And, even lower, "Half a mind to hop myself."

"Shit," Leef said, looking around their dusty room that smelled of horse piss. Rotten as this place was, with possible spies around every corner, they wouldn't bail on the others. Both knew it.

In the next room over, as Adam chucked his travel carryall containing paper, artwork, and supplies and his journal under the mattress ticking, he reflected that Roy was much more present as an absence than he had been while with them, he had become so isolated since he'd returned from his long sojourn in Bereth Ferian. Even his dreams had been shielded.

In the distance, the watch change bell clanged. Mealtime.

"Could writing about magic cause Roy to turn against us?" Adam asked Curtas as they descended the stairs through pungently humid air, Adam careful not to touch any object or surface.

Curtas glanced around quickly before answering. "Don't know, but maybe *he*'ll tell us." *He* being of course Detlev.

". . . go to Mearsies Heili and strangle him there, or drag him back here to be strangled," MV's voice drifted back.

"Why d'you think he'd go to Mearsies Heili?" Laban retorted. "Tutoring Clair was an assignment. Not an assignation."

"What's an assignation?" Noser butted in.

"Where two spies talk in secret," Silvanas told him when the older boys ignored his interruption.

"Shut up," David said to them all as they caught sight of a stream of stable hands heading in the same direction. He didn't want anyone overhearing talk about one of their own hopping the fence—a more bearable expression than betrayal. Treachery. *Turning his back on us.*

In spite of all his diligence it had happened again.

They broke into twos and threes to enter the mess hall. The place smelled, as always, of stale food and staler sweat. They kept to the walls, meeting no eyes. News of the loss of Five had to have gotten around, but judging from the lack of derision, rumor still hadn't decided who was to blame—or who was to take the fall. It could be dangerous to show partisanship to the wrong side.

The boys sat around the edges, where they could see one another. Pretty much as usual fish was the main dish, with pepper-and-carrot pea soup, and hard biscuits. Peas would be present in various forms at all meals, because dried peas stored in sacks practically forever.

David was halfway through his lackluster meal when Detlev's mental contact came, no more than an image of his office: he had arrived and finished his sweep—probably finding far more magical traps of various sorts than David and MV had.

David waited until he caught Leef's and Vana's gazes, touched his forefinger to his forehead, then shoved his overlong bangs back. Leef and Vana each turned to those on either side to spread the word.

A short time later they crowded into Detlev's office, where he leaned against the narrow table that served as a desk. Even in the small room Roy's absence was obvious. From a smaller room adjacent came the murmur of high voices: three-year-olds.

"Why'd he do it?" Laban burst out, elbows outthrust.

"You will have to ask him when you catch up with him," Detlev replied.

Noser grinned. "Is that our new orders? Hunt him down?"

Detlev cut through the mutters of approval, "No." And into the sudden silence, "David, you will need to broaden your studies in magic." He picked up a stack of papers from the desk. "Begin by mastering Roy's treatise."

David regarded the papers as if they were poisonous. "Is that some lighter maunder?"

Detlev's brows lifted. "Whatever was going through Roy's mind in recent months will not show up in those pages. It's a very thorough work, and you are not nearly advanced enough in wards."

"I hate it here," Noser spoke up. "Can we make another Den?"

Vana elbowed him—habit, no force. Noser was voicing all their thoughts, as he often did.

"For now," Detlev said, "you are here. Continue your drills, but unseen by the others. Listen to all gossip, but don't engage with anyone, at all, outside of yourselves. Yeres got her fingers shut in the door on Five as well as we did. No doubt she will be looking for someone to blame when she comes back out of the Beyond. You're ignorant, you're losers. Let's keep it that way for a while."

Then, without warning, to each via mind: *Your thoughts are no longer your own, unless you use your mind-shields waking and sleeping.*

He dismissed them, and Adam held in the urge to sigh. So mind-raids were now to be a way of life if the head snakes came out of the Beyond, were they? He knew how to keep his private thoughts private and to make his surface thoughts boring. His defense, developed when he was small, against the interest of the predatory was either stupidity and obliviousness, and it had served well enough. But as he followed back toward the barracks area preparatory to a practice session of some sort, he scanned the others, sensing sobriety, disappointment, and regret. Not in MV, of course. Anything was a challenge to him. But in most of the others, the regret was strongest in Rolfin and Curtas.

Is it going to be this place forever? Adam surprised himself with the depth of his own abhorrence.

A contact came from Detlev: *No. But it is a necessary transition.*

Adam frowned at the dusty ground. Life was good when they were all together, and it was sometimes good when they went Out, but. . . but. . .

Rapid memories flashed through his mind: Arthur's face after he found out that Adam was one of Detlev's boys. It shouldn't have mattered, for Adam's his words and actions spoke for themselves—didn't they? Clair of the Mearsieans didn't think so. *If you don't see the difference between us, then it's not worth discussing,* she'd said. And then: *But I hold you responsible for what Detlev does.*

His last conversation with Roy, before Roy's anger at David made it impossible for anyone to talk to him. *This is a false life we're leading, Adam. How long can we lie to ourselves?*

But I don't lie. And Detlev doesn't lie to us.

Yes—no. He doesn't outright lie, but he doesn't tell us all the truth, either. How long will you accept his perception of the world without questioning it?

David just after the disaster at the Den, bruised and dirty, still wearing the shirt ripped in his fight with Roy. He hadn't cared about losing the Den—then—or about the sudden and weird appearance of those crazy cave-dwellers, for the head snakes hadn't known, either. It was Roy's betrayal that had upset him.

It was worse this time than the last time they'd lost someone, because they all *liked* Roy.

What could be worse than losing one of the group?

What, then, were the stakes?

Once again Detlev answered: *Everything. It is time for you to get back to your far-sense exercises.*

Adam let the sigh escape at last, and caught a quick look from David as he said, "Drill time. You know where."

Adam didn't know what to think, and so he didn't think at all, losing himself instead in the comparative relief of immediate action.

Twenty-four

CLAIR WOKE TO A throbbing head. Every joint ached. She did not want to open her eyes to another dreary day in—

The side of her head panged. She fingered the bruise she got when she fell off the chair and hit the leg of the upturned desk. Because MV had slapped her. Because he wanted to know . . . Rapidly memory returned, bringing with it a surge of joy tempered with disbelief. They were really safe?

She had to find out.

She opened her eyes to an airy room. Greenery moved outside two long, open windows. The breeze drifting in brought fresh scents of wet grass, and cedar trees, sweet-peas and wisteria.

She was truly free.

A fresh surge of tears stung her eyes. She let them fall, then sat up, aware of intense thirst as well as the thumping headache. In reach a bedside table, a blue ceramic jug gleaming with moisture on its fat body, a cup sitting beside it. She slurped sweet, pure water, relishing the coolness spreading through her body.

She was free, but hard on the heels of that awareness rushed inexorable memory, and she lay back down, another surge of hot tears seeping from under her eyelids as she remembered Irenne's death. Even having seen Seshe couldn't assuage that. Clair stirred. She ought to find Seshe, but what would they say? Clair had cried out her heart over Irenne, and could not bear more of it, not right now, when she hurt so much . . .

She slid into sleep again.

When she woke up the second time, her head pounded fiercely. She sat up and looked around. There was more water. She drank, and decided she had to face the day.

She got up, wincing at how boggy her knees felt, how all her bruises ached, and her eyes burned. A cleaning frame carved in a pattern of trailing grape leaves had been set up in a corner. She had fallen into bed in her winter clothes, now twisted and grimy. But a step through the frame snapped away the ever-present dust of Five. Then she looked in dismay at the bed, now equally grimy, and—moving carefully—she yanked the bedclothes free.

Even though she still ached, she couldn't help but notice how much stronger she was now. The thought made her angry as she tossed the bedclothes through the frame, and watched the magic zap over them.

She'd just dumped the pile back on the bed when she heard a gentle tap at the door. "May I enter?" asked Lilith the Guardian.

"Please," Clair said.

Clearly Lilith had been monitoring in the mental realm. The old mage walked in, a comfortably plump figure with silvery gray hair swept up into a comb. She wore a long robe embroidered with spring leaves. "How do you feel, my dear?"

"Better, thank you," Clair said, conscious of resuming manners that she had abandoned while a prisoner. She sat down on the untidy bed. "Where's Seshe? And Terry?"

"Both went home. Your friend Seshe will prepare your friends for your coming, when you are ready."

"I'd like to get home, too, if I may," Clair said. "They'll need to—" Then memory hitched, as always: she didn't have any responsibility to Mearsies Heili. Mearsieanne was queen now. *Truth is, they don't need me.*

Lilith's gaze narrowed with concern. "You might like a chance to rest a bit longer. And I know that Roy would like to talk to you before you leave."

"He could come home with me, if he wants," Clair offered.

And at Lilith's expression, which had closed a little, Clair said fiercely, "If he's worried what people will say, anyone who gives him trouble will have to deal with me."

Lilith laughed. "You sound so—"

"Please don't say warlike," Clair cut in quickly, blushing hot.

Lilith's smile blossomed. "I was going to say determined, my child. And your friends will be eager to hear about your experiences."

Eager? Was that a warning? Clair said slowly, "You mean they'll want to pester Roy with stuff he can't answer? But they wouldn't—oh, yes they would. Leading the pack would be Senrid."

Lilith murmured, "Senrid still has a foot in each world, a stance the disadvantages of which you can probably see now better than most."

Since the subject was open, why not get it all out? Clair perched on the edge of the bed. "Senrid won't be the only one. When I first got grabbed, I was walking alone, thinking about why my friends' attitude toward the poopsies upset me so much. I thought then that what bothered me was my friends acting too much like those creeps, who are, after all, our enemies for a reason. Except for Roy, I mean—"

"Roy is not your enemy," Lilith acknowledged. "But you didn't know that at the time. Go on."

Clair shrugged. "Adam isn't bad, either, not really. At least I haven't *seen* him do anything awful. Curtas, the same." She shrugged sharply. "David—MV—especially MV—that horrible little Noser, they are all thoroughly evil. My friends see them running around doing terrible things and getting away with it, and it must seem they can do anything. But they can't. There are Norsundrians worse than them, and they all prey on each other just as much as they prey on us. It's a sickening, rotten system. That's all." She shrugged again, more sharply.

Lilith had been standing inside the door. At this she approached, and brushed her hand over Clair's shoulder, a gesture of tenderness that made Clair's throat unexpectedly tighten. It seemed to clear the last of the arid atmosphere of Detlev's compound from her spirit.

"Roy's waiting with a big breakfast," Lilith said. "Why don't I help you make up this bed again, after which you might join him?"

"So you don't think he'll come home with me?" Clair asked.

"You can always ask." Lilith picked up a sheet and shook it out as if she were some ordinary cottager, and not a mage from four thousand years ago. "I feel certain he'll appreciate it," she said as she and Clair each took sheet ends and stretched them over the mattress. "But I feel obliged to suggest that the readjustments Roy needs to make within himself might have to come first."

"What needs readjusting? He's now free of them," Clair said, as she tucked the quilt under. "He can do anything he likes, can't he? Go anywhere he wants? Although he'll have to watch out lest Detlev come hunting for revenge for what Roy did to help those cave people."

Lilith smoothed the quilt one last time, shook a pillow into shape, then laid her hand on the door latch. "If I may make a suggestion," she said gently.

"Of course."

"Remember, to you Detlev's boys are enemies— killers— but to Roy they were once friends. This means that they didn't leave him, he left them."

Annoyance burned through Clair. "Yes, like I said, now he's rid of them. What's the problem?"

Lilith lifted her hand from the door latch and drew a step nearer, her gaze earnest. "Let me try it this way. Supposing you had to leave your group, for whatever reason. Set aside the distinctions between Sartorias-Deles and Norsunder—"

"But why?" Clair protested. "Aren't those what this conversation is all about?"

"Yes, and no," Lilith said, her smile sad. "I wish it were quite that simple. You have to remember—surely you saw it— that for whatever reason, Detlev bonded his group together not with fear and threat, but with friendship and trust. Just like you and CJ and the others."

"But it isn't . . . the same," she muttered, knowing as she said the last two words that it was—for some nasty, twisted, typically twisted Detlevish reason—exactly the same.

"So they had a reason for their nastiness during the skills test?" Clair said. "Detlev tried to impose a new person on them, and they didn't want anyone breaking into their circle. Is that it?"

"You tell me," Lilith said. "But how would you feel if

someone interposed a new girl into your own group?"

"But why would —"

Mearsieanne.

Clair's head dropped forward. She had avoided thinking about Mearsieanne's appearance among them from this angle because it had always seemed disloyal. Now she forced herself to consider facts as facts, withholding judgment. The truth was, having a new person they were obliged to accept had changed things. And (Clair thought of dark-eyed Diana, to whom freedom was important, who hated fussing with dress and society manners, and who spent so much time roaming the woods) not all those changes were perceived by all to be good. Though Irenne had loved them.

Clair's eyes burned, but she fought the tears back. It would take time for *that* pain to go away. But right now the subject was not Irenne, it was Roy. Clair tried to imagine taking in some girl who acted like a friend, then turned against them, and ruined their plans on the way out.

Seen that way, twisted as it was, she could understand why Roy had hated her gratitude, why her comments about how glad he must be to leave, meant to brace and cheer, had probably had the opposite effect.

"In order to break away, he had to destroy their friendship, and of course he betrayed their trust," Lilith said, putting words to Clair's thoughts.

Clair remembered MV's vicious comment: *I'll rip his head off.* It was the only time during the whole nightmare that she had seen him really angry. And she'd paid the price for it when he'd slapped her clean off the chair.

She studied Lilith for clues, striving to understand. "So . . . if Roy left them, then maybe they feel a little bit as rotten about it as we felt when Irenne was killed." She pressed her lips together, *hoping* that David felt even half as rotten as she did. Again she searched Lilith's face, reassured by the kindness there. "Is that justice? Or is it merely retribution?"

Lilith said, "What do you think?"

Clair struggled for words. "I don't *know*. I'm always trying to figure out what justice actually means. Is a true sense of rightness one that everybody sees? But not Norsundrians."

"I don't believe people join Norsunder's various entities and armies out of a search for rightness, but I cannot say for certain," Lilith replied.

"Here's something I've been . . ." *worrying about.* ". . . thinking." Clair wrapped her arms tightly around herself. "That a ruler—a good one. I mean, one who tries to be good, but who talks a lot about retribution and justice for an entire kingdom, well, finds ways to spend lives to get it. Is that really just, for the ones who have to go out and die?" Clair was thinking of Tahra's angry, grief-stricken talk about murder and justice. But she couldn't bear to say that about an ally, someone she liked, and had traveled with.

"What do you think?" Lilith asked.

"I don't *know*. I guess it's stupid, talking about what-ifs, which can mean so many different things! Back to Five, and what happened. The only people who got a . . . a redress, or balance, were the cave people, though what they gained is a ruined world and a military compound." Clair drew in a deep breath. "And I got, oh, a little bit of justice. Seeing Detlev lose, for once. And I escaped." The old nausea boiled in her stomach again. "But even if Roy's now free, if he's anything like me, he'd feel like the world's biggest failure for not convincing them to go with him."

She spoke slowly, as the ideas emerged from the morass of emotions. "Adam said *Firejive* once, and then wouldn't explain. When CJ asked MV, he snarled that it was, ah, something disgusting. We all assumed it was typical poopsie arrogance. Meaningless. But there's something else. Isn't there?"

"The second part of that word is 'gyve', and it has a very old meaning: to fetter. To bind."

"Binding of fire. It's their bond. Isn't it?"

"Not just a bond," Lilith said. "Their retreat when young, in an extraordinarily harsh situation."

"Where did they come from?"

"Each has his story."

Clair shrugged. "Should I, well, say anything to Roy?"

Lilith tipped her head again, considering. "Use your judgment," she said at last. "I need to return to Aldau-Rayad, though I believe that Yeres of the Host of Lords, in trying to wrest that compound to herself in secret, seeded her own defeat. But that might not prevent one of the others from making another try, most particularly her brother Efael."

"I'd think the biggest fear would be Detlev coming back. It was his place, wasn't it?"

"One of them," she said. "He'd made it for the boys, a

shocker that has kept me in this time far longer than I have spent in millennia. Until he chose that isolated locale, I'd deemed the Al-Athann Valley people safe enough to check on once a century or so."

"I know you need to go, but what is that like? To only be in the world a little over many years?"

"It is . . ." Lilith lifted her gaze toward the window. "A bit like hearing a story, one whose beginning is only summarized, and whose end you can't see. But you can affect one part of it." She opened the door and walked out.

Clair knew Lilith wasn't telling her everything. That was fine. She wouldn't understand everything. Her mind went back to "Use your judgment," words she intuited had been deliberately chosen, and though her emotions underneath the relief at escape were still as tender as the skin on the side of her head, she felt immeasurably better. A sense of purpose realigning.

Clair followed Lilith into the hall. "Breakfast that way." Lilith pointed toward a far room filled with creamy-bright morning light.

High windows in twos along the opposite wall, reminding her of Bereth Ferian's architectural style, opened to a spring-bright blue sky; Clair had no idea where she was, and didn't really care. Soon she'd be home. Right now she was about to have what might well be her last chance to talk to someone who'd saved her — and whom she had totally and consistently misjudged. The worst thing was, if he was anything like her, he'd probably hate it if she maundered on and on about how sorry she was. Of all the nasty things to get thought at you, pity is one of the worst.

The room Lilith indicated smelled of fresh bread. It was a semi-circular room, tall windows overlooking a garden around a lake. Roy sat hunched up in a window seat looking out, wearing the same clothes he'd worn at the end. He looked taut with tension, his skin under the fading marks pale and tight. When she entered, he shifted his entire body, rather than twist, moving with the care of someone with cracked ribs.

"You look rotten," Clair said.

Roy's smile flashed. "That bouquet of colors in your face is quite inspiring."

"MV certainly enjoys slapping people around," Clair said as she spotted a table set with covered dishes. "At least he considered me too rabbity for an actual punch. Oh, hello," she added as she lifted lids to discover hot rolls, cold butter, shirred eggs, cheese-potatoes, spiced porridge, five kinds of berries, grapes, two melons, and oranges. To drink: Sartoran steep freshly steaming in a clay pot; fresh milk; a couple types of juice.

Clair began loading a plate. As if pulled by her enthusiasm, Roy got up and picked up a plate. But all he put on it was a roll, some eggs, and some grapes.

A table and chairs sat empty on the opposite side of the room, but Clair headed straight for the windowseat. She sat cross-legged, the plate before her, a mug of steep and another of milk beside her. Roy eased himself onto a footstool nearby.

For a time the silence was broken only by the click of cutlery on ceramic plates. Clair sipped the steep and encountered under the summery flavors the tart herbal bite of listerblossom. Some of her aches eased a little.

She broke the silence first. "You know you'll always be welcome wherever the gang and I happen to be." She remembered then that he'd had a gang, and added, "The girls, I mean." And at his wry side glance, wished that she hadn't.

"Thanks," he said as he turned an uneaten half of his roll around in his fingers. His knuckles were still mottled. "Listen, do you want to talk about any of the twists Detlev put on those memories of your world?"

Your world. "Um . . ." She bit off a retort that the last thing she wanted to think about was Detlev. But she sensed that Roy was trying to be helpful, and she had learned after being displaced by Mearsieanne that there's nothing more steadying than feeling you can be useful to someone, at least. "The nastiest, sneakiest part of it was that he didn't really say anything that I could disagree with. I was afraid that he'd do that by degrees—you know, keep graying and graying my views of people and events until I'd gradually go over to his view without knowing it. I was all ready to argue with him about all the unconscious wastes that lighters do, for he'd said that that would be our second session."

Roy grimaced. "But don't you see, you did it for him."

"You mean, thought up his arguments for him? Well, only to argue against."

Roy twitched a shoulder up.

"But I *was* still doing his work for him," Clair said. "Yes, I see it."

"Nobody wins an argument with Detlev — unless, for some reason, he wants you to," Roy said. "Believe me, I tried."

Clair thought she caught echoes of that failure feeling.

"Well somebody did, once," she said with a grin. "If all that gossip about him having been a hero back in the Ancient Sartoran days is true. He's certainly no hero now. Personally, I think he was always a fungus. Anyway, I hope he gets into lots and lots of trouble for not having figured out what you and the fifth-worlders were up to."

"He won't," Roy said with a morose shrug. "He was hardly ever there. When we trained there, it was mostly with Siamis. More recently, Detlev was off at Songre Silde doing what he was supposed to be doing, and then he was chasing Siamis along the border to the Land of the Venn, while Yeres double-crossed him. Efael and Yeres will, of course, take the defeat out on someone else."

Clair said, "I hope MV and David are at the top of the list."

"They haven't been overlooked, though not for the reason you're thinking."

This conversation felt all wrong, though Clair meant the best. Remembering Lilith's warning, Clair side-eyed Roy. His bleak expression made Clair flail mentally for a subject change, then Roy's gaze flicked to the door. "Mac is running around below, entertaining Leotay and her sister, but also looking for you."

"Mac!" Clair stood up, relieved at the deft subject change, and delighted at the news. "Lilith remembered! And I didn't even think to ask, but then I did see that Guem and the critters got left behind when all the snakes slithered off."

"That world isn't exactly overpopulated," Roy said. "My guess is, they'll be adopted by the cave people."

"But why are there some here? Are they hurt?"

"No, Leotay is a mage, and her sister is learning. Detlev won't bother with Five again — there's nothing there for him — but Lilith is afraid he will come after the artifact the sisters carry. As soon as they learn some Sartoran, at least one of them is going to Sartorias-deles to the mage school, while Lilith guards Five."

Feeling intensely awkward, Clair drank off the last of her milk. "I'll go find Mac." She stood up. "See you around, I guess."

Roy grinned. "Can't say it was fun, but I do thank you for your help."

What help? She forced a smile. "Come whenever you want. You'll be welcome." She dared an emphasis on the last word.

"Thanks." His cheeks flushed, then he looked away.

And that was that. Clair felt a vague dissatisfaction as she left. As if she could have made up somehow for her lack of insight. No, she wished she could use Lilith's calm and wisdom to make everything right for Roy. He deserved it. But the depressing truth was, though he was now free, he was equally lonely, with nowhere safe to go.

Clair walked along the hall to discover a spiral stairway leading down to a tiled floor in a green, white, and muted gold pattern, where a small boy showed off handsprings for a pair of tall, thin, silk-clad fifth-worlders.

"Clair!" Mac yelled, his voice echoing.

Two pale faces dominated by dark eyes turned upward. Clair walked down the steps. "I'm Clair," she said.

The elder of the two put her narrow-boned hand to her middle and replied in careful Sartoran, "I, Leotay. Sister Horsefeathers."

Clair was startled into a laugh, which she turned into a cough. The second sister's name sounded like a distorted version of the Sartoran words for 'horse' and 'feathers.' *Horsefeathers?*

As Leotay frowned, then turned to address her sister in a quick, soft language, Clair thought she caught some Sartoran words, only . . . different.

Then Leotay turned back to her. "I, I." She pointed to them both.

"We?" Clair asked, whirling her hand around to include them all.

Leotay's expression of concentration altered. "We!"

Clair took a deep breath. Lilith was obviously off being a guardian. Roy recovering. Seshe home safe, and she'd carry the news that Clair lived — and Irenne didn't. Clair felt it impolite to leave until Lilith said she could go; meanwhile here was something that needed doing, so why not?

"We. Talk Sartoran," Clair said, and the eagerness and relief in the two bewildered faces before her eased a knot inside her. Yes. She could teach them Sartoran. Clair did not have to go home yet.

Twenty-five

OVER THE NEXT STRETCH of days, the girls made rapid progress. They discovered that the house they stayed in was some kind of old mage retreat, with an extensive library, and even more extensive grounds. Once Mac discovered a pack of local dogs and a couple of cats, he was almost never seen, except when he did lessons with Roy in the mornings.

Clair watched them through the long windows a couple times. They usually studied in the garden, and the fact that they stayed alone — without inviting Clair or the two fifth-worlders — seemed to underscore what Lilith had said. Roy needed time to himself, except for feeling useful teaching Mac, pretty much the way she felt about her language lessons.

Clair accepted that as just. Her own grief over Irenne was never very far away (and for that matter, the sisters' grief for their friend Jeory was not either) but having a purpose felt good.

Leotay was quiet, practical, studious. Always working away at reading Sartoran when she and her sister were not practicing to speak; Horsefeathers delighted in a new world full of green, growing things. When taking a break from her own magic studies with her sister, or language lessons with Clair, she'd lie flat on the grass outside, long ribbons of silky black hair that had never been roughened by sun or wind spilling around her, as she smiled up at the clouds, or gasped at the flight of a bird or the flutter of a butterfly or the slow bumble of a bee.

Yet both missed their world, revealing it in little ways: wondering how this or that person might be doing, or comparing Sartorias-deles to home. *Home.* That word, how its meaning could change. But Clair would not let herself go down that mental road. Things changed. That was life. Mearsieanne was a better queen than Clair would ever be. Her friends were safe, and she would soon be among them.

She felt kind of sorry for Leotay and Horsefeathers, who'd risked their lives and the secret safety hoarded over countless generations, just to gain a barren, dusty world with only that tiny patch of arable ground at the Den.

Roy couldn't sleep until he was so exhausted he'd fall into bed, then jerk awake after three or four hours, heart pounding, memories pressing in. When that happened, invariably he'd get up and go outside to prowl the quiet garden, looking frequently up at the stars so different from those he was used to on Geth — and on Five, though that was never home.

Really, what was home? It seemed more an idea than a place. If he had to consider any of the places he'd lived a home, instead of temporary quarters, it would be their houseboat on Geth.

After this latest nightmare a tidal wave of memories in sight, smell, sound overwhelmed him and he moved out of the garden, through the glass door and into the lamp-lit room beyond. Here he found that someone had thoughtfully put out a ceramic pot of cobalt blue, fragrant steam rising from the spout. The sky over Sartorias-deles might still be alien to him, but one thing he'd become used to very fast was the taste of Sartoran steep.

He picked a cup off the stack and had just poured the fresh steep into it when the door opened behind him. He had relaxed enough to turn his back to the door, but the sound of it opening snapped awake trained instincts, and he looked back as Lilith walked in, followed by Siamis.

Roy recoiled, the cup flying to crash on the window seat.

Lilith held out both hands, quickening her steps. "Roy. This is a house of peace."

Roy didn't hear her. He stared at Siamis there in the doorway, lamplight gilding his hair. This was a nightmare made real. Siamis did not carry the ancient sword named Truth, though that did not make him any less lethal. It just limited his reach.

Roy's heart thundered frantically in his ears. "Why are *you* here?" he asked.

Siamis answered the real question he saw so raw in Roy's distraught face. "My enemy is Norsunder. I came to offer some advice on your next move. Truce?" He lifted his empty hands.

Roy swallowed in a dry throat, and nicked his chin down in an assent so tense his neck twinged. Siamis's smile deepened, and he walked in, keeping the room's width between them. Roy flushed, knowing that Siamis did that for his benefit. He braced up. "Truce it is. What can you tell me?"

Lilith looked from one to the other, then said, "I'll leave you to it. Young Mac is in another nightmare." She shut the door behind her.

Siamis said, "You left Detlev and the boys, and of course you want to make a gesture. My first guess is, you'll go after the Norsunder Base on Geth in some way."

Roy tried not to let his dismay show. Was he so obvious then?

"It's a good idea." Siamis's light voice gave away nothing. As always. "Excellent idea. But there are a few things you ought to know first."

Roy said slowly, "Detlev explained the wards as a teaching tool. I know them. I've studied how to break them."

Siamis said, "All true. And the place has been all but neglected, as you remember from your stay there. That was true until recently. One of Yeres's pet mages is there right now, busy laying traps."

"Yeres?" Roy whispered. "Why? Why now?"

"That I don't know, communications between us having ceased." Siamis's tone sharpened into irony. "And I'm exerting myself to keep it that way."

Roy knuckled his temples, trying to rub out the headache. "It has to be the marshes."

"It's always been the marshes." Siamis lifted a shoulder.

"But no one has succeeded in conquering that area yet. I suggest, if you don't want to abandon your admirable plan, you put in some time truly mastering mirror wards. And be prepared for some of those wards to be tied to Five. I'm sorry I can't give you specifics — my name is bound into some of those wards, or I would have been there before you — but I learned what I could."

He explained what he had discovered, and what he had not been able to find. Roy listened, but he wondered if he dared to ask why Siamis had turned on Detlev.

"That's it," Siamis said at last, and turned toward the door.

Roy surprised himself by exclaiming, "Wait."

Siamis paused, brows raised in enquiry.

Questions reeled through Roy's mind, and Siamis saw the conflict in him, the struggle to articulate the true questions — the deeper ones — to which Siamis could not give him true answers. He said, "I'm off to expose myself as target practice in Sartor. I hope you succeed, but do be vigilant."

"Why?" The question burst out of Roy, his voice cracking. He flushed miserably. "I mean — why everything?"

"We might have that conversation one day," Siamis said. "But not now. We both have too much to do."

And he was gone.

Twenty-six

Norsunder Base

I —

No, I believe the first rule must be: do not let the grass see you unless you've been ordered to appear.

Adam lifted his pen and studied the coded words, dipped the pen, changed his mind, wiped the ink absently on his pants and put pen, ink, and journal under his mattress. If you chose to roam Norsunder Base, you learned very fast to do it early in the morning—very early—before dawn.

When he recovered from the encounter resulting from his first late night exploration that blundered him into three hard-bitten brawlers looking for targets (at least he gave as good as he got), Adam rose before sunrise, and this time used his stealth skills to drift about unseen. He discovered the place mostly deserted except for the night guards. The one or two who saw him were too tired to make him a target.

As soon as the sun began to bleach the torchlight on the outer ramparts, the noise of the day shift stirring echoed down the stone halls. Adam ran when the rusty bell clanged to raise the day watch; he reached the stairs to their digs over the stable. He was about to turn the corner toward the cubby he shared with four others when he spotted dark-haired Leef, who sat in a window embrasure whittling something with one of his knives.

"Meeting." Leef pointed with his knife toward the last room, where David, Laban, and MV lived.

Adam found most of the others crowded in, two on the bed, two on the desk, and three sitting shoulder to shoulder on the floor with their backs to the wall. Someone had brought food, which they passed from hand to hand. That meant one meal they wouldn't have to eat in the mess hall. The general mood was not grateful, but irate.

Adam sat down next to Erol, who had folded his stocky body as small as possible. His jutting chin rested on a knee, his broad, palely sallow face often earning him from Norsundrians the "platter" epithet given so many Chwahir.

Erol's dark eyes flicked Adam's way. "B-bread-and-cheese." He handed Adam a napkin-wrapped bundle, still warm. "David."

David had been on the early morning duty as kitchen slub. The one perk was fresh food.

Erol pointed at Adam's eye ridges, which Adam could tell by feel were still purple and rose with greenish edges. "Can you see?" he whispered, as he often did to suppress the stutter.

"Yes. The thing about black eyes is, they always look worse than they feel."

Erol grimaced, and Curtas observed mildly, "Not true of smashed jaws."

A shuffle at the door broke the little conversations, as Laban stumbled in, shoved by David's impatient hand: he didn't know how long they had before someone nosed around.

David snapped his fingers, and Curtas and Leef moved off the bed. Laban sank down in their place. The glitter of magic around Laban's head testified to the agony he was feeling. He was not the first of them to get teeth bashed in and jaw broken, repaired by magic to hold the bone fragments in place until his body could reknit them and reseat teeth. Nothing helped the pain.

MV sauntered in last, hooked the toe of his boot around the single chair, then kicked it to the doorway. He dropped into it and leaned precariously back, one foot propped on the door frame. Now he could see inside the room and down the hall to the staircase. Leef stepped over bodies to the window.

David took in the waiting faces. This was it, ten of them besides him. Three re-assigned when they were young, because they couldn't keep up, and now two gone off on their own. "Of course it stinks up here," he said, and MV dropped his foot down to kick the mattress, jolting Laban, who winced.

David said, "The only one who can get away with saying stupid things to the regulars is Adam. And he doesn't always get away with it."

Noser crowed with laughter. Adam knew that many considered him stupid for stating the obvious, but that was fine. Being considered stupid had been his first discovery for successful hiding in plain sight.

"Laban seemed to think that Bostian's strike team captains were interested in his opinion." David sent an unsympathetic glance in Laban's direction. "Adam seemed to think this place is like the Den, where we went anywhere we wanted, when we wanted. They now remember the rules, something we were all told when we were small, and every time since when we've found ourselves in this shit-hole." David lifted his chin slightly in Ferret's direction. "Report."

Adam knew that his own exploration, far as he'd made it on his second foray, was as usual superseded by Ferret's abilities in sneakery and observation.

Ferret said, "Most of the place is empty."

The boys knew better than to waste time or effort exclaiming or giving an opinion. But quick and expressive looks relayed among them. The place was empty, and they were still stuck over the stable?

Ferret went on. "The old markings still keep north, west, and upper east wings empty. Dust this thick." He held up a finger.

Noser whined, "Why can't *we* get rooms there?"

"Turf war." MV grinned. "Those empty wings may as well be overcrowded."

"Did you really not listen last time we were here?" David's soft voice stilled everyone, even Noser. "All that space is waiting for the mages to find rift magic again, so they can shift Theronezhe's armies in from the Beyond. Every commander wants space for their own force."

"How would *I* know that?" Noser sulked, affecting injury.

"Nobody ever lets me anywhere near command."

"That's because they would slit your throat the first time you opened your yap," MV retorted — which Noser knew very well. But it made him feel important that they were looking out for him.

David went on. "Some of the claims are centuries old out here, because the commanders are still in Norsunder-Beyond, awaiting the rifts. Their supplies long since shifted out of time as well." To Noser's expression of interest, "And none of us want to meet any of them."

Noser sighed, as Adam thought about breads and cheeses and berry preserves grown, pressed, formed, and stowed away by hands several centuries dead. He wondered if the tastes of those things had changed over time. Or, in the Beyond, no-time.

Laban said, "But we all know what happened to the latest try for Songre Silde's rift magic. And who is blamed."

Everybody considered that, each in his own way. To Noser, Siamis was to blame for hopping the fence. Laban, Curtas, and the cousins considered the fact that since Norsunder couldn't reach Siamis, who had vanished off-world, whoever Siamis had been with would catch the debris. Adam and David both reflected back on the increasingly virulent arguments Siamis and Detlev had had over the past several years — witnessed avidly by half Norsunder.

MV mentally shrugged: Siamis had made it plain that he scorned them all. In a place where betrayal was an accepted tactical move in advancement strategy, who'd bother to ask why? He found it funny that Siamis's contemptuous rejection of them before his spectacular betrayal of Detlev had the unexpected outcome of sparing them retribution.

Curtas gave a shrug. Back to immediate things for him, as always. "But there has to be some space somewhere, especially as there are no signs of the mages being able to restore the rift magic. So we could be temporarily billeted in any of that space. Right?" Curtas leaned forward, his light gaze serious.

David lifted a shoulder. "Your point?"

"Only a question. We're stuck over the stable as an insult?"

"No insult aimed at us. We're rat shit, beneath notice. So they say." David's lip curled. "Insult to Detlev."

Noser scrambled to his knees, his belligerent expression half-hidden by the shaggy blond hair hanging in his eyes. "He won't fight for us!" His round urchin's face reddened as his top teeth gnawed his underlip, a disgusting habit nobody had been able to break him of.

MV leaned down and swatted Noser hard enough to knock him into Rolfin on Noser's other side, who grunted and shoved Noser back upright. "Idiot! If he challenges anyone on our behalf, then we're really Detlev's babies."

Curtas lifted his brows. "So we fight for new digs?"

"Since we've lost the Den, I think it's time. Ferret?" David tipped his chin again.

Ferret said in his flat, dull, unmemorable voice, "Rooms to spare in east barracks, underground, above the dungeon. Only command gets a window."

No one bothered asking how he knew. If Ferret wanted to get in somewhere, he got in.

Noser scowled. "So . . . if we grab ourselves those rooms in east barracks . . ."

". . . we're marking ourselves as warriors to be commanded. It's just a matter of who would want us." David cast a glance at the smaller of them. "Of course for menial tasks, as we're too young for *real* runs."

"Not for me, thank you. I'd rather the stink." Silvanas laced his fingers together and put them behind his head, his shiny dark hair fanning against his palms.

"There are also two rooms upstairs in the courier annex," Erol said.

"Near Detlev's office?"

"We wouldn't have to run across the entire fortress when summoned!"

"And the stable stink isn't nearly as bad as here." Laban whispered without moving his teeth.

"Nothing here is going to smell good," Curtas commented. Detlev had explained how the wards over Norsunder Base were layered so heavily that everything warped—time, space, stone. Living things. Those few things that survived; the entire region was a desolate space as those who'd built the Norsunder Base ages ago had chopped down every single tree to use, and to burn during winters, before firesticks were made. The topsoil had blown away, leaving dust and barren rock.

Noser jumped up. "So we fight our way there, is that it?" He was ready to start toward the door the moment David gave the sign.

"You leave the fighting to us." David's thumb switched between himself and MV, who cracked a brief, toothy grin, and creaked the chair far enough back that Silvanas, Curtas, and Leef made silent finger bets about it crashing. "Too much of it, and they'll think we're not too young after all, then we've got grass all over us."

They had code not just for activities ("swot" was a regular drill, a "dust" was a beating, or special training—which could hurt as much as a beating—"niff" meant hearing on the mental plane) but also for attitudes and people. "Grass" was lower-level command—the military and mage leaders who struggled for ascendance in Norsunder. "They" and "them" meant the Host of Lords.

The boys had learned not to make their codes interesting.

David said, "We're going to make the courier annex ours, a room at a time. No commander will care if the desk jockeys complain, so make 'em complain. Your job is to make noise coming and going from the two empty rooms. Lots of noise, but always busy and always under orders. Stick your head in every room, offer to sweep, can I get you anything, do you need weapons from storage, ask helpful questions. We want them sick of the sight of us. MV and I will handle the heat quietly, where no one notices."

Noser whined, "Why-y-y-y do y-o-o-o-u get a-l-l-l-l the fun?"

"Because you can't take on anyone with any size yet."

Noser yelled, "And why is that? Because Detlev won't *let* us grow, that's why!"

"You don't want to anyway," Silvanas reminded him. "And if you swotted half as much as you whined, you *could* take 'em on."

It was Adam's turn to speak up. "He told me before he left for the Venn border inspection that there's one more long plan to accomplish, after which we can do what we please about the Child Spell."

Some considered that, Laban wondering why Detlev hadn't made a general announcement. But what one was told, the others always found out. MV suppressed a spurt of amusement, certain that Detlev hadn't told *him* because he would have argued *why not now*.

"I hate swot," Noser muttered, but under his breath; David

was already impatient. Noser had become an expert in just how far he could push.

"Vana. Noser. You two're up for double-swot." He shot a look at Noser and Silvanas.

Noser pouted and Silvanas sighed.

David snapped his fingers. MV crashed the chair down (it was Leef's turn to sigh, having lost the bet that MV would fall, and Curtas grimaced, having lost his bet that MV would break the chair) and leaned over to pull Laban to his feet, as the others slipped past.

Adam lingered. MV and Laban were the last ones out. David turned an inquiring gaze Adam's way.

Adam said, "I wasn't really exploring. I tried to find a safe place to hide my journal."

"Are you still doing that?" David asked, making no attempt to hide his annoyance. "I thought you'd stop it once we left Geth." When Adam shrugged, David said, "We had private space in the Den. Even if we fight our way into a couple extra rooms here, we're still going to be sweeping for traps, tracers, wards, and windows every time we leave and come back."

Adam reached into his tunic and pulled the journal out. David took it, opened it, and ran his gaze down a couple of the pages closely written in a script no one had ever seen before. "Double-coded?"

"Triple, actually."

"You know if any of them find it—" A chin-flick over his shoulder in the direction of the rest of the fortress. "—they'll just beat the code out of you."

"The second level is all about food and stable duty," Adam offered.

"Which will fool maybe half of them."

Adam waited. David could hear his thought: *This is why I asked.*

"I'll find you." David jerked his thumb toward the door. "If you have that much free time, you can go to MV for some dust-up."

Adam ran off. David went the other way, scanning by mind then sight, as he ghosted toward the extreme end of command, next to the courier annex. The middle was where those who sought precedence wanted to be established, but Detlev had chosen an office at the extreme end, next to where the couriers stayed.

He was there. David entered. The furnishings were the bare minimum, not those the boys had made over the years in their lessons on patience and control. On the desk lay papers squared exactly the same way. All of them reports, but written by other people. Anything Detlev wrote remained in Norsunder-Beyond. The boys had discovered that when they were young, and spent a lot of sweat sneaking in to riffle them, before they realized he not only knew what they were doing, but the other commanders did the same thing, or as the boys said to each other, the grass blew over everything.

Detlev's gaze flickered. David knew he was scanning, and habit nearly made him relax in the old way, into the old trust that Detlev knew everything, that he was infallible. But he hadn't niffed those underground people on the fifth world — he hadn't niffed Roy's plan to break and run — and he hadn't known that Siamis would betray them all.

"Problem?" Detlev asked. If he'd sensed listening minds, he would have said, *Your report?*

David said, "Adam wants a stash for his journal. A magic one."

"And?"

David flushed. "That's a lot of work, to build a magic stash."

"Good practice."

Detlev's observation was offered in the same mild voice he used even when he was annoyed with them. David tried to use that voice when he was angry, finding it way more effective than yelling — once you'd proved you could back it up with muscle. Detlev had never raised his voice with any of them, though before Siamis betrayed them, they'd heard all that yelling in the map room up at Command Center. Maybe Detlev only lost his temper with Siamis.

Detlev said, "First, take a little time to settle in." David realized Detlev knew what was going on, and here was his tacit permission. "In addition to your studies, and kitchen patrol, you will also build Adam his stash. Your general orders are to keep drilling the others, out of sight."

And when would he have time to himself?

But Detlev was not done.

"After which, I want you as backup in tutoring duty with them." He indicated the inner door, where David heard two-

and three-year-olds playing. "Curtas and Adam are in charge, for now. You'll cover when they can't be there. Others will eventually take a turn."

David lowered his voice. "Here? In this shit-hole? They'll get stepped on."

Detlev's faint smile held no humor whatsoever. "Before I heed the summons to the Beyond, I'm going to do a shakedown here. Siamis got them at each other's throats — easy enough—and Henerek, with Yeres's willing help, made depredations they're all aware of. As for those babies, they'll be regarded as my new experiment, Aldon's sister's boy among them. *They'll* be safe enough."

The reminder of the real danger got David moving again.

Later, he lingered outside the old tack room that MV had chosen as their training area, for this was another thing they did out of sight of the rest of Norsunder, as much as possible. Some skills they practiced in public, like archery, and riding. Target practice with various weapons. Looking good was important, and everybody watched everyone else. But contact fighting, and some of their blade skills, Detlev and Siamis had trained them in private. When you're small, you need the unexpected on your side, he'd said. Like pretty much everything else he told them, it had proved to be true.

So why didn't he know about Roy?

David wrested his mind from the sickening reality of Roy's defection, though he was aware of the question lying there, still unanswered from before the rain of shit: why did Detlev set Roy to training that stupid Mearsiean girl?

Watching MV slam Adam to the mat again and again, David considered the fact that they had never seen Detlev training Siamis. Whatever had happened, nobody in Norsunder Base command could beat either of them.

Adam finally deflected one of MV's attacks and landed a couple of good blows. When MV released Adam, David cut the latter out on the way to the mess hall. "I'll make you a stash. Then all you have to hide is the token. What kind of token do you want?"

Adam looked around, then vaguely down at his skinny body. His muscles felt like cut string. "My belt buckle," he said in a voice of discovery.

David held out his hand. Adam yanked up his baggy shirt, pulled the worn blackweave belt from the loops, laid it across

David's palm, then moved away painfully, relieved that he'd soon have means to hide the journal.

David watched him go, tossing the belt on his hand, the buckle a plain square of steel, standard issue. The rest of the belt was so plain and worn, nobody would ever bother to take it from him. Adam never tried to dress distinctive — if anything, the opposite. Unlike Laban and his fine shirts, and MV settling on black in mockery of Bostian and Aldon, and Curtas in Colendi styles.

Siamis had told the boys repeatedly that anger was futile if you couldn't act. David couldn't act, and he was still angry — with Siamis, with Roy, angry that they'd lost the Den. He *hated* that. He was also angry at Detlev for not knowing about those people underground, and for trying to foist a girl on them, that white-haired idiot from Mearsies Heili.

David had done his very best to make her loathe them so much she'd cut and run the first moment she could. But then Roy had ruined it by taking his assignment as an opportunity to make friends with her. How long had he been covertly planning his betrayal?

David grimaced when he remembered trying to get Roy to organize a run, *any* kind of run, so that they could take Terry and the Mearsiean along and he could have worked it so even a pair of idiots could have escaped, but Roy . . .

A surge of fury made him want to smash something. But orders were orders. It would take a long time to do the magic necessary to make Adam's stash. Though David could not understand the need to keep a journal, the practice in complicated magic would make him faster.

So. Conclusion: Firejive — closed circle, now down to ten besides him.

He would not lose another one.

PART TWO
PRISON

One

Late autumn, 4748 AF
Eidervaen, capital of Sartor

AT BEST, SIAMIS WAS an embarrassment.

People who regarded themselves as just, merciful, and generous had to struggle with quite opposite emotions whenever they thought of him walking freely around Sartor's capital Eidervaen.

There were, of course, those who wanted him dead. They spoke passionately about justice, safety, trust, many not quite bringing themselves to bluntness, but all hoped someone would take the hint and kill him.

Tsauderei, the aged mage who was serving temporarily as head of the Sartoran mage guild, said privately to Sartor's high council, "Don't do it. I believe him when he says it was not his hand behind the murder of my predecessor and her chief mages mainly because he'd already obtained the information he sought. He'd moved on to Colend's king — where he got what he wanted, also without violence. The Norsundrian Efael murdered the mages, and assassinated the Colendi king."

"A regret this Efael didn't murder Siamis instead," a baras said, then glanced nervously over her shoulder.

No one argued, but Tsauderei reflected on the fact that Siamis had not only helped lay wards against Efael, but had also given them the names of all his chosen assassins in the Black Knives. Tsauderei made it a requirement for the senior students as well as the teachers to lay specific wards so vigorous that if these assassins so much as walked into the city, tracers would alert the mages on duty, who had stone spell tokens at the ready.

The small contingent of city guards did make certain to watch the guest wing of the palace as soon as Siamis took up residence there. For a number of weeks they even posted watchers armed with crossbows on the roofs surrounding the two doors Siamis would have to use.

Rel, one of the earliest members of the Young Allies, and friend to Atan, the queen, took this post a couple of times, and occasionally looked down at Siamis's familiar light hair as he came and went peaceably. Rel noted that Siamis didn't even wear the infamous sword named Emeth, or "truth."

One time, as autumn waned into bitter winds, Rel sat hunched over, pressing his gloved hands between his thighs and chest. He'd been watching his breath cloud until Siamis emerged, swinging a cloak around his shoulders. He glanced up, and Rel was quite certain Siamis saw him, though Rel had his mind-shield firmly in place.

Later, he said to the grizzled commander, "I think it's a waste of time to post guards on the rooftops. Siamis has to know exactly where we are. Whatever his game is, he's not going to start anything while he's playing guest."

The commander had his rank by virtue of age, and having survived the war over a century ago, when Sartor was removed beyond time. In the oldster's mind, experience and sense called for compromise. He knew that Rel had the most experience with Siamis, so if he thought the close watch useless, then it was probably true.

One thing for sure: no one liked that duty. Especially with winter coming on. "We'll leave him to the politicos, then," he said, and wiped the rooftop duty off the chalked roster. "Maybe one of them will break out and rid us of him."

And so, with universal relief, the guards relinquished the roof duty — but most made certain their rounds took them often into the first district, and over by that end of the palace. Just in case.

As for Siamis, Rel was unsurprisingly right: a couple practiced glances picked out the best spots for roosts, and Siamis saw the bobbing heads of the guards when he came and went. It did not take Dena Yeresbeth to perceive what people thought of him. Every time he walked into a room, he could see in tightened faces, angled bodies, the slight drawing back, how much he was hated by most, and how strong was the moral dilemma in others.

That was good. Moral dilemma was nothing new to him. Shaking the light magic world from its complacent moral superiority was only one of his current goals.

Two

Hostel, Western Drael to Mearsies Heili

FAR TO THE NORTH, in the secluded retreat, Clair gradually came to face the fact that she wasn't yet ready to go home. Irenne was dead. Seshe had gone ahead to tell the girls that Clair was alive, and there wasn't any great need for her, was there?

She never answered that, even to herself. She did not even like her mind going there. So she kept busy in that house, either talking Sartoran vocabulary to the sisters, or reading in the library. It felt good to study magic again—even though she'd come to the grim realization that her skills were mediocre. She'd let herself become complacent. Lax.

The very morning she woke up, finding herself restless for the first time, she arrived in the breakfast room to discover Lilith gathered with the others.

"I've been speaking with Leotay and Horsefeathers," Lilith said on greeting Clair. "You have done a commendable job teaching them the language."

"I think there might be some Sartoran roots in theirs," Clair said slowly.

"Oh, there is no doubt," Lilith said. "Their language does

share both words and structural elements with Ancient Sartoran, as there was frequent travel between the two worlds—which is why both were attacked concurrently back in my day. I'm certain the Scribe Guild in Sartor, as well as the mages, will be learning as much from Leotay as she learns from them."

"It makes me happy, to share," Leotay said.

"So Horsefeathers's name, it isn't an accident that it sounds a bit like the same words in Sartoran?"

Lilith smiled. "No accident. Though of course the meaning is vastly different—but you have met one of the indigenous beings who took horse shape."

"Hreealdar?" Clair exclaimed.

"Indeed."

"But Hreealdar doesn't have feathered wings. When he— or she, or it—takes flight, it's in the shape of lightning."

"That is true, except for his coat, which is actually down— very fine feathers."

"I never noticed that," Clair exclaimed. "I sat right on Hreealdar, so many times."

"You saw what you expected to see," Lilith said, smiling. "That's natural. Hreealdar has several forms, as you know. There were, however, winged horses in the mountains, who did have feathered wings. They were quite a bit smaller. I hope they fled elsewhere."

"Ours, all gone now," Horsefeathers said, sighing with a sixteen-year-old's impatience. "Trees, grass, all gone."

Clair had been about to ask if there were any others like Hreealdar living in Selenseh Redians besides the one in Mearsies Heili, but she fell silent.

Lilith lightly clapped her hands. "Everyone eat up. Then we shall all depart to our various destinations, shall we? I must return to Aldau-Rayad, until Leotay can return to her guardianship."

Clair went to get her food. When she came back with her plate, she found the sisters deep in conversation with Lilith, so she veered over to where Roy sat. Mac arrived a moment later to sit with them. "Are you going, too?" Clair asked Roy.

"Back to Geth," he said.

"I'm going with *you*," Mac said to Clair with an eager smile, and for the first time she felt enthusiasm. She'd wanted very much to bring Mac out of Five—had dreamed about showing him the locations of the stories he had listened to so eagerly — but when she saw him with Roy she had squelched those plans. When he saw her answering grin, he went on in a rush, "I want to see your secret underground hideout, and the bubble lake, and the white castle on the mountain. And Puddlenose, and Ben, who changes into animals, and Diana the forester, and *everything*."

"So you shall," Lilith said, laying a hand on each of their shoulders.

Clair loathed farewells with a secret and abiding passion. To her immense relief, transfer magic shrouded and squeezed them, unraveling a heartbeat later. Clair staggered as the smell of pine and clean water and wisteria gripped her: the smell of *home*.

A sob ripped up through her chest, which she turned into a cough, making the greatest effort of her life. For Mac looked up at her, wide-eyed, a homeless and family-less small boy between four and five, when no one ought to be alone. She forced a smile, but sensed his question in the mental plane — then she swayed, aware for the first time that she recognized the mental plane.

When had *that* happened?

She lifted her hand. "See the white palace? Just as I told you."

They had landed on the Destination before the terrace. Distracted, Mac tipped his head back, his mouth rounding as he took in the towers in their uneven heights spiraling upward, gleaming in slanting autumnal rays.

Clair knew that light. She knew the old-leaf smell on the wind: she had lost nearly a year as Detlev's prisoner.

"Come inside," she said, and when Mac's small hand took hers, she clasped his fingers reassuringly.

The broad arched doors stood open as they did nearly year-round, except during very cold weather. The magic in this palace was impossibly old — it was always warm inside, never needing so much as a firestick. Yet in summer it stayed cool.

It was late in the day, so Mearsieanne's morning court would be over. They encountered no servants in the foyer. Clair walked slowly, seeing her home through Mac's eyes: the upward vaulting, the glistening not-marble walls that were somehow all colors blended with infinite subtlety to white.

Smells drew them, though they'd just had breakfast, and as they approached the dining room, Mearsieanne emerged from a side hall, her long black hair ordered in a fall down her back to her blue and white skirts. At first glance she was young, no older than Clair, except when you saw her eyes.

Mearsieanne exclaimed, "You have returned! I am so glad. I'll summon everyone."

Mac's hand tightened convulsively on Clair's, and she remembered consciously that Mearsieanne was a very old woman in a girl's form. But that prompted the question, for the first time: How old am I, really?

She glanced down at Mac's waiting face, and her nerves shot cold when the thought occurred that she was old enough to have a child of her own.

Though Mearsieanne disliked the underground hideout, she was not averse to using the blotter that Clair had made for communication. She appeared again and said, "And who is this?"

"Mac was among the children I tended while I was a prisoner. I brought him back with me."

Clair so expected Mearsieanne to welcome him that when Mearsieanne's upper lip crimped, Clair thought she was in pain. Then Mearsieanne said, "Not, I trust, one of Detlev's spawn? Does he understand Mearsiean?"

Mac was looking from one to the other, clearly lost.

Clair said in Norsundrian—which Mearsieanne would recognize from her prisoner days— "It's all right." And to Mearsieanne, "Macadais likes to be called Mac. He's four. All he's been learning are his letters, and the sort of basics you'd get in garrison life anywhere."

Mearsieanne's mouth tightened to a thin line, and Clair sensed an emotion-charged tangle of memory image and jumbled words that her own mind translated out to: I don't trust Detlev not to do anything wicked.

"Mac has no home, no family. Detlev lost the fifth world, as I'm sure Seshe told you."

Clair hoped that mentioning Lilith might help—and her name might have with anyone else, except Mearsieanne. Who silently, and bitterly, resented Lilith for not having rescued her when she was yanked out of her own time and kept in Norsunder Beyond for one of Detlev's failed experiments. But Mearsieanne never spoke that resentment out loud, because everyone else revered Lilith.

"Very well, then," Mearsieanne said in the sprightly voice that Clair knew meant she was conceding, and hated it.

Clair had enough time to feel the inwardly sinking sensation of regret before the girls began arriving. First was Falinneh, red braids flapping on her orange and green striped shirt, worn with purple knee-pants. "Clair! You're *back!*"

Next was CJ, small, black hair flying, wide blue eyes beaming delight. Fierce, loyal CJ. "Clair! You're really okay? Hey! You brought somebody!"

"This is Mac. Rescued from the fifth world. He needs to learn our language."

"Oh, well," Falinneh exclaimed, rubbing freckled hands. "Let's start with the *good* words."

"He'll be pocalubing villains before the day is out," CJ promised, and to Mac, "Eat? Choc-o-late?" She made motions to her mouth. "Let's start with hot chocolate." She beckoned to Mac, who looked from CJ to Clair.

"That's CJ," Clair said to Mac. "Go with her. She's got a good surprise."

Seshe appeared, her gaze searching. "I'm glad you're back," she said in her quiet voice, but Clair sensed the question.

No, she heard the question on the mental plane. Now that she knew what that was, she had to stop doing it. Out loud she said, "I stayed to teach Leotay Sartoran."

Seshe's eyes widened in dismay. "If I'd known—I would have been glad to stay so you could come home."

"It's all right. I think I needed to stay," Clair said, and suppressed the words, *There was no need for me here.*

In a way that wasn't true, and sure enough, here came Gwen, her big blue eyes earnest, her curls bouncing. "Clair, I'm so glad you're back!" And in a low voice, "We waited. For you. We held a vote, whether to wait for you, or to remember Irenne right away. We all picked waiting."

Clair pressed her lips against a sigh. She knew that this was going to hurt all over again. "Thank you," she said.

Three

MEARSIEANNE STOOD ALONE, HATRED so intense it made her tremble.

She was at the window of her favorite room in the white palace on the mountain, but she did not see the fading autumn colors in the forest far below. What she saw was inward, imaginary: she relished the righteousness of her hatred of Detlev, and loved to imagine his humiliation before the Host of Lords for losing Al-Althan. Had they tortured him? She hoped so.

She knew that wishing someone tortured was wrong, but in this instance she wanted to laugh, loud and hard, at the image of him lying bleeding, with broken bones, blubbering for pity that would never be granted. She clenched her hands at her sides, though it drove her rings into her flesh, and reached for the impulse behind the flush of violent images. As if she didn't know.

Clair and her girls were in their underground cave, holding their long-postponed memorial for Irenne.

Mearsieanne shut her eyes. She had been ready to attend whatever memorial the girls wanted to hold, feeling that loyalty and duty obliged her to. Regret as well. Of all Clair's odd collection of strays, Irenne had been the one Mearsieanne liked most. She'd readied herself, mentally arranging her evening so that she could contemplate good things to say when it was her turn to speak . . . and over the course of the evening four of the girls had come to her, shyly, tentatively, earnestly, to invite her to come.

Yes. There was the reason: underneath the justified and righteous anger, lay *hurt*. You couldn't tell someone how much their invitation hurt, but the truth was, the girls didn't invite one another. It wouldn't have occurred to them. They invited her because they worked so hard—here was their loyalty and duty—to include her. She could not tell them that their very effort more effectively closed her out than mere rudeness, or girl-group silliness, could ever have done. She couldn't say that though she wished they would fill in that disgusting, stuffy underground cave, she understood that their memorial could be held in no other place. To them that was such a given that any words from her would have sounded like condescension.

She tested her unpalatable conclusion by staying away. And such was the girls' grief in their closed circle that none of them came to get her.

While she stared out into the night sky, down in the underground hideout, once Mac had fallen asleep in Puddlenose's room, the girls gathered around the colorful rug in the main room, some teary, others uncertain.

Clair said, "Thank you for waiting for me. Since we don't know when Puddlenose will return, or where Ben is traveling, then it's just us. And I think it's right, because we were the ones she lived with most."

CJ nodded, having worried this subject over for months, dreading news that Clair and Seshe, would also be reported dead. "We don't have any traditions about . . . about losing someone. For us," she said, scowling to keep tears away. "I hoped we never would. But Irenne was the first of us to get—"

"Second," Sherry whispered next to Clair, her huge sky-blue eyes sorrowful.

"Second," Dhana said tightly. "Jennet."

Only Sherry had known Jennet, Clair's first friend, a Chwahir girl she'd met when both were very small. Jennet had been a victim of Chwahir politics before they reached the age of ten.

"And Jennet," CJ said firmly, though she'd never met her. "Let's just see if we can even the score," she added fiercely.

Even the score and we lose, Clair thought. But she said nothing; she knew CJ. Angry as she was, CJ still couldn't bear the thought of really killing someone.

"We'll go around the circle," Clair said. "And share memories. Irenne never wanted us to know where she really came from, because she always liked pretending she was somebody else from somewhere more interesting, which was what made her so much fun. But I don't think she'd mind your knowing how we met. . ."

Clair went on with the story, and though she'd never been very good at describing, she managed to evoke Irenne in memory by unconsciously mimicking Irenne's hands-on-hips posture.

"And when she came," Sherry said with a tremulous smile, "she hinted that she was a runaway duchas, and I asked, what's a duchas? And we were great friends after that."

They went around the circle once, twice, three times, then four, talking until most were teary, and then they still stood, no one wanting to be the first to turn away. CJ's light blue eyes widened fiercely, framed by black lashes and expressive brows. Her short, slight form stiffened with emotion — anger, grief, sorrow. Uncertainty.

"So we're agreed?" CJ said, looking from one girl to another. "Clair, you weren't here, but we talked. A little. We won't touch Irenne's things for a year. Everything just as she left it. Then next year, on her birthday, we'll decide what to do. All right?"

Sherry wept quietly, shoulders shaking. Clair looked down, her white hair curtaining her vision so she couldn't see Sherry's stricken eyes, or Seshe's compressed mouth that didn't hide the trembling.

Clair's initial reaction was that she would never want to get rid of Irenne's things. But that seemed creepy, too. Would it be natural to maybe invite another girl? She remembered their blundering with Liere, and Devon before her, and winced. No, it would never work. No one could replace Irenne.

As the girls broke up slowly, some to collect the cups, others talking quietly, Clair looked around. The hideout really did seem . . . small. No. She was *not* growing out of it. She rejected that thought with her whole being. Her emotions were unsettled, because of Irenne, and that long imprisonment. That was all.

She walked down the tunnel and stopped outside Puddlenose's room, listening to Mac's light breathing. He'd loved the place at first sight. She smiled at that. What if some day she had her own child? She was old enough.

Another shake of the head. She was tired.

She walked back up, where she found Seshe and CJ both waiting, question in their gazes. "I'm all right," she said. "Get some rest. It's really late for you. I'll go tell Mearsieanne what we decided," and transferred to the white palace.

She walked softly down the hall, peering ahead for lights. She found her great-grandmother in her own parlor; Mearsieanne's head turned quickly. Then she had been waiting for them! Why hadn't she come when Clair had been so careful to ask her?

Mearsieanne never went down to the Junky on her own. Was that it, she found the place too repulsive even for a memorial? Clair decided that since any answer she could imagine was upsetting, she would not ask. "We decided to leave her things for a year."

"Very well." Mearsieanne touched her fine desk, with its magic-laden scribe blotter. "It's good to have you back. But I will never cease missing Irenne."

"Nor I. Nor I." Clair's chest ached, and her throat hurt, but all her crying had been done on the fifth world, and Lilith's retreat — and it hadn't accomplished anything. "Good night."

"Good night," Mearsieanne said, looking weary and . . . not old, as the Child Spell kept her contours round and youthful, but . . . sad.

Clair withdrew softly and returned to her room, which was exactly the way she'd left it so suddenly nearly a year ago. Her notecase lay on the desk. She opened it. Several notes lay within, all recent, and all expressing gladness that she had been reported safe, and all adding their regrets over the news about Irenne. The one from Senrid was the shortest:

Glad you're safe. Very sorry about your friend.
Report when you can.

Clair laid that down, reflecting that the Clair who'd gone away a year ago to Wnelder Vee would have angrily refused, insisting that such a horrible experience should be forgotten.

But you don't forget.

Clair's gaze touched the familiar objects in the room — the quiet blue coverlet, the froth of pillows that she'd added in a forlorn hope of reproducing the effect of sleeping suspended in air, as she had in Tsauderei's Valley of Delfina. You don't forget. You learn and . . .

She shook her head, glancing down at Senrid's quick, precise handwriting. Last year she also would not have perceived that what he really wanted was an insider's report on the enemy. But *that* could wait.

Knowing it was already day where Terry lived, Clair pulled a piece of paper from the waiting stack, and wrote to ask how he was.

Then she wrote to Arthur:

> *I'm back. I'm sure you'll be hearing about the fifth-world mage coming to study in Sartor. I wanted to tell you, in case you hadn't heard, that Roy is on our side. He always was, I think. He was there undercover as Lilith's eyes into Detlev's group.*

Clair hesitated about reminding Arthur of their ship journey, and the shared friendship. If she had not forgotten, he certainly would not have. That visceral, stomach-tightening sense of intruding where she might not be wanted kept her silent. She remembered how incensed he'd been at the discovery that Roy was one of Detlev's boys. Of course he had to have felt that Roy's friendship was fake, a betrayal. She'd felt the same, and she hadn't been as close to Roy as Arthur had.

When the notecase gave her that inward ting of a letter arriving, she signed hers, folded it, took out the new letter and sent off the one to Arthur.

The new note was from Terry.

> *Glad you're home again. Why did they keep you?*

> *Lilith the Guardian sent me on after she sent your friend. It was quite interesting to see who actually welcomed me back, who pretended to welcome me back, and who didn't even pretend. I prefer the*

latter. You don't expect anything from someone who hates you. I wonder how they'd feel if I told them that in many ways I'd rather be a horse trainer than a king? In both situations you're moving around something a lot larger than you are, but with the horse you get honesty, and they don't care if you've got a hitch in your gallop.

But as Halad points out, there are some good bits about kinging. Like, I can order my own horses to train, and I don't have to wand out the stable.

T.

Clair smiled and reached for a piece of paper to answer, then the notecase tinged again. It was Arthur, asking if he could visit.

Clair stared in surprise. Arthur must badly need to talk if he intended to endure two long distance transfers for a conversation. She wrote back an assent, and pulled a day robe over her nightgown to hide it.

By the time she got downstairs to the white palace's Destination, Arthur was already there, blinking away the transfer reaction. Arthur reminded her of a lighter-haired version of Ferret, except a bit older—he'd released the Child Spell sometime in the past year—completely unremarkable at first glance. But if one looked, the fold of the eyelid, the subtle bump in the lightly freckled nose, the rounded cheek curving down to chin, the light hair coming in light brown underneath, all were distinctive. Individual. And Arthur wasn't furtive, he was just absent.

"Mearsieanne has gone to sleep," she murmured, as her suite lay on the same floor. "We can go to the kitchen."

Arthur swallowed a couple times, still recovering from the transfer, but followed her.

"I take it Roy hasn't written to you?" Clair asked when they reached the empty hall, where night-dim glowglobes turned the hallway into a blue-white space.

"No," he said as they entered the kitchen.

Clair touched the glowglobe to full light, and steered around the big prep table, where cloth-covered breads were rising, filling the air with a yeasty smell.

She indicated the table where the servants ate, and Clair and the girls had also, before Mearsieanne came. Arthur sat across from her, his clothes rumpled, the edges of his cuffs ink-stained, indicating a long day of work behind him. Clair saw that he'd flushed red to the top of his ears as he studied his clasped hands. Then Clair remembered all his angry talk when they were all in Wnelder Vee chasing Detlev's boys. She'd seen a side of Arthur she hadn't known existed.

Arthur said, "I know you remember all my ranting. It's bothered me ever since I heard that Seshe was back, and you were safe." He looked down, then up again. "The worst thing about my raving," he said, "was, besides making you hear it, that I cursed Roy for what he might do. Not for anything he actually did."

"I get it," Clair said. "You—we all—were angry because we thought he'd pretended friendship in order to betray us. He told me he always existed between not very good choices."

"But from what I heard, he's made good ones anyway."

"He did at the end, yes," Clair said. "I can't speak to anything before we met him."

Arthur didn't know what to do with his hands, so he clasped them behind him. "So . . . is he coming back?"

"I don't think so. Yet. I think he's gone to Geth."

"That makes sense." Arthur looked away, strongly suspecting that Geth was probably preferable to meeting up with him and his self-righteous posturing again. Regret hurt at least as strong as those initial spikes of betrayal and anger. Though he'd really come in hopes that Clair would have something to say about Roy that couldn't be committed to paper, it was clear she had nothing. "What can you tell me about the fifth world and the magic that freed them?" he asked, to hide that regret. "All the mages are asking about that."

"Very little." She spread her hands. "When that was happening, I was sitting at the other end of the action, trying to recover my wits. But the mage responsible went to Sartor at the same time I was sent home. You can probably find a way to meet her. Hibern told me once that the northern magic school shares news as well as students with the Sartoran one."

"Thanks," Arthur said, sitting back, then he said to the opposite wall, "I hated him because I told him everything. I thought he was . . . a friend. The kind of friend who might be closer, when you're ready for that." His face burned, and he looked upward, then at Clair. "I always envied you because you have all those girls, like sisters, a family you made. Roy felt like that to me. Then it was all fake, and I believed he'd only been saying what I wanted to hear."

Clair ground her thumb against the edge of the table, back and forth, as she remembered her own sense of humiliation, the sickening sense that what she'd thought was friendship had really been lies, manipulation. That she'd been made a fool. Because what other motivation could a Norsundrian have?

She sighed, eyeing Arthur, unsure what to say. She was used to him being self-possessed, interested mainly in his books and magic. But everybody had feelings. Some didn't wear them outwardly, like clothes. She remembered Roy's anguish at the haven, and felt her way into words. "I don't believe that's true. At least, he might have said leading things, to find out whatever magic teachings he was told to learn. But the important things, the things that felt real. I think they *were* real."

Arthur's mobile mouth tightened. "You don't need to pat me on the head."

"I'm not. You didn't see him, at the end. I did." She shook her head. "He . . . took things really, really hard."

Arthur looked away again. Clair sensed that he was embarrassed at his outburst, maybe even his impulse to transfer so far, instead of just writing a note. He said in a less heated voice, "If you do hear from Roy, will you let me know?"

"I will," she promised, and walked him back to the Destination.

When he was gone, she returned to her room, doused the light, lay down . . . and fell straight into nightmares.

Four

TSAUDEREI FELT LIKE A student again when he received the summons from Lilith the Guardian.

Decades ago, when he was a journeymage, he had lain up on the dragon mountain—one of the highest peaks in the world, there on the Sartoran border—looking at the brilliant stars, and counted up the questions he would ask if he should ever meet the famous Lilith the Guardian. Over the years since, most of those questions he had either answered himself, or determined were unanswerable. About the only one left was, *What was Ancient Sartor really like?*

She wafted him from the southern end of the world to the north as easily as stepping through a doorway. He blinked at the short, dumpy woman in the draped robe who looked maybe twenty years younger than he, and exclaimed, "Teach me that transfer!"

"It requires Dena Yeresbeth," she said. "And has been impossible hitherto. But it is time for you to know that magic has strengthened enough in the world to permit other, oh, call them accesses to magic." She turned her head, and gestured to a broad window overlooking a lake.

Three figures could be made out in a sailboat, tiny at this distance.

"They are the ones I am concerned with right now," she said. "Will you take these two from Aldau-Rayad into the Sartoran mage school? They wish to study, and I think that would be a good idea, but my primary need is for the artifact one of them carries to be protected. I must return to their world to guard until they can return."

Tsauderei said, "Artifact?"

Lilith considered him. "It's from my time, yes, but from their world. I know nothing about it, except that it is not complete. They know nothing about it. I hope they will learn something as they study here."

There was, of course, only one answer to be made to that. "I'll do what you ask." Then Tsauderei gathered his courage — and she turned to look up at him. He remembered the damned mind-shield too late, as the fine, wrinkled skin around her eyes contracted to an expression of sorrow.

She said, "Your question would take a lifetime to answer. More, because life was so very different." She paused, then: "I understand how important it is. And yet now is not the time . . . Oh, I know how frustratingly vague that sounds. But truly, we would have to establish a vocabulary we both understood before we could even begin."

"Then use the words we both know," he said with heavy irony.

Her tone took his challenge as a serious question. "I will try — in certain regards. For example, you want to know the hierarchy of governing back then, but in a sense there was no hierarchy, not as understood now. Yes, we had a queen — it was always a queen, and even now that title carries more gravitas than king, except in a few places — but her duty was to lead ritual. She made no laws, and led no wars. We didn't *have* war. Monarchy was not at all the way it is understood now, evolved as it is from war chiefs, bolstered by law as well as military threat."

"You didn't have a military?" Tsauderei asked in disbelief.

"Yes, we did. But it was not made up of standing armies as customary in most places now. It was made up of those who prized, let us call it, the highest arts of physical exertion, one of which arts was the duel. Because we still occasionally had personal conflicts that could not be resolved through healing or the peace rituals, there was the duel—another ritual—and the military was there to see it carried out to its end so that the conflict did not spread."

"Who governed? Who held the power?"

She glanced out at the lake, whose waters slowly took on a pewter cast as a spring storm moved in. "Each polity had a family overseeing it, call it a clan chief. But they, too, answered to ritual. Power, ah-h-h. I can hear your next question about those who formed Norsunder, and why, and of course the answer to that is the accumulation of power, but even then there are reasons . . ."

She put her fingertips together, and pressed the forefingers against her lips. "So many questions lead in a direction that right now is so very dangerous. Let me say this: I was asked to remain because I, involved in ritual, knew all the progenitors of Norsunder, or almost all. Svirle is the only clan chief amongst them. That name, Host of Lords, is a mockery he brought back from his world-gate expeditions, we thought to travel and gain experience—for he had been perceived as idle, leaving responsibility to others—but actually he had studied human worlds and types of power. It was he who brought back those terrible children, Yeres and Efael. Not children in the physical sense. They were nearly adults, but so damaged that perversity was their pleasure, violence their method of expression, and they were willing—eager—to do what Svirle and Sfenaraec found beneath them. They will never be more than minions, though they aspire to equal power in that circle of wanton destruction. And right now, they appear to be making a bid to take that place."

Tsauderei thought—behind his unpracticed mind-shield— *At last I am beginning to learn something useful.* "And the rest of this circle of wanton destruction?"

Lilith shook her gray head. "Theronezhe organized the military force. Connanre was part of ritual—a musician, very high in the hierarchy, as music was so much a part of everyday life. A friend, I had thought, who would do anything for love." She shut her eyes. "That 'anything' is what made all the difference—that and the lover he chose. It was he who, from his position close to all, pointed out the best targets to murder for the widest effect."

"Are you talking about what we call the Fall?"

"You could say . . ." Lilith's gaze shifted away, her eyes

nearly shut as she gazed far into the past. "You could say that what you call the Fall began with the destruction of mutual trust and harmony during an important ritual, but there was a more personal, oh, change before that . . ."

Once more her voice suspended, and he wondered what it was that he was not going to hear. And why.

Lilith had not been there to witness the entirely human error, the tragedy of wisdom and moral scruple being seduced not just by transcendent beauty but the promise of unlimited power over which to extend that benevolent intent. She had only been there to see the result.

Tsauderei—while temporarily heading the Sartoran mage guild—had spent a good deal time deep in the dustiest archives that had been closed to him hitherto, and had discovered just how scant those were, and how deliberate the lacunae. As if the women—and in those very early days the chief mages had been only women—had conspired to eradicate something they did not want found.

He considered the possibility that even now he was being lied to.

Lilith lifted her gaze to his; she knew his thought, but also knew that to address it directly might confirm what was only nebulous suspicion. "Nay, the rituals were very important. This particular one was attended by the most people. Random, vicious murders, destruction and fires that caused more deaths, ripping apart the bindings of civilization we had grown up thinking so strong—that sparked anger, and a reaching for weapons, and it was then that they brought in the warriors. The soul-eater," she said bitterly, in the low tone reserved for repeating obscenities, "had a feast."

She stopped. "Already vocabulary is leading me astray, and yes, you have studied the forms of Ancient Sartoran, but so very many terms cannot be understood in their original sense. The war then was much as war is now—and the personalities are long forgotten. You want to understand more about the center of power, but the fundamental idea in our world was that there *was* no center of power, that all these forms overlapped to a purpose. But the strongest, oh, defense—the final, hmmmm, authority in conflict was the circle of Healers, the dyranarya . . ."

She whispered the word, then looked up, her expression chagrined, almost he would have said of anyone else, frightened. "I've already spoken too much. I am truly sorry, Tsauderei, to be so cryptic. I hope one day to have the leisure, and the freedom, to explore it all as much as you wish. But that time is not now. Events move far too fast as it is."

She had been coming to the world more often than any time in history. And because he could see the traces of sorrow — of profound loss — in her expression, and he was certainly old enough to understand loss, he said, "Thank you. So tell me about these two from Aldau-Rayad."

"That," she said gratefully, "I can do. In as much detail as you like."

While Lilith described Leotay and Horsefeathers, the sisters scrambled happily over the little boat, and Horsefeathers even climbed the slender mast to the top, where she could hang on and look below at the curve of the sail thrumming and flacking in the rising wind.

Leotay liked standing at the side and watching the way sky and sea knit together on the other side of the lake, and the way the weather marched across the sky unhindered. Sunsets were so beautiful that the first one had made her throat hurt and her eyes sting: she kept thinking of Jeory, and how he would have loved it.

It was then that the rain began.

The sky turned dark and water splatted on their faces and hands.

Water out of the sky! Leotay remembered Seshe's story about it, only this was even better than she had imagined. And this water, unlike ocean water, was good to drink. At first Horsefeathers squinched up her face and refused to try it, until she saw her sister lick it off her face with no ill effects.

Roy, who had taken them out, began to head for shore. Leotay was already shivering, but Horsefeathers laughed for joy.

Five

SOON AFTER SIAMIS'S TWELFTH Name Day four millennia ago, Efael ripped meaning away along with his innocence. Detlev saved him, at a cost that Siamis eventually understood had been far worse than his own experiences. In a place where there was no moral certainty, he still felt a moral burden, and his resentment had intensified with that understanding. Death in the Beyond was no escape.

"Meaning," Detlev eventually said as they stood alone (except of course they weren't, and they knew it) in the Garden, "is what you make it."

After that the training had begun, overt, then covert when they weren't being watched or under orders. The pleasure of speaking the entire truth, without calculation, he'd enjoyed so seldom that he was no longer able to.

Lies were the resort of the short-sighed, the stupid. Siamis always told the truth, but only as much as the situation required. Though he knew very well who was actively hunting him, and what would happen if he were caught, he reveled in this semblance of freedom.

He openly discussed his prospective jaunt off-world with

anyone who asked, but to no one did he give any hint of his real plans.

At Norsunder Base, the night-watch kitchen crew were the ones who had to get the dough rising for the next day's bread, and the peas soaking for the inescapable pease-porridge and soup.

David, Laban, and Curtas rotated volunteering for that duty, each staying in the empty room next to a courier, banging and crashing at night as one got back from a shift and another got ready. After several repeats of, "Sorry, we're trying to be quiet!" and a personal encounter with MV's fists in the stairwell, the desk jockey in that room decided life would be easier doubled up with a work mate—and they could both lie in wait and issue some creative retribution if they could catch MV unawares. They didn't.

The boys had begun on the next room over when that target abruptly vanished on assignment somewhere north, at Aldon's command. The boys promptly took over the room. They'd deal with the owner on his return, beginning on the basis that possession was half the battle, and the other half would be ten against one.

Four rooms! One more, and they'd be two to a room, with one extra. Bearable. Some even liked rooming together, like Adam and Curtas, the cousins Leefan and Rolfin, and Noser had been under Vana's charge for so long that it was habit.

They were quietly rejoicing when Ferret returned from kitchen duty dunking and stacking dishes. "Five-fingered some caraway bread," he said, pulling a fresh loaf out of his loose tunic.

Rolfin snatched it first, and began breaking off and passing pieces as Ferret murmured, "Heard Siamis is in Sartor. Did we know that?"

"We do now." MV looked up from sharpening one of his knives as Leef set his share of the fresh bread on one of MV's skinny, black-clad knees.

"And? We don't have orders about Siamis," David reminded them. "So far, we've not done real well going outside orders."

"But Siamis! Wouldn't it be fun to dust him?"

Everyone considered that. Curtas said, "If Detlev — or Efael — hasn't landed on him already, then my guess is, something's going on."

"Something's always going on." MV flipped up the back of his hand toward the wall. "Efael could be prancing around off-world, or in the Beyond. If we were to snake into Eidervaen and nab Siamis, not touching anything or anyone else — no one knowing we're there — what could possibly go wrong?" He spread his arms, whetstone pointing one way and the knife the other. "Detlev comes back, finds Siamis, or what's left of him, waiting in a cell . . ."

"You really think you can take Siamis?" David asked.

"I think he lost his mind," MV retorted. "Easier to believe than one day he wakes up and decides, good day to betray everyone."

"Not what I asked."

MV sighed loudly. "So, say, two or three of us? I'd say we have a chance. If we take him by surprise. And if we dropped him, wouldn't —"

"Dead or alive?" David asked.

"More or less alive, waiting in a cell, wouldn't Detlev be pleased? And more to the point, cut us into better plans, once we've proved ourselves?" MV sheathed the knife in his boot and picked up his bread. "Who's with me?"

"Count me in. Anything is better than this shit-hole," Laban muttered.

David held up a hand. "Just you two. Three. Ferret, you scan ahead, report to MV, then come back here. All of you, use the adjunct Destination. We'll have to divide up your chores so no one notices you're gone. Any more than three, they'll notice."

Laban sighed, because the adjunct, or outer perimeter sentry outpost Destination, meant a long, boring ride in the bitter late-autumn wind. But backing out would be unthinkable.

MV whacked his shoulder, and nicked his chin at Ferret. "Let's get in one last hard practice, then Ferret, you cut ahead and find him."

Mearsies Heili

Over the next few days, Clair's suspicion that bringing Mac back to Mearsies Heili had been a mistake became conviction.

Mearsieanne didn't say anything, but she winced at Mac's normal little kid noise and boisterousness, and she seemed relieved that Mac preferred staying in the underground hideout with the girls, who'd made a pet of him. How could Mearsieanne not like him? He was fun, he did what he was told, and though he loved pie fights — CJ and the girls gave him one every day, but they kept them strictly in the underground hideout — so did the girls.

Clair felt she ought to continue the tutoring that Roy had begun, so she showed him Mearsiean letters, figuring the sooner he could read words in another language besides Norsundrian, the better.

"Do you miss the other boys?" she asked him on the third day.

Mac's round eyes lifted to her and he shook his head so firmly his silky dark hair brushed over the tips of his ears.

"They didn't hear me. Like you do," he said, rubbing his forehead. "Except Sveneric, and he's barely got teeth. Can't do a handspring yet."

Clair remembered the still, small, brown-haired toddler painstakingly copying out his letters. Clair was fairly certain what Mac meant was that of all the critters, only Mac and the two-year-old had Dena Yeresbeth.

She thought of that when she wrote Senrid, and got an immediate answer back inviting her to come, adding that Liere and Lyren were there on a visit. Clair wrote back to say she was bringing a new young friend.

The truth? She was no longer in charge of Mearsies Heili, and though she now had complete free time, her days of bringing unwanted orphans or runaways home were effectively over — unless Mearsieanne approved first.

Clair worked very hard to make Mac a medallion like those she'd given the girls, with the Universal Language Spell, and wards against scrying — a defense against Wan-Edhe of the Chwahir that still seemed a good idea — but she hesitated about putting a transfer on it. Five wasn't a responsible age for transfer magic, was it? She'd ask Liere, she decided, and the next day very early, she and Mac took hands and transferred to Marloven Hess, where it was midday.

Liere was small and scrawny as ever. Dressed, Clair suspected, in the same old clothes Clair had last seen her in over a year ago. It was clear that she, at least, would never relinquish the Child Spell, and yet the Birth Spell had come to her anyway.

"How goes magic studies?" Clair asked. "I remember someone saying you'd figured out why you couldn't get the basics?"

"I could *get* them," Liere said earnestly, her thin face, as always, dominated by her enormous light brown eyes that looked in most lights like gold. "I have everything by memory." She tapped reddened, gnawed nails to her forehead. "I couldn't *do* them. Still can't."

"She needs another way to learn magic," Senrid said.

"But there isn't one." Clair spread her hands.

"And so I'm here with Lyren on a visit," Liere said, with one of her rare, sweet smiles. Her fingernails might be gnawed like Noser's, but otherwise there couldn't be two people more utterly different.

Clair watched Mac as he and Lyren eyed one another; Liere sensed them testing on the mental plane and finding one another, their curiosity mirrored. Her gaze shifted to Senrid, who looked around fifteen, as always, his blond hair worn clipped above the collar in a military cut, his plain white shirt rolled to the elbows despite the chill in the air; Clair had never paid any attention to such things before, but now she recognized in the shape of his forearms that he did some kind of drill, probably on a daily basis. The rest of him looked the same in uniform riding trousers of black with a gold stripe down the side, tucked into the tops of his riding boots.

Clair would never have thought Senrid and Liere could be friends, but they had been ever since Siamis's first appearance, when he'd enchanted a good part of the world in some Norsundrian experiment.

Mac said, "I can do three handsprings in a row."

"*I* can do three cartwheels," Lyren replied.

"You can do that after we see the exhibition," Senrid said. "I had the seniors wait, in case you might like to watch." This was said to Mac, who obediently quieted.

Lyren, who had a great deal of trouble with obedience, looked at him askance as they reached the stone spectator stands above the academy parade ground. Senrid lifted a hand, and on the field below, seniors in the Marloven academy galloped around in circles with their lances, passing one another at a canter and clashing the weapons together.

Mac, who Clair and Senrid had both assumed would find that interesting, was too busy chasing little Lyren up and down the stone steps. Of course, Clair thought. Riding and fighting exhibitions were nothing new to Mac. Far more interesting was someone exactly his size, who could meet him on the mental plane, where she was a lot more deft.

Clair watched the expert riders wheeling, charging, and handling the lances under the low, gray streaked autumn sky. She was not about to claim any expertise in military matters after ten months of extremely reluctant imprisonment, but she couldn't help a question. "What is the use of those things? They look impossibly clumsy."

Senrid flicked her a glance. "Right now? Practice in strength and precision. Militarily, the lance charge is only useful in limited situations. But within those, it can be devastatingly effective."

Clair sighed. She understood the general idea, which increased her feeling of ambivalence. On Clair's other side, Liere said, "Did you ever get a sense that Norsunder is preparing to go to war against us?"

"There was a lot of talk," Clair said. "Most of it bragging and gas, how much they want one, who will lead, hoola-loo. But it's not going to be next week. From what they all said, Siamis dealt Detlev a significant setback. But I haven't any more idea than you do about what anyone actually in command thinks. Especially since 'Norsunder'—when it comes to any sort of unified goal—is kind of like saying 'mages' to mean Arthur's northern school up in Bereth Ferian, the Sartoran mage school, and my hermit Aunt Murial, who doesn't communicate with either of them, and Erai-Yanya, who she does communicate with, but who is independent of all of them. And old Tsauderei. . . ."

And Mearsieanne.

". . . Oh, and Mondros, and, well, the rest of us who've studied magic. We all learned magic to help in general, but *how* we do it, we're all different."

Senrid, sitting at Clair's right, sat back, nicking his chin down in a minute expression of approval.

Liere gnawed absently at a reddened cuticle. Clair looked away, smothering a shudder. Liere jerked her hand down, and Clair remembered mind-shields *again*.

She carefully framed a thought. *I'm sorry.*

Liere's thought returned, clear as if spoken: *It is a disgusting habit.*

It looks like it hurts. Clair tried to control how her mental communication conveyed flickers of bloody flesh and her own revulsion, but she felt those things form around the words anyway. Nobody had told her that so-called coinherence was largely useless, embarrassing, and impossible to control.

She concentrated on making a mind-shield, and out loud, said, "When I got there, I thought they all wanted one thing, conquering for the sake of conquering. But . . ." She shook her head.

"Like us. Some like fighting for the sake of fighting," Senrid said, pointing down at the galloping seniors on the horses, mud flying up from ground saturated earlier in the week by rain. "Some are here because it's what their families have done traditionally. Some are here because they love the idea of command. Some want the adventure of an equal enemy. And some . . . like bloodshed."

"What do you do with those?" Clair asked.

"In peacetime, they'll be quartermasters, or some other job that limits their tastes. But if we do come to war, they'll be promoted, and they'll be leading that first line of cavalry chargers."

"Do it again!"

They turned at the sound of Lyren's voice. She was talking to Mac, completely oblivious to the dangerous expertise demonstrated on the parade ground below. Lyren was dressed in a lacy tunic tied with ribbon over matching trousers, her curly, gold-streaked dark hair tied back with ribbons.

Behind her tight mind-shield, Clair marveled at how different Liere's daughter was from Liere. She wondered what had caused Liere to try the Birth Spell while keeping the Child Spell—but then Mearsieanne had done the very same when she had Clair's grandfather.

Her mind skipped from Liere to Mearsieanne to herself. Loneliness had prompted her to adopt Irenne and the girls, the desire for a family. And from her to Mac to Roy. Surely Detlev's motivation had been a cruel contrast to hers, Liere's, and Mearsieanne's when he'd adopted all those boys. He wouldn't raise a family — the idea made no sense. He was probably raising his own cadre of commanders, who happened to more or less find a family in each other.

Mac turned two handsprings, coming perilously near the stone steps.

"Mac," Clair called, pointing to the step.

"I saw it," Mac called back. "I can do a handspring on a wall," he added proudly. "Though not backward. I need dirt for that."

"Show me how," Lyren said. "I want to learn."

Mac said happily, "All right."

Senrid wondered what it would be like to have a child around. Family. Except a son or daughter would be such an obvious target for someone like Detlev to snatch in order to make untenable demands. The thought of being forced to decide between his kingdom and his child chilled him, and he shifted on the stone bench hating the image. Hating the thought. Much better to be the target himself. Much.

A shout went up as the exercise ended. The seniors gazed expectantly at the stands, where Senrid turned his thumb up. As the seniors rode off crowing and whooping, Senrid said, "Watch change is coming. Who's hungry?"

"I am!" Mac yelled, the medallion Clair had given him swinging out of his sturdy tunic.

Mac and Lyren raced up ahead of the other three, then started a game of hopping over every other flagstone.

"Where did he originally come from?" Liere asked.

"I don't know," Clair said.

"Does Mac miss them?"

Clair lowered her voice. "I thought he might have nightmares or something, but he seems happy. He was happy at that place Lilith took us. He told me nobody at Detlev's base heard him here." She tapped her forehead.

"But Lyren does," Liere said slowly, and then they reached Senrid's study, where runners had set trays of hot biscuits, a thick, peppery green soup, and crumbling cheese.

Lyren and Mac pounced on their share, and retired to a corner, gabbling in their high, piping voices.

Senrid said, "I don't suppose you heard any of their short-term goals."

Well, Clair had known what to expect from Senrid.

"Detlev's boys? No. If they had any, they never talked about them around me. And Roy didn't say. I don't know if it was because David started to suspect him, or because Detlev was gone for so long, and they were waiting on his return. Then the fifth worlders took everybody by surprise."

Senrid sighed. "That would have been too easy."

Liere turned and said abruptly, "I wonder. If you'd consider." Her big earnest eyes searched Clair's. "Letting Mac come with us, just for a visit? It's not like your group is prepared for small . . ." Her lips moved, and to Clair's surprise, Liere's thin cheeks mottled with color. "I'll be traveling soon. With Siamis. You might have heard."

"What?" Clair said, staring from Liere to Senrid.

"I still think it's a terrible idea," Senrid muttered — then, as if regretting his words, he got up abruptly and walked out, saying, "Just remembered something I should have done."

Both girls knew he was leaving them alone, without making a fuss about it. Liere said, "You might be the very best person to ask."

"Not if it's about Siamis," Clair said. "I've only seen him a couple of times, and both times he put that enchantment on me."

"But. . . so many don't trust him, and yet Atan admitted to Erai-Yanya that he did nothing terrible to her, and he could have. Many times over. He taught her to ride, did you know that? Anyway, there is this plot to get Tahra away from the horrible wreckage of Ferdrian and Everon, and Siamis volunteered to take her off-world. He wants to investigate some magic or other that would ward Norsunder. He says. Anyway, he offered to take Tahra."

"And she's willing?" Clair asked skeptically, trying to picture odd Tahra, who counted her steps, and liked things to be exactly the same — orderly — going off-world to explore. "She's willing to go with *him?*"

"Siamis never did any damage to Everon. And as long as he's Detlev's enemy, Tahra will tolerate him. Everything is so, oh, either evil or pure with her."

"That I remember."

"But they think another girl should go along for Tahra to talk to, and I have so much trouble with our magic learning, and nowhere to be and nothing to do, so I thought, why not? Lyren loves to explore."

"Tahra likes you, that I remember. Admires you."

Liere gave her head a shake, ragged, uncombed hair flapping lankly against her cheek. "She admires Sartora." She pronounced the name with soft disgust.

Clair sighed. She would never tell anyone, but the second earliest memory of Irenne was when she found out Clair was a princess. She had simpered a lot of false flattery. But that had not lasted.

Clair said confidently, "Maybe this would be the very best way to get rid of the Sartora stuff in her mind. She could get to know you as yourself."

Liere's eyes widened. "That's *true*." A brief silence fell as she considered the fact that she'd be in places where no one would have heard of Sartora, the Girl Who Saved the World.

Clair's mind flitted back to "your group." Uneasily, she said, "Mac knows he's not forced to stay with us. If he wants to, of course he can go with you. He seems to love new places."

Senrid returned, and they got up to find the little ones. As soon as the question was put to Mac, he and Lyren looked at one another, grinning, and the other three knew a fast mental exchange winged back and forth.

"Can he come now?" Lyren begged, her round golden eyes puppy-like.

"Why not?" Clair forced herself to say when she saw Mac's eager face. "He's free to do what he likes."

"I want to go with her," Mac said, taking Lyren's hand. "Another world!"

Clair smiled at the two, hiding her hurt—but knowing it was for the best.

As soon as Mearsieanne heard what had happened, she smiled with obvious relief. "That is an excellent solution," she said, as if Mac were a problem to be solved, and not a person in need of a home. "And the timing is also excellent. As for Tahra, I was going to discuss this with you, Clair. I think you would enjoy this project."

"What's this project?"

"The main part is that people—some of us—are worried about Tahra. What will happen when she is gone. But I'll let Atan explain everything. I'll write to her now."

Six

Sartor

ATAN — QUEEN YUSTNESVEAS LANDIS V of Sartor — loathed
having Siamis as a guest with every nerve in body and soul.

But Tsauderei had convinced her that it was a diplomatic
necessity. Even though she had instructed her court herald to
invite him to Star Chamber events, and she herself had agreed
to public demonstrations of friendliness in accepting his offer
of riding lessons, the idea of him walking about Eidervaen
gnawed at her like a worm gnawing its way through a plum.

And so she sought any sort of distraction when she wasn't
involved in the complications of court and legal ritual.

Finding herself with a free hour, she glanced at the letter
from Mearsieanne, which had lain on her desk for over a week
now. Anything was better than the prospect of forcing herself
to diplomatic politeness for another riding lesson. But answering Mearsieanne would take concentration, and she couldn't
concentrate. She turned to the letter next to Mearsieanne's,
from Peitar Selenna, King of Sarendan. Maybe she wouldn't
answer that one, either. Instead, she might use one of her free
hours and go to Sarendan to visit Peitar, since he would not
come to Sartor while Siamis was there.

She sighed, looking out her window at the garden labyrinth the Sartorans since ancient days had called the Purad, so secluded and peaceful, and though she'd walked it once that morning, peace seemed to be as far away as summer.

A scratch at her door brought in one of her maids, who bowed and said in the formal manner the servants tended to draw on like armor when they disapproved of something, "Your majesty, the riding clothes are laid out."

"Thank you, Malias." Atan pretended that nothing was amiss, because she was not going to admit that she shared their misgivings.

"I am also to tell you that her grace, the Duchas of Ryadas, begs a mere six, and awaits your pleasure in the Queen Diantas Chamber."

Atan held her breath so she wouldn't sigh with irritation. "Thank you, Malias," she said again.

Malias must have heard something in her tone—or perhaps the poor girl felt crushed between two wills—for she dropped a curtsey and backed out hastily.

A "six" was the small sandglass. A "mere six" (or more often shortened to "a mere") was a pretense, a weapon of moral suasion so long in use that no one really expected so short a conversation. Very unlikely that the duchas would even finish her greetings in that time—which both knew very well—and in the formal chamber named after Atan's mother, too. Moral suasion indeed.

Atan took her time dressing. Finally she looked at herself in her mirror. It felt wonderful to shed the layered silks and velvets of queenship for plain riding trousers and tunic and cloak. She'd grown up with two outfits for summer and two for winter. But the tall, gawky girl who'd hidden in the Valley of Delfina had changed, except for those goggle Landis eyes staring back out at her. Even the brown hair was different—in those days, long because she didn't bother cutting it, dull and lank. Now it was just long enough to be done up in elaborate styles that supposedly suited her station. It certainly shone almost aggressively, cared for by one of her maids who had clever, gentle hands. Today those artful fingers had tricked it up in many braids forming a kind of coronet, steadied by a real coronet so that it would not come down while Atan rode—a coronet loaded with magic protections.

Her eyes ran down the rest of her. She'd relinquished the

Child Spell earlier in the year, and had expected her courses to begin right away, for she'd been nearly sixteen when she'd done the spell. To her surprise they had not yet begun, but her bosom seemed to be growing as much as her hips had begun to broaden. The beanpole of her young days was definitely gone; at least, she thought with a smile, her body was now in better proportion to her frog eyes.

What she didn't see was the high, intelligent brow above eyes so deep a blue that in the shades her wardrobe mistress favored, they looked violet, the straight nose, and the severe lips. She thought of herself as a very big, very broad brown-haired girl; she did not see her own regal presence, far more striking than mere prettiness would ever have been.

The chamber named after her mother was, according to the oldsters, where Queen Diantas once sat to receive court ladies in the morning during the seasons of low sun: a tall, white-walled room with ovals of robin's egg blue painted on all four walls, framed with gilding in acanthus and queensblossom chains. In each blue oval blossoms had been painted, one season per wall.

The duchas had chosen the least place of the circle of chairs, an appearance of humility Atan had learned was another courtly weapon of moral suasion: Atan knew it meant the duchas was quite aware that whatever she had to say was going to really irritate Atan.

But she was going to do it anyway.

When the duchas saw the riding clothes, her expression congealed. She was the age Atan's mother would have been, had she lived through the war the century previous, before Sartor was enchanted away from time. The skin around her dark eyes tightened as she bowed, her embroidered robes glistening in the weak light afforded by the four tall windows.

"Your majesty," she said and dropped into another profound curtsey. "I beg of you, please reconsider the riding lessons. No one can rest while you are in danger — "

"From whom, your grace?" Atan asked as she sat in the principal chair, set between the two sets of windows. "I thought we were agreed that Siamis is one of the most power-ful mages in the world, and no one in our guard can overcome him in physical conflict."

"From *him*," the duchas said, her lips tightening.

"But the world has accepted his change of heart," Atan

said, thinking of Peitar, and knowing how very hypocritical she would sound to him. She tried harder. "I feel I must remind you that before he came here, he spent six months leading the chosen mages to each of the weapons cache sites that Detlev had secreted against a future attack. Which, thanks to Siamis, cannot now happen." *In other words, he back-stabbed his uncle in coming to our side. For which I am required to officially express gratitude, because that is how diplomacy works. As you very well know.*

"Your majesty, if anyone else could serve as riding teacher—"

"But they did not," Atan reminded her. "For four years, I petitioned the high council, and indeed, the entire first circle on this matter. No one was deemed acceptable to instruct me, because of political implications, because the season was considered too cold or too wet for my royal person to be risked, because Norsunder might ride over the border any day, because a great company was necessary to properly guard me."

Her voice sharpened. "When my friend Rel offered, no one would accept him because he's not nobly born, he's not Sartoran, he holds no military rank that would somehow promise adequate protection. So I asked Siamis, who meets all those specifications, though the army he commanded was Norsundrian. But no one doubts his ability—and nothing has happened to me yet. The result? Finally," she finished gently, "I know how to ride."

They couldn't prevent her from using magic transfer, as she'd been a magic student before she'd become queen, but they'd boxed her tight in all other ways—as they never failed to assure her, for hers and the kingdom's good.

"Now," Atan said inexorably, "we have talked well past 'mere,' and I'm keeping him, and the horses, waiting. That cannot be good for the animals," she added with her own needle-prick of moral suasion.

She rose. Perforce the duchas must bow, and Atan walked out breathing with relief, though she knew that the duchas would be on her way to gossip with the rest of her cronies at court, and there would be repercussions. But there were repercussions to every action, Atan had discovered: you could try to please everyone, you could work yourself exhausted, strive to be as good and true and just as possible, but it would never be enough for some. Or right to others.

When she reached a corner under a vaulted ceiling, she stood, arms crossed tightly under her bosom, shut her eyes, and worked to form her mind-shield.

When she trusted that her thoughts lay encased in thick porcelain, like one of those Venn stoves, she continued on, and a short time later she entered the main square to find Siamis there, sitting astride one of the palace horses. A wooden-faced groom held the reins of the mount she'd chosen as hers.

The gloomy light silvered Siamis's fair hair. *Every* light flattered the former villain (Or, as most Sartorans agreed not-quite-behind Siamis's back, "former" villain), whose plain dun-colored riding trousers molded the curve of leg above his high-topped riding boots. The unadorned riding tunic of light gray set off the excellent line of his shoulders. Though she'd been trained by Tsauderei to be observant, it was only in recent months that she began to notice such details with a physical reaction, not just eyes and mind.

It was disconcerting, and interesting, how she was getting a peek through a door she had known existed but had considered irrelevant. But acknowledging the pulse of attraction and feeling attracted, at least so far, she had no trouble keeping separate. Siamis was handsome, slender, and strong, to appearances only a few years older than she—and she didn't trust him for a heartbeat.

But Tsauderei—distracted by overseeing the integration of Leotay and her sister among the mage students—had said, *Act as if he is trustworthy until he isn't.*

The mages had fashioned her coronet. She had also made her own preparations, beginning with a transfer token worked into one of her buttons. One touch, one word, and she'd transfer back to her room if Siamis so much as breathed wrong.

As she climbed into the saddle and took the reins from the servant, Atan had to admit that Siamis rode with an ease that added to his air of natural competence. The only other person Atan had seen ride that well was Senrid of the Marlovans.

"The rain should hold off long enough to reach Hodos Hill," he said. "Excellent opportunity to practice your gallop. But collect your mount first."

Atan straightened her shoulders and began paying attention to her seat and her hands. She had to admit that Siamis had been a good teacher. But the fact remained that he had been a Norsundrian. She was here because she'd seen a way to get what she wanted as well as do her diplomatic duty. She'd gotten what she wanted, but she'd promised herself that she would utter no diplomatic falsities. So. If his comment about the rain was an oblique hint about being kept waiting . . . "I was late," she said, "because another courtier tried to talk me out of riding with you."

"Did this person say what I was expected to do with you?" His eyes crinkled with amusement. "Or are these rides seen to be an opportunity for assassination, inexplicably yet unexploited?"

"It was not said," Atan retorted. "But I'm told that no one can rest for the duration."

"Let's hope that they'll find something sufficiently entertaining during this restless interlude," he replied equably, and offered some correctives to her seat, handling of the reins, the signals she sent the horse, and the gait, as they proceeded through the third district.

She would have liked to go unnoticed but her distinctive features below that golden coronet were too well-known for that; word ran ahead, as it always did, and as they rode toward the western gate, people backed out of the way, bowed to her, stared at him—some putting their fingertips beside their mouths in the spitting sign once his back was safely turned to them. Though he was alone, and didn't even seem to be carrying the infamous four-thousand-year-old sword, they knew what he was capable of.

Atan and Siamis proceeded sedately to the west gate, through that and the meadows beyond, on which many of the city's cows grazed peacefully. Once they'd cleared those, her mount tossed its head, ready for the expected gallop. Side by side they raced past sloping rock below crags rising steeply. North-facing slopes still furred dark green with cedar and pine, their tops mist-shrouded.

Lower down, she and Siamis passed a famous fir under which some of her ancestors had disported; it towered above the city's tallest roofs, with great garlands of lichen suspended from its boughs.

The trail led past massive, ancient logs thick with new growth—'new' being a century old before Sartor was removed from the world—and bordered with pungent shrubs. Few wildflowers were left, and even fewer berries, those black and withered, but still tasty to the birds who flocked scolding skyward as they passed, then settled back down after they had left.

Atan had always loved the world of nature. She breathed in the scents of duff and fir and shrubs as her mind kept a running tally of riding instructions. It would be long—if ever—before all this felt natural, but at least now she could ride. It wasn't until they'd slowed before the steep trail to the promontory called Hodos Hill that it occurred to her they had ridden in silence for a while.

They reined up as farther along the trail some creature rustled through the shrubs. Siamis glanced her way, appreciative of how hard it was for her to pretend a semblance of friendship. He admired how adroitly she'd managed to get around her self-righteous first circle in the matter of the riding lessons.

He had two purposes here. "I wanted to tell you that Tahra of Everon has added another traveler to our prospective jaunt away from Sartorias-deles: Liere Fer Eider."

"Liere?" Atan said, her eyelids flashing up. "What I don't understand is why you would take either of them." And there was the ever-present distrust.

"Your leading mages all agreed that Tahra of Everon could use a total change of scene. Since I'm researching other magical methods—which will be good for Liere to experience—I offered to take her. It 'll only be for a few months, at most."

Atan remembered that Tahra, who was one of the odder persons she had ever met, loathed Detlev as much as she admired Liere Fer Eider.

He said, "I wasn't certain how much Tsauderei told you, but I was informed by him that by revealing the caches, and submitting to the Selenseh Redian, I've shifted in her estimation from an eleven to a five, which can become an even number in fours, whereas Detlev remains eleven, odd number and evil."

Atan glanced sharply at Siamis. His tone did not mock Tahra's oddness about numbers. But then in his many years he must have seen stranger, and worse, things than Tahra's idiosyncrasies.

Everyone felt that getting Tahra away from Everon for a

time might break the pattern of grief and increasingly peculiar behavior that she seemed to have fallen into. It was Roderick Dei, Commander of the Knights and a family connection, who had written to Atan about his worries. He had also written to Mearsieanne, who knew Tahra as well as anyone did.

Of course, getting away and getting away accompanied by Siamis were two different things, many had said, at tedious length. But no one else had offered. Now, Atan reflected, the news that Liere was going meant that there would be someone who could anticipate trouble. Liere had that Dena Yeresbeth mind whatever-it-was, and she had even defeated Siamis once. Best of all, Tahra's getting away would give Atan time for her secret project.

While she ruminated, her gaze safely distant, Siamis used the time for another scan in the mental realm. And there was Ferret, who still seemed not to grasp that physical proximity did not necessarily correspond with awareness in the mental realm: Siamis had sensed him steadily over the past few days, after which he'd caught sight of him briefly twice. At this moment, Ferret was drifting toward the guest wing of the palace.

It was risky to reach toward another's mind while seated on something as unsteady as a horse, but all it took was a heartbeat. Ferret's intent was clear, to search fast and then report to MV and Laban. Ah.

The mist had begun to descend in a gray blur down the mountainside, every once in a while splattering them with fat, cold raindrops. Siamis and Atan turned the horses and rode back down the trail, Siamis reflecting that he had a couple of days to find suitable tasks for the servants assigned to him— the mages' spy, two spies belonging to separate courtly factions, and the royal heralds' spy—and to let the word get out that he would be alone before his departure from Sartor.

Seven

Outside Eidervaen

WHILE SIAMIS CONSIDERED THE boys, the boys considered Siamis.

"I learned two things, one related to Siamis and one unrelated to him," Ferret said.

"Siamis first," MV and Laban spoke at the same time.

Ferret's snub-nosed, unremarkable face didn't change. It almost never did. "There are five servants, including the guard acting as a porter at the door, put there by the city guard."

"The city guard?" MV repeated. "I thought they got rid of the guard. It's all magic wards and tracers."

"There is a city guard again," Ferret stated. "Old garrison. They patrol in pairs, three to each district. Rel's one of 'em. When he's in Sartor."

MV grinned, cracking his knuckles.

Laban and Ferret, successfully interpreting this gesture, said at the same time, "Stealth."

"Shut up," MV said, which for him meant, yeah, I know.

Ferret went on. "Every round by the guard, they stop by the porter there at the visitor wing, west side, north door.

Siamis is upstairs, overlooking the canal on the Grand Chandos Way."

"Got it. Night visit, then?"

"Not night," Ferret said. "Way too many watchers. Best time would be early morning. He always has breakfast alone, before whatever court thing he does."

"Court?" Laban smirked. "Siamis dances attendance at Star Chamber? They must love that!"

"*He* must love that," MV retorted. "Snor-r-r-e."

Ferret counted on his fingers. "Once a week, rides with the queen. Did that today, which is how I got inside to scout."

"Too bad," Laban exclaimed. "What a prime opportunity to scare the steaming shit out of the lighters if we grabbed the queen of —"

"Stealth." This time it was Ferret and MV, the latter adding, "She'd be covered in wards."

Laban crossed his arms. "Just thinking."

"Well, don't." MV elbow-jabbed him in the ribs, making his eyes water. "Ferret?"

With the conviction of one who had been watching for over a week, Ferret reeled off Siamis's schedule. Good thing? It was regular as bells. Bad thing, it was also very public.

". . . and today was his last ride with Atan, before he leaves Sartor."

"He's going away?" Laban said.

"That's what they said, the herald, *Two more days of this duty, and if nothing happens, I get three weeks' leave.*" He mimicked the herald's voice.

"Then we've got two days."

"We'll pay him a visit while he's loafing," MV said. "Five servants, you say?" He poured a handful of metal brads through his fingers. "That's six stone spells, one for each, and an extra for Siamis."

"Not if we have to carry him." Laban scowled. "There's no chance three of us could muscle him out of the palace stiff as a plank in stone-spell and not get dusted."

"Transfer to the outer Destination," MV said.

"Three?" Ferret asked, turning his gaze from Laban's vivid blue eyes to MV's narrow, yellow-flecked light brown. "You want my help?"

"No," MV said, having already mentally reserved the pleasure of a serious dust-up to himself, with Laban running

shield. "You said you learned two things. What's the unrelated?"

"That two of those hidden people from Five, the ones Roy
knew about and never told us, are here. With the mages."

MV hit his fist into his palm. How long had Roy known
about them? MV wanted to take them all apart. "Siamis first,"
he said aloud.

Laban had been watching him for cues, and shrugged. He
had no interest in those fish-faces on Five.

"Siamis first," MV repeated. "The idea is to take him by
ambush. Won't see us coming."

Laban laughed. Ferret also laughed, because he'd learned
that mirroring the others' reactions kept life smoother. He was
not going to admit to ambivalence; he had spent some time
with Siamis the previous summer, having seen no evidence of
betrayal. Or enmity. Questions he had, in plenty, but no anger.

MV clapped him on the shoulder. "You've done your part.
Get on back. Cover for us."

When Ferret was gone, MV said to Laban, "Right. We've
got a day to get inside the city undetected, scan, and plan our
approach."

Eight

FOR A COUPLE OF days, Clair thought the restlessness and the sense of a hole in her life was due to Mac being gone. She knew that was stupid. Mac didn't belong to her. He belonged to himself.

Then one morning after breakfast, she recognized the itch in her muscles, and recognized what it was. She'd gotten used to those morning drills, much as she'd hated them. Now she was missing the . . . exercise? No, she'd loathed it. She was missing the strength.

At least she knew how to fix that. Diana and CJ welcomed the suggestion of a forest run. To the surprise of all three, Clair outpaced them. That delighted Diana, and spurred CJ to try harder.

When Clair returned, morning interviews were nearly over. Mearsieanne liked her to be there—Clair knew she regarded their relationship as teacher and student—and Clair struggled silently with what she knew were unworthy feelings, but she hated all the fuss of fancy clothes and aristocratic manners. Mearsieanne said nothing about Clair's being late, and so Clair felt better than she had in days when the bell rang announcing the midday meal at its proper time.

Over that lunch in the formal dining room, Mearsieanne said, after a polite exchange about the weather, how each was feeling, and the fine meal, "That project I believe I mentioned once? Atan wishes to meet tomorrow in Ferdrian's royal castle to discuss it."

"Who will be there?" Clair asked, glad for anything that would get her away from another stifling morning court session.

"Many from your old alliance, as it happens," Mearsieanne said, carefully pushing back an errant lock of her long dark hair. Her hand looked like porcelain, the skin both young and old.

She didn't say more, and lunch ended with the usual semblance of tranquility. But as soon as it was over, Clair walked out onto the terrace under the broad balcony overhead, watching the silvery sheet of slanting rain blurring the dimming autumnal colors below, and considered. She'd had little to do with Atan ever since the alliance had gone to Geth. On that journey, Clair had discovered that Atan had taken a dislike to the Mearsieans, especially CJ. Mearsieanne either didn't know it, or considered it irrelevant.

Clair crossed her arms, reassured by the curve of biceps that she hadn't had a year ago. A lot had changed, mostly bad, but not all.

She turned around. Rather than get third-hand news, she decided the questions needed to be put directly to Atan.

> *Atan: I know we haven't had much contact since we all went to Geth, and I remember that some of us made mistakes that might go unforgiven.*
> *Mearsieanne wishes me to join whatever it is you have planned for Tahra. I'd like to help, but not if you would rather I not come.*

She signed it formally, which she rarely did. As soon as she sent it off, she remembered that Sartor was practically halfway around the world. It would be late — maybe almost midnight.

Well, she'd give it until lunch the next day, and if she heard nothing, she'd find some excuse for not going —

click The internal warning of a note.

> *Clair: I have been answering letters all evening. If you can bear the transfer, perhaps it would be better*

to talk in person. Atan.

Clair looked down at herself. She wore her green gown, which was very formal for her. If it passed muster for Mearsieanne, it would have to do for the queen of Sartor. She went to look up the Destination, braced, and did the transfer spell.

Three walls of the Sartoran Destination chamber were plain blue-white marble, a gilt sun dominating the fourth wall, with rays slanting down through three panels. Dragons wound upward through the two outer panels, flying upward toward the sun.

A boy about her age, wearing a dark blue robe trimmed with light green, brought a cup of what smelled like really good summer steep. He spoke formal words of welcome in pure Sartoran. Clair sipped the tangy, hot steep, which helped speed away the transfer reaction, then she said in careful Sartoran, "Queen Yustnesveas." Clair stumbled over Atan's formal name. "Is expecting me."

"Please come this way."

Clair looked around as they walked out. The air was cooler than that at home, with the faintest undertone of . . . was that herbs? And . . . *mildew?*

As she followed the servant, she looked up at the high ceilings, the curves everywhere. The Sartorans had plainly not liked box shapes any more than whoever had designed the white palace. In fact, this palace reminded her of the white palace. Not the stone, which felt rough, almost new, compared to the weird white stuff at home. It was the many styles of the formal rooms that they passed; only here, those spaces she glimpsed between open double doors had been modernized incrementally over the centuries, according to what Mearsieanne had once told her.

Clair certainly saw varying styles, and she could believe that everything was maintained to the extent of replacing worn fabrics with exactly the same thing. Clair reflected on the fact that at the white palace, in the upper reaches of the towers, no one replaced anything—ever. That's because nothing ever seemed to need replacing, which firmed Clair's private conviction that the rooms really did move in and out of time, somehow. You just never caught them at it.

Atan stepped in through the opposite door as Clair was let

into a study with a fine carved desk that ran halfway around the room, set on carved wood supports that looked like twisted tree branches. The wood was one of those rare colorwoods—the deep greens and golds and browns of verdigris.

"Welcome," Atan said. Atan wore a blue silk robe worked in a pattern of falling leaves, over a loose linen shirt and loose trousers. Her hair was bound up in a complication of braids above those startling Landis eyes, a distinctive shape with the droopy lower lid, so much like the terrifying, dangerous Kessler Sonscarna. Whose family had once married into Atan's generations ago, apparently, weird as it was to think of a Chwahir marrying into the Sartoran royal family. Or rather, the other way around.

She looked taller than Clair remembered, and larger. More grown up. Atan had clearly released the Child Spell, as Tahra had. And Terry, and Arthur. Clair wondered if the Mearsieans would be the only ones left who didn't as Atan spoke words of greeting. And again, deep within her, like a massive bell whose tone was felt rather than heard, she knew that one day, she, too, would lift that spell. But not yet.

"Come inside," Atan said, taking in Clair's stiff shoulders and her guarded expression, as if she wasn't certain of her welcome. Regret suffused Atan. She knew she was at fault here. "Thank you for writing to me."

"There's nothing to be thanked for," Clair said, and added plainly, "That summer at Tsauderei's valley, I know you didn't really want us. I know Mearsieanne means well, but she wasn't there. I don't want to make things worse."

"Thank you," Atan said, a sharper pulse of guilt causing her to speak with care, "for your candor. You probably have no idea how very rare that is. And what a relief. Have a seat."

The two arched windows whited, taking all the color out of the room, then restoring it as thunder smashed directly overhead. While the long, juddering rumble died away, Atan decided on some plain speaking of her own—such a luxury! "That summer I was at fault for judging," she said. "Anyway, your friend CJ made peace with Rel once we all reached Geth. As for her attitude toward Liere, she couldn't value Liere lower than Liere does herself."

"But CJ doesn't value Liere low." Clair leaned forward, her morvende-white hair swinging around her arms. "CJ would tell you herself that she struggles against unreachable expectations, especially for girls. She wants Liere to be a hero in all ways, and knows that isn't fair or right to expect."

Atan inclined her head. "I apologize for gossiping about your friend. I brought it up mostly to point out my own misconceptions. As to . . ." She hesitated, remembering a recent conversation between Tsauderei, Mondros, and Erai-Yanya.

Tsauderei had said, *Why did Detlev take to the fifth world a girl from Mearsies Heili, which no one has ever heard of?*

Mondros retorted, *No one has ever heard of, and yet in all the world it contains the only building located directly above a Selenseh Redian. The other six are far from civilization.*

Erai-Yanya had shaken her head. *Do you think Detlev taking Clair to his fifth-world citadel for nearly a year somehow has something to do with the accident of her home being above a Selenseh Redian? I think it's far more likely those boys grabbed her out of childish spite, as well as Tereneth of Erdrael Danara.*

To which Tsauderei had replied, *And Terry was promptly stuck in the stable, whereas she was kept away from him, and apparently tutored on a daily basis. You forget just how long Detlev's plans run. She might not even be aware of some compulsion, which could reveal itself in twenty years. Fifty.*

Leave her alone, Mondros had said. *Remember she was with Lilith. If an opportunity arises to talk to her, do. Talk, not interrogate. A hint of interference and those Mearsieans will close ranks and never trust you. They don't trust adults as it is.*

Atan said with an appearance of impulse, at which she had become adept, "Would you mind if this conversation included Tsauderei? He is very much a part of this plan I've been forming."

Clair's encounters with him had been brief, the longest that summer in the Valley of Delfina when they were all hiding from Siamis. She'd enjoyed the irascible old mage. "I'd like to talk to Tsauderei," Clair said, to Atan's relief.

Atan got up straight away and sent a note in her golden notecase, and was not surprised to receive an immediate reply. A sudden rattle of hailstones against the diamond-paned windows startled Clair as Atan said, "Let's go to him. He has trouble getting around."

Blue lightning flickered again, farther off, as they left that room for another across the marquetry hall. Here Tsauderei sat, gnarled hands on bony knees beneath an old-fashioned robe. His hair and beard as white as Clair's own hair, and as long. Better kept, too, Clair thought; she tended to forget about her hair after its morning combing, snipping the back ends when they got long enough to sit on, and the side ends if her elbows caught on them when she sat.

Tsauderei took her in, a sturdily built girl with a square face and sea-green eyes, with the white hair that indicated morvende among her ancestors. Not recent, as her hair fell in heavy waves, rather than being the cobwebby drifts of the underground city peoples, and her skin was a normal brown, if on the light side.

"Welcome back," he said. "I understand you spent some time with Lilith the Guardian after your freeing from Detlev's citadel on the Aldau-Rayad?"

"Lilith took us to a mage house," Clair replied. "You might know of it. I think it was somewhere up north."

"I know of a couple retreats there," Tsauderei said. "Beautiful places. I understand you were there with a boy who was once one of Detlev's? Roy?"

"He went somewhere else. Geth, I think." Clair's head came up, her brow puckered in wary question.

Tsauderei leaned forward. "Why did those boys take you when they fled Sartorias-deles?"

"Detlev told one of them to pick someone. For an experiment. He—Laban—picked me. I think because I happened to be walking alone. He had an arrow wound at the time. I bet he didn't want to walk very far, so he picked the closest victim to hand."

Tsauderei's bushy brows rose, and Atan bit her lip.

"What happened?" Tsauderei asked, and at the undisguised reluctance in Clair's face, he said, "What happened with Detlev? We don't need to hear about the petty cruelties of his followers."

"Unless you need to talk about it," Atan put in quickly.

"I don't," Clair said. "I hated it. Now I'm back. As for Detlev, I only had one real interview with him. He was mostly gone for months at a time, first at Songre Silde, and then tracking Siamis on the Venn border, or so I was told."

"What did he say during that interview?"

Clair flushed, remembering what that impassive mind voice had said about the people right in front of her.

"He said stupid things. Mean things. About everybody I care about."

Tsauderei and Atan exchanged looks. They were not surprised at that.

Tsauderei said, "Did he use Dena Yeresbeth on you?"

"Oh, yes. The entire interview was . . ." She tapped her head.

"Did he lay compulsions on you, by either suggestion or magic?"

"No."

"Do you think he could without your knowing?" Atan asked, fingers gripped together. What a nauseating idea!

Clair began to shake her head, then paused, her eyes closing. The others watched, wary, questioning. Clair thought rapidly, then decided against saying that she thought she might have Dena Yeresbeth, too. Or did you "have" it, like you had a cold, or two ears?

She opened her eyes. "I guess I wouldn't know if I didn't know. Does that make sense? But I don't feel like there are mysterious walls in my mind or anything." She finished candidly, "I don't think I was interesting enough for any of that. I was definitely a failure at their experiment of having girls in their group. I worked hard at that," she added with a brief, grim smile.

Tsauderei recollected his frustrating conversation with Lilith, and asked, "I take it you didn't hear anything about magical shortcuts? Different magic, that Detlev knows? May have taught his minions?"

Clair looked surprised. "I thought magic is magic. We use light, Norsunder uses dark—both the same magic, just different methods. The only magic talk, really, was with Leotay and Horsefeathers when we were doing Sartoran lessons. They sing their spells, but it didn't sound like a different kind of magic. Maybe you could ask Siamis, before he goes off-world?" Clair asked doubtfully.

"I had that conversation with Siamis very early on," Tsauderei said. "He was twelve when he was taken—and had not been taught magic, except for the daily magics, which he said were mostly the same then: the Waste Spell, Birth Spell, and so on. We have to remember that magic all but vanished after the Fall." He made a gesture. "Enough of that now. To Atan's plan. You may or may not be aware that some fear for

Tahra Delieth's sanity."

The rapping of hail against the windows eased as abruptly as it had begun. Clair let her breath out, aware that she'd turned red at the word *sanity*. "I . . . was worried. Last year. When we were all in Wnelder Vee. Tahra kept talking. About killing." Clair's voice dropped on the last word, an obscenity to her. "Even Liere couldn't get her to stop."

"Commander Dei, who as you probably know has fallen into the position of a Regent until next year, when Tahra will be considered of age, is worried as well," Atan said.

Tsauderei said slowly, "Everon needs stability after years of troubles. It has a young population, and they look to Hatahra as the last remnant of her family. Roderic Dei says that she demonstrates a good mind for the details of a struggling treasury, but she has no skills with dealing with people."

Clair nodded, knowing that Tahra much preferred numbers to people. But a queen couldn't only deal with numbers.

Atan opened her hands. "Here's where you come in, if you wish. While Tahra is away from Everon, we're going to do something about that palace, which she has kept exactly as it has been, fire marks and all, since it was burned six years ago."

Clair exclaimed, "I saw that. It can't be good for anyone's spirits to live in a ruin like that."

"And yet no one in Everon can, or will, go against her wishes. But *I* can," Atan said. "With the aid of her royal friends among the alliance. My idea is for her to come back to something new. Get her to put the past behind her. We'll make our plans tomorrow when we meet there."

"Meantime, Tahra is also with a friend she admires," Tsauderei said. "Perhaps Liere even can use her Dena Yeresbeth somehow," he added doubtfully. To him, poor little Liere seemed to need as much help of some kind as Tahra. He sat back, clapping his hands on his knees. "I realize that everybody is going to argue with me, but what I'm really hoping is that Siamis will help them both. Because in many ways Dena Yeresbeth has been more a burden than a boon to Liere."

"Yes." Clair breathed out the word.

"There has been no one to train those born with Dena Yeresbeth. It's too new in the world," Tsauderei said. "The rest of us don't even comprehend what it is, really. I recognize that Lilith the Guardian did help Liere in some ways when she was small, but that was mostly to guard her from being found by Detlev."

Clair wondered if Lilith, like Roy, sometimes felt she had no good choices before her. And so, when it was an individual or an entire world in need, she had to help the world and let the person flounder on as best they could. Not just Liere, but Roy also. She said, "Thank you including me in the plan. I'd like to help, and I've plenty of free time. I'll be in Everon at noon tomorrow."

"Excellent. You, and all your friends, will be most welcome." Atan smiled with relief and summoned the page.

Clair would rather have gone outside the room and used her medallion to transfer home, but she decided to be polite and do it from their Destination.

When she had been escorted out, Atan said to Tsauderei, "Well, what do you think?"

Tsauderei had been mulling. Of course he'd seen no signs of magical tampering in Clair. If Detlev had done something like that, what would it even look like to those who had no Dena Yeresbeth? In any case, nothing good ever came of precipitous action. "Clair seems unharmed. Perhaps time will tell. I hoped she might have made some sort of telling observation while Detlev's prisoner, but that was a very small hope. It sounds as if they had minimal contact—a blessing."

Atan agreed and retired as the last of the storm died away eastward.

And at the other end of the palace, Siamis withdrew from the mental plane, after having listened to the entire exchange; like most people, Tsauderei and Atan rarely remembered mind-shields when they were not in Siamis's proximity. They, too, did not comprehend that physical distance was irrelevant to those with far-sense. But listening so long while remaining undetected was tiring, and he had morning to prepare for.

Nine

SHORTLY AFTER DAWN, ATAN transferred to Everon, and one
by one Siamis's watchdog servants departed on their tasks,
gently chivvied by him when he sensed Laban—who was
impatient about mind-shields—on the approach.

Siamis set his sword aside and sat down to wait, as outside, MV and Laban approached cautiously. Both hid their
banging heartbeats beneath the cat-walk saunter that characterized the boys on the stalk. They scanned warily—rumor
had it Rel was a patroller. One glimpse, and he'd be calling for
reinforcements. They each had a transfer worked into the
middle button on their shirts, as MV was not deft with transfer
magic, and Laban didn't know it at all.

No sign of any guards as they approached the palace in the
center of the first district. They crossed the enormous central
square, which left them exposed in all directions. The only
glance they got was from some girl driving a cart pulled by
goats. Her gaze lingered, and MV's hand drifted toward his
wrist knife, when Laban waved her away.

The girl shrugged and drove on past. MV let his breath
out, a pulse of feeling stupid making him grimace. She'd
merely been hoping they'd hire her for a ride.

The garden looked desolate, the way gardens do when
poised between the last few withered leaves of autumn and

the snows of winter. The great double doors to the guest wing had been closed. MV filled his hands with the stone spell tokens, but the door guard did not appear.

At a glance from MV, Laban pulled open the door, and MV raised his hands, ready to throw the tokens, but the entry hall was empty, the marble floor smooth and polished. The boys advanced slowly, gazes running over tapestries, pilasters, gilding and vaulting, MV looking for threats, and Laban forgetting to look for threats. After the unrelieved plainness of the Den, followed by the unrelieved ugliness of the Base, the use of light, space, line, and color made him giddy—and livid with envy.

MV made a wide sweep with one long arm, knocking into a crystal candleholder on a table. It smashed on the tiled floor with a musical tinkling that made him laugh. "Ooops," he said loudly. "Anyone here?"

Laban spotted a statue of a crane just lifting its wings to take flight, and put the toe of his boot against it. They watched it topple with majestic slowness, catching the edge of a tapestry and ripping it across before the marble cracked against the older stone of the floor. "Someone has to hear that," he said, with rather more forceful bravado than needed, because he couldn't make himself look at the pieces of what had been fabulous art, a weakness he would never admit to out loud.

Then Siamis's door opened, and there he was, unarmed, wearing only shirt, riding trousers, and boots, as if he'd been planning to spend a quiet morning. He smiled. "Welcome to Sartor, boys."

MV dropped the tokens and attacked, Laban a heartbeat after.

The two had been trained to work as a team, but it was Siamis who had trained them; a step toward Laban, a sidestep, and Laban found Siamis on his other side, deflecting his first blow. His expected first blow. Siamis's fingers slid up his arm instead of recoiling, and tapped, with exquisite precision, the nerve nexus in his elbow.

Laban gasped as white lights shot across his vision. He stumbled but caught himself and valiantly launched a mirror attack to MV's—and again Siamis was half-a-heartbeat faster, as if he'd anticipated that move, too.

Laban gritted his teeth—and found himself knocked into MV. This time the tap hit a nerve cluster in his neck, making that side of his body flash red and then go numb, and he fell, knocking his forehead smartly on the outer wing of the fallen crane statue, as he gasped for breath.

Leaving the other two to face each other, exchanging a fast series of feints and attacks, strikes, twists, testing, reaching. Exhilaration threw MV back to the Den days when Siamis tirelessly scrapped with them, but that brought a memory of Roy, followed by the heat of ire. Because Siamis had betrayed them, too. "What could they possibly have offered you?" MV snarled, and attacked.

Once again Siamis was ready for him. "You have it wrong," he said, twisted, whirled, and tapped the side of MV's knee. "It was I who made the offer."

"Laban," MV gasped, his temper flaring, and he extended two fingers, lunging for a punishing strike.

Siamis deflected, and pain flowered at two nerve clusters, so precise that MV's heart stuttered. "MV, your lesson is to learn the error of underestimating those you do not respect."

His breath hissed in, and that was all the warning MV got. He managed one hit, though his knuckles grazed over a gut that felt like brick, so that Siamis could come in close, and . . . Pain flowered through MV, relentless taps over nerve centers, jolting him into stumbling, limbs like water . . .

Both boys lay stunned, Siamis standing over them, breathing fast. Laban was very good, but MV's skills were superlative. With some size and experience on him, he might soon be ready for the next level of training.

Siamis reached for one of MV's boot knives, made two quick cuts, then shut his eyes to concentrate as he transferred them to the spot he'd prepared as a Destination.

When MV and Laban slowly recovered their wits, they found themselves lying in a muddy field with no building in sight. The effort it took to turn over to hands and knees caused every joint to flare again. Laban sat up, holding his head with both hands. "Where are we? Ow."

MV forced himself to look around. To the east, hazy mountains jutting up. "I think we're at the border." Then he looked down at himself, and saw the middle button of his shirt neatly cut away. Laban's, too.

"Shit." He glowered southward and painfully began the long, dreary slog over marshy ground in bitter wind to Norsunder Base's perimeter outpost. "Shit*fire*."

Ten

Everon

THE DELIETHS' ROYAL CASTLE—or palace—or building mid-way between the two—looked even worse than Clair had remembered. No one had done anything to repair it since Kessler Sonscarna's strike team had set fire to the place a little over six years ago. All morning, as conspirators arrived, Clair found old friends who wanted to chat, look about making faces at the old fire damage, and say things like "Where do you begin?" and then chat some more.

Clair caught sight of Atan several times, dressed in a sensible riding outfit of super-fine linsey-woolsey, with a loose robe over it, edged with butterflies in gold stitching, and was glad that she'd dressed up. She was trying to repair the Mearsieans' reputations in the eyes of the others, and she knew she'd succeeded a bit, judging by the friendliness of Atan's welcome, but she still felt a bit wistful when she saw cheerful Lilah Selenna of Sarendan welcomed by Atan as if she were dressed in diamonds and lace instead of old riding trousers, tunic, and bare feet. Ah, well, feelings were feelings.

Things finally started happening when the wandering conspirators were herded together for a picnic lunch. Clair sat between Lilah Selenna and Terry, and when Lilah hopped up to speak to another friend, Clair was alone with Terry.

"Do you find yourself thinking about what is right?" she asked.

Terry didn't blink at the sudden question—he was used to Clair, who seldom chattered about inconsequentials. "Here's the problem. I don't really even know what 'right' is. I was what, seven or eight, and all I thought about was escaping lessons to go riding, when revolution broke out. To one side I was the prince. To the other, a target. To the desperate third, surely I'd been taught the location of ward protections."

Here he stretched out the mangled hand with its missing fingers. "It took a long time to convince them I was ignorant, and then they were going to use me as an object lesson, but got interrupted. I hadn't done anything to warrant either the title or the abuse. I happened to be born Prince Tereneth, and I was in the wrong place when the adults around me started fighting each other."

His voice was too low to carry, bitter with remembered pain. The contrast between the soft, swift words and the pleasant picnic lunch, birds twittering over crumbs in the background, made Clair feel a bit giddy.

"I guess I'm blabbing," he admitted, his head low.

"To you, maybe, but it makes sense to me," she whispered back, her heart bursting with emotion that had to get out. And why not talk to Terry? He'd been there on Five. He was a king because it was duty. She didn't dare confide in the other girls, because they'd take on the burden of her emotions without being able to help—and they'd have to live in Mearsies Heili every day. Roy was gone. Senrid would be great, except she knew he'd expect a trade in talk, and she was not ready to describe her experiences on Five to his too-interested face. If she ever would be. But Terry would understand.

She drew a breath. "The truth is, I hate the way Mearsieanne rules. I hate the hierarchy of duchas and counts and the like. But there is nothing I can do about it, short of violence. And I'd rather go volunteer to join Detlev than to lead a revolution at home. Thanks to what I was being tutored in, I even know how to do it."

Terry turned her way. "But you're not."

"I'm not. So?" She lifted a hand. "So I whittle away the rest of my life in doing things like this?" She turned out her hands, indicating Tahra's palace. "I'm not convinced it's even a good idea to redecorate someone's home without asking."

Terry shook his head. "Here's where I'm on solid ground. Tahra isn't like anyone else. You know that."

"True."

"She hates any kind of change. If no one acts, she'll live in a ruin forever. But if she comes back and finds things nice, with Atan heading the list of donors, she'll be so gratified at the attention that she'll adjust. And want a wager? She'll never alter a pin or pillow again, so we better make it good."

Clair let out a slow breath. "Yes. I think you're right."

"As for the rest, look. They kept us apart on Five for a reason, I'm thinking. Though I couldn't tell you what. But after MV handed me my ass, they all stayed away from me, except for Curtas. Who kept me busy in the stable. Want to know the truth? It was not a bad life."

She sent him a quick look as he absently coaxed a questing ant off his scarred arm and onto a blade of grass, then lowered the grass an arm's length away. "We argued. A lot. Or, I argued," Terri corrected, keeping his voice low. "Curtas isn't the arguing sort. Like Adam the painter. Laban loves arguing. Silvanas loves joking. I began to see that they're all different. Like us. My wanting to kill them, eh, in my own eyes that started making me indistinguishable from the worst of them."

Clair, who had been watching, saw Lilah break off her conversation and begin to head their way again. "So you're saying . . ."

"Nothing. Last person to offer advice," Terry whispered — he'd been watching, too. "You peaceably handed off your kingdom to Mearsieanne."

"It was hers, by right."

"You could have said it was yours by right. Years ago, Puddlenose could have said it was *his* by right, because wasn't his mother older than your mother? Don't you see? You and Puddlenose chose the peaceful way. It's still peaceful, isn't it?"

"Yes. Yes." She breathed out again. "It is."

"Well, it seems to me, that's where you begin. It's where I had to. Everything else is compromise," and when Lilah thumped down on Clair's other side, he said, "I don't have to ask if your friends were glad to see you." He chuckled.

Clair said, "Very much. So did you start your stable?"

"No time." He rolled his eyes. "But I've discovered that threatening to start it, and to staff it with my more obnoxious nobles, has had an interesting effect."

Clair laughed, and Lilah said, "You were stuck in a stable when you were a poopsie prisoner? I thought all they had was dungeons and torture chambers!"

Terry spent the short remainder of the picnic telling funny stories about his lack of skill in learning to curry a horse, sending Lilah into gales of laughter.

After the last dishes were carried off, Atan stood up. "I know how busy everyone is, so let's gather in a group and take a tour."

Clair found herself walking next to Lilah, who seemed to know everyone in the alliance and to have made friends with them with her indefatigable letter writing.

"First thing, stonemasons," Atan said as they began walking along the front of the building on the enormous parade ground that Prince Glenn had had put in.

They tramped across an inner court, where dry autumnal grasses tufted up between the cracked tiles. "Local?" Terry asked.

"Oh, most definitely local," Atan said. "I see you're thinking the way I am: local work, local business, can only help here. If Commander Dei agrees, this entire parade ground that once was a garden can be put back and replanted. That would employ even more people, and not even be costly."

"Dei," Clair repeated. "I wondered about that. Are they related to the Dei family you read about in Sartoran history?"

"Yes," Atan said. "But there was a split in the family a while ago. And some trouble." Her voice dropped a note.

Clair's new sensitivity detected Atan's extreme reluctance to talk about that subject as they passed through the smashed inner doors.

Lilah pointed, exclaiming, "Oh, that was once a beautiful chair. Why would someone smash up a *chair*?"

"Why would someone attack a country that threatened no one?" Atan said, glad to abandon the subject of the Dei family.

She touched the fine gilt along the edge of the smashed wood. It looked like some Norsundrian had picked it up and crashed it against the carving of an archway. It bothered her less that Tahra hadn't replaced the chair than that she hadn't permitted anyone to repair it. This evidence of violence felt too much like someone keeping a wound open so it would continue to hurt.

A deep, short breath. Focus! "Peitar wants to help, and Arthur, and even Senrid, though none of them could be here today. But I'll write to them—"

"I will, too," Lilah said cheerfully. "And of course I'll be telling Peitar *everything*."

Atan smiled at her. "We both will. My thought was, everyone takes responsibility for a room, that is, donate funds to hire a local to redesign a room in local styles. Or you could redo their kitchens, say . . ." She turned to Clair.

"I don't know anything about kitchens," Clair admitted. "A playroom?"

Atan said gratefully, "Splendid idea! Eventually Tahra will have children. She kept repeating something someone said to her, that her staying alive was the best revenge against Norsunder's determined effort to wipe out her family. Yes! Give her a nursery, with replicas of your favorite toys."

Clair walked through the door into what was now the only garden left, now wildly overgrown. "I don't want to sound like a wailer and whiner, but I actually never had any toys. The other girls did, though! Some of them. They can put it together. Yes, that's what we'll do. It'll be fun to find toys from local artisans as well as from home—we need such a project. We'll make a splendid nursery."

"Excellent! So! What rooms can we assign to Shontande Lirendi?"

"You mean, someone has actually heard from the mysterious new king of Colend?" Lilah interrupted, eyes round. "Thad said that regency council was keeping him practically a prisoner."

"They don't dare circumvent *my* letters," Atan said with such relish that there were some smothered laughs. Then her smile faded. "Once he gets older, I'm going to insist he be sent to Sartor to visit my court, as was traditional in both our families. Let's see them keep him sequestered in my city—oh!"

Atan stumbled to a stop and toed away the dirt from a gleam of greenish color, revealing tiles with figures worked into them in mosaic. "Oh-h-h-h-h," Atan breathed, crouching down. She used her hands to shove aside the dirt from an expanse of mosaic.

Clair bent. "Dancing . . . is that a turtle?"

"This is extremely rare," Atan observed, sitting back on

her heels. "And so close to the castle." She leaned on one hand to stare up over her shoulder at the gap-toothed windows and doors. "Once a tyrant took the throne. No one could topple him, he had such a grip on Everon. People resisted by reminding him — in indirect ways, of course — that he'd die one day, in which case they would dance for joy. The dancing turtle represented the triumph of time over tyranny. He ordered death to anyone who made a turtle in any form, which of course made him ridiculous."

Clair grinned. This, she had to tell CJ.

Atan turned back to examine the mosaic. "I wonder who laid this down, and if the tyrant was meant to discover it, or did discover it."

"It's entirely possible that they made it in secret," Terry said.

"And put dirt and plants over it, knowing he would walk over it every day," Lilah added.

Atan chuckled. "And so the weather has eroded the soil away from it. Well! Tahra might find that interesting." She looked around. "Someone good at gardens is needed, who can discover and preserve such things. I think I know whom to approach."

"When is it to be done by?"

"Let's aim for the end of winter," Atan said. "I got the impression that they'd travel for at least a season." She rose and whacked the soil from her clothes. "When Tahra comes back, I mean for her to find a home waiting. A real one." She bent and yanked up a weed grown between the steps to a side entrance. "People need to live."

Everyone agreed with that, and seeing the light fading, they began the transfers home.

Eleven

ONCE THE TRANSFER REACTION faded, Atan ran to her private chamber, buoyed by the satisfaction that comes of doing good. Gehlei, her steward, was waiting. A tall, middle-aged woman with a furrowed brow and a grim look; though she proudly wore the green, silver, and violet of the Head Steward, there was no mistaking that posture for anything but a bodyguard.

"He's gone, all right," Gehlei said, the guttural emphasis on "he" making it clear she meant Siamis. "Ruined the place before his going."

"What?" Atan exclaimed.

A jerked chin, and Gehlei said in a slightly less hortatory tone, "Morning. Just after you left. The crane statue, given to the first Yustnesveas, smashed. Same with a crystal candle-holder. Scrapes, furnishings kicked awry. We left it untouched, in case you might want to see for yourself."

"I do indeed. Where's the page? Let's summon the city guard, whoever's on duty."

"Already done," Gehlei said. "Rel has a team of guards cordoning off that end of the wing."

"Was anyone attacked? Where are the residence wing servants?"

"None of them were present. All sent off to other tasks."

That sounded both deliberate and mysterious.

Atan hurried straight to the residence wing, heart pounding—in part because of the news, but also because one of the deepest pleasures of her life was getting to see Rel. And there he was, towering head and shoulders above two pairs of city guards. At the sight of her he turned, and his deep-set eyes met hers. Light flared inside her, and she smiled, but said nothing, aware of the cluster of palace servants waiting in the background with buckets, dust clothes, and brooms to clean up.

Atan gestured to Rel to join her, as the rest trailed behind. Atan took in the scuffed-up marble, the debris, and the inside of the guest room where the furnishings had been kicked about. There was no sign of Siamis otherwise.

"This wasn't done by one person. At least two. Quite a fight, I'd guess," Rel said, hunkering down to examine the scuff marks, then raising his gaze to the askew tapestry above.

"A fight?" a waiting servant repeated, her hands pressed together under her collarbones as she looked about. "Are we to be attacked again?"

"My guess is that they must have come after Siamis," an older guard said. "What's more, he expected it, seeing as how the servants were sent off."

Atan turned to him. "And the morning patrol saw nothing?"

"I was morning patrol. We were on the opposite side of the Great Chandos Way," the older one said.

Rel added, "Which is probably why the attackers moved when they did."

Atan turned to the waiting row of servants, who bowed like reeds in the wind. "Please restore this area. The rest of you can go off duty."

The guards departed. The servants began setting things to rights, overseen by Gehlei. Atan gave Rel an inviting glance, and he joined her as she began the long walk back to the other side of the palace. As soon as they were out of earshot, he tipped his head back toward the residence wing. "Evidence we really need more guards?"

Atan wished she did not have to deal with this now. "Come with me."

Rel was tired after a long day, but that brief smile of hers banished it. Anticipation sparked instead as he regarded her with question.

Atan misinterpreted that question, her mind on Siamis and violence and what, if anything, she ought to do. She led the way out a side door to the private garden, at one end of which lay the royal Purad, the labyrinth barely visible in the starlight. They passed on by. It was not appropriate to talk while making the *napurdiav*, or walking the labyrinth, and so she paced along the rows of tightly clipped rose bushes readied for winter as she said, "Rel, I was a part of the argument to expand the guard, as you well know. I thought Chief Veltos and the mages were being arrogant and, well, it doesn't matter anymore."

She hated to say anything against Chief Veltos, who had been murdered by the Norsundrian assassin Efael.

The truth was, Atan had never liked Chief Veltos, but she had respected her as a dedicated, hard-working mage guild chief. Veltos had been embittered by the Sartoran defeat in the war with Norsunder that had resulted in Sartor being removed from time and physical access for nearly a century. They were still recovering from that removal, more than a decade later.

"I didn't tell you this," Atan admitted, stopping so she could look up into Rel's face. Tall as she was, he was a full head taller. "Because it . . . the time never seemed quite right, especially since you volunteer with the guard, who are all volunteers, good people every one, doing their best in spite of the high council and the first circle despising them. I thought it was because they hadn't protected us when Norsunder invaded, even though the mages hadn't either."

Rel waited patiently, his anticipation dying to frustration, which he struggled to suppress. Friendship they had, a strong one. It meant everything to him. Almost everything: he wanted more, but nothing that she wasn't ready to give.

"While you were traveling, after Chief Veltos died, I got hold of the city records before the war," she said. "Including records of the guard, and about them, and, ah, though they did a good enough job against thieves and the like, there were also complaints about them. Bribery, blindness, bullying. The guard commanders had inherited their position, because to Sartorans inheritance is orderly. One grows up knowing the expectations of one's position, right? And how can I argue against that?"

With an ironic gesture, Atan touched the thin gold coronet bound around her brow below her coronet of brown braids.

Rel said, "From what I've seen, expectation without being answerable is a recipe for bribery and the rest. But the fact is, there are not enough of us to catch the likes of whoever it was who attacked. I understand that no one wants a militarized city, inherited position or not. So what's the solution?"

Atan shook her head. "That's what bothers me. I don't know what to do! The guild chiefs want this, the nobles want that, the city wants to be safe, and to be left alone to live their lives. And nobody wants to pay any taxes to insure that."

She went over the familiar ground as they walked back to the state wing, and he listened, because that was what she needed from him now. As always, he suppressed the wish to take her hand, to turn her head up to his. To kiss her. But she walked with her arms crossed, her head bent as she wrestled with her dilemma. The truth was plain: she wasn't any more ready than she had been when together they released the Child Spell last year. Either that, or he wasn't the right person to spark desire in her.

As they parted at the double doors, she turned to watch him walk away. He really was tall, and so broad through the chest. And he looked so strong. What would it feel like, to have his arms around her? Heat flashed in a shivery way through her, and she tightened her forearms across her ribs, lost between longing and fear of where it would lead.

Fear won, though she understood it as caution. She had spent all last winter reading her forebears' personal records. So many of them had fallen in love (they thought) forever, only to lose interest, or to be betrayed, and in every single record the most passionate made rash decisions they later regretted.

Tsauderei had taught her since she was small to think ahead to the future, to make decisions after considering consequences. Love, in those records, was so overwhelmingly *present*—so *blinding*. Just like now. She became aware of herself standing in the doorway, arms tight against her chest. She turned, and there were two servants waiting at a respectable distance.

Humiliation prickled nastily through her nerves as she forced her expression to smooth, her hands to drop, and her mind to return to the schedule that never, *ever*, relented before all those watchful eyes.

Rel kept walking fast, wishing for a good blizzard to cool him down. She's not ready. How stupid he'd been to assume that they'd reach for each other at the same time, just because they'd ridded themselves of the Child Spell together.

He turned his steps toward Blossom Street, and the pleasure house where Hannla Thasis, one of Atan's friends from the enchantment days, lived with three generations of family. It seemed a lifetime ago that Hannla had offered to take him upstairs, and he'd turned her down flat. He hadn't really understood what she meant, except in the general sense.

He did now.

The pleasure house lay halfway down the street, light spilling from the diamond-shaped glass windows bowed on either side of the door. Downstairs, musicians played lively dances, people crowded in the center leaping and turning, surrounded by an even bigger crowd, the general mood one of hilarity in the way people did when they felt winter looming. Hannla, in her late twenties, circulated opposite her aunt, each watching the smooth flow of custom, and noting who had gone upstairs and who was still available.

Rel stepped in, ducking his head slightly as the top of his thick, glossy black hair brushed the lintel, and Hannla paused. When he lifted his head and met her gaze across the room, she stepped back, every nerve alight, her breath short. He's woken up, she thought. And he was every bit as searing to the senses as they'd guessed he would be.

In spite of the crowd, somehow her feet got her to him despite a drumming heartbeat, and he stood there inside the door, gazing down at her from those long-lashed, deep-set eyes, as he whispered, "You said once . . ." He half-lifted a hand in a gesture of appeal. She grasped his wrist—life! He really was strong—and tugged him into one of the side rooms.

He blinked, then said in that deep, chesty voice of his, almost a growl, "Hannla, you once said you'd, that when I was ready, to come to you."

Rel would never know how many tears she'd spent over

him when she first met him, she sixteen, and he a year or so younger, before he did the Child Spell. But that was then, and this was now: she was three months with child, with a steady relationship that might very well someday be marriage. She used her hostess voice. "I'm glad you came. I'll find you the perfect partner."

His eyes widened. "I thought . . ." His magnificent cheek-bones—rougher cut and more heroic than those on the statue of King Connar on his rearing horse in the middle of Triavos Square—reddened. "But if you don't want me . . ."

They both could hear the *either* that he bit off short. And now she had it. He'd come straight from the palace.

"It's not that at all," she said low-voiced, barely audible over the laughter and tinkle of music behind them. "First of all, I retired from upstairs a year ago. I'm taking over management of downstairs, as my aunt is ready to retire entirely. And even if that were not the case, we both have emotional entanglements that would be awkward, when what you really need, I suspect, is the ease of the heart-free encounter. Yes?"

He met her gaze at last. "Is it wrong, to be here when I have feelings for Atan?"

"Have the two of you exchanged vows of exclusivity?"

"We haven't even kissed," he said. "Or talked about, well, any aspect of that."

"Only the two of you can decide what's right for you, but if she's not ready, she's not ready," Hannla said, and watched some of the tension ease from his face. "I suspect she'd be the first to say that it's sensible to get rid of frustration. Romance will come in its own time. It can be as unpredictable as the flight of a butterfly."

He jerked his head down in a nod, then shifted from foot to foot uncertainly.

"Wait here," she said.

She poked her head out, catching aware glances from every one of the staff. Rel would never know how much speculation there had been about him after his visits to share news, cakes, and hot Sartoran steep. She scanned the parlor. Four of her staff, two men and two women, signaled their willingness. Hannla beckoned to her cousin Fiar, a merry redhead who looked nothing like Atan, and who was famed as an excellent first-timer.

Hannla introduced them, Fiar invited Rel to share a drink of punch with her, and Hannla left them. Even if Rel changed his mind and decided it must be Atan or no one, Fiar would at least talk things out with him. He was going to need that, if he was heart-given to Queen Yustnesveas Landis of Sartor, watched jealously by her entire first circle of nobles, who expected her to make a splendid match among the world's princes.

Atan had scolded herself into focus, though at the cost of a warning pang at her temples, by the time she trod upstairs. She was always sorry to part from Rel, but she did their best to bribe palace servants to spy on her; she firmly turned her mind away, leaving that aspect of things to Gehlei, who was fiercely protective. If she caught one blabbermouth, that person would find themselves at the border with a boot in the behind to send them off faster. But all it took was one blabbermouth to get rumors doing.

When she reached her private salon, she found Tsauderei waiting. She greeted her old guardian and mentor, though feeling that the day had already been far too long.

"Siamis is gone," Tsauderei said.

"I know. I just came from his rooms." Atan went on to report what she'd seen, finishing with, "Rel thinks there was some kind of fight. Bethros—one of the older guards from the old days—thinks that the servants being sent away was no accident, that Siamis expected to be attacked."

Tsauderei said, "I can corroborate the servants being sent off. My own watchdog was one of 'em, sent on a supposedly necessary but entirely spurious errand." He looked ironic. "You're angry over that? Angry over something."

"Not angry." She was unsure how to express the sense that she'd missed something important in her conversation with Rel. It felt like missing a step that she hadn't know was even there. If he had anything to say, wouldn't he have said it? They had always talked plainly—that was one of the comfortable things about Rel. He said what he thought, and he listened to her, without trying to tell her what her duty was, or what to think, or what he thought she might want to hear.

Unlike her court.

Her mind flitted back to that annoying interview in the Diantas room, and she gave herself a hard mental shake. "Just tired." Time to get her thoughts away from Rel. "I need to talk to Peitar Selenna. He sent Lilah to Everon, but didn't come himself. And he could. His style of kingship gives him all that time to study magic. He could have come if he'd wished. I know he's angry that Siamis was tolerated here. I was very careful to explain how much I hated that, that diplomatic needs had to be put ahead of my personal preference."

Tsauderei stroked his long mustache with a finger. "I haven't seen him for weeks –" His white brows shot up. "Longer. Much longer. We've been writing, always about magic. But now I'm aware that I've let time slip away while I've been mired here."

Atan rubbed her temples. "I was thinking that he might like to meet Leotay and, ah, her sister." Her voice faltered as, unbidden, she thought of Rel again. She bent her head to hide her unease. She *had* missed something with Rel. But what? The pressures of duty must be to blame, making her forget, or overlook something, the way Tsauderei felt about not visiting Peitar.

Tsauderei grunted a laugh, for once completely misinterpreting her faltering voice. "If it helps, Horsefeathers seems to have been an honorable name among them. Had a meaning very different from the old-fashioned implication of gullibility in our language."

Atan straightened up, and did her best to look interested. "I remember reading that in Colend, they call a crooked merchant a seller of horse feathers."

"Other nouns have also lost meaning and found their way into Aldau-Rayad names, Leotay told me: Snow, Dawn, and apparently one of Horsefeathers' friends is called Rancid. Rather suggests that they lived so carefully that nothing was permitted to go bad, so the word lost its meaning."

"I look forward to talking more with them, when the entire court isn't intimidating them."

Tsauderei grinned, then shook his head. "Do invite Peitar. I've been remiss. The sooner I can shed the mage guild, the better."

Atan sighed. "I wish I could shed tomorrow's meaningless tedium, but I can't, and my reward will be another tedious

Name Day up on Parleas Terrace."

Tsauderei's tufted white brows drew together. "I've nothing to say to your nobles and first circle obligations up on Parleas Terrace, but Atan, it grieves me to hear you slander tomorrow's guild interviews. What's more it would hurt Peitar if he thought you were beginning to think yourself too busy for ordinary people."

"That's not it at *all*." Atan flushed. "The Name Day will be just as tedious and meaningless . . ."

As she said the word, she knew that she was making excuses. Name Day celebrations weren't meaningless. She might not like half the attendees—and she knew they only wanted her presence as queen, not as Atan—but celebrating the birth of a child was a time of joy, and hope for Sartor's future.

Tsauderei's gaze was steady. "This might be the last time I can act as guardian, and I'll accept it if you send me to the right-about, your majesty, but even if you spend an entire day listening to people whine about their guild leaders, or their calling, or each other, lay blame and make excuses, the one time you hear genuine grievances ought to make it all worth it. You might be the only recourse someone has to justice."

"I know." Atan pressed her hands to her eyes. "I *know* that." She sighed out her breath yet again. "And there are fewer people who will remind me of what I need to hear, rather than flatter me with what they think I want to hear."

Tsauderei heard her genuine contrition. "I'll also scold myself for disparaging the Sartoran mage guild with my 'shedding', though I know they've several quite capable candidates to replace me. What I regard as political maneuvering they assuredly see as taking steps to make the right decision. At least they'll be glad to be quit of me!" He levered himself up. "I'll wish you good night."

Twelve

TSAUDEREI WAS SUFFICIENTLY DISTURBED by the fact that he had neglected King Peitar Selenna of Sarendan except for occasional and cursory exchanges about magic books. He spent most of the night in disposing of much of his desk work, and forced himself the next day to endure a transfer to Sarendan.

As he recovered in the Miraleste palace Destination, a young page emerged from a hall. "Oh, it's the mage! Please come this way."

She couldn't be more than ten, probably some orphan Lilah had discovered somewhere and promptly adopted, giving her a livelihood and a place to live. Tsauderei remembered that the palace was full of strays whom both Peitar and Lilah had absorbed after the disastrous civil war the summer before Sartor emerged from the enchantment.

The page scrupulously led Tsauderei to a room that was blessedly nearby, sparing his creaking joints. It was a cheerful room overlooking the lake below the row of hills the city was built on. Then Lilah herself bounded in, her tilted eyes characteristically crinkled with humor, her short rusty-red hair flying about her ears as it had since she'd done the Child Spell at age twelve.

"Tsauderei! It's been *ages!*" Lilah carried a toddler on her hip, his wispy dark hair and tilted eyes Peitar's in miniature.

"Too long, certainly," Tsauderei said. "I've been kept busy in Sartor."

At the mention of Sartor, Lilah's smile dimmed.

Tsauderei, guessing successfully at the cause, said, "Not just watching over Siamis, but I've been serving as the interim head of the Sartoran mage guild — a position I trust I will be able to relinquish soon — and supervising the integration of a mage and a mage student from the fifth world, a delightful pair of sisters I expect you would enjoy meeting once they settle in a bit more. Is this Prince Darian, then?"

"Ian's already turned two somersaults in a row," Lilah said proudly.

At this, the child wriggled and Lilah set him down. Ian already looked more like Peitar than like his aunt: he was slender, dark-haired, and bid fair to be as handsome as his father. At some months older than two, he was as equally unaware of it.

Ian turned unblinking eyes up to Tsauderei, then his gaze shifted to the door, feathery dark curls flipping around his head. "He's got that DY stuff," Lilah said. "Always knows where we are."

"Da," the child said, a small hand lifting. Then he took off, running on his toes as they often did at that size, though he was more deft than most.

"Peitar's in his work room," Lilah said. "The page went ahead. I know he'll want to see you."

"How are you both doing?"

Lilah matched her pace to Tsauderei's as she began to talk. "Everything is good. Ian just started using words. We couldn't get him to for the longest time — he was telling us in our heads. It was the weirdest thing! Kinda like a bird chirping in your ear, except inside. We all thought it was cute, until Peitar said that Ian needed to talk. So we had to do mind-shields. It was awful, until Ian caught on," Lilah said. "Here we are! Is it something fun, or magic stuff?"

"I'm merely here to catch up," Tsauderei said.

Lilah opened the door to the king's study, glanced at her brother, and grimaced at Tsauderei. "That means boring magic talk. When is it anything else? I hope you stay long enough for dinner." And she flitted off.

Peitar glanced up from his desk as the old mage entered,

and Tsauderei experienced a cold shock: for a heartbeat Peitar looked exactly like his deposed uncle. It wasn't just the finely boned face framed by softly waving dark hair, it was that expression of cold reserve.

But this was not Darian Irad, emotionally and physically scarred ex-king—and as Tsauderei got his shaky old limbs to lumber up to one of the chairs, he recognized wary tiredness where Irad had been only warily angry.

Wariness. Tsauderei would never betray Peitar's passion for Atan to her, but her innocent observation that Peitar had not been communicating with her had given the old mage a severe jolt. For years, Peitar had studied with Atan, corresponded with her, and visited.

Tsauderei also had to protect Peitar, who seemed to believe his unrequited love unobserved. Peitar was as sensitive as he was private, so Tsauderei leaned back in his chair and said, "I could apologize for not having seen you for so long, but that goes two ways. I trust you were not avoiding Atan because she felt obliged to invite Siamis as a gesture? I will not say of what," he added wryly.

Peitar's lips twitched. "Not avoiding. Atan wrote to us to explain when he first arrived in Sartor. We understood her position. But I'd reached my own decision."

He rose and came around the desk to lean against it, the old limp that had made his life so painful now a slight hitch in his walk. "Since Atan was forced into a position of truce, shall we call it, I would not break that. But if I see him outside of Sartor, there is a matter of justice. I owe my people that. Promised it."

Peitar was very nearly the age his uncle had been when he, driven to militarize a starving, angry populace in an effort to prepare for a Norsunder war that had not come, had instead faced that populace rising against him—led by the rabble-rouser Derek Diamagan, who had ardently believed the only good noble was a dead one, with the exception of his best friend Peitar Selenna.

Right before he lost the kingdom, Darian Irad had felt himself forced to put Peitar—and Derek, but there'd been no regrets there—on trial for their lives. And his handpicked jury had voted for death. Tsauderei was aware, and knew Peitar was aware, of the heavy irony underlying his words when he said, "A trial, eh?"

"No." Peitar breathed the word, reddening along those fine cheekbones. Then, with his gaze dropping away, "Aside from the question of whether such a trial can ever be truly just, their remains the fact that Siamis shot Derek dead, before four witnesses. Whatever reason he might offer in his defense would mean nothing to anyone in my kingdom."

Tsauderei looked at that averted gaze, the tight mouth, and decided that any kind of discussion about Siamis would be a waste of breath.

Or about Derek Diamagan.

"Speaking of your uncle," Tsauderei said, though they both knew he hadn't been. "Are you two still in communication?" That relationship was one of the stranger ones Tsauderei had ever seen in a long life: Peitar had not only protected his uncle from execution, which was all too frequent in the history of violent throne changes, but he'd insisted that if his own kingship failed, his uncle should return. No one understood that agreement except uncle and nephew.

Sure enough, Peitar said, "He's still in Geth-deles."

"So that worked out?"

Tsauderei remembered something about Darian Irad going to their sister world to help organize a defense. He'd thought it a terrible idea—and yet convenient to get the ex-king well away, both of which opinions he'd managed to keep to himself.

"Quite well." Peitar went on, "In fact, he's been so successful that he has garnered me good will. I've been trying to obtain information about a new kind of magic, and the mages on Geth seem willing to communicate with me."

Tsauderei was glad he'd sat down. "New kind of magic?" He thought of Lilith's exasperating hints. "What is this?"

Peitar glanced aside, one long hand resting on a stack of old-looking papers. "Vagabond magic."

"Oh," Tsauderei said, sitting back in disappointment. "That's mere illusion. Fit for children to play with."

"So I thought, until I discovered that someone—a young man named Leskander Rhoderan—did his best to keep the spread of it a secret, as he was in the midst of creating a child army in order to defeat a Norsunder incursion. Before he was murdered by one of Detlev's boys."

Tsauderei said, "You haven't mentioned any of this."

"Because everyone thinks I'm chasing shadows," Peitar

said. "It was admittedly a side project—one of many—until this past year. Until I began receiving records from Geth, both ancient and recent, the latter raising questions. Like, why would Detlev get involved, even through his minions, in something completely frivolous? There's a lot missing that has me curious." Peitar's expression hardened, bringing Darian Irad forcibly to mind again. "As I found out during our revolution, sometimes there's nothing more frightening than a child soldier."

"Seeing everything in black and white, swayed by emotion rather than reason. Spending their own lives as quickly as they take them, if the weapons are sufficient," Tsauderei said. "I can point to some histories."

"I know them," Peitar said—as Tsauderei had rather thought he would. "More to the point, why would this Les Rhoderan, whatever his intent, think vagabond magic a weapon? And why would Detlev send his boy assassins to take him out unless there's more to it?"

"I don't know, but I'd be very interested in your findings," Tsauderei said, and wondered how much of Peitar's kingship had been delegated in order to permit the young king to do what he loved most: research.

Peitar moved away from his desk. "And to answer the question about Siamis that you so bluntly didn't ask, yes, I plan to act summarily. But I can't justify killing him cold, so I've prepared a stone spell, one of the old ones, from the days of Gardens of Shame."

Peitar plunged his hand into a pocket, his fingers closing around a worn wooden shank button. Derek had left behind few belongings; he'd felt that owning anything went against his common origins. He'd even refused to wear better clothes than the old homespun shirts of his wandering days. After his assassination, some of his followers had found his winter jacket packed away in a trunk, and had cut off the buttons, sharing one each with his closest followers, Peitar being given the first, as his oldest friend.

Enchantments were spells chained together onto some sort of artifact, place, sometimes a person, though that was always a danger. Peitar felt that the means of justice belonged on Derek's wooden shank—and once the stone spell was triggered, he would drop the shank into a fire so that the artifact would be out of reach, assuring that Siamis got his full hundred years before the spell wore off.

He gripped the button as he said, "Siamis can stand as a statue in a secluded garden here. Whoever follows me a century from now can decide what to do with him. But he'll harm no one in the interim."

Tsauderei shrugged, not about to remind Peitar that mages did not interfere in political matters, because they both know that Tsauderei *had* interfered, bringing a summer storm before Peitar's and Derek's executions could take place. While it could not be called direct interference—the storm had conveniently covered the palace guard running a rescue—it was the sort of indirect interference that could have caused trouble between government and magic community in many places.

"You won't see me shedding any tears if Siamis meets up with the consequences of his actions," Tsauderei said. "But he's no longer in Sartor."

"Good riddance. I'll find him eventually," Peitar promised. "I owe Derek that much of a semblance of justice."

Tsauderei bit back a comment. Peitar was not asking for advice. He hadn't asked for advice for some time, which might be one of the reasons their communication had dwindled. So he said only, "Atan will be inviting you to visit, and to meet the two mages from Aldau-Rayad, the fifth world, while they study at the Sartoran school. Their magic is, eh, another metaphor, let us say, than ours. We both thought you might be interested."

Peitar's entire demeanor brightened, evoking the Peitar of the old days, however briefly. "Ian is coming." Then, "I look forward to it."

As little Prince Darian pattered in, yelling, "Da, da!" and waving a bright red feather that he'd found, Tsauderei said, "Bring the youngster. I'm sure Atan would love to see him again. I don't believe she has since his Name Day."

"No," Peitar said. "She hasn't."

Thirteen

WHEN MV AND LABAN reached Norsunder Base at last, humorous commentary by the bored outpost sentries still burning fresh in their ears, their bruises had begun to yellow. The moment David saw the two trudging soddenly in from the stable, he said, "Office."

Laban and MV exchanged looks. They'd scarcely finished a cold, wet ride in thin rain just this side of sleet, their feet caked in dun-colored mud. *Of course* Detlev was there, though he'd been away for months.

David said as they began crossing the stable yard toward the command wing, "We tried to cover for you."

Laban grimaced, and MV began cursing. They reached the office to find Detlev waiting for them, seated on the edge of his desk, hands clasped loosely around one knee. His unreadable hazel gaze shifted from the big bruise on Laban's forehead to the marks on MV's visible skin.

"You had general orders," Detlev said. Always, when he spoke the obvious, they knew bad road lay ahead.

Laban's temper flashed. "We went to snatch Siamis. For *you.*"

"Shut up, idiot," MV breathed.

"What made you assume I wasn't capable of giving orders to that effect if I'd wanted Siamis snatched?"

"But he was *right there*, swanking about in Sartor," Laban protested, angry at the vast unfairness of it all. "He *turned* on us, and of *course* they rewarded him for it. Next thing you know he'll be crowned King of Sartor," he finished bitterly.

"Ferret scouted for you?" It was posed as a question, but it wasn't one, and both knew better than to lie. They nodded, and Detlev said, "Yes. Ferret is so used to regarding himself as invisible he never remembers a thorough mind-shield. Siamis was waiting for you."

It was another not-question. Detlev saw assent in Laban's dropped gaze and MV's tightened jaw, and went on. "Surely Ferret, at least, spotted how many guards they had hedged around him, even if he couldn't sense the interlocked wards and tracers? But MV, you ought to have detected those."

MV jerked up a shoulder. "We were moving too fast, and I figured, any wards would be laid against him. Not us."

"My point is, the evidence is there, Laban, that they don't trust Siamis much past his next heartbeat. You may assure yourself, if it comforts you, that he is not likely to be wearing any crowns in the near future."

Laban rolled his eyes, lip curled. *Of course* Detlev was watching Siamis—somehow—from a distance, contemplating the right moment to drop like a hawk on a bunny.

And sure enough. Detlev said, "From what I've been able to discover, there've been at least three covert operations intended to exact justice. Three that I know of: as you're probably aware, I'm warded from entering Eidervaen, and now, after Siamis's vigorous aid, Efael, Yeres, and the Black Knives—those whose names Siamis was able to furnish—are warded as well."

Laban whistled. "The three attempts. Ours or theirs?"

"Does it matter?"

Laban flushed. "Only if they succeeded. And we know they didn't."

Detlev's expression didn't change. "As well Siamis considered you too negligible a threat to get your names added to the wards." Both boys grimaced at that. "The general orders still stand, and you and I will discuss them presently." Laban flushed even brighter, his lips tightening mutinously. "You may trade off with David in tutoring duties." With a flick of his eyes he dismissed Laban.

When the door closed behind him, Detlev said to MV, "Your experience?" When he said that, he was asking to see the memory for himself.

MV let his breath out in a short sigh. If he refused, then Detlev would just say, in that bland tone, "Your report?" And all the questions would go where Detlev wanted, and MV didn't want, anyway.

The memory was faster, and as always, it wasn't just the memory of their decision and the journey and the fight, but bleeding in — impossible to stanch — the memories and emotions motivating all that, how MV couldn't even sharpen his knives without remembering that stupid girl Irenne twisting in his grip, right into the knife, the stiffening of shock in her muscles half a heartbeat before his own disbelief, how there was nothing he could do to stop a major artery from gouting out her life's blood because he knew exactly where to lay the knife for the most threat but she'd been *stupid. Ignorant.*

"It was a game to you," Detlev said, because of course he was going to talk about that, and not Siamis at all. "And a game to her. But not the same game."

Definitely not the same game, but how was he supposed to know that? So he sharpened his knives twice as much, and maybe when he'd scraped away that memory life would be fun again.

"What have you learned?" Detlev said.

"That the lighter girls are stupid," MV burst out.

Detlev said, "Then you haven't learned anything after all."

As soon as the words were out MV regretted them, and there was memory: his fight with Dtheldevor, how he rarely got one that good, and his impulse to nab her, maybe turn her, but as a result she was scragged by some of Henerek's rats among the guards.

Two impulses with stupid consequences. "Shit," MV muttered.

Detlev's eyes narrowed, as if he were bringing a distant subject into focus. "It appears you could use some work on self-discipline. You might as well learn something while at it."

Here it comes. And the worst of it was, MV knew he deserved whatever was going to happen. But first, "Ferret said there are a couple of those people. Who were hidden in the mountain. Right there, in Eidervaen, with the mages."

"I know," Detlev said—unsurprisingly. "When you recover from the transfer I'm about to give you, ask for Owl."

"*Owl?*" MV then burst out, "You're letting Siamis get away with ratting us out?"

"Siamis and I will meet again," Detlev promised, as he touched MV on the arm and began the transfer spell. "Timing," he added as the world began to dissolve around MV, "is everything."

At the end of the hall, David lounged in the doorway to the critters' room, waiting for MV to come out. Laban sat on the floor with the critters, who watched with fascinated delight as Laban finished building a castle then commenced a breeching attack with some of the wooden soldiers that Leef had carved. Laban provided a range of voices, well livened with groans, and shrieks, and crashing noises as the boys giggled.

Two of the boys.

David looked around, then relaxed when he noticed Sveneric on the other side of the room, lying on his stomach, short legs sprawled out, a chalk held in one small fist, that steady hazel gaze narrowed as he tried to sketch the toy castle. The sketch was eerily good, better than David remembered Adam's being when he was twice that age, and certainly superior to anything David could make. Yet Sveneric's frequent glances back and forth, and his protruding bottom lip, revealed how disappointed he was.

The round head turned, so all David saw was feathery light brown hair, but to his eye Sveneric was so obviously related to Detlev. A weird idea, that. Until he was born, the usual pattern was the sudden appearance of a newcomer, anywhere from infant to about age four. No explanation, until the boy got old enough to ask where he'd come from. Then Detlev always told him as much as he wanted to hear, after which he could tell the others, or not.

Sveneric lifted his head, his steady gaze turned David's way. "I am now thwee," he said, his soft, high little voice precise, even though he still had trouble with some consonants.

David had been thinking of him as older for a while, and wondered if his thoughts had somehow leaked. He knew he needed to work on his coinherence skills—keyholing the mind-shield, sensing identity, and managing single-contacts. Better dream-walking. He still regretted how badly he'd stumbled in attempting to break Roy's dream boundary.

Adam, it turned out, was far better at dream-walking than any of them had had any idea; they hadn't even known when he'd made his coinherence. Like Roy. But Roy had kept his secret because he was a traitor, and Adam . . . was Adam.

"Adam," Sveneric said. "Can Adam make the people?" He pointed to his drawing.

David sighed. Looked like there were two with better coin-herence skills than he. It was time to get back to those exer-cises Detlev had given him, though when he was to do that —

The door to the office opened, and Detlev walked out alone.

"Where's MV?" David asked as Detlev entered the room.

"In the harbor at Star Island," Detlev said, then bent down to examine Sveneric's drawing.

"Wong," Sveneric stated, as David thought, isn't Star Island infested by pirates?

"Not wrong," Detlev said. "Incomplete." He reached for the dark chalk, worked it between two fingers, smudging both, dropped the chalk, then leaned over. One hand briefly cupped the back of Sveneric's head, then with his forefinger he touched the drawing, roughing a line along one side.

"Oh," Sveneric exclaimed.

"There are two ways to convey dimension, shadow and perspective. Your shadow is on this side," Detlev said. "Be-cause the sun is over there. When Laban takes you to the stable, I want you to see where the shadows lie in reference to the sun. And when you get a little older, Adam will show you perspective and reference point."

David remembered he was at least ten before Detlev had taught them perspective and reference points in their report sketches. Although Adam had seemed to know it already.

Detlev stood, and flicked his hand through the nearby cleaning frame to clean the chalk off. "David, come with me."

Neither spoke as they walked out, down the stairs, and into the cold rain. Detlev continued in silence, splash, splash, until they reached the back of the stable. The thin rain had increased, a bitter, sour wetness. Neither spoke until they stood under the windows of the boys' old rooms, now empty — they both checked mentally —

Detlev said, "Find that artifact in the shape of a flute that the two Al-Athann Valley people brought to Eidervaen's mage school. Swap it with this." He held out a flute made of some wood David didn't recognize. As his fingers closed around it, he felt that bee-feet prickle of very heavy magic. "Get it before Yeres and Efael find someone to."

David's nerves chilled. "Are either of them hunting it?"

"They will be as soon as they emerge from the Beyond and figure out that it's loose in the world. One of the artifact's attributes is that it's invisible to Norsunder-Beyond. The moment they find out about it, they'll come out hot. Get in ahead of them, covert if you can, blunder if you can't. But make sure their minions find this substitute."

"Aren't Efael and Yeres warded against entry into Eidervaen?"

"How long," Detlev said, "do you think the lighters' wards will keep them out if they are truly determined? Or their hirelings?"

"Right. Blunder. Are we still using our stupidity ruse?" David asked.

"Yes. The rest of you will run decoy. The only chatter I want to hear about you is your incompetence. Send Laban and . . . Rolfin. Leef, too. They are to argue and complain, then fail as noisily as possible. Create gossip and scorn. I'll give you a list of targets and specifics on how to fail them so that failure will set events in motion, again without drawing Yeres or Efael."

"So we're clowns." An impulse of bitterness prompted him to say, "Still."

"You are," Detlev corrected, "to look as if you still need training." David saw the *Which you do* in the humor narrowing Detlev's eyes. "Remember the long view," Detlev then said. "An appearance of competence outside of scrapping down in the yard is sure to result in, ah, let us call it recruitment coercion."

Unwanted, memories of Efael breathing, *You think you are so strong, sweetheart, so brave, so smart* into David's ear before he bit it bloody, then licked it, caused David's skin to crawl with revulsion. "Right." He breathed the word.

"That'll be your second task, to oversee these various runs. Your third task is specific: the time is coming when we're going to need to move around without being tracked. Do you recollect the enemies book made by the King of the Chwahir?"

David sighed. Didn't the King of the Chwahir have

nothing but enemies?

Then he remembered, and looked up. "Tracks the transfers of people, right?"

"Yes. It was harmless enough when it merely tracked his enemies, most of whom numbered among his own people, mages like Tsauderei, and locals he had grudges against. But Jilo has the book now, which probably means your names are in it. More to the point, when Efael does decide to release Wan-Edhe, the first thing he'll want is that book. Get it."

"So we're definitely running against Efael now?" David guessed, trying to hide the intensity of his angry joy. He'd always hated Efael, who had made it clear from their first encounter how much he despised "Detlev's babies," but now that hatred was personal. Though he was going to be very hard to beat. Maybe too hard.

Detlev said, "What's your first thought at the mention of Efael's name?"

"Stink," David said, his throat thick with disgust and loathing. "The stink of his sweat and sex."

"You're supposed to equate his name with fear, with power," Detlev said.

David spat into the mud.

"That your first thought is of his proximity during his games demonstrates that Efael is both petty and predictable. Therefore a weakness. First thought of Yeres?"

"Lies. Even her name is a lie."

"It's supposed to be ironic," Detlev said drily. "But it reveals her obsession with Dena Yeresbeth, more specifically with mind control. Efael and Yeres desire to claim an equal standing with the rest of the Host of Lords. It amuses Svirle to permit them to try, while they run all the petty errands he would prefer not to come forth to execute himself. And their antics entertain him."

Detlev so rarely talked about the Host that David forgot his animus against Efael, and was going to ask what Ilerian thought, but that was a stupid question. No one knew what Ilerian thought, only what he did. And no one wanted him to come out of the center of the Beyond, because where Ilerian went, death spread out in widening rings.

Bringing up the old question: what exactly happened between Detlev and Ilerian so long ago? And how could Ilerian have the form of a morvende, when they hadn't even gone down into their caves until well after the Fall of Ancient Sartor?

David was concentrating on his mind-shield, because Detlev did not like sloppy habits, but something must have shown in his expression, because Detlev said, "That narrative will mean little without context."

In all their years of growing up, Detlev had answered all questions except about his life before they came to live with him. David ventured a question. "When will you give us the context?"

"That'll come with experience. To the present matter: Efael is attempting to gain the Host's attention. His current plan is to retake Five. And, of course, he and Yeres are laboring to shift blame for the lack of awareness about the hidden indigenes to me."

"They didn't know, either," David exclaimed indignantly.

Detlev flicked his fingers to lower his tone. "What they fail to see is that the emergence of ancient protections such as the artifact from Five is no accident."

"So it ties in with the emergence of Dena Yeresbeth?" David asked, a new plane of thought opening up. "Which Efael and Yeres don't have."

"Yes," Detlev said.

"And so we're going to flank them by getting the artifact first."

"Correct," Detlev said, then glanced upward. "Watch change is imminent. You have your orders. I'll send your decoy target list presently. Write nothing else down."

"Done."

Detlev transferred, and David hotfooted back inside, and when the boys were alone again, with sentries posted to watch for ears, David related all that they'd said, and added in a low, triumphant tone, "I think Detlev's going for that place in the Host. At last."

"Stepping on Yeres and Efael to do it," Rolfin said.

"They've stepped on us long enough," Curtas said.

The boys dispersed, most of them sure they had the inside line of communication at last, a glimpse of the big plan. Only Adam thought something was missing, but even after he'd written all his thoughts into his journal, he still had no clue as to what.

Anyway it was time for Sveneric's drawing lesson.

Fourteen

Star Island Harbor

MV FOUND HIMSELF STANDING on an outside Destination square under a hissing deluge. The shock of sleeting rain intensified the transfer malaise, and he stumbled off the streaming tiles, peering under a hand at what appeared to be a horseshoe-shaped harbor nearly obscured by the slanting torrents.

He sloshed toward the nearest building and ducked under a low awning. The pounding shower lifted abruptly, roaring on the awning overhead. He stood there dripping as he caught his breath, his boots clean as the last of the tan-colored dust streamed in rivulets to join the water rushing down a brick quay toward the gray ocean beyond.

His tunic-jacket was thick, and had kept most of the wet out, but his pants had soaked through, and rain had dripped down his collar. The middle button on his shirt was still missing. He thrust his hands into his pockets to keep them from numbing in the cold—he could see his breath—and considered his options.

He had nothing, not even his knives. Siamis had relieved him of all his weapons before transferring him outside of Sartor. Detlev hadn't given him anything but the order to seek this Owl.

MV looked down at the smooth bricks. He could actually do anything. He could even transfer. He knew the spell, though he had to think it through, and concentrate on Destinations. Where would he go? Not back to Norsunder, if he was under orders. That left the rest of the world, and him on his own.

Punishment or test?

Both.

He'd start with this Owl. Decide from there.

He glanced along what he could see of the quay. The few people walking about leaned into the deluge, moving swiftly. Ships rode in the harbor, anchored down. Midway along the curve a big, rambling building of two, no, three stories in haphazard construction gave off a glow in its many windows. Had to be an inn, probably the main one on the harbor. There was always someone at an inn who knew what was happening, and who was making it happen.

He started toward the inn, then was nearly blown off his feet by the wind whooshing between buildings. He ducked under the low, broad eave of the inn a short time later — not short enough to keep him from becoming wet through to the skin.

He stood dripping inside the door, spotted a damp towel apparently left out for wet guests, and used it to mop his face and the worst of the drips. His clothing shifted icily at every step as he dropped the towel back on its hook and made for the enormous fireplace on the other side of the room. At least three fire sticks burned in it. A crowd of people gathered around at small tables, bent in low-voiced conversation, with occasional glances at the big windows across the front, through which could only be seen the solid gray sheets of rain, with indistinct shapes beyond. From the pungent aromas rising, they were drinking hot, hard cider, and wine spiced with cinnamon and cloves.

MV had no money, and he'd already been hungry when he and Laban had finally reached the Norsunder Base gates. The smell of braised fish and garlic potatoes caused a cavernous yawning inside him. His mouth watered as he edged up near the fireplace, where a couple of other wet standees steamed, smelling of wet wool. A woman, obviously a sailor, eyed his blue lips and his tight-armed shivering, then grunted and shifted over half a step.

MV moved in toward the fire, relishing the heat on one side. He shut his eyes and thought it through. As if there was really any choice. No, there was always a choice. What did he want? He'd never considered that. Life was fun, especially when they had a run. Detlev would give them better runs as they gained better skills. And—?

MV turned to toast his other side, which gave him better access to the room. Judging from the frequent glances at those windows, the talkers appeared to be waiting out the storm as they nursed those drinks. What activity there was centered around a spare red-haired man on the other side of the room, who sat with a tall girl, while a half-circle of watchers waited a few paces away.

The girl got up, smiling, and went off in one direction, then the next in the half-circle sat on her chair. That was an interview. MV's gaze transferred to the man's face. This had to be Owl.

When MV's clothes were bearably damp, he made his way to the end of the line. A grizzled man glanced back at him. "Is he Owl?" MV asked.

A grunt of assent, and the man turned a thick, hairy neck and shoulders like barrels to MV. When MV got within earshot, he heard Dock Talk—no surprise—as red-haired Owl asked, "Name? Can ye hand, reef, steer?" Owl was recruiting for sailors! MV grinned at the thick, hairy neck in front of him. He loved sailing, and had missed it badly ever since they left Geth-deles. MV couldn't hear the mumbled answer, then Owl said, "Have ye had weapons training?"

MV's interest sharpened. Was Owl a pirate? Detlev had never expressed anything but contempt for pirates. Another test, oh yes. Some were sent one way, others another. Barrel Shoulders lumbered away cursing, which meant it was MV's turn at last.

Owl beckoned wearily, and sighed with relief when he saw no one behind MV. "Last one, good," the man said. "I'm a watch overdue for my grub. So. Ye ever sailed?"

"Yes."

"Where?"

MV had thought out his story. If you didn't want questions veering off into territory that would either lead to a complication of lies or trouble, you answered as vaguely as possible, in hopes they formed their own ideas on the details. "Islands," he said, with a wave of his hand. He figured there had to be islands lying somewhere in every direction.

Owl gave a short nod. "Name? Hand, reef, steer?"

MV said, "MV. I can haul ropes. Raise sail. I'm used to two-man skimmers among the islands." He'd figured small boats had to look like small boats whatever world you were on.

"Good enough. Some don't know that much. What about weapons training." He leaned forward, eyes narrowing as he took in MV's bruises. "You a troublemaker?" His tone had shifted to suspicion.

MV felt himself at another of those crossroads. A smart answer would probably get him sent after Barrel Shoulders. And then what? Detlev wanted him here. Best to figure out why. "Training accident," MV said, touching the biggest bruise along his cheekbone, and anticipating the next question, "Which is why I'm here looking for work."

And watched Owl draw his own conclusions about a mythical brutal taskmaster: his brow furrowed, then shot upward in decision. "Well, the truth is, we're badly in need of crew. We lost many to injuries in that dust-up—" He nicked his head behind him at the harbor, still obscured by rain. "And the captain's planning something bigger."

Dust-up?

"Get some food into ye. Soon as this lifts, ye'll get to work with the other new hires. We'll make a final decision before we sail." And when MV didn't move, he said, "What, no money?"

MV spread his hands.

Owl snorted a laugh. "Join those three over there. I'll talk to the innkeeper." He indicated a table near the fire.

MV walked over and slid into one of the empty chairs. He was the youngest, he saw at once, but not by much. The others looked at him, then looked away, and continued their conversation.

"I heard he took the *Zathdar* with only two mates. Two," the oldest of them, a weather-seamed sailor with a long, grizzled gray braid said, leaning forward with two blunt fingers held up, as if the listeners needed the extra help in comprehending "two."

Zathdar was Sartoran for *thunderstorm*, MV translated to

himself.

The light-haired girl, who appeared to be about seventeen, said, "After eyeballin' them hulks out there, you get no argument from me."

The third, darker of skin and hair than Leef and Rolfin, sat back, spiced wine held in both hands. He looked maybe twenty. "What I heard was, they took a sizable treasure off 'em."

"That's what I heard, too," Grizzle said.

"Everybody's talkin' about that treasure, but I ain't seen no sight of it. Zathdar, when I seen him, his duds're older than I am, looked like."

MV bit back the instinct to ask questions. They were ignoring him and talking freely, which was the easiest way to gather information. He glanced to the side, aware of the light changing, and discovered that the storm was moving out fast, as hard storms usually do, leaving a clear view through the windows of a startling sight: the three closest ships, all narrow-built, rake-masted schooners, showed extensive fire damage from masts to hulls.

And now he understood the urgent tone of the conversation, the wide glances at the windows. This was after-action exhilaration. In the last day or so, a fairly hot fight had taken place here. Pirates against pirates? Nobody had mentioned cargo, whereas he'd heard the word treasure.

As MV watched, parties of sailors were already plying boats through the choppy waters toward the ships. They had to be repair parties. He wondered if Detlev was sending him to survive among pirates. He'd already survived Efael and his Black Knives. Mere pirates? Eh.

By the time loaded plates of braised fish, garlic potatoes, and buttered cabbage were plunked down in front of each of them, he discovered that some especially hated pirates had taken the harbor the previous summer, and had been trying to grab the entire island. Those not involved in the fighting had run for the hills, which included several of the hires. The winners included Owl, who was first mate for Captain Zathdar—which also seemed to be the name of his ship.

They'd mopped the last of their food with fresh biscuits when Owl appeared and said, "The four o'ye get down to the quay in front. Ye're now larboard watch waisters on the *Jumping Bug*, under Second Mate Tuzsin."

When they got to the *Jumping Bug*, Tuzsin, a tough-looking woman of forty or so, promptly ordered them into grueling work. Sometime between his being part of a rope-hauling line and swinging outside the hull to scrape charring from bulkheads, MV discovered they'd set sail.

When at last Tuzsin bawled, "All hands for'ard!" MV looked around to find out what that meant, and discovered everyone gratefully finishing up whatever they were doing. They stowed tools and line, the latter neatly flemished, and reported to the foredeck, where they stared at a rowboat approaching.

Seated in the sternsheets was what appeared to be a clown, or a traveling player. In the waning light, the fellow's purple shirt was still bright under a long green vest, worn over red and white striped sailors' trousers, tied with a yellow sash. As he approached with his rowers, MV, standing tiredly at the rail, saw a face maybe Siamis's age, or a year or two younger. His head was tied in a bright red bandana, from which a hank of dun hair straggled.

He might have looked like a clown, but the way he vaulted up the side of the ship wasn't clownish, nor the way he glanced fore and aft, then upward — while everyone waited, noise dying away.

"Looks good," he said finally, and a cheer beat the air, sending sea birds squawking. Then, "To you newcomers, I'm Zathdar. As you know, we recently cleared out Star Island Harbor."

Another cheer.

Zathdar flashed a grin. MV spotted the extra bulk of bandaging under the flowing sleeves, and around one knee in those striped pants. "The harbormaster promises we can use the harbor as home if we keep the pirates on the hop, and I intend to do just that."

And they cheered again.

So this Zathdar preyed on other pirates, then.

"You newcomers probably heard what the shares were for all hands after our brush with 'em. Word is, there's more of 'em along the Chwahir coast, setting up to drop on anyone coming down the strait. Including an enterprising band out of Ghanthur, where they seem to grow pirates like the hull grows barnacles. Let's give them a hot time, shall we?"

An even more enthusiastic cheer this time preceded his

saying, "Then morning watch, we'll see how you handle yourselves, hand to hand and then working the ship. We'll return to harbor to finish loading supplies, then sail north on the morning tide."

Star Island Harbor, MV thought, mentally considering the map he'd had to draw so many times, Siamis saying, "You'll discover that when you need a map most, there won't be one to hand." If MV remembered his archipelagos right, he'd ended up not very far from Geranda, where he'd been born.

He had no intention of telling anyone that. As far as Geranda was concerned, he'd croaked years ago, after Detlev winkled him out of slavery—complete with iron collar—in the stable, where he'd found himself after political infighting among his elders. He'd been four years old at the time.

He half-wished he'd made up a name, but the initials MV could stand for anything. No one needed to know about the Gerandan preoccupation with the Venn, their ancestors; in Geranda, Mal Venn was a pompous name, assuming a straight line from some king or other, which probably wasn't even true.

Being the youngest on his watch, he found himself thoroughly ignored that first evening, as they crowded down below for their first mess—a thick pepper soup with fish and onion—and then were told they'd get six hours in their hammocks until the watch change. The other crew got to do the loading.

The next day, they departed on the morning tide, tacking against fitful, cold winds, but Owl kept them warm by making them drill laying aloft, reefing and sheeting home over and over again, as Zathdar flashed signal flags from his ship, where the sailors could be seen scrambling up the lines to the yards, and then down again to haul the big sails up and down. Once MV learned where to put feet and hands, and how to lean into the lines against the sway and pitch of the ship, exhilaration burned through him. This was a thousand times better than those two-person skimmers on Geth!

From listening to the chatter around him, he gathered that they would all either fight or sail the ship, depending on their watch, but the best of them would be reserved for defenders.

After a sweaty, muscle wringing morning at ship drill, they ate a big meal of cornbread slathered with leftover soup, then both watches gathered for weapons drill and hand to hand combat. Zathdar rowed back for this, and he and Owl set the pace by a sword fight, cutlass against what MV recognized as a cavalry blade.

MV hunkered on the weather deck, watching intently. He was sure he recognized Zathdar's fighting style as Marloven; Detlev had forbidden the boys to interfere with Marloven Hess, but MV and David had executed a sneak the summer after their arrival back on Sartorias-deles, riding into the capital in the wake of a big jarl party to join the audience watching the Marloven academy games, after which they'd ridden out again, no one the wiser. They'd been incorporating what they'd seen into running their own drills ever since.

Zathdar and Owl pulled up their blades with a mutual salute, making it plain they'd been setting a standard. They began pitting the sailors against each other, first in hand to hand, no weapons. MV watched with intense interest. Most were adequate at best, and he recognized a couple different styles, but so far, Zathdar was the only one whose fighting style appeared to have been shaped by the Marlovens.

At last MV was beckoned up, and paired with someone more or less his size and stature. Three strikes and he had the boy down flat, a hand at his neck. MV grinned, ignoring some side-eye from new and old recruits alike. This was fun!

Owl said, "Pick a weapon."

MV preferred double-knife fighting to any other form. He grabbed up a couple of battered wooden blades, not all that different from the ones Siamis had started the boys on long ago.

Owl also picked up two knives, but three exchanges in, he said, "When were you at the Marloven academy?"

"Wasn't," MV said.

Owl's interested gaze narrowed to wariness. "Who taught you that style?"

MV had been about to claim that he'd learned it at the Khanerenth academy, but just in time he recognized Owl's familiar accent. Khanerenth! MV knew very well the style taught at their academy, which was mainly brute strikes, depending on numbers for effect. MV said, "Swordmaster southeast of Marloven Hess." He didn't say *how* far southeast, Norsunder Base being one continent over from Halia. He let the implication suggest itself: someone Marloven-trained in one of those kingdoms that used to belong to the Marloven empire.

Owl's brow cleared, and MV suspected that he was no longer regarded as a renegade Marloven. "Let's see how you do with a boarding blade."

MV chose a lighter cutlass, sturdy but not heavy enough to ruin his speed, and he and Owl set to. He could feel immediately that his training was better than Owl's, but the man had both strength and experience on MV: his blocks and blows were the basics, but hard and fast. They ended in a draw, MV horking for breath, his entire body wringing with sweat.

Zathdar had been busy testing other hands, but watched now as he wiped his brow.

Owl said, "I thought he was a Marloven."

"That," Zathdar said from where he leaned against the rail, "is not Marloven style."

MV shrugged, then wheezed, "Swordmaster never talked about his past."

Zathdar had already turned away; he leaped over the side into the boat and began rowing back to his flagship. Owl clearly accepted MV's finesse, as he'd hoped. Everyone knew how bad Marloven history had been in the past couple decades, under the old Regent. Of course some had run over the border.

Owl said, "Whatever that style is, it's very, very good."

MV put the cutlass back in the rack, grateful not to have to make up some lie that he'd have to remember. He truly had no idea where Detlev and Siamis had gotten their training. Even Noser hadn't been able to wheedle or whine them into talking about their past.

"MV, want to fight some pirates?"

"Sure."

"We'll put you in the defenders on the *Mulekick*." Owl jerked his thumb over the far rail, at a ship floating a cable's length away. "You have a problem with that?" Owl asked, his eyes narrowing.

MV wondered what the man had seen in his face. "It's just, I want to learn how to navigate one of these big ships."

Owl laughed. "Oh, you'll learn plenty. Every watch works the ship. But when we have to attack or defend, you'll be right out front."

MV shrugged. "Sounds fair to me."

Fifteen

Dyavath Yan (New Year's Week) 4749
Sartor

THROUGHOUT SARTORIAS-DELES, NEW Year's Week is actually eight days long, which gets the moon cycle realigned for the fresh year, and permits each year to begin on the first day of the week.

In most southern countries, the initial days of New Year's Week are given over to traditions and rituals — Oath Day, Debt Day, Tax Day, and so forth — and, as Senrid, king of huge, troublesome Marloven Hess once remarked to Leander, king of the tiny country next door (and mostly free of problems — if you discounted Marloven Hess on its border), the last part of the week is for recovery from those first few days.

For everyone else, the remainder of New Year's Week is observed as time for family and relaxation, and to brace for the rest of winter. Except in the most stringent households, this time off includes service personnel: much of the preceding weeks, for example, have been spent in preparing food that needs only warming in the winter-bound south; servants go home on New Year's Firstday (or the last day of the year) and the rest of the week, people of whatever rank mostly shift for themselves.

Once the ritual days were observed in Sarendan, the nobles were expected to retire to their estates to celebrate with their people. By Fifthday, Peitar granted the entire staff of the royal palace time to go home to their families, leaving the place nearly empty, to be enjoyed by a skeleton crew with even more freedom than usual.

Peitar and Lilah had begun a tradition of retreating up to the Delfina Valley where Tsauderei lived, to spend the rest of the festival week in the old family retreat. In this way, they both escaped the tyranny of a battalion of aging great-aunts still determined to scold Peitar into advantageous marriage, and Lilah into releasing the Child Spell so that she could be scolded into advantageous marriage. But this year, Lilah was thrilled to discover, they were going to Sartor to visit.

Peitar transferred first, then little Prince Darian—known to everyone as Ian—then Lilah. Safely arrived between his father and auntie, Ian seemed to recover first, looking about him with wide eyes. Lilah wondered if he felt the weight of all that history in his Dena Yeresbeth, then scolded herself. Ian was *two*.

She skipped along behind the gliding servant in soft green, holding one of Ian's hands, Peitar holding the other. Lilah was so used to her brother's silences when they were anywhere outside of their own private rooms that it never occurred to her to notice the tension in his stillness.

Peitar had long since schooled himself against any expectations with regard to Atan. The pain had slowly begun to fade, for which he was grateful: they both were shackled by the expectations of their ranks. Neither would leave their home kingdom.

Still, though Lilah drew in a breath of sheer pleasure at the beauty of the white and gold reception hall, with its tall trees under domed glass ceilings, they could have been in a barn for all the notice Peitar paid. His attention arrowed straight to Atan. Who had clearly released the Child Spell. He tried not to stare at the magnificent young woman she had become, and in forcing his attention away, his gaze then shot to the person who otherwise dominated the room, merely because of his size: Rel.

Without a trace of self-consciousness—with a smile that made it clear how much she expected Peitar to be surprised and pleased—Atan exclaimed, "I'm so glad you came! And here is Rel!"

"Rel! You're here!" Lilah said cheerfully. "I thought you were still on the other side of the world."

"I was, but now I'm not," Rel said, grinning, and dropped down on one knee so that Lilah could introduce him to Ian.

The little boy gazed up at Rel with solemn eyes, then hid his face against Lilah's leg. Rel guessed that his size intimidated Ian, and quietly moved back.

Lilah gasped. "There's Hinder! And he brought Sinder! I haven't seen her for ages!" Lilah left Ian to Peitar and skipped to the other side of the room, where two slim white-haired morvende stood with a teenage, brown-haired girl, the three admiring the indoor tree.

Someone with more humor than heart might have been amused by the similarities and differences between the Queen of Sartor's two suitors standing there together, Peitar not sure how to gracefully withdraw as his son clutched at his legs, keeping him still.

Both Peitar and Rel were tall, dark of hair and eye, Peitar being slender, with the slight hitch in his walk that remained after years of healer spells and patient and painful work retraining muscles, Rel taller and broader, especially through the chest. Peitar gazed out at the world under winged brows, the lines of a lifetime of endured pain etched in his face making him look older than his years. Rel's strong bones and deep-set eyes also made him seem older than he was. The close observer might notice a similarity in habitually mild expressions, for Peitar was passionate about peace, and Rel, though trained in the arts of war, much preferred getting along with his fellow being.

In a further twist of irony, had Atan's council any inkling of Peitar's feelings, they would be clamoring ceaselessly for a state marriage, for of course Sartor would dominate Sarendan if the kingdoms were to be combined—whereas the sooner Rel left, the better, as far as the more ambitious were concerned.

Atan—as yet unaware of either's desires—smiled at her two oldest friends, then knelt and tried to coax a smile from Ian. Across the room, Lilah's voice rose. "Hinder! Your talons are gold!"

Hinder stuck a bare foot out and wiggled his toes, on which the talons were freshly painted. "Handsome, aren't they? Match my eyes."

Lilah didn't think they matched his eyes at all, which were a light brown closer to amber in his pale face under cobwebby white hair, but taking people as they wanted to be taken was one of the reasons she was liked everywhere.

"They're beautiful! It's so good to see you! It's been much too long. Seems like ten years instead of . . . two? And you? You are . . . familiar," Lilah said, shifting her gaze to the brown-haired girl a little taller than she, with those distinctive droopy eyes like Atan's. She had not dressed in her best, like everyone else. She wore forester garb—a tunic and sturdy woolen trousers. "Oh, wait. Julian?" Lilah asked.

"I remember you," Julian said, grinning. "You were with us when we freed Sartor."

"I don't think I've seen you since Geth," Lilah said slowly, remembering how Julian had followed Siamis around for a time.

Julian paused to take a glance at the rest of the company, whose attention was safely on each other. "I mostly live in Shendoral Forest," Julian said to Lilah. "Atan promised if I learned to read and write I don't have to be a princess, or do any state stuff. I mostly stay with the foresters, guarding Shendoral."

A bright smile lit Lilah's freckled face. "Are Rip and the Poisoners still there?"

"Yes they are. Still experimenting with their cookery. You should come back with me for a visit."

"In winter?" Lilah wrinkled her nose.

"This is Shendoral," Julian reminded her.

"Oh, yeah. Time is weird there." Lilah was seized by a longing for summer, which might even be possible in the forest's depths. "Yes, I'm definitely coming." And, her mind rushing on, "I bet the other Sharadan Brothers would enjoy it, too, and I could bring Ian, maybe. When he gets a bit older," she amended, with a glance Peitar's way. "Maybe when Deon gets back."

Julian asked, "Sharadan Brothers? Deon? Isn't that usually a girl's name?"

"We pretended to be brothers. In disguise. We were spies, during the revolution. Against my horrid uncle." Lilah's voice dropped on the word "horrid" and she sent another anxious glance toward Peitar.

Lilah was not ordinarily vindictive or grudge-holding, but her uncle, then King Darian Irad, had been the chief terror of her early life, and that impression had worsened during the revolution, when the king had tried to force his disintegrating kingdom back into order.

"Spies? Why do I not know this story?" Julian asked, plopping elbows onto knees, as from the other side of the room, Atan watched with a sense of relief as she crossed the room to greet a trio of nobles just arrived.

Julian still bore the emotional damage from the days of war and then enchantment more than a hundred years ago, when her ruthless mother had cruelly attempted to use little Julian against her royal cousins. Julian preferred to live in the forest watched over by the indigenous Loi, whose magic made the forest into an anomaly both dangerous and utterly safe.

"Oh, yes," Lilah was saying. "Kids make the best spies, because who pays any attention to us?" Lilah's freckled hand took in herself, Hinder, Sinder, and Julian. "Anyway, Deon sails with Dtheldevor's crew, having adventures."

Julian's jaw dropped. "Dtheldevor? Really? Can anyone join?"

"Oh, yes. Dtheldevor has an island hideout, where lots of kids on the Wander stop. Some sail with her, and some don't. Some stay, some move on. Deon loves it so much I think she's pretty much left us." Lilah heaved a comfortable sigh. "But she does sometimes come back to visit, if Dtheldevor is having the ship repaired."

Shipboard travel, without adults! That was *exactly* what Julian had been craving — and far, far away from boring Sartor with all its stultifying, smothering traditions. While Julian and Lilah quickly cemented their friendship, and Atan was called away by one of her courtiers, Rel asked Peitar how Derek's brother Bernal was doing. Rel was a traveler, not a courtier, and Peitar reflected that Rel — unlike courtiers — would not ask for political or social reasons, but because he wanted to hear the answer.

"He's gone north to raise horses," Peitar said. "Too many people tried to pressure him into politics, which he never wanted."

"Good." Rel's deep-set eyes crinkled and his chin, chiseled in the heroic mold, lifted in honest pleasure. As Rel went on to describe his discussions of horse breeds with Bernal, Peitar thought: Rel the Traveler. Friend to kings and commoners alike. A new idea bloomed. Rel was in so many respects the perfect person to ask. "Rel, have you ever heard of vagabond magic?"

"A little," Rel said, glancing upward and frowning — though he recollected people and places, he rarely listened to talk about magic, a subject on which he was completely ignorant. "Something about Geth?"

Peitar said, "If *you* haven't, then regard me as completely confused about the claim that this is magic for travelers. 'Vagabond.' How would magic differentiate?"

Rel's thick brows lifted over his deep-set, dark eyes. "I thought magic was inert, like water, or stone. It has . . . thought?"

"I doubt it, but I've been wrong before. Have you ever had any interest in learning magic?"

"I'm willing to learn anything I can turn my hand to." Rel lifted a massive shoulder. "But I assumed magic was something one must begin at an early age. I thought I'd be much too old. And I was never very good at sitting still at a desk." The strong planes of his face shifted as he flashed a grin.

"Would you be willing to travel to Geth as an experiment, and report back what you learn?"

Peitar's impulse was primarily because he knew Rel's report could be trusted, but he was aware of a despicable wish to get him away from Sartor, and Atan.

While he struggled internally with awareness of mixed motives, Rel glanced across the room at Atan, smiling and talking to an ambassador and a duchas, her coronet gleaming in the light of the floating glowglobes overhead, her silver gown shimmering. Leaving Sartor for a time might be a good thing.

They currently saw each other often, as he enjoyed coming to the palace as guard liaison — but they both knew the formality and brevity of their visits a sop to the watchers in Sartor's court who wished to see each of them keep their respective places.

That conflict was merely irritating. He could ignore it. Less easy to ignore was the fact that he didn't know what his place really was; he still had not come to terms with his own origins. And so he had not told Atan about his mother. Even thinking about that, and about how much he longed for Atan to reach for him as more than a friend, sparked the old restless yearning to be on the road.

Peitar's question gave him a perfect excuse. "Certainly," Rel said readily. "It sounds interesting."

And that's why Rel is liked wherever he goes, Peitar thought.

Atan approached with tall, gaunt Tsauderei leaning heavily on a cane.

Peitar said, "You survived your diplomatic guest?"

Atan's lips thinned, then she looked guiltily around as she led the way to a grouping of cushioned curule chairs carved with acanthus and wheat motifs, set against a tall window overlooking the frost-touched palace garden glowing in the moonlight. "We survived."

"As did Siamis." Tsauderei sank down with a grunt, followed by a hiss of breath and a grimace. Another winter to live through.

"What do you mean?" Aware of angry exhilaration, Peitar asked, "There were attempts on his life, then?"

"One obvious one, the day he left." Atan lowered her voice. "Otherwise, Rel and the guards tried to make certain there would be no violence."

"And failed," Rel observed, crossing powerful arms as he sat back. Rel had always been big, but now the lamplight along the strong line of his jaw caught the contours of skin subtly stippled by the beard spell.

Peitar stared, recognizing that Rel had lifted the Child Spell as well as Atan.

"*Not* your fault!" Atan whispered, hands on her hips as she turned to Rel, then back to Peitar. "Tsauderei felt obliged to lay magical wards and protections." Atan indicated the mage.

"Though his were far superior," Tsauderei said. "And I noted he never entered a room without using a tracer rather more powerful than any I've ever constructed."

Peitar's hand tightened on Derek's shirt button in his pocket. "There really was a different kind of magic during the days of Ancient Sartor? That isn't the hyperbole of old records?"

"I still don't know that," Tsauderei said. "Lilith isn't talking, and Siamis was a child. His future was not magic, but government—or what passed for government in those days—

and what he learned in Norsunder was the dark magic we fight against every day."

"Has he talked about his governmental training?" Peitar asked skeptically, wondering if Siamis had been measuring himself for a crown—Sartor's crown.

"No. He says there's no use, as circumstances are so very different now. Lilith actually corroborated most of what he said, or I wouldn't waste the breath repeating his words."

"Example?" Peitar asked, glancing under the table, where Ian had begun playing with an exploring kitten.

"For example, they both attested to the fact that there were no geographic boundaries the way we regard them, no notion of kingdom loyalty, and the word 'treason' was unknown. The monarch of Ancient Sartor was entirely symbolic, a little like the sort of symbolic kingship of Bereth Ferian nowadays. Real power the way we understand it now was balanced between rituals and local interests. Therefore his training would mostly be in ritual."

"It's that way in records," Atan said, leaning forward, elbows on her brocade-covered knees. She sat exactly as she had when she sat up in the hermit's cottage in Delfina Valley, wearing castoff shirt and trousers, talking enthusiastically of magic and history. "I found a really old one, barely legible. Lilith was interviewed by a mage guild Chief centuries ago. And when she was asked about the Old Magic, she said that it was nearly destroyed in the Fall, and was so different there is no reference point."

Peitar said, "I've been learning that Geth has a different magic system than ours. But while their records go back to the days after the Fall, when some of our ancestors fled there, they wrote nothing down. It was their progeny, after they'd mixed with world-gate travelers, who wrote down their ancestors' histories in what amounts to story form."

Tsauderei stroked the braided mustache folding into his snowy beard. "Yes. Larger than life figures. One pure evil, one pure good, the most beneficent being Charlotte, who purportedly started that old library at Isul Demarzal. That is, she was apparently a real person, though I doubt that she was all that wise, good, and powerful, or she might have exerted that power to squash the evil one on sight."

They all laughed, then Atan exclaimed, "It isn't until you read history that you understand how much of our lives are expressed in metaphor. And when the context is lost, the metaphor becomes obscure."

"Poetic," Tsauderei said, wiggling his brows.

"Another word for obscure," Peitar said.

"Well, I can promise you one delight who is anything but obscure, Peitar," Atan said as a distant bell bonged musically. "I think you'll enjoy talking to Leotay."

"When do we meet?" Peitar asked, as he bent to retrieve his son.

"Tomorrow. Maybe late, depending on the incoming snowstorm," Tsauderei said. "We thought it better to let them accept an invitation one of the senior students extended to celebrate New Year's Firstdays with her family. But the seniors always return by Sixthday, so that the instructors can plan the winter classes."

"Let's go in to dinner." Atan rose as the double doors opened, and Peitar noted that Rel went to Tsauderei's elbow, not to Atan's.

Atan and Rel might have passed over the threshold of adulthood, but the subtle signs of lovers—the glances, the secret smiles, the touches and angled bodies toward the other—were notably absent. Atan moved as she always had, with a brisk, unselfconscious ease. Atan's smiles in Rel's direction could be those for a brother.

". . . and after we eat," Atan was saying, "we've a play I think you'll like. Julian chose it, and tomorrow morning, if it's clear, I can keep that promise I made to you at least two years ago, to take you to the Purad . . ."

Sixteen

THE NEXT MORNING, PEITAR met Atan at dawn. His motivation was mixed, partly to spend time with Atan alone — though he knew that nothing whatsoever would come of it — partly out of historical interest, and partly to keep a promise he'd made a long time ago.

He would finally see a real Sartoran labyrinth, as opposed to the ordered and clipped gardens some of the older estates in Sarendan boasted, claiming they were modeled on the Sartoran plan. He was expecting a geometric, aseptically pristine garden laid out in a hexagon, or some such pattern, and from a distance the thing looked pretty much as expected, dominated by a lot of trees of varying heights, the deep green of pine marking a border of a kind.

As they paced alongside a wall to the older side of the sprawling palace, they talked about the play — an old favorite about Jaja the Pirate Queen out-foxing a snotty Colendi king — until the ancient path opened to the tree-sheltered Purad. It was larger than he'd thought it would be, apparently comprised of loops. Its start and finish were marked off by smooth pebbles.

"You begin with the right-hand path," Atan said. "Or, I suppose you could go left. It's just that I was taught to always go right." She extended a hand for him to precede her.

Peitar set determinedly out, wishing he'd brought a cloak. He'd thought it would be a matter of marching around in a small circle, and so had worn only a winter tunic over his heavy trousers and walking shoes. He trod the first loop, self-conscious at first, aware of the crunch of his steps on the little stones smoothed on the path. Aware of his breathing. He wondered what he was expected to see when the space was open to view, no surprises hidden among the ancient silver-barked trees, now winter-bare.

Halfway around the circle he saw that the Purad encompassed four groups of triple loops — called leaves — the outward shape a little like clover-leaves, twelve altogether. He found himself wishing as he finished treading the first leaf that twelve had not had such importance to their ancestors, or that the builders of these things could as well have stayed with four, or three rather than their multiple, but perhaps they'd had more free time for the luxuries of contemplation.

As his footsteps closed off that first leaf, he sneaked a glance back for Atan. He'd thought she followed in expectation of his reaction, but he was alone. One walked this thing in solitude? Yes, that matched what he remembered from records. The exception being ring-marriages, for life: it had been a fashion for a time for each partner to walk half the Purad, and exchange rings when they met at center. Music and spoken words along the way optional. In other centuries they walked all twelve together, sometimes exchanging poetry or vows at each point, other times in silence.

At least alone he need not think out polite praises that didn't sound too trite, too false, for something that she found so meaningful. Instead, he contemplated the truth: how Sartor, and Sartoran history, seemed an ever-widening divide between them, culturally, historically, in time as well as place. Emotionally, ever since Atan found it proper to accept the villain Siamis as a diplomatic gesture of peace. Why not accept all of Norsunder, then?

No, that was mere spite. He forced himself to breathe out, and he even turned around and walked back to the beginning of the first leaf to begin again. He must not walk this thing in anger, seeing himself as wronged. The pain was personal to him — and to Sarendan — not to the rest of the world, who probably did not know, or care, that Siamis had murdered Derek Diamagan, Peitar's oldest friend and most ardent supporter through the soul-sickening days of the revolution . . .

A revolution Derek had begun in a gesture of desperation and anger.

Peitar had to acknowledge that anger, because here it was welling up again. For the fourth time he retreated to the start, and set out firmly. These labyrinths were supposed to be places of peace and meditation. If he could not contain his anger, he might as well give up the whole thing, tell Atan he had done it, and say whatever she expected him to say.

But he would try once last time. He took a step, his foot squeaking on the light covering of snow. He breathed in the pine-scented air, and took another step, working to empty his mind. He contemplated the snow-crowned trees so still and silent to either side, arching their branches overhead, and let his mind wander to the upward reach of wedding arches, and of window arches in trefoil, ogee, lancet, reverse ogee and inflex — each leading the eye upward, toward sky, sun, and stars.

Today those winter-bare fingers lifted toward the pale blue serenity of a cloudless sky. No, not fingers. He would not sully the trees by seeing them as human. He must see them as they were, a pleached geometry, natural beauty. Each subtle turn changed the view, enhanced by shadow and sun and the textured pattern of stone underfoot. What would be the sounds and smells, the feel, the colors at the height of summer, trees in full leaf, or in spring, full flower? How about the brilliant colors in golden light, the smell of old leaves on cool autumn winds?

Turn and turn, and he discovered he had finished all three loops within the first leaf. He'd read once that sometimes there were four loops within three leaves, and wondered if there was a hidden meaning to the different division.

His breathing matched the rhythm of his steps. He sorted the scents: cedar, a hint of water in the cold air; a lingering of herbs, and flowers.

As he set out to assay the second leaf's second loop, he smiled at the pattern of tree roots rippling a subtle tracery beneath the smooth pebbled path, the stubble of herbs and flowers slumbering beneath the soil until the sun returned from the north, and the crunch of his own steps, now a rhythm counterpoint to his heart, his breath. A sudden, absurd urge to hop, to leap, even to dance seized him and he was surprised, for he had never before felt any such impulse: for so much of his life, walking meant enduring inescapable pain.

The pain that never completely left even in sleep was still there, but faint, a reminder only, a twinge in hip and knee as he walked. He satisfied himself by swinging his arms, and finally, at the midpoint—between the second and third leaves—he paused and bounced on his toes, laughing softly, then watched in pleasure as his breath clouded and began to fall in countless tiny pinpoints of light.

Air—sound—the feel of the pebbles beneath his feet—the twelves of trees, for he knew instinctively without counting that here were twelve twelves, young and old. Who planted them, who tended them? Who placed the pebbles, hands recent or long gone? Perhaps put down by other kings, who could come here and be only human. *As we all are, as we truly are. Kingship is no more than shared delusion.*

He had nearly completed the first loop within the third leaf. By now the ever-changing subtleties of trees and sky had woven a boundary around him, enclosing him in peace and harmony, setting his mind free to wander its own paths, doubling back through present and memory, and venturing into an infinitude of possible futures. But each time he found a path leading toward anger he pivoted in thought as his feet pivoted on the pebbles, and there expanded in him the heady sense that he had begun climbing to a height where the air was clearer, purer, sharper, granting a wider vista.

And when his feet began the last leaf, they climbed the pattern they had learned while his mind soared into the heights, peering beyond the horizon to the shimmer of clouds, and beyond those, as he reached for the sound of singing—no, of instruments uncounted, all playing a chord of complexity and perfect harmony.

He climbed until he could climb no more, and perched on that pinnacle in perfect balance as he strained to reach that distant, faint music, so sweet, so beckoning . . .

Until urgent, unmusical, insistent, a voice intruded, and he tumbled from the heights—

And gasped, and staggered, and looked around, dizzy, bewildered, his thoughts squashed remorselessly back within the confines of his skull as he gazed without recognition into a pair of droopy eyes under a puckered high forehead.

"Peitar?"

"Atan," he murmured, astonished at having almost not recognized her. His voice seemed to come from someone else, and he coughed and wrung his hands, to discover they tingled unpleasantly. He shivered, aware that the light had gone, shadows melding into the blue of sunset, and it was very cold.

"Peitar, you've been here all day," Atan said. "We thought you had transferred home, or gone away."

Peitar looked around, and found himself not five paces from the starting point.

He clawed his numb hands up his face, and blinked. "All day? I . . . I hadn't realized. I'm sorry."

"Why should you apologize? Come in and drink something warm," Atan said pleasantly, though privately concerned at the paleness of his face.

He'd been gone all day, everyone assuming he was either at the archive, or the mage guild, or the Tower of Knowledge—places they expected him to want to tour—until one of the servants reported up the chain having discovered him standing near the Purad finish point, completely motionless, staring upward. All had refused to go near him.

They said he had a ghost-light around him, Gehlei had reported to Atan in private, with the bluntness of the guardian—though in front of anyone else, she was a stickler for protocol. *We don't know if that's bad or good, but in any case, he's a foreign king, and your guest, and no one else dares walk it until he moves. So it's better if you go out there and make certain he doesn't freeze, for it's not been what anyone would call a warm day, but it's getting colder now the sun is going down.*

Atan said aloud, "So . . . did you enjoy the Purad?"

"What was that music?" Peitar asked, blinking. Atan seemed to be blurred. No, not blurred, but a faint greenish light reflected off her. He tried to blink it away.

"Music?" Atan repeated, wondering if someone had been playing somewhere outside the walls on the Great Chandos Way. But that would have had to be fairly loud.

"You don't hear music when you climb?" He wound his hand in a circle.

"Climb?" she repeated, her puzzlement vanishing. Of course he was speaking metaphorically.

He glanced backward at those flat paths neatly inscribing their circles, his perception wheeling. He drew in a deep breath to steady himself, aware of the thud of their steps on the cobblestones, so different from the crunch of those pebbles, the rustle of his clothes against his flesh. Distant sounds: the rattle of wheels as little goat-pulled chariots bowled along the stone street, the unmusical cheer of a conversation whose words were too blurred to make out, but Peitar sensed their laughter as a mixture of gold and peach glow at the side of his awareness.

His skin hurt. Sounds, touch, even the lights all pained him. He cleared his throat again. "How old is it?" he asked.

"It?" Atan repeated as a footman opened the north-side palace door for them. "Do you mean Rive Dian?" The name came out quick, habitual, blurred as these oval-worn steps underfoot.

Rive Dian—was it Riveh Dian, or Rivay Dian, what was the name originally—no, he could figure out the roots—His mind raced from thought to thought, then crashed when he caught up with the sense of her question. "Not this palace," he said. "The . . . labyrinth." How could such a mundane word, that evoked curved hedgerows and children's games on nobles' estates, compass what had happened to him?

"Oh. Like the Tower of Knowledge, it goes way, way back. You could say Rive Dian grew up around and between them both." Her voice was cheerful, calm, the same voice he'd known, but for the first time in years he heard it merely as a voice, and saw her as a young woman barely out of girlhood in spite of her height and breadth through shoulder and hip, her cheeks still round, her brow clear of any lines. Her broad, blunt-fingered hands smooth. She was still surrounded by faint light, which he found distracting.

He cleared his throat again. "You told me you go there every day. Is it always the same?"

"It's never quite the same," she said obligingly. "The light is different, depending on the weather, and the time of year, and of course in spring and autumn various things are in bloom."

"But the sense of walking up steep stairs—the music—"

"Music?" she repeated, and her straight dark brows snapped together. "That area is supposed to be quiet. Was someone disturbing you?" Her voice changed tone. "Even though Colend insists on keeping the Sartoran Music Festival from returning to Sartor, we do get street musicians, but very seldom at this time of year. It still means something in some places to say that one played the streets of Eidervaen. But they usually stay away from the Purad, which is supposed to be a place of quiet and reflection."

"It wasn't that," he said, aware of a sharp sense of disappointment. Did she really not hear it? How could she walk that labyrinth every day and not hear it? At that moment they approached a stairway, and he stumbled against the bottom step. For a heartbeat the stones seemed to be moving, and he swayed, fighting vertigo.

"Are you all right?" She peered at him, concerned.

He caught himself against the wall, cold sweat prickling in his armpits and the back of his neck. "Thank you. I'm fine. A little cold."

"Well, of course. If you were there all day—well, come straight inside." No wonder his remarks seemed so random. It was dangerous for anyone to be out in such cold, and she knew that he had always been frail of health. "We must get you warm again."

He lifted a hand, startled, and a little disturbed by the yearning that gripped him. This was different from the attraction he'd felt for Atan: it was more of a sense of loss, a hunger. "I'm fine."

Atan gave him a worried glance, clearly not believing it, and the faint shimmer around her changed to a dark blue, almost violet—the same color as her eyes. "I'll order something hot at once. There's a concert tonight, but perhaps you'd prefer to rest? Tomorrow we'll be meeting with Leotay."

"I'll need to check my notecase, in case affairs at home require my notice," he said, making an effort to pull his thoughts back to the present, duty, expectations.

"Of course!"

They parted at the guest wing, and a servant brought him hot steep. He sat over his empty notecase, trying to claw his mind back to the present. There had been no messages. He was proud of how much he had delegated—how he had kept his promises to Derek.

Lilah appeared. "There you are! Where were you all day? Gehlei found some other little ones for Ian to play with. Now we're ready for dinner. We're starved!"

He bowed and smiled and uttered politenesses through dinner, though that odd blur of emotion-charged light that he'd experienced on the walk back to the Residence Wing of the palace crowded his awareness. Lilah's reminded him of the spark of the lake in the sunlight, and the morvende were more like the brilliance of the night sky, Sinder's a cooler, distant starlight, Hinder's merry and golden, like a harvest moon.

Julian's was the most disturbing, an ever-changing spectrum of color that he tried to shut out, until some mention of Sarendan caused Lilah to exclaim, as she often did, "Oh, I wish Derek could see that!" And then, from Tsauderei burst a virulent, storm-green glow of poisonous dislike.

Peitar was so startled he dropped his fork with a clatter, and murmured an apology as he gazed at the mage. Tsauderei looked benign, as if nothing was amiss, and the poisonous green faded to the green of spring. And from Atan there was — blessedly — no glow, as if she had a mind-shield.

Da? There was Ian, bright as dawn, innocent of pain and disappointment, love his natural state of being, the brightness so intense, the sweetness so poignant that Peitar had no defense. His heart ached, and his eyes stung, but he would not weep in the middle of a state dinner! He concentrated on forming a mind-shield — and at once all the glows winked out.

Mind-shield. Could it be? No. Peitar was too old for Dena Yeresbeth, was he not? And he heard none of the mental voices Liere Fer Eider had spoken of. But what had caused that ugly green from Tsauderei when Derek was mentioned? No, impossible. He had merely missed something in the conversation. He was unaccountably stupid this evening.

By the end of dinner, Peitar was aware of a throbbing headache. He was glad that Atan had arranged for a concert, because that meant no speaking would be expected of him. And though the concert was no doubt very fine, the music was noise against the memory of that vast harmony he had caught so faintly at the pinnacle of the Purad.

When finally he was able to lay his aching head down and shut his eyes to sleep, he dreamed that he floated upward, until he looked down at the city like a bed of fireflies, then the universe wheeled and he gazed again at the infinity of stars . . . Frightened by the intensity of his longing to fly out and out until he could find that music, he pulled himself along the tether back to his body, and its responsibilities. Then he slept oblivious until morning.

The next day, the eerie glows around people were still there.

Seventeen

THOUGH LEOTAY APPRECIATED EVERYTHING the Sartorans were doing for them, she longed to go home. She was anxious on behalf of her people, and she missed Quicksilver badly. She was also tired of trying to deal with the strange foods, and furnishings, and remembering shoes, and she hated the bitter weather.

Horsefeathers was the opposite. Time, youth, and distance had helped to ease the sharpness of her grief at Jeory's death. She never tired of chattering to Leotay about how friendly everyone was, and how cute the boys and girls were—so many to choose from—and how wonderful and different all the buildings were, and she wanted to go inside every one, and look out of the windows. She was fascinated by windows.

After their stay out in the country, and their trip through snowy fields—all that pretty white—they returned to Eidervaen. Horsefeathers pressed her face against the carriage window, glass steaming from her breath as she tried to see everything. Statues! She wanted to know the story of each one. Corbels and cartouches, carved vines and pilasters, even the acorn and acanthus patterns along eaves seemed to beckon silently, promising a story, and she thirsted to know them all.

She was thrilled to be going to the royal palace again, to meet a king and princess from another land, as her sister braced for it as if readying herself for those cold blasts of wind in the outside, but this time she had to acknowledge, the new people — in spite of their titles — were far less intimidating than the Sartoran courtiers.

Lilah and Horsefeathers took to one another at once, and Leotay found the quiet King Peitar easy to talk to. He even looked a little like people at home, except for the brown skin. They talked over how they approached controlling the basics of magic. Atan and Tsauderei both watched as Leotay demonstrated her birdsong method of magic.

As for Peitar, he noted the warm shift of hues surrounding Leotay, then found that if he concentrated hard enough he could shut out those distracting haloes. It was a little like squinting internally, and it made his head pang, but he would soon be home, in the quiet of his study.

Atan watched the tension in his face smooth, and she breathed easier. She blamed herself for having left Peitar at the Purad, but who would have known he would not come in after walking it, and nearly freeze himself to death?

Since Tsauderei had retired with the senior mages to plan specialized tutoring for the fifth worlders, plus security, Atan walked around as the fifth worlders described their world. Having already heard this story several times, she let her thoughts range outward.

When she'd first taken up the duties expected of the only remaining Landis, she had found herself not just intimidated, but resentful of the enormous staff required of a queen. Dealing with them had been bewildering, the traditional complexities of their interactions daunting, but now she appreciated how each contributed to a constant state of order and peaceful existence. Every pair of hands did meaningful work, from those who slowly rounded the palace year after year, dusting, polishing, and repairing ancient furnishings and art works, to Tsauderei and the mages wrangling with the inexorable pressure of threat from Norsunder.

Everybody in the magic realm, north and south, expected Norsunder to come on the attack. Why now, this generation? If it related to Dena Yeresbeth, she found herself resenting the danger of a thing she would never have. She forced the subject away, and returned to her guests.

Horsefeathers sat down by Peitar. Atan listened as he asked a few polite questions of this twig-like teen who, in her turn, was clearly delighted to meet a king. She babbled happily about snow, and language lessons, and how funny she found it that people at home had names that turned out to be for things—and how funny her own name had sounded to people.

"But I'm told that horse feathers were special things, long ago, on my world," she said earnestly. "And Jeory had even said something like."

Peitar had heard "and Jeory said" several times already. So he asked kindly, "Jeory?"

Horsefeathers' huge eyes shuttered, and her mouth downturned. "The enemies killed him. Well, they hurt him, and he, oh, he wasn't very strong. Our healer said that someone else might have survived, but he always forgot to eat, especially after he found out the Thing made music."

"Thing?"

"The Thing That Does Not Burn is a *flute.*" She fingered something hanging around her neck, half-hidden by a panel of her silken over robe. "We didn't have music things, we only sang. But they had music things long ago, and there is so much magic on this one. It's fallen to me to study it, but I must be very careful. If I play softly, it makes my head buzz like bees are inside—aren't bees *wonderful?*—only it's more like music, only far, far away," she said. "So they told me, if I learn ordinary flutes, maybe I can better learn its magic."

At the words *music, only far, far away,* Peitar's idle attention snapped to the earnest face before him. Horsefeathers wasn't looking at him at all, but down at the patterned carpet before her bare feet, her thin fingers twisting as she struggled to express herself in Sartoran. Her mental aura glowed incandescent as candlelight. She whispered, "They won't let me play the Thing itself, except in a warded room, for of course it is very powerful, if it truly is what we need to heal our world. But powerful as it is, I still cannot see what Jeory saw, the light beings. All I can hear is that music, only it's so far off."

Peitar's head buzzed, but from elation. "Only when you play that instrument? Was it made before the Fall?"

"Fall? Oh, yes, before the enemies destroyed the world." Horsefeathers blinked up at him. "It was prisoned in a spell for generations and generations, until Jeory broke it. Lilith told us she thinks the white horse made the spell break."

Peitar had no interest in white horses. "Then there was another kind of magic on your world?"

Horsefeathers said, "I don't know. I'm not very well trained yet, you see. Well, none of the others can use the Thing, either. Some said it gives them a headache, or makes them dizzy."

"Might I try?" Peitar asked.

"You might, but you must know that it is dangerous," Horsefeathers said, but she made no move to take whatever it was out of what he saw now was a silken case strung on a sturdy silk cord. "So very dangerous. You must listen, only, and play soft on a single note."

"To listen is just what I wish," Peitar said, shrugging off the idea of danger. He would face any danger to find that music again. "Might I try now? I have to return to Sarendan tomorrow."

Horsefeathers said, "If you like. They said I must not take it out, even, unless in a warded room, and Leotay says it must never be let away from me. We must therefore go to the warded room to make it sound."

Leotay whispered to Atan, who sent a page to Tsauderei. The old mage was surprised by Peitar's request, but he was always in favor of magic inquiry, even late at night in the middle of a gathering, and Atan said only, "I trust it won't give you a headache the way it did me, and I scarcely breathed into it. Felt like I was struck by a hammer. Be warned."

They crossed a narrow alley to the mage council headquarters, Tsauderei's cane tapping. When they stepped into a windowless room deep in the building, Tsauderei warded the door. Then Horsefeathers took the silken case out from under her over robe, and slipped out a flute carved from a silvery wood. It was fashioned on a model he'd never seen.

Peitar pursed his lips above the hole as he'd seen flute players do, and blew gently across it. His head buzzed. He put his fingers over the holes and blew again on a longer note as he strained to listen for that distant music.

Color chased across his vision as the walls appeared to ripple, then vanish, opening him to a space much wider than the entire building — than the city. His ear caught echoes that couldn't be contained in the small, plastered room. Giddy, he backed up and sat down abruptly on a waiting chair, dazed, his mouth open as he fought to control the disorientation.

"You did much better than I," Tsauderei commented presently.

Peitar slowly shook his head, and held the artifact out to Horsefeathers. "Can you . . . play it?" *Play* seemed the wrong word entirely.

"I'm not very good yet. Some of my lessons are in music falls, ah, notes," she said, and raised the flute to her lips. She played softly, slowly and carefully running up a chord, as Peitar shut his eyes.

For a heartbeat or two his sense of the physical world dropped away, and he seemed to be suspended high above the world, echoing his experience in the Purad. Then he was himself, his breath stuttering. Horsefeathers looked at him with wide eyes.

He sorted the impressions as he pressed the heels of his hands against his eye sockets. Powerful it was, and he could not possibly guess what the magic pulled him toward—but it was not the same as whatever had happened to him in the Purad. That had a specific origin. This flute music washed against some vast ward.

"Well?" Tsauderei said.

"I don't know what to think," Peitar responded finally. "There's a ward. The magic can't get past it. Or that's the sense I get."

The old mage narrowed his eyes. "Better than the rest of us."

Horsefeathers said solemnly, "Our oldest records say it will make our world whole again, but did not say how. Some think that might be symbolic." Her smooth, mobile teen features did not hide her skepticism.

"It . . . it does have an effect," Peitar said, trying to blink away the auras around the other two, now so bright their physical beings were almost reduced to silhouette.

Everyone seemed to be affected in some way, at least. Tsauderei and Horsefeathers waited patiently until Peitar had once again forced the auras to dim, then wink out.

He thanked the two, and they returned to the gathering.

Next day, the Selennas returned home.

Eighteen

Marloven Hess

WHENEVER HE THOUGHT OF it, Jilo made an effort to get away from the toxic magic binding Chwahirsland's royal fortress. The problem was, he thought of it very seldom. Ever since Wan-Edhe, who had ruled with a fist of iron for nearly a century, had been taken to Norsunder, Jilo had been doing his best to dismantle the toxic wards not only over the royal fortress, but over Narad, the capital.

He still hadn't been able to find and dismantle the tangle of wards that prevented Mondros from entering the kingdom and giving Jilo the aid he needed so desperately — but he could sense increments of success. (Though sometimes those were measured by the words *Not killed today*.)

Relying on reminder letters from Mondros didn't always work when Jilo was deep inside the warped space that he thought of as Wan-Edhe's personal Norsunder; weeks, even months could go by on the outside that felt like a day or two inside, before he thought to check his notebox. He'd learned to check his fingernails, and if they began looking gray, and he could not remember his latest meal or when he'd slept, he knew it was time to get away from the poisonous effect of the time-distorting, life-draining magic over Narad, which, while lessening, was still potent.

They were gray now.

He wrote to Senrid, and as he had hoped, received an immediate invitation to visit Marloven Hess to see the New Year's Week exhibitions.

New Year's Week!

Jilo was too used to the distortions between time outside and that which he endured inside Narad to be disturbed by the apparent jump from summer to winter, but he regretted having missed the Chwahir Great Hum, now that they dared do it again, after decades of enforced silence.

Bad weather had postponed the Marloven exhibitions for a day, bringing them to the very end of New Year's Week. As a result, Jilo sat next to Senrid in the stone stands overlooking a muddy field, his toes numb in his boots, his front teeth absently gnawing his knuckles as the Marlovens got a look at their first Chwahir.

Jilo was completely unaware of the covert stares at his scarecrow figure slouched like a rusty blackbird on the stone seat as he took in the feats of horsemanship. He looked, and was, completely absorbed by the Marlovens' skills as they leaped from horse to horse, then tossed spears back and forth as the animals galloped, and last, shot from horseback, no one missing the center of the target as the horse streamed nose to tail across the parade ground, and then out.

"Fighting on horseback," Jilo said. "Can they do that?"

"They usually do, but the mud is icy, and while they can knock a spear off course if their mount slips, that's harder to do in exhibition fighting, which is not considered worth watching unless they strike sparks with the steel."

"Oh," Jilo said.

Senrid said as they walked inside the massive castle, "If you want, I can send Captain Stad home with you, if you'd like to experiment with some different fighting styles."

Jilo's toes had begun to needle painfully as they defrosted. "No," he said. "They'd kill him."

"They'd try," Senrid retorted as they trod upstairs.

Jilo struggled for the words to explain. There wouldn't be any duels, nothing outright. It would be covert, because the Chwahir had been living covert lives for nearly all the century of Wan-Edhe's terrible reign. If they moved publicly, it was in the safety of huge blocks, all at the same time in the same way.

But Senrid's quick retort—his obvious belief in the superiority of his Captain Stad over the many thousands of Chwahir he might encounter—silenced Jilo.

It might even be true. That, too, was a result of the poison of Wan-Edhe, who was still alive somewhere in Norsunder, a nearly intolerable threat to people gradually, doubtfully, accustoming themselves to slivers of relative freedom.

Senrid considered Jilo's silence, his bent head as he shuffled along in his peculiarly flat-footed way, and heard an echo of his own words. He heard the tone, the easy assumption of superiority, and regretted it. Jilo faced worse problems than Senrid had ever faced, always with the awareness that the worst king in the entire world could return at any time, and here Senrid was, on the strut about one of his captains, whose expertise he could in no way take any credit for.

"Tell me about your fighting style in Chwahirsland," he said.

"Foot warriors," Jilo mumbled as they walked into Senrid's study, to find hot coffee waiting for them, the servants knowing the rhythm of the exhibitions from long experience. "I think we also used horses long ago, before the droughts made it difficult to grow fodder. We always depended on numbers, but Wan-Edhe requires the warriors to move in synchrony, in squares and walls, every man the same as the next. Shield wall perfectly measured."

Senrid said, "That sounds rough."

Jilo nodded soberly.

"And when attacked?"

"Still the same, moving to the call. Every step in synchrony."

"They'd die in droves if lancers broke the wall."

Jilo shook his head. "We haven't attacked anyone for years. The invasion of Colend a few years ago doesn't count, as the mages united against Wan-Edhe before there was actual bloodshed. The most important thing to Wan-Edhe is seeing those thousands move only by his will. Individual belongings, likes, dislikes, even emotions, were forbidden."

That suggested to Senrid an arrogance far beyond insanity, but he already knew how loathed Wan-Edhe was by the Chwahir. Feared as well as loathed.

Jilo set down his cup and frowned. "If you don't move in perfect synchrony, do you attack in melee?"

"No. Chain of command is important here, too, but wing commanders down to riding captains are all trained to know ways to carry out their orders. The idea being, warfare usually moves faster than communication once the attack commences, so the fewer orders needing to be passed down, the better. The commander can, say, signal the skirmishers to an oblique attack on the left flank, and the flight captain in charge of the skirmishers—light cavalry—knows how to carry it out. The commander doesn't have to signal each move. Nearly impossible, according to the records, once battle is commenced."

Jilo nodded his head several times, one hand swiping absently at the lank black hair hanging in his eyes. Senrid noticed his nail beds were an odd color that had nothing to do with the nail paint popular at the other end of the continent. Chwahir didn't paint their nails, as far as Senrid knew, but he'd seen that gray before in Jilo. Good food and water, sleep in pure air, would restore some human color.

Then Jilo said, "We probably need better training, but it would be useless until we're rid of Wan-Edhe. And even if that should happen, that doesn't solve the problem, which is that the only respected work for men is army, or navy to a lesser extent. Right now, I can get them to repair some of the worst damage caused by time, neglect, and Wan-Edhe's concentration of what wherewithal we have on his prize commanders and their armies—to the cost of everyone else. That's interim work. They all know it. They'd rather be carrying on the endless competitions to move in precise synchrony through these impossibly long sequences. But how can I change the century-old belief that everyone else exists to support the army?"

"*That* problem," Senrid threw his hands wide, "I understand. Every Marloven believes that when Norsunder attacks we have to be ready. The thing to do is to make life better for those outside the army."

"Yes," Jilo mumbled, his gaze wandering blindly from object to object, then he blinked at the food in front of him, slung back the lank hair hanging in his eyes, and picked up a hunk of bread.

Norsunder was a distant threat compared to the dangers Jilo lived with every day. And Senrid knew that. He watched Jilo tucking into the food as if he was starving—which might very well be true, judging by how skinny he was—and wondered when Jilo had last had his hair cut.

No, "when" was a useless question in relation to Jilo and the seemingly insurmountable task facing him. When Senrid first met him early in the alliance, their skills in dark magic were roughly the same, but since that time Jilo had doubled his knowledge in the area of wards, and perhaps that yet again. He was living with the end result of dark magic's reach, at least eighty years of parched soil, poisoned air, and a people so warped by fear that when they did rise, it was going to be felt all over the world. But holding them in its grip was the pocket Norsunder in the capital, which Jilo was quietly — heroically, a word Senrid never used ordinarily — trying to dismantle singlehandedly. Just because it needed to be done.

And no one could help him, because of the tangle of lethal wards Wan-Edhe had surrounded himself with, that only Jilo could navigate.

What could Senrid do? At least he could feed Jilo, listen to him ramble on, and maybe get the garrison barber over to cut his hair for him.

Nineteen

Sartor

REL CONSIDERED THE CONTRARINESS of human emotions that first week of the new year, as everyone returned to the regular rhythm of winter life. He packed his travel kit, aware of a sharp sense of regret, almost what others described as homesickness.

Yet Sartor wasn't — quite — home. That is, he liked living in Eidervaen more than he had anywhere else in all his years of wandering, but he understood home as the place where everyone must accept you, and he knew that much as his friends at the guard and in the city accepted him, he was — at best — watched askance by Sartor's more ambitious first circle nobles.

They might like him personally, but it was his friendship with Atan that they mistrusted. He wanted more than mere friendship, and they wanted that less to an equal degree. He knew what they feared most: that Atan, who'd spent her childhood taught by Tsauderei, would shrug off the diplomatic and economic necessities of royal marriage ties and choose someone totally inappropriate. Like Rel. Once she was safely married to the prince of their choice, she could entertain herself privately with anyone she wished.

Which left him with what? At best, life as a future favorite. He'd take it if offered, but so much would depend on the prince she married. And — Rel would never admit this out loud — he loathed the idea of sharing her, he loathed the very thought of that unknown prince, who in any other circumstance might be a friend. And he did not like who he was when thinking down that road. Others had no problems navigating between favorites, friends, and marriage ties. There were all kinds of relationships, but people of rank were expected to marry, if anyone, a representative of the other gender, to symbolize gender parity. Which was why many royal marriages were entirely diplomatic.

It was time to get away, and let his feelings cool down.

He said his farewells to the other guards, who wished him good journey, then he walked out and over the bridge toward Blossom Street, where he found most of the family up to their ears in flour, turning out cakes for a party.

Hannla was out in the main room busy with duster and polish rag. She looked up, tucking a curl behind her ear. "Rel! Now is a terrible time, I confess. The joiners guild hired the entire house for a betrothal."

"Just came to say my farewells. I'm off."

"Oh." Hannla cast down her feather duster, and wiped her hands on her apron. "How long?"

"I don't know."

"You never do, do you?" She smiled. "Include Aunt in your farewells, and you might net a hot cake for your walk. Good journey!"

He said goodbye to Fiar and the others, most of whom were gathered in the back room for their breakfast. Then he poked his head into the kitchen, and sure enough, was soon on his way to the palace, eating a freshly baked little six-layer spice cake. He finished it before he reached the great square, dusted his hands, adjusted the sword strapped over his back, rehitched his travel bag over the other shoulder, and crossed to the side door.

The nobles might have misgivings, but Gehlei, the head steward, liked him, and looked on benevolently at his popularity among the servants of the royal palace. If it was at all possible to get to Atan, she was sure to waft him past those who had been waiting for hours. And so it was, with the contrivance of two scribes and a fleet little page.

"I'm off to Sarendan," he said to Atan, who'd followed the page down the connecting servants' corridor.

She'd just come from a very irritating court interview with a duchas, which had turned out to be a pitch for Atan's marrying "within Sartor," — that is, the duchas's nephew.

Rel's heart thumped hard at the sight of Atan ruddy-cheeked, wearing white brocade decorated with tiny pendants of wheat sheaves in gold, a contrast to the muted golden highlights in her high-dressed brown hair.

She stared back, surprised at the intensity of her disappointment. She bit back a sharp, "Already?" She reminded herself firmly that she had no claims on Rel but friendship, and that meant acknowledging that he had the freedom to come and go as he willed.

But the brief tightening of her expression betrayed her to Rel, who was sensitive to every subtle alteration in her face or voice. Even her breathing. He said, "Peitar asked me for my help, and Tsauderei made me a cross-worlds token."

Atan got her face and voice firmly under control. Smile, smile, smile. "You're really going off to Geth? That ought to be interesting!" In her own ears the laugh she forced tinkled like broken glass.

"First to Sarendan, but yes. And I promise to report back on whatever I find. Even if it turns out that I'm not the sort of vagabond who can learn vagabond magic."

She saw his smile in the deepening of the long dimples on either side of his generously curved mouth, and the quirk of his deep-set eyes. She forced her own answering smile. "If there really is such a thing as vagabond magic, I'd think you'd be a candidate, after all your travels. I hope you find it quickly. And safely."

"Do my best on both counts." He waited, hand half-outstretched, saw her stiff posture, and lifted his hand all the way, turning it to a farewell wave. Then he walked out.

She fought the urge to fling herself on him and hold him fast, but caught herself up and watched his broad back retreating, a horrible hollow sense inside her. What if she begged him to stay, offering him . . . what? She could offer herself, but what would that actually mean once the immediacy was over?

She turned away, leaving the question behind, and sped to her second meeting, where she knew a room full of people awaited her.

Rel walked out, not looking back, though that same hollow feeling, twin to hers, opened inside him. Yes, it was time for some distance. He turned to the Destination chamber, and waved off the mage on duty. "Have my own token," he said.

Why this Destination — one of the oldest and most frequently used — never seemed to get that hot sword smell, he didn't understand, but he was glad of it. After the expected wrench he stumbled into the familiar Destination chamber in Miraleste, the capital of Sarendan.

The air smelled different in Miraleste, though it was difficult to characterize how. Here, a glance out the long window showed the winter snows had begun in earnest. Once the transfer reaction had faded he looked around the chamber, mildly surprised not to see at least a student on duty, but the Sarendans were far less formal than most anyone else except maybe the Mearsieans. And that was changing, ever since Mearsieanne returned to the throne she'd sat on over a century ago.

Rel crossed the empty room, anticipating Lilah's happy greeting, and interesting conversations with Peitar. A girl stepped in the doorway. She was dressed only in a knee length, armless cotton tunic, her arms and feet bare, a garland roses and lilies crowning her head, ruddy-highlighted auburn hair framing her lightly freckled face.

"Autumn?" Rel said, remembering her from an early adventure with the Mearsieans.

"Give you good winter, Rel," Autumn said, her voice betraying the fact that her human form was not quite the same human as most, though he could not have said how he knew. "Rel. You have before you a choice."

Rel stopped where he was, hand ready to reach for his sword, for all he could imagine was some lurking danger. Autumn smiled

When she did, her eyes seemed to brighten — not just her eyes, but a subtle light glowed below her skin. "I have heard that you seek the way they are calling vagabond magic."

"Lilah told you?" Rel asked, laughing as he dropped his hand. He knew that Lilah wrote to everybody in the alliance.

Autumn nodded, her hair spilling around her bare arms. "Lilah, and CJ, and Arthur up north, and Hibern far off in Roth Drael. You can go to Geth, where Dak will see that you are introduced to his friends, and they will be happy to include you in their group. Their restricted group. And you will be taught the restricted forms that their leader taught them."

"Or?" Rel asked.

"Or," Autumn said, "you can come with me, and learn it our way. There is no politics here." She said the word *politics* slowly, emphasizing each syllable, and he suspected that to non-human Autumn, the word was synonymous with *taint*.

"But you have inherent magic," Rel said. "I remember that. You and your sisters, you *are* magic."

"So it is," she said. "And that part you cannot learn. But we understand that which wakens in the world again. Which is it to be?"

Rel considered about two heartbeats. "What must I do?" he asked. "Shall I speak first to Peitar? He's expecting me."

"Words." She sighed. "So necessary, and many times, so misleading. Leave here the token he made for you." She indicated the bench in the Destination chamber where he'd sat to recover from transfer reaction.

Rel dropped the token. Autumn reached into her garland and pulled out a white rose, which she laid beside it. Then she touched his hand, and he stepped from that chamber into a forest glade on the other side of the world, feeling not even a ripple of air.

Twenty

UNDER A LOW, DREARY sky, the brats napped in the far room. "Brats" having evolved from "critters" mostly due to one of them being temperamental and constantly determined to destroy himself. But Detlev didn't permit beatings. He expected the older boys to use wit and words to corral the three and four-year-olds, who seemed to be equipped with maximum liveliness and minimum wit and words. Except, of course, for Sveneric, who only had to be told something once.

Now—so rare—all three were asleep, Paolan having screamed himself into exhaustion after a tantrum over his wish to kick apart the block city Sveneric and Ki had made.

David had no excuse not to practice his DY exercises. He and Adam made a contrast as they sat in chairs facing one another. David sat squarely on his chair, booted feet planted on the floor, knees apart, hands gripping the chair arms, his shoulders and arms tight. He wore only a heavy tunic shirt, unlaced, over his riding trousers. He rarely felt cold. Adam lay curled in his chair, his body cocooned in a thick blanket, a besorcelled handkerchief clutched in one hand, into which he honked juicily every so often.

Except for Adam's recourse to his handkerchief

punctuated by crashing coughs, there was no noise. This exercise took place entirely in the mental realm.

Caught you again, Adam sent, and held his breath against the sluggish tickle deep in his chest. This cold seemed inevitable after breathing Norsunder Base's dust for longer than a month, the effect intensified by the cold.

Wrath tightened David's gut. Adam sensed it, but his own control was too strong for any reaction to reflect back.

While Adam burrowed in his blanket, eyes closed, David let out his breath, then sucked it in again as he forced his worming stomach to settle. Sweat prickled along his hairline and in his armpits as he concentrated, and carefully formed the image of an invisible finger. Detlev and Adam called these focus images *tendrils*, but David found that disorienting. The best he could do was an invisible finger, attached to an invisible arm, attached to his invisible self within his real self. But that, he found, was even clumsier than tendrils.

Furthermore, distance was distance! Mental connection was so much easier close by, easiest if David had physical contact. Useless for Detlev and Adam (and Siamis in the old days before he lost his mind and turned traitor, double that for Roy, damn him to Norsunder-Beyond and Ilerian's tender mercies) to say that geography was irrelevant. David knew better. If he reached too far, he felt his mind slipping back into Geth's marshes a world away.

He replanted his feet, regripped the chair arms, shut his eyes, and concentrated on being in the Marsh. Got it. Then he lifted his nose, sorting the scents, familiar and unfamiliar . . . and reached for MV.

MV only bothered with a mind-shield when he had to, and he obviously saw no need now. Sight, sensation, scraps of thought flooded David: *heat, the taste of brine and sweat, exertion, MV's running laughter as he feinted and struck lightly with his blades — the deck swaying underfoot, partner slamming down —*

And David nearly fell out of his chair as his body tried to compensate for the rise of a ship on the swell of a wave. He ground his teeth against a surge of nausea, and held his breath as his mind punched back into his body.

:Forgot your stealth in your retreat, came Adam's thought, tranquil and effortless. *:Caught you again.*

David sent back an image of a steaming pile of horse droppings, but Adam merely honked into his handkerchief, coughing. David resettled himself, and this time reached for Ferret. This was both easier and more difficult. Ferret half-shielded his mind naturally, somewhat the same way he concentrated on making himself unnoticeable. A glance at Adam's expectant face, and David muttered a curse, making an effort to slip past that half-shield. David could see what Ferret watched—from the angle, he sat on a rooftop looking down at the Sartoran mage school as he waited for Leotay and her entourage on their daily round.

One by one he checked the rest of them: Noser's unsettling, stuttering mind busy with horses as he and Silvanas worked at the duchas enclave where Leotay and her sister sometimes visited one of their mage student friends. Erol newly joined the kitchen staff at the mage school—the one place they were careless about checking personal history—currently dipping stacks of dirty plates in cleaning buckets, and restacking the clean ones.

Curtas working with a tailor across the way, seated by the window as he stitched: David saw the street under its fresh snowfall through Curtas's eyes, and the golden lights in mage school windows three stories up. David caught the surface of Curtas's mind as he tried to remember the verses of some Colendi satiric poem, and how slyly the symbols had been worked into the stone carvings over the windows.

David breathed against the boiling in his stomach, and checked Laban, who also didn't bother with a mind-shield. Cold hit David, who saw what Laban saw, and felt what he felt as he crouched behind a boulder on a cliff, sketching winter army maneuvers down below on the fields of Ralanor Veleth. At least that one didn't make David seasick, though Laban's bitterness took a few breaths to shake off. Detlev was going to have to deal with that.

Next: Rolfin, at that moment gloating quietly as he led one of Bostian's spies deeper into the chaos of the Port of Jaro. David stayed with Rolfin long enough to see him raise his eyes and spot Leef on a rooftop, giving him a hand signal indicating a vector. Rolfin kept pace until he passed a street seller hawking hot pies, then ducked under the decorated wagon, waited until the trackers ran past, and reversed his direction, to be rejoined by Leef.

By then David's head throbbed, but he'd done it. He opened his eyes.

Adam coughed, snorted, then said, "Niffed you six times."

David's response was as pungent as the images he'd sent, then he said, "We'll put in some time in the yard before I take my stint tutoring."

Adam sighed as he got to his feet. "You're going to take those six out on me, aren't you."

David had rocked out of his chair as if released from prison, but at this he whipped around. "What?"

"You're annoyed," Adam pointed out. "Your wrath keeps you tied to the body, and you have to fight twice as hard to make and shield your —"

"Piss on your *tendrils*," David snapped, then forcefully expelled his breath, trying to shed irritation with it. Adam was the teacher here. He was doing what he'd been ordered to do. In a more normal voice, David said, "Useless image. And 'niffing' is useless as an action. Let's go."

Adam stood where he was, clutching his blankets. "It's what I learned," he said, eyeing David, whose heavy eyelids and habitual half smile usually made him look studious, even indolent. When the anger surfaced it the change in his expression was sudden, and startling. Ever since David's time with the Black Knives he seemed an island in the midst of a seething, simmering, bottomless sea of rage.

Adam said, "What did Efael do to you?"

"Nothing," David said, low and savage.

The mental onslaught that David didn't bother to hide felt like walking straight into a furnace, but Adam walked anyway. "That's obviously not true."

"If I say nothing, then I make it nothing. It never happened," David retorted, hands flexing.

"All right," Adam said, knowing that pushing beyond certain limits would only rend instead of mend. "I'll accept your nothing. Especially as I'm certain Efael would hate that, after all his effort. I'm used to niffing for reach and focus. It's almost smell, instead of the focus of light, or the tendril of touch. None of them are right, because they relate to other senses. Don't use any of them if you have something better. But you need to work on this sense, just the same."

David snorted. "Get some shoes on those ugly feet. Time to work up a little sweat before those brats wake up."

And there the subject ended — on the surface. Why didn't Detlev pursue it?

Adam was aware of a growing sense of being unmoored, ever since the ease of "us against them" blurred. They were used to Detlev being gone for long periods, but until recently there had always been Siamis overseeing them. Now, sometimes, it felt as if they were forgotten, but at other times he could discern a wake in the ever-changing seas; Roy was the second one to leave — third, if you counted Siamis — and some wanted to run independent, Laban especially.

Adam stilled the ripples of worry. He could wait. Watch. Learn the true goal, the one he was certain sailed just beyond the horizon of perception, leaving its trace only in its wake.

As David ran downstairs, Adam wrote that out in his journal, blotting and smearing the words in his effort to be fast, then went through the complicated process of storing it again, the spell tied safely and securely to his belt buckle. He rammed his feet into socks and shoes and leaped down the stairs.

David checked briefly when he saw the snowy ground outside, then deciding against running up again just to fetch a coat. He'd be warm soon enough. He scanned the practice area for tracers, and began swinging his practice sword — the black one stayed upstairs under his bed, with an illusion over it.

Your wrath keeps you tied to the body. David had been avoiding the coinherence drills because he wasn't certain of his control, how much of his memories Adam would see. How much mental focus would stir up everything he worked hard to shut behind a steel door. To forget, to truly make it nothing. But no practice meant weakness, obviously. Just as in the physical realm. And Efael would win if David didn't build mental strength. Adam was right.

Adam appeared, bundled up against the weather.

"Let's keep it smooth and tight. Hand through the water," David said, as Detlev had habitually begun drill sessions.

They took up position side by side and moved in silence through Detlev's sword warm-up, low (man to man) then high (ground to mounted), right hand, left hand, then against two low and high, before they faced off.

From now on, every day. No, twice a day, he promised himself. *Just like the sword drill.* "Everyone's in place in Eidervaen," David said as they exchanged a few blows to get the rhythm. "Once I snip the tracers and wards, we just need half a heartbeat's inattention from the watchdogs."

Adam defended himself against two feints and three attacks, high, low, high. "We're off to Chwahirsland next?"

"Not we. Me. I'm done reinterpreting orders."

Adam thought back to their disastrous stay in Wnelder Vee, which had begun so well and ended so disastrously.

"And I won't go all the way in if I can avoid it. Bad enough when I went there to grab Kessler. Has to be worse now, with wards and tracers lying for me. Flush Jilo out if I can."

Adam said nothing as he returned an attack, to be driven back three steps. He paused to cough, his forehead now as sweaty as David's had been during the coinherence exercise, and once again David pulled his point to wait out the coughing spasm. Then Adam wiped his nose across his sleeve and straightened up as David came on.

"You've met Jilo, right?" David asked as they exchanged a flurry of feints, blocks, strikes and more blocks.

"Once," Adam said, coughing again, then holding his breath against the tickle. After it subsided, "When he handed off the blood mage text to Senrid."

Another fast, hard exchange, and David said, "If he's fended Kessler Sonscarna off, then he has to be tough enough to take on all of us. Chwahirsland's usually been run by the Sonscarnas, right? But Jilo isn't any relation that I can tell. What's his hold? Tell me something I can use."

"I only saw him the once." Adam paused to turn aside a complicated attack, which took all his concentration and most of his strength, then he said, "Um, he doesn't look like he's tough enough to take Kessler. Or anyone, really. But I know looks can be deceiving. Like me." He gave David a seraphic smile, then attacked.

David fought him off, then said, "You look like an idiot, and you are one." But his tone was one of approval for the exertion he'd been put to.

Adam accepted that with another attack, low and inside.

"Now you're waking up." Another exchange, then David said, "Anything you observed that I can use?"

"He knows Hibern of Roth Drael."

"Nah." David tossed his sword to his left hand. "No chance I'd be able to set up a trap in Roth Drael."

"There's Senrid." Adam also switched to left.

"Even worse. You know the hands-off order there."

"And Leander Tlennen-Hess. To a degree."

"Ah. The one with the mouthy sister, right? Vasande

Leror, a pimple stuck on the butt of Marloven Hess."

"Yes." Adam crowed for breath, then came in hot and hard. He ached all over, knowing that the fever was coming back, but maybe a good workout would sweat it out. "Leander was learning wards with Roy and Arthur."

"Damn." *Clang! Clash.* Jilo had to have balls of brass; the reputation Kessler had left behind at Norsunder Base, where only force was respected, had put him beyond even Aldon and Bostian for bloodshed both in contact fighting and tactical command, much less the lower level grass.

Kessler could have gone up against Bostian or Aldon—he could be commanding the Base now, but he'd skipped out of Norsunder altogether, *after I slammed him into the dungeon here. Which I'm sure he well remembers.* If Kessler was Jilo's rival for Chwahirsland, David might have a chance. If Jilo was Kessler's errand boy . . .

David shuttered useless questions. They still had the fifth worlders and their magical artifact to bag, without the switch being detected. Ferret, Erol, and Curtas seemed to be invisible to the Sartorans and Norsunder spies, judging by the total lack of rumor around the Base; so far what little rumor there was had been derision about Roy's betrayal, and how Detlev couldn't seem to keep the brats in his nursery, and more laughter at Detlev's expense over Rolfin's blundering about in the Port of Jaro. All according to orders. And when that died down, Laban would furnish the next topic of gossip, once he was exposed as a spy by some ambitious lord in Dantherei.

David knew Laban was having fun prancing around pretending to be some baras's heir in Dantherei's glittering court, while laying out lures for Lord Galacki. Sometime in the next few days this ambitious Galacki should be searching Laban's room and discovering Laban's "spy notes" on Ralanor Veleth's army, but until then, Laban was effectively out of reach.

David only had Silvanas and Noser, who he'd bring in as backup at the last possible moment, if it turned out the snatch got complicated.

Adam feinted, stepped out of line after blocking, and tipped his head back, his cloud of curly hair hanging in sweaty ringlets. "Brats woke."

Reminding David that Adam had his own strengths.

"Your turn," David said. "I'll put things away here."

Adam tossed his sword in a lazy arc, and David caught it

by the hilt, an old game.

Upstairs again, Adam stopped in the alcove where the downstairs couriers had coffee steeping in a steamer over a firestick. The stuff was vile, especially as they just added water when it got thick, but it was hot, and kept one awake.

He filled a mug and eased upstairs without spilling, pausing only to kick his shoes into his room, then he set the mug down and shot into the nursery in time to see Paolan attempting to bash Sveneric over the head with a wooden wagon. Sveneric sat cross-legged on the floor, eyes closed, his small hands lying loose in his lap.

But before Adam could cross the room, Sveneric raised his right arm to deflect the toy. He didn't move his head, or even open his eyes.

The back of Adam's neck crawled. Surely that had to be Detlev's awareness somehow taking cognizance of Sveneric's surroundings, as the two communed in a lesson over unimaginable distance, though how he did it when he could not possibly be seeing through the boy's closed and averted eyes, Adam did not know. But surely Sveneric wasn't niffing around himself. He was so *small*.

Adam caught up the wagon and set it on the floor. He gave it a push as he said, "The wagon is a toy, Paolan. Weapons are in that box. And we wait until our partner is ready."

Paolan's lower lip popped out. He picked the wagon up and in a fast overhand throw that would have been impressive in an eight-year-old, hurled it at Adam, who caught it and put it up on a high shelf out of reach.

Paolan sucked a breath to let out a shriek. Adam braced for a repeat of morning's tantrum, but then Paolan stopped, and gave Sveneric a puzzled glance.

Sveneric met the older boy's gaze, then looked away, and Paolan turned to the basket of wooden balls. He spilled them out, sending them rolling in all directions. He and sleepy-eyed, pale blond Ki began batting and kicking them as Sveneric trotted to the shelf where his chalks and paper were kept. He brought them back, looking at Adam expectantly.

That was Detlev monitoring somehow long distance. Wasn't it? Adam began mentally composing a journal entry, hiding his thoughts behind a hard shield. Out loud, "What shall we make?"

Twenty-one

Winter 4749 AF
Everon

ON THE WESTERN SIDE of the continent, an iron frost set in. The eastern side seemed to be getting all the snow. The windows were white, huge, soft clumps patting the glass like giant cat paws, as the conspirators walked around Tahra's ruined royal castle commenting, inspecting, talking about the progress of their various reconstruction projects—by mutual agreement spending time before bracing for the wrenching magic transfer back to their various homes.

Surprisingly, everyone seemed to be in a good mood, except for Lilah Selenna—the person most likely of all the Young Allies to be counted on for good spirits. Lilah was upset that her older brother (who rose before dawn to study magic, worked all day at the necessary tasks of kingship with grim discipline, then retired to more magic studies until late at night) apparently had no time for coming with her to Everon's capital, but he did have time to vanish on unexplained journeys. At least these were short. But he came back looking exactly as tired as he was at home.

"I wish Derek was still alive, and he was here with us," Lilah said to Bren, who perched on a table inside the library, which featured a long picture window that looked out over the frozen lake. He was drawing the trumpet lilies climbing up a trellis framing the big window, the blossoms perfect. Was that because they grew inside, where there was no wind?

"So do I," Bren said. "But saying it every day, every year, isn't bringing him back."

"I know." Lilah kicked her bare feet moodily. Life was good—except when she worried about Peitar. But they had promised not to interfere in each other's lives. He never asked her to relinquish the Child Spell, so she couldn't nag him about how he worked all the time.

No, about how he wasn't *happy*.

"If Derek were here, he'd talk Peitar out of this whatever it is that makes him squinch his eyes up like he bit into a rotten apple, and then disappear."

Bren turned to stare at Lilah, absently wiping his chalky fingers on his pants. "Disappear?"

"He says he's going to those Sartoran labyrinth things. But why would he do that? They're just mazes. Not even nice in the winter."

Bren lifted a shoulder. "Sounds like more of his magic stuff," he said, obviously losing interest, and went back to drawing.

Lilah sighed, and decided that, though she couldn't nag outright, she could *invite* him to Everon next time, to see the progress himself. Maybe getting together with friends would shake him out of this strange compulsion of his. She wrote letters to CJ, who in turn wrote to other friends, and a date was agreed on for an inspection.

Peitar's expression shuttered when Lilah told him, but he kept his word, and they transferred early on the appointed day.

"He studies all the time, and only stops when Ian wants to play," Lilah confided to the Mearsieans as soon as Peitar walked off with Atan to inspect the progress in Tahra's throne room, which the Norsundrians had used as a stable during the attack in '42.

Clair said all the right things, but CJ—intimidated by Peitar—ran off to the nursery wing to find a huge finished central chamber, cleaned and plastered and dried, ready for art. She stood, arms crossed, glowering at the blank walls. Her enthusiasm had steadily waned since Clair first brought her to

Everon to inspect the nursery, at which time CJ got the idea of painting a forest glade. She'd mentioned that idea to many people over the weeks of slow but steady repair progress since then, and though several had said that a mural sounded nice — that there were a lot of fine artists — not a single person had exclaimed, "Great idea! You should paint it!"

Mearsieanne had pointed out sensibly that so much brown and green would darken the room, making it gloomy in winter, and anyway, Everon was covered with forestland. The future Delieth children could just go for a walk if they wanted trees.

Falinneh had — of course — said, "It has to be funny! You know how much kids like to laugh. We'll all help! We can put in drawings from our silliest adventures."

CJ had stared back, appalled. Falinneh couldn't really draw, nor could Gwen or Sherry. And while their additions were great in the girls' underground cavern, how would it look in someone else's royal palace, where everyone else was arranging for fine arts in wood and paint and plaster and tile?

Sherry said, "How about lots of butterflies?"

Seshe suggested figures from famous tales — both funny ones, like some of the Peddler Antivad stories — and heroic ones from Everon's own history.

Diana said, "What about an ocean scene full of ships? I know, you could paint Dtheldevor's ship, the *Berdrer*!"

"Everybody loves butterflies," Sherry said wistfully, her big blue eyes round and earnest. She amended hastily, "We can put in what everybody wants, and add the butterflies."

That conversation occurred right after New Year's Week, when the local hires had just begun scraping out the burned places, and redoing floor, walls, and ceiling. Since then, any time CJ brought it up, everybody seemed to have a different idea of what to paint, and who should paint it — but no one mentioned her. Finally it occurred to CJ that what they were all hinting, but not quite saying, was that they didn't think her painting was as good as she thought it was.

First, she couldn't believe it, then came the hurt. Which prompted a bitter comment when they transferred to Everon earlier that month, just after the plastering was done and still wet, "If it had been *Adam* wanting to paint a mural they would have been *thrilled*." The name "Adam" came out in corrosively angry sarcasm.

"But he was really great," Falinneh said, perfectly innocently.

"Not was," Seshe said. "He's still alive, as far as I know."

"But he's a poopsie, so he doesn't count anymore," Falinneh retorted hastily, as if she'd said something disloyal.

"Well, the plaster won't be dry until our next visit. There's plenty of time to decide," Clair had said. "And we still have all the toys to gather."

She had been seeing to that part. CJ helped, as did all the girls, but her heart was in her mural idea. And now they were back again. The walls were dry, and blank. Jenel Sandrial, head steward for the Delieth family, followed CJ in. "They did a lovely job, didn't they?"

CJ nodded, slowing taking in those blank white walls, like a gigantic canvas. She could just *see* her beautiful forest glade. What kid wouldn't want a room with forest all around?

Jenel was a friend, even if she'd grown up. CJ made a last desperate try. "Do you think that a forest scene—a *bright* one—would be nice? I can really see it, after a lot of experience painting trees."

Jenel put her hands on her hips and squinted up and around all four walls. "The style the old queen had chosen here was flowering vines, with spring blossoms over the door, summer green under the ceiling there, and autumn leaves around those windows, and snowflakes under the ceiling over there." She gestured with her hands. "They call it framing. There's a painter down in Treaty Road famed for her beautiful framing."

CJ forced out the word "Thanks," though her throat hurt and her emotions jangled, but no one seemed to notice. And maybe they shouldn't—maybe she was wrong, but it still, she grumped to herself, left her madder than a cat during Dog Week.

Jenel went out again. CJ could hear her voice in the hall as she began talking to Lilah about the library. Ordinarily CJ would have been interested in the idea of rebuilding a library, but she stayed where she was, fiercely blinking back tears. Though it had been a long time since she'd escaped Earth, the emotional scars remained, and she shivered against the old, sick dread of a beating if someone thought she might be whining.

She tried to scold herself. No one was going to take a belt

or a wire hanger to her. Except thinking that didn't help. If somebody did take a belt to her, she could feel like a victim when it was over, and she could hate the somebody as a villain. But she wasn't a victim. Others simply didn't notice, or care, that she really wanted to do the painting herself. And they weren't villains.

Even worse, she knew that Atan hated her. CJ had tried hard ever since those awful days when she'd slanged Rel without knowing that he was Atan's best friend — she'd even had daydreams about rescuing Atan from some terrible villain, maybe masked, and then revealing herself, or arranging some stunning surprise, so that Atan would gasp, and say —

Say what? Atan was always going to despise CJ for nothing but talk and teasing. It wasn't like they were truly enemies, and CJ had been trying ever since to be super friendly every time Rel was even mentioned.

She scowled and dug her bare toes into the floor. Clair and Atan entered right then, Sherry following behind, and CJ started guiltily, as though Atan somehow knew her thoughts. Atan certainly looked tall and intimidating in her embroidered layers.

Clair came to CJ. "Peitar and Lilah got Tsauderei and Arthur to donate books. It'll be a good library for them to start with." She looked around the fresh white walls. "What kind of paints do we need to get for our part?"

"Well," CJ said, her shoulders tight as she sidled a look Atan's way, for she could not resist one last try. "My thought was a forest glade — a *bright* one, not the *least bit* gloomy — with lots of flowers and butterflies and stuff . . ."

Atan nodded. "I have a list of local painters that the Sandrials put together for us. We can visit their studios."

"I thought I'd paint it myself," CJ said airily.

Atan's heavy brows lifted slightly. "Of course you should sketch out your ideas. It's your gift, so the artist ought to paint something that you like." But those eyebrows had given her away.

CJ stood still, holding her breath.

A lot of thoughts streamed through Clair's mind, beginning with the inescapable fact that Atan still didn't like CJ, or maybe didn't trust her, which was almost the same thing. She wasn't going to say any of it, any more than she was going to admit how much she distrusted the direction Mearsies Heili was going in. But not everything was about Clair; she wrenched herself back to the present. "CJ, didn't you say you'd rather paint it yourself?" Clair asked.

Atan said nothing. Sherry's brow puckered as she looked from one to another.

Clair held her breath; the pause became a silence, which no one broke until CJ said, struggling to sound brisk and careless. "Oh, it's so cold and wintry, I think maybe we should go ahead and let some local artists paint it."

"I'll go find that list," Atan said.

Clair stayed where she was, troubled by CJ's hunched shoulders and averted gaze. "CJ," she said in a low voice. "*We* all love your painting. How about you do a new mural for us at home? But maybe here, it might be best to pick a local artist. Remember, the idea was to create work for locals. There has to be a new artist eager to get their reputation established."

CJ whooped in a breath, and said in a brittle, airy voice, "Right, that was the idea, wasn't it?"

"I'm sorry about Atan," Clair said. "If I could fix her feelings about us, I would. I don't even think she means to be mean."

"No, she sees us differently. I get it." CJ's usually expressive, often fierce blue gaze gleamed with unshed tears before she looked down at her hands. "Here's the weird thing," she said slowly. "I think . . . I think . . . friends, *real* friends, don't just 'accept you as you are.' I mean, everyone says that, but what does it really *mean*? I think it means that they go, okay, so you blew it, when you do something stupid, and as long as you don't do it again, well, life goes right back to normal. You still belong. Right?"

"Right," Clair said.

"But with some people, even when you try really hard and behave perfectly to try to be their friend, it's like every time you see them, you're having an audition. They might accept you *this* time. If you go along with everything they like, everything they do, *this* time. But if you mess up once, they never forget the mess-up, and the rest of the time, no matter how good you behave, you'll never, *ever*, be good enough." Her voice wavered. "Or maybe I really am not good enough." She sighed hard. "No, don't tell me I am. I know you guys like my art. I have to accept that nobody else does. I'll look at the list, and go visit artists." Her voice wobbled.

"We're paying, so we get to pick. And of all of us Mearsie-ans, you know art best," Clair said.

CJ walked out, and half the light in the room seemed to go with her.

"I still miss Adam," Sherry said wistfully. "The *old* Adam, I mean, not the poopsie Adam. He loved art, and it was fun when he and CJ did drawings of us."

Clair knew what Sherry meant. She, too, missed the friendship they'd had before . . . she didn't even know what to call it anymore. *Betrayal* seemed uncomfortably self-righteous, and what CJ had said about mess-ups and forgiveness made her even more uncomfortable. Adam hadn't actually done anything wrong. It was his group who'd done it. It had also been clear to her that Adam's feelings about them all had never changed, though how he could reconcile being a Norsundrian, she still didn't understand.

"Hey," she said to Sherry. "How about going along with CJ? She could probably use someone liking her choices."

Sherry brightened at that, and trotted out.

Clair left the nursery, and began wandering.

Twenty-two

EVERY THREE WEEKS OR so, Senrid had been dutifully visiting Everon to see how the rebuilding of the royal palace progressed. It'd begun as an alliance obligation that Leander had talked him into, until he got involved in discussions of styles of architecture—how to angle windows to catch the winter sun and mitigate the summer, and so forth—and watched as CJ of the Mearsieans consulted everyone she could catch about her ideas for the nursery wing.

Where CJ went, Clair wasn't far behind.

Senrid hadn't given up trying to get the details of Clair's imprisonment. Much as he loathed Laban and the rest of them, he had to admit, if only to himself, that he respected their training. And he wanted to know the details of it. After all, what better way to eventually face Norsunder than by using their own tactical and strategic training against them? But though he remained intensely curious, Clair seemed equally— adamantly—determined not to discuss it. Senrid watched for an opportunity, figuring the best way to catch her would be away from Mearsies Heili and Mearsieanne, who hated him purely for being a Marloven.

The first time Senrid entered Everon's royal suite, which the Norsundrians had used as an auxiliary armory, it still bore the tang of rusty steel. Now the room was beginning to look like something someone could live in. Senrid moved to a window alcove to glance outside when he heard footsteps and the soft murmured cadences of magic. He leaned out and glimpsed Peitar Selenna murmuring tracer spells. Senrid was fairly certain he'd seen Peitar doing that earlier. Idle interest, or intent?

"Looking for something specific?" Senrid asked when Peitar finished a spell.

Peitar turned sharply, tilted eyes squinted under steeply slanted brows, one hand plunging into a pocket in his long coat. Then his expression smoothed, and he said in greeting, "Senrid." Peitar's hand withdrew from his pocket. "I wonder if Siamis will bring Tahra and Liere back himself."

"*If* he does," Senrid retorted.

Peitar gave him a considering glance. He still had difficulty shuttering those distracting auras around people, but he'd become accustomed to Lilah's bright gold, and Ian's luminous light. Senrid's was like the reflective surface of steel. Peitar was distracted by memory, being told that Senrid had Dena Yeresbeth. Was he *seeing* a mind-shield? He forced aside that thought. "You think he won't bring them back?"

Senrid crossed his arms and leaned his shoulders against the wall. "Well, I thought their going off with him a bad idea, especially taking Lyren, but Liere seemed to think there was no danger. Even though she was more of a target than I was when Siamis hunted us both during his first attempt against the world."

"Tsauderei tells me that that was more in the nature of an experiment, or a test." Peitar's tone was reflective.

"If that was a test, then I don't want to see what it was a test for."

"I believe," Peitar said slowly, "that is to come."

Senrid snorted in amusement. "You think Siamis's hop over the fence is fake."

"I think it's a ruse." Peitar backed to the wall, his hand still in his coat pocket. "Nothing else makes sense."

Senrid understood in that moment that Peitar Selenna didn't want it to make sense. And he knew why. He'd been there when Siamis shot Derek Diamagan, Peitar's closest and most trusted friend. The memory was still vivid, how Derek had flung a dagger at Siamis, but Siamis was faster.

Peitar went on slowly, "I cannot fathom whether Siamis

really is Detlev's enemy—running on his own—or under his command." Then he shook his head, and his tone changed. "I suppose it doesn't matter. There is still no justice either way."

"I think it does matter," Senrid stated. "Detlev is far worse."

Peitar made a gesture of acceptance. "I know so little about how things truly operate in Norsunder. There has to be a command structure."

"There isn't."

They both turned, and there was Clair, standing in the doorway.

"Oh. Hello. What did you learn while you were in Aldau-Rayad?" Peitar asked.

Senrid bit his lip. Clair had refused to talk to *him* about what had happened to her while Detlev's prisoner, but maybe she would to Peitar.

"Not much," Clair said flatly. "But you can't help hearing things. Unless one of the Host comes out, everybody is competing to be a commander. You get power by grabbing it."

Peitar looked around slowly, taking in the enormous suite that had belonged to King Berthold and his queen. The artists hired to do the carving and painting were half done. Only two pieces of furniture had been brought in. The rest was bare.

"What I don't understand is, why did Norsunder turn and leave again after Kessler Sonscarna conquered Everon that summer?" Peitar asked, tipping his head back to study the fresh molding under the ceiling, and the half-painted ceiling of stars against a blue field. That way he didn't have to see the steel-bright intensity of Senrid's aura, or the dull blue of Clair trying to smother emotions she obviously did not want to feel.

"My guess is, couldn't hold it," Senrid said.

"Or wouldn't," Clair muttered, her head bent as she examined the beautiful pattern of wheat sheaves edging the new table. Her white hair swung forward, covering her face and nearly making her invisible against the equally snow-white window behind her.

"Wouldn't?" Peitar repeated.

Clair straightened and crossed her arms again. When she didn't speak, Senrid said in his Marloven-accented Sartoran, the consonants precise, "If what Clair said is true, and I believe her—I've heard similar speculation—none of the other head snakes were willing to commit their own forces to holding

Everon against whoever was bound to come against them. The smart ones knew it was going to be a belt-tightened winter anyway, as Kessler's slaughter-and-burn strategy had destroyed so much of the ripening harvest. So Detlev ordered them to pull out—as we found out from Tsauderei."

"And thus we come back to what Detlev plans and when," Peitar said, clasping his hands behind his back as he gazed at the snow-blinded window. "In every record I can find about Ancient Sartor, they claim they'd almost eradicated our instinct for violence. But then Norsunder came, and sparked it into flame."

Peitar lifted his gaze away from the window, studying Clair and Senrid before repeating, "Flame." His expression tightened. "Flame burns clean. Violence is dirty. The Fall was dirtier. Our ancestors were knocked back to scrabbling for enough to eat, and so began four thousand years of crawling back toward civilization. At this end of the continent we've enjoyed the Covenant of Civility, as huge wars have given way to a combination of diplomacy and mostly marching and maneuvering. Now Norsunder wants to take it away again, even though we have yet so far to go."

Senrid looked down at the floor. Both he and Clair sensed Peitar's intensity, though not the emotion driving it.

"But real war with or without arrows is just as dirty," Peitar said to Senrid, as if he'd spoken, the bleak winter light harsh along his cheekbones, darkening his eye sockets. "I saw it in my own land when we revolted against my uncle. We'd rid ourselves of kings and nobles, but could we settle in peace as everyone had expected? No. Everyone wanted to be what amounts to a petty king, shouting one another down at every gathering until they formed into a mob to tear at one another."

His voice sharpened. "And when we tried to get them to choose someone to speak for their guild or group, even Derek, with all his persuasive powers, could not convince them to vote for the best representative, rather than the handsomest, or the one they liked the most as a drinking friend, or who'd bribed them with promises no one could fulfill. And so my uncle took the kingdom back again, and it was only happenstance that he lost it to me. It seems we're incapable of ruling ourselves, though I've been trying, slowly, to put decision-making into more hands than mine."

"But it *can* work," Clair said, and Peitar's austere gaze

turned her way, as again he fingered whatever it was in his pocket. "It can work. At least, in Mearsies Heili. It took a couple of generations — like anything, people need to learn how to do a thing. After the nobles lost power in my grand-father's day, people did learn how to govern themselves. I know I'm a queen but really, the provincial governors — chosen by the guilds and farm enclaves — have the most power. I'm a last resort if someone doesn't like a decision, a tie breaker, and I . . ."

Clair faltered, recollecting that Mearsieanne was slowly altering things back to the way they had been in *her* day, with all decision-making flowing back to her capable hands.

Clair flushed, but didn't want to share her doubts about Mearsieanne's unspoken strategy to regain power for the crown, a strategy that Clair had only begun to perceive since her return. Since she didn't want to talk about Mearsieanne at all, she tried a subject change. "There are other places where people choose. Anyway, what you said about mobs tearing each other apart. I keep thinking about what I read about mobs in this book Roy gave me, about training in tactics, strategy, and supplies. It was in the chapter about strategy."

"Strategy," Senrid cut in, gaze distant. "I wonder if they stole the Gand text." He snapped his fingers, and looked up. "It's a distillation of Inda's teaching, eight hundred years ago."

"If you mean Inda as another name for the Fox, or the Elgar, I thought that was mere legend." Peitar looked askance. "I myself have seen at least three separate origin stories, all from different lands."

Senrid sighed, and Clair let her breath trickle out: subject successfully changed.

"You've been talking to Leander." Senrid made a wry face at Peitar. "He keeps hitting me with those three origin stories as proof that Inda never existed, though we Marlovens *know* he was a real person."

"My objection is to the concept of an elgar," Peitar said, with a smile too sad to be mocking. "An elgar being somehow set apart from the worst of Norsunder, though both are known only for the effectiveness of their killing."

Silence followed that, except for the soft pat of snow against the window.

"I'm not," Senrid said finally, "going to justify Inda to you. I don't know enough myself, except that he defended Marlo-

ven Hess of old against the invading Venn. And then he refused to fight anymore."

At that Peitar's head came up and his expression changed
to remorse, red staining his cheeks. He pinched the skin
between his brows, then dropped his hand. "Forgive me. I'm
being simple in my judgment, in a situation that was anything
but simple. From early childhood I believed that the evilest
thing anyone could do is take the tools of making from a
carpenter, or a repairer of pots, or a painter of ceramic, and
put a weapon in their hands instead. Then train them to march
over borders to kill people like themselves at the whim of
some king. But Derek pointed out that these people should
have the right to defend themselves, and the wherewithal to
take up their tools again when the peace was regained."

"Nothing wrong with that," Senrid said, and to all their
relief, he turned to Clair. "I interrupted you. I know what
Gand wrote about mobs. What did your text say?"

"It's an odd thing." Clair's forehead puckered. "You'd
think, if Detlev wants everybody dead, he'd be fine with mobs
and their destruction. Anyway, it said that the military is
about how to organize and contain violence. Mobs have no
structure, so they can be worse than any invading army."

"That's the Gand text, word for word." Senrid turned up
his hand. "Either everyone agrees to the sharing and expression of power, or else the military is there to enforce it."

Peitar said, humor flashing in the deepened corners of his
mouth, "Sartor has whole buildings full of writings on
statecraft — the origins of law, of justice, and how we mutually
agree to keep the peace, and to protect the weak, and how we
should put armies to work maintaining roads and bridges."

Senrid snorted. "Nobody volunteers to do that stuff,
though they might be ordered to by a captain. As for statecraft, even we Marlovens have some books on it, though more
than half of 'em are fart noise justifying this or that king as
being superior to everyone else. Especially the ones from —"
He cut himself off before saying *Sartor*.

"And so," Peitar said, "we come back to our natures as
predators. We fight it, or ignore it, or create elaborate traditions and rituals to control it. But it's there, and Norsunder
knows it. I see it in myself," he added in a low voice, and
Senrid watched his arm flex as his hand tightened on whatever he carried in his pocket.

Twenty-three

Sartor

DAVID CROUCHED IN THE lee of a massive stone acanthus flower corbel. He and Adam perched on the narrow ridge running around the second story of the building housing the tailor's shop, across from the mage school in Eidervaen. The corbel didn't give them much shelter from the sleet battering the stone, but he was grateful for what he could get.

They'd spent the past two weeks in cat-shadow stealth while they waited for the right weather, after both Ferret and Erol had reported to David that the protection detail around the sisters had become so ingrained in habit that they never looked around anymore, especially when the weather was nasty.

David wanted the grab-and-swap to go as clean as a single wood-curl when he carved a flute. Which he'd been doing to keep his hands busy during this tense yet dull wait for the perfect sleet storm. Dull when he had to sit and watch, tense when he prowled the perimeter, watching for anyone watching *them*. It wasn't the Sartorans he watched for. The itchy feeling between his shoulder blades might only be from not being used to action without MV on his flank, ready to back him with either magic or steel. But MV was somewhere along the strait, fighting Ghanthurian pirates; since Detlev had sent him directly, David dared not pull him back. His next best muscle, Leef and Rolfin, were somewhere on the road south, keeping Bostian's spies on the run. Curtas had gone back to Norsunder Base to take over watching the critters, and Laban was about to be exposed as a spy on another continent entirely.

David and Adam had ridden in from the border, as had Silvanas and Noser. No magic transfers, so no risk of tripping tracer wards. They'd walked peacefully into the city to join Erol and Ferret, who had swapped off spy duty. David put two to work patrolling the outside perimeter, two inside. Four weren't enough to cover all possible avenues of approach. But they were all he had.

Ferret, barely visible around the corner at an angle, lifted his hand in the flat-handed signal *They're coming*, and a fast pair of heartbeats after, the fist meaning *No change in the order of their approach.*

David and Adam slipped down from their perches, and moving fast hand over hand, used the carvings as a ladder until they dropped to the street. They separated to either side of the narrow alley that opened into the back of the mage guild building, below the floors of the school. They were in place before the tramp of feet slogging through the slush echoed up the stone near the corner. David gripped the pebbles he'd prepared with stone spells, and half-bent, batting the icy water off his coat as he glanced sideways. As he'd expected, the husky mage students appointed as guardians to the sister with the flute were hunched each into his or her coat and hat, leaning into the gust of wind blowing sleet at their faces. They gave David the barest glance.

Ferret drifted up behind them unnoticed. David waited for the last of them to pass him, then he moved swiftly, tapping a stone to each back, as Adam stepped up to the tall, reedy girl who had to be the fifth worlder. Even bundled in a coat, she was thin as a reed. The students plopped heavily into the ice-clogged gutter, face down.

"I'll take that," Adam said, reaching for the cord around the sister's neck.

"No," she whispered, but Adam caught hold of her arm, knife held to cut the silken cord.

David reached for the first bespelled student guard in order to pull their noses out of the water. Ferret moved to help, but David said, "Perimeter!"

Ferret splashed up to the other end of the alley and disappeared around the corner as David began slinging the stone-spelled students to the wall to keep them from drowning helplessly in the gutter running down the center of the alley.

"No, no, no," the sister cried, struggling violently to free herself.

Adam tripped her expertly over his hip, nipping the flute from the swinging bag. His breath caught at the weird sense assailing his Dena Yeresbeth the moment he touched the thing.

The girl fell to hands and knees at his feet, scrabbling fruitlessly on the ice as she tried to get her feet under her. He was about to drop the fake one from his sleeve when a footstep splashed at the other end of the alley. A tall young man sauntered out, holding Ferret high against him by the arm bent behind his back, a dagger at his throat.

"Loyand." David breathed the name.

Aldon's best tracker was notorious for exacting hard prices for his services. Aldon hadn't been seen for a year and more. Someone had sent for Loyand. Dejain? *No, Zhenc.* Loyand smirked, gaze on Adam, who had frozen, holding the flute, as Horsefeathers struggled to get to her feet, slipping on ice that she was still unused to.

"Neat work," Loyand said, and to Adam. "I'll take that. Or." He gestured with his chin at Ferret, and his hand tightened. Blood, dark in the gloom, began trickling down Ferret's neck.

"Take it," Adam exclaimed hoarsely. "But don't blow on it." Even with Dena Yeresbeth tightly leashed he could feel the flute loaded with wards so strong that the magic scraped seductively over the contours of the bones in his hand.

Loyand snapped Ferret away, expertly holding his wrist until his elbow joint fractured. Ferret fell to his knees, silently cradling his broken arm and Loyand snatched the flute away from Adam. And with a contemptuous glance at Adam, he twirled the flute, handling it like a horn, and blew into the mouthpiece.

The note emerging from the flute, high and hard enough to

crack glass, blended horribly with Horsefeathers's sobbing, and another higher, raw, throat-scraping scream — from Loyand. His distended eyes stared blindly upward, his mouth a rictus of pain, the hand holding the flute blistered red. Blood trickled thinly from his nose, eyes, and ears. Adam dashed up, letting his sleeve fall over his hand before he grabbed the flute from Loyand, and as everyone stared in horror at Loyand, Adam dropped the fake from his sleeve, and replaced the real one with it.

Everyone else, including Horsefeathers, stilled as tiny black lines spread from Loyand's eyes through the rest of him and then outward into the air, like ink in water. They thickened and slowly, then more rapidly, began to whirl in a vortex around him, like slashes in the fabric of the world. When they tightened in and coalesced around his body, he stood — a still silhouette — then he fell into dust that the rain scoured away down the gutter, light gray against the wet gray stone.

Three of Loyand's trackers approached from behind, led by Zhenc, Dejain's chief rival among Norsunder's mages, a tall man with a shock of gray hair. Two held Erol and Noser, both looking bloody and disheveled. Their gazes stayed on the space where Loyand had stood.

Without glancing Adam's way, David said to Zhenc, "You saw what happened. Wasn't us."

"We'll take it anyway."

Zhenc's pale gaze remained on the spot where Loyand had stood as Adam held out the false flute, still with his sleeve over his fingers.

"Bag," Zhenc said — he clearly wasn't going to touch it.

Adam bent, flexing his arm to hold the real flute within his sleeve. He cut the silken cord hanging loose as the trembling Horsefeathers tried once again to get her feet under her. Adam slid the false flute into the bag and surrendered it. Then Zhenc lifted his chin minutely, and the trackers released Noser and Erol.

"Now," David said to his boys. They transferred out one by one, and so did the Norsundrians.

Horsefeathers collapsed sobbing, heedless of her numbing hands, as the first of the stone-spelled student guards groaned, shivered, and then began to cough and retch helplessly into the now empty alley.

At Norsunder Base, David fell into Detlev's office, water running off him to puddle onto the floor, the stink of hot metal making it plain that transfer anywhere in the fortress was still volatile. Transfer reaction felt more violent than ever before. He was glad he'd only risked himself, though he knew the others would curse having to ride in from the far perimeter.

David changed, then forced himself to go to the brat lair. Curtas was there reading.

"What happened?" Curtas asked as he set aside the book. "Brats?"

"Out. I put them through one-on-one then ran 'em out on the field until they were ready to drop. Got food into 'em and . . ." He jerked his thumb over his shoulder to the smaller alcove where they slept. "Bad?"

"Zhenc somehow got Loyand and his band. They had us pantsless—moved in just as we were making the grab." David gave a succinct report as Curtas's pleasant face tightened.

"Did Adam make the switch?"

"I didn't see—I was watching Loyand," David said grimly.

"Close. Too close," Curtas said. "Zhenc obviously let us do all the work before moving in."

David's fluent execrations were his answer.

Curtas shook his head slowly. "D'you think Detlev expected that to happen?"

No answer, of course. Detlev questions were mostly rhetorical.

"I should have been there to help," Curtas muttered. "I hope Adam didn't touch the thing."

"He did. Nothing happened to him. Which makes me worry that he mixed up the two, and handed off the real one. Not that I'd blame him for getting rattled, after what happened to Loyand. Anyway. Not a chance I'd leave Noser alone with the brats. He wouldn't be able to stop himself if Paolan started yelling. It was a close run with Zhenc. Could have been worse. Now it's done." David ran his hands through his hair, slung the water onto the floor, then said, "I'm going for coffee. Clear my head while we wait for Adam."

The storm had moved south enough to fall in a thin, cold, needling rain when Ferret and Adam showed up, Adam half-carrying Ferret, who was white-faced from the pain of his broken elbow. "Other two are right behind us," Adam said hoarsely, shivering from the cold.

"I'll get him to the medic," Curtas said, sliding an arm under Ferret's good arm, and taking most of his weight.

Adam dropped the flute from inside his coat sleeve onto the table.

David said, "Which one is that?"

"Real one."

David expelled his breath in relief. He could have sworn he'd seen Adam touch the thing without harm, them shrugged it off. Didn't matter. Real or fake, they were getting rid of the damn thing as fast as they could. "Drop it in Detlev's office. Without getting it anywhere near your skin."

Adam said, teeth chattering, "No chance. It's . . . *weird.*" Even through the fabric of his shirt sleeve, he'd felt the powerful magic on it, a resonance in his bones.

"You taunted Loyand into blowing it. Did you know that was going to happen?"

"I did not." Adam blew out a breath. "I could feel the magic on it. So very much magic. I thought it would jolt him — confuse him — so I could palm the switch while his attention was not on me."

"What kind of magic?" David hated sharing on the mental plane. But he refocused his shield in a way that had become easier after weeks of gritting through practice, and Adam shared images, a torrent of white hurling outward from mountain steep to steep, sun spinning its light outward . . .

An abrupt halt of the images rocked David on his feet. His awareness, rammed back inside the limit of his skull, found brief release in painful intensity of all five senses: his clothing scraped against his skin when he shifted, and he fancied he could feel the warp and weft of each thread; the smell of old stone; the roar of rain on the slate roof; the taste of the dusty air.

He opened his eyes, to meet Adam's. Despite the dark circles under his eyes, Adam's assessing brown gaze had lost none of its acuteness.

"I don't understand the magic part at all," Adam said. "But it seems to center around a specific place."

"Mountains a component. Who, or what, were the white things?"

Adam shrugged, hands out. "It feels like . . . almost like . . . a world within a world." Adam had closed his eyes, then opened them again, his musing tone more practical. "Part of it is missing. I think. Also: I don't know if it matters, but I saw blood on Loyand's hand. Under his nails."

A wail from one of the brats echoed from a far room. David sighed. "What a life!"

"I'll stash the artifact, if you deal with Paolan," Adam said. "I have to get out of these wet clothes."

"Done." David laughed as Adam used a paper to scrape the flute onto another paper, and then picked that one up by the corners.

They separated, one to the tend to the little ones, the other to Detlev's office.

Twenty-four

TSAUDEREI LISTENED TO THE clamoring voices talking over each other. In the background, Horsefeathers sobbed angrily, her long, thin fingers still clutching at a broken silken cord at her neck as if the flute would suddenly reappear in its bag. She sawed the cord back and forth with her fingers so that the cord began to cut into the back of her slender neck.

"Stop that," Leotay said, dropping to her knees and grabbing her sister's hands with both of hers. "Cease. You will hurt yourself."

"I deserve to hurt myself," Horsefeathers retorted fiercely, in their own language. "I lost it! I should have left it, as they said they would protect it, and us —"

"I agreed to it, too," Leotay said in a soft tone that caused Horsefeathers to sniff, and look up, her puffy red eyes watchful.

They both had agreed that these foreigners, though kind and everything that was good, would never care as much as they did for an artifact they did not own, or understand. Horsefeathers saw that there was some extra meaning in her sister's gaze, and compressed lips. Something unsaid.

Hiccoughing, she sat up. "What is it?"

"A thing I did not tell you, as it has gnawed my heart, and I saw no reason for it to gnaw yours. But the Sartorans are not the only ones to lose that of importance." And at Horse-feathers' fearful, questioning gaze, she said, "Lyal is missing. Lilith sent a message: while she was at another world, where the enemy also strives, he vanished from our kin. It is said he climbed the wall daily, looking outward. And one day, he was no longer there. It is believed the enemy got him."

Horsefeathers thought of Jeory's sweet-faced brother, youngest of the knife fighters. "Got him or killed him?"

"We do not know. But this, now, has decided me, I must go back. Do you go with me, or do you stay, and learn?"

Some of Horsefeathers' ferocity returned. "I will not go back without the Thing."

Leotay became aware of a silence, and straightened up, to find Tsauderei's acute gaze on her. He had dismissed the miserable, guilt-ridden and sodden mage students to sleep off the headaches caused by the stone spell.

Leotay said in Sartoran, "I must return to my home. But my sister wishes to stay, and learn."

Horsefeathers sat up, looking from one to another as her long hair drifted over her arms. "And perhaps, if there is a way to recover the Thing?"

Tsauderei spoke at last. "I believe Horsefeathers would do well at the northern school. And she wouldn't be here if these wretched minions of Detlev's decide to return for another try at either of you."

Horsefeathers bowed her head in acceptance.

Early Spring, 4749 AF
Everon

Peitar had decided not to trust to the tracers he'd laid over Tahra's palace. If he was to waylay Siamis, he needed over-lapping preparations.

The last time he accompanied Lilah to Everon, he sought Jenel Sandrial, the Delieths' head steward, and asked if he might give her a message token to be used the moment Siamis came back with Tahra and Liere. Her face showed no reaction to the request, but her aura blazed up into bright green as she promised to keep the token with her. Peitar had no idea if that green meant enthusiasm, resentment, or surprise. But she kept her word.

Spring had begun fuzzing the ground and trees in Everon when she sent the token. Peitar immediately transferred north. The moment the magic left him, he stumbled out of the Destination, stomach churning, his hand closing tight on the stone spell token he had carried with him all this time, just to discover Liere, Tahra, Lyren, and Mac alone in the antechamber to the Destination, recovering from world transfer.

Siamis had escaped him.

Peitar backed away before the girls saw him. And though the transfer reaction still gripped him—he knew he would be returning to Everon again with Lilah in short order—he forced himself to transfer back home, to recover in isolation from the bitter fury that made his breath short and his hands tremble. He hated this lingering, futile rage, worsened by his lack of success with his other pursuit. Every Purad he had tried since New Year's had been empty of music, leaving him aware of his impatient steps over soggy half-frozen ground, his mind stuck in a circle of conjecture that seemed never to provide answers.

Back in Everon, the new arrivals recovered.

Tahra's throat closed at the familiar aromas of home, overlaid by the fresh loam smell of spring. Then she forgot the smells when she walked out of the Destination antechamber, and looked around at the familiar space with its unfamiliar paint, decorations, mosaics, and furnishings.

New paint, decorations, and the rest.

Lyren ran off, Mac following as she shrilled, "Jenel! Jenel! We're back!"

Liere stepped out next. As she recovered from the transfer spell, she watched Jenel Sandrial pull a plain wooden disc from her apron pocket and whisper over it before carefully laying it down again as if it were made of glass.

"Magic?" Liere asked.

"The queen of Sartor gave it to me," Jenel said, and with mild triumph, "There were two monarchs who wished to know right away about the return of our Queen Hatahra. I already sent the one to the King of Sarendan."

Behind her, Tahra wandered in amazement from room to room as the conspirators—duly contacted by Atan—began transferring in from their various kingdoms.

Clair was the first. She halted just outside the Destination, startled when she saw Tahra, tall, long-faced and sallow; though it had only been a few months, Tahra had definitely left childhood behind. But at least she was smiling, something Clair hadn't seen for a long time. In contrast, Liere looked unchanged, her pale hair hacked off raggedly. She most definitely had not lifted the Child Spell. No, almost the same. Her fingernails had grown, the skin around them healed. It seemed she had ceased gnawing them. But there was the old, happy smile when Senrid walked in from the Destination chamber, and stopped beside Clair.

Senrid greeted them both, then said to Liere, "Where's Siamis?"

"I don't know. I thought he'd transfer with us, but I guess he didn't."

Senrid's eyebrows shot upward. "Why did he take you off world in the first place? Whom did he visit? Of course it's a ruse of some sort. But for Norsunder or against them?"

Liere stared at her oldest and best friend. Everything she'd heard and seen, people and observations she had piled up, she'd looked forward to sharing with Senrid. And here Senrid was, but he wasn't asking about her. He wanted to know about *Siamis*.

"He wasn't always with us," she said. "I don't know if he's got other plans. He would probably not tell us if he did. But he chose places and people we liked — first Geth, which I did not want to go to, after that horrible time I was a prisoner there, but it turned out to be so much fun . . ."

Senrid heard the drop in tone, saw the disappointment in her face, and caught himself up. Of course Siamis would hide his purpose. Senrid had always been two steps behind Siamis. Two steps? More like ten. No different now. He understood that he no longer had the inside line of communication, if he ever had had it — but worse, he'd managed to disappoint Liere, whose bright smile had vanished the moment he said Siamis's name.

He exerted himself to ask questions about people and places he had never seen, and wouldn't ever see, and had no interest in, because Liere seemed eager to talk about them. His reward was a gradual return to her old self.

Lyren and Mac reappeared at a run, Mac brightening when he saw Clair. He ran straight to her, and started gabbling in Norsundrian, as Liere and Senrid broke off their conversation. Mac didn't notice their startled expressions at the sound of that language as he gave Clair a disjointed, typically little-kid version of his travels.

Lyren then showed up. "Mac! Sartoran! That language is *disgusting.*"

"Why disgusting?" Mac shot back. "It's just words." But he made the switch to Sartoran, after which he and Lyren got sidetracked into a squabble about words. They sounded like brother and sister.

At the other end of the palace, Atan walked out from a side hall, her brocade over-robe rustling. "Ah, there you are!" She greeted Lilah and Peitar, who were just stepping out of the transfer Destination.

Tahra turned Atan's way, reddening to the ears. "What — was this your doing?"

Atan lifted a hand, but before she could speak, Lilah pressed forward, bouncing on her toes, her thick shock of rusty hair flapping around her round, freckled face.

"It was us all," Lilah exclaimed, arms thrown wide. "We *all* took rooms. Come on, see the library! That was Peitar and me! He picked out the books himself. And I added a lot of good ones about adventuring princesses, with CJ's help!"

Tahra willingly let herself be led on a second round of inspection. The truth is, she scarcely saw the handsomely fitted out rooms, gilt, painted, carved, plastered, tiled. Those things mattered little, other than small places needing squaring. It was the deed she struggled to compass. Wonder and gratitude swelled her heart, and emotions she couldn't name, except that they hurt but felt good at the same time. She paused in the royal suite, which was plainly decorated, most of the art in the carved furnishings. She turned to Senrid. "My brother would have liked this very much."

Senrid heard the sincerity in her voice. He also remembered how frustrated Tahra had been with Glenn's obsession with war as he got older. Senrid couldn't bring himself to mouth out the hypocrisy that lighters seemed to require for politeness, so all he said was, "It's yours now."

Tahra looked around once more, then her sharp chin jerked down. "Yes," she stated in the voice of decision. "Yes, it's time. I was going to . . . on his birthday . . . or Mother's, but you're all here, and what you did, well, it's only right for you to see. And I can feel it . . ."

"Feel what?" Lyren asked, clapping her hands.

"The Birth Spell," Tahra whispered.

Jenel gave a faint, scandalized shriek. "Not without — " She fled, her apron flapping as she called for her daughter and nieces to fetch nursery linens.

When she returned with a row of servants carrying loads of blankets, diapers, baby dresses, and a young knock-kneed nephew solemnly bearing a cradle, it was to discover Tahra and Liere — the only expert in the room — holding two naked, squirming newborns.

Jenel gave another faint shriek. "Twins?"

Tahra nodded at the cradle, looking a little shaken. "They can share it. Meet Princess Mersedes Carinna and Prince Berthold Jessan."

At a quick shooing from Jenel, a delighted Sandrial daughter and her cousin came forward with the linens, and the babes were surrendered to be dressed.

"Those are long names," Lyren said, looking around at everyone with the smile of a little girl who loved being the center of attention. "Though not as long as mine."

Tahra smiled her way. "We'll call her Carl. Just like my mother. And he can be Jessan." She faced the circle of conspirators. "Will you all stay for their Name Day?"

Clair and Liere, who understood the sudden demand now placed on the Sandrials to not only come up with an instant nursery staff but a party, turned in question to Jenel, who proved to be mistress of any domestic situation. "If you will finish up the tour, your majesty," she said with a grand curtsey, "we'll have a celebration within the hour."

CJ had airily said to Clair that she had a little headache and couldn't face a transfer. Clair understood what remained unsaid, and so it was she alone who led the party to the nursery wing, where everyone admired the many toys, for children from babyhood to older, and then finished with compliments to the graceful painting under the ceiling and around the windows.

"It was CJ's plan," Clair said firmly, though she knew Tahra had little interest in forests, and suspected that Tahra was hearing maybe one word in ten. "She would also liked to have given your children a forest scene on these walls, but she heard that the fashion in Everon was this."

Tahra didn't even hear that much. Her astonished gaze kept moving from one to the other twin, but then she turned slowly around and proclaimed in a thin, hieratic voice, "I am going to fill this room with children. Norsunder did its best to destroy my family, so I'm going to make it as big as I can. *Lots* of children, as many as possible."

"Are you getting married?" Lilah asked, eyes round.

"Never." Tahra's thin, sallow face tightened with disgust, and those who knew her remembered how she loathed being touched. "If they don't come in the Birth Spell, then I'll adopt them."

Everybody exclaimed appropriately, few believing that her passionate words would be remembered much past a week — all except for Liere, who had begun to understand Tahra while they were traveling, and knew a vow when she heard one. But she said nothing, and followed along as they moved again through all the rooms more slowly, taking the time to listen to each donor tell the story of the choosing and making of each piece. They fetched up in the library, where Lilah gave a tour of the books. Clair found Liere walking next to her, the great golden eyes observant.

Liere said, "Is everything all right?"

Clair habitually kept a mind-shield now, so whatever Liere had seen had been in her face. But she wouldn't expose CJ's private struggles. She gave voice to a worry she hadn't meant to discuss at all, "Bad dreams."

"Detlev? And those horrible boys?" Liere asked, with ready sympathy.

Clair couldn't have said why she felt it necessary to correct her, but she said, "No. Not them. But that world. It's . . . I don't know, I don't think my mind believes I'm done with Aldau-Rayad. I keep dreaming about the caves of the mountain people, though I never even saw them. And lava, and breaking rock, and oh, you know dreams. Never make any sense."

"But they can still hurt," Liere said softly.

"Yes," Clair said.

Lilah bounced up, rubbing her hands. "Jenel Sandrial ordered spice cakes! And pear cider. And Lurei says there's hot custard for the cakes. Come on, let's be first in line!"

While they talked about him, Siamis was looking around a village a day's journey from the market town of Sayin at the northwest end of Telyerhas. Those months away had effectively broken all the wards and tracers on him that he had agreed to in his truce with Tsauderei. Now no one in the world or outside of it knew where he was.

By the time he reached the capital, he intended to have a solid identify established among scribes, who had the most comprehensive network of communication in the world.

It would take time. That was fine. He had a secondary goal. This one was personal.

Twenty-six

Summer 4749 AF
Norsunder to Norsunder Base

"ZHENC WAS FASTER THAN you were," Yeres said, after having summoned the mage Dejain to her favorite lair in the Garden of the Twelve. "Even Detlev's babies were there! Though none of them were fast enough in spite of Loyand's stupidity, Zhenc said. I'm not surprised. There's a reason Efael didn't want Loyand in the Black Knives. But Dejain." A low, cooing tone, sweetly chiding. "Why didn't you find that artifact first?"

"Because you wanted me laying traps for Siamis. In case he showed up at Norsunder Base," Dejain said humbly. The old habit of meek servitude, low voice, deferent manner, the right words avoiding the speech of power, saved Dejain's life — she could see it in the roll of Yeres's eyes. "Whatever Destination he used was not one we've warded."

"Which is why we must have that book Wan-Edhe made that tracks enemies. We know it exists."

"But no one has been able to get into Narad's citadel," Dejain said. *Including you.* She didn't dare say it.

"Then beat Zhenc to it." Yeres said. "You know he'll be back there again. Prove your worth to me, Dejain, and I'll take care of you."

The sense that she had to rely on these stupid, clumsy people frustrated Yeres, but she was not going out into the drag of time until absolutely forced to—and that would be only right before they were sure to break time forever. She snapped her fingers, made a gesture of dismissal, and Dejain slammed back into the Destination at Norsunder Base.

For a heartbeat, the room wavered, the hot stench of burning metal causing her to sneeze violently. She threw herself out of the space before the Destination could implode, and landed painfully, her brittle bones jarring.

Slowly she picked herself up, trembling in every limb. She gestured an illusory gate across the doorway. If others were smart, they would heed it, if they didn't smell the volatility first. She made her way to her lair that was no lair. All her careful wards had vanished when Yeres forced her away. It would only get worse if Yeres possessed Wan-Edhe's enemy tracking book. Dejain summoned a lackey to bring food and hot drink, and sat to think out her next move.

Independence was an illusion. Efael and Yeres had decided to go to war against Detlev, which ordinarily would amuse Dejain, except that they were grabbing whoever they wanted and forcing them into subordinate labor. Loyand was dead—Dejain wagered that Zhenc had promised to get him entry into Efael's elite assassins. Zhenc's influence was growing.

Late that night, while Norsunder Base was hammered by a last blizzard in what northwards was a cold, late spring, she crossed over to the courier annex, where she knew Detlev and his irritating brats had their lair. She felt the interlocked rings of tracers, and did not attempt the stairs. Sure enough, within a short time one of them appeared, a tallish blond teenager, the one with sleepy brown eyes whom she often saw fetching and carrying at the mess hall: David, one of the two Detlev had trained in magic.

"Detlev isn't here," David said, making a move to step past her.

She blocked his way.

He waited.

Dejain looked around Siamis's age, except when you studied her closely. All the signs of dark magic age retardation were there: everyone knew the Child Spell only worked before puberty. After that, age was possible to retard, but only through the force of dark magic, and he was seeing its cost. Dejain was old, and though she kept her dainty chin high and her posture adamant, David could see in the tightness at either side of her mouth, her stiff shoulders, and the shadow of a forming bruise at one wrist that she was feeling the effects of age.

And while she was strong enough a mage to have survived on top of the heap of magic workers at the Base for years, she was not strong enough to have won recourse from time in the Beyond. Or she'd been too smart for the compromises they demanded.

"I know," she responded, stepping past him into the outer chamber. She gestured, warding the room.

David recognized the webwork of spells that she had prepared and seemed so effortlessly to position around them. "I want you to get a message to him," she said. "Yeres wants that enemies book in Chwahirsland's capital before Zhenc gets it. If one of you gets it for me, there will be a commensurate reward."

"Right," he said.

She took that as assent, as he'd hoped, and exited.

David stared at her retreating back. Shit, shit shit! This is what he got for lazing around when he had orders. He ran back upstairs, to where Adam was watching Sveneric trying to draw a horse from memory. Curtas sat on the floor with Paolan and Ki, building an elaborate structure with the wooden blocks, watched by Laban, who had just brought a meal.

David caught their gazes and jerked his head toward the door. The three got up and followed him to his room, leaving the door open behind them. "Dejain was just here. This is what you need to tell Detlev, her words exactly." And he repeated them.

They listened, having been well trained to convey messages as given, but Laban drawled, "And so, what, you're running off because of Dejain?"

"No," David said as he rolled the clothes and stuffed them into a knapsack. "Because I should've left for Chwahirsland last week. Earlier."

Adam said, "Ah."

Laban crossed his arms and leaned against the door, a lock

of curly dark hair falling on his brow. "You see some meaning here? How about enlightening the witless?"

"I don't know why Detlev gave that order to David," Adam said. "But he issued it before Yeres threatened Dejain. That suggests to me Detlev has reached a point in his plans where he doesn't want anyone else having that book. Or maybe he needs it."

Laban said derisively, "And that's your evidence that Detlev has a grand plan?"

David dropped the bag on the bed, threw open MV's trunk, and began picking through the impressive collection of cloth-wrapped daggers, knives, and swords.

Curtas observed, "MV won't like you taking his steel."

"He's not here to complain." David jerked a shoulder impatiently.

Laban snorted. "If he doesn't come back from his stint as a pirate with an entirely new collection, I'll do your house chores for a year."

No one took him up on that wager.

David said, "If I have to go into Chwahirsland alone, I'm going strapped." He chose MV's best wrist sheaths, then bent to yank up his trouser cuffs. As he slid the best two throwing knives into the loops in his riding boots, Laban said, "I still don't believe there's any grand plan. I think Detlev's running a defense, but it's disintegrating around him, with us galloping about pretending to be idiots. For what? Covering the fact that Siamis — Roy, even — really *are* idiots? Or are they the smart ones, and we're the idiots?"

"Do you really believe that?" Adam asked.

Laban's splendid coloring deepened as he flung back his head, blue eyes wide and angry, his luxuriant, waving dark hair spilling like silk. Laban didn't actually posture, but strikingly handsome people draw the eye dramatically even when totally unselfconscious. "All he sees fit to tell us is *nothing*. And now he's off in the Beyond playing hide-and-find with Efael, or Aldon, or who-the-shit-ever. While keeping us from doing anything *interesting*. And meanwhile, that idiot Tahra Delieth is now bringing more Delieths into the world to ensure another generation of mediocrity . . ."

They'd heard it all before. David cut into the flow. "Laban, you know as well as I do that when you're not sulking, you like a ruse better than any of us."

Laban delivered a pungent opinion of ruses — and David. As if in response, Paolan yelled, and Ki howled. Curtas turned to Laban, whose turn it was for brat patrol. Laban cursed louder as he ran back down the hall.

Adam said to David, "Have you come up with a plan for getting into Narad?"

"No," David said, shaking his loose cuffs down over the wrist sheaths. He hesitated over taking the black sword that Detlev had given him, its provenance only known to David. He was going alone into *Chwahirsland.* Of course he needed all his weapons. He fastened the sword over his back, grabbed a cloak, hitched his pack over his elbow, and said, "You and Curtas are in charge."

He didn't wait for an answer, but picked up the transfer token he'd made while hoping he'd think of some brilliant plan that would obviate his having to use it, and transferred to the mountainous border of Erdrael Danara, a day's walk from Chwahirsland.

He recovered from the transfer in bitter cold. The border was still piled with snow at that height. There was no hiding his deep footprints. He wanted to make it across the border before the Danaran Mountain Guard found him, but just in case, he'd better have an alias and a story worked out, something so dull that the Guard wouldn't want to take him back to Terry. Stealth meant not getting himself into kill-or-be-killed situations; if Terry found out that David was anywhere in his kingdom, he'd be forced into exactly that choice.

David kept his sword loose in the scabbard and forged on long past sunset, until he felt the weird hum in his bones that indicated he had crossed into Chwahirsland. Wan-Edhe's lethal wards persisted, testament to decades of effort. But David did not try any spells, and so he was able to enter the kingdom without detection. David walked until he couldn't see anything, found a place to hole up, and half slept through a long, icy night.

Twenty-seven

THE NEXT DAY, HE located a Chwahir mountain patrol outpost, thankfully empty. He found stores there, stale way-bread and dried fish. He settled in for the night as sleeting rain poured steadily. Once he was certain a patrol was not going to come in and find him, he composed himself and reached on the mental plane, an exercise far easier now.

Several months of hard practice had proved that Adam was right. Geography was indeed relative, more often mis-leading. He had never met Jilo, but he'd learned to search by niffing for self-awareness; he still could not dream-walk unless he knew the person well (and their mental-shield was gone) but unshielded thoughts he could now find.

Jilo was in reach, though he seemed impossibly far away, as dim and distorted as the sun at sunset when the horizon was clouding up. That was not distance but magic, David rec-ognized now. Jilo was present in Narad. And though the distortion was far too thick for David to discern thoughts, it was clear that Jilo was not intending to come out any time soon.

The next morning David loaded up his knapsack and began the long tramp down the mountain. Even an empty belly couldn't put any taste in the Chwahir travel food, but it kept him going, and a few days later he descended far enough to walk in mud instead of slush, and then — finally — stumbled onto an ancient road, long unkempt, as he got his first glance at Narad hulking grimly below.

The strangest thing of all was how remainders of what had once — thousands of years ago — been a magnificent city could still be glimpsed here and there. Between the bleak, narrow alleyways, a hint of an upsweeping corbel caught the eye, and at the north end, barely discernable from the unrelieved blocky masses of granite that the Chwahir had used to build for so many centuries, a single rooftop of bilateral symmetry.

In the oldest records, Chwahirsland was often called the Sleeping Dragon, an odd name considering how dragons had actually lived on the highest mountain tops and in the deepest sea waters. Detlev and Siamis had once taken the boys to the heights above Sartor, where it was always brutally cold and windy, and the air thin. Those vast rock walls were somehow exhilarating, though the dragons had vanished millennia ago. There was no evidence of dragons, except in the glassy smoothness of the walls where their fire had scorched, no evidence and certainly no art. And yet the horizontal lines here and there in Narad's oldest buildings, with their carving suggestive of sinuous flight, called dragons to mind.

These intriguing details were more noticeable at a distance. Inside the city gates, the burden of life-taxing magic dimmed vision to the space around one, conveying impressions of gray murk. What little sunlight filtered from the ever-present clouds seemed dirty.

David slipped into the slow foot traffic that mostly comprised groups of four, usually women, bent against yokes as they pulled wagons loaded with wares. He wrapped his dark cloak around him, keeping his light hair well covered, and his head bowed in the manner of the Chwahir as he plodded up the main thoroughfare toward the castle.

The press of dark magic wards intensified, creating a sense of compression on the lungs, as if he'd been swimming too long, or staying underwater past the time he needed air. He breathed open-mouthed, and noticed he was not alone in that.

The crowds slowly thickened, and David decided to inspect the perimeter of the castle first before attempting the walls, but scarcely had he rounded the first corner when a trace of licorice reached him. Humans possessing functioning eyes always think of sight first, followed quickly by sound, but smell is truly the fastest warning: David knew that smell.

He stepped behind a wagon and glanced ahead. Sure enough, Zhenc was already here. The licorice chewer was Suttir, one of Bostian's trackers; David caught sight of his heavy, sloping shoulders as the man sauntered up the street. Typically arrogant, he did not bother to look behind him, but David dropped back ten paces, keeping well behind a wagon full of turnips.

Suttir veered, and joined another familiar figure, tall, gray-haired Zhenc. David cursed himself for not having tackled this loathsome task the moment he'd returned from Eidervaen — and he cursed Zhenc for being so damned sedulous. It was clear he was slavering for the chance to kill someone, if only some miserable, half-enchanted Chwahir.

A third Norsundrian joined them from the other end of the street, obscured by the others, a short, pale older woman who used to be Henerek's tracker. The three held a short colloquy, Zhenc gesturing with a stiff hand toward the gate, a shock of gray hair falling over his high brow.

Suttir peeled off and followed a pair of Chwahir patrollers — but when he tried to go through the gate behind them, greenish light flared. David felt the metallic singe from his distance, as Suttir recoiled, nearly falling on his ass. Someone had warded Suttir by name.

The flare of triumph lasted less than a heartbeat, doused by the reflection that David surely had to be warded as well, after his having successfully laid that trap here for Kessler Sonscarna. David had hoped never to have to set foot in this place again. But he was here, and he had orders. He forced himself to attempt the first gate he reached, knowing that if one was warded, they all were — and he walked through.

His surprise cooled into suspicion. The ward against him was somewhere else, that was all. He drew in a deep breath, fighting the faint panging in his head that he remembered from his previous stay.

This time the enormous crowd of guards seemed more awake and aware. He risked an illusion, the lightest magic possible, creating the vague effect of another Chwahir. As long as no one studied him, it would get him across the court and into one of the side doors.

He forced himself to walk at the deliberate pace they all used, as if the entire population of the fortress shared the same headache. When he reached the shadowy entrance with its thick walls and mossy stone that gave off a wet, sour smell that made him grimace, he looked around and made for a stairway. Third floor, that was Jilo's lair.

Halfway up the stair leading to the third floor, the bone-scraping warning of a ward halted him with one foot not quite touching the next step. Tracer ward — against him, or general? David reached tentatively. Magic buzzed over his hands, but did nothing worse. It was not the lethal one Suttir had encountered at the gate. This was only the first layer, then apparently abandoned. Either that or the lure to a lethal trap further on.

At least David was inside, where Zhenc and the trackers could not get. He might as well take a look around in case Jilo came down for meals, or interviews, or whatever.

Sentries patrolled endlessly with a slow, deliberate tread. They were easy to dodge, sparking a thought on the futility of a complex guard system that failed to keep out intruders. Wan-Edhe (or Jilo) probably put all these people to work keeping watch on one another so they wouldn't escape the ever-present lour.

He poked into room after room, many empty, the stale air in some bearing the faintest metallic taint of old blood. The sparse furnishings did not promise comfort, being massy, ugly, barren of covers, much less cushions. The wood looked centuries old, nearly petrified.

One would assume that the third floor, the royal lair, would have all the light and comfort, but David had been there when lying in wait for Kessler, and it had been exactly as dark, far drearier, just with more of the ugly furniture.

He encountered a basic illusion of wall. A gesture and he spied the door the illusion hid. He entered and found a table covered with scry stones set up on either side of a slate window. Magic-sense stank of rusty metal in the still, stale air. David recognized what he was seeing: spy stones.

He walked up to the table and touched the slate, which looked at what had to be a military command center, from the maps and the dispatch trays lying on a long table. He touched each of the stones in turn. When he let his fingers linger, the scene in the slate changed after a short time, say the count of twenty: overall, from this table, one could see pretty much every intersection, court, entrance, and exit in the fortress, and all along the wall outside.

And there was Zhenc with Suttir and Henerek's tracker, now joined by a fourth: Bostian's pet Ris Fon, whose specialty was interrogation, or torture.

". . . find a way in, you can have the first cut," Zhenc was saying to Ris Fon.

David slid his butt into the tall wooden chair set before the table, and reached again in the mental realm for Jilo's self-awareness. If David had needed any proof that geographic distance was unreliable, he had it here — though he had to be, at most, two floors away from Jilo, his mental presence still seemed impossibly far off, and so distorted David could not perceive sensory details, much less thoughts.

But there was one difference: Jilo seemed to be on the move. David's consciousness returned. A held breath, a moment of disorientation, and he walked out, grimly glad of all that practice. He paused in the doorway, braced himself, and checked again on the mental plane to get a vector on Jilo, then set out to intercept him. The illusion reformed behind him.

He had no idea what to expect. Adam had reported a skinny boy of around fourteen or fifteen when he'd briefly seen Jilo early in the alliance days, but time had passed since then, and Jilo could be the size — and strength — of Rel. David was expecting such a threat, or how could Jilo rule this land and stave off the likes of Kessler Sonscarna?

At first he thought the scrawny, shambling boy at the other end of the corridor was a servant, except that the general outline and the baggy clothes corresponded exactly with the memory image that Adam had shared.

"Jilo?" David said.

The shambler stopped and turned, then put out a grimy hand to clutch at the wall. He blinked shadowed eyes as if having difficulty bringing David into focus. David had positioned his right hand to grab his sword and his left to spring a knife from the wrist sheath, though he didn't relish a fight in this breathless atmosphere. As Jilo blinked at him, looking vaguely puzzled, David's gaze went to the black grime on his fingers. "Inked chalk?" he asked, and then, "You were *drawing?*"

Jilo said in a creaky voice, "Don't know when I sketched last. Too much to do." His gaze dropped to his hands, as if they belonged to someone else. "Ash," he said. "Burned some.

. ." He let the sentence drift.

David eyed Jilo, who seemed weary and bleary, and risked the truth: "The enemies book?"

Jilo sighed. "No. Torture. Wan-Edhe's mind experiments."

David said, "Did you know you have four Norsundrians trying to get in?"

"Norsundrians?" Jilo repeated, obviously bewildered. David wondered if he was always that gray-skinned, or if his apparent witlessness was the result of some insidious spell. Except he could feel the pressure of layers of magic on his own skull.

"Among those after that book is Yeres. Of Norsunder." Since Jilo was, so far, absolutely nothing that David had expected, he took another risk. "Where is it?"

"Hidden," Jilo retorted, quickly enough.

David repeated what he'd overheard, then added, "How long after the first cut do you think you'll hold out?"

Jilo blinked. "Wan-Edhe warded everyone in Norsunder. Kessler added to the names. None of them can get inside here."

As he spoke, he was trying to remember who this newcomer was. Had they met before? He seemed familiar, or maybe it was just that he was tall and blond with a military haircut. Sent by Senrid?

David said, "They're determined. Are you sure everything is warded? Underground escapes? From what I've read about the Chwahir, there have to be a couple of tunnels here, at least."

Jilo's eyes widened, then narrowed. Wan-Edhe had actually not known about the dungeon tunnel, which Kessler had used when he'd escaped with his life. "Warded. So you came to help me?" Jilo asked warily. "Senrid can never stay."

David thought that leap interesting. "I've had training. I'm here to help you ward Zhenc of Norsunder," David said. That much was true, and wouldn't have to be remembered in this skull-cracking environment.

"Come upstairs. Wait. Wait. What did I come down here for?" Jilo pinched the skin between his eyebrows. "Oh. Food."

"I have some right here," David said, elbowing his pack.

"Then come on."

David followed close behind Jilo up the stairs, and when he felt that internal burning and smelled the singed metal that meant he was near the ward, he bumped into Jilo's scrawny form, grabbed his elbow and half-pushed him up the next step; he was ready to spring back at the first sign of internal heat.

His gamble paid off. The ward was only a single layer, and broke at David's physical connection to Jilo. But that effort left David gulping for air.

When Jilo turned to give him a wary look, David dug into his pack and pulled out strips of dried fish. As he'd hoped, Jilo was immediately distracted. He took the offering and munched absently, bending forward like an old man as he continued on up the steps. The thick, oppressive atmosphere closed around David, worsening as they gained the third floor, which David had spent time in before.

Jilo said, "How much do you know about mirror wards?"

"Some study." The atmosphere made it difficult to hold onto the simplest thought.

Jilo made another of those vague gestures with his grimy hands. "I finally found the underlying structure here. It's a perfect mirror ward."

David stared. "Perfect" had nothing to do with art or ethics. It meant lattices of odd numbers bound together in repetitions of another odd number, forming a number only divisible by the first number. Norsunder Beyond's more accessible outer layer was based, Detlev had told him, on a perfect mirror ward of eleven-strand lattices bound eleven times, the perfect number being one hundred twenty-one.

There was one of those *here?* And Jilo had found it under the morass of distortions and accretions? He was astonished that Jilo could even think, much less work, with the most powerful and dangerous spells in this lethal murk.

David tried to niff Jilo's mind, and then shuttered his consciousness when Jilo flicked a puzzled glance his way. David learned two things in that brief contact: that Jilo had made his coinherence without knowing what it was, and though he had no mind-shield, he'd constructed a mental framework to protect his thoughts from the corrosive atmosphere. The image was like a glass cage let down into water, from which one could see in all directions.

It was instinctive, easier to maintain than a mind-shield, and entirely effective. David shut his eyes and carefully formed his own mental glass cage. The vicelike pressure on his head eased somewhat. He could perceive the insidiousness still there, and his body still moved as if slogging through mud, but he could focus.

"Let me explain," Jilo said. "It might take some doing."

David gestured assent. The plan here was obvious: help Jilo enough to gain his trust, ask to see the book, take it. Get out.

Twenty-eight

Between Chwahirsland and a Northern Glade

DAVID — LIKE REL — WAS unaware of time drifting by, during which the Young Allies pursued their various activities.

In Everon, Tahra Delieth accustomed herself to life in the home that other hands had made new again, centered around the twin scraps of humanity in the nursery, and the duties required in guiding a once-devastated kingdom slowly back to stability.

In Mearsies Heili Clair continued to fight her pillow in increasingly persistent dreams about distant white mountains and winged creatures.

Liere moved back to Bereth Ferian, where she began magic studies with the beginners once more, but next to her sat Horsefeathers, while mage guards tightened security around the northern school and the surrounding city. Inside the palace, the marble halls rang with Lyren's and Mac's voices as they played.

Rel and David were completely unaware of the other, but in the light of later events, their efforts ran parallel before meeting up, so I will shift between them.

After being intercepted by Autumn, Rel had stepped from

the winter-bound palace in Sarendan to a leafy glade somewhere in the north as if stepping from one room to another. Magic transfer had never been so effortless, leaving him full of questions. He was not alone — three other students stood in the glade besides Rel, all looking as puzzled as he felt.

Autumn smiled guilelessly. "My sisters and I enjoy our human forms. In some ways we will be sorry when the time comes to change them for another form, in the way of our kind. But in other ways, it will come as a relief, for human senses can be so very limited."

She waited, but Rel remained quiet, as was his habit. The oldest student, a woman wearing the mage robe of the north, folded her hands inside her sleeves. A dark-haired girl of about sixteen, wearing the brown of a courier, crossed her arms. The skinny fair-haired dawnsinger, wearing a long belted tunic over loose trousers in a Colendi style, made a quick, very Colendi gesture of politeness. Then he smiled all around.

Autumn said, "Humans blunder through the world, unaware of the chaos of their wakes. You will not be able to gather the magic and use it if you persist in these habits. You are going to learn to listen, and to hear, and to move. Then you will learn together."

She indicated a pool nearby fed by a trickling waterfall, and began to wade out into it. "Your first lesson is to understand currents."

When Rel saw that he was expected to enter the water, he unslung his sword harness and laid aside his weapons on the grass. As he did, he caught a glance from the courier, a sharp-nosed girl whose mouth pruned as if he'd belched in her face.

Over the next two weeks, the four students spent most of the day in the water, repeatedly holding their breath and suspending themselves below the surface as they learned to perceive the slow ripple and drift of currents by the way plants and little fish moved.

Each morning after he woke, Rel took his weapons away to a glade by himself and worked through the Sartoran guards' daily sword drill until his muscles were warm and loose, as the dawnsinger went to another glade and danced to his own humming. At first, on Rel's return to their central gathering place, he caught disparaging looks from the courier girl's dark eyes, though she ignored the dancer. The mage, once she discovered none of them had studied magic, had nothing to say to any of them, and kept to herself.

Aronis Harper, the Colendi half-dawnsinger, chattered to them all, his lilting Colendi accent and cheerful demeanor making charming what might otherwise have been annoying. Then Rel recollected the Colendi style of politeness, conveyed through seemingly inane questions about comfort and shared likes that established one's status. Colendi had more strata than any social group that Rel had ever encountered, far more complicated than Sartor's first, second, and third circles.

It was Rel who was getting the most questions, which surprised him. As always when he traveled, he'd settled into his ready-to-hire wanderer self, without realizing how many subtle clues he betrayed about how much he had seen and experienced.

But he didn't mind the extra questions from the Colendi dawnsinger—he had learned long ago that the sort of Colendi he was drawn to were no more arrogant or superior than anyone else. Their complicated social strata sorted into specific verb tenses, types of address, and where they stood in a room, everyone gracefully going to their socially mandated place so that the whole agreed with harmony and order.

Through Aronis's chatty efforts, the students began to be less four separate people and more a group. The night before they left the water for the last time (everyone now able to discern the currents) Aronis sat next to Rel when they gathered in the treehouse where they slept. They shared around the basket of warm nutbread and fruit that they found waiting for them each morning and sunset, though so far, no one had seen the dawnsingers who brought it.

To forestall closer questioning under the guise of friendly chat, Rel said, "How is it you can say you'll be a dance teacher, when you are not yet a professional dancer?"

Aronis grinned. "It is the Sartoran, so limited in many words. Ah-ye, I cannot find the true translation, except to say dance-teacher, or love-guide."

"Love-guide?" Rel repeated.

Aronis gracefully flung his hands apart in the bird-on-the-wing, an untranslatable Colendi gesture that managed to convey astonishment, surprise, and acceptance. "How to say it? Perhaps in the dance. I could study merely dance, and yet, I find people are more interesting. They are the art. And so, as the teacher shows the prospective lover how better to find the beloved, the better dance teacher teaches not just the steps, but the . . . the peaceable self who makes the steps."

Rel sorted those words, then said, "You'll teach people courtship?"

Aronis opened his hands, then said, "Yes, and yet not quite yes. For some, 'courtship' I am told is to conceal, but we wish to teach how to reveal."

Reveal, taught by a Colendi who could not—like his countrymen—say the word *no*. Rel hid an inward flutter of laughter. He thoroughly enjoyed Colendi, who reminded him of dancing butterflies, but he would never go to one for advice about simplicity or truth.

The next day, Autumn set them to sorting scents, eyes closed.

Again, they spent days at it, remaining still as they sniffed the air, detecting not just obvious scents, but moisture waning and waxing, warmth and coolness, the subtle alterations of objects in and out of sunlight.

Next the more difficult task of sorting currents of air.

As one month slid into two, and their sensitivity to evanescence in water, light, and air defined and sharpened, it was time to learn to detect the currents of magic in the world.

As they struggled to put their new knowledge to use, the old divisions fell away: Morat, the courier, got used to Rel's size and morning drill, ceasing to think of him as a brutish warrior bent on using this new magic for some warlike purpose; Brith, the mage, had to accept that her years of discipline and study did not put her ahead of the others in this new form. Aronis Harper said little about his own motivations or intentions, but instead laughed at his errors in the same easy, unselfconscious way he laughed at missteps in his dancing.

The mage was the first to perceive the natural flow of magic—without the work of signs and spells of customary magic.

Rel struggled. Autumn's explanation seemed so simple. Too simple. Finally he retreated to the water again, and reviewed her instructions while watching the currents.

He was sitting in the water, his skin pruning, when he came up for air to the sound of Morat sobbing. He hauled out at once, splashing rapidly across the thick, grassy duff, and fetched up when he saw her sitting on a log, her fingers nipping the air then opening—and illusionary butterflies flitting upward before winking out. Her sobs turned into breathy laughter as she gazed skyward.

"I see it," she cried. "It's all around."

Aronis stood on the other side of the glade, his mouth shaped in an O. He rubbed his fingertips together as he pulled at the air, mimicking Morat's gesture, his forehead tense with effort.

When his fingertips began to glow, he stilled.

Rel also looked around, but now that he knew the others had found it, he expected to perceive it, and there it was, a glow that was not sight, or hearing, or smell, or touch, but a combination of all four in some way he couldn't define.

He raised his hand slowly, almost fearfully, and sensed the current flowing gently around his fingers. He rubbed his thumb and forefinger together, aware of the inward glimmer of blue.

Later that night, Aronis said softly, "It is all changed. Everything is changed: not the what of what I do, but the why."

Yes, Rel agreed.

Twenty-nine

DEEP IN THE OPPRESSIVE atmosphere of Narad's fortress, David discovered the only way he could hang onto his focus was by keeping his mind-shield tight behind that glass cage, though that took extra effort in concentration.

As he and Jilo began sifting through the layers of interlocking traps, David drew on not just his dark magic studies, but what he'd learned in Geth while lost in the marshes, and how to discern something of intent behind the spells. In this way, he detected traps where Jilo only suspected, and was forced to find more laborious methods to discover them so as not to give himself away.

Meanwhile David began to perceive the latticework of the mirror ward. Looking too hard felt like chasing a mirage. No, like chasing vapor, which has substance, whereas the mirage doesn't. He knew there was some connection here, but that atmosphere dragged at linear thinking the way water dragged at a heavy coat should one fall into a lake in winter. David had to fight to keep a simple focus, and even then, his perspective couldn't be trusted: objects seemed flat, far away, shifting and distorting in a smearily vertiginous way when he was very tired.

Detlev had taught them that Norsunder's understructure was a latticework of enchantments linked tightly, and then chained into larger links. Masked by traps, mirror wards, and lethal distractions, that same structure lay here—in physical space, but so distorted that the word "physical" almost lost all its meaning.

He sensed Jilo following him. This was not why he had come, but he could never resist a puzzle, especially one predicated on threat. Until, at last, he pointed—somehow—and indicated the first lattice.

:Yes, I see it now, Jilo said in the mental realm. It was easier than speaking, and they needed to spare themselves the slightest unnecessary effort. It was difficult to *think* in that atmosphere. But somehow it was important to tease out the first link in that lattice, with excruciating care. When it broke at last, they both felt a lessening of pressure—a weakening—no more than the hitch of breath in a hiccup, but it was enough to propel them back into themselves.

They sat on the floor in a grimy hall covered with black mildew that had never been scrubbed away. David frowned, trying to remember what he was supposed to be remembering, then gave up. He needed sleep, that was it. Or maybe another meal. Or . . . he gazed vaguely in the direction of the stairway.

Jilo's eyes had closed. He wrenched them open, then jerked his hands to his eyes as he stared intently at his fingernails. "Gray," he whispered.

David couldn't imagine what that meant, and right now didn't care. Jilo got to his feet, wandered out of the room, and found his golden notecase. The gray had jolted him into remembering his promise, and he wrote to Senrid:

> *I think I need to visit but should I bring David? He's*
> *helping with the mirror ward deflections. I see it*
> *now. There is so much to do, so much.*

In Marloven Hess, Senrid was dressed for riding. His horse had been saddled, his overnight gear packed. He stopped in his study for a last look at his notecase before departing with the academy for a week of fun out on the plains.

"Damn!" he yelped, and sat down abruptly, staring at the note in horror. *David?* It was a common enough name across the continent, in various forms—even right there in Marloven Hess. But coupled with mirror wards?

The timing couldn't be worse.

The only people in the alliance who had studied dark magic long enough to learn about mirror wards had been himself, Jilo, and Roy — who was not in Sartorias-deles, the last Senrid had heard. And though the entire academy was waiting for him down in the parade ground, he grabbed his pen, looked at that scrawl, and cussed steadily. He knew what Jilo was like when he emerged from his labors, barely able to remember his own name.

Senrid dashed to the door and poked his head out. The duty runner leaned on the wall outside, studying the signal flag book. "Halrid," Senrid said. "I've an emergency. Tell them to ride out, and I'll catch up."

Halrid saluted with one hand and with the other crammed the book inside his tunic, then bolted down the stairs.

Senrid returned to his desk, opened a drawer, and took out two of the transfer tokens he'd made specifically for dealing with the miasma of Jilo's fortress, with a time-transfer worked into it so he wouldn't inadvertently find himself having been there for days or even weeks. It would wrench him back within an hour.

He checked to see that his knives were loose in his wrist sheaths. Ought he to grab a sword? He hesitated, thinking of how little practice he got in. Especially in the poisonous atmosphere of Jilo's castle, the only danger of waving a sword around would be to cause the likes of Detlev's boys to laugh themselves sick.

He took the tokens in his left hand, put his right to the knife hilt in his sleeve, and transferred. When he staggered into the noisome gray stone hall, he spotted Jilo standing nearby, slouched over his golden notecase as if he would wait until the end of the world. Jilo was not alone.

He was worse off than usual, by the looks of him. As Jilo blinked in vague surprise to see him there, Senrid whispered, "Get your book and get out." He pressed a transfer token into Jilo's hand, which would take him safely to Marloven Hess.

He pulled both blades from his wrist sheaths and stepped past Jilo, who was swaying on his feet. What had they been *doing?* He blinked in the weird, shadow-clogged air at David sitting on the floor with his back to a wall. Several weapons had been piled nearby. David looked almost as gray as Jilo, greasy hair hanging on his forehead, a grimy shirt open at the neck, under an unlaced winter tunic smeared with what looked like mold from the walls.

Senrid took a single step, bringing his blades into guard, though he wasn't sure he could win any fight when he had to concentrate on breathing, and on keeping his balance. His fingers tightened when David's eyelids flickered, and he turned his head toward Senrid.

Senrid's sudden appearance shocked David out of a fugue that he hadn't known he'd entered. Threat, incipient fight—instinct got him to his feet, steel in hand, though his head reeled. He groped mentally, finding Senrid's thoughts as loud as a shout.

Senrid watched as David's eyes narrowed as if he had a headache. "What did you do to him?" Senrid said.

"Nothing," David retorted.

Senrid felt the *paff* in the air behind him as Jilo transferred.

Good. With the book as ordered, Senrid hoped, doubting he could win any fight in this place—

"No," David said with all the bluster he could muster, "you can't."

Senrid then remembered his mind-shield—nearly impossible to concentrate on here—but David moved again, faster than Senrid would have thought possible in this atmosphere as he swept up the sword and two knives from the ground. There was the infamous black-steel sword, and Senrid knew he hadn't a chance against it.

He sidestepped, muttered the transfer, and vanished.

David sagged against the wall, the sword clattering to the stone with a dull clank. For a time all he could concentrate on was breathing. He stared down at Jilo's transfer Destination, knowing he had to ward it before either Jilo or Senrid returned. No doubt Jilo had taken the book—which would make separating him from it easier, now that he was away from this sinkhole of a stronghold. But only if David made some effort first.

Every joint ached as he moved to Jilo's table, flipped open one of the magic books to a blank page, and ripped it out. Then he tore it into strips. Ordinarily a scrap of paper was the worst token to bind a ward onto, but air never moved in this place.

One by one he warded each scrap, though concentration became exponentially more difficult with each. With painful slowness, he placed the scraps all through that upper hall.

A weird red miasma edged his vision when he finished, and he leaned on the table with both hands wide to steady himself as his vision swam. Now for the border. That ward was the flimsiest. Jilo would be able to break it easily. But he would have to walk in to do it, without being caught in one of Wan-Edhe's lethal traps.

David drew an unsteady breath, picked up his sword, and transferred.

He thumped to his knees on the wooden planks of the old, abandoned dawnsinger tree house in Wnelder Vee that the boys had adopted as a hideout, as he fought clouds of darkness. That much sustained effort had nearly caused him to pass out, right there in Jilo's fortress, with Senrid ready to gut him.

He dropped his weapons and pressed his hands against his knees as he struggled to stay conscious. It took many slow breaths — he counted each one as if the number was vitally important — and finally sank down, weary, lightheaded. Sick.

Instinct had brought him to this rat-hole. The air smelled sweet. It slipped easily into his lungs. Norsunder Base . . . he knew he hadn't the strength for that transfer. David barely had enough strength left to grope for one of the blankets in the chest. It was musty with dust, but dry. He curled up in it, so exhausted that his mind insisted it was still late winter, though the air was balmy, and the canopy overhead thick with the deep green leaves of late summer.

He slept through the rest of the day and night, waking hungry, thirsty, and completely disoriented.

It took all his strength to sit up, as the world hitched and slid, hitched and slid. His gaze moved slowly from object to object as he tried to figure out what to do next. Since the day he and the others had transferred to Five, the wind and weather had swept away nearly all their supplies, except the heavy chest. In its lee lay a half-finished flute he had been carving. He stared at it, trying to find meaning in the two holes he'd hollowed out.

After the sun had shifted the shadows from one side of the chest to the other, he stretched out fingers that shook, and closed them around the flute. He turned it over in his hands, staring stupidly at it. Hunger and thirst clawed at him, worsening that shaky feeling in his hands and knees. He had to get back — to report.

He dropped the half-finished flute, which clattered to the wooden floor and rolled away to drop off the edge. He pressed his thumbs to his eyes, then slid his fingers down his grimy clothes that stank of stale sweat and mildew.

His stomach heaved, then settled, too empty to turn itself inside out in retching. He found his transfer token safely in its pocket. Sheer instinct had brought him here. As well, because he knew he hadn't the strength to bespell a transfer, or to make a token.

As it was, this transfer might kill him, but he was too tired and nauseated to care. He closed one hand over his weapons, grasped the token in his other hand, said the word — and magic yanked him mercilessly away and flung him onto the stone floor in his room.

The familiar stink of Norsunder Base closed around him as black spots swam before his eyes. He heaved himself up long enough to drop his weapons onto the bed then sank down again, struggling to overcome the feeling he was going to pass out right on the floor. His nose was too clogged for breath; warmth ran out of it, and red dripped down onto his hands. He needed water, and food. And a bath — though he wasn't in any shape to cross over to the baths. A cleaning frame . . .

But first, where was everyone? He made an effort to walk the length of the rooms and back. Empty, empty, empty. There was of course nothing to eat there. He made his way to the jug of water they kept outside the nursery, drank his fill, then on the strength of that started down the stairs — to find himself confronted by four gray-jacketed couriers, one old, one young, two somewhere around thirty, all looking at him with grim anticipation.

"Told you I heard one of 'em clumping down the stairs," the oldest one said, grinning up at David's blood-smeared face. "We got ourselves one of 'em."

"It's a start," the biggest one said, and cracked his knuckles before pulling a long knife from his side sheath.

David leaned against the doorway at the foot of the stairs, aware that he hadn't the strength to run back up. He niffed them fast, seeing himself through their eyes. To them, he appeared a wreck, lounging there against the door frame, blood splattered down his grimy clothes. Easy win.

Detlev had ingrained lessons in defense for those smaller

and weaker than opponents. David waited where he was, conserving his last scrap of strength, as his strategy assembled from their stances and the way they gripped their various weapons: a run and step up the short one, side-kick to Knife Hand's knee and a snatch at the blade, a whirl to Horse Face with the weapon—no more than six hard, fast moves, if he didn't pass out first—

"What have we here?" A familiar hoarse snicker.

"MV." David sagged against the door.

"You didn't learn anything from the last time you tried to jump one of us?" MV asked the couriers, who whirled around, far less menacing now as MV and Rolfin sauntered up, Laban and Curtas at their shoulders.

"Who wants first crack?" MV asked—and attacked before anyone could answer.

David didn't move as MV and Rolfin each took on two, dividing them expertly, as they'd been trained. The four would-be brawlers, whose idea of training was circling a single enemy and kicking him into bloody immobility, went down hard, clutching at joints that throbbed as if stabbed by lighting.

Laban collected their cudgels and knives as Curtas came David's way. "You look terrible," he said, peering into David's face.

"Worse than they do," MV commented, as he stepped over the groaning Knife Hand, who clutched broken fingers against his chest.

Rolfin bent over Horse Face. "Next time, we'll break both knees." He slammed the outer door on the would-be ambushers.

David wiped his nose on his sleeve and said to MV, "I thought you were off with some pirate fleet. When did you get back?"

"Weeks ago," MV said, lip curling. "When said pirate fleet decided to go political over in Khanerenth. Where've you been? We thought you'd been sucked into the Beyond."

Warning flickered in David's mind, some connection that he was too tired to grasp. He lifted a hand in a vague gesture.

Curtas said, "You look like you could use a meal."

David's look was so eloquent that Curtas muttered, "Right," and took off at a run.

"You also stink." MV stepped back as he shook his cuffs

down over his wrist knives. "Want help to the cleaning frame?"

David pushed away from the door frame propping him up. "I'll manage. What's with them?" His body seemed weighted with stone, and the steps to go on forever.

MV followed right behind him, and David knew it was in case he fell. He looked that bad. Great.

"Tried three times now to gang up and jump one of us. Get their space back. We just got back from practice, heh. Nice and warmed up." He snickered again, as Laban rolled his eyes and jerked his chin, flinging back sweat-damp hair; MV had, as usual, worked them until every muscle trembled.

"Everyone else?" David asked, at last attaining the top step. A few more paces and he thumped onto his bed next to the weapons, which clanked unmusically.

"Erol and Ferret on the move. Leef out on the training field, being us." MV mimed a slow, clumsy block and strike. "Vana's training new horses, and the Nose has perimeter outpost stable duty. Adam and the brats are somewhere." MV shrugged. "Probably slung out before I got pulled back."

"Detlev?"

MV shrugged again. "I came back, the brats and the shrimp were gone. No one saw him."

Tired as he was, David knew that the brats were the two annoying critters, whereas the "shrimp" was Sveneric, who might be uncanny now and then, but was never annoying. That was part of his uncanniness.

He turned his head as Curtas walked in, carrying a battered wooden plate with boiled greens and peas, bits of fish, and a hard roll. It was a measure of David's hunger how tasty the half-congealed food looked.

As he wolfed it down, MV talked about a couple of sea battles. His uncharacteristic prolixity—unasked, yet—indicated how much he'd enjoyed his months as a pirate fighter. He ended with a description of the boat he was going to own one day, which no one listened to. They were waiting for David to speak.

MV kept up the chatter as he watched David's color slowly become less corpse-like, though his bloodshot eyes remained crimson. When David had scraped up the last of the grayish-brown excuse for sauce, MV said, "Where were you?"

David set aside the dish. "Chwahirsland. Lost Jilo. Senrid

turned up and took him."

"To Marloven Hess? Let's go." MV rubbed his hands.

"Against a direct order?" Laban drawled. "I've had enough mountain top for a lifetime."

MV offered a pungent observation about Laban's opinion, and turned his gaze on David. MV was so sun-browned his light gaze seemed fiery by contrast. "If a quarry bunks for there, and we're supposed to chase, that supersedes, right?"

"No," David muttered. "If Senrid doesn't have us all warded by now, I'm a—"

"Horse's ass," MV muttered. "We can't let this go. Were you a prisoner?"

"No. Wan-Edhe's magic. Anyway. I warded Jilo," David's voice dropped to a whisper. "Has to walk into Narad, and his castle. We can catch him at the border. Erdrael Danara."

MV grinned. "Home of Two-Fingered Terry, who loves us like brothers. That should be fun—"

David shut his eyes. "In. And out."

MV cursed again, then made the mental shift to stealth; if he couldn't go in fighting all comers, then he'd sneak past everyone. Same game, different rules. "All right, but Senrid and Terry are tight. He'll have the entire Mountain Guard on the watch for us, if he thinks we're messing with Jilo." He flashed a toothy grin. "Yeah, that will definitely be fun."

"Just give me a couple hours to . . ." David's eyelids drifted down, his eyes rolling underneath.

They all stared at him. A lot was missing from his story. Gone for half a year, but not a prisoner? In more practical matters, David was normally as fastidious as Curtas and Laban, he just didn't care what he wore. But it was always clean. It was impossible to say which was filthier now, he or his clothes.

Laban was the first to move. "No, you don't." He grabbed one of David's arms and jerked him upright. "Your reek will stink us right back to the stables."

David's eyes opened at that, and he made an irritated but futile attempt to pull away. "Is that stench me? Thought it was here."

"Both," MV said grimly. "You're worse." He jerked his chin at Laban and the two of them hauled David to his feet, frogmarched him to the cleaning frame, then thrust him through.

Green magic flared so bright it crackled.

Curtas thoughtfully picked up the weapons from the bed before the other two let David flop down again. David drank more water and collapsed, bloodshot eyes squinted upward. "Wake me in two hours. Be ready to go."

Two hours later, Curtas, who had been tasked to waken David while MV assembled the others, went into David's and MV's room. He came out again, meeting the rest in Detlev's empty office, which was the best-warded room.

"He getting ready?" MV asked.

"Dead to the world." Curtas shook his head.

MV pushed past him, walked back to his room, and frowned down at David, who lay open-mouthed and boneless. He *looked* dead, that weird grayish color having replaced his usual golden tan.

MV nicked his chin down. "Two more hours." He noted that David—usually as light a sleeper as he was—didn't stir. He backed out, and said they might as well get a meal in.

When Curtas returned after a couple more hours had passed, he found David sitting up. He grimaced and rubbed the heels of his hands into his eyes, then squinted at the others crowding in the door. His eyes were still red, but some of the darkness beneath had faded.

"We're ready to move," MV said. "Talk to us."

David closed his eyes and mentally considered Jilo, who'd shuffled about like an underfed, slope-shouldered hound-dog, the definition of unprepossessing. But he'd been enduring that excruciating atmosphere for how many years?

David opened his eyes. It took effort. "He's coinhered, but I don't know how much control he has. It seemed he had none. But now, I'm wondering if he influenced me. Or maybe it's that place. I knew my orders. Remembered 'em. But somehow, it was more important to work on loosening the lattice."

MV's head came up at the word *lattice*.

David shrugged, and sat back against the wall, trying to hide how much effort it took to talk. "Never mind. Here's the point. Before he got distracted with the lattice, he'd been trying to break Wan-Edhe's border wards. Wan-Edhe's spell-book was right there. Easy enough for me to add Jilo's name to the wards. Won't last long once he walks inside—he'll break 'em in a blink—but he has to get inside the Chwahir border first, on foot or horse, and then inside Narad before he can destroy those spells."

MV said, "Easiest to catch him this side of the Chwahir border, then."

"Right. If he gets past it, the chance of him falling in with one of his patrols makes it tougher for us. Closer he gets to Narad, more likely we'll lose him, probably for good, if he's putting it all together the way we are now. So we need to get there first."

"You don't think he's already there?" Laban asked.

"If he feels anything like me, he's still sleeping."

No one argued with that; David looked better than he had, but far from normal.

David rubbed his eyes again, then dropped his hands. "Keep your minds shielded. We'll avoid Terry's people, catch up with Jilo, separate him from the enemies book, send him on his way, and we're done."

"I have the map right here, and made a set of transfer tokens," MV said.

David shook his head, then winced. "We have to remake them. If we all transfer there, Zhenc will smell something. We'll take it in stages. Each to a different city, one big enough to lose spies in. Wait an hour. Then to Erdrael Danara."

A general groan went up at the idea of two long transfers when one was bad enough.

"Shut up." MV snickered hoarsely. "This is going to be fun."

Thirty

Marloven Hess

SENRID RODE HARD ACROSS the plains in an effort to catch up with the academy, who he knew would be setting up camp somewhere to the west.

As he rode, he scarcely saw the countryside or the clouds building up on the horizon. That nagging sense he'd forgotten something caused him to mentally review the long day. He done everything expected of him. This week's all-academy war game was a centuries-old tradition, planned for by everybody. His going along was not traditional, but he'd begun doing it a few summers ago. His few remaining tasks had either been delegated or postponed until his return.

He'd seen to it that Jilo was put to bed, customary when Jilo emerged from the vile fastness of Narad and its pocket Norsunder. Jilo usually slept for a day or two, ate well, and once he'd recovered, he would always transfer himself back, and vanish again until he needed another dose of real air, water, sleep, and food. Again, nothing new.

Detlev and David couldn't get into Senrid's capital city. Detlev'd been warded for centuries, and by mages far more powerful than Senrid. Those wards were linked down deep. Senrid had added the names of Detlev's boys as he learned them.

So what was it?

Senrid reined to a walk as he frowned down at the trickling stream they rode beside. Once again, he mentally reviewed each step of his day. When he got to the side trip to Chwahirsland, he reached the obvious: he'd left David in possession. Most likely David couldn't do much damage to Wan-Edhe's vast snarl of lethal magic, assuming he would even want to.

But he'd had enough wit to threaten Senrid. And he could ward Jilo's return transfer, which would make it so much easier to go after that damn book the instant Jilo left Senrid's citadel.

That was it.

"Damn. Damn. Damn!" Senrid pulled up, and wheeled the horse. Choreid Dhelerei lay far to the east, barely a smear on the horizon.

He hesitated, fighting against his conviction, but he knew that had to be it. Surely David had been there to get the enemies book. There was no other reason for anyone to enter that noisome pit. Why he hadn't come long ago, who knew. It didn't matter. He was sure to be laying on wards to prevent Jilo from transferring back. That's what Senrid would be doing. Jilo was all-powerful in that citadel that only he understood, but outside it he was about as helpless as a two-year-old.

Senrid dropped the reins, and the horse began to canter back toward Choreid Dhelerei, while Senrid mentally considered and discarded plans. First, waken Jilo . . . no. Senrid remembered how terrible he'd looked. He wouldn't make it five steps, even in summer, in those rugged mountains high up near his border.

The only advantage Senrid had going was that David might not know how weird time was in Narad's fortress. Weeks might pass and he wouldn't be aware. Of course that meant that he'd still be there when Jilo turned up, but Jilo would know what to do about that. He had the magical advantage; whatever damage David tried would be superficial compared to what Jilo had been wrestling with as long as Senrid had known him.

So, first thing: contact Terry. Get him and his Mountain Guard riding out in force to the western border, which was the closest to Narad by a matter of weeks. Then personal protection for Jilo, people he trusted. Who would that be? Senrid himself — Terry — Leander — oh, and Rel . . .

Sarendan

Autumn walked Rel through the invisible door between spaces and left him at Miraleste's royal palace Destination, from which she had taken him.

Rel told the startled attendant who he was, and then wandered outside. After living outdoors for months, being confined inside drove him instinctively to seek light and air.

He found a terrace where a fresh summer breeze rose off the deep blue sparkle of the lake below. His attention shifted from the taut arcs of sails, like new moons, to a statue a few paces away, gazing out to sea. Rel recognized something familiar in the lines of the marble-carved figure's jawline and shoulders. He stepped closer, and he found himself looking up into Derek Diamagan's face.

The sculptor had caught a characteristic expression — intent, smiling with that quirk under his eyes that made it seem as if Derek shared a joke with the viewer. A fleeting moment made eternal.

"That was sculpted from one of Bren's sketches."

Rel turned as Peitar approached, squinting as though the sun was in his eyes, though it was behind him. Rel gazed up at the statue, hands clasped behind him as he observed the subtleties of a magical current drifting in the air. "Bren is a very fine artist."

"That he is," Peitar said. "So quick to capture the variety in human faces. He is not so observant about nature."

Rel indicated the statue and its eternal gaze over the peaceful lake below. "But Derek was?"

"No, he had even less interest in nature's beauties than Bren. His passion was entirely taken up with the cause. The statue is here because this is where the revolution began." Peitar gazed outward in the same direction of the carved marble eyes above, his expression so different from the shared humor of the larger-than-life statue on its pedestal: reflective, a little melancholy. "There are times when I wish we could go back and undo the events of that day . . ." He stopped and faced Rel, the reflective mood gone. "And so? You vanished so abruptly last winter."

"Autumn left a rose beside your token. Said something about words not being trusted."

Peitar turned his hand in a circle. "At first we overlooked it, except as a strange thing to find there in winter. But when it did not fade and die, I consulted Tsauderei, who said the rose was a symbol of good faith among the dawnsingers, and to wait for your return. Lilah planted the rose in the garden as soon as the ground thawed. The rose thrives. It's already half the height of a tall man. What can you tell me? Did you learn vagabond magic?"

"Yes." Rel had been sensing the magic drifting over the lake, blurred ropes of light constantly streaming and shifting. He pulled some of it to him and cast an illusion—a rose tree that he'd seen in the glade near he and his fellow students had stayed.

"Excellent!" Peitar's entire demeanor brightened. "Do come inside and tell me everything you can. Beginning with, why vagabonds? Does the magic really differentiate between travelers and stay-at-homes?"

"No," Rel said. "The magic is here." Rel lifted a hand, his fingers tracing that drifting current, then he dropped his hand when he saw Peitar looking puzzled. "Finding it is another matter. I was told that it's easier to learn magic the customary way. What Autumn taught us was to find it by using our senses . . . and . . ." Rel tapped his forehead. "Hard to find words. But using it takes memory."

They sat down in Peitar's private office, an austere room that overlooked the lake, the only furniture an orderly desk and several chairs.

Rel continued. "It took us weeks to perceive it, first in water, then with the other senses. Then we had to learn how to shape it. We don't really have the vocabulary. And it does have limitations—as individuals, we can use it for illusion, at most for bringing a spark for fire. In a group we can transfer a person at a time, but we have to know the Destination to send them. We can bring someone into a group, if we know them, and they are amenable. The transfer doesn't hurt."

"How does the magic know the person is amenable?"

Peitar leaned forward.

Rel shook his head. "It doesn't. It's more that if the person rejects or refuses the transfer, the magic falls apart."

"Doesn't hurt. What they said about the Old Magic," Peitar murmured. "Did Autumn mention that? Or take you to labyrinths?"

"Labyrinths?" Rel repeated. "Do you mean the Sartoran Purad?"

Peitar shut his eyes again, exerting himself to suppress the auras. Rel's was so intense it made his head swim. "Yes, but I feel there might be some connection, if only ephemeral, and way in the past."

"Autumn said nothing about labyrinths. What she did tell us was that the magical currents are rising, but 'rising' isn't the right word, either," Rel said after the pause began to grow into a silence. He wanted to return to Sartor — to Atan — though he knew it would be to walk right back into the same problems. "We kept coming up against the limits of the language. And maybe human limits."

"So, vagabonds. If you can only transfer to and from places you've been, then of course this type of magic would appeal to those who travel."

"Yes. That's it exactly. And we can only make illusions from what we've seen."

Peitar said, "Will you teach me?"

Though his request was that, and no command — he never had succeeded in overcoming his discomfort with the prerogatives of kingship — the intensity of his gaze, the inheld breath and still posture, caused Rel to mentally alter his plan to return to Sartor. "I can try. I don't know if it'll work. It took me weeks to see the currents of magic, and then to reach for them. I guess this is different from the magic you practice. Like I said before, you don't perform spells. You just . . . take it and weave it."

As he spoke, he concentrated, and there between them curled, like drifting smoke, the glimmering green of magic. Rel still had to use his hand to focus, but he drew it to him, shaped it into a ball, then "saw" a miniature of the statue of Derek.

The statue sat on the desk, blurry as if seen through rain, but Peitar stared, recognizing it, then squinted again, shaking his head.

"See the currents," Peitar repeated, memory taking him

right back to the Purad on that first amazing walk. But that had been sound, surely?

He swallowed as he fought the nearly overwhelming urge to smite trade agreements and petitions and messages from his desk—all the dreary detritus of a kingdom that, given the liberties it had desired so badly, seemed always fractious. And he made a furious effort to slam a lid on the aura, which had coruscated with sun flares when Rel made his illusion. "I have some time now, if you would like to begin."

Before Rel could agree, Lilah pelted up, bare feet slapping the ground. "Senrid is here! Looking for Rel!"

Peitar and Rel walked out again to the terrace, and found Senrid Montredaun-An wearing the grimace of one recovering from transfer magic. Water splashed nearby, little Ian playing in a fountain with his tutor nearby.

"Rel," Senrid exclaimed with obvious relief. "Are you free to help Jilo?"

"Jilo?" Rel repeated blankly.

Senrid opened his palms up. "He only trusts maybe three people, and you and I are two of them."

There was only one answer to be made to that. "I've got my travel gear inside," Rel said, and cast an apologetic glance at Peitar.

There was nothing Peitar could say. His inquiry could scarcely take precedence over a demand for help. So he had to let them go.

When he reached his room, he looked down at the ancient, crackling text he had been translating so painstakingly. It was a history of a Sartoran ruin, and now that he had taken a break from the drawing in the old scroll, he saw what he had missed before: the entire building was laid out in what could be conceivably called the Purad form. Or was that illusion?

The important thing was that the ruin lay at the west end of a river valley in Sartor. Since he had cleared the morning for lessons that would not happen, he might as well transfer to that ruin himself, and see if it hid a Purad that would bring back the mysterious music.

Thirty-one

Erdrael Danara

TERRY REALLY HOPED SENRID was right.

He thought he'd gotten over his miserable experience on Five, but the moment he comprehended that Detlev's boys might have the arrogance to invade his territory, the furnace of his hatred for Noser, MV, and David flared as bright as ever. The others he could live and let live. But the killers? The world would be better off rid of them.

He burst out of his tower retreat, yelling for a page to fetch the Mountain Guard aide-de-camp, and had a stream of orders mentally organized by the time the page discovered the girl halfway through a meal.

He gave out the orders—including precise descriptions and names of every one of Detlev's boys—ending grimly, "And tell the Guard to wear every weapon they've got."

"All?" the aide-de-camp repeated, eyes round. "Bows? Arrows?"

Terry didn't flinch. "These are Norsundrians. Nobody pays attention to the Covenant when Norsunder threatens. They can disable the rest, but those three, shoot to kill. And anyone who downs Noser, MV, or David will come into a reward. *Big* one."

Surprised and somewhat dismayed by the bitterness in Terry's voice as well as the bloodthirsty nature of his order, both of which she would have thought foreign to his nature, the aide ran for the stairway.

Shoot to kill? Reward? Young as she was, she knew Guard history. The Mountain Guard hadn't done kill practice since the bad old days when the Chwahir used to attack. All their practice was to avoid violence — guide lost travelers back to the road, discourage hopeful brigands trying to prey on traders, and to process the miserable Chwahir who'd managed to survive climbing the barren mountains with their sparse belongings, hoping for a better life elsewhere.

She sped down the long stair again, and burst into the stable to demand the fastest mount.

Erdrael Danara lies roughly eight hours to the east of Marloven Hess, and a goodly way north.

After a short night, Senrid rose earlier even than usual, dealt summarily with a few tasks, then gathered tokens for experiment. As expected, he'd been warded from Chwahirs-land, which meant that Jilo had to be as well.

He ordered a hot meal, by which time Rel showed up, and together they went to the guest room, where they found Jilo buried in the covers. But he woke at the sound of his name, and blinked owlishly at them. "Rel?" he said.

"I've ordered breakfast," Senrid said. "Let's get each other's stories while we eat."

Jilo got up easily enough, but he seemed as thin as ever, unchanged since their first meeting. Senrid waited while he gulped down water, then said, "You have the Child Spell on you?"

"Dunno," Jilo said. And as Senrid's brows shot upward, Jilo blushed and mumbled, "Kwenz insisted when he first began teaching me. Keep Wan-Edhe from looking for hints of conspiracy and executing me. Puddlenose did the same. But I don't remember if I took it off when I removed all the wards he'd laid on me."

That was grim. Senrid reflected that Jilo's existence in the nastiness of the upper story of that fortress probably couldn't be measured in any kind of time that mattered.

As they sat down in the dining room, Jilo looked as animated as he ever did at the prospect of hot oatmeal with cream and honey, then poured another full glass of water and drank all of it before Senrid said, "What happened with David? Did he threaten you?"

"No." Jilo passed hands over his face. "Helped me with the wards . . . then he showed me . . ." His hands groped in the air. "Haven't the words. But we broke the first lattice."

The back of Senrid's neck crawled. He knew Detlev had to be teaching at least some of his boys the darkest magic. If David had stayed behind, working lattices, maybe he was wresting Chwahirsland's pocket Norsunder to connect with Norsunder Beyond. And if that happened, Norsunder would surely be able to bypass rift magic altogether, and bring armies over. Senrid didn't know enough, but there was no one to ask about that deep a level in dark magic — except for going straight to Detlev.

He'd rather be put against a wall and shot.

Senrid wrenched his mind away from that useless trail. Not enough evidence meant he could be adding one and one together and letting emotion make the sum out to be eleven. "Rel here is going to see to it you get back inside, all right?"

"Sure," Jilo said, with a bony-shouldered shrug. "But I can walk. I did, once. All around my kingdom. Learned much from doing so."

The other two the way he slumped in the chair red-eyed and pale as he drank more water. He didn't look as if he could walk down the hallway without a couple of stops to rest. But no one argued.

They tackled their meal, as in Erdrael Danara, the Mountain Guard scrambled to assemble for the largest hunt in any of their careers.

And while they divided up and prepared for the trap they'd been ordered to set up, David and his group — minus Adam, who was still missing — transferred in one by one, paired up, and began to disperse through a chill, misting rain to cover the likeliest routes to the border.

Aware that he was still recovering both mentally and physically from going into Chwahirsland at the end of winter, and coming out — after eating one or two meals that he could remember — in very late summer, David put MV in command. He couldn't trust himself to lead when his body felt like it'd been in prison for ten years.

No, he thought after a very long slog into the increasing rain. *Twenty* years. "I have to sit down," he said, tipping his head back and staring up through the trees at the gray sky beyond. The air here was pure, but thin; he tipped his head to breathe past that grab at his lungs, as if he couldn't get enough air, which was the normal state in Narad.

"Here," Ferret said, pointing upward. "This oak do?"

David unslung his bow and handed his arrows to Ferret, then pulled himself up. "A few breaths."

Ferret's forgettable face was ruddy in the rain. "I can move faster without you." His lip curled on one side; they both knew MV had put Ferret with David to slow him down. MV wanted to be first to the find.

"Go to it," David said. "I'll be ready when you return." He said that to himself as much as to Ferret.

Having granted himself a respite, he leaned his back against the bole, and—without having to concentrate on walking—let his mind range freely, as he drew in the pure air. It was nearly second nature now to keep consciousness intact, and yet be able to niff beyond that barrier. Jilo had—David saw it now—been struggling to learn on his own what Detlev, and Adam, had so painstakingly drilled David in practicing.

David knew there was a risk that Jilo might choose the long route, or even remain in Marloven Hess to recover. But was as certain as he could be that Jilo would not do either. Jilo was driven by his goal, so driven he endured that shithole of a fortress in Narad in order to reach that goal. He wouldn't laze about in a comfortable bed.

David shut his eyes, reached out in the mental plane—and there he was. The contact was brief, then Jilo instinctively closed himself off, but not before David caught a glimpse of woodland similar to what surrounded him now.

He reached again, and there was MV, moving fast parallel to the border. David sent a thought: *Jilo's here. I want to talk to him. And set your mind-shield.*

MV's response was predictably pungent, but he vanished from easy reach on the mental plane. David waited, and one by one the others did as well.

He found he could still track them by the, ah, call it a shadow where they ought to be, but that was because he knew them. As an experiment, he reached for Roy, but got nothing. Except maybe a whiff of the Marshes. Real, or memory, he had no idea, but Roy was too shielded to reach. He resettled, fighting a mild wave of dizziness, and reached for Adam.

:*David?*

It was as if Adam sat beside him. Relieved not to have to make the effort to form words, David shared memory of his recent experiences, then, :*Where is everyone?*

:*Aldon took Paolan away. Detlev took Ki somewhere on Geth-deles, and that flute to the Beyond. The shrimp and I are in a tent in the wilderness. I think at the west end of the Sartoran continent. But we'll fall back to the Base as soon as Detlev returns. When he does, shall I share what you gave me?*

:*Yes.*

Adam was gone. David remembered the old summer camping trips, though they had never come anywhere near Sartor. Why Sartor, and why now?

Think about Adam, not that lattice . . .

But of course as soon as he decided that, he was thinking about the lattice. Specifically, what MV had said: "We thought you were in the Beyond."

But I *was* in a Beyond. David shifted on the oak branch, the idea so disturbing it wormed its way into his already consider-able physical discomfort. Now, as he struggled toward the connections that had evaded him, a cold thrill of fear — of finding himself far outside the comfortable boundaries of the world he knew — pooled to ice in his gut.

He faced the truth. The cause was not Wan-Edhe's magic. Disturbing as that was, it did not concern him. It was how the Chwahir lattice reminded him of those lessons about Norsunder's structure. He was used to the excitement and challenge of weapons training, lessons in stealth craft, and the fun of infiltration. This connection — the very idea of attempting any kind of interference with Norsunder's magic — could not possibly go unnoticed by the powerful central figures of Norsunder, especially the soul-eater himself. Even thinking about him was dangerous.

David tried to scoff himself out of the funk. His conjectures were nothing more than guesswork. Anyway Jilo's goal had nothing to do with Norsunder. Of that he was sure. But as he listened to the rustle of wind through the trees, for the first time he began to consider the future. He had no goal. What *would* he be doing? Detlev had never said what his long plan was, though they all knew he had at least one.

There had to be a reason why they had better training than anyone else at Norsunder Base — and kept it hidden.

While he frowned upwards at the splat of rain on the broad, yellow-edged leaves of the oak, and for the first time, contemplated his future, MV covered ground fast, he and the others moving noiselessly and printless over the thick, rain-sodden late-summer duff in their forest mocs.

He'd already fitted whistles onto his signal arrows, but he meant to send the single-shot *come to my aid* only if they did spot their target. A low rumble of thunder somewhere in the distance, and an abrupt change in the quality of the light, both deepening and sharpening the greens, heralded an oncoming storm.

MV and Erol ran parallel tracks, barely in sight of each other as they pushed west as fast as they could cover the ground. These mountains were treacherous in the extreme, one river valley being the most commonly used connection between the two countries, the river carving its way through the sky-scraping peaks toward Narad below.

Erol's head came up, then his palm: halt.

MV stopped, turning his head in all directions — ah! Over the sound of the increasing rain, the steady rumble of horses. A lot of horses.

Lightning flickered. Thunder crashed across the sky, muffling the hoofbeats. They waited where they were for sound to return, giving them direction, then far to the south whistled a signal arrow, quickly followed by another: *trap.*

MV faced Erol downslope some hundred paces away, his pale, round Chwahir face all he could see beyond the veil of steady rain. MV tightened his fist then flattened his hand: *flank and take cover.*

By now they could hear the riders again, pounding steadily eastward along the slope. The two took to the trees and waited as the company passed about fifty paces below Erol.

MV's breath hissed in. Twelve, fifteen, twenty riders, and in their center, shrouded in a hooded cloak, a skinny rider. Jilo? He and Erol could easily shoot the escort, but this was supposed to be a stealth snatch. What was the trap?

MV heard a soft rustle at his left, and turned, knife out — Ferret's skinny form. He crept up, head low. MV relaxed, appreciating Ferret's skill in knowing exactly where to make a sound so he wouldn't get himself gutted.

"That's not him," Ferret whispered, his face blotchy from the chilly rain.

And that was the trap, a decoy ruse. Good for you, Terry, MV thought. Put some fun into it.

They watched as the company passed to the east into the rain, the jingle of harnesses and gear barely audible above the rising roar of the storm. MV noted the tension in the outriders, gazes sweeping constantly left and right. The number of hilts along with strung bows. His gut tightened. They had orders to kill. That means he and the boys did, too. He smiled; a full company—maybe more—against ten seemed acceptable odds, changing things up to be interesting.

So, back to the goal. As Erol bounded up the slope, MV pivoted to regard Ferret. "The hood? That wasn't Jilo? How could you tell?" MV had to raise his voice as thunder crashed once again.

Erol lifted his chin in Ferret's direction. "You s-saw it, too."

Ferret wiped rain out of his eyes. "Remember what David said? Shuffler. Clumsy. And if he's as wasted as David—"

MV stood up, peering under his hand against the rain. The Danarans were no more than a blur now, but memory was sharp. "You're right. He's a good rider. What I saw," he added, "was their gear."

Erol said morosely, "Th-they. Wanna. D-draw us."

"They're hunting our blood." MV grinned.

Both the other boys knew that grin, and with no more than a flicker of glances between them, Ferret was chosen to take the heat.

"We still have orders for a clean grab," Ferret said.

MV knew why Ferret stated the obvious. He reached for arrows, then dropped them back in the quiver. "Let's get David."

They ran. A short time later they joined David, who swung down from his tree. A short report, and David leaned back and reached into the mental realm again. The equivalent of little lights flickered, but with all the steadiness and meaning as sunlight sparkling on water. When he reached for Jilo, he was there, bright and clear—unshielded again. Probably fast losing what little strength he had.

David caught a flicker of conscious thought about rain and

mud and cold. David had guessed that much right, and attempted to glean a location from Jilo without making contact, which he suspected Jilo would feel. Jilo wasn't paying any attention to his surroundings. His focus was entirely on staying upright. So David had to fall back on trying to triage his general direction with respect to the moving lights of the boys.

His focus was broken by Leef pelting up, Curtas at his shoulder, both hoarse for breath. "Spotted Jilo. With Rel. Heading up toward a ruin." He pointed toward the top of the rise on the other side of the river.

The sudden shock of cold rain, the prospect of the hunt, infused David with strength. He knew it wouldn't last—he had been run to the point of dropping enough times to gauge—but if they were quick, he could endure until they made the snatch and smoked.

Every muscle ached as he pulled a signal arrow and shot one: *On me.*

Thirty-two

WHILE THEY PLUNGED DOWN the mountain toward the rushing river, in Telyerhas at the other end of the continent, Siamis felt the inward prod of a tracer spell while following a line of scribes on their way to breakfast. Defensive awareness had been crucial to his survival since he was twelve; between one step and the next he returned to himself and stepped out of the line on the pretext of wanting another pen.

He sat in a deep, tiled window-seat. The morning sun warmed the side of his face as he shut his eyes, and soon had it all. He got up, shoulders hunched, feet shuffling awkwardly as he retraced his steps. The senior scribe looked up in mild surprise.

"It seems that some former pupils of mine require a tutoring session," Siamis said in the nasal, droning voice he'd developed for Amid the Scribe.

To the senior scribe, such a breach of order and decorum could only mean the rich acting on whim, at the inconvenience of everyone else. "I trust at least you will charge a thumping fee," she said.

Siamis rubbed his slackened jaw. "Oh, I doubt very much that I will be paid at all. My satisfaction must derive entirely from restoring order."

He bowed, and shuffled out, leaving the senior scribe to

observe to her assistant, "He may be slow, but he's thorough. And dedicated. Imagine doing anything for no pay."

The assistant assented, but with a sigh, as she knew who would probably get stuck with Amid the Idiot's work while he was busy harassing someone else with a list of rules. *Boring* work. He, being the newest hire, got all the tedious stuff no one else wanted—but she had to admit he never complained. He probably didn't even notice.

Siamis shuffled through the rambling building, which covered two sides of the town square. This being a free town, the local government was all here, rooms added on as needed. Though he knew he was not being followed—no one was thinking of him at all—one never relaxed vigilance.

Past the hall with people on benches waiting for their turn (". . . well, I was told that in Colend, they eat baby mush behind curtains." "Really? Did they all lose their teeth?").

Past busy guild offices ("No, if your village thinks it needs a bridge, you need to speak to the provincial Road Guild, not us . . .") (". . . and bring it back with a real sved. Yes—it's a perfect likeness—shows your skills in paint, yes it does, but the guild magistrate doesn't have my sense of humor, and the sentence for falsifying . . .") (". . . you can insist on seeing the magistrate, you can even go to the capital and apply to the Royal Bench, but they'll all say the same: you can invite musicians to your wedding, but the moment you say, 'Hey, friend, how about a tune?' they cease to be guests, and become performers. And guild fees apply. Do you think you're the first, or even the twelve-hundred-first to think of this? I can tell you, the Royal Bench might decide to fine you triple, they're so tired of this one . . .").

And through the kitchen, where the baker's deep voice sang out rhythmic nonsense words, "HUM-ah nah nah, SHOO-lah nah nah," echoed by the treble voices of his young apprentices, "HUM-ah heela-hee!" as they beat and flipped long, flour-dusty rolls of dough.

Siamis reached the residence side, where a number of low and mid-level artisans and pen-pushers rented rooms. His room was on the top floor, with two exits, and the next roof a heart-stopping jump away if a third was to be necessary. He straightened his posture and stepped through his cleaning frame, which snapped away the oil greasing his hair to a dull light brown.

He unsashed his scribe robe, dressed for forest work, sealed his trunk by magic, and concentrated on a transfer.

David shook himself as he clambered out of the icy river, then hopped about swinging his arms violently as he tried to get his blood moving again. They'd been taught physical control. They breathed to increase their inner warmth as they moved.

MV cursed steadily as he and the rest shook like dogs, then everyone checked their weapons. Their bows were effectively useless. MV cursed some more, as David threw back his head, peering against the gray curtain at the tossing pines moving like a dark green sea up the slope ahead.

He wound a hand then pointed, and they started up a tiny animal path that streamed with golden mud. Rolfin and Laban waited at the top of the first curve, and joined them. "We saw a company riding past, with — "

"Someone at the center, hooded," David finished. "I think there are four companies like that." He tapped his head. "You didn't chase?"

Laban's splendid cheekbones reddened. "I was ready to take them on. Rolfin said it was a ruse."

"He was right," David said, and pushed on past.

Laban sighed as MV snickered, and they started up the mountain into the hard rain. they didn't get very far before they came to a stop as a girl wearing a summer tunic, bare armed and bare legged, stepped out directly into the path. Though rain sparkled in the flower garland she wore on her head, and ran down her hair and bare arms, she somehow managed not to look sodden or cold.

"Uh oh," Laban said.

"Greetings of the day." Autumn smiled down at the boys.

David didn't trust her or the situation for a heartbeat. He signaled the others, who obediently spread out in a semi-circle facing the girl, who stood alone.

Rolfin raised his knife and took a step toward Autumn to get her to retreat. But Autumn raised a hand, palm flat out. "You cannot go this way," she said.

"Says who?" Laban muttered, blue eyes wide as he and Rolfin stepped closer.

"You may call me Autumn," she said, looking right and left, without retreating.

David joined the others as he said, "We have orders. You'll have to stop us."

Autumn lifted a hand. She glanced skyward into the rain, then around, nipping at the air with thumb and forefinger. With the other hand, she plucked a rosebud from the garland on her brow and cast it at the ground before David and Rolfin's feet. The air blurred, a fresh scent rising, and the bloom shot roots into the ground, then tangled up and out into a thorny rosebush about waist high.

That was definitely weird, but not very effective. David drew the black sword and hacked the thorn bush off at knee-height, but then it grew back in a twinkling, twice the height it had been, and very much thornier.

Autumn hadn't moved, spoken, or made a sign. David's blood chilled in his veins, a reaction that had little to do with the summer storm. Memory: Geth, chasing Les Rhoderan and his child army, who used illusion in the same way.

He leaned out, touching a thorn. Pain shot through his finger, and blood beaded then washed away in the rain. This was no mere illusion.

"What are you?" David asked.

"A vagabond?" She made it a question, and then laughed.

"Vagabond magic is illusion," David said, as MV ranged up behind his shoulder.

She smiled and extended her hand toward a bend in the trail leading down. Her assurance irritated MV, who nicked his chin at Rolfin — the only one who'd thought to bring a dry string for his bow, kept in a waterproof pouch. He restrung obediently, but flicked a question at MV from dark eyes. Really? Shoot down an unarmed girl? MV lifted his chin, and Rolfin understood: warning shot. He raised the bow and aimed a hairsbreadth above her shoulder.

Autumn opened her hand like a flower, and the arrow thumped to the soggy ground a couple of paces in front of her bare toes. Arrow? It had transformed into a twig, from which green tendrils sprouted. As the boys watched, the tendrils wormed eagerly into the rich, wet soil, and the arrow-twig stood upright, sending out fresh green shoots.

David jerked his chin over his shoulder: *Retreat*.

MV led the way, with a couple of considering glances

backward as they took off along the path Autumn had indicated. But only until they lost Autumn from view. Then David bolted up the steep cliff, barren as it was from some fairly recent landslide, slipping and slithering in the liquid mud.

Eventually they made it back to the original path, but it took far longer than it should have, with the rain increasing to a punishing downpour. Furious, David knew they'd been delayed, and pushed himself to the limits of his endurance.

At the top of the rise, Rel peered grimly into the worsening downpour. As many times as he'd crossed back and forth between Erdrael Danara and Chwahirsland along this route, he'd never paid any attention to the heights other than looking for signs of danger. But humans are predictable, and he was certain that a crest above a river at a border would surely have some sort of outpost on it.

Was that gray more intense than the blurring gray of rain? Yes. Relief propelled him on as Jilo plodded next to him, head bent, bony arms crossed over his middle. They emerged from the fir shadows at the side of a crumbling tower, found a gaping entrance, and plunged inside a dank, dark room. The sudden cease of the pounding rain made breathing easier, though they were both aware of their sodden clothing squeaking at each step.

"Take a seat, Jilo. I'll explore."

Jilo dropped heavily onto a bench, after looking around with not much hope for a jug of water.

Rel slipped his hand into his pack and came out again with a fire stick. He murmured the word to light it. The ruddy flame threw the shadows back, revealing a table with benches, some bales of moldy hay used for all purposes now that it was no good for horses, a barrel, on top of which sat a cold lantern.

Rel dragged a bench closer for Jilo to sink wearily onto. The flame on the fire stick streamed and flickered, jittering shadows about the room, against which Jilo shut his eyes. Rel spotted a couple of sticks bound with oil-soaked ropes. He lit one, tossed the fire stick into the fireplace, and waved his hand to bring the flame to the maximum the spells on it permitted.

Then he took his torch to explore. After traversing a web-hung hallway strewn with moldering leaves and dust, he found another room that boasted a stairway. Guessing that this led to the one undamaged tower Rel had glimpsed, he ran up, skipping four stairs at a time.

Here he found a surprisingly tidy room with a fire-blackened walnut table central in the round room at the top. Wavery, thick glass had been plastered into the deep, narrow arrow-slit windows all around the room, affording good lighting. Here, too, was a fireplace. Rel looked at the door, reflecting on how much easier it would be to defend that narrow entrance if he had to, rather than the archway downstairs with the door at the other end, and the old shutters at the two windows.

A short time later he had Jilo established in the tower, with the fire stick now warming that space. Rel retreated back downstairs with the idea of airing out the warmth, and using the old hay to mop up their puddles and prints. He doubted that his attempt at hiding their presence would really fool hunters, but he still tried it anyway.

Up in the tower, Jilo struggled inwardly a short time, then removed the damp enemies book from inside his clothes and put it on the fire-scorched table. He watched morosely, knowing that he hadn't a hope of defending himself from Rel if the latter decided to take it. But if he left it in his clothes any longer, it wouldn't matter anyway, as the wet was sure to penetrate to the pages, reducing them to sodden blobs blotched by runny ink: Wan-Edhe, in making the book, had undoubtedly never dreamed it would go outside of his warded, guarded work room. Jilo relaxed on his bench, his clothes gently steaming as he warmed up.

Rel trod back up presently. "I think I see some blue in the west," he said, moving to one of the windows. "We should be out of here in an hour."

Jilo felt the pull of his lengthy labors, now that—at last—he understood the form that had so long eluded him. Lattice. Yet another area of study Wan-Edhe had taken great care to hide. Jilo permitted himself a cautious hope that maybe, perhaps, possibly, there might be a breaking at last of that interlocked desolation of lethal spells. He wanted to be at it. And yet it felt so *good* to sit and breathe real air, and not worry about tracers or traps or . . .

Oh. Right. Faint alarm brought his head up. "What if they

come?"

"If they do, they won't take us by surprise," Rel said with a grim smile. The watery, gray light striking the strong bones of his face made him look startlingly dangerous. Jilo blinked slowly, then gnawed at his knuckles while he stared down at his shoddy, scrape-heeled boots.

Rel went on, "I wedged that heavy door shut. If they try to open it again, it'll squawk like ten mad parrots." He unlimbered the sword he wore across his back. "And I'll be waiting to greet them."

Jilo tried to understand why the same David who had helped him with the lattice, and the wards, and who had come to warn him about the Norsundrians at the gate, would hunt him down. Oh, right, the Enemies Book.

Jilo blinked rapidly, knowing that he needed sleep again, a meal, and most of all water. If only he wasn't so thirsty! He looked at the rain dribbling down the windows, and wished he could lick the droplets, but instead shuffled his feet, listening to the squishing sounds they made inside his wet boots, as new thoughts proliferated like the distorted flowers of his worst dreams. He watched Rel prowl the perimeter of the room, his attention on the windows, and never once look at the Enemies Book lying right out there. Finally he burst out, "Prince Kessler. You know him. Right?"

Rel's head turned sharply, his deep-set eyes narrowing. Danger curled inside Jilo as he stuttered, "It's just, you sometimes come. At the same time. And . . ."

Rel, as always, was unaware of the effect of his countenance. He hated lying, and yet he was not ready to tell anyone about his connection to the Sonscarnas through his mother. She, he was proud of. The rest of the family? Not the least. He glanced Jilo's way, saw the anxiety tightening Jilo's too-pale face, and answered what he suspected might be the real question, "I don't trust him past my next breath. I suggest you keep your distance—"

A buzzy sense, a sudden pulse of air that smelled of olives and red spice—and Siamis stood in the room.

Rel's sword scraped halfway out of its sheath before he remembered Siamis's putative alliance. Siamis brought up his hands. Rel saw that Siamis had no weapons in sight; while he might have a knife or two hidden in his green and brown forest clothes, he was not carrying his sword. Rel let his own sword slide back into its sheath, but his gaze measured the distance between Siamis and Jilo, as Siamis's lips twitched in a smile of awareness.

"What are you doing here?" Rel asked, glad they weren't in Sartor, so he didn't have to pretend diplomatic politeness.

"You're about to sustain visitors," Siamis said with a tip of his head toward the window. "I thought I might even the numbers a bit."

Rel was going to ask how he knew, then shrugged. Siamis would probably lie. More important was the threat. Rel had been trying to keep watch, but he was only one person, and no one could monitor all directions at once

"Room directly below," Siamis said gently. "I've been following them."

Damnation, Rel thought in disgust. "Them?" He'd missed more than one? "Detlev's boys? All of 'em?"

"Ten," Siamis said. "Adam appears to be elsewhere."

"The least threatening," Rel said sardonically.

"Don't underestimate Adam," Siamis said with a rueful smile. "He had to defend himself the most while growing up. But no, I doubt very much he'd be inclined to attack either of you in this situation." He held up a hand, and nodded toward the door. Then flicked his glance toward the left.

Rel saw what Siamis wanted, and moved to the other side of the door.

Which banged open, and MV started in, Rolfin and Vana flanking him — and stopped as if they'd slammed into an invisible wall when they saw Siamis.

"Who's first?" Siamis said invitingly, hands wide. "Or will it be a three-for-all?"

Before anyone could move, another flicker and a swirl of cool air presaged transfer, and Autumn appeared on the other side of the table. Her clear gaze took in the room. "Ah," she breathed, barely audible above the rumble of thunder outside. "There it is."

A quick weaving motion with her hands, and the book lying on the table flashed green, then settled into ash. Another wave of her hand, and the ashes swirled to a window, which opened wide. The smell of burn faded away to nothing as the ashes dissolved in the rain.

From below came the sounds of rushing feet: it was Senrid, with a company of the Danaran guards. MV turned to David, who leaned against the door frame, having arrived in time to see their goal vanish to ash.

"Out," David said, and the boys all transferred to their respective decoy cities.

As Senrid and his troop labored up the stairs, Siamis turned to Autumn. He shaped a thought that only she would hear: *You do see that the magic in Chwahirsland is killing him?* With a glance at Jilo.

He was surprised when a thought returned, bell-clear, and focused: *The evil has poisoned the vital waters of his being.*

No time to consider what that meant: here was Senrid in the doorway, flushed from a hard run in the rain. He looked around distrustfully, then he, too, stopped abruptly as if he'd hit a wall, a vein beating in his forehead. "Siamis."

Behind him, the Danarans on the landing and below on the steps all the way down to the ground floor hissed the name in question, disbelief, exclamation, like a rustling of snakes.

Siamis's smile deepened with appreciation. He touched his forefinger to his brow in ironic salute and vanished. Senrid's astonished gaze fell next on Autumn's calm demeanor. He remembered encountering her the first time he ever left Marloven Hess. He'd had warriors at his back that time, too, and had intended summary execution. And he strongly suspected that she was remembering as well.

Feeling badly off-balance, he forced himself to turn to the captain of the Danaran company he'd pulled after him when he'd spotted David's group earlier. He said, "They're gone. Someone report back to Terry, will you?"

Surprise—here and there dismay—rippled through the Danaran ranks before their captain saluted, fingers tapping the opposite shoulder. Sharp disappointment was now the mood as they thumped and clattered back down the stairs, and began the long, empty-handed withdrawal. There'd be no rewards for this one, and it would be a long, cold ride back.

Senrid kept watching the spot where Siamis had been as he said to Jilo, "Want help getting home?"

"You may leave that to me," Autumn said.

Senrid regarded her, protest forming. But after all, none of this was his business, and he knew that Jilo wasn't in any danger from her. He transferred back to Marloven Hess, where he shed his soggy clothes, ran down to the stable, and took horse to join his academy out on the plains.

Thirty-three

BACK IN THE TOWER, Autumn studied Jilo, who was still staring at the table, trying mentally to grasp that the enemies book was gone.

He wasn't certain how he felt. With it had gone the gnawing worry of an enemy getting hold of it, but gone too was the relative comfort of looking into it to see if Wan-Edhe had emerged from Norsunder.

Gone was gone.

He tried to shrug it off, and to remember all the other wards he'd put up to warn him if and when Wan-Edhe reappeared, then he shut his eyes. It felt so good to sit merely there, listening to the rain, even if he couldn't drink its pure, clean water.

He was scarcely aware of the room filling with a kind of warmth, only fuller and fresher than anything he'd ever felt during those half-forgotten days when he used to sneak into Mearsies Heili to sketch the trees, the waterfall, the mountain covered with snow and its weird castle beyond. The air smelled astringent, like crushed early-summer herbs. He breathed deeper, wondering if his vision was blurring or if that really was the moisture in his clothing rising and drifting out the window in a silvery mist. Rel's as well.

Then a tingle worked through him, a little like biting into

wintergreen, which he'd done once while traveling on Geth-deles with Rel and Puddlenose. Wellbeing suffused him. "Oh." He looked up, startled.

Autumn seemed to be drawing in the air, light shimmering from her fingers and spreading outward in a misty glow. She said, "Humans are made of water as well as flesh. Did you not know?"

"I . . ." Jilo's thoughts suspended.

"Your vital waters are pure again. I will send you home."

"You can't," Rel said quickly. "We're here because David managed to lay a ward against Jilo at the border."

Autumn waved her hands in a circle. "Perhaps, but you know the vagabond transfer as I make it: he will be here, then there, and this terrible magic will know it not."

She touched Jilo before he could speak, and he stood in Narad again, in his transfer square. The stale, close atmosphere settled around him, but he felt . . . he felt he could think. David had obviously laid down some wards on those scattered papers, but those would be easy to break.

Jilo got right to work, as back in Erdrael Danara, Autumn turned to Rel. "Where wish you to go?"

He knew where he wanted to be, but that was superseded by where he ought to be. "I promised Peitar Selenna," he said.

Autumn glanced at the window, where indeed, the storm was breaking in the west, the silvery light catching golden highlights in her auburn hair, and outlining her profile against the stone. Her expression seemed pensive, almost sad.

"So shall it be," she said.

He took a step and found himself on the terrace overlooking the lake below Miraleste, now a steel gray reflecting the bands of underslung clouds as a summer storm brought a wash of rain.

Elsewhere in the palace, Peitar Selenna, who had given orders to interrupt him immediately upon Rel's return, was interrupted by a breathless page. He handed off a crowded hall of petitioners to one of his traveling agents to deal with, and met Rel in the royal study. "What happened?"

"Senrid was right," Rel said as Peitar shut the door. "Detlev sent assassins after Jilo."

Peitar did not know Jilo, but he knew *of* him. He leaned forward, his brows slanting at an inquisitive angle as Rel gave his report. When Rel paused to draw breath, Peitar said,

"*Autumn* was there? Autumn, teacher of vagabond magic, who in some wise governs Bermund on the strait, required you to come to the aid of a Chwahir?"

Rel considered how to answer this, then said, "Jilo has been trying to take apart the dark magic destroying Chwahirs-land."

"I see. Go on."

Peitar closed his eyes so he would not have to deal with auras as he listened to Rel's description of what happened. He kept his patience through mentions of the Danarans, Jilo, and Detlev's boys, but when Rel got to the end, Peitar's lips compressed into a line, his thin cheeks red with anger. "Siamis was there, and this Autumn did *nothing?*"

"I don't think human affairs matter to her —"

"Of course they do," Peitar whispered, eyes still closed. "Or she wouldn't be there. So she exercises her power on behalf of a Chwahir, yet does nothing against a murderer. Are you certain she's not an agent of Norsunder?"

Peitar's fury seemed to fill the room, a beating presence that Rel could felt as a band of pressure around his skull. Rel had heard a great deal about Peitar's passion for liberty and peace, how he had survived an exceedingly violent revolution without once putting his hand to a weapon. And yet he sensed danger, and tensed into readiness.

Then Peitar dropped his head, let his breath out, and the tension in the room eased. "Clearly I must take my questions to Autumn. If she ever gets the courage to face me." He looked down at his hands, determined to master his anger. His uncle had let his anger rule him because he believed it justified — and he had nearly destroyed the kingdom. In a much calmer voice, he said, "To her magic. What can you tell me about her method of transfer? It's obviously unlike what we use, bringing me back yet again to my old questions."

"All I can say is that it seems as easy as stepping through a door . . ."

Peitar listened to Rel in silence, thumb running along his lower lip, back and forth. Finally he dropped his hand and looked up, squinting past the incandescing aura around Rel. "The more time passes, the more I'm convinced that your vagabond magic is an elementary form of something far more powerful. And Autumn — who is not really human — interfering twice convinces me that there's a secret here, questions of justice aside. Bringing me back again to the need to get away from Sartorias-deles altogether, and seek some answers in Geth."

Silence fell between them, as Peitar thought about that ruin he'd recently visited with such expectation, just to find a jumble of moss-covered stones, long overgrown. If there had been a Purad, it was long gone.

Rel was considering what he'd seen in the Danaran tower. He still had not resolved his feelings about Chwahirsland — what, if anything, he ought to say, or to do. And meantime, Peitar was right. There did seem to be a mystery behind this vagabond magic. "You still want me to scout for you?"

"Now that you've actually been taught, if anything your insight would be more valuable. And my first question will be — I will even make up message boxes, with world transfer magic worked in — do the vagabond mages walk labyrinths in Geth? Do ordinary mages?"

Rel nodded. "Put together whatever you want me to use, and I'll do my best not to lose it. Though I've had little success hanging onto golden notecases."

"Perhaps you can put the question early on," Peitar said. "It is very important to me."

"I'll make it a priority. I'm curious as well."

"Excellent." Peitar's tone lightened. "Thank you. I suggest you get in a night of rest while I work. It will be ready by morning."

Rel remembered the effects of a world transfer, and there would be no Autumn to waft him through this time. Just as well to take it easy before enduring it. Besides, he wanted to send a letter to Atan. It wasn't nearly as good as seeing her. The rest of the world only saw her court face, but he saw every expression except the ardency of desire.

Yeah, a letter might be best, because that made it easier to fall back to their old friendship, which proximity made so difficult. And so, as Peitar turned to his magic books, Rel walked in the other direction to seek Lilah and borrow her golden notecase.

Thirty-four

Sartor

ATAN SET DOWN REL'S letter and turned away, then picked it up to read again, even though she'd already read it twice. This time through it hurt in the way of poking at a bruise. Rel hadn't even gone to Geth yet — he'd learned magic — he wasn't *here*.

She forced herself to retire, knowing that the next day would be full, and woke to a beautiful day with bleakness in her heart after a night of bad dreams.

All day she walked through her schedule with her mind far from crown affairs. She was evolving a plan. And why shouldn't she? This was her city. She had been friends with Hannla since before Sartor emerged from the enchantment. She used to walk with Julian to Blossom Street all the time, because Julian had liked to ply a broom and eat sweet cakes and listen to the musicians downstairs.

So Atan had stopped going there after Julian got old enough to start wandering. Everyone knew the queen was busy, right?

Atan finally stopped arguing with herself — imagining what everyone would say — and instead of using her study time, told the palace guard that she was going for a walk to enjoy the beautiful day.

The guards felt it their duty to go before her, and so when a local child ran into Blossom Street shrieking, "The queen is coming this way!" Hannla heard her through all the doors open to the fresh breeze.

Hannla set her daughter on her feet, hands on little shoulders to keep Hlareas steady. Then Hlareas trotted off in the distinctive tiptoe of toddlers, her wispy honey-brown curls bouncing, the morning sunlight lancing low through an adjacent window catching in one of her little ears that stuck out from the side of her head. How could the sweet curve of a child's ear cause such a hollowing inside one?

Hannla didn't know, but she blinked against a sting along her eyelids at the brief reddish-pink glow of light on that ear. Then Hlareas tottered toward the kitchens, Hannla following after. She relaxed when she heard Staneth's voice. "Ho, there, little daughter! Where are you escaping to?" Hlareas's giggles followed.

Hannla joined them as the front door opened, and then Atan walked in, tall and queenly, but tense around the eyes. Hannla noticed, and knew Atan noticed, how all conversation stopped abruptly, and though the household merely nodded in greeting as they would to one another, it was self-conscious. The lack of protocol was something Atan had insisted on during her early visits with Julian, but she'd had to exert all her royal authority to achieve it.

My poor Atan, Hannla thought as she stepped forward. You can never be the girl in the forest again, with only a single care: freeing Sartor from enchantment.

Everyone tried valiantly, but the conversation was stilted as Atan labored equally valiantly to restore a sense of normalcy, during which time Hannla exchanged glances with Staneth, wordlessly handing over Hlareas's care from one parent to the other.

"Julian has not visited us for well over a year," Hannla's mother stated, an oblique way of finding out what the queen wanted.

Atan smiled. "I know. She's off adventuring in the waters off the northern continent, with Dtheldevor and her crew."

"Dtheldevor is real?" That was fourteen-year-old Amitu, looking up, though his hand didn't falter in slow-stirring the custard he was making.

"She is indeed. I've met her."

The household exchanged looks. Of course the queen of Sartor would meet any famous person still alive.

Atan's gaze shifted to Hannla, and her mother read that. "Come now, back to work. We're opening our doors in an hour," she said, making shooing motions.

Staneth hoisted Hlareas to his broad shoulders, where she promptly grabbed the jug-handle ears that he had bequeathed to her, and off they jogged, Staneth making pony noises to Hlareas's delighted squeals.

"Come into the accounts room," Hannla said. "It's the sunniest room in the house this time of year. Would you care for steep, or fresh berry buns? They just came out of the oven."

"I've already breakfasted," Atan said, "but a hot berry bun? Thank you."

Hannla snagged two, sliding one onto one of the finer plates that she had helped decorate herself, and led the way to the little square room added on at the back, currently filled with warm sunlight, though the air outside was brisk with autumnal chill.

The scent of buns filled the room as they each took a bite. The oven heat had already dissipated, leaving a mouthful of tart warmth that melted on the tongue. Hannla thought happily that Amitu's baking improved by the day.

Atan closed her eyes. "So delicious. And different from the berry buns the palace cook makes."

"Don't try to winnow the recipe from my aunt," Hannla warned. "She'll bring out the pitchforks!"

Atan laughed silently, finished the bun, then sighed, loosely folding her hands around her plate. Hannla noticed that she still kept her nails blunt cut and only buffed, not painted, though paint had come into fashion again in Sartor's first circle.

Atan sat down, then raised earnest dark blue eyes. "Hannla, you were one of my first friends when Lilah and Merewen and I first came to the forest, chased by that horrible Kessler Sonscarna."

"That I was," Hannla said, waiting patiently.

"Sometimes I miss those days," Atan said.

Oh, yes. Here it comes. "I don't," Hannla admitted, and when Atan sent her a startled look, she went on, "Oh, life in the enchanted forest was fine enough. Except when Irza was trying to rule us all. And except when our guardian vanished. And except for us all wondering and worrying about our families—I didn't know if anyone lived. Or if and when the enchantment would be lifted. And what we would find when it did." Hannla swept her hand around in a circle, including the entire house. "I didn't know if Blossom Street had been destroyed."

"You're right," Atan said in a low, chastened voice.

"Atan, our worries then seem small now because it's the past. We mourned the dead, we rebuilt, and now life is quiet again. But your life is only quiet on the surface. You walked into that palace untrained for queenship, and your worries have never ceased to multiply, even if you get some of them settled. Which is why I wouldn't change places for anything."

Atan straightened up at that. "Hannla, I don't know what to do," she whispered.

Hannla thought it was time to shut the door. She rose to do it, noted Atan's blush, and knew that the time had come for *that* conversation.

Atan said, "Has Rel been coming here for . . . going upstairs?"

Hannla sat down again, saying with amusement, "You mean time for the mattress-dance, pillow-jigging, whoopee, and other assorted euphemisms for sex?" At Atan's crimson-faced stare, she went on, "You know I can't answer that question. I told you that years ago, when you first asked me what to expect about the monthlies, and what it meant. Have you forgotten everything we talked about?"

"Most of it," Atan admitted. "It seemed . . . irrelevant at the time. When not awkward. Funny. Even kind of disgusting."

Hannla noted how the young queen's hands had tightened to white knuckles, and said gently, "You've forgotten that we might mention who's been seen downstairs, as people usually come to be seen as well as to listen to music, or watch a play, eat, or dance, try their skill at games, or just to socialize. But as soon as they go upstairs, their presence or absence becomes theirs to talk about or not, for much the same reason we wear clothing. Our bodies have public and private faces. You can see that, can't you? How if we, in this house, once have loose tongues, no one would come back?"

"Good," Atan said, bringing her chin down. "That's what I

thought. So . . . if I were to want to get the first time over, then no one would know, and bruit it about who it was, what I did, and so on?"

"Well, now, that's a different matter. You're a public figure. People talk about you. At one time, when Julian was little, you were here frequently, but since she's begun her wandering you're here, what, once a year, maybe? And it should be so," Hannla hastened to say, patting the air between them. "I know how much your day is filled with duties. But what others see, well, the last time you were here was for Hlareas's Name Day, not quite a year ago. So if you were to suddenly begin coming weekly, or even monthly, people *would* notice. And speculate."

Atan grimaced. "Which will weaken my insistence that marriage is too far in my future to be thought of. If certain court figures know I'm visiting pleasure houses, they'll begin diplomatic negotiations abroad, and badgering me—always for the good of the kingdom, order, and continuity, you understand—at home. I'm trying to keep that at bay as long as I can."

"That makes sense. You walk about the city freely, which you ought to be able to do, as it heartens people to see you taking as much interest in their lives as they take in yours. And we don't have a private door, as do some of the places your first circle nobles visit. Their business is predicated on discretion, and ours is on our music and food. Upstairs is secondary to that—our stairway can be seen from the west end of the common room. Our custom comes from local people who have no influence or expectations in courtly circles."

Atan began twisting her hands inside out in a way that looked painful to Hannla. "I just want . . ." Her heavy brows twitched together as she sorted words. "I guess I need to *know*. And to plan ahead, to avoid making the mistakes so many of my ancestors did. Maybe I'm backward because I did the Child Spell."

Hannla sighed. "I can't speak to the Child Spell, as magical things are out there." She waved a hand. "Not in my everyday experience. But I think you got your courses late because you were still growing."

"Really?" Atan's brows shot upward. "I . . . wasn't aware." She looked at the cuffs of her fine linen gown, dyed a deep green, with its gold braid edging and tiny opals stitched at intervals along the braid.

Hannla could not prevent a sardonic smile. "Atan, if your dressmaker and dresser had permitted you to walk around with your hems or cuffs too short they would have been turned out of their positions. You can be certain they check the fit of your clothes, and when something is too snug, it gets replaced with another garment just like it that isn't."

"I didn't even notice that," Atan said, obviously disturbed.

"Yes, because you have other things on your mind. That's what's on *their* minds. We all have our work, and we don't necessarily pay close heeds to others' work. Part of their job is to make certain you don't have to think about your clothes, since you clearly aren't all that interested."

Atan blew out a breath. "All right. I've let myself get distracted. Here's the truth. When Rel is around—nobody else, just him—I get a tangle of feelings. Physical feelings. It feels like fire, at once warm but threatening to burn. I want to touch him, but I don't want him to see me wanting to, if that makes any sense. Because of all these other obligations, and the arguments I know I'll have to endure."

"Understood."

Atan's voice lowered. "And yet I find excuses to step near him, when he's not noticing, so I can sniff him. Is that weird?"

"Normal."

A sigh of relief. "When he's away, I find myself wondering what it would be like to kiss him. And . . . other things. That's normal, too?"

"Completely." Hannla opened her hands, palms up. "Here is what you need to know. There's a wide variety of things that are normal. Wanting to experiment with a new partner every day is normal. Not wanting to know their name because you don't want to get entangled here." She put her fist to her heart. "That's also normal. Not being able to bear the idea of closeness with anyone but the one you care for, also normal. Not wanting anything to do with anyone at all in that way? Normal. There are a range of things that many would consider not normal—"

"Like?" Atan leaned forward, eyes wide.

"Well, one example, a person might like being tied to the bedpost with silken ribbons while their partner plays with their body as he or she wills—"

"Ugh!"

Hannla laughed. "Well, if both partners are agreeable, then it becomes normal for them. Curiously enough, that one, I hear, seems to be more popular among persons of power. Anyway, do you see what I'm saying?"

"Ah . . . my coming here feeling I ought to get the first time out of the way so that I'll be less confused when Rel returns, but the idea of it revolts me, is that normal?"

"You might be one of those who has to have fire here," the fist to the heart again, "before the fire ignites down below. Normal!"

Slowly Atan's fingers began to loosen, as Hannla went on. "Most who come here for the first time to get it over with are already feeling the fire, but they don't have a partner yet, and are not sure how to find one, or they don't want to be clumsy, or they are shy about asking someone and being turned down. But you know, there's nothing amiss with figuring things out with a partner you care for. Anyone with half a thought knows that nobody is an expert at anything the first time."

Atan's gaze was now stark. "But what if the fire becomes overwhelming? And it's all one can think of? I can name every one of my forebears who made terrible mistakes while over-whelmed with love. It seems . . . *dangerous*. And that's without considering the entire high council's disapproval of my getting too close to Rel the Shepherd's Son. I suspect they'd even be relieved if I were coming here regularly, as long as I didn't have a favorite who might interfere with their political plots."

Hannla sighed. She didn't pretend to any wisdom, but she did have experience of people in all the magnificent, messy spectrum of love, lust, and what they thought were permanent or ephemeral states of both. She also didn't pretend to predictions about relationships, but this she did know: Atan and Rel laughed in the same language, such a rarity, so precious. But the shackles of state pulled on one of them while thrusting the other away.

She chose her words with care. "Atan, I can talk to you about the wide varieties of intimacy, but the political dangers are as foreign to me as is talk of magic. My only suggestion is, when Rel returns, you talk to him. If your feelings—both of you—are still the same, then you go from there."

"You make it sound so easy," Atan said, low-voiced. "While I—I have learned that the simplest conversation, even the simplest words, can go so very wrong." She caught herself then, thanked Hannla for her time, and went out to greet the others.

Everyone parted on friendly terms, full of good will, but Hannla felt a strong sense of failure as she watched the tall figure walk alone except for her respectfully distant guards toward her huge palace and the invisible, inescapable weight there.

Thirty-six

WHEN THE BOYS GOT back, they found Adam had just returned. He looked dusty, his face sun-tanned. "Sh," he murmured, pointing to the inner room. "Sveneric is asleep. We had a long walk today."

"Long walk?" Noser's scowl cleared as he gloated, "You got a mountain-top? You?"

"No," Adam said. "It was me and the shrimp on an extended camping trip."

"*Camping* trip?" Noser repeated. "You got *rewarded?*"

Silvanas regarded him askance. "You hate camping."

"I do not! Anyway, it's a thousand times better than what *we* got!" He glared at Adam. "What for, if it wasn't a reward? Were you spying?"

"Nobody within days of us," Adam said, and MV, Curtas, and Laban noted — each with different reactions — that Adam didn't say what the trip had been for. Though they'd always had at least one goal when they'd camped as small boys.

"We finished the hike when we found transfer tokens waiting," Adam went on. "And this." Her jerked his paint-stained thumb at the opposite side of the room, where they discovered a basket of fresh fruit, mostly varieties of summer berries, a loaf of bread, a wheel of cheese, and a pan of freshly grilled fish that smelled of wine, olive oil, and herbs.

As the boys fell on the food, Adam murmured to David, "The shrimp will be glad you're back."

David lifted a shoulder. Tired as he was, shrimp duty was just another duty. Though the shrimp was getting more interesting as he got older, he was also getting weirder, which David thought made Adam the better tutor. Weird for the weird. He picked up some bread and cheese, aware that his hand and arm were almost too heavy to lift. A few bites, then he trod heavily in the direction of his bed. He set the bread down, shucked his clothes, and dropped onto his bed. He was asleep in two breaths.

MV had thrown together a massive sandwich. With that in hand, he went after David, expecting a debrief. He stopped in the doorway and glared at that oblivious figure. Irritated, he set his sandwich on his weapons trunk, grabbed David's sodden clothes, and put them through the cleaning frame so they wouldn't mildew and stink up the place. Then he yanked the blanket off his bed and tossed it over David, grabbed his sandwich, and returned to the office, annoyed with the questions buzzing around in his head like bugs. No one to answer. Especially annoying as that basket of waiting food made it clear Detlev was observing them from somewhere.

The watch bell clanged, echoing off the stone walls. MV looked around at the others sitting along the floor with their backs to the walls as they devoured the last crumbs of the feast. "Back to usual. Keep your traps shut before the grass. And if anyone yaps any question at you, lie, report who, and what they asked." Pointing at the empty basket, "*He* will want to know."

The reminder got everyone out the door except Adam, who was still on shrimp duty. Seeing him relaxing over his stupid scribbling, dry and content after a luxurious campout that must have been livened by feasts, brought back all Noser's resentment in a rush intensified by a sense of injustice. As he followed MV out, he whined in a tone of ill-usage, "You just stood there like a turd in the road, blocking the door. You could've at least let *us* in to attack, if you were scared of Siamis."

MV sighed in disgust. "He and Rel could've held that door all day without breaking a sweat. You really didn't see it?"

"You also didn't seem to hear Senrid and his horde coming up behind us," Laban drawled. "Don't be any more of an idiot than you can help." He pushed past Noser and stalked off toward the practice field.

"You," MV said to Noser, "stop your yap and wand the horse stalls."

"It's my turn to train!"

"You're arguing with an order?" MV said menacingly.

"No! But *why-y-y-y-y?*" Noser whined.

"Because you're so annoying that if I see your stupid face again today, I'm going to use it for target practice." Thus MV pushed his own bad mood onto Noser, who stamped off in the direction of the stable.

He circled around behind, risking the officers' riding court because it was a shorter route. He saw no one there, and pelted across the stones, fetching up when a woman stepped out of a shadowy alcove. "Halt right there," she said.

Dejain the mage! Noser hated mages, but he also respected their powers. "What do you want?" he asked, belligerent to cover his fear. "I got duty."

"You can answer some questions," she said. "Like, where Detlev is, and what he's planning next."

"I dunno. He doesn't tell me *anything*," Noser snarled.

"Whom does he tell?"

Anger and resentment made Noser snide. "If you want to know, ask his *favorite*. I'm sure he knows *everything*."

"Oh?" she asked. "Who is that?"

"Adam," Noser replied, and ran away, his shoulder blades twitching, but she didn't turn him into a tree stump. Hah. Let Adam have to dodge that stupid mage's questions. Maybe she'd turn *him* into a tree stump.

By the time he reached the stable, and saw how much awaited him, his bad mood shifted to the work ahead.

After a long shift, he tromped back, to find David awake. "Anything to report?"

Noser had forgotten all about the mage and her questions, but at David's question it all came back—along with MV's orders to keep lips buttoned. Uneasiness prompted irritation, but Noser knew better than to lie. David always found out. "That yellow haired old mage stopped me to ask a lot of questions about Detlev's plans and where he was."

"What did you tell her?"

"How could I tell her anything? I don't *know* anything," Noser yelled. "Nobody tells *me* anything!" He stomped past, and dashed to the cleaning frame before running off to the mess hall.

David turned back to Detlev's empty office. He still hadn't slept enough, but his sleep had been fitful, and he knew the cause: those unsettling questions about the future. Everything they were now doing raised questions. He understood the covert training that they hid from the rest of the world, and had always loved it. It made sense, when you were smaller than everyone around you to have some powerful training that no one knew about.

But what was it supposed to lead to?

David recuperated for a couple of days, intermittently downing what felt like a river of water, and traded off tutoring duty with Adam. Sveneric did everything David asked, his quiet delight in having his chosen favorite back apparent to Adam, to Curtas, to Laban (who found it irritating) — everyone with the interest or awareness to see, except for David.

Adam saw, but said nothing. His nature was not a jealous one, and he knew that attachments couldn't be ordered or forced, they just were.

Meanwhile, when he wasn't tutoring Sveneric, David ran the boys through extra drills, taking them all on in order to restore himself to normal the faster. But everything maddened him: the airless heat, the slanting light that swiftly shifted from late-summer heat to the gloom that promised another long, cold, dark, bitter winter. The unanswered questions.

Finally, during a pre-dawn drill, he thrashed his way through every one of his partners, ending with MV, who cursed when David hit him too hard, and backed off, hands up, saying, "What's chafing your ass, shit-for-brains?"

David looked at the puffy flesh around MV's eye that was going to be black and blue by midday, and sighed. He had better control than that.

He ought to apologize, but what he heard himself say was, "I'm going to Geth, to find Roy."

PART THREE
MISPRISION

One

EVERYONE STILLED AT THAT.

"Roy?" Curtas repeated.

"You know for sure he's on Geth?" Laban crossed his arms and leaned against the stone wall of the stable back, a bruise fast purpling on his jaw.

"Not for certain. But whenever I try to reach him . . ." David brushed his fingers over his forehead. "I niff Geth's marsh. I'll start there."

"And then what?" Erol said in his quiet voice.

David said recklessly, "Rip his reason for betrayal out of him. Then go from there." And at the various expressions of skepticism and shock, he said, "We finished our orders. The rest of you can maintain the fool schedule. I want to do some scouting."

"Ripping Roy apart is scouting?" That was Silvanas.

"It's fun. But only if we get to see it," Noser said, wiping his hair out of his eyes with a snot-smeared, freckled wrist.

David couldn't say the truth: It would be scouting if he could choke some answers out of Roy, beginning with why he ran—and if he knew what was coming next. He said, "If I don't find anything, expect to see me back soon."

When he spotted Sveneric's hopeful face at breakfast, he said, "Laban. You take over tutoring while I'm gone." And he turned away, without seeing the hurt that lengthened

Sveneric's mouth, before the small boy shuttered his expression.

David had stalked to his room. He looked at his few belongings, then shrugged. Geth was much warmer than most of Sartorias-deles, except along the islands at the belt of the world. All he'd take would be his weapons. Everything else he'd scavenge. It didn't escape him that the only two who could make a reliable cross-worlds transfer token had been Roy and him. That brought back the question of just how long Roy had been planning his betrayal.

You'll answer soon, David thought.

He braced himself. David didn't trust himself to an open Destination in a world transfer, so he'd set his Destination for the houseboat that had been their den while in that world.

The transfer was as excruciating as expected, leaving him crowing for air, his body aching in every joint as he dropped his weapons on a table and bent over, hands on knees, fighting against nausea. The reaction faded at last, leaving him in his empty room, which looked smaller than he remembered it. The air was agreeably warm, the houseboat—made of the familiar iridescent undersea wood that looked like melted candy—and the pungency of brine and marsh grasses bringing up old memory.

Senses alert, he tested the quiet sway of the deck under his feet, knowing immediately that he was alone on the houseboat. Pretty much as expected. The cove Detlev had chosen was difficult to navigate into, and MV and Laban had practiced their magic lessons by laying illusions to hide the mouth of the inlet, and to make the water from the outside appear to be toothed with rocks and other dangers.

Nearly all the islands in this long, serpentine archipelago had coastal inlets of various types, generally on one side the steep cliff coves, and on the other, marshy, flat estuaries and tiny bays. Learning to navigate the currents had been an early lesson, two boys per rowboat before they were allowed to put up sails. Navigation by sun and stars, and then charting, had taken up summers.

David knew the coast well. He'd come because it was a familiar place from which to start a search.

But first, they always did a sweep. He prowled from room to room, gaze moving slowly right to left as he'd been trained. Not much left behind, of course, but what little there was brought up memories he'd thought he'd forgotten. Like the carvings in the wood supports that he'd made from Curtas's drawing the second time Detlev let Curtas design a new roof, after both the old one and his first attempt had both blown off during typhoons. There were the bars Rolfin had put in his doorway for pull-ups; Noser's battered toy horses, and in David's room, still sitting on his worktable, a row of flutes he'd carved as practice, each tuned to a different chord.

He picked one of them up, tested it, and grimaced at the sound. Yes, that's why he'd left it there. Smacking it against his hand, he proceeded on, halting outside the kitchen when he smelled spices: sweet pepper and the sharp scent of yellow-glass.

He stepped inside, hand to knife. Nothing was out of place. The familiar fragrances hung in the still, somnolent air.

He peered through the slats of the kitchen windows. No one in sight. He unlatched them to the air, and stepped out the back door onto the ramp that the boys had made after lashing together ancient rowboats, then smoothing and hammering the tangleroot trees they'd chopped away from the shore so they could afford a clear field of vision. It was in that cleared space that they'd put in their kitchen garden, now overgrown.

David stepped out to the edge of the ramp where it met the rich reddish-brown soil, and looked out over the neglected kitchen garden that had supplied all their vegetables and most of their herbs. At first it looked undisturbed, and if David had cast a brief glance, he would have assumed no one had been there. But he assessed the garden, spotting gaps here and there. Wildlife? If so, there would be prints.

He stepped out, his feet sinking into the spongy ground — and he saw where someone had been smoothing away his or her footprints in and out of the garden. Animals didn't do that.

He turned back, aware of Geth's blazing sun beating on the back of his neck. Someone had been fetching food from the garden. He looked around more carefully as he retreated into the houseboat. No signs, of course. In the distance, the orchard, and beyond that clumps of greenery fading toward the dark green of the forested ridge, beyond which lay the Norsunder fortress a hard ride in the distance.

It was too convenient to assume that the trespasser was Roy. It could be anyone. There'd been no boat tied up in the inlet—not surprising, given the illusions protecting the seaward entrance. But the back end of the bay, where the houseboat floated, was open. Norsunder's presence on the other side of the forest had kept Geth wanderers away from this end of the island. Maybe it was a scout. Or a deserter. That brought David right back to Roy and his betrayal.

He retreated to his room and opened his trunk. His Geth clothes lay undisturbed: loose trousers, and a thin, airy long tunic-shirt with no sleeves. He changed, feeling instant relief, but hesitated over the mocs. It was much too hot for boots, and this was the wrong terrain. In the old days the boys had gone barefoot, except when on assignment. He slipped the mocs on in case he had to move fast.

He was so close to the Marsh. He could feel it tugging at his consciousness. It would be so easy to slip into that weird mental plane to scan, but he might find himself stuck in the Marsh, as the divide between the mental and physical plane was thin and ever-shifting there. Which was one reason why most humans who wandered there never recovered from Marsh madness.

He had, after being unconscious for weeks. He'd had to learn to keep the mental realm and the Marsh world separate in order to survive. He breathed slowly, now glad of all that practice with Adam: he closed off everything but the mental realm that had no connection to the physical world, and reached.

No one familiar anywhere nearby.

But he wouldn't sense anyone shielded. Instinct insisted it was Roy—but he knew he wanted the intruder to be Roy. So. Instead of a search, it was time to do some stalking.

Before he left, he hesitated. During the days the boys went out on longer stalks, they'd devised some simple signals to leave behind for one another. A truce had been two stones left on the windowsill of target or chase, meant for exchanging vital news before resuming to the chase.

Should he?

He walked outside—as he was watched through a field glass from behind a thick fern on a rocky hill near the mouth of the inlet.

Roy always scanned ahead.

Though he'd separated himself from Detlev, Norsunder, and the boys, he hadn't separated from the habits of training.

Like vigilance. Tired as he was, he'd dropped behind a fern, which would keep the field glass from winking in the sunlight, and swept the inlet around the boat, as he did every single time he returned.

The houseboat was not rocking on the mild current the way it did when empty: someone was inside. The difference was subtle, but they'd all learned to see it. He tightened his gut against hunger and waited. To his surprise and dismay, it was David who emerged, leaped up onto the bank, and examined the ground. For Roy's footprints, of course. He knew his sweeps had been cursory at best.

David bent down, picked something up, and tossed it on his palm. Rocks.

Roy scarcely breathed as he watched David run back over the ramp to the kitchen. Roy was aware of his palms sweating as David gently set two stones on the windowsill, then backed away a step. Two stones: truce.

Roy kept the glass trained on David's face, as David himself considered what he was doing. In the old days, the signals (at the cost of some bitter fights) had become sacrosanct. But he was aware that he was lying. If Roy actually turned up, there would be no truce.

And Roy, watching his profile, saw the gentle little smile that always meant violence.

He slid back down the rock, and with shaking hands replaced the field glass in his pack. He had no idea why David was here, now, dressed in Geth clothes, but this much was clear: the houseboat had become off limits, and at the worst possible moment, the hunt was on.

Two

Geth-deles, Isul Demarzal

REL HAD BEEN TO Geth-deles once before. As it happened, he'd been brought to the same island, and the same city — ancient Isul Demarzal, the oldest human city on the world — but the circumstances were wholly different.

On his previous visit, the city had lain under enchantment. Rel and the Young Allies entered covertly, in illusory disguise, in order to cause a distraction so that the warded mages could work together to break Norsunder's enchantment.

This time, he appeared at a Destination outside the city, overlooking a beach of soft white sand, under a tiled roof held up by eight columns nearly hidden by flowering vines. He'd gone from Miraleste's late lakeside summer to a strong mid-summer on a wide bay beside the sea. He blinked against a crucible of liquid light sparkling on the cobalt blue ocean. The bay brimmed with all manner of ships and boats, from kayaks and two-person canoes to tall, narrow-draft fore-and-aft rigged schooners.

Rel breathed slowly as the transfer reaction diminished; from the edge of the bay rose above the general hubbub a man's brassy shout, "Ho! Deeyo Ho-dio, holo ho HO!"

A chorus rose, "HO!" as from behind one of the schooners six or eight long, low craft shot into the bay, rowers lifting and dipping their oars in cadence as they answered the caller, "Ho! Holo, HO!"

The caller sang the nonsense rhythms, which carried on the breeze, the rowers—people of all ages, some with baskets and bulky packages sitting before their feet—responding "Holo HO!" on each pull of their oars. They skimmed over the water, approaching a distant rocky point. Before they reached it, flashing silver shapes, smooth and finned, leaped from the water to arc over the skimming boats and splash on the other side. The faint chorus altered to a new song before boats, and dancing sea life, vanished beyond the rocks.

Presently Rel was approached by a man wearing a bright green sash over one shoulder, who spoke in Geth.

Rel hated the Universal Language Spell. When he traveled, he did his best to learn enough vocabulary to get around—and in places where the root language was Sartoran, it usually didn't take long.

Here, he had to rely on the Spell. He knew that Sartorans had escaped here after the Fall of Ancient Sartor, but the language seemed to have evolved from other influences, for Geth held very few similarities to any of the variations of Sartoran he was familiar with. At least the Universal Language Spell was significantly improved from that last visit—someone had been adding words to it. But nothing could prevent the brief, irritating lag between what one heard through one's ears and what one heard in one's mind.

"You wish directions, traveler?"

"A mage named Hosha, in Isul Demarzal."

The man smiled, his white teeth a cheerful contrast to skin even browner than Rel's. "Isul Demarzal is all around you! For mages, I suggest you go along to the Char and ask. Most of them go through there. This street will take you to the gates."

"Char"—Rel remembered the impossibly vast, rambling one-story complex called "Charlotte's Palace" after some long-ago immigrant, the first to start keeping records. But—the alliance had been told earnestly— the complex was pretty much known as the Char.

Rel's guide waved behind him, and Rel squinted against the brilliant light past the throngs of people and barking dogs and little goats. Most of the people wore loose clothing in light colors. Rel had forgotten how the buildings, all wooden, looked like they'd been poured from golden candy and chocolate. Very few reached over two stories, and all had awnings and canopies. Flowers grew everywhere, a riot of color that added pungent scents to the air.

Rel turned his back on the sun-splashed sea and started walking up the sand-colored brick of the street. He was soon sweating, the bright sun beating down on his head.

The gates stood open, carts, horses, and walkers going in and out in a steady stream. He remembered that the building itself was a rambling affair so large it would be easy to get lost.

But relief came first when he reached the shade of a corridor, and then when one of the green sashed people said, "Hosha? You'll want that wing there."

Pages? Heralds? Rel knew better than to impose categories of people and work over situations where customs might utterly differ. The green sashes were worn by men, women, and children. They were seen everywhere, leading goat carts, giving directions, sweeping, nipping dead flowers and leaves off the many, many vines trailing up columns, trellises, and walls.

Rel took one last look around, much preferring this busy, crowded scene to the emptiness and threat of his last visit, then passed indoors. The walls had been painted white, and shallow pools and fountains were visible in squares off the awning-covered corridors. Air ruffled over these with a cooling effect, but still, Rel was glad to find the archway he'd been sent to. Getting out of the sun was a physical relief.

He entered a crowded antechamber and resigned himself to a long wait. It was one thing for a king to be corresponding with a mage; even mages from another world were more likely to drop everything to answer questions from a king, but an ordinary traveler expected to wait.

"I'm here to speak to Hosha," he said, and watched the weedy, green-sashed page narrow his eyes and wrinkle his snub nose. No doubt from the lag of the Universal Language Spell at the other end, because then his face cleared, and he said, "Through there."

Rel glanced in the direction the freckled hand pointed and walked through a door — to surprise an older woman in the middle of packing scrolls and pen cases into a satchel.

"Hosha?" Rel asked. "I was sent by Peitar Selenna."

"Yes, I've been expecting you," she said. "I'd hoped you would be timely, for I am needed elsewhere. And if I am correct, it is not me you wish to speak to anyway."

She waited for him to process the translation of her words to his, then went on. "For some reason, your king believes that the children's play magic is connected to something more serious. We believe that is because over there—" She gestured toward the sky. "You heard about Leskandar—" She pronounced it Less-cahn-dair, with the swallowed 'r' sound typical of Geth. "Les Rhoderan and his child army, who claimed intent to free this island from the oppression of adult rulers, and then march against the Northwest Island to rid us of the Stones."

"Stones?" Rel asked.

"Nor-sun-dair, wear gray, stones." She wove her hand in a circle on each point. "You have many names, too, for them, yes?"

Elevens, Rel thought. Nightlanders. And, of course, soul-suckers.

Hosha capped an inkwell with brisk movements and tap-ed her reed pens into a neat pile before sliding them into a silken sheath. "Leskandar Rhoderan is dead, and many of our Jayuns—"

The word translated as *young wanderers*.

"—regard him as a martyr to the cause of youth. Whatever that might be. You would do better to speak to young Dak about it all, I think. He is your best guide, though to tell you the truth, I think your king is mistaken about their play magic." Her lips curled, her eyes crinkling. "Eh! From even a world away, I suspect it never does much good to tell a king he is mistaken."

She rose, hefting her satchel. "Dak will arrive by sundown. Bide here. If you have thirst or hunger, to ask is to have. I must be about my affairs."

"One last question: do you have labyrinths?"

The hesitation between what he said and what she heard seemed a heartbeat longer, then she murmured in a voice of mild perplexity, "Mazes? Many build those in gardens, or other places, for children to play in."

"But they are not connected to this magic?"

She shrugged. "I suppose if the children make illusions to add to their play? But there is no import in it, if that is your question."

He thanked her, and she left.

Rel went out to one of the benches that overlooked a square, so he could watch the comings and goings, listen, and maybe catch a few words. So far, the information was disappointing.

But he could be patient.

While farther east on the island, Dak, their guide from their previous visit, sat with his brother Cath and some friends in a sharron treehouse as a brief thunderstorm rumbled over the eastern mountains, pouring rain down on the awning made of overlapped broad leaves.

"Apparently this Nightside king sent another representative," Dak was complaining to a Rowen friend, Tarsa Mdarenda. "This one wants to snout into vagabond magic. And the Char mages are unloading him onto me."

Below the sharron platforms a group of traveling Rowens had gathered to sing through the storm, staccato voices punctuating in stuttering counterpoint the never-repeating melody sung by deeper voices.

Mdarenda wanted to get back to the sing—he enjoyed thunder sings—but he'd shared adventures from island to island with Dak, a generous and entertaining friend, so he sat and let his friend complain. *You don't empty the bitter river unless it pours though another's ears*, his grandfather had said once. *Dak needs to pour as much as the sky does. Both the rain and the rant shall pass.*

"I don't *mind* talking about vagabond magic," Dak continued, his square, cheerful face earnest. "Or making illusions. But . . . kings?" A green snake head slithered out from Dak's frayed cuff, its tongue testing the air. Still too damp. The snake withdrew, and Dak's shirt rippled, then stilled, as Dak said, "Nothing but trouble."

Mdarenda wondered how many snakes Dak had on him this time, as he said, "But you're not a king. And this representative isn't one, either. So, if he starts ordering you around, you leave him a boat, an oar, and a direction. Maybe leave out the oar if he pretends to kingly offensiveness."

Dak tipped his head, then scowled. "But this king's uncle is the commander of the defense up north. What if he, the king I mean, gets insulted, and sends Commander Irad to the attack?" Dak spread his fingers across his chest, eyes wide below his unkempt pale hair.

"Why, then you run for Fya Rya, where they cannot get in," Mdarenda said, laughing.

None of this advice was new, or even that useful, but Dak needed reassurance. He didn't like change unless he went looking for it, but when it snuck up behind him . . . well, that was different.

As if sharing a thought, both he and Mdarenda glanced at Dak's brother Cath, sitting on a branch not far away so he could peer out into the meadow the trees grew around. Cath had reached that odd age between little one and not-quite teen, which in most was awkward. But Cath had never been awkward, even as a baby.

Cath had shut out their conversation so he could watch the pattern of the long-tailed swallows swooping, rising, circling and diving. Swarm was such an imprecise word, he was thinking. "Swarm" was like calling music "noise," taking out all the beauty and feeling, and most of all, the sense of it.

He was very certain that the swallows were singing back to the Rowens by weaving and looping, diving and soaring. Could he catch their song with his reed-flute?

Dak saw that his brother was oblivious and gave a silent sigh. "As soon as the rain lifts," Dak said. "We'll get it over with."

The rain was already passing as he spoke, and so they were soon on the road west, tramping over the raised bridges as people still working the rice fields in the shallow, sky-reflecting waters to either side sang the slow songs of lengthening day.

Dak found himself tramping in time to the song, and at one point Cath brought out one of his flutes and played softly in harmony, so the sound barely carried over the water. He did not seem to notice the occasional heads that came up from stooping over the rice, or the faltering of melodic call and answer melodies sung by the workers as they stooped and straightened, stooped and straightened. When Cath's music tumbled, airy and graceful, over the water, they listened enthralled, heads turning as they watched the boys pass.

Maybe their captivated expressions meant nothing to Cath. Dak had watched over his younger brother ever since they left their farm, but he seemed never to come closer to understanding him.

They reached the Char as the sun was sinking into the sea, throwing dramatically long shadows of bare masts to crawl back and forth across the main street.

Dak's spirits lifted when he recognized the off-worlder in the tall, black-haired fellow who'd led the group of off-worlders during their visit. Rel's quiet competence had earned even Cath's regard. And here Rel sat without any hint of impatience, surrounded by illusory animals that shimmered as the brothers approached.

"You already know vagabond magic," Dak exclaimed in rudimentary Sartoran.

Rel smiled his way, then banished his airy creations with a wave of his hand. They vanished in a green sparkle. "I've made a beginning. I'm hoping we can compare what we've learned. Maybe you've more to teach?"

Dak said, "Indeed. We might begin by meeting up with some friends, if you don't mind a long walk upland."

"I like nothing better than travel," Rel said, mentally resigning himself to a longer stay. At least he was likely to learn something.

Three

IF IT HAD BEEN Ferret at the houseboat, Roy reflected a few days later as he slogged hip deep up a stream, he would have been smoked by now. David was bad enough.

When Detlev's boys first began playing at stalking one another, they'd been immensely impressed by the cleverness Siamis demonstrated in laying down what they called breadcrumbs, or false trails.

Breadcrumbs were their default—the more the better—until David and Ferret first began looking past trail sign to intent.

Roy decided to hide his identity by laying the subtlest of breadcrumbs—maybe two tracks, maddening and time-consuming as that would be—to some other targets, one of which at least had to make sense to David.

What else was there but the Norsunder fortress and the Marsh? Roy hated the Marsh, so dangerous in so many ways. He'd never had marsh sickness, but that didn't mean he wouldn't. Some went blind, others lost hearing, or even their voices, and many lost their lives. David had been sick for weeks, scarcely eating, running a low fever while out of his head. Siamis and Detlev had traded off sitting with him . . .

Roy shook off the old memories, the old loyalties. It seemed so impossible for anyone to understand that there could be loyalties formed around a center that could only be described as evil. He could not explain it himself. But there it was.

He knew he was nearing the Marsh when the air began to whiff of dankness and soft drifts of fog slipped eerily along the unraveled coils of murky waterways bounded by a forest of reeds and marsh plants. The hairs along his arms rose and he took the warning, turning west . . . and again turning west. . . and where was west?

Thoroughly frightened, he backtracked until he could breathe easily, and there was the innocent sun, sitting where he'd left it, though it seemed he'd been gone hours. Mud caked his clothes to the armpits, slimy and veined with old grasses.

As he floundered toward higher ground through bulrushes, wild rice, and floating colonies of water lilies of a thousand hues, bending low so as not to create a silhouette above the cattails and rushes, across the Marsh David walked, eyes half shut. Unlike Roy he knew where he was, and further, that another human toiled somewhere on the extreme western border. David cut north, moving swiftly, his mind joining him to the space he needed to be.

Roy emerged into the wider, firmer finger of land between marsh-hugging rows of tangleroot, the weird complexity of their bare roots as complicated as the twisting branches above.

And when he cautiously ventured beyond the pleached tangleroots, he gained a clear field of vision. A distant figure paced steadily along a low ridge.

Familiar? He squinted, straining to recognize details, but the light was too hazy and full of glare. He froze there, half-hidden by the bole of a tree, but visible from the far end of the spit, just as David emerged from the Marsh. David spotted Roy through his field glass, and grinned.

"Got you," he breathed.

But what was Roy watching so intently? It wasn't David — his attention lay far to David's left. David swept the glass away and up onto the ridge, then stilled as one of Efael's Black Knives snapped into view.

From either end of the spit Roy and David both watched as the man paced, stopped, carefully laid something on the ground, straightened up, oriented himself, then began to pace. Counting off steps?

Yes. At three hundred, he bent and put down another something. This was preparation for some sort of perimeter ward, which meant that either Yeres or Efael, maybe both, were coming with some powerful magical intent.

They had to be shaping some kind of attack. Roy had to abandon his plans and warn someone. Who?

As he began his turn a warning prickle tightened the back of his neck, and he spotted a wink of light on a field glass, held by David, his sword strapped to his back.

David swung the glass toward Roy. As a flock of birds on the ridge took wing with a clatter and a scolding caw, Roy and David regarded one another, too distant to see faces, but each recognized surprise in the lineaments of the other.

Rage ignited in David. He wanted to transfer there and knock Roy's teeth down his throat, and then choke the reasons for his betrayal out of his bloody, mumbling mouth—but that Black Knife had to have been sent by Efael. Rage hardened into cold anger. David was here without orders, but this was something he knew he needed to report.

David watched the Black Knife until he disappeared beyond the ridge. When he returned his gaze to the spot he'd marked, he was peripherally aware that Roy was gone. As expected. David kept his glass trained on the spot the Black Knife had marked in some way and advanced up the ridge, staying close to cover.

A little searching in the thick, tough, shiny grasses disclosed a bead. David didn't touch it, but squatted down, fingers hovering over it as he tested the magic.

It was definitely a ward perimeter marker.

He looked back at the place where Roy had been. Chasing him was going to have to wait.

Roy shifted by magic to the inlet above the houseboat and hid up, scanning the houseboat in case David transferred back, as he considered whom to approach. He couldn't shake off that image of David standing there. It was something Roy had dreaded since he and Clair left Five—and it had happened.

One day, he knew they would meet. The prospect made him feel sick.

Then he forced his mind to the urgency of Black Knives and wards. Somebody needed to know. But who would listen to him? He considered all the people he'd met during the days the boys were learning to infiltrate and gather information, before the Les Rhoderan mission.

Dak? Mdarenda? Solomay Winda? All friends, trusted friends. Once. That was the problem, trust. He could go to them all and say he'd broken with Detlev and the group, but he knew what would happen: at best, polite listening, doubt, suspicion. "Prove it," Mdarenda would say. "Another ruse," Les's sister Caris-Merian would say —

He rolled onto his back, staring at the sky as he thought about trust. The irony was, he had now managed to break it with both sides. Only Lilith knew the truth, but she was busy with the bigger battle, watching over three worlds. He'd insisted he would make his own way, and so he must.

As he watched an army of little clouds slide in low overhead, bringing up the moisture in the air, he remembered the old lessons: Detlev had told them time and again, if one track was empty, find another.

So . . .

Of course.

He sat up. Trying people he knew would be useless, but what about those he didn't?

Four

REL LEARNED PLENTY.

Dak was friendly, cheerful, and garrulous. At first there was a lot of showing off with vagabond magic illusions, complicated tricks and games that Dak and his friends had been trading back and forth for a while. Amusing, but useless.

But as they made their way across many low bridges over marshy land, much of it planted with rice, and then began toiling up switchbacks toward the not-so-distant hills to the east, the conversation dipped into history: Fya Rya, the city of children—Dak's many friends—circling back around to Les Rhoderan.

"The readers tell us our history is tied to Nightside history," Dak said as they camped one night, Dak having snapped up a spark and fed it carefully with dried reeds before it caught on the pile of dried peat they'd stacked up. They were now high enough up for the night to become chilly. "Those old mages thought that evil entered men around the time they sprouted beards. I guess some of that was in old Nightside history?" He paused the glance over at Rel, the firelight beating in his eyes and bleaching his hair of color.

"Yes," Rel said.

"Well, all I can say is, it may or may not be true, but those traitors of Detlev's are an argument against. We almost destroyed Fya Rya over them," Dak admitted. "They'd already ruined the feel of safety. They were there. Among us! And not a sign of a whisker among any of us—the magic would keep any such out!"

"You never had evil people in there before?" Rel asked skeptically.

"If someone did something nasty, the others would throw them out," Dak said. "But no *Stonebacks*." He sighed. "And then the day came when Les got too old, and a lot of people wanted to break the magic just for him so it could be his secret headquarters, but we couldn't. No one seems to know enough."

"Did Les want you to break it?" Rel asked, trying to decide what he thought about this hero Dak mentioned only with praise.

"Of course." Dak spread his hands, and a snake head popped out of his sleeve. Absently he put the hand down on the ground and the snake slithered out and away on its own errand.

Rel's gut tightened with disgust. He didn't mind snakes living their lives as he lived his life—apart from one another—but he didn't want one roaming about in his clothing. He was fairly certain Dak had more than one in that baggy shirt.

"Then we'd always have a retreat from the enemy," Dak said cheerily. "Except of course for Detlev's boys. Whose leader stabbed Les." His cheer faded as he poked at the fire.

At that moment Cath fitted together the silver flute he carried, and began playing a series of notes that sounded like . . . like what, a waterfall of silver on glass?

Rel had always been aware of how music pulled at the emotions, from the days when he tended Holder Khavnan's sheep and listened to the field workers singing planting songs in spring, and harvest songs in the late summer. Since then he'd heard all kinds of music in many lands, and had once gone to the Music Festival in Colend, until he discovered how much even referring to "music" and "Colend" in the same sentence grieved the Sartorans.

It was rare that he'd heard anyone play such heart-catching, memory-evoking music as this Cath. He and Dak ate their rice rolls and fruit while Cath played, then Cath put his flute on his knee and reached for his share of the food.

"What do you call that last one you played?" Rel asked.

Cath rarely spoke. He raised his eyes, his gaze more oblique than ever in the firelight. "Music."

"Who wrote it?"

Cath's brow furrowed a little. "No one *wrote* it. I *play* it."

"He's been with the Rowens a lot," Dak said. "They don't write any of their music down, because it always changes."

Cath said, "If you had an alphabet of thousands of letters, and you put them together for words, then take them apart again in the air, it's like that."

"There's a music festival on my world," Rel said. "I think you might like it."

The corners of Cath's mouth lifted in the first smile Rel had seen, almost the first expression he'd seen. Cath was as beautiful as a statue — and about as expressive.

"Let's bed down," Dak suggested. "We can be off at first light. I think that'll put us with Caris-Merian and them by sunset."

The boys didn't seem to think that the night would bring rain. Rel trusted in their intuition, as the weather patterns here were different — maybe closer to what he'd experienced while sailing along the Fereledria, the belt of the world on Sartorias-deles.

He rolled up in his blanket and lay back to watch the unfamiliar stars in their slow wheeling . . . and woke to the sound of Cath's flute. The air was still blue, the sun beyond the horizon. It was pleasantly cool, promising a hot day.

They were soon making their way down the hill to a meandering river. While they ate breakfast they walked in silence, but as soon as he had licked the last of the sweet-nut juice off his fingers, Rel said, "Tell me more about Les Rhoderan and vagabond magic?"

"Let's get on the raft first," Dak said.

A small raft had been tied up at a rough and ready pier. They stepped down onto it — and as they did, the pure morning sunlight gradually faded to a white glare.

"Uh oh," Dak said.

Rel sat in the middle as the brothers expertly poled their way across the river. Then Rel helped them tie up the raft on the other side.

"Quick," Dak said, squinting against the glare of the sky.

They scrambled up the switchback path to one of the round cottages that looked like they were made of poured honey and chocolate mixed together, the odd, shiny wood fitted in interesting patterns.

The storm broke as they pelted inside. Rain roared down in sheets, silvery gray through the windows as the edge of the storm did not obscure the morning sun. Rel watched a flock of long, crimson-necked birds flying low over the pewter-colored river, then lift as one and wing up over the treetops on the slope of the terraced hill they were shortly to climb, as he considered what he'd heard so far.

"We hope Les is dead," Dak said, as Cath pulled out a plain reed pipe and began low, whispering atonal threnodies. "We hope he's not in the Stones' Beyond, but we never found his body. And we know, if he'd been merely wounded, he would have come back. We were going to get the entire island's children to rise, and throw out the corrupt High Council. . ."

Rel heard in Dak's disjointed story what sounded like oft-repeated phrases about exploitive or corrupt governments whose taxes were onerous, whose laws for child labor infamous, and so on.

What began to emerge was that Leskandar Rhoderan had promised, once he and his followers had succeeded in using vagabond magic to take over the entire island ("Magic would keep the takeover blood free, see? Only if some fought back, well, we had to defend ourselves, and we had people training for that!") a tax-free existence, with money outlawed. The forcibly shared-out wealth of the rich would guarantee shelter, food, clothing, and freedom for all.

And Caris-Merian, Les's sister, the one they were going to meet, had been Les's first recruit, and his hardest worker for the Cause. Rel listened, thinking that Les Rhoderan reminded him a lot of Sarendan's Derek Diamagan, except that Derek hadn't wanted to make himself king. And he'd had no interest in magic.

"This storm won't last long," Dak said. "We might as well eat while we wait." He dug into his basket and handed out cloth-wrapped rolls made of sweet-nuts, carrot and cabbage shreds, with ginger and peppers, wrapped in an almost translucent rice skin. They were savory and spicy, with just the right amount of crunch.

When he was done eating, Dak looked out at the sheeting rain, then rubbed his hands. "Now, watch. This is great for travelers. You polish the air above you . . ."

He began pulling magic and making smoothing motions overhead, as though cleaning a bowl. Then he moved out the open door into the rain, and Rel watched water stream over an invisible bowl—

"Yow!" Dak yelped, as a trickle went down his neck. He hopped back inside, then dropped his hands. "You have to make sure you weave *all* the air above you," he admitted. "If you miss a spot, you get wet. Some are much better at it than I. They even make invisible tents at night. I'm not that good yet. Try it. We'll dry out fast if you get wet. It's going to be a scorcher."

Rel didn't outline a circle, as Dak had. He began the way he would do a search, starting at one point and working out in tight spirals, as he concentrated on polishing the air. When he stepped outside, the rain splashed all around, but the spell began to dissolve fast. Hastily he began polishing again. Too late. His spell collapsed, and he was promptly drenched.

They retreated inside, Dak laughing. "Just like me, just like me!"

A stab of sunlight slanted down between the breaking clouds, spangling the flowing river as if someone had scattered shards of liquid sun across it.

"Here we go! Short, just as I thought," Dak said cheerily.

The storm was moving on, leaving a double rainbow arced against the sky as crystalline drips fell everywhere.

They splashed out onto the pathway. Cath said, "Who is Derek Diamagan?" He said the name perfectly.

Rel's neck hairs rose.

Dak stopped, hands on hips. "Cath, did you get that out of Rel's head?"

"He was thinking it right *at* us. And I didn't go into his memories, so I asked."

Rel snapped his mind-shield into place.

"He led a revolution on our world," Rel said. "For freedom, no kings, no taxes."

"That's wonderful," Dak exclaimed. "Did he win?"

"For a while. But it wasn't wonderful. It was very, very bloody."

Dak's smile wavered, then he said firmly, "Les would have

used magic. He promised, no killing."

Rel thought about what he knew of governments, and kept his thoughts tightly protected behind his shield. That would have to be some miraculous magic not just to take, but to hold. Memory brought up Derek's brother Bernal, met twice. Bernal had been part of Derek's revolution, but Rel had come to the conclusion that that had been out of loyalty to his brother, and to Peitar, as the only time Rel had seen enthusiasm in Bernal was when he talked about horses.

He wondered if Les's sister would be the same, and was ready to sympathize with someone dragged into politics who would rather have done something else with their life.

At last they approached what looked like a cliff, but Dak walked straight into the rock and vanished: illusion.

Cath and Rel followed, the faint brush of strong magic stirring the hairs on his body. He found himself looking down into a little cup valley, fed by a waterfall at the far end, where the hills reached up to form what to him looked like low mountains.

A small village had been built in the valley, around the edges, mostly hidden by greenery. It was difficult to see what was house and what wasn't, as the conical roofs were mostly covered by ferny tree branches, and the walls were all made of that smooth wood that looked like it had been poured out of a chocolate pot.

At first he thought it was several houses, but as they got closer to the bottom of the valley, it became clear that there was one large, rambling house that curved two thirds of the way around, and a couple of smaller ones across from it.

As they approached, a girl with long red hair streaming behind her danced out. "Dak! Cath! They said you were coming!"

Rel appreciated the unseen lookout in that "they said" as Dak greeted the girl, and even Cath smiled.

"This is Winda, a traveling player," Dak said to Rel. "She's the best at disguises I ever saw."

Winda's expressive face flashed a smile, then she waved a brown hand. "Come within, before the rain catches up."

In the gathering gloom of twilight, Rel hadn't even looked up. Good smells greeted the travelers as they walked into a big room of an odd shape. Rel scanned quickly, as he always did, looking for weapons and attitudes of attack, then lines of retreat.

Maybe eight or ten people sat there, Cath the youngest, and a couple full grown. But the angles of sitting made it clear who was the center of attention, a girl who looked about fifteen, but had that indefinable something about her that indicated the Child Spell. Rel still couldn't articulate it.

Surprise flickered through him at her familiarity, as her wide-set eyes under a high brow gazed unwaveringly back with no recognition whatsoever. No, they'd never met.

"Welcome," said Caris-Merian. "We were told you wish to learn the vagabond magic, to defend against Detlev's scum?" She made a spitting motion to one side.

Rel stared back at Caris-Merian's long, narrow face. Her dark hair had been pulled back into a long braid, and she wore practical clothing in dark colors, which stood out from her fellow Geth natives in their bright, light shades.

Interpreting his gaze, she said, low-voiced, "When my brother is avenged, then I shall wear light again. Until then, the world is dark."

Rel had met that kind of intensity before—in fact, the very same hatred and thirst for revenge—in Tahra Delieth of Everon. That had to be the familiarity, he decided as he sat on the cushion indicated.

By now he had a fairly good grasp on the language, thanks to Dak's constant chatter. "I came to learn vagabond magic," he said. "If you've found a way to use it in warfare, this would be news to us. Magic is useless in war, so I've always been told."

"It's useless for war," Winda agreed, as she set down a big tray of baked fruit that smelled of tart spices. "But defense? Illusions, tricks? We can use it to get away."

At that moment a shape hurtled in through one of the wide, open windows, somersaulted, and landed nearby. This turned out to be a boy wearing an old shirt from which the sleeves had been cut, and pants sawed off above the knees.

"*I* can get away on my own," he piped, striking a pose.

"Everyone knows that, Nataun," Winda stated. And to Rel, "On his island, kids are born able to fly. But only till they grow."

"Can anyone get that magic?" Rel asked, remembering the flying spell over Tsauderei's mountain village—which in ancient days had been a retreat for old mages.

Heads shook. "Only those born on Yafa."

Rel said, "Well, I'm here to learn what you have to teach. But a question first. About labyrinths. Is that part of your magic, especially vagabond magic?"

A room full of "What?" expressions met him. Rel then said, "So where do we begin?"

At last, once they showed him a room, he sat down and wrote to Peitar:

I've begun lessons in earnest, but all are agreed: No labyrinths here, except the ordinary garden type.

Five

ROY DID NOT WANT to risk a transfer to a place he'd never seen. But the distance wasn't all that long, a hard walk of just under a week.

As he traveled, he considered his approach. He knew that the former king of Sarendan, deposed in a bloody revolution that he very nearly won (indeed he lost by trickery), had been exiled rather than executed. Peitar had made it a condition of kingship: any more killing, and he wouldn't take the throne. This in spite of wily old Tsauderei's strenuous counsel.

Roy had understood better once he met Peitar, while he was studying magic with Arthur. Not only was the new king of Sarendan determinedly pacific in nature, but it became clear that Peitar found kingship a burdensome duty. His capital exhibited the least rank awareness Roy had ever seen. By preference Peitar would clearly have been one of the world's mage archivists.

It was while corresponding with Geth mages that Peitar had worked a trade with the full cooperation of his uncle: the Geth mages sought someone who knew something about land warfare against a new Norsundrian incursion, Geth's warfare usually being maritime, and in turn Peitar had received some very old records that even kings would have been hard put to afford.

Darian Irad agreed to go to the northwest corner of the island, to marshal what forces the islanders could come up with and create a buffer between the newly reoccupied Norsunder fortress and the rest of the island.

Darian Irad had been maintaining that buffer for six years. As Roy approached, he noticed with approval the roving lookouts, then the outer perimeter, at which he was stopped, searched, and questioned.

He was passed to the inner perimeter — word obviously going ahead by magic communication — and finally to Irad's semi-permanent camp. Tents lined neatly along the bank above a stream, under a row of shady banyan trees. Elsewhere the ground had been cleared, and volunteers of all ages, mostly young, engaged in weapons practice. In a far field, fenced off, people worked with horses, which were rare on the islands. Others labored at various chores, and at the far end an armory had been established, with a smithy, smoke curling into the air.

Roy passed on to the center.

Detlev had said once that personal guards often reflected the command style of the commander: a brute surrounded himself with bullies, a slacker with idlers, the pompous choosing their guards for size, or similar coloring, and then outfitting them in elaborate or impressive uniforms.

Irad's inner perimeter was alert, dressed comfortably, and heavily weaponed. Roy submitted to a second, more thorough pat-down, then was waved to what the islanders called a mackerel-wood hut — driftwood planed and fitted together — with tent wings and an awning.

Roy ducked under the thick foliage of the mighty banyan, which cut the sun's burn in half. The building had been tucked up amongst the many rootlings becoming adjunct trunks of the tree, the tent's side walls open to let in what breeze there was. A detailed map had been laid out on a table, with the Norsunder fortress at the center. As Roy ventured inside, he scanned it quickly: the drawing went all the way to the coast on both sides, but the inlet where the houseboat lay hidden depicted the false obstacles, and it was otherwise unmarked. It had been scanned from the sea, as one would expect from Geth people.

Roy's gaze lifted from that to the interested gaze of Darian

Irad. It was a shock to see how much the man resembled Peitar Selenna. Roy would have guessed they were father and son, the only differences being Irad's long queued hair was gray at the sides, and his eyes a startling light blue.

The exiled king spoke. "You are?"

"Roy." He hesitated, intuiting that Irad had heard enough jawing about evil kings. Surely here was the time and place to begin speaking the truth. "I was trained by Detlev, but I cut myself free."

"And you're here on this island because?"

"I'm planning to make my position clear by taking down the magical wards on the fortress, so the locals can do whatever they want about Norsunder's presence. But I made a discovery I thought someone ought to know about."

Irad lifted his chin briefly. "Stand down."

And two armed, ready-to-shoot guards stepped from the wings where they'd stood with loaded crossbows. Both had tight mind-shields; Roy had only sensed their possible presence because of the way Irad had positioned himself toward the back, affording a clear field of fire.

The man loosened the bolt and set it and the crossbow in a waiting rack to the left, then vanished. The woman, slender as Irad, with a vivid face and short curly hair the color of sand, also loosened her crossbow and stashed it, but then she dropped down onto a cushion next to Irad's.

"Talk to me," Irad said.

Roy said, "Have you heard of Efael?"

Irad's expression tightened briefly. "By reputation."

"You know his personal guard call themselves the Black Knives? I saw one of them on a ridge between the northern border of the Marsh and their fortress. He was laying down tokens that I believe indicate a magical attack being prepared."

Irad said, "The mages insist that Norsunder cannot send over armies anymore."

Roy shook his head. "Probably not, but are you certain they don't have a force waiting elsewhere in the world?"

"I am not." He glanced at the woman, who nodded, then he said, "We can ask mages about that aspect. Go on about the Black Knives."

"They prefer acting alone, covertly. They are less likely to bolster other Norsundrian commanders, as they don't willingly ally or share. Their usual strategy is stealth attacks."

Darian Irad brought his chin down minutely on each point, with no change in expression, until a little girl burst in. The girl's blue eyes were the same shade as Irad's, tilted at the same angle, her sandy hair flyaway. Selenna's expression lightened as the girl approached.

"I was to say, supplies are in," the girl piped. "Who's this?" Those wide, blue eyes turned Roy's way.

"He's from my home world," Irad said.

Roy did not correct him, though he wondered which of the three he had lived on he would call his home world.

"Ah, so! Do you know Lilah?" she asked Roy—blithely assuming that he would know everyone on Sartorias-deles. She looked about five. "Da says I have a cousin with red hair."

"We've met," Roy said. "You'll like her, I think."

The girl beamed, her resemblance to the woman next to Irad pronounced.

"Run along, Miri. You're free to play," Irad said, and the girl hirpled out, her high voice echoing back as other young voices joined hers.

Irad got up, rested a hand on the edge of the table with its map, and said, "Show me."

Roy looked down at the map, then pressed a finger to the spot where he'd been. Irad frowned at it, then looked up. "You think this indicates the likelihood of a magic attack being prepared?"

"I think so. I can't tell you what kind of magical attack, but it's almost certainly some sort of ward, probably preceding military action."

"Right," Irad murmured, his gaze ranging over the terrain. Then he looked up. "The first condition of my command here was that the volunteers would not be led into battle without the permission of the mages and their alliance. We're here as a defensive line. And yet—if you were to carry out your mission, and we carried out a surprise attack at the same time, we might come out with less loss of life than if we wait for them to choose the ground."

Roy said, "That makes sense to me. But I'd have to figure out what kind of magic that Black Knife was laying down there—find the token and test it—and scout if there're others. It'll take time."

"I can work up some plans and drill my volunteers as we wait for word. Bekani?" Irad faced the woman.

Bekani said, "I can transfer to Isul Demarzal if you lay everything out clearly so that non-military minds can understand the problem."

Roy expelled his breath. It had worked! "I'll do whatever I can."

"All right, then," Irad said, without any change in tone, but Roy could see in the direct gaze, the subtle tension of his movements, that he was trying to hide how much this prospective battle afforded him a sense of purpose.

Six

Late Autumn, 4749 AF
Sartorias-deles, Sarendan and Sartor

PEITAR'S FIRST REACTION TO Rel's short communication about the lack of labyrinths on Geth-deles was sharp disappointment, but that evolved into a sense of intrigue.

There *had* to be some connection between these old forms of magic. He was certain of it. Too many hints seemed to promise connections, if only he could find them.

He might have given up except for his experience during the previous New Year's Week. As the last of fall waned swiftly toward winter, and Atan issued another invitation to visit Sartor, he surprised her by accepting, to Lilah's delight, and Ian chattered away, echoing her delight, and repeating something that sounded like *rimpy*.

"What is that, son?" Peitar said. "Slow down."

Lilah said, "He has an imaginary friend he calls Shrimpy. Says he'll be there."

Ian's eyes narrowed to slants as he looked from father to aunt. "Shrimpy's not imaginary," he articulated. "Lives over the mountains."

"All right," Lilah soothed, obviously not believing him in the slightest, because how would a toddler know anyone who had not been introduced to him in the palace? "But I don't think you'll find Shrimpy in Sartor. Or maybe you will," she added. "If you want him to be there."

"I do," Ian said, eyeing Lilah's fond smile with an air of question.

Peitar was sharply aware of his own inadequacy. He knew that Ian had been born with Dena Yeresbeth, as Liere had told them so, but what that meant was anyone's guess. He reassured himself with the fact that no one at such a young age could possibly be talking to anyone — anyone real — far, far away.

His love for Ian burned strong as the sun. But growing alongside the baby fast turning into a child was Peitar's awareness that blithe innocence inexorably propagated its own view of the world.

At any rate, Ian abruptly clammed up about Shrimpy, and so the end of the year slipped away.

Peitar focused grimly on getting through his responsibilities so that he could spend more time on the project that increasingly obsessed him. Lilah gloated that their great-aunts would not be able to force a lot of prospective wives onto Peitar. All three, for different reasons, looked forward to New Year's Week in Sartor.

When the day came to depart, and Peitar looked at Lilah and Ian, a hot, fierce happiness welled up inside him. He loved them both — he wished they would never change.

Of course they would. Even Lilah would, despite the Child Spell. Peitar understood the ferocity of his feeling as poignancy, painful because life was so very fleeting: too soon, Ian would not want to climb into his father's lap, would turn to his friends rather than his family during his free moments, he would have experiences, and inevitably secrets, that he would not share. It was natural.

It was painful.

Then the transfer magic wrenched them away, one by one.

Those first couple of days in Eidervaen, it snowed so hard that Peitar could not visit the Purad. It was entirely covered when he checked. Besides, there were entertainments the Sartorans had arranged, the inevitable diplomatic exchanges and mage friends from the north to talk with, and between all those, he was peripherally aware of the determined search by his son for a boy who was not there.

On the third night, Ian broke. He was so rarely disobedient, or even unhappy, that his father and aunt were stunned by this sudden heel-thumping, crimson-faced temper tantrum when he refused to go to dinner.

At first Lilah thought that he was coming down with a fever. "Shrimpy's not *here,*" Ian cried over and over, face flush-ed, eyes streaming tears. "You *said* he'd be *here!*"

"Can't you pretend he is?" Lilah asked.

"No!" Ian shrieked. "'s not a *doll!* Shrimpy's a *boy!* Like me! But a *big* boy! He's *five!*"

Peitar knelt. As long as he could keep the disappointments of the world away from his young son, he would exert every power at his command to do so. "Tell me where to find him," Peitar said. "I promise, I will try to find him, and bring him to you."

"I don't *know!*" Ian howled. "He said, over the mountains, an' Lilah said that's *here!*"

"Sartor is over the mountains from us," Lilah said reason-ably. "And so is Gyrn, and Ar Mardeth, and —

Ian let out a wail of frustration and disappointment, drowning out her voice.

Lilah gave up, and whispered to Peitar, "A lot of stories begin that way, 'Once a long way away, over the mountains of Sartor.' Maybe he means some story about Dtheldevor's gang? But there's no Shrimpy in any of the stories I've told him, and Deon hasn't mentioned anyone by that name."

This helpful aside only upset Ian the more, causing his breath to shudder, and tears of frustration and disappointment to escape his tightly shut eyes.

Peitar raised a hand to halt Lilah's well-meant musings. "When did you talk to him?" Peitar asked his son. "Do you remember?"

"When I sleep," Ian said emphatically.

"In your dreams?" Peitar looked up at Lilah, who tried not to sigh — she remembered her own imagination games when she was little, and how real they had seemed.

"Yes," Ian said in relief.

Peitar said, "I cannot find a boy you only know in your dreams. I'm sorry, Ian. You'll have to be dream friends. Do you understand?"

Ian's lip trembled.

"Dream friends mean you can see him anywhere you go," Lilah said in a coaxing voice.

Ian cast her a doubtful look, sensing her lack of belief, but unable to express it. He looked from her to his father, struggling to grasp the fact that the people he loved most could do nothing to bring him together with the boy he'd known as Shrimpy for the past year.

But his father's arms were out. Ian climbed into his lap and pressed up against him as Peitar's arms closed around him. His chest still heaved from the aftermath of sobs, but he accepted that there was no finding his friend in this strange place that smelled funny, and he was tired, and his head hurt, and his dad's arms were warm and tight and safe.

Over his head, Peitar said to Lilah, "Go ahead to dinner. Tell Atan Ian isn't feeling well. She'll understand."

Lilah nicked her head down in a nod and scampered out, her rusty thatch of hair flopping as she vanished through the door.

Peitar held Ian until he said he was ready to go to bed. He'd go to sleep early, if it meant he could find Shrimpy.

Peitar stayed with him until he slumbered, sitting by Ian's bed in his good clothes. Dinner was over by the time he rejoined the others, but Peitar wasn't hungry. Dutifully he went with them to Atan's private theater, and though the play was excellent, all he could think about was Ian's disappointment — which slid into his own apprehensions, for he meant to try the Purad on the morrow, using Rel's lessons about state of mind for vagabond magic.

After a restless night, Peitar bundled up and slipped out before dawn. In the weak light the ancient city was defined by shadows, depth perceivable by the dim starlight reflecting off the ancient white tower at the west end of the palace, its top visible above the roof.

As his footsteps squeaked on the freshly fallen slow, he worked on what Rel had taught him about emptying his mind of concerns and expectations. He knew he had it when he could reach up and pull a trace of magic from the air, setting it to sparkle and dissipate. Mere illusion — utterly useless — it was the state of mind he must keep hold of.

He found the Purad by its bordering trees, and stopped,

aware of damp palms in spite of the bitter cold.

His footsteps crunched on the cold ground, brushed free of snow by some unknown walker who had clearly been there even earlier. He could see the looped leaves now. The stars overhead had faded into blue on the eastern horizon, Eidervaen rooftops etched sharply against the bowl of the sky.

He stepped into the first loop of the first leaf. No thought of the past, no thought of the future. Only the now, in the quiet of winter, his footfalls a soft chuff. Breath clouding.

He reached in his mind for the shimmering strands of magic around him, and as he paced steadily, the strands wove around him, blending and broadening into ribbons and then rivers as the past and present blended in the circle. Round and round again, and there was that sense of climbing, no, ascending. Body and world dissolved, and oh, there, *there* it was, the vast sound, larger and richer and more painful and more joyful than mere music, the place westward and —

His joy shot like a comet through the mental realm.

At the far end of the continent, Siamis jerked upward, uttering a curse in Ancient Sartoran in a voice so unlike his persona that the elderly scribe sitting next to him was startled into dropping his reed pen.

"I'm sorry," Siamis said, careful to reassume his nasal whine. "I forgot a book I owed . . ."

He dashed out, relieved to find no one in the hallway, and risked the most dangerous sort of transfer, stepping from one space to another a few paces from Peitar Selenna.

In the blue light of dawn, Peitar stood motionless in the balance point (did he know that?) of the four leaves, his sightless gaze turned up toward the last glimmering stars.

Siamis backhanded him across the face.

Peitar toppled like a lighting-struck tree, then lay there gasping as his mind crashed back into his body. Pain rung outward in throbs, then the face bent over him stopped spinning, and snapped into familiarity.

Siamis watched Peitar's gaze go from blank to astonishment and then white rage. "You *idiot*. Do you really want to invite all Norsunder into your mind?"

"What?" Peitar's lips shaped the word.

Siamis gestured, hands to either side, his scribe robe stirring in the rising breeze. "These old grottos act like echo chambers in the mental realm. I heard you from another continent."

Peitar flushed, then he sat up, one hand trembling as it scrabbled feverishly through his layers to where he had faithfully kept that enchanted button all this time. "I don't have Dena Yeresbeth," he said flatly.

"It's not a thing you have, it's a thing you do. Call it cohesion, or coinherence," Siamis stated. "And your mind was bellowing across the entire mental realm."

"I've never heard mental voices," Peitar snapped. "I don't believe anything you say."

Siamis shrugged, hands still out, though he watched Peitar's searching fingers. "Then let Norsunder invade your mind. Matters nothing to me. I thought for Lilith's sake I'd warn you."

Peitar wanted to shout, *How dare you hide behind her name*, then his fingers closed around the enchanted button. He got to his feet. Thoroughly unsettled after that transcendent experience, he spoke from the heart, though he knew as the words hit the icy air that they sounded merely petulant: "You murdered Derek Diamagan. And walked away free."

While he spoke, Peitar was slowly withdrawing the button, knowing that Siamis was watching. Suspecting Siamis knew what it was, what with all the mental realm talk. But he was still going to take his chance.

"I saved you the trouble," Siamis retorted. "And it would have been trouble."

Peitar stilled. "What?"

"You really were that willfully blind?" Siamis asked. "Under Diamagan's enthusiastic guidance Sarendan was busily becoming another version of the military kingdom that you and your friends slaughtered half the population to rid yourselves of. How long," he added cordially, "do you think you would have lasted if you'd stood against Diamagan's vision of an armed and ready Sarendan?"

Peitar wavered, then the fury was back. "Even if it were true, that was not your decision to make."

"A defense," Siamis retorted, "I've trotted out since I was twelve years old, and no one listened to me, either. Stay out of the labyrinths until you learn an adequate mind-shield, or you will wake up and find yourself a mouthpiece for the Garden of the Twelve."

And he was gone a heartbeat before Peitar hurled his

enchanted token.

The thing spun through the air and landed in the snow with a soft chuff. Peitar bolted out of the pathway, the peace ruined, and bent to scrabble in the snow for the button. He spied the dimple where it had landed and burrowed his fingers down to retrieve it.

If it had connected, and Siamis had been transformed to stone in the middle of the Purad, would Atan leave him there for the hundred years? Peitar backed away, for the first time considering the fact that no one outside of Sarendan had agreed to his judgment.

Where lay authority here? At home, as king, his uncle had always heeded the rules for judges and hearings, at least superficially. Peitar still occasionally had nightmares about the trial at which he and Derek had stood accused of treason, and had been condemned.

He had passed judgment on Siamis himself. One could argue that a king could do that, but he had used that very argument *against* kingship. He tossed the button on his hand, sustained an impulse to hurl it away, but he returned it to his pocket, and forced his mind to calm. To facts.

Fact. If he saw Siamis again, he knew he would try, and keep trying, until he was withered and old, because Derek was still dead. Therefore, questions of authority could wait.

Fact. Norsundrians lied. Therefore, he refused to believe anything Siamis said.

Fact. Peitar had found the music, what's more, it had a direction. That meant it had an origin, a place.

He tried to breathe out his anger. If he didn't get another chance to commit Siamis to justice, then someone else might. More important, right now, was the music, and finding it.

When he reached the guest wing, Ian was waiting, still in his nightdress.

"Did you find your dream friend?" Peitar asked, making an effort to recall his son's small dilemma—though not small to him.

"Yes. He said he's too far away," Ian murmured, looking sad. "I want to go home."

"We will," Peitar said, pulling him into his lap. "As soon as Lilah wakens."

As he rocked back and forth with Ian in his arms, he thought back to that encounter. Why was Siamis wearing scribe robes? Spying, of course. Those robes were so universal that Peitar couldn't even send a warning to whoever ruled where Siamis had retreated to, warning them of the evil lurking in their midst. Or did they know? He thought of Atan, housing Siamis for so long, and giving him his freedom. Bitterness surged, but he forced it away.

He had the stone spell button.

There was still a chance for justice.

Seven

"THERE IS STILL A chance for justice," Peitar said to Tsauderei on a mild Restday morning a week later, the first opportunity he had to get away from the iron gall of duty. He repeated the entire conversation with Siamis.

When Tsauderei didn't respond, but sat there stroking his long, silky mustache with one age-spotted, gnarled finger, Peitar said, "You've never actually said anything about my decision."

"There's nothing to say." Tsauderei's hand dropped to the arm of the chair. "I consider that a political decision. Out of my sphere."

"And yet you brought a thunderstorm over Miraleste the morning Derek and I were to be executed."

Tsauderei's brows lifted. "I never claimed consistency."

"Please be inconsistent now, because I need wisdom from someone who knew Derek, to counteract Siamis's poison." Peitar's voice was raw. "Is that how Norsunder gets as far as it does, smearing the memory of everyone good and true with doubt?"

Tsauderei's gaze shifted out over the pewter-colored frozen lake below his window. As Peitar began to wonder if this was reflection or reluctance, Tsauderei said slowly, "Doubt happens when you allow for the possibility of a different view of truth."

"What has that to do with my question?" Peitar got to his feet, then sat down again. He was too tired—he had not been able to sleep well ever since he'd found the music again, along with a conviction that there was a physical source. And even when he slept, he still heard Siamis's words, and in those dreams, he threw the stone spell token, just to see it spinning uselessly through empty air. "Speak plain. Do you believe Derek would *ever* have betrayed me?"

Tsauderei said, "I believe . . . that had Derek lived, you would be facing very different problems now." And as Peitar flinched, a subtle tightening of muscles as if Tsauderei had hit him, he spoke firmly. "Speculation is useless. It merely disturbs you. The only part of what Siamis told you that I'd heed would be the advice about mind-shields. Dena Yeresbeth is too new, and I'll never have it. Or do it. But I'll say this, his advice corroborates what those we trust tell us about it: mind-shields keep out the predators able to invade minds."

"Like Siamis," Peitar retorted. "You don't think he was spying on me in some way?" Said out loud, the words sounded ridiculous.

And Tsauderei's bushy brows shot upward. "Why would he do that?"

Peitar rubbed his gritty eyes. "My instinct, which I don't entirely trust right now, is that he was keeping something from me, misleading me. I can't say how or why."

"You hate him for the murder of your closest friend," Tsauderei said. "Of course you distrust him. Look, why don't you forget all the rest, and work on the mind-shield part. One thing we both know for certain: you do *not* want Detlev invading your mind."

"No." Peitar breathed the word.

"As for your music, I believe you perceived something. There're too many records claiming such experiences, though I never felt anything remotely that unsettling or profound the many, many times I've walked various labyrinths. It was considered a fashion in my youth—usually for courting, or for confidential conversations. I'm not saying it's not real, what I'm saying is that your mind might have tried to find a way to express the intensity of your emotions, whatever the cause, and chose music. The way another person might express it through art."

Peitar felt that this was not right, but he had no proof, and his strivings to find proof had been completely unsuccessful.

Tsauderei saw his doubt. "Here's the truth about the Ancient Sartoran records: there are so few of them, and many of those are not true artifacts, but bits that have been translated and retranslated over the centuries. Lilith warned me once that we don't actually have the true meanings of many of those words, but life was so different then there's no utility in correcting them."

"They were human. We are human. How different can it be?"

"That's my own thought. But custom can vary from place to place in our own time, and we are, after all, talking about four *thousand* years ago. Think about how many changes in language and culture have occurred in your lifetime. Consider the changes you've read about over the past century."

When Peitar's expression tightened to wariness, Tsauderei said, "My point is, it is easy to take those scraps, many couched in figurative terms, and put, as Peddler Antivad does in the children's stories, one and two together to make twelve."

"Then you think it's all in my head."

"I didn't say that. But—since you asked me to speak plain—let me give you one other observation, and you're not going to like this any better. You yourself have acknowledged how much you are like your uncle. Both of you spent yourselves in working toward something you were convinced is right: your uncle, in forcing Sarendan to be able to take on Norsunder whenever it does come to the attack. You have this magical goal, and I can see the effects of your long nights of labor in how tired you are. You are close—very close—to burying yourself entirely in your magic studies and forgetting the rest of the world in exactly the same manner your uncle pursued military goals to the cost of everything else."

Peitar wanted to argue, to deny. But he knew it was true. He did delegate what he could, and spent every hour he could get away from his duties. Not from his family. Never from them, and yet, he had to acknowledge in his secret heart the relief he felt when Lilah and Ian had gone to sleep, because he was then free for as many hours as he could force himself to stay awake—never enough time, never enough.

He winced and shifted the subject. "You really think that

the Purad music, and vagabond magic, are not connected to something we lost?"

Tsauderei said gently, "I'm the oldest mage in the entire world, I believe. Got two years on Igkai the Hermit. And I'll also claim to be among the most well-read. A few months ago, after you told me you send Rel off to learn about vagabond magic, I gave the senior journeymages a project to seek specifically through the northern as well as the southern archives for a lead on any connections. I didn't tell you because I thought it would be a nice surprise to give you what they found. But they found nothing. I'm sorry, Peitar. I believe you're chasing a mirage."

It took Peitar an effort to find his voice long enough to force out words of thanks. He knew Tsauderei was telling the truth as he saw it, and many of his points hurt with the sort of pain that only comes with hearing inescapable truth.

He walked out of the cottage and stood on the grassy verge not three paces from where Derek had died. But he did not look at that grass, for once. Instead, he gazed up at the mild sky with its slow tumble of clouds in the distance.

He could not face his loving, anxious family, or the never-ending demands of duty. And so, though he recognized it as a return to childhood, he took a step, made the sign and whispered the word, and lifted into the air.

For a little while, he promised himself. Then, back to duty. Maybe it was even time to give up this quest that no one else seemed to believe in.

No, it hurt too much to think that. He put his hands together and dove down through the air, pulling up a short distance above the quiet blue waters of the lake. There, he flipped over and lay quiescent, eyes closed against the sun. He was so tired, body and soul, it would be such a relief to drop into sleep here, suspended between water and sky. When he was a boy, in the terrible years after his accident when his broken leg was painfully mis-healing, the only true sleep he'd had was here in the air, where his hip, leg, and ankle touched nothing, and the inexorable weight one felt everywhere else but while flying did not drag at his misaligned joints.

His thoughts ran free, skirting the borderland of sleep. It was the same peace he felt in the Purad. Hadn't Rel said something about . . . yes, that was similar, too: one had to empty the mind of all other concerns, and just reach for the magic. That much, he could do. But what was the use of sensing fine strands of golden, glowing magic, when spinning them together only made toy illusions, tricksome light?

What he wanted and reached for was —

There.

Shock jolted him, and his arms and legs pinwheeled, nearly propelling him into the lake. He caught himself an arm's length from the lapping waters, and he formed his mind-shield, lest Detlev smite him on the mental plane.

That much, Peitar believed. Was it possible that Siamis told the truth after all? Only enough to get him to accept the rest of his lies, Peitar was certain. Though he had no proof either way, it no longer mattered.

Because he'd found the music.

He didn't need the Purad after all. He just had to completely empty his mind, and with it somehow *reach* . . . He grasped his transfer token and braced for the wrench back to Miraleste. He had plenty to do before he searched for its physical location.

Eight

Geth-deles, Main Island

OVER THE FOLLOWING WEEKS, Rel's life settled into a pleasant routine at the hideout on Geth, highlighted by rafting down white water, introduction to fruits he'd never tasted, and lots of vagabond magic. Most of what people did was illusion, a complexity that tested imagination but didn't really accomplish anything beyond games or entertainment.

The exception was learning how to transfer people in a group. For some reason no one could explain, the magic was easier to draw on at sunset, sunrise, and full moon—either of the Geth moons. When both were in the sky, the magic was strongest. Magic couldn't have to do with light, or noon would be the strongest, right?

No one knew, they just knew it worked.

Rel scrupulously wrote to Peitar, reporting everything he'd learned. He heard back occasionally, always with more questions to ask the Geth people, but most of the answers weren't written down. Or if they were, no one knew where.

Dak vanished on a boat trip to another island. People came and went, Rel's most frequent company being Solomay Winda, or just Winda, the pretty actor who knew unlimited numbers of poems and plays by heart. She was mid-teens, and she throve on attention — especially from boys — though she'd not quite reached the age to do anything about it. She was popular with everyone, friendly, interested, and full of humor.

After Caris-Merian's initial conversation with Rel, during which she discovered that he did not know structural magic, and yes, he was familiar with Detlev's gang of killers, but he hadn't seen them for an appreciable time, she didn't seem to have much to say to him, and he seldom saw her after that.

He asked about her once.

"She studies magic on her own," Winda said earnestly, while taking a break from planning a play to be exhibited the next rainy night. "She is *so* dedicated! Even more than Les was. But the Ones won't take her, it seems."

"Ones?" Rel asked, having learned that Winda liked gossip at least as much as she did humor.

Winda looked around, then lowered her voice. "The real mages. They know *everything*. Word is, when you go study with them, you leave behind your identity, and your former life. They would never have let her take off if she'd heard that that David was back." Winda wrinkled her nose. "And I'd be the *first* to tell her. He was always *horrible* to *me*."

"If," Caris-Merian said, coming up behind them, "the Ones are attempting to teach their students to rise above personal concerns to the extent of ignoring the seeking of justice, then they have nothing to offer me. In spite of their secrets, I believe I can learn magic elsewhere. It just takes longer."

She rubbed her eyes, as Rel wondered if he'd just stumbled on the source of the magic that Peitar wanted, and Rel could not find. "The ink on that book is so faded I can scarcely see it," Caris-Merian said.

"Maybe someone should copy it out," Winda suggested, shaking back her long red-gold hair.

Caris-Merian's earnest face lightened briefly, no more than a quirk of humor at either side of her mouth. "That's what I'm doing, so the next person won't strain their eyes."

"Good," Winda said. She reverted right back to David, exclaiming with gleeful horror, "He once cut off a lock of my *hair!* As a *joke!*" She lifted a shiny curling lock that was merely elbow-length, and brandished it like a trophy. "Right *here!* I got him *good* for that. And Dak was going to help me steal that ugly black steel sword that he brags about so constantly, and we were going to throw it into the deepest ocean."

"Why would he brag about it?" Rel asked. "Did he take it from someone?"

"No, but Detlev probably did. David used to bore on about how it was centuries old and belonged to some idiot on the world we think of as Nightside, or Darkside." She shrugged.

Rel's mind went to the only historical mention of black swords that he remembered, but shrugged that possibility off. Too long ago, and wasn't it a knife?

"In any case," Winda went on, "whatever else that ancient fool did, he doesn't seem to have been able to hang onto his sword. Of course, it could be a fake, or maybe that wicked Detlev stole it from the man before killing him, and he's got a warehouse full of stolen swords somewhere in Norsunder, to give away to his minions to impress them. But anyway . . ."

She launched into reminiscences. It was clear that she'd very much enjoyed her feud with David, judging by how often she went after him to retaliate with pranks intended to sting, but not necessarily to drive him off. Halfway through her recitation, Caris-Merian, whose countenance had withdrawn into extreme reserve, got up and noiselessly left the room. Winda settled deeper into her cushion, her pretty chin still lifted with outrage, but the curve of one hip, the relaxed hands and feet were not indicative of anger, rather the opposite.

Then at the very end, her attitude of comfortable indignation faded, and her arched brows drew together as she said in a different voice, lower, "And then we found out he'd taken a knife to Les . . . and, well, everything turned really –"

Caris-Merian rushed back in, eyes wide. "Norsunder is preparing to attack," she said, waving a curled piece of paper. "They're calling for volunteers to go to the fortress to help."

Winda sprang up, her long drapery fluttering. "I'll call the message dogs!"

Caris-Merian turned to Rel. "I suspect no one will be here."

"That's all right," Rel said. "If you've got a fight on your hands, let me volunteer, too."

She smiled, a real smile at last, for she had seen him out in the secluded garden doing his sword drills. "You will be most welcome."

Spring 4750 AF
Sarendan to Sartor's Western Border

Back in Sartorias-deles, at the other end of Rel's infrequent reports, Peitar buried himself in archival searches, aware that he was following the trails of Tsauderei's journeymages. In fact, a couple of archivists cheerily told him so, rare as visitors were. But he knew that research you are assigned to do and research that you truly want to find the answer to, can result in different approaches to reading. He would not skim a blotted or age-spotted word, no matter how old-fashioned the hand.

He still found nothing. So thorough a nothing that a person could be excused in wondering if there had been some conspiracy of silence formed centuries ago, but even he couldn't sustain that trail of thought. There was simply too little left from Ancient Sartor in the major archives. It was time to venture into those more obscure.

He received a couple of brief reports from Rel, consistent with some of those Ancient Sartoran scraps that Tsauderei had insisted were mere poetic hyperbole. Maybe they were, but the echo of that music in his dreams was so persistent. No matter what the rest of the dream was like — the usual random symbols — that much was always specific: he had to go west from Eidervaen.

When doubts threatened to overwhelm him into disbelief, or a conviction that he was slowly going mad, he would wait until very late at night when all the world was asleep. Though his body clamored for rest, he would compose himself the way he had in Delfina Valley, relax the mind-shield he had dutifully made habit, and listen in that way he could not find the words to explain, for it was both inward and yet outward at the same moment, a perfect balance.

He knew when the balance was perfect because three times, he caught that faint chord like nothing any instrument he had ever heard played or sung by living voice. It was powerful. And . . . infinite. He longed to sink into it forever, but each time he heard it, he kept it just long enough to know it was there, then forced himself to shut himself behind the mind-shield lest he be attacked by Siamis again, leaving an ever-increasing hunger to find its source.

As winter howled its way through the dark days, that hunger grew, and he knew he was going to leave Sarendan to seek it. Not someday, but soon.

He wrote back to Rel with questions to ask of their mages, and waited for answers while he delved into old books he'd ordered, at terrific expense, from far corners of Toar, Goerael, and one that purported to be an old record kept by the mountain people of mysterious Skyhaven, the island-continent up in the northern seas that otherwise had nothing to do with the rest of the world. Their primary language had roots in both Ancient Sartoran and Chwahir.

The only time all winter long that Peitar Selenna permitted himself a break from the stream of kingship demands and his quest was when little Ian wanted him. Then he dropped what he was doing to make time for his son, his rare smile lighting his face.

The problem — if you could call it a problem — was that Ian was not a baby anymore. He was about to turn four, and he had discovered how much he enjoyed playing with others his age. He was always wanting to run down the hill into the city.

Lilah was glad to see him making friends, but everyone in the palace noticed that if Ian didn't ask for his Da, then Peitar might not appear at all. He'd work from before the sun came up until very late at night. And they told Lilah, earnestly, hopefully, warningly, even reproachfully, because the only one who could do something about that was Lilah. There wasn't much she could do during the drear of winter, but this year, first thaw came to Sarendan early, so she decided they could eat outside.

It seemed the entire capital city had the same idea. The sun still arced far in the north, and the air in the shadows retained winter's bite, but the sky was clear, the sunlight relatively balmy, and everyone was outside who could find a reason to be there.

The small royal family ate on their favorite terrace, near the statue of Derek Diamagan gazing eternally out over the lake, quiet and still as he rarely had been in life. Lilah ordered all Peitar's favorite foods. Her brother had always been thin, but the hollows under his cheekbones seemed sharper, and the shadows under his eyes darker. She knew he had been throwing himself into one of his magical searches, reading far into the night, and rising early the next morning with grim discipline to get through all the king duties he couldn't delegate, so he could be at his precious studies again. This was the worst one ever. Yet she couldn't do anything about it.

While they ate, they were as happy as she had hoped they would be. And yet Peitar was so quiet. She frowned out over the lake, where a fish leaped out of the water and splashed down again as she tried to find subjects that would interest Ian and Peitar as well.

She turned to Ian. "Heyo, do you still have your story friend?"

Ian dropped the sloppy piece of cake he'd been eating, looked puzzled, then his expression shuttered. "Shrimpy," he muttered, picked up his cake again and bent his head over it.

"That's right, Shrimpy!" Lilah exclaimed, and to Peitar, "After New Year's. I wrote to CJ, and she said that Liere was visiting with Lyren, and she knows Shrimpy, too. And they say Carl and Jessan in Everon also do, it's like a game they have together. I guess you can do that when you're born with Dena Yeresbeth."

Ian muttered thickly around his cake, "You're not *born* with it. Like blue eyes. You *make* it."

Where had Peitar heard that? *Siamis, at the Purad.* His skin crawled. "Who told you that?" he asked sharply.

Ian looked up, startled, his cake dropping in jammy clumps. Then his face shuttered again, his aura going from a bright flash to a dim blue. "Nobody. We just all know."

"Who is we?" Peitar made an effort to speak more gently, and once again shut out the auras.

"All of us. Lyren and Jessan and Carl." Ian dropped his gaze to his plate.

Lilah looked from one to the other, sensing tension. Just when things had been going so well! "If you'd like us to invite Jessan and Carl for a visit, we could write to Tahra," she said coaxingly.

Ian's demeanor brightened at once. "Can we go up to Delfina and fly?" he asked, grinning around his cake.

"Sure! I'll go with you. I always love flying," Lilah said. "We might not be able to swim in the lake. It'll be really cold. But in a few months, we'll have perfect swimming weather."

The tense moment passed, but when Ian trotted off to wash his hands and return to lessons, Peitar gazed after him. That blank face—he knew that expression. He'd used it on his own father to hide his friendship with Derek, when he wasn't much older than Ian. And Lilah had used it, too, until she trusted Peitar enough to admit that she had been sneaking into Riveredge Village to play with the youngsters there, in spite of their father's rule that they stick to their own rank.

Did Ian already have secrets? Why would he have secrets? Peitar let him do pretty much anything he liked. There had never been bad moments between them, except the misunderstanding about Shrimpy and Sartor at the beginning of the year. He said to Lilah, "What's he hiding?"

"Nothing," Lilah said, then her brow puckered. "I don't think. You think he was hiding something? Why?"

"That's what I don't know. I'd hate that. I thought we had a better understanding with him than you and I had with our father."

Lilah grimaced at the mention of their father, the Prince of Selenna, murdered in a riot at the beginning of the revolution. Right after an argument with the two of them, he'd died trying to protect Lilah. Then she rallied. "Ian might have some kind of game with his friends in the city. You know, pretending to be thieves like the Sharadan Brothers, or something. Tsauderei told me on his last visit that I shouldn't show Ian all the secret passageways, that I should let him have the fun of discovering them himself. It could be something like that."

Peitar let himself be talked into that because the sun was warm, the winter had been tiring, and he wanted it to be true.

But the memory of Ian's lowered gaze and shuttered face nagged at him as a few days passed. He struggled inwardly, searching for the source of his discontent, and striving to eradicate it. Sons could no more help their natures than rivers could choose to flow backward: he and his own father had never understood one another, though both had tried. In the years ahead, Ian would become more himself, and it was right and good that it should be so, but that did not guarantee that he and his father would agree about things.

Peitar had to comprehend the truth: Ian was already learning to turn to his friends for things he could not, or would not, share with his elders.

The pain of that inescapable fact drove Peitar deeper into his quest for that place of harmonic peace. It was not enough to hear it. It would never be enough. He had to find its well-spring, for the sense of direction never wavered. And once he found it, there would be no need for the limitation of the mind-shield, right? He could immerse himself in its transcendence, whence he would at last reach the peace he had craved all his life, above the profound but inevitable disappointments of human limitations.

With spring's longer days and melted snows, the conviction gripped him that the time had come. Now, while Ian was busy with his city friends and his secret, while life in Sarendan was quiet, people busy with spring planting and all the customs around it, he could delegate his few tasks and take a few days — alone — and go on his quest.

He set about preparing very methodically, telling no one. The night before he left, dinner together with Lilah and Ian was all the sweeter, though the food was nothing special, the chatter unmemorable. He looked back and forth between his sister who would never grow up, and his son who was becoming his own person, and knew that this moment was perfect.

But it was only a moment.

He despised the melancholy emotion underneath the thought. He would return soon; at most he'd let himself stay away a week. Then life would go on as usual, and there would come other perfect moments, and he would treasure each. Yes, one more search, and if it was unsuccessful, he'd give up this quest for ever.

As they finished their tarts, Ian and Lilah playing a childish hand-clapping game in rhythm and snickering, he teetered there between what he loved and what he craved. And there it was, the truth. Even if to no one else he must be true to himself: he would never give up the search.

The next morning dawned warm and clear. He dressed in sturdy riding clothes, took up the bag of Sartoran coins he'd set aside, left a note on his desk explaining that he expected to be away for a week at most, and transferred to the Guild Destination in Eidervaen, where he would merely be another artisan.

He found an inn on the extreme western end of Eidervaen, outside the ancient gates, on the well-traveled road. Here, he hired a horse, turned his back on Eidervaen, and began to ride west.

Nine

Geth-deles, below Norsunder Base

DAVID HAD KNOWN THAT it was going to take weeks, if not a couple of months, and it did.

But he could never resist a challenge, especially if it seemed nearly impossible, and held out the prospect of thwarting Efael.

He dared not transfer back to Sartorias-deles. Too many eyes and ears, and anyway now there was only MV who knew enough magic to help him, and—unlike Roy—MV hadn't studied mirror wards.

He was on his own.

He began that first day with the bead he'd seen the Black Knife lay down. He captured it on a broad leaf, careful not to touch it, pulled a button from his shirt and whispered a location spell on it. Then he pressed it into the ground where the bead had lain, and transferred back to the houseboat, where he laid the captured bead on the boys' old worktable.

Examining it was going to require careful, painstaking effort. He discovered that the transfer spells that Detlev had purchased for bringing food from a service on a faraway island to the houseboat still held. The water barrel magic had faded, but that was one of the first spells David had learned.

He was all set. Now to work.

It took two weeks to sift the layers, with many rests, and a couple hasty trips to lie up and hide when he sensed someone coming overland in his direction, though no one discovered the cove. As he labored, he was aware that his experiences with Jilo made his work a lot less arduous. Maybe made it possible. He still had trouble remembering everything that had happened in Chwahirsland, but it seemed somehow he recollected in muscle memory, like sword drill.

When at last he defanged the traps and disclosed the links, he'd put together enough clues to determine that Efael — or possibly Yeres — planned an enormous, and lethal, mirror ward, aimed at anyone who tried a magic spell once they crossed the line.

David prowled around the empty houseboat, which floated gently on the current under a soft fall of rain, so soft that the droplets rang outward in little circles. He watched the rain, wondering why Roy had been there in the first place. He couldn't have known about Efael's plot. He'd looked as surprised as David had been to spot that Black Knife. But Roy had been working his way in the direction of the Norsunder fortress. Why?

David tried to imagine his next step, supposing he gave Detlev and the boys the back of the hand. He'd want to make some gesture. Like?

He wandered restlessly around the houseboat again, until he halted in the door of his room. He looked down at his half-finished reed pipes, made when they all —

No, not *all*.

Memory flooded back: the days with Les Rhoderan, listening to vagabond magic theory and playing music to the admiration of those in Fya Rya, until Dak and his little brother showed up, and skilled as David was, Cath had far surpassed him in spite of being so much younger. Cath's small hands made perfect flutes, attuned to the chords in half steps — something David had been attempting so badly here. His music . . . brilliant.

David laughed at himself, swept up the half-finished reed pipes and chucked them out the window, then returned to the bead, and began putting together a webwork of wards to lay over it.

It took five days.

When he finished it, he transferred back to the spot he'd first seen the Black Knife. He watched, listened, then transferred again to his button. He replaced the button with the bead, then straightened up and looked around.

Now he faced the most tiresome part of this mission: he had to find the rest of the beads, not knowing how many had been laid down, or whether they formed a line or a circle.

Typically, the weather stayed humid, rainstorms coming through followed by brilliant, baking sun. He had to work out in a tight spiral before he found the next bead, which took the rest of the week. That gave him enough of a vector to shift to a zigzag search for the third. That took a day, and he now had a tighter vector. He lived in stealth mode. Ferret, of course would be faster. Probably Leef as well. But more people meant more risk of discovery. This was *his* mission, to prove . . . what?

He'd decide that after he proved it.

And time it took.

Norsunder abruptly began sending out more spy patrols. David packed along journey-bread and cheese, just in case, and was midway in placing some newly corrupted beads back in their positions when he was nearly caught between two patrols. He went to ground moments before the low gray clouds overhead hammered the entire region with a deluge.

He was forced to lie up for a week, sleeping on a broad tree branch in sodden clothes; he could not risk a transfer back to the houseboat as he sensed tracer magic. *Something* was up.

When at last he'd finished replacing the beads going southward, he had to collect the rest of them going north from the original bead. This meant belly-crawling through the mud left by the week-long storm, painstakingly eradicating any traces of his presence behind him as he searched.

David had stalked and stealthed the ordinary guards long enough when the boys had lived in the area to know how to avoid them, but he dared not leave any trace, physical or magical, that might cause them to make a report to the Black Knives. So far, he hadn't seen any, which suggested that this might either be a diversion from a larger plan, or abandoned altogether, but he dared not assume that.

And so, though it took weeks — one bead every eight or nine days to find, carry back to the houseboat, strip of magic and re-enchant, then to return to its spot — he kept at it.

One hot, thundery day, it seemed he only took two steps before squawking birds or rustling foliage indicated that yet another search was going out, and he'd have to lie up. Over and over. How many more beads awaited him? At this rate, it was going to take up a year —

A warning sense at his mind-shield. It was habit now, the tiniest break for a niff. And there was Detlev: *Go to ground.* And a mental picture of two of the worst Black Knives closing in on him.

He was trapped, and had completely missed the signs. Cursing under his breath, David bent low and used his Marsh-sense to weave between stands of leddas and marsh-weed, until he found a thin canal barely wide enough for a trickle of water to flow over thick mud. He threw himself headlong into the bog, sinking down with a slurp except for his head.

Twisting to the right until his neck twinged, he spotted the two silhouettes dodging the sparse tangleroot trees and coming fast. Fifty paces, forty — then a figure dropped from a tree behind the pair.

Maybe once a year, if that, Detlev had sparred with the boys. It had mostly been Siamis, sometimes (if he was there) Detlev watching and making comments when they trained. Occasionally demonstrating a move slowly, to show the right and the wrong posture from foot to angle of head. David had never seen him actually fight.

Detlev had armed himself with two daggers. From David's water-level view, the fight was nearly too fast to follow, a blur of snapping dun-colored sleeves and whipping tunic flaps, further obscured by the gently nodding grasses. Twice Detlev stepped between the pair and shifted minutely, precisely, hip then shoulder.

A hooked foot — feint, slash and step, one Black Knife spun away, fingers clawing at a neck opened from ear to ear. Then both of Detlev's daggers drove into the second Black Knife, one in the gut, the other slashing a backstroke across the throat. Detlev yanked the knives free as the man staggered, struggling to kill with his dying breath before thudding lifeless to the ground.

Stay hidden, came the mental command.

Silver glinted. Transfer tokens? Detlev and the corpses vanished.

Shit. David lowered his head until his nose poked above

the murk. He'd very nearly walked into the stupidest trap. Sure, he'd been checking, but—he realized now—more and more perfunctorily. And he would have lost that fight. He closed his eyes, reviewing what he'd seen, before memory pulled him farther back. David hadn't been able to take a single Black Knife. Their cruel hilarity at his efforts still burned.

That had been his first real proof of Siamis's old warning that speed wasn't everything. Training, either. The Black Knives possessed those, and strength.

Here he'd just witnessed proof of a later warning: Detlev was not only fast and strong, but it was very clear that he could both fight and scan in the mental realm, reading enemy intent that fraction of a heartbeat before bone and muscle could act. David hadn't believed that was even possible, though Siamis had told them repeatedly to practice keeping the mind-shield open while fighting. But all that did was distract one—painfully—and David and MV had both thought his words the equivalent of the teacher moving back the target as your aim got better, and thinking you didn't notice.

Now he knew there was yet another layer to training, one none of them had been exposed to.

David lay there in the bog, bleakly wondering why.

Ten

THE BOYS (MINUS DAVID and Ferret) had begun taking Sveneric along to their private drills and sparring. There, looking like the others in miniature, Sveneric swung and blocked in Detlev's fourfold sword warm-up, a throwing knife instead of a sword in his small hands.

Some thought his determination funny. Others found him disconcerting in the formidable concentration that he brought to everything: riding, drill, and above all, drawing.

Adam was the only one who saw how hard Sveneric tried to mimic what he remembered of David's style in defensive training, and heard how often Sveneric's precise treble voice would begin a sentence, "But David said . . ."

Though Adam was the one who most often saw to it that Sveneric ate, had clean clothes, encouraged his drawing, and made certain Sveneric had remembered his mind-shield, it was David who Sveneric wanted to see back.

Sveneric shielded his mind all the time, even in his sleep, after Adam found him dream-walking, and taught him how to both navigate and shield. Sveneric had vanished altogether from the mental realm, unless you were very good at sensing quiescence.

After drill, when it was time to spar, Adam and Laban set Sveneric to lunges and cuts at a wooden post while they squared off to spar, banishing the last of winter's cold air — muddy slush still lay on the lee sides of buildings — until they were sweaty and string-muscled.

Ferret had vanished not long after David, unsettling those with enough awareness to question. They still did not know if he, like David, had gone off on his own mission, or if he'd been pulled. If he'd been pulled, why hadn't they been told? What was going on?

"But that's the pig pen as usual," Laban snarled one night. "Corralled and fed scraps, so we shit manure to aid other people's gardens."

Yeah, they were getting restless.

Then came a dreary, cold morning, prompting a longer than usual scrap. Erol peeled off, heading for duty on the chow line, which meant he'd return with fresh gossip. When MV, who invariably went first, got to the top of the stair, he froze, smelling the acrid sweat of hard fighting, mixed with the tang of blood. Detlev's door was open.

All it took was a glance, and the others crowding in behind stilled as they followed him. Detlev had clearly just arrived. They saw two daggers, both gore-smeared, cast on the table.

Filthy, sweaty, and blood-splattered, Detlev walked along the walls, touching each as he whispered. Magic briefly glowed at each touch, and MV's hackles rose at the intensity of the wards. As the last of the boys filed through, MV shut the door and put his back to it, moving only when Detlev approached to seal off the room. This is it, MV exulted. Detlev didn't want anyone hearing what came next. Surely that had to mean that they were about to retake Five.

Then, still not speaking, Detlev stepped to the far corner and walked through the cleaning frame, which hummed and coruscated briefly. He came out the other side, wearing camouflage clothes of dull brown and green patchwork, still damp from the blood and sweat — now mere water — and marked with sharply cut gaps, the biggest one over Detlev's right arm below the shoulder. Below it, the flesh began bleeding as Detlev bent to rummage in the drawer of the desk.

Curtas was the first to speak. "Want help wrapping that?"

"It'll keep." Detlev pulled out a handkerchief and wound it around his upper arm.

MV eyed the angle of the wound.

"Who and how many?" Noser demanded.

"Black Knives. Two," Detlev said, into a profound silence. It was so very rare that Detlev told them what he'd been doing. That meant something had changed, something important.

Two, MV thought, whistling silently. He eyed the cuts in the baggy tunic, putting together what must have happened: a totally insane move, leaving that shoulder open to draw them as Detlev stepped between a pair used to working together. Strike upward with one hand, downward with the other, both backhand. If you weren't lightning fast, there you were, caught totally open between a couple of angry enemies. In double-knife Marloven style it was called "the seed" but the boys called it "pincushion" — a move they only used in drill.

"They won't find the bodies," Detlev added as he cleaned the blades.

They all knew that, by the inexplicable rules binding certain kinds of magic, you couldn't Disappear someone you'd killed. That meant he'd had to transfer them somewhere, one at a time, and bury them.

"Two down," Noser crowed.

"Efael will replace them fast enough," Detlev said. "Preferably with one of you."

His tone shut Noser up, and Silvanas, to make certain he stayed shut up, trod on Noser's nearest foot.

"Failure," Detlev said, "can sometimes be a strategy . . ." He paused, and the sidled looks and nudges became focus. "It seems that Connanre is moving against me in aid of Yeres and Efael. Your safety was always relative, and now it hinges on separating yourselves from me."

Their focus intensified.

"Does that mean we can get rid of the Child Spell?" Laban demanded.

And for the first time ever, Detlev said, "Yes."

There was no time for reactions because he kept right on talking. "Efael's spies are reporting that my experiment with you is a failure."

There were some covert glances, and Noser scowled.

"This and the news of Siamis and Roy being the latest to break away might succeed in keeping you from any more special invitations. Might," he repeated.

The warning in the last word wiped the grins, except for Noser's shrill snigger.

"What's in play?" MV asked.

With no change of expression, Detlev said, "You've grown up hearing speculation about when Norsunder will make a second run on the world, using the ships and armies caught in the deep Beyond. Efael and Yeres want to make that run now."

The questions shot fast.

"Why don't *you* take command?"

"Are we being forced to take their orders? I don't want to take their orders!"

"It's more fun running *against* Efael! I hate that soul-sucking turd."

"Can *we* get Five back?"

Detlev said, "You may do whatever you like. I won't stop you."

If anything, this was stranger than hearing that they could lift the Child Spell at last. Some grinned, others felt . . . unmoored.

"If you stay with me, your training will be much harder, and you run the risk of becoming a target, if Efael makes me a target. You now know what being his target means. As far as he and Yeres are concerned, you're presently a failed experiment, splintering off. The more noise you make about it, the better you slide beneath his interest."

Curtas said, "What would our orders be if we choose to stay together?"

"Vana, and Noser, you two want control of the strike force stables, so you'd be sucking up to Bostian, as he's currently in command here. If Aldon were to show up, I'd order you to switch allegiance to him, because I want eyes and ears inside his command."

Noser rubbed his hands as he whispered to Silvanas, "*We're* gonna be running that war. Wait and see!"

"First there's Yeres and Efael to get past," Vana reminded him. "Shut up."

Detlev was speaking again. "Erol, you'd stay where you are. For now. No one is better at catching stray rumors."

This rare praise caused Erol to blush, his somber mouth twitching into an almost-smile.

"Curtas, you would be designing and building a house."

Detlev leaned back and reached into the desk drawer, pulling up a pouch that clinked promisingly. Curtas's face flushed with elation that he tried to hide.

Noser forgot the prospective war. Here was fun right now, and he was missing out. "Why can't *we* go undercover? We can do it! We can!"

"We *are* undercover," Vana muttered. "Shut *up*."

"Not with a *real* disguise," Noser protested, jerking his thumb at Curtas. "We're just wanding stables. As usual."

"Shut. *Up*."

Detlev raised a hand, and the buzz of noise halted. "Noser, when you can write me a treatise on when the Sartoran builders shifted from third story trefoil window arches to the ogee style, and why, you may go undercover and build a house, too."

Noser groaned, Laban rolled his eyes, and Curtas grinned as Detlev handed over the heavy bag. "A big house?" he asked.

"We will discuss the details presently," Detlev said, and turned to Laban, who sat back, arms still crossed, his vivid coloring emphasizing his lip-curled scorn.

Laban fumed. All this talk of failure and false fronts, it was more stupid game playing. Either he left the group — became a Roy — or he remained stuck under Detlev's orders. What he really wanted, he knew he would get no help with. Only unwanted advice.

Maybe even direct interference.

"Of course you won't let me go back to Geth to scout," Laban said insolently, too angry to pretend there was a real choice.

"No." Detlev's tone was mild. "Yeres has summarily annexed Dejain, so I could use your skills there. My orders would be to return to magic studies, after which you'd let her recruit you. She's very angry over Zhenc betraying her once he got the information about the flute from her. On the surface you'd be studying, but you'd act as her liaison with me. She has a weakness for handsome, well-behaved youth. Which you would do your best to become."

Noser crowed, and a couple of the others guffawed.

Detlev cut through it all. "You'd learn, carry information, and I'd provide the information that you ignorantly let slip to her."

And there was the lure. Laban had to laugh inside. Detlev knew he'd enjoy that, and he did want to study magic again.

"All of you," Detlev said, taking in the circle. "If questioned, you may revile against me as much as you wish, adding that I never tell you anything."

This time everybody laughed.

"First of all, if you're with me, then nothing of this discussion is ever to leave this room. Don't talk about it among yourselves unless you are absolutely certain you are alone." Detlev glanced inside, to where Sveneric still lay asleep. "Especially before him."

"He should be safe from Efael," MV protested. "He can barely run, he's so small."

"Siamis was small, too," Detlev said. "Efael prefers a challenge, but if he believes there is any emotional attachment to a target, that changes the game. It adds extra pleasure, that of dominating two people instead of one, through a single act—the one he violates, and the one forced to witness. This is why I've been absent as much as I have. To the spies, I've lost interest in what you called critters. Aldon took his, I fostered one out, and abandoned Sveneric."

Adam bit his lip; only he seemed aware of Detlev and Sveneric's contacts on the mental plane.

"Leef," Detlev said. "One of Bostian's captains has been trying to recruit you for light cavalry skirmishers, am I right?"

Leef ducked his head in a nod.

"Let them recruit you." And on his second nod, "MV, I understand you met Tsauderei once."

MV reddened to the ears. Until now he thought Detlev hadn't known about that idiotic venture. "I didn't get far," he muttered.

"On the contrary," Detlev retorted, still mild. "You got all the way to his valley, which is formidably warded. That means he took an interest in you."

Ignoring the chorus of hoots and cracks from the others, MV said, "All he did is insult me."

"Interest is interest. My orders would be to try again."

This time when Noser crowed derisively, Detlev leveled a glance at him. Noser fell silent, and the others as well. Detlev continued. "But first, you'd take a month to establish yourself somewhere else. A new life."

MV regarded Detlev with wary interest. He had no interest

in leaving the group, but he wanted a clear strategy, and it was obvious no such thing was forthcoming. As usual. "You said training harder. When Laban and I took on Siamis, I saw it, there's another level to training. Good as Zathdar is, he doesn't have it."

"There is," Detlev said.

"And we're getting it when?"

"When this is over. Unless, of course, we're all dead. Until then, what do you want to do?"

Fiercely disappointed, MV said recklessly, "I want to buy a boat."

"Do so," Detlev said.

"A yacht." MV stretched his arms up and crossed them behind his head in oblique challenge, though his body remained taut as wire. "Big enough for a crew. But that I could sail myself if I had to."

Detlev said, "An independent method of movement should magic transfer be compromised is an excellent idea. Try Jaro. There's a popular ship agent holding a yacht that might fit your requirements."

MV's black brows shot upward. "A yacht, unless it needs to be rebuilt, is going to cost a whole lot more than I have in my sved from Zathdar's fleet."

"So you sign up with one of the passenger services and work off the rest. Then sail down the coast toward Sarendan. While you sail, you'll be studying Roy's comparison on forms of magic."

"That mess Roy wrote before he turned his back on us?"

"The very same. It's scrupulously exact."

"It was also heavier than a brick. We had to order paper twice while we were holed up in Wnelder Vee, just because of Roy." MV groaned, but inwardly he was thinking that Detlev had it all planned. Even the yacht. Then he rallied. Well, of course; it wasn't any secret how much MV liked sailing, and he'd always wanted his own boat.

Detlev said, "You're on your own, and since none of the magic schools will take you, you're starting at the top in looking for a tutor."

Everybody laughed.

"Further, if Tsauderei tried to turn you, you'd let him. Not too easily or too swiftly."

MV grinned. "And so, if he questions me, I can feed him

misinformation, right?"

"You'll have to gain his trust first. If you can." Detlev cut through the scoffing. "Those who want to accept their orders, go ahead."

"Without knowing the real target," MV said, crossing his arms.

"Remember what I told you. If you stay with me, even peripherally, the risk is there. Right now there's nothing more to know than what I've told you."

They knew the rule: What you don't know can't be ripped out of you.

Noser scowled. "Where's Ferret?"

"Where he needs to be."

Noser elbowed Silvanas as they turned away. As soon as they got through the door, he whispered, "If Ferret's on a spy mission, that has to mean that Detlev's planning to take command of the war away from Efael."

Silvanas muttered, "Who's to say we'll be in it? Don't you get it? We're being split."

"It's a ruse," Noser said, voice high as they clattered down the stairs. "It's only a ruse. Isn't it?"

"Shut. Up!"

Those left were Curtas, still waiting for his instructions on his house assignment, Rolfin, and Adam.

Detlev turned to Curtas. "Why don't you fetch your sketchbook and chalks, so we can talk over some ideas."

Curtas walked out, light-stepped with anticipation.

Detlev turned to Adam. "Sveneric still asleep?"

"Yes," Adam said, surprised that Detlev didn't check mentally. Maybe he was too tired. Or a hidden message lay here.

"Good." Detlev turned his head. "Adam, your first far-sense monitoring mission: you are to track Peitar Selenna in the mental realm."

Adam's eyes widened. "For how long?"

"Should be no more than, ah, three days."

Adam walked out slowly, considering where to hide up for three days, as Detlev shut the door and crossed to the desk. Rolfin, aware of being last, watched as Detlev carefully removed something rolled in cloth. He opened it, disclosing a crossbow bolt made of silver, with the greenish tinge of very heavy magic roiling over it.

"You have two days to find Peitar Selenna and shoot him. Directly over the heart. With this," Detlev said, and handed the bolt to Rolfin. "You have only one shot."

He waited as Rolfin's expression altered from doubt to horror to wary question.

"Peitar Selenna's a king." Rolfin spoke slowly. "You want me to hunt down and shoot a king."

"Yes." Detlev looked askance. "Your objection is to his rank?"

"No," Rolfin stated. "Oh. Maybe some. Only because he's popular. His people like him. He's not a bad king. And he's no ally to Efael. Or Yeres." He fingered the blunt end of the cross-bolt. "There's no point here. This is going to *hurt*." When Detlev didn't say anything, he thumbed it again, noticed the fuzziness of magic, and looked up, puzzled.

"There needs to be at least one civilian witness," Detlev said. He opened the door, where Curtas — waiting patiently outside with his sketchbook and chalks — stood, ready to come in. Rolfin passed him by and walked toward his room.

He passed by Adam and Curtas's room and saw Adam writing in that grubby book of his. But the moment Rolfin's gaze touched Adam, the latter glanced up, slammed the book shut and slid it inside his tunic.

Adam took in Rolfin's expression, the long knife scar on his dark face tight. Rolfin passed on into his room and began methodically packing up his saddlebag, followed by Adam.

Adam said, "I think there's something else going on."

Adam could be inscrutable when he needed to be. Rolfin had not coinhered, nor had he contracted Marsh madness, or any other kind of extrasensory perception, but he had grown up with Adam, and wondered if he struggled with the same . . . no, no use in thinking of it. They stayed together. *Firejive.*

No use whining about it. He knew he'd carry out an order he hated because the group was more important than anything.

Rolfin hoisted his gear over his shoulder. "Can you locate Peitar Selenna for me? I can make this a lot faster if you would."

Adam said, "Already did." And he went about the elaborate process of hiding his journal.

Eleven

DAVID HAD BURIED HIMSELF in a bog.

There he stayed, with little things crawling into his clothing, until Detlev's mental contact: *Return and report.*

Mud sucked at David as he pulled himself out of the quagmire. He sloshed into a feeder stream and splashed vigorously until the worst of the grit and crawlies vanished, then hauled himself out, slung his sword behind him, took hold of the token he'd carried with him all this time, then braced for the wrench between worlds . . .

. . . and found himself back in the familiar smell of dust, moss, mildew and sweat of Norsunder Base, as Geth water dribbled off him. He swayed on his feet, fighting transfer reaction, and as soon as he could get mind and mouth to work in unison, turned toward Detlev. Then blinked at the camouflage clothing, and the red-stippled handkerchief bound around Detlev's arm. "I had to go, because—" He caught himself.

He was offering excuses, not a report. He summoned his wits, began with his observations on his walk into Chwahirsland from Erdrael Danara, and saw from the minute alteration in Detlev's expression—a slight lift of the chin—that he'd got it right. He finished up with the Geth journey, the mirror ward beads, and scouting on Irad's defensive camp. "I was nearly done. And avoiding the patrols."

"Ordered out there to deflect you," Detlev said. "You were tired, focused on the finish, and your sweeps became perfunctory." His tone was even—mere observation—and David knew it was all true.

"This," Detlev said, "is why I assign complex missions to pairs or teams."

David began to justify himself, but Detlev cut him off. "Whatever Roy's motivations might be, he's interfering with Efael's plans."

So Detlev had been watching Roy as well. *Of course he was.*

"There'll be time to catch up with him later," Detlev said as he stepped into the bedroom alcove beyond, and only his voice emerged. "Assuming he succeeds in destroying that fortress, and survives the consequences. That's no longer your concern. Let's talk about the lattice you found in Chwahirsland."

David swiped his hand over his face, which was already drying in the arid atmosphere of Norsunder Base. The gesture was instinctive, a recoil from the remembered sense of profound stupidity and physical exhaustion. "Is that why Wan-Edhe was yanked, because he was creating his own Beyond? Jilo said he'd been at it for years. Decades. How'd he get taken anyway?"

Detlev reappeared, wearing an old, loose tunic that hid the bandage around his arm. "Wan-Edhe made the mistake of leaving his citadel to go overseas on conquest. He forgot he wasn't protected by his border wards. Efael wants the blood mage texts that Wan-Edhe hoarded all these years. Yeres wanted the enemies book. Wan-Edhe has been in the process of using both to broker a deal."

"And we lost it." David shrugged. "I don't know how Siamis knew."

"He had his own tracers, of course," Detlev said without any discernible emotion. "The book is gone, which suits our purposes well enough. As for Wan-Edhe, Efael can't kill him because all his secrets would die with him."

"Jilo expects him to return."

"That's the deal on the table. Efael will send him back. Yeres will give him some of the power he craves. But he'll be on a leash."

David was not surprised. Jilo had been fatalistic about

Wan-Edhe's eventual return from Norsunder, but still he toiled, nearly at the cost of his life, to destroy as much as possible of what the evil old king had striven so long to make. David did not know whether to admire or despise such a labor of faith.

"In beginning the process of weakening Wan-Edhe's pocket Norsunder," Detlev said, "it appears that Jilo has been remarkably successful in lessening the effects of Wan-Edhe's lattice framework. That process left Jilo unprotected against the effects of the lattice wards."

"It was killing him," David said, chill crawling up his back to tighten his neck.

"He seems to have recovered. No," Detlev raised a hand, forestalling the obvious question. "I'm still warded at the border, but I've someone on watch. From Jilo to you."

The "you" was plural, David understood as Detlev gave a brief report on the others' assignments. Then he forgot that when Detlev came last to Rolfin. "*Peitar Selenna?* Why? I never met him, but from all I hear he's never so much as picked up a sword. He can't be any kind of threat." He eyed Detlev, wondering if this was some kind of test, the kind that Efael required of his potential Black Knives: the murder of random people, the more harmless and well-liked, the better.

"You," Detlev said, and David now heard the singular, "could not be more wrong."

Questions — unanswered questions — detonated into the heat of fury. *"Why?"*

Detlev looked around sightlessly for a long pause. David's righteous anger at being eternally kept in the dark curdled into fear. He'd never seen Detlev at a loss for words. Ever. But the man, always seemingly invincible as well as composed, far removed from the messiness of emotion, looked very human now, tired, stressed, even grieved.

Finally, he turned David's way. "You know what Efael's recruitment methods are like. Do you want to experience his interrogation techniques?"

"No." David exhaled the word. "There's a reason."

"Here's what I can give you: what would have been Siamis's job in the next step."

No answer about Peitar Selenna, but David didn't really care. What he did care about was the increasing conviction that there was a plan. Further, the news that their participation was voluntary was a sign that the danger had intensified exponentially.

Detlev turned his hand outward and there was a doorway where none had been in the solid granite wall. This doorway opened into night. Detlev stepped through and David followed, finding himself in the airless pressure of the outer Beyond, at the archive, which the boys had all seen before when they were learning to write reports. The doorway was gone, of course; his surprise was entirely reserved for how painless the transfer had been.

He turned to Detlev, startled. "The slide," he said. "It's real."

Detlev's eyes narrowed in amusement at the term the boys had made up for the way Detlev seemed to transfer back and forth without showing any physical effect.

Then David remembered the Geth chase after Les Rhoderan and his underage army whom he was teaching vagabond magic. It had seemed a stupid form of magic to David. Still did. But there had been one useful spell, accomplished by people standing hand in hand in a ring: they could transfer someone in that ring to a site all knew, and it was a painless shift. He looked up at Detlev, startled into question. "There *is* a connection."

Detlev showed him a book.

"*The Emras Testament*?" David said, disappointed. "MV and I slogged through that ages ago."

"No," Detlev said. "Take it."

David did, looking skeptically at the spiky Sartoran handwriting on the cover. It was the same old-fashioned language he remembered.

Detlev said, "You read part of it, the part the Sartoran Mage Guild has. I believe you're ready to comprehend the part they've never seen. Do not," Detlev said, "let it leave your hands. If you do, it'll vanish to a protected space. You will not be able to trace it."

David exulted—this had to be about the lattice wards. Excitement thrilled through him, and wariness: this was the stuff Norsunder-Beyond was made of.

"When you're done, let it go, then . . ." Detlev pointed to the shelves around them. "Read every report. Every one. Remember what you read, noting errors in fact, but write nothing down. And keep that mind-shield tight."

He summoned a door with a gesture, and vanished, leaving David alone. The angry frustration rushed back, but diminished slowly as David looked around the airless space. This was the Beyond. So much of it was in the mind: his body was not his real body. He made an effort and depicted a hammock and himself in it as he considered what he'd heard.

The comment about Siamis was interesting. On the surface, it would seem to underscore Siamis's betrayal, except why would David be given a job that Siamis the betrayer had been assigned? Detlev of all people would know that a betrayer would find a way to either destroy a plan or make it into a trap.

That suggested Siamis's betrayal . . . hadn't been.

It was then that the obvious hit David. Here he was, trying (as usual) to winnow out meaning from Detlev's typically sparse explanations, and yet Detlev and Siamis has been so loud, so acrimonious in their arguments all over Norsunder Base, with never fewer than half a dozen spies busy earing in, then gleefully gossiping. Exactly the way the boys were supposed to be complaining about Detlev . . . Right. It had all been a sham.

Failure can be a strategy.

David locked his mind-shield tight, uttered a few pungent curses, and opened the Emras book.

Twelve

Sarendan and Sartor's Western Border

IN SARENDAN'S ROYAL PALACE, the day wore on. They were all so used to their king being sequestered in his study that no one noticed that he was missing. He'd taken care to delegate his roving agents, or listeners, to various tasks, he kept no court, and there were no guild meetings until after Flower Day.

The first to discover him gone was Lilah, who as always thought about her brother's meals, as he was prone to forget. He considered more than one reminder a day to be nagging, but accepted one as a compromise, so when dinner was served and he still hadn't shown up, she ran to ask the steward if he'd eaten.

When she was told that he hadn't gone down to the kitchen much less ordered a tray, she sped to his study. Empty, the desk covered with the usual lexicons, ancient texts and scrolls, translations, and miscellaneous bits of what she thought of as king papers. She backed out and checked through the entire palace. When she didn't find him, returned, and this time ventured closer to the desk. Her gaze went to a single piece of paper lying in the middle of a bare space.

She bent over it, then ran to the dining room, where she

found Ian halfway through his dinner, some of his dolls lined up next to him. "Your Da is gone," she said. "He went somewhere."

Ian shut his eyes, and the corners of his mouth lifted. "I know."

"You know? Did he tell you he was going somewhere?"

"No. I can hear him," Ian said. "He's reading."

Of course that had to be little-boy imagination. Lilah smiled and nodded. "Oh. Good. I hope he's happy."

"He is. But he misses us," Ian said matter-of-factly, and straightened a sailor doll on the chair.

Imagination, Lilah thought firmly, and tucked into her dinner. Maybe it would be good for Peitar to have a nice ride somewhere, though it was a bit odd for him to go out like that and not tell anyone. She hoped he remembered to eat dinner.

As Peitar rode that first day, a kind of euphoria gripped him, a sense of escape. He scolded himself mentally: he had a purpose here, an important one. If he was right, it could surely benefit the world. After which he would return to his family and his duty. This was no mere escape, like a spoiled child running away.

But underneath the words persisted a sense of freedom, one he had only felt while floating in the air of Delfina Valley. It lasted through the day, lessening as he and the horse both tired. He had not ridden for hours since the old days with Derek Diamagan; his bad leg throbbed faintly at first, and by nightfall all the way to his hip.

Arrival at last in a little crossroads village did not mean an end to effort. He still had to muster strength to attend to the simplest things. As far as these village Sartorans were concerned, he was a traveler, not a king.

Much as he resented the yoke of kingship, he discovered to his disgust that he'd become accustomed to the willing hands who took care of all the little details of life. He'd forgotten the continual toil of those scrabbling days of the revolution, not the dramatic exertions of warfare or great magery, but the constant demand of effort and decisions about necessary things: stabling and currying the horse, carrying the bags, finding a place to eat, waiting one's turn to inquire, and then waiting again for the food to appear as those who had come in previously got their share first. He endured the long waits by reading.

When at last he was done with it all, he retired early, lying still on a narrow, lumpy bed in a small room that he was to share with two others, as the throbbing in his hip slowly settled to dull ache. He stared at the square of light on the plain board ceiling from glowglobes across the little street, and listened to voices rising and falling in tuneless singing, often breaking up into laughter and chat.

Then he shut them out, and composed himself to check on the direction of the mystery music. . .

Nothing.

As a boy at Selenna House, he'd been adept at finding secret passages. Eventually he discovered the old treasure room, by his father's day an empty space surrounded by stone. He'd hidden there once in total silence and darkness. That was all he sensed now. Obviously he was too tired. He'd try it again come morning, after rest.

When he woke, he opened his eyes to a strange room, and after an effort remembered where he was. One roommate was already gone, the other slumbered heavily, the stale scent of beer breath heavy on the air.

Peitar got quietly out of bed, straightening slowly. His entire body ached, the old wound, mis-healed for so many years, throbbing in a way that threw him back to those bad days in his early manhood.

He stepped through the cleaning frame, made it downstairs, and asked for a Healer. After a meal and listerblossom steep, he'd sufficiently masked the pain to force himself to get back upstairs again in order to pack up his saddlebag again, there being no servant to do that for him, much less carry it back downstairs.

First, of course, he must clear his mind for another try at locating the music. Surely, now that he was in Sartor, proximity would favor him? He sat in the little chair beside the bed, closed his eyes, and let the mind-shield relax. Then he imagined him-self floating in the air between lake and sky, the winter sun warming his face, and listened. But it was the treasure room all over again, the sense of stone enclosing him in darkness and silence.

Very well. He'd ride on and begin asking about older laby-rinths.

Midmorning a storm slid over the white-crowned mount-ains high to the west. The road had bent northwards along the face of a mountain. By noon, the wind had turned icy, with chilling fog. The horse was already drooping, so Peitar looked for shelter.

Then the storm burst.

It seemed an eternity, so slow was their pace, until at last they reached a traveler's shelter, old and mossy. Peitar rode into it, and dismounted onto ground running with water down the middle, but at least now he could employ magic: he carried a glow globe in his saddlebag, and a fire stick.

With light and fire, he staved off the bitter cold, but he had not thought to bring food. Next time, he promised himself as he stroked the animal's nose. The storm battered the shelter through the rest of the day, the sleet turning to snow in the night, and then to sleet again, as the horse lipped at sweet grass, seemingly inured to the cold.

Peitar slept fitfully, wrapped in his cloak as he lay on a stone bench uncounted centuries old. In the morning, he tried once more to reach for that which he sought, and once again found nothing. His mind seemed enclosed within stone walls far thicker than those of this shelter.

Peitar set out into a dripping world the next day, the trail liquid with slush; only the stone beneath kept them from sliding down into the thick firs from which drips trickled and plinked musically.

As the horse climbed slowly, hunger and ache and cold angered Peitar. There was nothing keeping him on this trail — nothing keeping him from transferring home, to his beloved son, his loyal and loving sister, to the duties that he had made his peace with. Nothing, and yet he avoided the pocket in which he'd slid a transfer token, as if its touch might wrest him away.

As at last he crested the rise and gazed across a wind-swept plateau. Here he paused to drink from a cold stream, and to water the horse.

Nothing kept him here, except for the quest for meaning.

I'll guard from here.

That was Detlev's thought, and Adam, who had never sustained so long a watch in the mental realm, gratefully withdrew, and opened gummy eyes. He lay curled up on the mattress that he'd dragged into Detlev's heavily warded office, the only safe place to leave his body while his mind traveled so far and so long.

He forced himself to rise, and to drink from the water jug that Detlev kept there for when he returned from the Beyond. Then he collapsed gratefully onto the mattress again, burrowed under the quilt, and tumbled into sleep, mentally composing the journal-code for the questions he couldn't answer, until letters and numbers blurred into the oblivion of exhaustion.

Some distance northwest, Rolfin patiently stalked Peitar.

You had to believe, Rolfin mused, that Detlev had some purpose behind ordering this assassination — with a blunt arrow, yet, which would do more damage as it smashed past ribs than a sharp arrow would. He'd never talked about killing for the sake of killing, unlike many of the braggarts around Norsunder Base who jostled and strove to prove they were bigger and badder than anyone else.

But two things shook Rolfin's his confidence in that purpose. First, remembering those who'd left: Roy and Siamis. Not that the boys really knew Siamis. He'd always been a few years older, an impassable divide when you're really small, and he had always seemed so effortlessly competent. Siamis had never told the boys anything about Ancient Sartor, or what had happened after, nor had he shared his inner thoughts, not even what he did when he was away on assignment. When he'd come up with his enchantment experiment, the boys had been as surprised as the lighter mages had been.

Oh, they'd all heard about the vicious arguments between Siamis and Detlev after the enchantment failed, held mostly in the command center of Norsunder Base where they were surrounded by avid witnesses, but none of the boys had been among those witnesses. They heard the gossip third and fourth-hand.

Everyone's speculations — mostly that Siamis wanted power and his uncle wouldn't let him have it — weren't corroborated by either Siamis (before he was gone altogether) or Detlev. They hadn't talked about such things at all. The only sign that something was wrong was that henceforth the two were never in the same space at the same time, at least that the boys saw. But they were used to Detlev being gone for lengthy periods between brief visits.

The second thing was Detlev himself. What did someone that old really think about the value of a life? He'd been in and out of real time for centuries. He couldn't possibly know Peitar Selenna as anything but a name.

You don't either, Rolfin imagined Laban saying.

He struggled back and forth as he rode onward, through bad weather and good. Peitar's trail could have been followed by a blind man. He didn't even try to hide, other than not using his name. The first day darkened to night, and Rolfin gnawed trail bread, changed horses, and moved on.

A bleak morning, broken by a brief meal of dried turkey-jerky, revealed Peitar's trail leading off the main northern road and veering westward across a plateau, and then gradually around and southward again. Mindful of his orders about a witness, Rolfin hired a guide, a venerable codger who said he'd been traveling these roads for a half a century before Sartor was removed beyond time. If Rolfin decided this was a lost cause, he could always tell the guide some lie or other. As long as people got paid, they generally didn't look beyond that.

Thirteen

PEITAR WAS LOST.

The second day he dismounted and walked, holding onto the reins, a hazy idea in mind that the horse might founder because he had no fodder. Half-delirious from hunger, he kept drinking at every stream in order to trick his belly into feeling full, as the horse cropped at spring grasses.

He tried to walk toward the setting sun, mind-shield forgotten as he used all his strength to reach for what he knew, he *knew*, lay out there somewhere. He would not return until he found it. But all he got was that empty silence.

He was still on the plateau, gazing out over the peaks and valleys under the peachy light of the sun, when the wind brought the sound of another horse, and two riders. He turned, making out the silhouettes against the rising sun, as one figure unlimbered something from his pack.

Rolfin paused at the edge of range, far enough away so that he would not see Peitar's eyes. Because it came down to this: if he didn't follow orders, he'd have to run, and he'd be forever alone, cut off from the others. Leef was family, but so were the rest. He'd shoot straight, and hope the pain wasn't too bad, or maybe the magic on the dull point would do the work that a sharp arrowhead would.

Ignoring the startled question from the guide, he

assembled the crossbow in a few fast, trained moves, slapped the bolt into it, cranked it, and leveled it.

Peitar raised a hand to block the sun as he peered at the lineaments of threat, and yet he could not assemble any sense out of what he saw. Why would anyone else even be out here, much less threatening him with a crossbow, when he had nothing?

His thoughts were consumed by resentment of the limitations of flesh that kept him from connecting with that unity somewhere out there, bathed in the hazy light of morning. It was there, it had to be, but ever since yesterday he could not find even a hint of it. But then, abruptly, the stone walls around his questing mind vanished, and there was the music, so strong that surprise, even rapture, swallowed him whole

Rolfin aimed and shot. As ordered, right over the heart.

Peitar never saw the silver glint of the bolt that struck like lightning. He spun around, and then he was gone in a flash of light before he could even fall.

Rolfin ignored the bleating horror of the guide as he kicked his horse into a gallop. The guide looked between him and Peitar's horse, and duty forced him into action. By the time he caught the reins of the loose horse, his hire had vanished down the trail. He began leading both horses back the long road to home, mentally assembling the words he was going to say to the local road guild agent, and shivering in fear lest that murderer reappear and come after *him*.

"Da!"

The shrill scream ripped through Miraleste's royal palace.

Lilah had never heard Ian scream like that, not even the time last summer when he'd cracked his collarbone in a fall from a tree. Fast as she was, old Lizana, gray and wrinkled, was faster, wordlessly clasping the shivering boy against her. But three generations of her boundless love and comfort were only perceivable in the physical sense, of which Ian was unaware.

"He's gone! He's gone!" he screamed over and over. "Da is *gone, DA!*"

He didn't hear the voices rising in question around him.

His chest heaved in deep, shuddering sobs, then he stilled, as abruptly as he'd uttered that first scream.

"There, there," Lizana crooned. "All better. Were you asleep? Did you have a bad dream?" she murmured, not expecting any answer.

Lilah knelt on the rug next to Ian's small table and chairs, surrounded by the papers and books he'd scattered as his tutor stood in the background, hands at a helpless angle. "He was working on his sums, then he just stopped, and screamed," the tutor said.

Lilah gazed at Ian's staring eyes fixed on some point beyond the confines of the room, and thought helplessly that it was that Dena Yeresbeth stuff again. She still didn't know if that was bad or good or even real, in spite of all the stories about Liere's feats. To Lilah, poor Liere was a skinny girl with ragged, chewed nails, even more ragged hair and clothes, who needed extra kindness, the way simple people and animals did.

Ian leaned against Lizana, his mind shut within the beehive that his friend Shrimpy made around them both. Other little lights—new bees, Shrimpy said, giving Ian the image—had joined them, but these bees could only hum. They didn't have words or pictures yet.

Within the beehive, Ian could bear to share what he still had no vocabulary to explain: his father riding farther away, his mind too distant, but there. Then he turned, seeing someone level a crossbow at him, and a glint of silver, and then Ian was alone in the mental realm. He could no longer see his father's thoughts, but he remembered the feelings right before the end. *He was happy to go away from us.*

No, he was happy to find something.

What was that he found?

See it again, and keep it secret.

Ian understood that Shrimpy didn't have the words yet either, but it seemed important to remember. In the beehive he was safe, and he could look, and it didn't hurt so much, because of the way the shooting star made him feel in his chest, a little like some of that light got in there.

Always remember the happiness of what he found, but never tell anyone.

Or the crossbow would shoot at *you.* That had to be what Shrimpy meant. He always made sense, sometimes more than other people did, but that was because he could get into the beehive and see memories.

Are you all right? I have to go, came Shrimpy's thought, and Ian knew that his friend had to hide. He hid a lot.

Ian also knew he wasn't going to be all right, because Da was gone. But he had Lilah, and Lizana, and his tutors, and his friends, and he also had that secret thing that had made his Da so happy, even though he had to go away to find it.

He opened his eyes, to see two of the faces he loved most bent over him. The third one was never coming back, and yes, here came the pain of that. His eyes filled with tears.

"What is it?" Lilah whispered.

"It was a crossbow, and then Da was gone," Ian said, and when Lilah asked a stream of questions he couldn't answer, he shook his head, and Lizana let him crawl into bed, where he curled up, still crying as he examined the memory again and again, striving to understand what it was, and why Da had to go away to find it, why he couldn't find it here.

Of course Rolfin got away. He was too good at stealth not to easily escape through Sartor. But he couldn't escape his thoughts, specifically the growing sense that this order had been another test.

Rolfin had used the group to avoid thinking about consequences, but the consequences were happening anyway: he knew he couldn't tell Curtas, or Vana, or even Laban, what he'd just done. He wasn't even certain that Adam knew, or what he'd think if he did. Adam was so odd that rarely did he make any sense anyway.

While at Norsunder Base, Adam woke at last, and when he could, poured questions he did not dare ask into his journal

Aldau-Rayad, Al-Athann Cave

Yeres and Connanre tramped through the abandoned cave, examining stone stairs softened by generations of feet, and tattered tapestries in garish colors that had been endlessly repaired, each time losing more sense of the original patterns and depictions, until the figures and figurative had blended into a mess that looked to her like a child's finger painting.

"Utterly. Disgusting." Yeres's gaze flicked from object to object.

Connanre, walking behind her, had been more interested in watching the sway of her blue and red patterned peplum, and the way the silken cord bound around her long, supple torso caused the fabric to mold to her curves in a way more alluring than mere nakedness. Though he hoped that would come, now that she was actually in time's flow again, so very rare.

She was so beautiful, so dangerous. Like fire. He'd broken a government and ripped his beautiful life to bleeding ruin, just to hear her sigh his name, and he'd do it again. And again.

She glanced over her shoulder, straight black brows meeting over black eyes. "Nothing to say?"

Connanre's mobile face altered to hilarious dismay as he kicked the tapestry lying on the stones at their feet. "Think how *I* feel! I am very, very certain that was my flute, the one I gave Neolea."

"She's probably the one who bound the world," Yeres said spitefully.

"No, no, she was quite dead by the time Aldau-Rayad was bound. I saw to that. She was much too powerful." He sighed with real regret. "And too difficult to persuade."

Yeres looked away at the cavern, uninterested in the messy last days of a battle that no one won. "Generations!" She threw up her hands. "*Thousands* of years! Steadily breeding, crawling around in here, while we sat in the Garden unaware." That was the drawback of the Beyond, right there. Oh, for the key to true immortality!

Well, Ilerian had promised that as the reward for success. But success had to be worked for. Therefore, back to work.

Everywhere she looked was an affront. "We should have known." She turned her head to pin Connanre with an angry stare. "No, you lot with your vaunted Dena Yeresbeth should have known! *I* don't hear minds a continent away."

Connanre sighed. "Yeres, my darling, my life. I have told you repeatedly that the mental realm is not the equivalent of the airless reaches between worlds. It has its walls and doors, or its layers, whatever metaphor you wish to employ. The truth is, they were shielded. And Lilith seems to have emerged every so often long enough to renew that shield."

Dena Yeresbeth has limitations. Of course those with it would call it something besides weakness. That was an important distinction, one to share with Efael when he was done playing around with his interrogation of that local boy. She already knew he wouldn't learn anything of import, but then Efael was always seeking new worshippers—they had to be fast, attractive, deadly, and obedient, and Lyal, the boy Efael had managed to pluck away from that guarded and warded compound on the plain below, was definitely the first three, young as he was.

"Let's get out of here."

Connanre turned from his scrutiny of the oldest of the tapestries, having failed to detect any hints of who had circumvented him, and how. In his experience, humans had to gloat, in some form or another. But wherever the evidence was, it did not seem to be here.

They slid into the Beyond and out again on the plateau that Yeres had marked as a Destination, from which the compound below could be seen, a shimmer of protective magic as well as a dust pall obscuring details. All the powerful protections that Detlev had laid over that compound—and Yeres had even contributed, when she'd intended to take it as hers—now protected those cave people. Irritation shivered through her.

A flicker of movement behind one of the huge boulders caused Connanre to step back. Yeres formed a stone spell, advanced—and exclaimed with irritation when she spied Detlev, looking rumpled and unkempt, the singe of magic all around him.

"Haven't you broken the wards yet?" she exclaimed. "You laid them!"

"And Lilith altered them. I've been working on it for two days," Detlev said.

Yeres rolled her eyes Connanre's way, then shut them as she inwardly gathered her strength. She was thinking that it was always good to remind Detlev that he was a minion, and further, that his objective was pointless. Useless. *Immaterial,* after nearly five thousand years.

Connanre was thinking that yes, Dena Yeresbeth had its

limits, but the dyranarya had always experienced the least of those. And Detlev was a dyranarya. He was given a freedom by Ilerian and Svirle that no one else had because Detlev could sense what Ilerian wanted most. Gone, these five thousand years—gone forever, Yeres was so certain that she had drawn Connanre out of the Beyond to Sartorias-deles today. And thence here.

"*I'll* finish the ward breech," Yeres said, and with one of the imperious gestures that Connanre found so winsome—chin high above the delicate curve of her collarbones, one long, curved hip cocked—she did.

The spell smashed into the ward below. Power buffeted them, enervating and dangerously metallic in feel. Then dissipated, leaving the ward below intact.

A flash of light drove them back another step, and there stood Lilith. Yeres struck fast, then uttered a snort of irritation. Of course this was an illusion, a mind projection.

"The ward will hold," Lilith stated, chin up.

"For now," Yeres retorted, glancing at Connanre and Detlev, as if to say, *Do something with those mighty mind powers!*

Connanre shrugged. Lilith and her band had always been opaque to him. But Detlev narrowed his eyes, and the other two watched as the projection of Lilith actually blanched. Then vanished.

Yeres hated to give Detlev the satisfaction of asking, but Connanre, ever curious, said, "What was that?"

"Made her a promise," Detlev said, "if she continues her interference." And transferred away to the Beyond, which always left its distinctive whiff of hot metal.

Yeres turned to Connanre. "He'll be back to finish up. Leave the minion to min." She took hold of the front of Connanre's tunic, then traced her fingers down his chest, and pause at his waist. "You can see, can't you, that Detlev knows the disirad is gone forever, and his only hope of gaining power is to betray us, and take command of the invasion. Make himself indispensable. But he isn't indispensable. We really, really want to dispense with him."

"You won't see any grief from me," Connanre sighed into the curls on the top of her head. "But you know there's nothing I can do. His orders come from Ilerian."

"But there *is* something you can do . . ." Yeres whispered, and let her hand drift down and down. "And after that, find us a place with time drag, where we can still have fun," she whispered.

Another flicker, and they vanished, leaving the wind to scour away the scorch of their magic.

And Siamis, the watcher, transferred away undiscovered.

Fourteen

Geth-deles, Northwest Island

INITIALLY, ROY HAD FIGURED his plan might take as much as a year, but he had nowhere to go or to be. That was before he spotted David and the Black Knife—after which he'd made his way to Commander Irad.

Roy stayed with Irad long enough to listen to the development of contingency plans, then withdrew to select a hidey, where he waited patiently, watching that spot where he'd seen the Black Knife, and David.

Three days he waited, and was rewarded with the sight of David appearing after a transfer, sinking below the level of the grasses and moving in zigzag search pattern. He was clearly searching for whatever the Black Knife had been doing. That meant he was not troubling with the fortress, which was Roy's target.

Roy jettisoned any notion of investigating what the Black Knife was doing, as David was clearly stalking, for whatever reason. He scrambled off at an angle, never moving upright until he was half a day's distance. Then he ran, camped, and ran, until he spotted the towers of the fortress on the horizon.

He knew how to get inside. Fortresses don't change much, even those built more from the odd, melted-looking wood common on Geth than stone. Stone there was, especially in the perimeter walls; the boys had played on them, and inside the courts when first learning basic drill, until a day when Siamis went away on some unknown errand and a gang of bored liberty guards decided to while away a dull, rainy day by trying to thrash the stutter out of Erol.

When Curtas and Leef had stumbled in, shocked at Erol's bleeding body, arms and legs worming helplessly as the guards kicked at him, they'd run to Erol's rescue—and to what might have been slaughter, had not Siamis returned abruptly and broke some ribs, arms, and one leg among the guards, without saying so much as a word, as the boys beetled with Erol back to the bunk room.

After that, the boys had begun to learn stealth in earnest, the way you do when you discover that the world outside your group is not your playground.

Roy used that stealth now, taking his time to sense ahead. Efael was not about, nor were his Black Knives. Still, Roy waited for nightfall before attempting to breech the walls. Two storms came and went before he decided to move, an hour before the watch change: the night patrol would be most tired, early morning patrol still a-slumber.

He'd just begun his infiltration when the hairs on the backs of his arms and neck lifted. The noiseless, internal buzz of very powerful magic seized ground and air, a barrier ward!

That meant no one could transfer in or out. Good thing. If Efael or Yeres were not here, they wouldn't be able to get in. Yet. Roy had no doubt that Yeres, at least, could break the barrier ward if she worked at it. But she'd have to be present in the world and time to do it.

Bad thing: if anyone saw him, he wouldn't be able to transfer out. It was just him, his stealth skills, and his wits, now.

He ran low and slow, so his footsteps wouldn't splash in the warm rain. He remembered the way to the old tunnel, which still existed, though filthy, and a very tight fit now that he was no longer ten. When he reached the basement of the west tower at last, he gritted his teeth against the slimy mold, and the things crawling into his clothes, and forced himself to wait. To scan ahead—

Two minds. One familiar, angry over laundry duty. Laundry duty?

The man's name was Vindot, and he swore violent retribution against someone. Roy grimaced in memory; that much had not changed. He contained his thirst as he waited, and after what felt like a century the basement emptied.

He crawled up against the stones and pushed. A heartbeat of panic when one stuck, but it was only the dried mud from the last time the boys were here. He chiseled at the old mud with his knife, then pushed the stone out, and the next. Another moment of panic when it seemed he'd grown too much to get himself through the narrow crack—his ribs creaked warningly—but he made it, warm dry air ruffling over him.

He replaced the stones, ripped off his shirt, and used it to clean up the telltale mud. Then he straightened up to scan. A ceramic stove had been put in, with firesticks roaring, burning the moisture out of the air.

Instead of the old, unused snow equipment that some long-forgotten commander had put there in case, the place held three big washtubs and was filled with drying racks full of sheets and pillowcases and towels. This was clearly an adjunct laundry room, which indicated more warriors had been brought in, one by one, either from elsewhere or off-world.

He sat long enough for the chill to wear off as he planned his next step.

He couldn't count on everyone forgetting mind-shields, not until he knew who was running what. The fact that a Black Knife had been there was enough of a warning to take his time: first listening on the mental plane, then using physical senses. Door, stairwell. All the way up to the bell tower. Here he waited until sundown, crouched low, hands pressed tight against his head when the rope quivered, but even so the reverberations of the huge bell hammered his skull and shook his teeth.

Another storm slanted in, giving him cover, but making the roof slate slippery. He had to worm his way along the roof pole, holding an illusion spell around himself. Another agonizing century of that, until he reached the north tower.

Here, he was not surprised to find the jumble of old and broken equipment and furnishings jammed in tighter than the last time they'd been there. He felt around the ceiling of the tower until he located the loose slats, and soon he was in the

attic that the boys had built themselves. It had been Siamis's
last assignment, to put an attic in the tower, unnoticed. He'd
maintained that no one would ever inquire why one tower
had a ceiling. And no one had.

By the time they'd built it, Curtas had learned enough
architectural principles to design a sturdy support. It was dry,
dusty, and of course warm, as Geth very seldom got cold.
Candle stubs waited inside the four lanterns, each with a cover
to keep light from shining upward to the covered air vents.

Nothing had changed, except thickened dust. Vivid memory images: Curtas's delight in designing it, MV proving to be
not just deft with saw and hammer and nails, but enjoying it;
Roy remembered his brief smile, the quirk in his pale eyes as
he talked about building a boat someday; David perched on
the trunk containing their blankets and pillows, carving a
flute, and occasionally blowing softly through the holes as he
cocked his head . . .

Roy shuttered that thought away. He was surrounded by
danger. He was going to have to steal food, and spy for
roaming mages, as he took apart, layer by layer, the protective
lattice of the fortress's magic.

And so, while outside the fortress, David had slowly worked
away at corrupting the ward beads, within the fortress, Roy
meticulously and carefully warded himself, removed a single
binding link, and waited for the effect—and to see if anyone
noticed. Then again, and again, until, after uncounted days
had turned into weeks, quite suddenly time ran out.

He knew he had to get out when he spotted two Black
Knives being let through the gate. They strode, angry and
arrogant, toward the commander's office. Roy knew better
than to niff them. Instead, he concentrated on mental
assessment of the gossip propagating out in their wake. A
search? And a fleet for invasion?

Searching for whom? If they searched the fortress, they'd
be thorough, unlike the guards, who were lazy and careless.
He couldn't transfer away because of that ward, and he'd
never be able to outrun them. He had to leave, rather than risk
accidentally leaving some subtle clue that would catch their
interest.

He tightened a ward around himself one last time, and
then bound a veiling ward around the remaining links, soft as

fog. Once that was secure, he delved down to the bottom layer of the protection spells, sweating from the mental gymnastics: one wobble, one touch on any of those protective supports would be lethal.

And there it was, the object the fortresses wards were bound to: a mirror image of . . .

Shock poured through him, icy cold.

He knew that object. It was the flute he'd last seen in Horsefeathers's hands. How was that possible? This fortress on Geth did not date back to the days before the Fall, when the Al-Athann people had gone into hiding.

This was no happenstance. He knew he had stumbled on a trap, maybe centuries old, or even older.

I'm done here. While Efael's errand boys enjoyed intimidating the commander with their exploits, Roy carefully retraced his steps, and under cover of a storm, withdrew into the night and away.

A flurry outside Irad's tent caused Bekani to take a look, then return to tell her husband, "Roy's back. The outer patrol has him. Shall I run interference?"

Darian Irad looked up from the hundreds of tasks demanding his attention. "Please, please."

Bekani strode out to meet the two patrollers assigned to bring Roy in. She was shocked at how thin he was, and grubby. "Password was an old one," explained one of the escorts.

"I'm glad you're vigilant," Bekani said. The two husky boys looked relieved and withdrew to rejoin their patrol. "Come in, Roy. I'll send my daughter to fetch something to drink."

"Maybe some bread?" Roy asked. "Mine disintegrated in the rain. Really, anything will do."

Bekani spotted her daughter playing a circle game with some of the other camp children and dispatched her. Then she said, "Sit down. You look weary."

They withdrew to a log that someone had planed, and he sank down. "Had to run. Couldn't transfer."

Bekani looked concerned. "You know that ward's to keep

Norsunder from transferring enemies in."

"It has," Roy said, and though he hadn't eaten for three days and looked it, "I'll be fine. But listen, there's a fleet coming to reinforce the Norsundrians. Be landing in a day or two."

Her eyes widened. "But we've scout ships —" She paused, and her lips thinned. "Caught, of course. Caught, fought, shot. Come inside. Darian needs to hear this *now*." She cast a grim look over her shoulder as she batted aside the canvas flap that served as the door. "At least war on the sea is something we know *plenty* about."

Roy followed Bekani inside, and his eyes adjusted to the cool darkness. He stopped short, shock flaring his nerves when he recognized Rel, whose head nearly brushed the ceiling, profile bent as he listened to someone else talking. Surrounding him, familiar faces all: Caris-Merian Rhoderan, lips a straight line, Dak, tossing back his messy hair as he described what sounded like a mad gallop of a journey.

All attention was on Dak. Roy backed out again, too weary and light-headed to face the condemnation of Les Rhoderan's inner circle — people he'd once studied, traveled, eaten, sang songs and danced with. His gaze roamed the busy camp without him taking anything in, until he heard a quiet footfall crunch the ground. He sidestepped, hand half-raised to block, then he dropped the hand when he recognized —

"Rel?"

Roy swayed, blinking.

Rel stared as well, stunned by the change in Roy. But all he said was, "Clair of the Mearsieans told us what you did on the fifth world. It might not mean much here, but it did to many of us."

"Arthur?" Roy asked, unable to keep the bitterness from his voice.

"Can't speak for him," Rel said. "You know he's the least likely to pick up a sword and start swinging."

"He might want to drop a stone spell on me," Roy retorted.

Rel lifted one of his powerful shoulders, then said, "If you want, I can carry in your report."

Rel understood military reports. In a few succinct sentences, Roy conveyed the gist, then paused.

"What do you need?" Rel asked.

"I need to return, once those Black Knives are gone. At least they never stay in one place long. Otherwise I have everything in readiness at the fortress, except for the last layer of magic, which will keep Norsunder from easily reestablishing the grounding wards. The surface magic was all laid fairly recently by a mage named Zhenc. I don't know what his aim is, but my guess is that he's involved with Efael or Yeres." Roy blinked grit from his eyes, aware that he was babbling now.

That flute. Who made that trap for whom, and when? The sense that Roy had stumbled onto a very ancient, very dangerous web had kept him awake even more than the steady rain that he'd had to sleep in during his three-day run. He braced himself, then said, "The short version is, there's a step that involves something that I think is still in Sartorias-deles. And since I can't transfer out." He let his voice drift.

"Then ask for help," Rel said. "Can someone at home help?"

Roy's gaze strayed to Caris-Merian, Dak, and the others who had once been friends, and now, he knew, would listen in stony disbelief. And David was probably still lurking out there somewhere. Back on Sartorias-deles, it was much the same, Arthur at the beginning of the list of those who —

Then it hit him. "Clair," he said on an exhaled breath. "But we can't even send messages because of the ward."

"Talk to Bekani. They've been sending messages, I think, from a distance out to sea. Don't know how. Magic's still a mystery to me, though I'm getting better with the vagabond version."

Rel? A vagabond? Roy wrenched his mind away from that, and to the urgent tangle of problems at hand. They'd found the limits of the ward. Good. He would have to use the world transfer token he'd been keeping for emergencies in order to send his message.

Rel went inside to fetch pen and paper for Roy; Darian Irad had not missed Roy's horrified expression and his quick retreat. He walked out to meet Rel, while Dak was still talking to Bekani and the other captains.

While Roy wrote, Rel relayed his report to Irad, whose only comment was, "Can you fight?"

"I can hold my own," Rel said.

Irad looked him up and down. Rel definitely looked big

and dangerous, his voice a rumble in his chest. He could turn out to be a lumbering dolt, as so many big men were, but if he wasn't an outright coward, Irad's new plan required someone who looked like a serious enough threat to distract Norsunder's lookouts.

"Good," Irad said. "Because my frontal attack is now going to become a noisy feint. You lead it. And while you dash around looking valiant, we're going to flank 'em from the west wall up the river, and put our main force at the harbor to meet and greet the newcomers . . ."

Fifteen

ROY DISPATCHED HIS LETTER from the beyond the edge of the ward, and by nightfall was on his way back to the marshland and the fortress. He had eaten, at least, though he still hadn't slept, and his mood was somber. He knew it was cowardice that kept him from confronting the old Les Rhoderan crowd.

Well, call it avoidance. He knew all the arguments about trust. He'd wrestled mentally with them for longer than any of them. He also knew that trying to explain would be so much wasted air, because they'd hear the names of people he still missed, and every word afterward would be *enemy-enemy-enemy*.

In the springtime woodland of Mearsies Heili, Clair looked down at her bare toes scrunched in the soft grass, then up at the sun-browned face of her cousin Puddlenose, newly arrived from another sea voyage. "I'm not ready yet," she said low-voiced. Then, even lower, "But I can feel that it will be right to release the Child Spell. Some day. But not now."

Both Clair and Puddlenose glanced through the quiet forest glade in the direction of the hideout, though of course it could not be seen, as they'd run halfway along Clair's usual route.

"You're going to wait for CJ, aren't you," Puddlenose asked. He squinted upward at the trees, gauging the direction of the wind, which ruffled his sun-bleached brown hair.

Clair turned to her cousin. "It means the most to her. Falinneh and Dhana are from magic races. Gender doesn't mean anything to Falinneh. Gender *and* age mean nothing to Dhana—she's a girl because we're girls. She could dance just as well as a boy. Or a being that is neither. Gwen will be happy doing what everyone does. I think Seshe would like to relinquish the spell someday, and I know Irenne was going in that direction. As for Diana, she's another like CJ. Maybe the inward scars are too great for them to ever trust relinquishing the spell. But one day, whatever they decide, I hope those two will be all right with me relinquishing it. Then I can."

Puddlenose grunted acceptance.

Clair looked at him. "You want to?"

"I can wait. I've decided what I want to do with my life, which is to be a ship captain. Maybe even take over from Heraford, if he retires someday. But that means I can't look fifteen forever. I will when you do," Puddlenose said, flashing a quick grin.

And that, she knew, was as much serious talk as he could tolerate. Like CJ and Diana, he, too, had endured a terrible early childhood, as Wan-Edhe's hostage-prisoner. But everyone had his or her own way of coping with those scars.

He took off running, leaving a whoop echoing back through the glade. Clair faced the other way and began to run again, vaulting over mossy logs and boulders. She slowed when she neared the rough, rocky area that sheltered what the girls had always called the Magic Lake.

This pool was where Dhana's people lived, the huge, wobbly bubbles that rose and fell being one of their forms. Apparently other such lakes—much larger—existed elsewhere in the world, all up north. This was the only one in the southern half of the world. That Clair had heard about, anyway.

It was also the only one near a Selenseh Redian, wherein Hreealdar dwelt. Or so the girls had thought, when they also assumed that the mysterious caves were just caves full of weird gems that glittered like fires had been lit inside, and that make the air feel — as Falinneh said — like you were hoopled, though you hadn't drunk a drop.

Clair began to run again, casting a quick glance at the lake, then up to the entrance to the Selenseh Redian, a little way from the waterfall fed by the mountain top. She had grown up in the white palace, whose rooms seemed to appear and vanish; she had played beside this lake as a small child, and had wandered into the Selenseh Redian, coming out again heady with euphoria, half-hearing chiming voices. These things were just a part of home. It wasn't until she traveled that she began to understand not only how very rare they all were as separate items, but how extremely rarely they were found together. Yet no one elsewhere in the world seemed to know.

"And that's the way we want it," she said aloud, panting the words in time to her steps.

Above her, a crimson-tufted bird scolded, another hidden higher up in the tree trilled, and in the lake a hundred bubbles rose, rainbow hues trembling over them, then fell to vanish in the churning waters below the trickling waterfall.

Three rare magical things: the castle, the cave, the lake. What about the fourth? *Hreealdar.*

She touched her medallion, and whispered the words to the spell that used to call the magical being to the girls.

No reaction.

Hreealdar had not reappeared since taking Seshe to Five, something no one could explain satisfactorily. Maybe the horse-being had decided to stay on Five. Aware of a sharp disappointment and regret — surely she'd missed an important clue — Clair turned her back and raced back to the hideout.

She slowed when she neared it, proud that at least she could run all that distance and arrive back only a little out of breath. Remembering her talk with Puddlenose, she looked down at her bare feet, wriggling her toes in the soft spring grasses and the mud, still warm from the first pleasant rain of spring. She ran her hands down her baggy tunic top and her cut-off riding trousers and breathed in, listening to the sough of the trees in the rising wind. She had made her peace with Mearsieanne as ruler — yes, she had (she reminded herself every night and every morning) — and she was proud that no one knew of her inner struggle. The girls, who would sympathize, were helpless to do anything about it. Anyone else, she suspected, would curl their lip in scorn. No one felt the least sympathy for ex-rulers, especially those who saw only the trappings, and knew nothing of the life behind the parade, the satisfaction of a knotty problem worked out, the trust.

What could she say? *I miss being queen, even though I wasn't a very good one.* She wouldn't blame anyone for scoffing. It was time to find something else to do with her life, that was all.

She clambered down the tunnel into the main room, which was filled with enticing aromas. "I'm back. Do I smell crispy potatoes?"

CJ ran up from the lower tunnel, black hair flying. "Clair? Oh, good, you're back! Your notecase chirped!"

Clair had bespelled her notecase with the trill of a lark. She usually left it on the little desk beside the underground lair's kitchen, so she wouldn't forget it, she got notes so rarely. It was unexpectedly heavy. Something filled the entire box. She opened it, and found a paper folded around a coin. "It's from Roy. He's on Geth, and needs us to contact Horsefeathers. For her artifact."

CJ's blue eyes rounded. "Norsunder got it."

Clair's lips moved. Then she stared down at the letter, and up again. "That part I think I'd better tell him in person. He seems to think even mentioning it might get eleven-tentacles oozing up to grab us. And there's other stuff going on that he seems to need help with, in getting rid of a Norsunder base."

"He needs *us* to *fight*?" CJ asked, looked incredulous.

"No, it sounds like he might need talking help, or maybe magic help." Clair looked down doubtfully. "He's sure hinting around a lot."

CJ made a horrible grimace. "The best person would be Boneribs for magic help against Norsunder *or* with fighting junk."

Clair had to agree. Senrid was definitely the best of anyone in the Young Allies when it came to dark magic and military questions. "I'll write to him. Seems Geth needs everyone they can get. But Roy also wants me to talk to the Geth kids who know vagabond magic. Thinks they won't listen to him."

CJ's expressive black brows knit. "And people talk about *me* being a grudge holder! After he helped rescue all those people?"

"The Geth people might not know what happened on

Five—on Aldau-Rayad," Clair said, correcting herself.

"If it's kids in trouble, I think we should go," CJ said.

Seshe said, "I agree. But should we send a message to Horsefeathers?"

Clair bit her lip, then shook her head. "No, not yet. You remember how horrible she felt after her flute thing was stolen. Let's not tell her until she has to know. It's only going to make her feel worse if someone needs it and she doesn't have it." She scowled at the paper, as if Roy's oblique hints might clarify themselves if she squinted hard enough.

Then she considered the eager faces before her. Falinneh, Dhana, and Diana had been living more and more in the underground cave, as they felt out of place in the increasingly formal atmosphere of the white palace, which Mearsieanne believed upheld the prestige required of her royal rank. Clair looked at CJ, who was fiercely loyal, and charged into trouble firmly believing that the right cause would win out.

The truth? Clair knew she had no authority over anybody anymore, outside of what their own loyalty inspired them to. But she wasn't going to ask Mearsieanne's permission, either. Whatever Roy had going had nothing to do with Mearsies Heili's government—and, though she accepted Mearsieanne's authority as queen, Clair did not accept her authority over Clair's own movements.

She said, "If you all want to come, then let's go together. But we need more world transfer tokens. Roy only sent me this one. And I don't want to write to Arthur. I think he's still sore about Roy."

"If you ask grownup mages, they'll tell you for your own good to stay home and be a nice kiddie and let the adults do everything," CJ said sourly.

"Tsauderei wouldn't." Clair shook her head. "I'll ask him if he can get us world transfer tokens for all of you. Pack up whatever you think you'll need."

Tsauderei had been friendly every time Clair had seen him, and she knew he was a favorite of Lilah's—practically family. She wrote to ask, only to receive a very short answer:

> *Clair: Events here are not going to leave me the time to make transfer tokens to Geth-deles. Erai-Yanya is the one to ask. She might even have some already made.*

Clair showed that to CJ.

"Wow," CJ said, her blue eyes wide. "I guess ol' Tsauderei *really* hates Roy. How come everybody else gets to be a grudge holder and no one says a thing?"

Clair chewed her lip, and reread the letter. "I don't think that's it. I think something else might be going on."

CJ's eyes narrowed, and the belligerence leaked out of her stance. "You think they've had bad news?" She whirled around, black hair flying. "I'm writing to Lilah!"

While Clair crafted a carefully polite letter to Hibern, CJ scrawled a note to Lilah, who could be counted on for all the latest alliance gossip.

And as the day turned to night, and then passed, it was Clair who received a small box of tokens. CJ received no answer at all.

Sixteen

Sartor

THE NEWS ABOUT PEITAR Selenna's assassination began with the guide, who was not very articulate. He dutifully reported to the local road guild agent, who listened skeptically to his slow, rambling tale.

She, in turn, felt obliged to complain (in the guise of a report) to her duchy chief how ill-trained guides were these days.

> *Thunderford seems to hire the people no one else*
> *wants — with reason. The guide reporting a murder*
> *made little sense.*

> *If he's to be believed, the guide's hire absconded*
> *without trace (with a horse! How does one remove*
> *traces of a horse?) after shooting a random traveler.*
> *The hire, described by both the guide and the*
> *Thunderford road guild agent (they only have one,*
> *and he's ready to retire) could fit anyone: dark hair,*
> *age anywhere from fifteen to twenty, plain riding*
> *dress.*

As for the mysterious traveler whose body was
mysteriously Disappeared by being shot (I thought
that this was impossible, and the local mage agrees),
all we have is a saddle bag with a few clothes, and
some books written partly in some language no one
can make anything of, and partly in the Ancient
Tongue, up and down. And a name at the front,
'Peitar Selenna.' The Yosta road agent, here on a
visit, thinks this a name more common over the
mountains. We agree that he might have been a
foreigner, so we're sending what we have on to you.

It was Peitar's saddlebag that got passed (along with responsibility) to the road guild chief, who in turn brought the bag, and the questions, to Atan, as he had to report to Eidervaen for the monthly guild audience anyway.

He was considerably surprised, after the pleasantly somnolent regularity of the meeting in the beautiful hall, to see the queen blanch when she heard the foreign name, and hold out her hand imperiously for the battered, much-written-in book, which she took very carefully. "When did you get this?" she asked, all politeness forgotten. "Where did they *find* this?"

The road guild chief stared witlessly up at the queen, who was half a finger taller than he. He'd never had occasion to notice before, but her eyes were so dark a blue they looked violet. They, with that goggly Landis aspect, together with her size and height, seemed to pin him back like an arrow right through the forehead.

"A week ago, maybe a bit more," he said—knowing that the saddlebag had sat next to his travel bag for half a week. But really, if the mystery man had been someone important, why didn't he travel with an entourage, the way important people are supposed to? And what would *anybody* be doing out in the middle of nowhere, days from the most remote village?

Atan stared at the bewildered face of the chief. "You say the guide Disappeared Pei—the traveler?"

"No, the guide told the Thunderford road agent that the man vanished the moment he was shot. Never hit the ground. There's only the one guide in those parts, and him over eighty.

But experienced!"

He threw his hands out wide, and when the queen's eyes narrowed even more, he hastened on. "The Thunderford agent took a couple locals up to where the guide said it happened, and they found the prints right enough, the weather having held off. No other prints around, just the three horses. The hire who did the murder rode off down the trail, but the prints vanished among the rocks in a valley, where snow seldom sticks because of the hot springs nearby. And a loose horse was found downstream a day or two later, saddled but otherwise carrying nothing helpful. We've written his description into the record, the shooter, that is, not the horse, under the Suspicious Circumstances heading, in case he's seen in these parts again."

Atan stared at the book in her hand, her mind pinwheeling. This was Peitar's own mage journal, something no mage ever let out of their possession. It was that, more than anything else, that convinced her of the unpalatable truth.

She looked up, and the bleakness in her gaze made the chief step back. "I guess you will be the first to know," Atan said heavily. "It'll be all over soon enough. But the man was King Peitar Selenna of Sarendan."

"A *king?*" the road guild chief repeated, and only his respect for the queen kept him from exclaiming, "Impossible!"

"Keep it to yourself, please, until diplomatic channels establish how Sarendan wants to release news that affects them so vitally," Atan added.

The chief agreed with heartfelt sincerity and bowed himself out, happy to leave that mess well behind him. The only time you wanted to be caught up in the affairs of kings was when they were handing out rewards. The death of one, even foreign, under suspicious circumstances, was not going to bring any rewards, only trouble.

Atan breathed a sigh as the door closed behind him. She retreated through the far door as she considered what to do next. Her throat tightened at the thought of contacting Lilah. Oh, this was going to hurt so, so much.

She turned to her steward. "Cancel everything else."

It would be stupid to act without full knowledge. What if some thief had stolen Peitar's mage books? It could happen! That made more sense than his going off to the middle of nowhere — wait, hadn't Tsauderei said something once about

Peitar's odd quest, something about illusory magic and a theory about "old" magic? She needed Tsauderei.

She clasped the saddlebag in her arms and ran through private byways up to the sanctuary of her private room. There she wrote a note to Tsauderei. The answer was immediate:

I think you had better come here.

Atan was surprised to be summoned like the student mage she'd been as his ward up in the Valley of Delfina. He was usually so careful about protocols, at least publicly. She sent a page to her steward, went down to the Destination with Peitar's bag, and endured the bone-wrenching jerk of transfer while carrying something. She didn't dare send it ahead.

When she came out in Miraleste's royal palace Destination, she plopped onto a bench, swallowing repeatedly to keep the nausea down. Transfer was so much worse carrying this bag. An attendant brought listerblossom in a tiny cup, and she slurped it gratefully.

By the time the warmth of the brew had reached her middle, the worst of the transfer reaction had begun to fade. She made her way to the parlor off the terrace, which was a short distance away, and a favorite place for the family, though they had nearly as large a palace as she did. Odd, that, she thought as one of the servants went ahead. Humans were such creatures of habit.

The Sarendan servants were an informal lot, something Peitar had not only preferred, but insisted on. The girl poked her head inside the parlor and jerked her thumb sideways. "It's the queen from Sartor."

She gave Atan a gap-toothed smile, then scurried away.

Atan entered to find Tsauderei in an armchair, looking very old and worn. Lilah's round face was almost unfamiliar — Atan had last seen that anguish when Derek was killed by Siamis, and she'd had to struggle to hide how little that death had affected her.

Shying away from *that* memory, she held out the bag. "Is this Peitar's?"

Lilah bolted toward her, freckled hands reaching to clasp the bag as if it was Peitar himself. "He went away days and days ago," she exclaimed. "Without telling anybody! Just a stupid note! Then, a week ago, Ian got upset and said he was gone! We didn't know what it meant."

Atan looked around. "Where's Ian now?"

"In his room. He's been staying in a lot, saying he wants a nap, or to play alone," Lilah said. "We think he's doing that thing again, with his imaginary friend, or with Tahra's kids. I don't really understand it. But it makes him feel better."

Atan stiffened her resolve. "Lilah, in the bag there's a book. Would you give it to Tsauderei while I tell you both what was reported to me?"

She would rather have written a letter, only she knew she would have agonized over it for days. She fell back on repeating the report by the road guild chief, and she addressed it to Tsauderei, because she knew if she looked once at Lilah, she would never be able to finish.

She made it halfway before Lilah cried in a frantic voice, "Ian was right! He was *shot!* Someone *shot* him? Did they catch the killer? *Why?*"

Atan turned to her. "What's this about Ian?"

"We thought it was imaginary," Lilah wailed. "But it must've been real. He must've somehow heard it up here." She dealt her forehead a slap. "Though he says he's not like Liere, hearing everybody's thoughts." She gulped, saw Atan's confusion, and started again. "Ian was having lessons, and then he screamed, and said Peitar was gone, and later, I don't know how, he said that somebody shot him. With something silver. Did your guild agents tell you that?"

"Only that he was shot with a crossbow. The bolts can be metal, can't they? The guide the killer hired to help him on the trail witnessed it, then brought Peitar's hired horse back to its stable. He didn't chase the assassin. I gathered the guide was somewhat slow, being aged."

Tsauderei said wryly, "No doubt carefully picked for that very quality by the assassin."

"Anyway, no one found the assassin. All we know is that he was young, maybe teenage, dark of hair."

"Detlev's poopsies," Lilah exclaimed.

Tsauderei said, "We cannot assume that every random bad deed done in the world is due to those boys."

"Assassinating a king?" Atan rubbed her eyes, then flung her hands out, palms up. "Not precisely random. Though why anyone would want to kill Peitar is beyond me."

"I don't know, either." Tsauderei scowled, and during the

silence that resulted, Lilah began keening, rocking back and forth, tears bouncing down her cheeks to fall on her forearms crossed tightly over her chest. Atan's throat closed, and she turned to Tsauderei in helpless question.

"I told Peitar that quest was useless," Tsauderei said, running a trembling hand over his face. "I thought he agreed to let it go. But it seems to have taken over his mind."

"What do I *do*? What do I *do*? What do I *do*?" Lilah wailed.

Atan might not have been able to answer that when she first became queen—but now she said, "Is there panic at his being gone?"

"No," Lilah quavered, gulping on a sob. "He parceled out a lot of things to the listeners, and guild people, and other things usually wait for after Flower Day. People are waiting for him to . . . come back," she whispered, and a fresh spurt of tears coursed down her face.

"Then I suggest you take the time to . . ." *recover*. "Figure out your next step. You don't always get that time," Atan said with the inexorable conviction of one who had steeped herself in family history. At that, she exchanged a look with Tsauderei, who nodded briefly.

Lilah gulped again, then said in a watery voice, "I—I think I need to . . ." *Be alone*. Her bare feet slapped on the marble floor, and the door slammed behind her.

Atan said to Tsauderei, "What now? I know that Lilah was adamant about being left out of the succession. And I remember that strange threat Peitar made when he first took over: that if anything happened to him, and there was no adult heir, he would leave his throne to his uncle, the former king."

"That," Tsauderei said, "is now law. He was equally adamant about it—had it written up. Got the nobles to agree."

Atan kept her opinion about Peitar's decision to herself. "Maybe Darian Irad should be apprised. In case?"

"Except," Tsauderei rubbed his face again with a gnarled hand, "he's right in the middle of a war with Norsunder. Rel is with him," he added.

Then, to her surprise, he reached inside his robe, and pulled out a sealed letter. "All things considered, maybe I ought to give you this now. It's to be opened if he doesn't come back."

Seventeen

Between Sartor and the Northwestern Island on Geth

ATAN RECOGNIZED REL'S HANDWRITING, and the word "war" echoed in her ears. Sick with apprehension, she forced herself to slide the letter into the pocket of her over robe, but she could not make her fingers let go of it.

"I would suggest that you don't read it," Tsauderei said wryly, "but I know you will. I trust he'll return, and demand it back, and I'll tell him you have it, and the two of you can rant and storm and make up again. And we can all laugh. Unless we're embroiled in something bigger."

Horror suffused Atan. "Do you think this is the war everyone is dreading? Beginning over there?"

"I don't know."

"And Rel's somehow in it, though he went there to learn vagabond illusions? Of course he is," she whispered bitterly.

Tsauderei shook his head. "I'll stay here. But any advice as to Sarendan's succession has to come from you. Nobody wants a mage's fingers in governmental affairs," he said wryly. "I suggest you keep your notecase on you." He pulled his out of his robe's side pocket, then put it back again.

Atan had no answer. Her mind streamed with questions, and when her gaze fell on the mage journal Tsauderei still held in his other hand, she knew that Sarendan would be stunned by Peitar's death. Quiet and reserved though he was, he had always been respected by his guild leaders, and much loved by the common people he had walked among, and listened to, before the revolution and after—until the study of magic swallowed him.

She transferred home, and—still keeping her hand on Rel's letter lest it vanish—spent the rest of the day dealing with matters that could not be put off. But she gave them scarce attention. All she saw was the writing on the letter, from Rel, who so very rarely wrote letters: *This is for Atan, in case I don't return.*

After a night of internal battle, she decided she would let herself read a bit at a time, after each onerous duty was performed. That would get her through the drag of hours the faster.

On Geth's island below the Norsunder Base, Rel and his force ranged up along the soft ground with all the grasses and cattails flattened down. He glanced back, his gaze caught by the pure white of Clair's hair among all the various browns and blacks and yellows. She stood among the vagabonds, who had accepted her and the Mearsiean girls with enthusiasm all the stronger for CJ's fervent reviling against Detlev's boys. CJ, in her imaginative and lengthy vituperation, had left out Roy's name, as had Clair: only those two knew that Roy lay up somewhere in or near the fortress looming ahead.

To Rel's right stood Senrid-Montredaun-An, wearing a grim sort of smile that Rel couldn't interpret.

Senrid had agreed to come, because he still believed the alliance was a good idea, truncated as it was. But unspoken was his determination to test himself by leaving Marloven Hess now and then, to prove to himself that he was not indispensable, that Marloven Hess could get along just fine without him—and that he was not going to come back to an assassination team lying in wait.

There was a third reason: his interest in witnessing a battle not on home ground, risking people he knew. His anticipation had nothing to do with entertainment. He knew the cost of violence, had seen it, had suffered it. But not war. And he had to learn, because when Norsunder did come, he was certain that the sword's edge would strike first at the world's militarily strong kingdoms, among which was Marloven Hess. And he had to be ready.

Then there was the anticipation of talking to one of Detlev's boys at last, one who moreover had not just the military but magical training. Only not long after their transfers to Geth, Roy had taken Clair off somewhere to talk, after which he'd vanished on a magic quest of his own.

Well, Senrid was here, and on the front line, at Rel's right. He'd been impressed with what Darian Irad had done in shaping up a scattered gang of volunteers; he had one company at the harbor, closing a pincer around Norsunder's arriving "surprise" fleet, as Geth put a massive navy behind to crush them. Another company—led from the front by Irad—was coming around to flank the fortress.

All they needed was the signal that he had begun.

A volunteer, still wearing his cobbler's apron as protection, stepped up on Rel's left and muttered behind his hand—as if the enemy could hear him— "I only see a few of the stonebacks. You think they're all at the harbor?"

"No, they'll be crouched down behind the wall, is my guess," said Senrid, leaning across Rel. "They'll want to lure us closer by looking undermanned."

"Oh. Right." A confused look. "But . . . aren't we going closer?"

"On the signal," Rel said, pretending not to notice the sweat at the man's hairline, and the way he kept wiping his hands.

This was the worst moment, he'd discovered, the wait. When they began to move, emotions would ignite like dry tinder, and time would speed to a gallop, leaving no room for dread, though fear would never go away.

Atan: I've started this letter five times, until I understood that it would take a lifetime to describe what you mean to me. I'd have to begin with every memory of you, from the day we met in the morvende cave, then when you'd newly regained your kingdom, and you stood there in that gown you'd made yourself, and me in my old work clothes, and you gave me the sword that rests here by my hand.

*Shall I tell you the truth? That I would rather have
had a kiss, even young as we both were? But I would
have been happy with a shepherd's crook, or a pair of
good walking shoes, because they would have come
from your hand.*

A flaming arrow shot skyward from the northeast corner
of the fortress: Irad and his elites had breached the wall at the
back.

Rel raised his arm and tightened his fist. On the far left,
horns winded, and Senrid was first off the mark, Rel a step behind, pulling the rest in a flying wedge as they charged,
screaming.

As Senrid had predicted, Norsundrians popped up from
behind the wall, bows nocked, and let fly.

"Shields!" Rel roared, not that he had to — but it imposed a
pretense of order on the chaos around them. They had drilled
this a hundred times only yesterday.

Everyone along the line jerked up the shields in right or
left arms, each one blurred by the vagabonds to be difficult to
see from the walls of the fortress. Arrows thudded into them.
A few people fell, unused to the shock, but scrambled up
again. Or tried — there were those whose shields had lagged a
heartbeat. They did not get up again, arrows standing up from
their still figures.

"There's the mage," Senrid shouted to Rel

At the extreme right, a man stood next to the tower. Rel
could see his mouth moving, and a faint greenish trace in the
air as he swiped his hand, destroying the illusions over the
shields.

Rel turned his raised hand — again not necessary, as the
Geth archers lifted their bows and shot high into the sky, the
arrows coming down well behind the wall, each arrow with its
bespelled tip that spurted an oily, putrid vapor on contact.
Shouts and curses rose, and the mage vanished to deal with it.

Senrid jogged a few paces away. His head turned sharply
as he muttered, "Ram."

Rel had come to the same conclusion a heartbeat behind
Senrid. He waved, and behind the Geth lines, a whooshing
noise indicated the hay-covered cloths being tossed off the

battering ram suspended between two wagons. They still had to cover the ground to the gate . . .

Rel's magical sense roiled, and he knew two things: that the mage was discovering that the vapor was not illusion, and that every magical spell he used to banish it strengthened the smoky stench, and that Roy — wherever he was — had begun to undo the wards.

The Norsundrian archers along the top shifted their aim to the ram crew. The cobbler gave a hiccup, and fell beside Rel, an arrow in his neck, the arrow having cleared the top of his shield by a finger's breadth. On the other side, several paces away, a woman dropped to her knees, pawing at the arrow buried deep in one thigh.

Now, Rel's commands were needed. "Advance!" he roared, leading the way. "Advance! Shoot!" he bellowed at those who were supposed to be providing covering arrows.

Ragged but determined, his company rallied as Rel's words imposed a veneer of order on the horrifying chaos. And the battering ram teams lumbered toward the gate . . .

But life seems always to lead me back to steel, so here I am, writing by candlelight in a tent, knowing that tomorrow we storm a fortress. I hope I will be sending another note to Tsauderei to tell him to tear this up. Or maybe I'll be able to come back, and we can laugh together over my awkward hand with a letter.

Caris-Merian shrieked, "Wood!"

The vagabonds with the specially prepared arrows aimed at the gates, and shot. Some arrows fell short, others flew over the gate. A few hit the iron reinforcement, but eight or ten thudded into the wood as over the gate, the Norsundrians kept shooting at Rel's team. One by one people fell, some yelling, others in silence.

Then the gate gave a warning creak, and a thousand root-lings exploded out, snaking up and out and over the walls, curling over every obstacle, human or stone, and tangling it tightly.

A gasp of shock from behind, and Rel heard Dak's voice, "I thought it was s'posed to make the slats separate! Who did *that?*"

The archers over the gate pulled swords and began hacking madly at the roots — as the battering ram team ran the last few steps, and boom! Crashed into the gate, which fell into a clattering of iron pieces and young trees blindly seeking to take root.

Rel swallowed. *Now the worst of it begins.*

He had an instant to realize he would never make a commander — he saw nothing but chaos around him — then he noticed Senrid scrambling up the rootlets to get to the wall. Maybe he'd be able to see what was going on and make sense of it. Rel knew one thing for certain: he could charge.

He began to run. Irad's warriors, seeing his tall figure charging, veered to join him in a flying wedge, screaming as they ran. He was the first through the gate, meeting a wall of defenders head on, sword humming in a deadly double arc before him.

> *But if I don't, I want you to know that I will carry those memories of you with me into eternity if I possibly can, because I know that is how long I will love you.*

Arrows hummed in the air, thudding into flesh. Rel's blood thundered in his ears as his vision narrowed to this enemy, and when he dropped, the next. Screams — distant — arrows that dropped to the dirt took root, snapping up into trees that threw out curling tendrils to trip the enemy. Norsundrians shouted in fear, some madly ripping the trees free again, then recoiling as rootlets wiggled in the moist air, seeking soil.

Whose magic was behind that? Rel glanced aside, sweat slinging off his face, to see shock in Caris-Merian's wide eyes. The vagabonds had not made these wooden shafts come to life again. They couldn't. But someone had, and though they were utterly benign, there were so many that the enemy archers wavered as their arrows writhed in the air, dropped, and began to take root.

The two forces met in a snarl of swords, knives, vines and roots.

Then an enormous *C-R-R-R-A-A-A-C-K!* shocked everyone.

The tower at one end of the blood-smeared, tree-strewn

court shot branches skyward, huge boulders falling with deceptive slowness to crash on the ground.

Two horns blared — Norsundrian and Geth — sounding retreat as the wood, several centuries old, stirred to life and threw aside the binding rock.

"Retreat!" Senrid yelled, in Sartoran, and then in Geth. "The fortress is coming down!"

Both sides bolted madly for the gate. Rel tried to spot wounded to help, but others grabbed arms to drag those who could not run, as cracks and booms and crashes resounded behind them, dust shooting skyward.

He felt the transfer ward vanish, the pressure of constrained magic lifting, and the dark magic wall loosening its hold. Rel ran, spotted Irad's young flag bearer, and gestured her onto one of the abandoned wagons to signal the place as a rallying point. He'd gather a perimeter . . .

In Sartor, Atan finished her day, and her tenth reread of the letter, then busied herself far into the night until her eyes burned, and she could not think.

But there was no chance of sleep.

She read through Rel's letter yet again, making a stream of promises to herself, if. *If* he lived. *If* he returned to her. If.

Which fear is worse? Fear for yourself in the middle of agony and violent death, or fear for someone you love as much as life itself? All she could think as she sat at her open window with her head in her hands was how ironic it was, that she had become one of the most respected people in the world, yet she could do nothing whatsoever to bring Rel back safe.

And so it will be when war comes here, an insidious whisper breathed a carrion stench through her soul. *And so it will be here.*

Eighteen

THERE WERE TIMES WHEN Dhana struggled with ambivalence about having taken human form.

Violence was the first and worst, desert air being a far second. Considering how deadly dry desert air was to her kind, it is a measure of how deeply disturbed she was at the violence of war.

She understood the celebration of relief now that it all was over, but not the savage joy that many expressed while standing about staring at the ruined fortress and gleefully discussing the possibility that it had caught Norsundrians in its fall.

She slunk along the perimeter as messengers ran about, clean-up parties marched purposefully, and people in twos and threes walked back and forth staring and exclaiming and telling each other where they'd been standing when the walls fell, and what details they'd seen and how they felt. She didn't want to hear any of it.

Shoulders hunched about her ears, she mooched around in the ruined fortress until the rainstorm tumbling in a dark gray-blue band across the sky finally arrived. As soon as it formed puddles, she was able to transform to her native self and go from splash to splash until she had determined that no human life lay struggling under the jumble of stones and broken trees, whose roots had slowed in their growing once they had buried themselves in the rich soil. The only human forms were the dead who had been killed by other human hands.

She zipped back across the puddles steaming in the sun, transforming to her human self when she reached higher ground. She caught one of the wagons going back to Irad's camp, and brooded.

It had seemed a *good* idea to add a little life magic to the vagabond arrows, especially when she saw CJ and Clair both struggling so hard to understand the vagabond magic, and failing. Dak had told them that it took a while to understand the concept, and Dhana had seen how disappointed they were not to help, especially CJ. So Dhana acted for them.

Stupid idea! She could have caused deaths. Yes, they were Norsundrians, but what if some were like Roy — someone who would leave Norsunder if they could? The answer was simple: she must never bring home magic to wood while she was human. She was both too limited and too volatile in that form.

When the wagon reached the camp, she slipped off like a shadow and sped toward the far end, slowing when she spied Falinneh's bright red hair and brighter clothes. Falinneh was galumphing around with a small child on her back as she squawked like a chicken. A circle of small children laughed and clapped. Dhana flitted past them, looking around until she spied Clair's long white hair. There she was, walking with Roy. When those sea-green eyes turned Dhana's way, Clair left Roy and waited for Dhana to catch up.

Clair said, "The vagabonds are upset. They don't know if that root magic was an effect of their doing, or Roy's. He says he had nothing to do with it."

Dhana hunched more. "Are they going to attack Roy?"

"No, no. Lilah's uncle and Bekani the mage made it real clear that Roy's an ally, and that he ran away from Detlev. Cath was talking to him, and Dak, too, just before you got here. I think they'll work it out. But . . . well, Roy wants to have a private meeting. With us."

"Us?" Dhana asked guiltily. "Us Mearsieans?"

"The allies," Clair said. "CJ went to find Senrid and Rel."

Clair's manner was calm and easy — too easy? Dhana turned, to discover Clair studying the ground, when usually she met your eyes straight on. That usually meant Clair was trying to find the right words. And that meant something serious.

Dhana was not ready for serious. She sidled away, relieved to join Gwen and Sherry. "What's the game?" she asked.

CJ, a short figure in the distance, hopped and waved madly, and when they neared, she pointed at the tent that the Mearsieans had been given in the hastily-expanded camp. "I found Boneribs," she said, pointing at Senrid. "But Rel was talking to the grownups."

They entered the tent as Puddlenose, who had volunteered to be Irad's messenger to the harbor fleet, was finishing up his tale. ". . . all lateen-rigged, narrow draught vessels. They say they have big square riggers that go across the ocean to far islands with trade, but in this archipelago, it's all fore-and-aft rigging, see, so as soon as the word went out—they were fast."

Senrid said, "It's been too long since I sailed. Can you put what you saw into land terms?"

Puddlenose scratched his head through his thatch of thick brown hair. "I can try. Call it a cavalry gallop, the smaller, faster sail up front, carrying smoke boxes. Don't ask about the magic—"

"I know the magic for those," Senrid said. "Surely Norsunder had a mage to dispel 'em?"

"That's just it, they didn't. It was supposed to be a surprise attack, and they couldn't get a mage there, on account of something they called a ward. So the small sail threaded among the enemy ships, arrows going every which way, most of 'em fire arrows. Looked like a rain of falling stars from a distance, until the smoke got too thick. But not so thick they couldn't see the big ships coming. Then came ramming, boarding, fighting. They were jammed up so tight that the warriors sent to the harbor over land climbed right over the rails, and . . ."

He smashed his hands together, grinning. "When that ward thing disappeared, the Norsundrians who had transfer tokens used them and abandoned ship. After that it was a mop-up and putting fires out." Puddlenose grimaced. "A lot of ships burned. Both sides. They let a lot of them burn. They don't have a wood guild like at home—I guess there is so much wood here, underwater as well as on land, that it's easier to build new ships."

"What can we learn?" Senrid asked.

Puddlenose scratched his head again, looked at the sea salt griming his nails, and grimaced. "That, you'll by rights have to get from one of their captains. Too different here from what I'm used to. Roy! Glad to see you again," Puddlenose said with his ready smile.

And though Roy had been bracing for any kind of reaction, from hatred to awkwardness, somehow Puddlenose's easy acceptance set the tone.

"The elevens scattered like bugs. Good riddance," CJ said, rubbing her hands. "Is it time to plan a party? We taught the little kids about pie fights, but nary an eleven stuck his ugly mug around to receive a spoilt-egg-overripe-cherry supremo." She mimed splatting someone in the face with a pie. "But if we can teach the Geth kids the art of the pie . . ." She looked from Clair to Roy, and her smile vanished. "Uh oh."

Roy had leaned back, eyes closed, his homely face so drawn with exhaustion he looked ill.

Clair said to Roy, "Tell them about the fortress magic."

Roy opened his eyes. "I dismantled everything to the first layer of the lattice. But I couldn't take it all the way. They can rebuild if they want."

Senrid snapped his fingers. "Foundation artifact wasn't there, right?"

The others shifted so that Roy sat in the center of a semicircle, a thin, weary looking figure, his clothes still mud-splashed. Roy said to Senrid, "Siamis warned me that it might be mirrored."

Roy took in the reactions, but only saw whispers and sour looks at the mention of Siamis, except from Clair, who stared into space as though something of import lay in the air.

"Where's the original, do you know?" Senrid asked, his fingers drumming restlessly on his knee.

"Yes." Roy sat back, seeing complete confusion — except in Clair, who studied her hands. "Siamis told me. It's in Norsunder-Beyond. And I think I know where."

CJ's expressive black brows drew in a line as she stared at Roy. "Won't they squelch you if you turn up there?"

"Probably," Roy said. "But I don't see anyone else volunteering. And I wouldn't ask," he added hastily. "None of you know how to deal with it, and none of you are non-human. At least I've been there a couple times."

Senrid said, "Wait. What's being non-human got to do

with Norsunder-Beyond?"

"The wards and traps are for humans," Roy said. "Not sure why that is. Detlev never told us."

The mention of Detlev got grimaces and spitting motions from the Mearsieans, then CJ said in a tentative voice, "Could it be that dark magic is ineffective against the magic races?"

Senrid said, "Or it's a trap."

"But what if the non-humans don't have any magic in their human form?" CJ asked, sidling a glance from Falinneh to Dhana. "How do they protect themselves?"

"They don't," Roy said. "I just mentioned it as an existing condition, something else that Siamis told me. I'm hoping I can find some clues to . . ."

Dhana slipped out and ran.

She hated remorse. Her fingers brushed over her ribs under her thin cotton tunic. There were times she hated being human because of the tangled emotions you couldn't reach in and yank out.

Somewhere far to the right, music began, a waterfall of sweet silvery tones as someone played on an instrument made up of tiny bells. Then some glaziers, who were mourning fallen volunteers, tapped on a glass instrument with silver hammers, and Dhana shivered. She had first been drawn out of the water into human form because of music. In human form she could *hear* instead of merely feeling its air currents. She could dance it out. But her feet would not fly now, though the music beckoned.

"Dhana." The deep voice startled her, and she looked up. Rel was coming her way, having left the briefing in the command tent.

"Hi, Rel," she said.

"Have you seen —"

Rel broke off, startled by a puff of air that smelled of home, and Lilah Selenna dropped to her knees, the faint sparked of transfer magic blurring her outline then vanishing. Her freckled brown skin blanched to a sickly shade, and she breathed fast.

When her puffy, red-rimmed eyes opened again, Dhana said, "You're too late if you wanted to be in the battle. It's done."

Lilah was too distraught to hear her. She looked up at Rel. "Tsauderei said he'd use the notecase Peitar gave you as a

Destination." Her voice cracked on her brother's name.

Rel put his hand to his inner pocket. "Does he want it back? I know I haven't sent any news. I was waiting to learn about a possible new effect of vagabond magic —"

He stopped when Lilah shut her eyes, her mouth trembling. Fresh tears glimmered along her eyelids and tracked down her face. She gulped a sob, then said, "Where is my uncle?"

Rel gazed nonplussed, then pointed. "Right across there, in that structure. Shall I take you?" he added kindly.

Lilah jerked her wobbly chin down in a nod. Dhana trailed behind, wondering what she ought to do or say. Lilah's woe was a disturbing distraction from her inward struggle.

For Darian Irad, who had not seen Lilah since they'd parted on the border between Sartor and Norsunder Base after they'd escaped, Lilah's appearance was a shock. The fact that she hadn't aged since then threw him back emotionally to those terrible days, a jolt rather like the occasional mild quakes that shook the islands, rattling things and throwing one's balance off.

He was too tired for question. "Lilah?" he said, straightening up from the map.

"Peitar's *dead*," Lilah wailed.

And that brought the hard jolt, causing him to sink back onto a camp chair. "What?"

Rel's first thought was that he was done here. But a sharp jab of regret kept him from moving. Peitar, dead? He had to know what had happened.

Lilah sobbed out what little she knew about Peitar's disappearance, as those in the background left quietly, leaving only those from Sartorias-deles, Miri, and Bekani, who held hands while watching the speakers. They did not comprehend any of the words. It was the distress in Irad's face, and Lilah's frantic sobbing that kept them there.

Lilah's voice rose. "You promised," she cried unsteadily. "If . . . *if*. You would come home."

Darian Irad stared at Lilah, his heartbeat hammering as hard as it had during the height of battle. For an instant that seemed to stretch infinitely long he stood poised between two utterly different roads, one so overgrown he'd all but forgotten it. Then he had to breathe, and the noise of the celebrative (and mourning) camp roared in his ears. Bekani gazed at him, Miri at her side, both with wide, questioning eyes.

At first he wanted to shield himself behind his command here. Except that the task he'd been hired for had ended with the falling of the fortress and the scattering of what was left of the Norsundrians. Oh, the survivors would no doubt reappear again, and there was the half-burned harbor, but these were all problems for the locals.

He was now a free man, with a wife and child and the prospect of making a home. Peitar's promise had once been an exquisitely bitter irony, as Peitar would have been his heir if Derek Diamagan had not come along. But he had. And Peitar had believed Diamagan's idiotic rhetoric—and after about as bloody a civil war as any in Sarendan's history, Darian Irad had gone into exile, with Peitar insisting that if his kingship failed, Irad was to return.

Death was the ultimate decider.

Darian Irad regarded Lilah in silence, loathing the thought of resuming a burden he had gradually come to believe better left behind. And yet one could not eradicate memories of one's earliest home—the good as well as the bad. He was aware, as one moment streamed into one hundred, that in some part of his mind he was already sorting out the priorities.

"Very well," he said to Lilah, after that painful pause. "Under conditions."

Lilah gulped, wiped her eyes on her sleeve, then dropped a coin into his hand. "Tsauderei said to give you that. It will bring you to us."

Rel glanced from Irad to his wife and daughter, then back to Lilah. "How about something to drink before you face the return magic? I know the Mearsieans would like to see you." He led Lilah away.

Irad didn't even notice them leave, though Miri watched Lilah until she vanished among the tents.

When they were alone, Bekani said, "It's Sarendan. They want you back?"

"Yes."

"Though once they would have been glad to see you dead."

He gazed down at the map without seeing it. "A lot has changed since then. More than I knew. My nephew was assassinated while traveling. Something to do with magic."

His tone sharpened. The old hatred of magic was hard to shed. His wife was a mage, and he worked hard to make his peace with that which he did not understand. But old habit died hard.

He saw her stricken expression. "I promised Peitar once. But I won't stay," he said quickly. "I might be back by nightfall if there's resistance to my turning up again. Certainly won't fight for it. But Peitar's boy is still a baby. And though much has changed, not everything. I can guess which families would love to put up a regency, for all the wrong reasons."

Bekani's eyes blurred. She knew it was unlikely the unknown people of Sarendan would return him to her. She would need time to prepare their daughter for the prospect of life on another world, once he deemed it safe for them to come.

She said, "Close the outside entrance. There is no danger, and no need: before you go, we shall have a little time to ourselves."

Nineteen

DHANA SLUNK ALONG BEHIND Rel and Lilah, the latter uttering a disjointed stream of details between chest-wrenching
sobs. Dhana's steps slowed. She didn't want to hear more.
They slowed more when she saw Clair standing alone, as the
rest of the Mearsieans closed sympathetically around Lilah.

Clair didn't say anything, or do anything. She stared down
at the ground.

Dhana made it all the way to her, and still Clair didn't look
up. Dhana said, "You knew it was me?"

Clair raised eyes the color of spring leaves. "I know the
feel of the Lake magic," she whispered.

Dhana's shoulders jerked under her ears. "I thought it
would stop things. Not make the walls crash down. I don't
know anything about how buildings work."

Clair looked down at the shiny grasses, nearly blue-green,
in the rich reddish mud. Then she said, "I would never ask it
of you. But you do have protection that no one has."

Dhana glowered. "This is not our world. Horsefeathers'
world is also not ours. None of it is our problem."

"But it *is* our problem," Clair said in a low voice. "Anything to do with Norsunder is everyone's problem. And this . .
. Dhana, I've been having nightmares about Five, and flying
horses, and lightning, and when Roy asked about the . . . the

thing he doesn't seem to want to even mention, I *knew* something was tying it all together."

Dhana grimaced. "You think I should go with him."

"That's up to you. He seems to think the presence of someone like you can protect him. I don't understand it, and I don't think he does either, but it sounds a bit like . . . like the vagabond magic, I think," Clair said slowly.

Dhana's face prickled with shame, because she knew very well exactly how vagabond magic connected, but she didn't have the human words for it. "I'll do it," she said quickly — before she could run away and dive into the ocean.

It made separation slightly easier when the first aide-de-camp let back in to Irad's command center reported that a big celebration was being planned, with Irad to be guest of honor.

Bekani could see how much he loathed the idea. "Go ahead," she said.

Irad gripped her shoulders, touching his forehead to hers. "You sure?"

"Miri will be distracted. It'll be fine," she murmured, doing her best to smile. "Just send for us as soon as you can."

Irad peered into her face. "You're sure about that? You'd come to my world?"

"We're a family," she said, though she did not want the babe growing inside her to be born in a foreign world that sounded so cold and terrifying. "And perhaps it will not be for so very long."

"It might not even be a day," Darian Irad said, kissed her hard a last time, hugged Miri and tousled her hair, then spoke to the people waiting outside. "My second in command will take my place. I have to see to some matters on my home world."

And, with her kiss still on his lips, and the touch of his daughter's hair on his fingers, he used the transfer token.

It hurt as if he'd been hurled from the back of a galloping horse. When he came out of it, he found Tsauderei waiting, looking older and uglier than ever. "Still alive?" Irad wheezed out the words as soon as he could speak.

Tsauderei's myriad wrinkles shifted into lines of silent

laughter. "Every day I wake up is a surprise," he said.

By then the transfer reaction was beginning to wear off. Darian Irad became aware of the Destination tiles, and the room, and the familiar structure of the royal palace, though it had changed considerably from his day. But nothing could change the subtlety of scents: those struck deep in memory to his troubled childhood, and all its ambitions and expectations.

He met Tsauderei's gaze. "I don't want to be here. I'll ride out if they want a fight."

Tsauderei looked tired. "The nobles signed agreement to Peitar's proclamation. You are king if you want it. Or even if you don't. Most of them will probably be relieved to have you back. Things are . . . different these days."

Darian Irad said, "Regent. And, we'll see."

He refused to discuss politics with a mage, especially this old enemy, who he knew had worked against him despite all laws separating magic from politics and agreed to by both mages and kings.

He turned his back and walked out, pausing only to ask a red-eyed servant, "Is Captain Leonos still here?"

The young man looked confused. "You mean Peace Chief Leonos?"

Darian thought, why not begin with Leonos, whatever he was called now? "Yes."

"You'll find him at the Peace Patrol's wing," and waved in the direction of the old city guard barracks.

Ah. Same place, maybe some of the same people, different title. Darian crossed the palace, stopping at the offices behind the kitchen, where he startled a knot of older servants, younger ones looking at him in puzzlement. His gaze sought Mirah's tall, gaunt, long-nosed form. She was now as gray as he was. She wore a steward's robe.

Her gaze widened when she saw him. "Come with me for a conference with Leonos?" he asked.

She looked around at the uncomprehending faces, then set down the chalkboard she held in her hand. In silence he and Steward Mirah paced side by side the short distance across the back court to the old city guard garrison, where Leonos sat in his former office.

When he saw Darian, he leaped to his feet with the alacrity of one of his young recruits, despite the distinguished silver hair receding from the top of his domed head. "Your majesty,"

Leonos whispered, eyes stark.

"Not yet," Darian said. "Probably never if I have my way. Sit down, you two," he added, taking one of the chairs that sat before Leonos's desk. "Let me be plain. I don't want to be here. I have a good life on Geth now. I have a family. But I made Peitar a promise once, one I never thought I'd have to keep."

He didn't give them time to comment, but turned to the steward. "Mirah, I didn't understand until I lost my crown how much a steward comprehends everything going on that is invisible from the throne."

Mirah pursed her lips.

"You were instrumental in undermining my government."

She blushed, but did not deny it.

Darian turned to Leonos. "In spite of the trickery at the end that felled me and my command, I'm convinced we could have survived it but for you turning on me, and taking the entire guard over to Diamagan's rabble."

Leonos stirred, old anger flushing up his jaw.

Darian waved a hand. "I know why you did it. I'm not raking up old history to point fingers of blame. I'm convinced you threw yourself not behind Derek Diamagan so much as behind Peitar. Am I right?"

Leonos's brow cleared. "Yes."

"That's what I thought. So, to my questions. First, I refuse to come back as king. If the two of you can't accept me back as regent until Peitar's boy is old enough to hold a throne, then I'm off, and I wish you well. But if you can, I need a frank report on the state of the kingdom."

Mirah pursed her lips.

Leonos shifted in his chair again, cleared his throat, then said, "Permission to speak freely?"

"Right now, we're just three people talking."

Leonos met Mirah's gaze. She brought her chin down in a nod, and Leonos said, "Here it is. Things could be worse. It was looking that way for a while, before Derek was killed. We were becoming an army, all to fight Norsunder. Like in your day, but . . ."

"Let me guess. The nobles were to pay the taxes to support this mighty army, and they were readying for civil war on their estates. And Peitar was probably the last to know what was going on behind his back."

Leonos's brows lifted. "Yes! That's pretty much a fair summation. Then Derek was assassinated, right after a very nasty battle at the southwestern border. Many people lost faith in the army idea." He paused to rub his jaw. "This is hard."

"Tell him about the courts," Mirah muttered out of the side of her mouth, as if Darian wasn't sitting right there, listening.

"Fact is, my guard—now peace patrollers—are disheartened. We can arrest malefactors, but they have the right to challenge before a court of peers, and the only ones we can hold are capital cases. Mostly, it works out all right, but a purse snatch over two tinkets can tie up a court for days, if you get arguers. And some places, well, thieves have learned how to argue."

"What authority do you have?"

"None," Leonos said bitterly.

Mirah said in a tone of reproof, "Peitar's laws are based on restitution. And those arrested for anything but murder are free until their case is called. We don't have huge prisons. People can go back to work while waiting."

Leonos sighed. "The courts in some places are backed up months. Some say years. It can take ages before a smart thief is called up, and then *we* must find them. On some of the estates, the nobles are taking the law into their own hands—"

Darian waved a hand. "I already know how, and who, are acting like petty kings. I also know how to deal with the nobles. All right. If you two are behind me, Leonos, you will have the power to arrest them, and keep them. You can put them to work—*hard* work—while their case is pending. I could see from a single glance over the walls that repairs are neglected. Arrestees for capital crimes can start there. Petty crimes, put 'em to work in the kitchens, the fish docks, the guard stables."

A big grin spread across Leonos's face.

Mirah, whose staff heard what the nobles said behind Peitar's back when they gathered in court each New Year's to repeat the vows that about half didn't believe in, permitted a small, grim smile to curve her lips.

Darian looked from one to the other, then hit the tops of his knees with his hands. "That's a start at your end. I'll go get rid of the mage. Get the heralds to send out criers. Summon court. Let's clean things up a little, eh?"

"Peace at last," Mirah said with satisfaction, rising to her feet.

Darian thought of the warnings about Norsunder, but that could wait. One problem at a time.

He left the two there to confer — and no doubt pull in their cronies for a good gossip — but he was fine with that. Get the word out faster.

He returned to the palace alone, to be stopped in the kitchen courtyard by an old woman, instantly recognizable to him, though she had aged: Lizana, once his sister's nurse, then Lilah's. They had had a difficult relationship, but now, with the perspective of experience — of parenthood — he recognized the wariness in her lined face, though she stood respectfully, and bowed at his approach. "Lizana," he said.

He did not know what she heard in his voice, but her expression eased fractionally. "I came," she said, her voice thin, "to understand, if I can, your place in Ian's life."

"Will it make a difference to tell you that I left a little daughter behind, to whom I hope to return?"

"Yes," she said. "Yes." She bowed again and turned to go.

He said, "Three generations, now. Have you not earned honorable retirement? There are surely plenty of young nannies."

She smiled. "Nannies, yes. But I believe every young creature needs a mother. Or as near as can get."

Not until middle age had he come to understand what she meant: it had less to do with age or gender than with the unconditional love and tenderness that he himself had been denied by a grandfather determined to raise the ideal war king. "Yes —"

The patter of footsteps forestalled further conversation, but they understood one another well enough.

A small boy irrupted into the court, and slowed to a stop, head tipped back as he studied Darian earnestly. "Are you my great-uncle? Did you come back?"

Darian took in the small, earnest face so much like Peitar's. Ian's intelligent, inquisitive expression, still with the echo of grief puckering his brows, evoked Peitar when he was not so very much older, and he'd lost his mother, the sister Darian still missed. "I am."

"A big boy shot my father," Ian said. "I don't know why."

"Tell me about your father," Darian said to his namesake as he dropped to one knee beside him. "What was he like?"

Twenty

REL STAYED UNTIL THE Mearsieans had calmed Lilah down, got her to eat and drink, and then surrounded her to wish her well as she braced for the transfer back to Sartorias-deles.

Rel checked the command tent, and discovered that Darian Irad was gone, leaving Bekani in command, their daughter sitting unhappily on a cushion beside her.

Rel walked out again, and spotted Roy in earnest talk with the Mearsieans. Whatever it was about, Rel doubted he could help. He was finished. Promises kept, orders fulfilled. He retrieved his travel pack, pulled out the transfer token that Peitar had given him, and braced for transfer.

No surprise that it took him to Sarendan. Peitar would have wanted a debriefing. Rel shook his head in regret as he drank down the infusion the page brought, then handed the cup back, and said, "Is the mage Tsauderei here?"

"Oh, yes," the sober-faced page said. Her eyes were puffy and swollen. "He's still here."

Rel found the old mage surrounded by papers and books. "I'd like to go back to Sartor," he said, and on Tsauderei's nod, "but first, what happened? Lilah's story had more holes than a net."

"And I cannot fill them." Tsauderei threw down his quill and sat back, rolling his shoulders. Rel heard pops and cracks.

"There is no reason for Peitar's murder. He was on some kind of magic quest that was doomed from the start. It made no sense to anyone but him—" And Tsauderei gave a fairly accurate summation of his conversations with Peitar.

"Music on a single note from a physical location?" Rel repeated. "Do you think he was going mad?"

"It's a possibility that I will no longer raise," Tsauderei said, waving his hand toward the rest of Miraleste's royal palace. "It'd achieve nothing useful, so we're saying he was taking a small trip to visit old ruins and get away from the pressures of kingship."

Rel said, "That casts no aspersions on his memory."

"Exactly. It's entirely possible he wasn't mad, only his quest was. He knew as well as any of us that the Ancient Sartoran records are misleading because they're full of metaphor, and we don't understand their context." Tsauderei gave Rel a brief smile. "The matter's done with. You did your part. Go home, Rel. Atan is waiting. I'm on my way home myself."

Home. It was so simple a word, but the implications could be so very complex.

Tsauderei sent him directly to the private Destination in the residence wing of Atan's royal palace. When he shook off the reaction, he walked out, spotted Gehlei, the one-time guard who had saved Atan's life as an infant, and was now the royal steward. "There you are," Gehlei said gruffly.

"I'm back," he said, hands out, and at her grim smile, "where's—"

"Gehlei, the transfer ward alerted me—*Rel*?"

He turned to face Atan at the other end of the hall. She started toward him, lips parted, hands outflung.

Rel dropped his gear a moment before she impacted him chest to chest, driving him back a step as he gave a laugh of surprise. Heat flared through him, and his arms closed around her.

It was a crushing hug, but she was tall, big-boned and strong—she gripped him back, and lifted her face. Their noses met before their lips did, for she—raised by Tsauderei and Gehlei, who had never had children, and had deemed it right to keep an appropriate distance from Sartor's young queen— had no memory of ever having been kissed.

The idea of it had always seemed dubious, she'd once

thought, but that was before the touch of Rel's lips against hers, warm, then devouring, sending fire scorching through every muscle and nerve. She kissed him fiercely back, her breath shaky, and everywhere his tongue touched lit her mouth into urgency. Still holding him, she backed toward the door to a room. They stumbled, neither letting go, their bodies pressed together, hands spread to touch everywhere at once.

Gehlei followed, smiling grimly to herself; she didn't give a spit for the first circle's expectations concerning their queen. Rel was what her duckling wanted, and at last, it seemed, her duckling had fledged up.

Gehlei listened with deep approval to the frantic noises of passion, and shut the door on them. Then she went downstairs to summarily clear Atan's schedule. She would be dragged back to duty again much too soon. Today was hers.

And his.

Twenty-one

Geth-deles and Norsunder-Beyond

"I'LL GO," DHANA SAID to Roy. "I'm not really human. Only wearing this shape. What do I have to do?"

Roy was sitting in a big tent with the Mearsieans and Senrid, eating savory rice-flour rolls stuffed with crunchy greens and a delicious fish sauce. Rain thudded into the tent walls and streamed down.

Dhana longed to escape and dance in the rain, but she stood firm.

Roy set aside his plate and squinted up at her. "You sure? You don't look sure. And nobody should be pushed into going with me."

"I'm sure. Yeah." Dhana couldn't explain that Lilah's grief, and her own guilt, had prompted her offer. "Tell me more so I know what to do."

"I was about the ask the same thing," Senrid said. "The first of several hundred questions."

A few laughed, and Senrid smiled, but he wasn't joking. Roy knew it. He was far too tired to deal with Senrid, whose simmering energy could be felt across the tent.

"I don't know much for the first question, and I can

probably guess at the second: I don't know why Siamis left, or what he's doing," Roy said to Senrid, then turned his gaze to Dhana and the rest of the Mearsieans. "But I believe what he told me, especially as so far, it's proved to be true. He warned me about the mirrored artifact, and the connection with Aldau-Rayad, contrived by a now-forgotten Norsundrian warrior-mage centuries ago, who thought to build a power base on both worlds. Siamis also said that he cannot enter the inner levels of Norsunder Beyond again without risking wards bound to his name. But there are none for me."

He paused, frowning into the distance, and Dhana felt everyone's gazes as a moral weight.

Roy glanced up. "He also told me that there's a, uh, call it a door to the outer reaches of the Beyond, and I know where it is. What he didn't tell me—maybe he doesn't know either—is why my going in contact with someone non-human will make me invisible in those outer reaches. He thinks it has something to do with those at the center, where your physical form really is not there, but in . . . call it a holding continuity."

Everyone stirred at the mention of the "center", evoking the old, horrible stories about soul-eaters who dwelt there, a ceaseless unsleeping evil existing beyond time.

He cleared his throat, then said, "The sooner we get it over with, the better."

"Someone has to be reporting what happened," Senrid said.

Roy knew that if it was Efael they were reporting to, they might be showing up any time. "All the more reason for in and out. Now."

"In and out," Clair said, her voice rising a little, and to Dhana, "we'll be home, waiting."

Senrid then said, "I hope when you come back, you'll stay long enough to report. Whatever we can learn can only help."

Roy doubted that—but he agreed, figuring that if he survived, he'd deal with the inevitable questions, or Senrid would pursue him until he got whatever it was that he wanted.

Roy studied Dhana, a girl of about twelve with bird bones and short flyaway hair. He hadn't known her background, only that she liked to dance, and that she danced unlike any trained dancer he'd ever seen, less muscular skill and focused grace, and more natural, somewhere between a bird and thistledown on a breeze. That was its own type of art, and he appreciated art, but what kind of mind lay behind it?

"We have to make a short transfer first," he said to her. "Ready?"

He saw her brace up her thin body under its loose tunic and trousers. She, as did CJ and several of the other Mearsieans, went barefoot most of the year round. He remembered that CJ made a virtue of it for some reason, but this girl wore her thin, loose clothes like a sop to custom.

They transferred to the hidey near the houseboat so he could scout. He left her there, and then came back when he'd determined it was safe. No sign of David anywhere. Dhana looked around, giddy with delight. A house right on the water! Not quite a ship — it didn't seem to be going anywhere, as it had no masts or sails — but water all around. How she loved it!

Roy walked around it quickly once more, then returned. "Dhana, how much do you want to know about the Beyond?"

"I don't want details," she said quickly. "Enough so I don't get caught."

He rubbed the side of his thumb against his lower jaw as he stared out the window, then he said, "Here's what you need to know. It's a playground for those who made it. Time and distance can't be trusted. Nothing can, because the nature of the magic is to use your own emotions against you. Memories, if the magic can get that far. Try to remember that it's akin to a dreamland, where nothing is real."

"Got it," she said.

"This is the next most important thing to remember: we can't speak when we're in the Beyond. Too much of a chance of being overheard, and we'd never know it." He wasn't going to explain about the traps called spider webs and windows, that caught sound and movement. "Do you know how to do a mind-shield?"

She dipped her head in a cautious nod.

"Can you imagine a door opening in it, and me on the other side?"

"Yes," she said. "But first we have to have a garland."

"A garland?" Roy repeated.

Dhana dipped her head again, her flyaway, sand-colored hair drifting down by her pointed chin. She had learned from Child of Autumn how to weave a protection from living flowers, after which you put the blooms back into the ground and let them take root. *The humans say that flowers are innocent,* Autumn had said. *We know they just are. Their magic is life, and life their magic. They breathe out purity, and will give you strength when you are in the human world, and protection against life-destroying magic.*

In those days, Dhana hadn't been human very long, and the word "innocent" seemed silly, or rather obvious: you didn't do, or know, a wicked thing, you were innocent. It was one of the many words she still didn't truly understand, or even think about. But protections, she did understand.

"Put around our hands. Protect us," she said.

Roy glanced out the open windows toward the bluff, where wildflowers bloomed in profligate colors after all the rains.

Dhana flitted out, her footsteps barely audible, and in a breathtaking leap, cleared the ramp entirely. She landed in the grass, twirled around, arms raised and palms turned upward as if receiving the light drops of rain beginning to fall, then she dropped to her knees and began gathering flowers. Roy watched, wondering if different plants contained different properties unknown to mages and others alike. After all, herbs contained various health properties.

But she didn't seem to have any other criteria than long stems. Once she'd gathered an armful, she brought them into the houseboat and swiftly wove them together into three garlands. She held one out to Roy, plopped one on her own head, where it dropped rakishly over an ear, and then kept the third about her wrist.

At her glance upward, he put his garland on his head. It smelled fresh and sweet. He didn't believe it had magical properties, and she certainly hadn't been weaving spells – that he'd seen, anyway. But the sweetness would be a good contrast to the dead, stale air in the outer Beyond.

"This one goes around our hands," she said. "To keep them together."

He would only be invisible while touching her. He welcomed anything that helped keep their grip solid. Dhana held out her thin, grubby hand, still covered with the rich soil from the bluff. He took firm hold, said the spell that he'd hoped he would never in his life use, and they stared at the black door that opened.

He straightened his shoulders. Fear crawled in his guts, making his forehead prickle with sweat. He was tired, but dared not take the time to rest. She sent him a troubled look — he shifted his weight to take the step — she gave a little hop — and they were through.

She curled her toes under her, trying to look everywhere at once for the danger she knew threatened. Worse, she dreaded seeing all the ugliness of Norsunder and that's exactly what hit her: a vast plain strewn with the devastation of war. In all directions, burned houses, rubble, dead people lying mangled. She would have jumped back except that the dark door was gone, and Roy tugged at her hand. His profile was grim, his eyes narrowed as if he had a headache.

Instinct caused her to close her mind inside a shell, lest it be ripped away in a howling wind of fury and despair and malice. She knew it was out there; she could feel it through every nerve ending.

This is what it is to be truly human. The thought whispered from somewhere. Memory? They passed by a tumbled wall of dry stone, a fortress, it looked like — devastated in some war — and when she turned her head, cringing in expectation of dungeons, instruments of torture and the distorted results, there it was in merciless detail. She recoiled, nearly losing Roy's hand, which tightened around her fingers. She gasped in the dry, lifeless air, feeling that already her body withered.

Roy gave her hand a shake. She turned her head. His brows lifted in question, and she remembered she was supposed to leave a mental door open. But what if this was a trick, and he was one of them after all, and he would send that howling wind to scour out her mind and she would wither away to ash?

He stopped, his tense face worried. She could see by the flicker of his eyelids that he was trying to think past her mind-shield. She braced herself and tried to imagine the tiniest knothole — and there was his thought: *What are you making yourself see?*

That surprised her: *Making myself?*

:The weapon here is your own emotions. They want you seeing what you fear most.

The killing dryness — the war and devastation — the ugliness humans have made, the ugliness humans are . . . She tried not to let the thoughts run the foul images through her, but she couldn't stop them. Couldn't catch them.

:Water.

That was *his* thought: *See water all around you.*

She opened her eyes onto a sea of red, thick, clotted, lapping at her toes. It was a sea of blood. She sucked in a breath to scream, remembered about sound, and choked it down to a whimper.

:Dhana. Whatever you see, your own fears give you.

She shaped an answer: *You don't see an ocean of blood? All their wars and torture filling it —*

:Your magic is keeping us from moving, Dhana. We could wander here in the outer Beyond forever. Fight the images with good memories. You have good memories! See those.

But she couldn't. When she looked at memory, the first image was Irenne, who she'd enjoyed squabbling with, now dead, and that silly Prince Jonnicake and all the tricks they pulled on him, without realizing that he was a victim, too, of his horrible, selfish mother —

She wanted to weep for all the mean things that she'd done, just like Norsunder, she was human and evil — she hunched up, cowering down, down —

She smelled life.

She opened her eyes, which were half-blinded by the garland that had slipped down over her forehead, and here were the flowers about her wrist. She buried her face in them, and she remembered her lake, seen through her newly human eyes, the quiet waters rilling outward from the waterfall, bubbles floating on the air, trembling with iridescence while CJ's pretty voice rang through the woods in a ballad.

Dhana smelled life.

Her garland breathed fragrant life. *Oh. This is the purity Autumn meant.*

She opened her eyes again, looking down at her hand twined with Roy's, at the garland wreathed in soft light.

His thought came: *Your magic is stronger than mine here. We could navigate forever among our fears here unless you can see your way out.*

:How do I see my way out?

:I'll do that. Siamis told me how to navigate. You just see good memories. I can do the rest.

See good memories? If she were home, her magic would be strong! But it had been strong — too strong — at that fortress.

She tugged the garland down to block her eyes altogether, gathered the blossoms' light to her, then flung it outward over that sea of blood still lapping at her toes, and the light expanded in a ring of glory, banishing that terrible sea.

A deep boom, too deep to hear, trembled through them.

Roy had expected to be thrown back into memory, and had been. Everything as Siamis had warned, though no one can ever truly predict how much pain hurts. But he looked on those memories of the boys—those still there, those who had left—and walked through them all, banishing each with a firm thought: You *are deceit*.

Now they stood in what appeared to be the compound on Five. Only the quality of light, somewhat flat, and the way dust hung suspended in the air testified to the falsity.

He walked into Detlev's office, ignoring the furnishings, the obvious place for traps. Instead, he stepped to the window, and was going to reach through when he felt a slight tug from Dhana. He stilled, looking her way. Her head had turned. Her lips parted, then closed, and he heard her inner voice: *Someone's here.*

:*Where?*

:*I don't know. I'm afraid to look.*

:*Is the someone moving?*

:*No.*

:*Can you show me?*

To his surprise—and sharp dismay—she tugged him toward the door, through that, and in two steps they had crossed the wide lawn and entered the building that housed prisoners on Five. Roy looked from Dhana, who stood with the garland hanging over her resolutely closed eyes, to the door, then cautiously extended a tendril:

:*Leskandar Rhoderan?*

It had to be another deceit, a trap. Les had been mortally wounded by David. They'd never heard anything more about him, so had assumed he was dead. Roy made an effort not to see the door, which would be a trap. He extended his inner sense, and saw the ward surrounded Les Rhoderan. He considered how to break it, then caught himself. This is not real space, this is not real space, this is not real space.

Treating the ward as if it warded real space was a trap. Everything was full of traps. He made an effort and imposed a different space, the garden of windows that Detlev had

created to mirror the Garden of the Twelve, and stepped into
it. This was where Detlev had brought the boys to teach them
about the untrustworthiness of sight and sense in the Beyond.
Roy reached through one of the waiting windows, extended
his hand toward Les Rhoderan, and now there were three in
the garden.

Rhoderan had been sitting on his haunches, head on his
knees, the remnants of his clothing tattered and bloodstained.
The edge of his jaw was too defined, and one of the splendid
cheekbones so sharp it was skull-like. Roy could tell that Efael
had let his Black Knives loose on the young man, and nothing
healed here — ever.

Roy's head throbbed. That pain was real, and mounting
steadily with his effort to concentrate. He used the window,
and reached for the shimmery, carved-wood flute whose
mirror he had seen under the fortress. He sensed that the last
fingers to touch it belonged to Detlev. Warning flared through
Roy, and he shouted mentally at Dhana: *Out, out, out!*

He touched Les Rhoderan, then the three of them fell
through to the deck of the houseboat.

Dhana lay where she was, breathing with the flowers
mashed to her face, but her breath was fast and unsteady.
With a wild look, she sprang up, launched through the
window into the water, and vanished.

Roy threw himself onto his knees beside Les Rhoderan,
who had curled up, bleeding sluggishly from at least ten
wounds — besides the stab wound that David had given him,
which he could see now, with further training, was actually
not mortal. But it had carried the blood-knife magic, which let
Efael get to him before Detlev could.

With an infinite effort, Les Rhoderan turned his head, his
gummy, blood-crusted eyes cracking. He gazed up at Roy,
who gazed back, unsure what to do.

"Roy." It was a voiceless whisper. "Tell Caris . . ."

"What?" Roy bent closer.

Les's bruised, cracked lips moved. Was that "brother" or
"other" or even "cover"?

Roy waited, but no more came. He reached mentally, but
Les was already straining against the blood-knife binding. Roy
broke it with the spell Lilith had taught him as a safeguard.

And with a last breath of ineffable relief, Les Rhoderan
died.

Roy gazed down at his body, utterly wrung. So many questions streamed through his mind: what Detlev had really wanted when he'd sicced the boys onto Les; what Efael wanted, besides to thwart Detlev; how many lies either of them hid, how much truth they'd twisted. And now Roy had a new responsibility, thought there was almost nothing he desired less. But someone had to be told about Les — and he knew that Caris-Merian and Les's loyal followers would want to gather for the Disappearance ritual.

He was beyond even the shortest transfer, beyond any effort. But he had to make one anyway. He looked down at the flute that he had gone into Norsunder to fetch. It blurred, doubling in his pain-hazed vision.

Roy sat down heavily on a wooden locker, looking away from Les Rhoderan's still form, took the flute in both hands, and gathered the last of his strength. He found himself hoping that the spell wouldn't work, because it would make the resulting questions so much easier. But the moment he finished the spell, he felt the snap of inward magic that completed destruction of the fortress wards half a day's travel away.

That flute had been hidden on another world for four thousand years. The Geth fortress was first laid down maybe eight or nine centuries ago, its protective wards anchored to a copy of this flute, which had somehow been removed, with a mirror to replace it — a feat of magic at a level Roy could only guess at. He had no idea where the replacement was, or who was maneuvering in the background with century-old artifacts, but the sense of floating adrift in deep currents and dark waters intensified.

He shut his eyes, striving to focus on the immediate. Now that he had no further use for it, the flute needed to go back to its owners, and fast. And he had to send Dhana safely home. He heaved himself to his feet, then a surge of water outside the window resolved into Dhana.

She landed on the deck, shook water off, stared at Les, then away quickly as she said, "They're here, a pack of nasties. I felt them splashing that way, that way, and that."

She pointed in three directions. He didn't have to look to know that he'd waited too long, that he was beyond his last vestiges of strength. He pressed the flute into her hand — noted that she didn't react to the weird, numbing sense of heavy magic—then pulled from his pocket his emergency transfer token. "Get it back to Horsefeathers." He slapped the token into her other hand, murmured the words to change the location spell to Mearsies Heili, and she vanished.

Roy still couldn't see whoever was closing in on him, which gave him a chance. He was far too exhausted to risk a transfer spell without the aid of a token, so he had to run. He turned toward the window, intending to dive into the water—and saw the black door open.

Dejain walked through. "They want their prisoner back."

Instinct was faster than thought. Roy indicated Les Rhoderan as he backed toward the open window—and then, too tired, too late, felt a stone spell close around his body. He fell heavily, gazing up helplessly.

Dejain looked around with disgust. "*This* was your hideaway?" She held her skirts fastidiously away from Roy as she sat down in a chair one of the boys had made, "Yeres will probably discover Efael's playtoy gone any moment now. You left a magic trail as wide as a king's highway leading straight to here." She kicked him. "Focus, idiot. I have to talk to Detlev without spies. You find him."

Roy closed his eyes. "He'll kill me," he muttered through magic-numb lips.

"I don't care," Dejain said. "I want to talk to him. Now."

Roy lay where he was, beyond laughter at the horrible irony of his life now.

"It's either a fast death with him or whatever Efael is going to do to you when he gets back. *Something* is happening on Five, and Efael is on the rampage. It doesn't help that you stole his playtoy and then finished him off." She toed Les Rhoderan's body.

Roy closed his eyes. They didn't know about the flute.

Yet.

"I'll do it."

"Smart boy," she said, holding her skirts closer. "I'll wait."

It's all very well to resign oneself to certain death, Roy thought as he lay there unable to move. One's body and spirit still fight hard against the mind lying to itself. One thing he knew: he was too tired to sustain a mental contact and still maintain his mind-shield. He listened outside his mind-shield for Detlev—

And there he was.

Shock radiated through Roy, but he suppressed it and formed the thought: *Dejain wants you.* He tried to keep "at the cost of my life" from Detlev but it leaked through anyway. Or maybe Detlev could hear beneath Roy's disintegrating control.

Give her this Destination, came the answer in that familiar, effortless mental voice: *You and I will speak later.*

Roy opened his eyes and repeated the Destination details to Dejain. She looked as if she might say something, but then glanced through the windows. "And there they are. Too bad for you." She vanished.

Roy lay there, utterly unable to transfer, even to move, his body a mass of icy numbness, and waited for the horror he could not escape. But then air ruffled over him, bringing the familiar air of . . . Bereth Ferian?

He opened his sticky eyes to gaze up into Siamis's smiling face. "Good job taking those wards down," Siamis said. He whispered a short series of spells, and the air crackled with magic. Then he stooped and pressed a token against Roy's forehead.

A wrenching transfer, and Roy lay on cool tiles. "Black Knives," he croaked. It took the last of his strength.

"I think I left behind enough surprises for them to deal with. They won't trace us here."

Another face joined Siamis's. "Arthur?"

It was Arthur, though the bones of adulthood were beginning to emerge from that once-round face. Arthur smiled. "Welcome home, Roy. Welcome home."

Twenty-two

Delfina Valley

TSAUDEREI HAD SCARCELY EATEN his first meal in his own cottage after his extended stay in Sarendan when one of his tracers alerted him to a trespasser in the woodland at the base of the mountains. He reached for his scry stone, and his eyebrows shot upward when he recognized the long, lean form waiting with hands on hips. It was Detlev's arrogant youngster, the one who dressed in black and wore a lot of weapons.

Tsauderei had thoroughly enjoyed trouncing this boy's assumptions around the time Siamis had made his truce.

Wondering what the youth wanted now, Tsauderei murmured the spell to bring him the long way. And while MV soared up the slope of the lower mountain, Tsauderei dealt with some defenses, then sat down to prepare mentally.

He would have liked some rest time, which obviously he was not going to get. It was difficult to see Darian Irad back again, but so far, at least, affairs seemed to be progressing as well as could be expected. The entire kingdom was in mourning, as profound as that after Derek Diamagan's death. More so, because a great number of the nobles missed Peitar, whereas pretty much all of them had utterly loathed Derek.

Tsauderei had departed on a note of truce with Irad, but

he knew his relations with the Selennas would never be the same. His mood souring, he forced his attention back to the scry stone, in which he saw his prospective visitor swooping and diving with obvious pleasure.

Tsauderei dropped his dishes in the bucket, stacked them on the far table, then retreated to his chair to prepare for some diversion, as, at his end, MV recollected that flying was just as great at he'd remembered.

He now knew the limitations of the magic. He had relative freedom, as long as he progressed southward, up to the higher peaks. He experimented, thoroughly enjoying the speed as he considered his approach. The most obvious course would be to throw himself on Tsauderei's mercy. Surely these lighters would fall all over themselves to reclaim him from his evil companions. He wished he knew how Siamis had managed it—and why. And whether his hopping the fence was some long-range ruse for some snake in Norsunder.

No chance of finding out. Anyway, MV was not certain he could stomach faking the humble, pleading demeanor of the sort the lighters would expect. Though that would surely get the quickest results. He was still undecided when he spotted the cobalt blue lake down below, and the magic brought him gently to the grassy area outside the cottage that hadn't changed since MV's last visit.

The door swung open, and MV walked inside, casting a fast glance around. The old mage sat alone before the big window that overlooked the lake, bookshelves on every other wall.

"Well, come in," the old man rasped. "You're the one who wanted to see me. I'm here. And busy, so spit it out."

MV shrugged. "You did invite me back."

"No," Tsauderei stated with heavy irony, and MV decided against gaming the old geezer with pleading and error-of-his-ways, though he'd thought up a fine, heartrending speech during the last part of his flight. "I said I'd see you again. It more in the nature of a threat than an invitation." He laid aside his lap desk. "So. Detlev has blundered in Aldau-Rayad, and apparently also in Geth? I gather this is some desperate new ruse to scrape up some new and nefarious plan, using you little shits?" His teeth showed on the word "shits"—long and white.

MV's brows rose.

"Excuse me, you poor, misunderstood lads," Tsauderei corrected. "Sit down." With a gesture of irony, he indicated the only available chair.

MV remembered that chair. Matching Tsauderei's irony, he sat down with meticulous care, thinking that the old skunk was enjoying himself far too much. "Shits is fine," MV said. "What makes you think Detlev was involved in Geth?"

"I assume he has his sticky fingers everywhere. But do tell me more," Tsauderei said, and in an unsettling echo of MV's earlier thoughts, "Please. Correct my ignorance."

MV was very glad after that "poor, misunderstood" crack that he'd foregone the "errors" approach. Adam might have brought it off (though he'd probably slit his own throat before trying such a greasy ruse) but MV felt Tsauderei's derisive gaze like a drill through the head. He knew the old mage had not coinhered. What he had was nearly a century of hard experience, lived every one of those days, because for him there was no escape to a Beyond. "Geth seems to have been one of Efael's plans. I don't know. We don't talk," MV said acidly.

Tsauderei's grin was brief, then the humor faded. "Efael. He's the one who murdered Carlael of Everon, and the mage guild Chief in Eidervaen, yes?"

"Among others," MV said. "Many others."

Tsauderei had been watching closely. He was certain the hatred in MV's voice was genuine, however if the young fool thought he'd shifted the subject, he was mistaken. "Prince Glenn of Everon was murdered by one of you little shits, am I right?"

"That was a duel, forced on—"

Tsauderei cut in. "But you, if I am correct, didn't challenge that little Mearsiean girl to any duel, as she was not armed when you slit her throat in front of her friends."

MV reddened to the ears. "She was *stupid*. A hostage in a war game—*anyone* should know not to move with a knife pressed to that artery."

"Any number of exceedingly intelligent individuals not trained in killing would not know that," the imperturbable voice went on. "And, very recently, you were no doubt crowing over the successful assassination of Peitar Selenna of Sarendan. Who incidentally never held a sword in his life. Sounds like a pattern there, striking at the weakest and most peaceable." Tsauderei's voice ended on a biting tone.

"What?" MV exclaimed. "If it's even true, that certainly wasn't me!"

Tsauderei's gnarled fingers sketched a sign, and magic closed around MV. "I don't," Tsauderei said, "believe a word coming out of your mouth. This partial stone spell is worked into that chair. It will last as long as I wish. I also have here a hefty dose of white kinthus." He tapped a heavy ceramic cup sitting on the low table next to his chair.

MV made an intense effort, to find himself frozen fast. It took effort even to breathe. But lighters didn't do this kind of thing! In a husky, strained voice he began swearing fluently.

Tsauderei talked over him. "I could probably find half a dozen eager volunteers to pour this kinthus down your throat. Rel, I'm sure, would agree in an instant. Or I could starve you out, until you beg for it. But that would leave you here polluting my peace for days. And Rel has better things to do. Furthermore —"

MV uttered some especially pungent vituperations.

"Furthermore," Tsauderei drawled, raising his voice, "I find no desire whatsoever to listen to the no doubt sordid, dreary details of your miserable excuse for a life."

"That *wasn't* me. I didn't know anything about it."

"Tall. Dark-haired. Your age. One shot with a crossbow, which indicates familiarity with that kind of weapon — which leaves out most of this half of the continent," Tsauderei stated. "Who still observe the Covenant. Description matches perfectly."

"It matches several of us. As well as hundreds of other people! As for your so-called Covenant, there are people training with bows all over the place."

"I'm not the least interested in your opinion of the Covenant. Where were you these past weeks?" Tsauderei caressed the ceramic mug. "Lie to me, and I will manfully overcome my distaste for Norsundrian tactics."

"I was on my boat."

"Your boat?"

"Yeah. I like the sea. And the study of magic." MV added sarcastically, "But neither of the magic schools would have me."

Tsauderei's tone was still skeptical. "You claim to be a sailor?"

"I am one. Ask Captain Zathdar of the *Zathdar*. I sailed with his fleet for a season, fighting pirates up the Elgar Strait. Wanted my own boat, which I got a month ago. Trying to pay it off by taking passengers, while I study magic."

"Where is Detlev in all this?"

"Who knows?" MV tried to shrug, and couldn't. "He's never been gabby with the details. He cut us loose," he added. "Seeing as a couple were already gong off on their own."

"You want me to believe he just let you go."

"Believe what you want. I can show you the sale papers on my boat."

Tsauderei fixed MV with an unnerving gaze, then said, "I've been needing a diversion. Let's see what you *do* know — damn, there goes the notecase. I wonder if it's about you or your master." He began rocking back and forth, building up enough momentum to rise with a grunt of effort.

MV said, "There are spells for that."

"You think I'm not aware?" Tsauderei shot him another of those sardonic glances. "This is about the only exercise I get."

Tsauderei fetched a notecase from a side table. He took his time opening it and unfolding the three notes inside. MV watched, irritated and amused both. He knew the old geezer was toying with him. He could wait. This was nothing compared to being toyed with by Efael.

Tsauderei opened the last note, and his expression shuttered in a way that shot a pang through MV. Something big was going on. Tsauderei gazed down at Clair's note, took in MV's wary, interested expression, and thought, this is not a coincidence. But he could not even imagine how the two events connected.

For a heartbeat or two, he was tempted to actually carry out his threat and dose that fiery-eyed tough of Detlev's. However, he knew that even frozen to the chin, MV would still fight against swallowing, and Tsauderei no longer had the strength for such methods. Then there was the poisonous strength of white kinthus. One or two doses, most humans could absorb over a lifetime, but that was about the limit. Tsauderei would need more evidence that MV was really a vessel of evil before resorting to such tactics.

He threw the note into the fire, tossed the notecase onto the table, and resettled himself into his armchair. Then he began a grueling examination into the reading MV had done while sailing down the coast.

MV answered readily. It had been enlightening reading in a sense; he'd always despised light magic for what he'd regarded as its tiptoeing, fussy cautions. Dark magic was fast and powerful. Yes, and volatile. When he'd finished reading Roy's comparison, he had to admit that at least light magic spells always held, if done correctly, and without waste.

He learned through Tsauderei's searching interrogation into what he knew and what he didn't that the logical conclusions that Roy had so painfully built, step by step, were mere elementary assumptions to the old fart. And every time MV had to admit he didn't know something, Tsauderei grunted, clearly unimpressed. His questions reached deeply into dark magic, which also surprised MV. He'd thought the lighters considered themselves too morally superior to touch any knowledge of dark magic.

At the end, Tsauderei sighed as though stuck with a wearisome burden, and said, "If you really want to learn, the next time you show your face, you will have your wood guild sved. Which every beginner presents before moving on to the first level of real training."

MV exclaimed, "What? Making fire sticks? I've been beyond that level for ten years!"

"Five hundred of them," Tsauderei said, with obvious relish. "And when you're done, the basics of light magic will be second nature. You will also, for the first time in your life, no doubt, have contributed something worthwhile instead of merely destroying others' work."

"But—"

"If," Tsauderei cut in, "you attempt to fake the sved, I guarantee you won't like the consequence. Because your second lesson is to learn that every action, every choice, has consequences."

Then he snapped his fingers, and MV wrenched in abrupt transfer. When the reaction cleared, he found himself where he'd started, at the base of the mountain. At least it wasn't in some miserable port on another continent.

MV cracked a laugh. He'd thought this was going to be easy. And boring. But he had to admit, the old geezer was something of a challenge. He liked challenges.

Twenty-three

Bereth Ferian to Mearsies Heili

HORSEFEATHERS HAD LOVED BEING on this world until she lost her world's most important magical thing. She'd punished herself by insisting she stay until she found it, but the truth waited like a shadow ready to pounce every night: no matter how hard she studied, or how tired she made herself: she had failed. And every time she gave in to the sorrow and cried herself to sleep, she woke with a clogged nose and an aching head.

She knew it was stupid to let regret overwhelm her. She had important work to do, and she did it diligently—but no matter how tired she was, as soon as she dropped onto the bed that remained unfamiliar, with unfamiliar smells in the air, and unfamiliar sounds, the tears would come.

Guilt was a small part of it. Very small: Leotay did not blame her for losing the Thing. Nor did she blame the Sartorans, especially after people at home had managed to lose Lyal, Jeory's younger brother, one of Quicksilver's best knife fighters and Horsefeathers' own age. They were certain the enemies had taken him, just as enemies had taken the Thing. There seemed to be little defense against evil and malice, no matter how watchful one was.

She tried to think of good things as she walked to class the next morning. She loved the light-barked trees that swayed in the wind. She loved wind, too, the sound it made soughing through leaves and rustling grasses and dancing the dangling chimes people had on their houses. She loved the scents the wind carried.

How exciting it was, to wake up and discover the leaves on the trees turning brilliant shades — though some stayed deep green in contrast — and the many, many types of leaves they grew! She would never be able to learn the names of so many trees, but she liked looking at them. She also liked the way the wind chased those leaves along the walkway, and it amazed her to think that in Sartor's half of the world it was spring, with new leaves coming out on the tree branches, and new flowers from the soil.

As a male silhouette emerged from among the trees, the slanted sun of morning edging his cheekbones, she enjoyed the kindle of warmth inside her as she recognized Arthur. She relished attraction to handsome young people, found it easier to smile when they met on the pathway, but her smile faltered when she saw how tense he was, how searching his gaze. "Tsauderei sent a message. They found the artifact."

Horsefeathers gasped, every nerve shocking to ice. Then joy suffused her. "Where! When can I have it back?"

"That's what he wants to ask you about. Remember Seshe and Clair and them?"

"Of course! Our first friends, I could never forget!"

"Well, one of them has it. We figure it's as safe a place as any to send you and find out what you want to do."

"I will be happy to go to the home of Seshe and Clair!"

Her studies forgotten, she followed him back to the Bereth Ferian Destination — she didn't care if she ever saw her extra scholar's robe or the borrowed books again. She had learned enough to understand how her Hildi magic translated over into the Sartoran words and phrases. They were simply different methods of harnessing the same magic.

Full of expectancy and joy, she soon stood in Mearsies Heili on the Destination outside the enormous palace of softly glistening white material. As she recovered, she gazed upward, wondering if this edifice was made of moon. It glowed in the same way as moonlight.

While she gazed upward, inside the palace, Mearsieanne

did her best to control her exasperation at how Clair and the girls went straight to the kitchen to celebrate Dhana's sudden appearance weeks after she had gone off with that Roy.

Dhana sat in a hunch-shouldered heap, with CJ and Clair hovering protectively, as Dhana tried to assimilate the fact that the others had been home for over a month since she and Roy entered the Beyond. She'd thought she'd been gone an hour or two. A horrible hour—endless while enduring it—but neither thirst nor hunger had marked time the way they usually did while she was in human form.

She'd been very upset about Roy, all the more because she knew no one could do anything about rescuing him. At least Clair understood how she felt, and she knew CJ tried to, but Mearsieanne had given a sharp little shrug, muttering, "Detlev's boys deserve exactly what they get," and turned her attention to getting everybody out of the kitchen and into a proper sitting room.

Mearsieanne sighed as the gong toned, indicating an arrival. She was not pleased to see Senrid. Marlovens could not be trusted. Senrid passed her by in his usual brisk walk, and while he exchanged greetings with the others, she did her best to signal Clair in a quiet way to remind her that they had two empty drawing rooms waiting for visitors, with plenty of furnture that would encourage people to sit in a civilized circle, instead of parking on floors and tables and counters.

But the gong toning again caused her to go to the door. This time the visitor was well worth the effort. Here was Tsauderei, newly arrived from the Destination.

Mearsieanne adopted her formal mode. "You will find a comfortable chair in here," she said with a slight increase in volume, and turned to lead the way, noticing with relief how the others obediently trooped behind her into the bigger waiting room.

Then Puddlenose drew the Marloven over to the window, where they sat on the window seat. Mearsieanne turned away, hiding her disgust—there were plenty of empty chairs. She debated saying something when the gong announced yet more arrivals. Here was Arthur, half a hand taller than the last time she had seen him. Another releasing the Child Spell! He would need the beard spell in a couple of years, she thought, shuddering. With him paced a thin girl in the blue of a mage student, with sick-pale skin and enormous eyes that glanced around in wonder.

Mearsieanne advanced to greet them, as in the drawing room, Puddlenose and Senrid talked about sea travel on Sartorias-deles and (what little Puddlenose had seen) on Geth. Senrid was trying to decide if he was going to transfer straight back home. Roy clearly wasn't with Dhana, so once again Senrid wasn't going to get the chance to question him. When he saw Tsauderei and Arthur, he decided to stay. Something was certainly going on—centered on the flute thing Dhana held. He could feel the magic on it from across the room.

The fact that it came from another world didn't necessarily make it any more interesting; objects as protections were such a bad idea. Yeah, you could hide them, but that meant they could be stolen. Or lost. His most powerful protections—like the one that kept Detlev from entering Senrid's capital city, and now his boys as well—were bound to the stones at the foundation of his castle.

Arthur went straight to Dhana. "Roy's in Bereth Ferian, resting. Thanks for backing him up."

Dhana barely had a moment to express her relief before Horsefeathers rushed into the room, exclaiming, "Oh, Seshe, Clair! It is so good of you—"

Her gaze zapped straight to the object Dhana held out. Horsefeathers took the flute from her, and clutched it against her skinny chest, her eyes closed, face upraised in silent, profound reprieve. She stood in the middle of the room, barefoot, her silky black hair hanging down her back in a wind-tangled waterfall, and because she could not bear to wait any longer—she had to know if it was unharmed after being in the hands of the enemy—she raised the flute to her lips to blow one brief, soft, tentative note.

And everyone with Dena Yeresbeth, or who knew magic, turned sharply toward one wall.

"What was that?" Arthur asked, startled.

Horsefeathers knew she ought to ward the flute, but Tsauderei was there, and Arthur, and she could keep the magic within bounds by confining her playing to a single note. Soft as a whisper—she breathed the Note of True.

"There's something echoing . . ." Clair began, brow puckered.

"Answering it, like." CJ shot to her feet, bounded to the door, green skirt swinging, then glanced back at

Horsefeathers. "Can you play a louder note?"

Horsefeathers said, "It is not for playing loud. It . . ." She hesitated. "The magic—the images—they are very strong. Loud and hard, it . . ." She brushed her fingers from her heart to her head. "Hurts. Hildi told me before she died that it is very dangerous. Jeory was the only one who could play it safely, and he taught my sister, and she taught me."

"Then play softly? But longer?" Clair asked. "Did you hear the echo?"

Horsefeathers looked doubtful. "I thought that was in my head only. When I play, my mind goes . . ." She shrugged expressively and waved a hand outward.

Clair and Mearsieanne exchanged looks. What in the white palace could possibly have anything to do with an artifact from Aldau-Rayad?

Horsefeathers lifted the flute to her lips, and this time played the Note of Shade, which to the others sounded like a breathy, liquid trill half a step higher.

CJ pelted off, followed by Clair. They didn't have to go far. To both girls' astonishment, they were drawn to Clair's room, where a high, singing note trilled back. They converged on Clair's plain dressing table, which only had one object on it: her little carved wood treasure box containing her few pieces of jewelry.

They ran back to the drawing room, where Clair set the jewelry box on a low table, flipped it open, and looked up expectantly at Horsefeathers. Once again, she played her note, soft as a whisper. In the box, an object on a chain glimmered with white-blue iridescence as it echoed the note. Clair picked up the chain. "My shell?"

"That's a shell?" Arthur asked doubtfully. "It looks more like some kind of wood."

"It's shaped like a shell," Clair said. "So I thought of it as one."

Senrid's skin crawled, and anger boiled in him as Clair said, "Puddlenose gave it to me."

"I did?" Puddlenose exclaimed. Then he grinned. "Well, I've given you a lot of stuff I've picked up while traveling. I don't remember them all."

"*I* remember," Senrid said flatly. "I was there. It was when we first met." Not long after they'd encountered the magical figure named Erdrael, whose actions Senrid still could not explain—except for the old conviction that he was a piece on someone's game board in a game he couldn't see, for stakes he could not guess. *How* he hated it.

Puddlenose shrugged.

"I wear it because it's unusual, and I like the magic feel to it," Clair said.

"I remember that," Arthur put in mildly. "When we were in Wnelder Vee. You were wearing it. I could feel its magic across the room."

Tsauderei had been squinting at the object dangling in Clair's hand. He gave a grunt. "There are several of those around. With that central spiral."

Everyone turned his way.

He said, "The world is full of things like this. Well, not exactly like this. Those of you who haven't learned magic, you probably know enough to have heard that spells put together for a purpose are called enchantments, and they're usually bound to an object. Easier to deal with that way."

"It was the same for us," Horsefeathers said. "It was the work of the Hildis to renew the magic on them."

"Well, some need renewing here, too. Only over the years—sometimes centuries—their original purpose is forgotten, or superseded. A lot of them end up in drawers, archives, boxes, collections, and archives, north and south."

Arthur nodded. "I think we have at least a couple that have that spiral, one smaller, also wood, one carved red-rock, about this size. That's going to be one of my future projects, determining, if I can, what the purposes were of the forgotten ones."

Tsauderei's lips twisted in a brief, ironic smile. "In the south, they put the second-year students to work combing through the collection at the archive, and any whose magic has faded away get handed off to the herald-archivists to deal with. Jewels get sold, objects . . . ah, I'm straying. The thing is, there's at least one artifact very similar to this in the archive in the south, and its magic is quite strong."

"As is the red-rock one," Arthur said. "I thought someone had renewed it but neglected to note the renewal in the archive ledger."

"The southern one hasn't been touched, at all, for millennia," Tsauderei said. "It lies in a special room where such things are kept." He turned to Puddlenose. "Where exactly did you get it?"

Puddlenose shrugged again. Senrid said, "I can tell you that. Remember when Everon lay under enchantment? It appeared to be a desert. No buildings. No people. We were crossing it in search of the standing stones that would permit us to cross into the true Everon, when we met an old woman. She gave it to you."

Puddlenose sighed. "As I said, I get stuff, all the time. I never keep it. Rarely remember it."

Senrid gritted his teeth, alert in every nerve. The old woman could have been a magical construct; he was convinced that none of this was coincidence, and he loathed and distrusted being associated with it.

CJ had been studying the flute and the shell, then the flute again. She said, "These ridges and things."

"Decorative carving," Arthur said.

"But . . ." CJ, the mostly untrained artist, saw space differently than others. She pointed at a complicated working of leaves around an indentation. "What if the spiral-shell is supposed to fit in this spot here?"

Horsefeathers glanced from the shell to the flute, then said, "Oh. Let us try."

She shook the shell free of its chain, held it over the indentation—whereupon the shell and the flute acted like magnet and iron filaments, and snicked together, the join then vanishing in a fluorescence of magic.

And before anyone could react, a transfer sent air circling around the room. Horsefeathers gasped, as that draft of air smelled a little like home, then Lilith said, "You must come away from here. Now." She took hold of Horsefeathers' wrist, and the two vanished.

"Okay, that was kinda creepy," CJ said into the sudden silence.

Senrid was done being a game piece on a board he couldn't see. He vanished as well, leaving everyone else to question and wonder and come up with no answers, as Mearsieanne commented about the bad manners of those who were too self-important to step out to Destinations, like civilized beings.

Twenty-four

SENRID STARED GRIMLY AT the beautifully written letter he'd received from Shontande Lirendi, prospective king of Colend. Though it would be difficult to find two kingdoms more different from one another than Colend and Marloven Hess — each at opposite ends of the long Sartoran continent — they shared a few similarities.

Both had young rulers. Both young kings had dealt with, or were dealing with in Shontande's case, a controlling regency. Senrid had managed to survive a deadly regent, which inspired Shontande, who was still very much under the control of his regency council.

Not that they were deadly. Far from it. They exerted themselves to make certain their young king was protected, to the extent that everything he wanted to do on his own was considered a possible danger. He was surrounded waking and sleeping by an army of well-trained, soft-voiced servants who would give him anything he wanted to eat or drink, or wear, or play with, as long as he remained within the palace or his fortress retreat at Skya Lake. As for governing, the regency council sent him daily reports on what they had done in his name, and if he ventured any question, he was gently but firmly told why his elders knew best.

Shontande and Senrid didn't write often, and when they

did, it was mostly about magic studies. Shontande had another secret correspondent in Thad Keperi, thanks to Senrid's intervention. Shontande relied heavily on Thad's friendship. But Thad knew nothing about magic.

Senrid unfolded the paper and stared with a pulse of appreciative humor at the exquisite handwriting in pure blue ink. So very Colendi! Then his smile vanished when he took in the first line.

> *You were correct. That tracer revealed them tampering with the notecase they gave me. They must have spent a fortune, and of course if I reveal that I know, I am certain that I will hear about how it's for my own protection, and how much they admire the grace of my correspondence, and my correct use of the forms.*
>
> *I had already, on your advice, taken great care to hide this notecase, but now I have added a layer of magical protection. And I am building backwards to discover how the unknown mage compromised what I regard now as my public notecase, beginning with a tracer . . .*

Senrid suspected the Colendi regency council had no idea what Shontande was doing with all his free time.

He laid the letter down. At that end of the Sartoran continent, the day was already advanced, though on Senrid's side, the sun would not come up for two hours. Senrid usually used this time for personal correspondence (what little there was) and then for training in knife work or contact fighting, as he never relaxed his vigilance, and only the credulous completely relied on personal guards for their own safety.

The one martial skill he lacked was sword work. He'd been denied any training by his uncle; he could practice archery on his own, and knife throwing, and he'd been able to arrange for contact fighting lessons, which were not noisy and could be instantly abandoned if he was intruded on, but you couldn't hide the clang of steel.

Since getting rid of his uncle, other priorities always seemed to push ahead. He had a sword lesson arranged for that very day—and here he was again, contemplating sending a message through the night duty Runner that he had an emergency. Because it *was*. Shontande—a lighter—had proved what Senrid had known all along. They would have to listen now!

He sent a note off to Tsauderei; if the old mage answered, then Senrid would cancel the sword lesson If he didn't, then he'd go downstairs and struggle with his own inadequacies, while knowing that if assassins ever came, he was unlikely to be handily equipped with a sword, and if he had to command a defense, he wouldn't be leading from the front. He had trained captains for that. It would be his responsibility to sweat it out from behind, with the maps and stream of reports.

He was surprised to receive an immediate response from Tsauderei, and a token to come directly to the mage's cottage.

Senrid sent a runner to release the sword master, picked up Shontande's note, and transferred. The valley outside Tsauderei's cottage blurred with early spring, snow lying in blue banks in the shadows of the high peaks, though down below spring was in full bloom, most of the continent (outside of Marloven Hess) readying for Flower Day. In Marloven Hess, spring was acknowledged by the beginning of the academy season.

Tsauderei regarded Senrid somewhat in the same way he regarded thunderstorms: could be beneficial, or harmful, and always unpredictable in where lightning would strike. In his experience, Senrid was never frivolous—would not know how to be.

Senrid entered with his customary quick he the Marloven boy and Tsauderei's current challenge, MV, had ever met. And what the outcome had been. The idea made him chuckle as Senrid held out a folded note. Even at a distance Tsauderei could see that the paper was beautifully made—had to be Colendi.

"I was right," Senrid said without any preamble. "Everyone insisted that the scribes protect the magic on the notecases, that they can't be compromised. Well, I was *right*. They *can* be compromised."

Senrid gazed in astonishment at Tsauderei's lack of shock and dismay. "Yes, if anyone would manage it in this generation, it would be that regency council," he commented.

"In this generation? You mean, the notecases've been

compromised before?" Senrid demanded. "*Everyone* insisted it was impossible when I didn't want one for this very reason. Everyone."

Tsauderei uttered an affirmative grunt. "As far as they know, it is." Which was, Senrid noted to himself, not quite a direct answer. Then Tsauderei leaned his elbows on his lap table. "Senrid, it's rare enough that when they are compromised, the mage guild usually catches the offenders. A good many of these culprits are still sitting under stone spells in gardens of contemplation," he added grimly. "The guild has its problems, but they take vow-breaking very seriously."

Senrid whistled. Then his brows twitched into a skeptical expression. "You said usually."

"True. But as is obvious, first someone has to discover the breach. And complain. Second, it takes so much effort, the motivation—and the funding—is almost always at high political levels, which we mages cannot interfere with, unless invited for a specific purpose. Here is your perfect example." Tsauderei handed back Shontande's note. "We can't interfere with Colend's governing council without invitation. My guess is, the prince will address this matter himself one day. I deem it wiser to keep silent and leave the Colendi to themselves."

Senrid sighed. "Don't you see it? If it can be done, it *will* be done when Norsunder attacks."

"But it's a very cumbersome process, to deflect letters then resend them," Tsauderei said. "You have to obtain the target notecase, then possess it long enough to alter the magic on it. That's no easy task, as you have to work the spell to deflect the contents before the tracer alerts the owner, or the owner will know what happened. It's far more work than reward, unless you're deflecting one owned by a king or important spy, and most of them use codes, I would imagine. I wouldn't worry about it."

Senrid scowled. "Look, I know that centuries ago these notecases were made in pairs and for the really wealthy in small groups, but now, with so many of them in the world, aren't there fundamental spells laid down for them all? Which, if altered, could at least potentially alter all the notecases made with those spells?"

Tsauderei said, "Of course there are. Layers of them, accrued over centuries, with the enchantment anchors secreted all over the world. If Norsunder attacks, they aren't going to be able to destroy the notecase magic in a day, or even a year."

"Unless they're already working on it," Senrid countered, and on a muttered breath, "*I* would be."

Tsauderei's brows shot up, and Senrid reddened to the ears. "I'm *not!* We don't want to invade anybody. I don't want another country's problems. I've got enough to do at home. But I can't help thinking ahead."

"Senrid," Tsauderei said, "there's thinking ahead and then there's scaring yourself by assuming that everyone else is oblivious but you. The branch of the mages and the scribes who oversee the making of these things do check on the fundamental magic as part of their regular process. Any sign of tampering — *any* — would have both of what even you ought to admit are the world's most powerful guilds quite stirred up."

Senrid's eyes narrowed. "I remember once we talked about the invasion of Sartor before that century of enchantment, and you said it was random. I don't believe any invasion is random. There was a strategy, a goal, what you'd call a reason — and that means a lot of preliminary work beforehand that no one saw. Norsunder had a goal. Maybe the goal was specifically limited to testing that enchantment, which you have to admit would make a tremendous defense against invaders: you enchant your own country so they can't get in. Did anyone ever investigate what kind of magic could possibly remove Sartor for very nearly a whole century?"

Tsauderei reflected that Veltos and her chosen few had been doing little else before she was murdered. While he considered how to answer, Senrid walked restlessly in a quick circle. "I'm not trying to turn this discussion into an argument. I just don't want to be taken by surprise."

"I appreciate that." Tsauderei brought his chin down in a nod, almost a bow, beard rippling on his chest. "And I thank you for bringing this to my attention. If you catch word of any more anomalies, please continue to tell me. When random begins to make a pattern, then we can investigate — or at least raise the possibility to governments who insist on overseeing their own magical affairs. I don't want to raise alarms unless I'm very certain."

"Right." Senrid flicked up a hand, produced his return token, and vanished, leaving Tsauderei to shake his head, then return to the one amusement he'd permitted himself: thinking up arduous, tedious, and above all, difficult elementary magic tasks to stick on that young spy of Detlev's.

He'd been surprised that MV had actually shown up at the firestick enchantment site, and was apparently doing a commendable job. Tsauderei had wagered himself the strutting young cock of the walk wouldn't show up at all.

Well, the game was certainly on!

He looked forward to their next tangle.

Twenty-five

SENRID'S MOOD STAYED GLUM after two long, rough transfers in early morning, and nothing to show for it. He'd already canceled his sword lesson. He knew the sword master would return promptly if sent for, but that was a slipshod way to treat a very busy man, bordering on disrespect, given the time of year. Oh, especially *this* year.

At that thought his mood shifted. This change (and it shouldn't even be all that much of one) was either going to be great or a total disaster, and not for the obvious reasons. But he'd promised to invite Liere if it ever did happen—and here it was, suddenly spring, and when had she visited last?

He counted back, astonished that it had been well over a year. A year! Really? He turned around in a circle, feeling as if he'd missed something he ought to have noticed. The sense was strong enough for him to brace himself for a third long transfer—to Bereth Ferian. It was after dark there, but they were moving toward winter, the hour still early. He walked out of the transfer Destination, then took a step back again when he saw the long rank of windows reflecting an intense, eerily fluorescing cobalt blue. Oh yes, the dancing lights.

A page led him to a parlor with a terrace outside glass doors. Lyren and Mac ran about on the terrace, their hands dripping illusory lights that trailed after them like bubbles full of sparkles in various colors. Three silhouetted figures stood inside the glass doors. No lamp had been lit, probably so they could watch the brilliant colors dancing and shimmering across the sky. The children's breath could be seen clouding and vanishing, but they ran without coats or hats or mittens.

Senrid advanced, the glow highlighting Arthur's features. He'd shot up rather tall, though he was still fair-haired. Next to him stood Liere — looking the same as always — and . . .

"Siamis?" Senrid stopped short.

The tallest figure turned his head, his hair gilt in the shimmering light as he shifted a sack carried in one arm.

"Senrid," Siamis said in greeting. It was that exact tone Siamis had first spoken Senrid's name when his handpicked bullyboys had brought Senrid to him as a prisoner, after days of extra rough treatment.

Senrid's heart banged wildly, and his hands slipped into his sleeves, gripping the rough scars around his wrists.

Liere said in a quick, apologetic voice, "I invited him, Senrid. It's all right. Why are you here? Is something wrong?"

"No." *Not with me, anyway.* He still believed Siamis's change of side was some kind of ruse, but the others knew what he thought. "Came to see you."

Liere's face brightened in the old way, and a tightness in his chest eased that he had not been aware of until that moment.

"Let's go talk in the other room. I'm getting cold anyway," she said.

Senrid cast one last glance at Siamis to make certain of his stance before turning his back — and made a startling discovery. The sack that Siamis held was a baby. The child gazed out at the lights, which reflected back in wide eyes.

Senrid stepped sideways toward the door. He'd almost reached it when Siamis said, "Senrid."

Senrid stilled, alert.

Siamis jiggled the baby, who waved chubby arms. Then he said, "Have you ever met your cousins?"

"Besides Ndand, I don't have any —" Senrid's teeth clicked shut. Of course he had cousins, on his mother's side. Though he had never met any of them. He'd never corresponded with them, a mutually satisfactory arrangement, so he'd thought. "No." And he forced the question out, because he believed in meeting threats and danger straight on: "Why?"

"Just asking."

Senrid did turn his back then, stepped through, and thrust the door shut behind him. "Who's the brat?" he asked, jerking a thumb behind him as Liere led him down the hall.

"Her name is Margerian Li," Liere said in a careful tone. "But everyone calls her Yanli. Siamis said she was recently orphaned."

"What's he doing here? With a baby?"

They reached the library, where Liere shut the door, clapped the glowglobes into light, and faced Senrid. "I can't control Lyren or Mac at all," Liere said, and he saw the old defeat and tightness. "They can sense any tutor coming and hide. They talk mind to mind and play pranks. Nothing awful, but they won't listen, won't learn. Siamis had said . . . on our trip . . ." Liere shifted her gaze away. "He'd said if I ever needed a tutor, to let him know. So I did. And he said the timing is perfect, because he found Yanli."

Senrid scowled. "There is a *whole* lot missing here."

"I know." Liere stiffened her thin shoulders. "When he first offered to get us away—to make the trip—I said to him that he'd recently done good things for the world and against Norsunder, but before that, everything he did was horrible. And he said, can we begin again?"

"Begin again," Senrid repeated, as the windows flashed with ruby-red light bright enough to dim the glowglobes, which reflected a ruby iridescence for a heartbeat or two. "What a convenient piece of hypocrisy."

As the ruby coruscated with silver, Liere said, "I thought about that, too. Here's what I can tell you. Siamis was so good for Lyren when we traveled, and even Tahra had a good time, and acted like . . . well, she wasn't so unhappy, always talking about the numbers, and colors of numbers. In fact, she didn't do it at all. And he showed me how to learn magic."

"You did tell me that much," he said. "How is that going?"

"Slowly. It's a struggle. It was horrible in one way, but not horrible in another way, to find out Dena Yeresbeth—mine, anyway—negates magic as done now. And knowing that doesn't make it any easier to learn, because I have to control two things. It's like, oh, one hand has to knit, but at the same time, the other has to carve filigree. How is everyone in Marloven Hess?"

Senrid said, "I wanted to show you something. At home. I

finally strong-armed the jarls into letting girls into the academy. Back into the academy. They've been in and out again clear up to my grandfather's day. He was the one to toss them out of command, though not out of the army."

Liere nodded, remembering bitter words from the stable girls during one of her stays: it had been a jarlan, and a princess, who had argued the strongest with that old king against the northern war. He'd exiled the first onto her own land, ordered the second onto an impossible mission from which she hadn't returned, and then—on the strength of her patrol's deaths—closed the academy to females.

"All of the jarls agreed?" Liere asked.

"Oh, no, of course not. Methden leads the 'tradition' pack—tradition conveniently meaning whatever they want it to, considering how many changes we Marlovens have gone through. He has a daughter, but I'll never see her in Choreid Dhelerei, you can be sure. I got the majority to accept it, at last Convocation. And here we are, with spring and first callover tomorrow. Want to see it? There's a Senelac among the scrubs."

"He's ten already?"

"Not quite, but he's big for his age, and more than ready."

Liere smiled, then her eyes narrowed. "I don't want to leave Lyren long, not with the new rules, and tomorrow is the autumn lantern festival . . ."

"Well, here's a transfer token," he said, and held it out.

She was there the next day.

Senrid took her upstairs to his study, which overlooked the big parade ground. The new scrubs always met in this one because it was easier for family members unfamiliar with the royal city to find.

He and Liere stood side by side at the window. It was just like the old days, which she treasured so dearly. But so much had changed since those days! Sometimes she wondered what the biggest change was. For a long time she had considered the finding of a friend—Senrid—as her watershed (how she loved that word, watershed), then it was learning to read (her father had insisted that shopkeepers' daughters had no need, and reading made them get above themselves), then it had been Lyren's birth, and since then it was the beginner coinherence lessons Siamis had given her to do while they were traveling to other worlds.

She was no longer her own worst enemy — so breath-takingly wonderful a lesson, still needing practice, mostly to overcome years of bad habit. But it was good to practice, especially standing next to Senrid. She could feel his good mood, and enjoyed that as much as she enjoyed the warmth of the strong spring sunlight, and the way the boys and girls ran around on the parade ground below, their excitement so clear.

The children were roughly the age she had been when she first met Senrid. Except for variations in hair color, the new academy scrubs all looked alike. She couldn't tell which ones were girls. They all had the squared-off military haircuts, and wore loose smock-tunics and riding trousers stuffed into blackweave boots.

Did these girls really want to fight in an army? Was that the height of their desire? If it was, she thought as the instructor down below gestured them into a straight line, they ought to get their chance, same as anyone else with any other type of learning. How much of what girls wanted and what boys wanted was actually inside you, and how much came from everything one heard and saw around you?

For that matter, how much of thinking yourself girl or boy was really inside, and not from the outside? She hadn't even thought about such things until they traveled to a world where you couldn't just go to a healer and endure the gradual magical change if your physical and mental gender identities didn't match, the way anyone could on Sartorias-deles.

Almost anyone.

She remembered her own horror, and Tahra's somewhat pompous *Well it's not backward on* our *world*, until Siamis had pointed out her ignorance of Chwahirsland under Wan-Edhe, and a couple similar tyrants . . .

One of the Marloven academy leaders came out and issued a command. The children scrambled into straight lines, unmoving except for the spring breeze ruffling shirts and hair.

"Can you see them?" Senrid asked. "The girls?"

Liere focused. Out of the entire line, there were six or seven standing straight as steel. "The ones with perfect posture," she breathed.

"Yep. Well, not all. Two of those are boys. But you can bet they've been drilling all winter. Oh, it's going to be a fun summer." He chuckled under his breath.

Twenty-six

Autumn 4750 AF
Norsunder Base

DAVID BECAME AWARE OF a gradual increase in pressure around his head, and a dryness so profound he could no longer concentrate. And concentration – alertness – was vital in the Beyond. He had been reading and listening with physical and mental senses for what seemed like hours.

Felt like hours. Nothing was as it seemed. He had to focus to hold the archive around him, with steel walls outside, and air within . . . Four times the letters on the page began blurring into mush, forcing him to begin again, before he understood that he had to get out. Get a drink of water. A breath of real air – or what passed for real air at Norsunder Base.

He stood, visualizing a black door before him. Detlev's office behind it. The pressure increased to a throb, but he held the image – stepped through – a hot buzzing flash as he and his real body rejoined. Giddy with vertigo, he leaned against the desk, then reached for the pitcher of water Detlev always kept on the desk. How many times had they seen him return, and drink down a full glass before doing anything else?

David reached, poured with shaking hands, and oh, the sweet, cold refreshment! Life ramified through him. He breathed, drank some more, breathed again, then ventured out, aware of the bite of winter cold. He saw Adam coming up the stairs behind Sveneric, looking taller and thinner, his cloud of curly hair more unkempt. David's first real clue that he'd been gone longer than a day or two was the dramatic change in Sveneric's size: he'd completely lost the compact proportions of a just-out-of-toddlerhood critter, and was now a skinny little boy.

Sveneric's face lifted, expressive of quiet inner joy as he ran past David to the inner room where he existed most of his life—kind of his own Beyond, in a way—to put away his practice weapons. Adam was right behind him, looking flushed and heavy-eyed, and smelling of sick-sweat.

"You're back," Sveneric exclaimed from the doorway, his wide hazel gaze looking very green in the dreary light. "Where were you?"

"Away," David said.

Sveneric's expression smoothed to reserve as he suppressed the sharpness of disappointment. His memory of David was the freedom of exchange. David had always answered his questions. "You cannot talk about it, or you will not?"

"There are some things you don't want to know," David said, laughing to hide his surprise. He had never gotten that kind of question from the shrimp before. He turned to Adam, whose brows went up.

Sveneric looked from one to the other, then down at the floor as he dealt with disillusionment. Somehow he had expected everything to be different when David got back, that at last the boundaries of secrets that he sensed would be lifted, explained, and he would see the truth. Not just the truth, but a good truth. There were some things they thought he didn't want to know, and yet they did them anyway. Coming at a time when he wrestled every night with doubt and decision, this thought struck with the equivalent of a door slammed in his face.

"Take over for a day?" Adam whispered. "I'll be fine if I can sleep it out."

David gestured to Sveneric. "Why don't you get your work, and I'll see where you are?"

Sveneric knew a dismissal when he heard one. He stepped inside, and closed the door with both hands, aware that he had made a decision.

Outside that door, David sighed with relief, and said to Adam, "Status report?"

Adam kept his jacket on as he walked into his room and sat on the bed. "Hunt on for Roy. Both worlds. He nicked that artifact we took in Eidervaen, and used it to destroy the fundamental wards over the fortress there. *Everyone* wants the kill."

"Are they after you?"

Adam shook his head. "Zhenc is insisting he has the real one — that there was only the one — and that Roy destroyed a mirror of the artifact, not the thing itself."

David said, "Zhenc's life depends on Efael believing that. He's insisting we're all dupes and idiots, right, and lost the flute to him?"

"Yep. Dejain was up here questioning me last summer. I told her I couldn't get rid of it fast enough, after seeing what happened to Loyand. And Zhenc and his team all saw me surrender the fake one."

"Which of course they have corroborated," David said. "So if a duplicate does show up, that'll put Zhenc in the midden. Couldn't happen to a more deserving turd."

Thanks to Loyand's spectacular end, no one had seen the switch, not even David. He'd wondered from time to time since then if Adam had really switched the flutes. Obviously even Detlev had been in no hurry to experiment with it — probably as a result of what had happened to Loyand.

Anyway. Real or fake, not my problem, David thought.

"Efael is sure to think Zhenc lied, once the second one turns up. That's exactly the sort of thing Yeres would do. Has done." Adam paused to cough juicily. When he'd caught his breath, "Still here are Leef. Vana. Noser. Busy all day," Adam croaked, his eyes and nose streaming. Magic flashed over the handkerchief that he mopped his face with. "Only one with daytime free is Noser. He plays with the shrimp, but we don't leave them alone."

David considered Noser's broken mind. "He growing?"

Adam surprised David with a shake of the head. "Thinks Detlev will give him covert work as a boy. I think he feels safer."

"Get some sleep," David said. "I'll take the shrimp to grab a meal, once we review his lessons."

Adam had kicked off his shoes. Still dressed, complete to

jacket, he burrowed under his and Curtas's quilts until his head vanished.

David sighed, resigned to boredom, though that would be a relief after the tension of the Beyond. His mood sharpened when he glanced into the room he shared with MV, which looked exactly as neat and utterly barren as always. But his clothes trunk, usually squared out of sight under his bed, was subtly askew: a message.

He dropped to his knees and ran a hand over it. His fingers closed over an ordinary shirt shank, buzzing with magic: a transfer token. Had to be MV's. He pocketed it, stepped through their cleaning frame, then joined Sveneric, whose warded space, guarded by them in turns, had changed startlingly. He had chalked what looked like a mural on every wall, as high as he could reach.

The perspective was shaky, especially in the upper reaches, and the dogs' legs looked more like horses' legs (there were no dogs at Norsunder Base, nor had there been any at Five, so where did Sveneric get this fondness for dogs? The walls were full of them), and the trees were all shaped like spheres on sticks, but otherwise, the detail was extraordinary, especially for someone who was . . . almost six?

A lot of it looked like what you'd expect of an almost-six — messy, distorted — though his attention snagged, forcing him back to what appeared to be a theater player, or clown, with hair sticking up in waves, above a face not yet sketched in, and a body that seemed to be falling below a very messy tree full of spiky needles.

No, those weren't needles. That was a tree full of hands. David stepped closer, and as his gaze turned to the central figure, phrases from a very old ballad coming back, sung by Laban, who had the best singing voice of all of them. It wasn't a heroic battle full of war and trophies, as most of them they'd encountered had been — this one was strange, with complicated internal rhymes, a nightmarish ballad about the empty-souled man with the crown of fire whose defeat came "at the hands of the many."

Who gave him *that* ballad? David frowned. At the Den — on Geth — they could read anything they wanted to, isolated as they were. But here at Norsunder Base it seemed unsafe to the point of madness to introduce a brat of five to a lament that essentially was a vision about the summary destruction of all

Norsunder. Did Sveneric understand that the figure crowned with fire was Ilerian of the Host of Lords, founder of Norsunder?

David turned away from the picture to find Sveneric seated at his small desk that someone had hammered together out of two barrel halves and the legs of a chair that had been taken apart. The boy was carefully adding up a column of numbers and painstakingly chalking the answers, his lips moving.

At Adam's request, David had mentally prepared himself for a stretch of boredom, but now he was intrigued. Sveneric's mind-shield was wholly impervious.

When Sveneric finished a column and looked up, David spoke. "What's this you've drawn here?" He tipped his chin toward the tree of hands.

"A picture," the boy answered.

"Of what?"

Sveneric laid his chalk down, and raised his eyes, his round, childish face expressionless. "A story," he piped, the consonants precise.

"About?"

"I forget." Sveneric's gaze shifted downward at his slate.

This cautious lie both disappointed David and sharpened his interest. Sveneric had always been his little shadow hitherto. It was odd, how—now that he wasn't a shadow anymore—David felt he'd lost something important.

Over the rest of the day and half the next, David exerted himself to restore them to the old status. In addition to being attentive over Sveneric's lessons, he offered to teach the boy games he didn't already know, and showed him how to carve wood.

He thought he'd made good headway until Adam reappeared, still soggy, but looking far less feverish. "I can take over now."

Sveneric's demeanor changed, and he began chattering. "Look at the carving I began. It'll be a cat, I think. One sitting down. And I made a new drawing over there. Can you guess what it is?" Pointing to the wall. "That's Antivad-the-cat, see the white patches on his back? I know we're not s'posed to pet them, but if I see him when we go to drill, he puts his tail up and I know he wants me to scratch his back . . ."

Adam's voice sounded like gravel. "You're not supposed to feed them, so they keep the rats from eating our food. And you have to remember not to let anyone see you petting one. Bostian, and certain others – if they see you liking an animal, they will hurt the animal in order to hurt you."

"I will remember," Sven Eric said.

"Now, where did we leave off in your reading?"

David left the room. Adam followed him to the door.

"Thanks," Adam said. "If you're busy, Laban should be back when Dejain lets him free. He can swap off with me and Leef." Adam didn't mention that Sveneric had stopped talking to Rolfin. No one was sure why. Rolfin himself accepted being ignored by the shrimp with a grim lack of affect.

David had started toward his room, but glanced back at Sveneric sitting so upright on his stool, his thin wrists – the line of baby-fat gone – bent as he concentrated on his lettering, his feet curled around the legs of the small chair. "Were we ever that spindly?" David asked.

"Worse," Adam croaked. "Much worse."

David went out to the hall, closed his hand around MV's transfer token, and there was the familiar inside-out-wrench. When he came out of it, he caught a glimpse of sky and sea, then fell on his butt.

He squinted against the brilliance of sunlight on water and peered down the length of a yacht. MV – half a hand taller, and a lot more muscular through the arms – laughed at him from next to the tiller. Though the air was brisk, MV wore only a pair of black pants, feet and torso bare and sun-bronzed. He looked like the beard spell was maybe a year or so off, a startling change.

When the transfer-reaction dissipated, David said in a tone of discovery, "This is your boat."

"It is?" MV's sarcasm was more habit than sting; he recognized transfer reaction when he saw it.

Sure enough, the glassy stupidity faded from David's gaze as he took in the sails on the single mast, the rigging, the rudder pole. "You can sail this alone?"

"I can, but you're going to put in some work helping, if you stay," MV said.

David remembered their little boats from their days in Geth. He'd never been on anything like this yacht. He pulled off his shoes and socks, then stood up. "Show me."

MV did.

After a highly technical stream of instructions, well punctuated by pungent curses when David made a wrong move, he found himself working hard. It felt good to stretch his muscles, even to sweat, after the arid nothingness of the Beyond, which he knew he had to return to. The harder he labored, the clearer his mind seemed to be. It had been good instinct to get out when he did. But he was going to have to work on his endurance.

However, not right at this moment. "Where's Detlev? He part of this manhunt for Roy?"

"I suspect he's tracking Zhenc, because anywhere Zhenc is, Yeres is sure to be maneuvering right behind him. But that's a guess, not a fact."

David looked upward. "Left in the dark. Again. Even the shrimp doesn't trust me," he said.

MV snorted. "Don't whine to me. I've put in the better part of a year working on water filter magic, bridge spells, even breaking down and restoring the Waste Spell dispersion—and that old geezer still takes obvious pleasure in letting me know he considers me a spy."

"Aren't you a spy?"

MV gave David the back of his hand, then said, "Tighten that sheet." And when the sails had been trimmed to his satisfaction, "Behold me, trying to be cooperative and eager. Tsauderei just laughs in my face."

"But you're sticking it out?"

"He's tough. I like that. He's thrown every damn beginner labor at me—every single one—and piles on history and essays and lectures about the meaning of magic, ancient cultures, and the like. I have to say, Siamis's old tricks for memorization while you're planing wood still work."

"And so?"

MV's eyes narrowed. "He's up to something, all right. Something big. I think those fools over in the Sartoran mage guild are all in on it. Or the head snakes anyway. But so far, I haven't gotten a sniff of what. He takes the books with him when he goes off."

"Curtas is not here, I noticed."

"Still off somewhere building something or other."

David wondered what that was all about, but he knew there was no use in asking until Detlev was ready to talk.

"You?" MV asked.

David breathed out. "I'm . . ." He searched his mind for

words to express the weirdness of the inner Beyond, the stale
tedium and overpowering sense of danger, the way nothing
could be trusted, especially if you reacted. Then they had you
ensnared . . .

The next thing he knew the sky had changed, the waves
calming. MV rapped his knuckles on David's head. "The last
thing you said was 'I'm.' You still in there?"

David shook his head. "It's . . . I'm only just beginning."
And to get off the subject of the Beyond, "I think you should
give Tsauderei Roy's text. See what happens."

MV's brows shot up. "Tell him I wrote it?"

"Sure. Why not?"

"Nah." MV leaned back with one foot on the tiller pole,
arms crossed behind his head. Yep, still no pit hair. That
meant he'd get even taller. David looked down at himself,
feeling like he was Noser's size in comparison.

"It's more fun dueling with the truth," MV said. "Besides,
then I don't have to remember lies, and he's fast with the
questions. Always trying to catch me out."

"Then tell him Roy wrote it."

MV studied David, eyes narrowed. "You thought about
Roy? Why he left?"

"Some."

"And?"

"What's there to say? He didn't trust us enough to talk it
out. I don't know if it was Siamis hopping the fence, or
something else —"

MV cut in. "Adam believes Roy was a plant. Out here,
there's nothing to do but think. Want to know what I think?"

"I think you want to tell me."

"I think Adam's right. Roy was always gonna run. He was
a plant."

David was going to ask by whom, then recollected the
tangle at the very end, before they left Five. "By *Lilith?*"

"Yup."

David snorted. "Adam's an idiot."

MV checked sea, sky, then pulled a rope over the tiller
pole, which kept the boat on an even keel. "Come below. Let's
get some grub."

David agreed with some fervor. He was starving. They
went below, and David glimpsed a cabin aft, with two built-in
bunks, shelves above and below, everything tidy.

"That's where the passengers bunk. When I have any," MV said, jerking his thumb toward the cabin. "I swing a hammock abaft the galley here. I can get two in, three at a squeeze, abaft, and a couple of hammocks in the cabin in addition to the bunks. Or just sleep on deck."

The galley was small, with swing-down prep tables that could double as eating tables. Above and below, food supplies were tightly closed into ceramic jars of various sizes, big ones below, small ones — mostly spices — above, with fruits and vegetables swinging in nets overhead.

A firestick under a tiny stove provided heat. MV already had a covered bowl with pan biscuit batter sitting on a sideboard. With the economical speed of much practice, he crushed an olive onto a flat sheet to oil it, plopped biscuits onto the sheet, and set them cooking as he chopped up some greens and sliced yellow cheese.

"If you want fish for dinner, you have to catch it," MV said over his shoulder.

David's mouth was watering, and he liked the boat — liked the sense of isolation. But he knew that was deceptive. That sense of urgency had been growing steadily. "I'd better get back soon's we eat." He leaned in the galley hatch, staying out of the way of those flashing knives. "What are Adam's reasons for thinking Roy was a plant? Besides wanting to believe Detlev is omniscient — which we know he's not. We saw that on Five when those cave idiots turned up, taking everyone by surprise."

"One thing you can say for Adam is that he's way beyond you or me with Dena Yeresbeth. In contact, in shielding, in place-reading, in dream-walking, he was always up there with Siamis, right on his heels."

"That's true," David said, remembering the two of them sitting cross-legged on the houseboat, hands on their knees, for hours. After which Adam would get up and fall into bed as if he'd been running their obstacle course while carrying a pack of boulders.

He also remembered the time when Adam couldn't bear to touch anything that anyone else had touched. That was David's first introduction to one of the rarer forms of coinherence, sensing memories from objects. He remembered that Adam had begun drawing all the time — always having chalk in his hands so he didn't have to touch things — until he'd finally learned to master it. Adam had been born with it all, to a degree that no one else understood, and his mind had always taken a side road from everyone else.

"Adam thinks now that Roy was beyond *him*, and hiding it all along."

David blew a fart noise in disbelief. "What convinces you Adam's right?"

"Because of the orders after we left Geth." MV's knife winked and flashed as he chopped, then he used it to flip biscuits. "I think, if Detlev did know — he's a dyranarya, which is an order of magnitude beyond even Siamis's talents — I think, if Detlev knew about Roy, it was because he was getting as much information, or more, than Lilith got from Roy. Incidentally, same strategy I'm supposed to be using with Tsauderei. Not that I've gotten anywhere. Yet."

David flipped up the back of his hand to Tsauderei. "Making Roy a double agent without his being aware?"

"Yup. And when Roy finally got good enough to maybe suspect he was being used . . ." MV's knife flashed up to point at his head, then he used it to flip the last of the biscuits. "Detlev began cutting him loose. Sent him up to Bereth Ferian to infiltrate that mage school up there. Gave him that project to write." He nicked his chin toward the galley cabinet where books and papers were stashed.

"Then Five happened. Roy smoked to Geth and took down the fortress magic to show us all up, especially Detlev."

"Right."

"And now he's got how many hunting him?"

"Black Knives for certain. Probably anyone else looking for fast promotion."

David was going to make a comment about Roy deserving whatever happened, but he thought about those last days at Five, when Roy was so tense and silent. If it were true that he'd been a plant, then he would have always felt like an outsider. And what would especially make him feel like a marker in someone else's Cards and Shards game? The awareness that he was being used by both sides.

"Damn," he said finally.

MV grinned. "Biscuits are done. Honey butter in that crock. Bought it fresh in Ellir Harbor two days ago. Eat up, then we both better get back to it."

David thought of the Beyond, and sighed.

Twenty-seven

Telyerhas to Marloven Hess

Marloven Hess lies squarely athwart the middle of the Halian subcontinent. Below it is Telyerhas, one of several former Marloven territories, now a kingdom of its own. It, in turn, was divided into different principalities. These all bore the prefix "Kren" or "crown," Senrid had learned — when the Marlovan empire began breaking up, the Cassad family returned to their Iascan roots, taking up that language again.

Senrid had debated this trip all summer. Once the academy Games were over, and the boys and girls went home, he had much more free time.

He traveled alone.

He'd discovered a taste for camping during his adventure with Puddlenose, so he took a tent with water-resistant spells, and had the kitchen make up food that he could warm over a firestick. He rode armed only with his knives, and a transfer token carried on his person. No use in offending the southerners by carrying a bow. If his knives and his wits couldn't keep him out of any possible trap that Siamis might have laid (and it seemed a lot of trouble to go to, when Siamis could just as well hunt him down anywhere else he went in the world), then he deserved whatever bad thing happened.

As he rode southward past his ancestral lands at Darchelde, now deserted and wild, still showing the effects of powerful dark magic devastation four centuries old, he peered around with intense interest. He hadn't been back since that terrible confrontation with Detlev and the Norsundrian force that the mystery-figure Erdrael had banished. Senrid knew he had yet to pay the cost of that "rescue" — once whoever had arranged it appeared. But when that happened, he planned to show them just how much he resented being used in a game he couldn't see.

The Marloven-Telyerhas border was quiet, the patrol catching him in a gratifyingly short time. But he expected no less from South Army and the Jarl of Methden's riders.

After that, the trip was memorable only for being unmemorable: scenery, weather, people uninterested in the rider, though some admired the horse. Krend Erel, the capital (it seemed to translate out to "new crown city") showed only traces of the old Iascan stone castles in walls here and there.

Senrid rode in at a walk, looking about with intense interest. His father had ridden here once, and met his mother. He tried to imagine that, and failed. They were such shadowy figures, his father briefly recollected as this impossibly tall, smiling man. Senrid couldn't recollect any images of his mother, but he retained the vaguest sense of a warm, soft hand cupping his cheek — a memory he had never shared with anybody.

His contact with Telyerhas had been minimal, strictly confined to border matters and trade since he'd come to the throne — a mutual indifference predicated from his side on his having been angry that they'd not warned him about the Norsundrians on his border during those terrible last days before he defeated his uncle. Of course they (according to Leander, all Senrid's neighbors felt the same) seemed to feel in those days that there was little difference between Marlovens and Norsundrians, and probably hoped each would wipe the other out. As little contact as possible had been preferred ever since.

The capital, like most on Halia, was laid out more or less like spokes of a wheel, all the main roads leading inward to the oldest part of the city, which had once been behind massive walls. Now that area was the center of government and trade. He'd traveled enough to recognize clues to what he might find — in Colend, the royal palace had been surrounded by the smaller, but equally fine, palaces of the nobles, and it had been separated off not by perimeters of stone, but complicated braidings of gardens, pathways, and canals.

Here, the roads converged from five points, with a park at the center. Senrid assumed the building that first drew the eye was their royal palace—until he got close enough to see the words and shield of the scribe guild. Opposite was a lower, rambling building made up of old and newer wings. He rode toward that, to be stopped at a decorative gate that wouldn't have halted a determined scout team for more than a few breaths.

A tall woman who carried herself well in her military garb, complete with decorative spear, held out that spear to halt him.

"Senrid Montredaun-An of Marloven Hess here to see Havlan-King Casarod," Senrid said in passable Iascan, and waited to see what would happen.

Not much. Her eyes narrowed, then she clearly decided he was someone else's problem higher up the chain of command. The first sign that they were taking him somewhat seriously was an awareness of being flanked, out of sight but not out of hearing. He gave no sign that he was aware as an older, roly-poly servant appeared, bowed with palms together, then said, "This way, please."

Senrid was bowed into what was obviously a work room, one entire wall fitted with drawers that might have contained anything from papers to weapons. worn over loose trousers, advanced around a desk. "It really is you?" he asked in very archaic Marloven. "You have a look of my sister Lesra."

Senrid's maternal uncle, then.

Senrid said, "I'll let the resemblance serve as credentials. I'd hoped to bypass days of ritual in order to be granted an hour or so of talk."

Havlan's smile was brief, and lopsided. "Far more likely you would have been put off had I not been at home."

"Then I would have come back. When I went to Colend, it took weeks of preparation to see the king. And that ended with riding an honor guard right up into their teeth."

Havlan uttered a laugh that stirred some very faint memory, impossible to catch, but unsettling. "Oh, well, Colend," he said, ink-stained fingers out wide. "We're a lot less formal, probably as a result of our days as part of your empire."

Another of those flaring, lopsided smiles. "So. Why are you here, Senrid son of Lesra?"

Senrid would have cut out his own tongue rather than mention Siamis (except as a target), so he said, "I thought maybe we should meet. In spite of what happened. I don't know much about my aunt, but my mother was popular, and my father was grief-stricken at her death. I don't know why my uncle killed either of them."

Havlan winced, then said unexpectedly, "I was too small to be involved, but even I knew that it was a very bad idea to send Caras outside the country. But she would insist on marrying at her rank or above."

Senrid knew that Uncle Tdanerend (himself extremely unpopular) had married Caras, who'd made herself equally unpopular. "My uncle destroyed all the records of that time. It's a habit among Marloven rulers," Senrid said. "And I was a baby."

Havlan nodded, wisps of pale hair drifting over his ears. "I know. We were glad when we heard tidings of your having overcome Regent-Prince Tdanerend. It seems you've done well since then."

"No plans for conquering armies, if that's what you're hinting around for," Senrid said.

Havlan tipped his head. "What happened to Caras's girl? We never heard about her again after you became king."

"My cousin Ndand ran away," Senrid said — which was true enough. "All I ever got was a letter saying that she wanted to study music, and she didn't want to come back."

Havlan's expression had blanked, but at that his brows shot up. "Music! That sounds like my mother, truth to tell. Yet they never met. How strange blood is, at times."

"Your mother was a musician?"

"She was probably the worst queen we'd had in a hundred years," Havlan said cheerily, "but the best composer. Almost all our most enduring musical plays are hers."

Senrid repeated, "Musical plays?"

"You didn't know that?"

"It's this kind of thing I came hoping to learn. Little as my uncle left behind about my father, there's no sign of my mother except a few pieces of art that she'd brought with her, that the servants hid away when my uncle took over as regent."

"How long can you stay? There is surely at least one of

Grandmother's works being performed somewhere in the city tomorrow, maybe even tonight," Havlan said. "You might or might not be aware, but we are the center of the musical arts in the south here. People come from Toth and Perideth, even farther when we hold the competitions for whoever will be sent east to Colend for the Music Festival. Shall I send a page to discover what might be available?"

Havlan seemed perfectly pleasant, but in the steadiness of his gaze Senrid sensed deeper question beneath the surface question.

"Yes," he said.

The page was duly dispatched, reporting back that there were two possible selections, one in a central theater and a reading at a popular inn.

Senrid shared a meal with Havlan and his family—a consort of about forty, balding, broad through the chest as if he did some kind of labor, a gawky teenage son who pelted Senrid with questions about the horse he'd brought, and a small princess who was more interested in the cats roaming in and out in search of tidbits than in the table conversation.

Afterward they all piled into a well sprung carriage to be carried a matter of eight or nine streets to the theater, where they were bowed into the best seats. Senrid understood not a one of the references that got people howling with laughter, nor did he care the slightest about the vagaries of lovers' quarrels (there were two couples to sort out), but he did appreciate the music, especially the way it underscored the emotions portrayed by the actors.

Senrid's real appreciation went to the stage mages' expertise. But he clapped when the others clapped, and agreed with all the praise on the ride back, the little princess having fallen asleep against one father's arm, her feet curled over the other father.

Lantern-bearing servants appeared and carried away the princess and took care of coach and horses. Havlan led the way inside, and the family politely took their leave. Havlan and Senrid were alone.

The king said, "I have been pondering what I ought to do about certain artifacts. We had pretty much decided that these belonged in the archive, especially given the Marloven proclivity for destroying the previous rulers' relics. But I'm wondering if that might be a mistake."

"Mistake?" Senrid asked. He'd been on the verge of excusing himself to depart—he was already mentally arranging for the return of the horse to the border guards, so he could transfer home.

"You have to understand that my grandmother, cloud-minded as she was, retained enough astuteness to have misgivings about the romance that sprang up between your father and mother. Because it really was one of those ballad romances, both taking to the other almost from the first day they met. But no one here really wanted to see her ride north into the Marloven . . ."

"Maw? Lair?"

Another flickering, one-sided smile, and Havlan raised his gaze to the door, where a silent servant stood, bearing a carved wooden box. A gesture of the hand brought the servant in to set the box down and bow herself out again, closing the door.

Havlan laid his hand on the box, which Senrid could see was carved with running horses around the sides, a Marloven motif. Or so he'd thought. Havlan said, "I've heard most of what I am going to summarize. I was too young to really be aware, except of the sounds of raised voices. No one in the guild councils wanted to see the future queen ride north, because there was no question of erasing the borders, of course. And I will say that your father never put that as a condition. Instead, they wrote letters."

The way Havlan breathed out those last three words made Senrid's neck hairs prickle.

"We don't have hers. Unfortunately. I'd like to believe that he cherished them the way she did his. But she had been raised by archivists, and so, when she did go north to marry, she left his letters behind." Havlan pushed the box forward. "We've made copies, of course. But I think it possible that you might like to have the originals."

"My father's letters?" Senrid heard his own voice, high and squeaky, as if it came from outside the room. "I would very much like to have them."

"I think—I trust—I hope—you will find them interesting. There are also her letters to our mother included. Few of those, given their relationship, which was, ah, more good will than actual understanding either way."

Senrid's eyes did not move from that casket as he thanked

Havlan. He said everything that was proper, he made arrangements for the horse, and he transferred back his travel gear. Then he transferred home, enduring the extra hard punch resulting from holding onto the casket. But he dared not send it first lest it vanish forever.

He fell down in his study, stomach heaving, limbs trembling, but the reaction faded at length. He let the duty Runner know that he was back, lit a lamp, and late as it was, opened the cask.

The letters were all written in Iascan, which caused Senrid to rejoice that he had put in the work to learn that language. The sight of his father's own hand in the faded ink made Senrid's throat tighten. It hurt only a little less to see his mother's headlong scrawl, which was actually a little more like Senrid's own hand than his father's squared lettering. She signed her letters Tiri, which he'd learned was the name of a small bird seen around lakes. It was strange, seeing his city through her eyes, learning the rooms she had adopted as her own, and it was even stranger to read about his own birth. He had known that his father's nickname was Evan, which was now the common nickname for Indevan. From the number of times she wrote *Evan and I*, he could tell that they did a lot of things together. But mostly she wrote about Senrid himself. It hurt in a way he'd never been hurt before to read about how miraculous he was as a baby, doing what he recognized as ordinary things: babbling, crawling, learning to feed himself. He could see that there was no miracle here, or rather all the miracle was in the loving eyes of his mother.

How it hurt! Especially when he deciphered a sketch she had made, the ink faint. At first it looked like two circles, one half obscuring the other, until the smaller circles below, and the five tiny ones at either side resolved into a sketch of a crawling baby from the back, the circle of a diapered bottom, with a round head beyond. Seen without context, he would have thought it ridiculous, but she'd clearly found something endearing enough to capture the image as best she could.

He'd barely begun walking and talking when the letters stopped.

He had to get out of the room for a time, but he was drawn back by a need far more powerful than magic, though he could not define it. He bundled her slim packet of letters carefully and turned to those written by his father. And though the

outer direction had been scrupulous as to titles and formal
names, each letter's header was some variation on *My darling
Tiri.*

Senrid read all night, unaware of the sun rising until he
looked up, the words dancing before his vision. He laid the
last paper down gently on his desk, staring at the open windows of his study as he tried to encompass what he had just
read.

It was going to take time. He had to put them in Commander Keriam's hands, but first, a reread. Funny, ardent —
he'd skimmed through the love stuff, which might someday
be interesting — and impassioned by ideas, headlong chains of
reasoning that scarcely paused long enough to come a close,
the letters were also freighted with historical reference. All
through them Senrid caught tiny glimpses of his mother
through quotations heading many of Indevan's replies.

These were the letters of a revolutionary.

This had to be why Tdanerend — who had not been popular, unlike Indevan — had murdered his own brother, and very
nearly lost the kingdom as a result. Oh, yes, there had been the
quarrels about the purpose of magic, and Tdanerend's
jealousies, and his obsession with precedence and glory, but
the astonishing thing was the vision that Indevan had put
forth, nothing more than total reorganization of the Marloven
way of life, by abolishing the standing army.

Senrid dropped the paper and shut his eyes, readying himself to reach mentally for Liere in case she was not completely
shielded, then he caught himself. He remembered that Siamis
was there.

Of course there had to be a reason behind that comment of
his. Senrid began pacing along the windows, back and forth,
tapping each sill as he passed as he flung his tired mind down
the path of memory. Could it be that Detlev had been running
Tdanerend from the beginning, to prevent this very thing from
happening?

In a way it didn't matter, not before this discovery that his
father had already come to the conclusion that Senrid had
been struggling to formulate in his own mind. But in another
way it did matter. Siamis telling Senrid — Senrid's own
experiences — everything pointed toward that bigger game he
sensed beneath everything else going on.

Senrid resented being used, being *ignorant.*

Twenty-eight

Spring 4753 AF
Dragon Peak on Border Between Sartor and Sarendan

A FULL YEAR AFTER his last visit to Tsauderei, MV stuck
gloved hands on his hips and stared around the vast cavern
gleaming coldly in air so bitter it searched deep in his lungs,
scraping in and out with the freezing burn peculiar to ice. The
smooth walls, scorched millennia ago by dragon fire, the sheer
scope, daunted him as much on this viewing as they had the
first time he was brought here. The surprise he felt was caused
not by the caves, which he'd seen before, but by the fact that
doddering old Tsauderei had mustered the strength to arrange
this outing.

The wind howled and moaned, making speech impossible.
The old mage braced against it, the blasts fingering his beard
and hair with ice. Then he made a sign, and they used tokens
and returned to his cottage. He didn't keep it overly warm,
but in comparison to what they had just left, it felt like an
oven. MV threw off the heavy coat that Tsauderei had offered
him, and shed mittens and hat, then stacked them neatly on
the table near the huge picture window.

"Sit down," Tsauderei said.

MV would have rather walked around. He hated that

chair, but Tsauderei was capable of dropping a spell on him anywhere in his cottage. So he sat, and suppressed the sense of going into a fight unarmed. He never brought his weapons to Tsauderei's valley. At first he'd come unarmed as part of his persona as hopeful magic student, but the previous autumn when he got careless and left in his boot knives, he'd found the steel heating up suddenly. He couldn't get them out fast enough—after which they vanished. As nice a pair of folded steel dueling daggers as you could ever find outside of Marloven Hess. They'd cost him the entire summer's earnings.

"Steep?" Tsauderei offered.

This was a first. "Why not?" MV could take or leave the stuff. But he was here as Cooperative and Eager Student, so he'd run as far as the old fart would let him.

"You'll find the fixings over in my kitchen corner." Tsauderei then issued a stream of precise orders about the proper making of Sartoran steep.

Another test, of course. MV carried out the orders with a precision that he hoped would convey its own sense of irony. Tsauderei made no comment, but when he took his cup and sipped, eyes closed, he nicked his chin down minutely, and said, "Not bad."

MV slurped, then lipped another taste. All right, this much he'd grant: it tasted far better if you didn't throw the leaves into the water and let them boil, the way the boys had done when camping in very cold weather.

"You were not surprised to see the dragon caves," Tsauderei observed as he set his cup down.

MV considered lying, and as always, snuffed the impulse. "Right." And, to avoid any further questions about Detlev, "Why'd you take me up there?"

"Did your master tell you why the dragons left?" Tsauderei asked.

Seemed they were going to talk about Detlev anyway, but he hedged, because why make it easy? "*Siamis* told us that they regarded humans as vermin. Though old songs and stories insist that we tended them."

Tsauderei chuckled deep in his chest. "That's the hint we get in the oldest records. We tended them, followed them around, carried off their shit and made treasure of it—and of course fought over it, as we fight over everything. Or nothing."

"Their shit *was* treasure," MV said. "I've seen dragonfire stones. I can see why rich people pay as much as a castle is worth to get one."

Tsauderei shrugged. "What I'm endeavoring to do here is introduce the topic of worldview. You've been showing up once or twice a year now for three years —"

"And I've done everything you asked," MV was goaded into saying.

"And you've completed every first-year student's task I've given you, though I know you are quite advanced. In certain areas. In others, profoundly ignorant. To return to my original point," the mage said acidly, "we've yet to broach a serious subject. You've been maintaining a pretense, shall we say, that you're independent of Detlev. If that were true, you'd have to have a reason to run. Unless he booted your skinny ass out of his merry band of assassins and murderers for incompetence or squeamishness, and I don't believe you're incompetent or squeamish. What's your worldview?"

"I don't have one." MV flipped his hands wide. "Isn't that the kind of question to ask someone closer to your age?"

"Everyone has a worldview. A five-year-old will say, 'I want to help people,' if taught to say it, and to mean it, as much as you mean anything at five. Or, likewise, 'I want to kill people.' I repeat, what's yours?"

"I don't think much past . . ." —*the target*— "my next meal. If that far."

Tsauderei pursed his lips and made a loud, fruity razzberry.

"Let's shift the question, then, since you seem to be incapable of rudimentary intent. What does Norsunder's errand boy want with me?" The old mage flashed up a hand. "What are you supposed to say to that question?"

"Nothing!" Too late MV perceived the trap, and snarled, "I haven't talked to Detlev since I left."

"Your instructions were to stay silent?" When MV refused to answer, Tsauderei sat back. "It's a shame, even a tragedy, that someone as well educated in magic and history as you can't think past tomorrow."

MV flushed, knowing he was being goaded. "I want to do something interesting."

"Norsunder's dedication to wholesale slaughter and destruction not interesting enough for you?"

MV said with disgust, "If I wanted that I'd be running to Efael's rein."

Tsauderei grunted. "Then let us try this. If you . . . *somehow* . . . come up with the answer to these two questions—what spells did Detlev use to remove Sartor from the world for a century, and why— I'll let you read any book in this room. And teach you whatever you want to know in it. Until then, read this, and we shall discuss it next time." He pointed to a thick book lying on a table.

MV suspected he knew what that book was, and frustration gripped him. He'd lost ground for certain with that inadvertent hint that he was still in contact with Detlev. "I don't know!"

"Tough to be you," Tsauderei drawled. "Since we're not to talk about advanced magic, while you are here, let me see you renew the water-resistance spells on those coats. I mean down to the fiber level." The mage jerked his thumb over his shoulder at the heap of cloth on the table behind him, then took another sip of steep. "Ah. Not bad at all. You learned something today!"

Twenty-nine

Norsunder-Beyond to Norsunder Base

WHEN DAVID FINISHED READING years of reports in the Beyond archive, his reward was even more dangerous: to learn to move without trace.

At first, it had taken concentration, and immense effort. Now, after immeasurable time, David moved rapidly through Norsunder, shifting through levels with a speed that would give anyone vertigo who tried to make sense of the surreal scenery. He never made the mistake of focusing on his surroundings, so he remained little affected by the crazy landscapes fluctuating around him in a blur.

The result was a trail very nearly impossible to follow, even for the ever-watchful creators. His presence lingered in a myriad of places, and since time was blurred in Norsunder, his trail looped back in circles. Norsunder was one place a person could be everywhere and yet nowhere.

Once he mastered that, he ventured deeper. He dared not try following traces of anyone except Detlev. Those turned out to be unsettling enough. Inevitably David tested historical veracity by finding the vast plain on which Ivandred of Marloven Hesea waited, the fox banner raised above the infamous First Lancers. David zoomed closer, but all he could see was shadow in the face of the exiled king.

From there David ventured into magic-captured memories and scenes, until he figured out that these could be falsified, again through magic. The one truly unsettling sight – and it was not false – testified to only one of Detlev's many schemes: the endless black ocean on which bobbed too many vessels to count. Again, David in his bodiless state swooped overhead, as always alert for tracers following him.

He looked down at what had to be pirate ships, the sailors dressed outlandishly. Far too many of those ships bore the scorched marks of fire, masts, hulls, and mariners alike spiked by arrows. The decks of many ran with fresh blood centuries old, but caught beyond time.

And there, bobbing on the water, a Venn-made craft fit for a king, again flying the fox banner, though this version was different – far more fox-like, less raptorish. At the helm, hands on the wheel, green eyes gazing into infinity, stood a tall, knife-lean figure, still irascible in old age: Fox Montredavan-An.

What possible use had Detlev had for these?

At the slightest hint of tracer, David shot away, diving through layers with the ease of familiarity, but though he was fast, he knew the lords of this creation were faster. His trail might not lead anywhere, but if for some reason they chose at any time to focus on him, he might come face to face with one.

And then –

And then I will learn the purpose of Detlev's plans from the Garden of the Twelve.

But still he kept moving. He could not pause long any one place. Always his mind listened, ready to block invasions except from one person. When Detlev sent the signal, he had to act. Fast.

How long had he been waiting? No way to measure time, but it seemed an eternity. He fought tiredness and kept shifting. The dark, weird landscapes seemed still to David's eyes, but the sense of something moving at the edges of his vision heightened the sense of danger.

He was nearer the center now, where it was difficult to navigate. Reality blurred as much as time did elsewhere, and David fought to keep his focus, knowing a heartbeat's weakness and he could find himself trapped by false images, to be preyed on by Yeres or Efael. Or the far worse entities at the very center . . .

Find me. It was Detlev.

David scanned through the hallucinatory images, focused and there he was. The scene flickered around them: they stood in a borderland, on a flat stone bridge.

"Efael now knows that Zhenc lied about the Aldau-Rayad artifact," Detlev said. "Events are moving too swiftly. I need you on guard at Norsunder Base for a short time longer; I'm going to attempt a distraction by freeing Yeres's prisoners."

"Events?" David asked. "I thought I was here for a purpose."

Detlev gave a short nod. "That can still happen. It will happen. But not yet: Yeres and Efael will do anything to get their war. I believe Connanre is about to turn on me, so I'm scattering you boys."

"Scattering? As in . . ."

"Time to jettison Norsunder." And he vanished.

David paused, looking around at the ugliness surrounding him. A wait did not matter unless he was caught; the time he spent here would not measure out There. He found that he was not precisely reluctant to leave, but close. He'd finally mastered the Beyond, without daring the very center — and now he had to get out.

Why the reluctance? Because scattering meant breaking them up. Within the limitations of Norsunder, they'd been free to do whatever they liked. Life was good if you were fast and strong and smart. Their only loyalty was to Detlev himself. David frowned, looking over the silent deadness of Norsunder's borderland as he considered the vast interconnection of obligations and expectations the lighters imposed on one another, seemingly all in the name, as MV had said contemptuously a long time ago, of protecting the weak.

What was it Detlev said? Out there everyone has a right to a life with as much meaning and happiness as they desire, and in here no one has any rights at all. What you want, you take, so you'd better enjoy the taking.

He and the boys had stayed tight, a defense against both worlds, Norsunder and lighters. Leaving Norsunder meant, first thing, the others could take off if they wanted. And some would.

Laban believed he'd be able to appear to the Everoneth and say, "Hi! I have blood ties to one of your infamous royal exiles, and I want to join the Knights of Dei," and be welcome.

Vana believed they'd go right back to the fun they'd had when they first joined the Young Allies.

Curtas wanted to resume his friendship with Shontande Lirendi.

Then there was Adam, who'd been fighting regret ever since Roy left.

And David didn't know where Rolfin's head was at, other than some dark place that niffed of regret.

David sighed, snapped a Gate into being, and stepped through.

Norsunder Base smelled dank and moist, the noise of a hard rain roaring on the roof. Had to be spring. The smell of old ice and the dankness of mushy, melting old snow mixed with defrosting horse droppings made him cough.

He stepped into the office, found water, and drank. As always, the sense of desiccation that the Beyond fostered began to ease. He glanced into the inner room, to find it bare, the walls scrubbed of chalk drawings. No little desk or toys remained.

He walked out and poked his head into the rooms, to discover evidence of them having been changed around. He sat on his bed, closed his eyes, and reached for MV: *I'm back. Report?*

Instead of answering, MV shared a memory of his recent conversation with Tsauderei. Then: *No contact with anyone else. Easier than lies. Meantime he stuck me with that old snore,* **The Emras Testament**. *We read that how long ago?*

The rainy season before Detlev first let us go under cover in Fya Rya. But that's the short version — the one the lighters have.

There's a longer one?

Oh, yes.

Memories flashed between them, far too quick for words: the fun of those days before they'd been separated off, David and his band to tangle with Leskandar Rhoderan and his covert thirst for kingship while he prated of equality. And because David had to sustain the contact — MV was not good at long distance — the heaving and tossing of a yacht on rough waters coming through made him end it.

He settled his inward balance, then went off to get a meal, to discover Adam, evidence of a couple years' growth only in the sharpness of his cheekbones, and sitting across from him, a skinny boy whose straight posture and neat brown hair were both familiar and unfamiliar. Sveneric had spurted up again.

They sat off to the side in the mess hall, where he discovered that Sveneric had been allowed into the general population. He looked maybe seven or eight. Detlev hadn't let the older boys out until they were over ten, and then in batches. But from the position Sveneric had chosen—with the widest possible field of vision, and three avenues of retreat—David guessed he was probably better at making himself scarce than they'd been.

"Ah," Adam said. "Geography, maths, and language roots. We just finished history."

David looked down into Sveneric's shuttered expression. "What year are we in?"

Adam's grin flared. "'53."

What events did he mean? David was used to thinking questions into the void of no answers, so was startled when Adam heard anyway. *I think it's Five.*

David didn't bother asking how he knew. Instead, he turned to Sveneric, and, keeping his voice a bland murmur, "I was sorry not to see art on the walls."

Sveneric's brows twitched, and David sensed a questing brush against the firm mind-shield that was now habit waking and sleeping. He kept his surprise from showing. Sveneric was good. At least as good as Adam had been at the same age.

"I'm not very adept yet," Sveneric said, his diction precise in that treble voice. "I mess up perspective. Chalk on uneven stone makes it worse."

"Do you need new things to sketch?" David asked, still in that bland murmur that would not catch attention from anyone else. And when Sveneric stilled, the pupils in his hazel eyes widening, David said, "How about the dragon caves up north?"

"Oh, yes," Sveneric breathed. "I would like that very much."

"Then let's see what you do with maths, and I'll set it up." David flicked his hands, meaning magical transfer.

"Will you explain the spell?" Sveneric asked.

Detlev hadn't taught them transfer magic, which was so very volatile, until David was at least twelve. But he said, "All right."

A week later, Sveneric lay dreaming.

He dreamed inside the dragon cave that David had taken him to, which in turn was enclosed inside a steel ball as large as the sun, large enough to compass the entire world. In this safe world, he could float between lake and sky the way Ian floated over the lake in Delfina Valley, or he could play in the soft sand along the riverbanks, as Jessan and Carl did, or he could lie along a tree branch on a summer's night and watched the dancing lights, way, way up in the north, at the other end of the world, the way Lyren and Mac did. Or he could step through world-gates to see how others lived, as Dirk — the one nobody had met in person, yet — did.

But inside this world, he had taken care to leave a mouse hole, that only those friends knew about. When Lyren appeared in mouse form, Sveneric knew that something important had happened: *Roy was here, and gone again, with Lilith, to the other world. Arthur just told Liere.*

Sveneric had learned enough by careful listening to understand that small events could change one's life forever.

He tested the idea: *It's today.*

He lay inside his dream world, though he was now conscious of thought, and of his body lying in his bed at Norsunder Base, still and straight, his hands relaxed, his face cool. One never knew when one of Them from the Beyond might choose to dive into his mind to skim his thoughts, as had happened twice. There was isolation in Norsunder, when its masters so chose, but privacy was as difficult to construct as safety. He turned his attention to his inner self. No evidence of excitement. No fear.

No joy.

When morning came at last, he had everything ordered in his mind. He swung his feet out of bed and got up, then stepped through his cleaning frame. There were his clothes, plain black and gray, neatly hung on their peg. He dressed and buckled his knife belt on. Stockings, boots.

The gray tunic-jacket also hung on its peg, but he left it there, then looked around the room once. Plain, gray, one window looking north at clouds and rocky plains. The desk neat. Papers lined next to magic books and pencils.

Then he walked out, his heels rapping as they struck the wooden flooring. Everything was quiet, in a place where there was no weather, no stir of air.

He shut the door behind him.

Down the hall was his father's room. He stopped outside the door and put his hand to it. No one inside. His father was truly gone. Soft-footed now, Sveneric continued on his way.

David was waiting for him in the command mess hall. Norsundrians came and went, carrying trays of food and the bitter-smelling coffee that so many of them liked. Some of them noticed him and nicked chins up in a brief acknowledgment; these all were the ones who worked for his father.

Bostian's commanders ignored him as if he did not exist, and the others only noticed him to give him sneering looks. They weren't the worst. That was Efael's Black Knives, but Sveneric stayed hidden whenever they appeared. If he were to step in the minor captains' way, the ones the boys called grass, he'd be knocked down, but he never stepped in anyone's way. Not even in the way of those whose fear shone in their faces when he or his father came near.

David sat alone at a table across from a knot of Bostian's strike troops, his blond hair gleaming in the diffuse gray light filtering in through the windows. David had a pile of papers by his plate and cup, and he wasn't wearing any hardware, but the warriors left him alone.

Sveneric contemplated that as he stood in line to get his food. You could always tell who won fights by the way their followers behaved toward the allies or underlings of other commanders. In the little area out behind one of the barracks where private feuds were settled, MV with grinning ease, Rolfin with powerful efficiency, and David with his thoughtful, instructive air had made the corridors safe enough for Sveneric. In Norsunder Base, one thing only gained others' respect: force.

And here he was expected to make his life.

That was going to change.

David was reading, but when Sveneric came in, David looked up, smiled a greeting, and then turned his attention to his book again. None of the others of the group were present.

Tutoring had been the best ever since David's return, but though they talked about everything else, David still wouldn't say where he had been, or what he had done.

Sveneric swallowed in a suddenly dry throat, then turned his eyes to the dusty stone floor. Once again he sorted through his outer and inner self, reminding himself of how Ian had felt when he saw his father shot by Rolfin. *That* was the life the big boys chose.

When Sveneric looked up again his face and surface-thoughts were calm.

The stable laborer in front of him got his tray, pointed at the things he wanted, got a serving of each, then he moved away. Sveneric grabbed a roll, was tempted to pass everything else by, except he never did that. He was usually hungry in the morning. Despite his snaky stomach he'd have to eat.

He pointed at the fish stew, which smelled of fresh cabbage and wine-braised onions and good spices, and got a bowl of it. Then he picked up his tray and moved across the room, stepping politely aside once when three of Bostian's captains got up and moved out, their heavy boots ringing and their hardware creaking and clanking. The first two ignored Sveneric.

Everyone knew everyone else's business at the Base — or as much as they could find out, by any means possible. But no one knew Sveneric's secret plans. Because today . . .

The last leader gave David a brief salute and received a slight smile in return. When David looked up, Sveneric saw the light change sharply on his face, sharper than it usually did. The planes of his face seemed somehow more angular. Taut skin — tension?

Did he know, then? It was possible he could set up a terrible betrayal. That's what you expected of Them: Svirle appearing out of the Beyond for the first time in centuries uncounted, or the languid and cold-hearted Connanre, or worse, the beautiful soul-devouring Ilerian. They'd somehow divine his thoughts, and mind-rip him, amid triumphant laughter. . .

:*Because I am about to betray those I love most.*

Sveneric schooled his face, then saw David rub his eyes and stifle a yawn.

:*He's just tired.*

Relief sparked an impulse to grin, and Sveneric let that come.

"Detlev is busy," David said. "He said to tell you that he'll be back as soon as he can."

The coldness returned to the pit of Sveneric's stomach; he's really gone. But of course, he had to be; otherwise he would see your plan in your eyes. "Magic stuff," Sveneric said out loud. "He told me there might be some."

"And I'm at liberty today, so what will we do?" David said, chin in hand, his sleepy brown gaze reflective.

Sveneric shrugged. "Whatever you want."

Thirty

SVENERIC AND DAVID SPENT the morning in the boys' private practice court at Norsunder Base, doing sword, knife, staff, and contact fighting. Then some archery, until a dust-laden, sour wind heralded a summer thunderstorm. For a time they shot against it, long after the new recruits being trained in the bigger court had given up, laughing when the wind took their shots wild. Once Sveneric thought he detected a watcher-in-mind, but when he tried to discern identity the tendril of awareness dissolved.

Once the storm passed, they had lunch sitting on the roof, and as they often had ever since David took over Sveneric's tutoring in everything except drawing, David questioned Sveneric closely on magic spells and rules. Always the hows, never the whys.

During the afternoon they went over some maps together, and some files on different lands. Dinnertime came quickly. They did not talk in line, and twice Sveneric had to close his eyes and do a sort-and-calm when David's attention was elsewhere.

After dinner, Sveneric worked to slow his accelerated heartbeat. But his face stayed schooled, and he kept his mind blocked against any questing thoughts from David. When Sveneric got up to leave, David flicked a hand over the top of his head. Tightness grabbed unexpectedly at Sveneric's throat, but he kept walking.

Sveneric passed by the barracks building and the main courtyard. He kept his steps slow, shuffling his feet through the fine gray-brown dust.

Sunset shadows had begun to distort shapes, blurring the dark stone of walls and arches with the rocky landscape where the soil had long since blown away, and nothing could grow. Sveneric picked up his pace, crunching across the gravel toward the stable. The stable hands saw him coming, one approaching with a streaming torch.

"I want Trieste," Sveneric said softly. "No saddle."

The Norsundrian bobbed his head, his eyes incurious. Sveneric dared a whiff of mind-touch: no suspicion. It was a common thing for Sveneric to ride the horse his father had chosen for his riding lessons, though it was rarer for him to go out so late.

As they brought Trieste out, Sveneric did a cautious scan. No one listening on the mental plane. He breathed slowly out, then in again.

And here was Trieste, a stable hand on either side, as Trieste wore neither saddle nor bridle. Nervous, the horse pawed the ground, striking sparks off the stone of the gravel with freshly shod hooves to protect his feet, wheat-colored mane reddish in the light of the torches. His dark coat made its outlines difficult to discern in the fast-falling darkness.

The stable hands held the horse with difficulty, until Sveneric touched Trieste's mind with calm, and stillness. No one asked Sveneric if he wished a hand up. He ran on his toes and leaped onto the horse's back. Trieste pranced, then started out the gate at a warming trot as Sveneric settled in the way he'd been taught, hands on the horse's withers from habit, though he no longer needed to balance himself. His own muscles adjusted to the horse's gait, a smooth opposition that created true balance. This, his father had said, was how they rode when he was young.

The cold wind blew hard in Sveneric's face. He exerted fierce control, forcing up his inner warmth so that he felt only the thrill of the wind and not the bite. Sveneric let the horse choose his gait. The road had been smoothed, inviting a warming canter. His spirits soared as they raced across the barren, flat land northward. He did not miss his jacket. The symbolism was too dear for that.

After a lengthy gallop, Trieste slowed, and walked at a sedate pace when they neared and then passed the last outpost. Sveneric rode well within sight of the unseen guards atop the tower. He raised his hand in a gesture. He knew they'd been apprised of his having left the main Base, and there had never been a rule against these occasional jaunts beyond this far perimeter.

His gesture was usually a greeting, but not today. This time it was a farewell, though they did not know that.

When he passed the outpost, he did not look back, even though he knew it was the last time he would ever pass that way.

For Sveneric had deceived Norsunder, his father, and the boys, and was riding for freedom into the land of the lighters.

Mearsies Heili

Far to the north and west, Clair of the Mearsieans felt peculiar, as if time had stopped, and yet she'd been seeing its flow all around her: the sweet flush of spring ripening into the spectacular green of summer, followed by the brilliance of autumn and then winter's cold, while the girls withdrew cozily into their hideout.

Midway through that same summer's day, Mearsieanne summoned Clair, a thing she rarely did anymore. They had drifted into an understanding, without venturing into the broken glass of words: Clair was free to do anything she liked, except rule, though she could sit in and learn Mearsieanne's style.

Clair had gone north to spend a year with Liere in the mage school. She had sailed with Puddlenose on the *Tzasilia* in company with Dtheldevor's gang, working hard on board. She liked being strong and quick.

This summons was a surprise, and of course Clair must go.

She was completely unprepared to see Horsefeathers — and Roy. Both had changed in two years, Horsefeathers looking more like her sister had, and Roy tall and rangy in build, only the familiar jug ears and long face with its lopsided smile recognizable. His dark hair, always messy and overgrown, was neatly confined in a tail, and he wore the long side-slit tunic over loose, light trousers that Clair had seen on Geth. "Horsefeathers! Where have you been? Roy! You're alive! We've been worried ever since Dhana came back so suddenly."

Horsefeathers and Roy exchanged glances, then she said, "Learning. I was in a place —"

"Wait." Clair held out a hand, her white hair swinging. "Can I get Seshe first?"

"That is an excellent idea," Horsefeathers exclaimed.

Very soon Seshe arrived at a run. When the rush of greetings was over, Mearsieanne said, "Come within the magic chambers. It is warded."

Having spent three very intense years doing nothing but learning, Horsefeathers had already seen to their safety, but she had learned circumspection as well as magic, and so she thanked her host, and they were soon ensconced in the library on the second floor of the white palace.

Horsefeathers perched on a chair, thin hands pressed around the wooden flute that had been the cause of so much anxiety and chase. "Lilith took me to a place. It is a cave of white stone. Like this. But it casts its own light," Horsefeathers said, glancing up at the vaulted ceiling. "In this cave is a pool, and also a place of study. It is here, four thousand years ago, that my ancestor came, with some of your ancestors, to store the means of learning. I was alone, but with the record of what happened. There is little use in detail, but I will tell you that the coinherence they once called in this world Dena Yeresbeth is awakening in our people, too. Jeory was the first, which was why he could handle this safely."

Her long fingers fluttered over the flute's holes with a swift surety that demonstrated uncounted hours of practice. "On my world, as you know, music is the means by which we control the use of magic." She paused, eyes closed. "This is more difficult than I thought it would be, because I keep feeling I need to go back to the beginning, to explain everything—and that would take a lifetime. All I will say is, when it became clear that no one could stand against the great enemy, the people escaped him through a world-gate, except for the Guardian, whose family dwelled in the village of my ancestors."

"The Story was true, then?" Seshe asked.

Horsefeathers lifted dark eyes, and everyone waited while she fell into reverie, then at last blinked. "Much. Much. What you need to know is that after the departure through the world-gate, the Guardian closed the world, too. As a safety measure, this magical artifact was broken. It could not be used until rejoined." She touched the end, where the spiral Clair had called a shell had fit into the flute's carving. "Because this part was kept on your world, there were many of them made, over the centuries, each hidden among people who lived near your Selenseh Redian, whose magic is akin to that on my world."

"So that old woman, whoever she was, gave it to Puddlenose to bring back here?" Clair asked. "That would mean she knew who Puddlenose was."

Horsefeathers spread her hands. "That part is a mystery to me. Perhaps she was guided by the one you call Hreealdar. They, too, came here from our world, and dwelt here in the Selenseh Redian until it was time to return. I suspect that these beings caused the shells to be made, and when one vanished, they made another, as they waited down through time."

Roy whistled softly. Clair, glancing his way, saw that he had left off the Child Spell, but he looked better than she'd ever seen him.

Horsefeathers held up the flute. "That time is now. I have been back to my world twice in the last couple of months, to make warded tests, then I hid in the cave again to practice what I learned. I am now ready to bring the artifact home for the last time and destroy the enemy's magic there. I wanted to know if you would like to come and see."

Seshe and Clair both leaped up, their voices blending, "Yes!"

"Then come. Lilith awaits us. She has chosen a place." Horsefeathers played softly what sounded like bird calls, and before the astonished girls a glow formed as if a million sunlit bees swarmed, then coalesced into golden light giving onto a cliff side, where a white horse with a mane floating like strands of gossamer waited behind Lilith's familiar gray-haired figure.

Horsefeathers led the way, Roy following. Clair and Seshe's fingers met and gripped. They stepped together and the glow snapped shut behind them, leaving Mearsieanne alone in her chamber. She returned to her tasks, as on that barren Aldau-Rayad cliff, Lilith said, "Come, my dears. Witness the rebirth of a world."

Horsefeathers raised the flute and began to play.

At first nothing happened. She played music in a complicated melody that their minds could not catch hold of, and the others gazed outward over the barren plain when from the distant mountains lightning shot skyward, like the flickering lights of the north during the long summer twilights. One, three, eight, then more than could be counted.

The luminous bolts arced across the sky to gather in shimmering brilliance around Hreealdar, whose contours had flared to effulgence.

Hreealdar joined the lights, who transformed into winged horses plunging and leaping in cadence. More and more joined them, deliberate as ritual, as the light incandesced so brilliantly that the humans had to shut their tearing eyes. Then the light vanished, and here on the mountain it was still winter, the slope below an expanse of feathered ice, each needle sparkling in a blue-green forest of snow-dappled fir towering above the long-leafed fern trees indigenous to this world.

Above, white crowned the mountain tops, waterfalls cascading in lacy veils as winter evanesced, promising a new spring. Directly below them, two great, long-billed birds spiraled up slowly from the water in a clapping of wings. Beyond, on the other bank, reeds broke through the cool bluish white of melting snow, as dark waters rushed past, flowing away to an unseen sea.

Clair began to cry, happiness and sadness bound together: Irenne's body had been Disappeared into its components down there, but that which she left behind no longer lay in a place of desolation.

Seshe whispered, "It's healed. Their world is healed."

On the mental plane, Roy said to Lilith :*Norsunder has to be watching.*

:*It cannot be helped. But neither can they interfere, without possession of the artifact now made whole. Its purpose has been fulfilled.*

Roy accepted that, and smiled to see the happiness in the others, but experience was experience. Yeres would see this as a defeat, and Efael would make someone pay.

Thirty-one

Marloven Hess to Delfina Valley

FROM THE NIGHT SKY of Sartorias-deles, most of the other worlds circling Erhal were regarded as stars: Songre Silde silver as a moon due to its opaque atmosphere, Aldau-Rayad dull and dim as the most distant stars, and of course Geth never seen at all, always on opposite side of the sun from Sartorias-deles.

Half the world was busy about its day; most of the eastern end of the Sartoran continent and the lower end of Drael across the strait lay under a thick band of summer storms, so they did not see the sky.

But far to the west, Halia was still a couple hours from daylight. This was when Senrid always rose. He had been good about sword fighting practice lately, though he still hated it. But he gritted through it twice a week as part of his duty, and that meant today. His mood was grim when he got out of bed, dashed through his cleaning frame, and reached for his uniform. He'd just pulled one sock on when the bedroom windows lit with a shimmer he'd only seen once, during the summer he'd spent up at Bereth Ferian with Liere, dodging Siamis.

He doused his glowglobe with a gesture, dropped the

second sock, and ran to his window. Senrid peered up in amazement at a star he didn't even recollect among the brighter blues, greens, reds, oranges, yellows, and whites. This one fluoresced with magic scintillation from horizon to horizon, which died away after a heartbeat or two, but remained glowing with unfamiliar sapphire brilliance.

"What just happened?" Senrid asked the sky.

Of course, there was no answer. Impatiently he scrambled around in the dark, hunting up that dropped sock, pulled it on, jammed his feet into his boots, and on second thought, not only put on his wrist knives but his boot knives as well. He bolted for his study, startling the night runner and the roaming sentries, who smacked fists to chests in salute.

"Did you see that?" Senrid yelped as he skidded by.

"The lightning?" someone asked.

They wouldn't know magic when they saw it—they looked for human danger. Senrid leaped into his study and scrabbled for his notecase. Where was it? Under an entire stack of reports, which he shoved aside with an impatient arm. And . . . nothing. Nothing? No notes?

Who would be awake? He did a quick mental calculation. Liere? No, she was up north with Siamis. Senrid was not going anywhere near Siamis.

Then he thought of Tsauderei. It was full day on that side of the world. If anyone would know about magic blasting across the sky from some other world, it would be the lighters' senior mage.

Senrid grabbed a return transfer token off his desk, shut his eyes, and muttered the transfer spell to Delfina Valley's Destination, hoping that Tsauderei had not decided to ward him. Or even to make him fly in from the mountains below, which would take hours. He passed straight through, dropping onto the grassy sward at one side of the familiar cottage. He stooped to recover, hands on knees, aware of movement at the extreme edge of his vision.

He glanced up, and shock ran through his nerves when he recognized that black-clad, sauntering figure approaching Tsauderei's door. That was the killer MV! Senrid pulled his knives and launched into action.

When MV heard the shivery zing of steel, he whipped around, his own hands going to his bare arms as a short blond figure ran straight at him. MV let out a crow of surprise, stepped in, whipped his right forearm up into a block, and snapped his left at Senrid's ribs. But the brat didn't go flying. He sidestepped, the blow glancing across his shirt, then whirled and attacked again.

Senrid didn't even come up to MV's collarbones, but he was unnervingly fast in the double-knife Marloven style. Mentally cursing his lack of weapons, MV put some muscle into his blocks and cracked his return blows with palm-heel strikes and the edge of his hands, no killing blows—not unless Senrid went for his throat—his intent to put the maniac on the ground—

"Halt!" Tsauderei roared.

Senrid recoiled so fast he staggered back and fell on his ass, knives flying. MV swayed upright, gently fingering a cut above his elbow that he didn't remember getting. Then he wiped his hair out of his eyes and laughed. "You're not a bad scrapper for a little shit."

"Get inside and show me some manners, or both of you will regret it," Tsauderei snarled.

Senrid protested, "I thought he was going for you!"

Tsauderei paused in the doorway. "And what, you thought the old dodderer too senile to defend himself?"

MV deeply appreciated Senrid's crimson flush of humiliation as he felt around in the long summer grass for his knives, wiped them, and put them back in their sheaths. When he followed MV into the cottage, he'd shaken down his sleeves, but MV cocked an eye toward Senrid and said airily to Tsauderei, "I think he's earned a dose of the chair."

"I'll decide what he has or hasn't earned," Tsauderei retorted, and dropped into his wingchair with a grunt. "Surrounded by twits," he muttered not-quite-under his breath.

MV left The Chair to Senrid, and perched on the old table, as Tsauderei said, "I take it you're here with a specific question, Senrid?"

"What *was* that?" Senrid waved a hand skyward in a circle.

"I had the same question," MV commented.

Tsauderei narrowed his eyes at MV. "I don't expect Senrid to know anything about it, but I did think *you'd* have some notion, if from the losing side: according to your old friend Siamis, Aldau-Rayad is now rid of the Norsunder ward over their world. After nearly five thousand years. Norsunder hasn't a hope of getting within a sniff of the place, not without starting over."

MV let out a long, low whistle.

"What," Tsauderei said, "can you tell me about that?"

Senrid sat absolutely still as MV frowned down at his hands, then said, "Efael and Yeres had plans for Five — Aldau-Rayad — and Geth. A lot of it hinged on old wards, most of which I know little about. Care less. Sounds like they took a fall. Couldn't happen to a worse pair of soul-suckers." His voice hardened, then he added, "I believe our ex-brother-in-crime Roy was a big part of that."

"If Siamis is to be believed, and the northerners seem to, he aided Roy, and has hidden him from searchers for the last couple of years. At this point, I'm willing to provisionally regard Siamis as a neutral party in our struggle against Norsunder. So where stands Detlev in all this?"

"Not with Efael and Yeres," MV said. "I'll swallow your dose of white kinthus and you'll hear the same thing."

Senrid looked from one to the other. "Why are you even listening to him?" he asked in disgust.

Tsauderei smiled grimly. "You seem to be behind the times, there in your Marloven citadel. MV here has departed Detlev's tender care, and wishes to become a mage student in light magic."

"And you believe that?" Senrid's voice nearly strangled, so strong was his disgust. The old mage really had to be senile. "They're assassins! The last time I saw this shithead was the day he slit Irenne's throat. And you can't possibly say that was a duel," Senrid added corrosively. "With a girl who never had a day of training in self-defense."

MV's mouth twisted. "I'm going to pay for that for the rest of my life, aren't I?"

"Irenne paid with *her* life," Senrid retorted. "Seems to me the only cost to you is a little inconvenience in convincing the lighters to believe whatever ruse you're running here."

"Peace." Tsauderei lifted a hand. "Peace, Senrid. He can never make restitution for that, ever, to the Mearsieans. But I'm waiting to be convinced he can to the rest of the world. One of the convictions I hold to — though I admit some days are more difficult than others — is the hope that individuals will choose to live better lives, even those who are very good at leading bad ones."

MV lifted his gaze at that, and Senrid sat back, crossing his arms in disgust. As he did, his forearm sheaths pressed against his chest, reminding him that he was the only one wearing steel in this room. The only one who'd drawn it. Though he still believed he'd been right to do so, he had to admit that rushing to judgment was, eh, call it problematical.

Tsauderei said, "My concern at this moment is Norsunder's intent. MV, what you say is pretty much corroborated by Siamis. What I want to find out is, where *is* Detlev in all this? Not with Efael, fine. But that does not explain why Detlev's been seen more in the past ten years than in the past five hundred. As far as I'm concerned, that is a very bad sign. Siamis says I ought to ask him directly. What do you say?"

"No!" Senrid shouted.

Tsauderei held up a hand. "Do I have to turf you out of here?"

Senrid sat back, struggling with anger — and wild curiosity.

MV sat there staring down at his empty hands, one booted foot swinging slightly, as outside the open windows the breezes rustled through the long grasses, and in the distance sheep bleated gently. Then he looked up. "Want me to ask him?"

Tsauderei was hiding how his old heart hammered against his ribs. He knew it wasn't good to be this stressed. He could feel a tremble in his wrists, but kept his hands in his lap. He had a cottage full of wards and traps. Triumph helped him breathe. At last, the truth. "Do it."

He waited for MV to produce a token, or some sign that he'd been reporting to his master, which he'd always believed. But MV just shut his eyes. When he opened them again, he said, "He'll come."

Tsauderei breathed against the flash of pain down his left arm. Breathed again, and felt his heart ease in its slamming. "Shall I make him fly?"

MV gave a crack of laughter. "He'd probably like it."

"But time," Tsauderei said, "I am convinced, is short. Senrid, go sit on the window seat."

MV grinned. "You're gonna give Detlev The Chair?"

Senrid muttered, "What's all this about 'the chair?' It's just a chair."

"You can bet your ass he's getting The Chair," Tsauderei stated. "And if you say a word to warn him, out you go, never to return."

Senrid sat on the window seat, hating the situation, but far too interested to leave. He watched as the air shimmered. And there Detlev was on the grass outside the cottage, looking the same as he had in all Senrid's nightmares since that terrible day on his border, when Detlev had taught him the cost of power: a man somewhat above medium height, mid-thirties, in fighting shape, long side-slit gray tunic coat over black riding trousers—very much, many would say, like the old Marloven uniform. But then gray was practical, an easy color for vast vats of dye.

Detlev walked in and glanced around, a brow twitching when he saw Senrid, who fought the impulse to drop through the window and hide. Tsauderei said, "Have a seat."

Detlev did, and as the stone spell closed around him, Tsauderei flung his hand up, a shimmer of magic closing on MV, who froze in place, except for his head. "Aw, shit," he slurred. "Really?"

Tsauderei said to Detlev, without taking his gaze away, "You've a partial stone spell on you."

"So I'm aware," Detlev said.

"I realize you can kill me with a thought," Tsauderei said. "But I'm assuming you can't murder two at once. Senrid. If I drop dead here, will you cut his throat?"

"In a heartbeat." Senrid's teeth showed.

Tsauderei said, "What's Norsunder's intent?"

Detlev said, "That is very nearly a useless question."

Tsauderei waved an impatient hand. "I realize that you and others fight each other as much as you fight against us, if not more. Fighting being your reason for existence. Is Norsunder—any part of Norsunder—coming against this world now, as a result of what happened to Aldau-Rayad?"

"That I can answer," Detlev said. If he was in discomfort, frozen there with his hands on his knees, it did not show in his voice. "Efael and Yeres have suffered a profound defeat, the result of which we all have seen in the sky. But there's a part that no one has seen: while they've been chasing after young Roy, and Zhenc, a mage you may have heard of, I've been releasing their prisoners as I find them in the Beyond. They should be discovering that about now. 'Now' being a relative term in Norsunder-Beyond, you realize."

"You're fighting against them?"

"Yes."

"What is your intent, to lead a war yourself?"

"No," Detlev said. "My intent is to withdraw from Norsunder entirely, and live quietly in retirement."

"What?" three voices barked.

Detlev's lips quirked. "I've caused a house to be built. That's a side issue, I realize. To the second part of your question." All the humor faded from his expression. "Some part of Norsunder will no doubt be attacking, in some form, possibly within the next five to ten years."

"Why? Why now?"

"Did you not answer that question yourself? Because it's in the nature of some to do so. But it will not be by me. Once I return to Norsunder Base, it'll be for the last time. I've individuals to release from there, too. No one in Sartorias-deles will take any harm from them; many will be going elsewhere."

"Then you are back in the flow of time for the rest of your life?"

"However long that might be, yes," Detlev said.

Tsauderei said, "I need to think. And there are others who'll have questions."

"Appoint a time and place you feel is safe," Detlev said. "I will probably need to address Sartor's queen as my house lies in the west near Sartor's border, though quite distant from any settlements."

Tsauderei pinched the skin between his brows. He wanted to blame Detlev for the confusion of questions making it impossible to think, but he knew it was surprise—shock—the need to reflect. "Very well." He dropped his hand. In a tone of deep irony, "Would you have any objection to meeting Siamis? I trust him just enough to warn us of mental trickery."

"Siamis and I have achieved an understanding," Detlev said. The humor was back in his otherwise bland face, a hint at the corners of his eyes. "Arrange it as you wish. MV can contact me with time and place."

"It'll be sooner than later," Tsauderei warned, regretting the avalanche of letter writing ahead. But it must be done. "Tomorrow, many will want. Three days, most likely. A week at most."

Senrid could not believe Tsauderei was rolling over so easily. He should do the world a favor and slit the throat of the worst threat the world had known in millennia. One hand tightened on the hilt of one of the knives. Reluctance at the idea of killing someone who could not fight back conflicted with the urgency of that old memory —

There is work to be done, some of it by you.

Senrid started violently. He'd had his mind-shield in place! Hadn't he?

While he wrestled inwardly, both MV and Tsauderei were startled by the alteration in Detlev's face. It was subtle, no more than a tightening from blandness to intense focus.

Then MV felt Detlev's contact *:Dejain.*

And — with shocking abruptness — magic shimmered over Detlev. He vanished.

Tsauderei cursed. "He'd warded the partial stone spell all along, and I fell for it." He waved a disgusted hand, and the antidote spell shimmered over MV, who promptly toppled from his perch on the edge of the table.

"Ow." MV sat up, rubbing his limbs.

"So that news surprised you, too," Tsauderei said.

"I knew about the house. That is, I knew of *a* house. I had no idea *he* planned to live there."

"He didn't trust you little rats much more than I, eh?"

MV stood up, clawed his hair back, then said, unsmiling, "It's not trust. It's that what you don't know can't be ripped out of you."

Tsauderei grimaced. "I don't want to find out if that was figurative or literal. Both of you, go home, or wherever it is you lurk, MV. I know how to reach you. I have a lot of letters to write." But first a scry-session with Mondros and Erai-Yanya.

"I want to be there," Senrid started heatedly.

Tsauderei waved a hand. "You and a hundred others, no doubt. I warn you now that it'll be mages first, then kings. If there's room. But you're the acting mage in your country, eh? A terrible idea, that. I can give you histories that prove it's a very bad idea for one person to have all that power — yes, I can see you about to argue. Save it for some day when I have the time to hear it. If. Right now, go home. I'm tired, and feeling my age, but there's going to be no rest for me."

So Senrid did. For a time he walked around his study, wanting to smash something. Then the first faint lifting of dawn reminded him of the time, and the dawn watch bell rang. He ran toward the garrison, looking forward very much to bashing a sword around.

Thirty-two

DETLEV HAD TOLD DEJAIN to get out of Norsunder Base before vanishing off somewhere, peremptory orders that she
resented.

She took her time. She'd nearly all her work packed up,
and angry as she was — and tired, oh so resentfully *tired* — she
felt ambivalent about leaving for the world where she'd been
an insignificant member of an insignificant family. At
Norsunder Base, she'd had significance, even if it had to be
fought for.

She was sitting in her favorite chair, reflecting on the
sweetness of power struggles between those she disliked,
when a flicker on the edge of her vision sent a warning shock
through her nerves.

Cold terror flooded her as she looked up into Yeres's face.
"I hate old women," Yeres stated peevishly. "They're ugly. I
only tolerate them when they're useful. You've been
singularly useless, and we might just have to investigate why,
but I'll give you one more chance. Zhenc didn't last nearly
long enough. Died before we got anything useful out of him.
Efael wants information. It's either from you, or someone else.

You choose."

MV returned to his boat, but scarcely had he begun lifting the anchor preparatory to loosing his sail when he felt the inward tick of David in long-distance contact: *I think you better come.*

MV let the anchor go again, and transferred to Norsunder Base. As soon as he recovered, he banged open the door to Detlev's office, took in the circle of tense faces, and snapped, "What happened here?"

Laban sat on the floor, arms crossed over his bent knees, head on his arms. "Sveneric went missing last night."

David slouched on the corner of the desk, face marked with tiredness and tension. "Erol and I started a covert search through the entire fortress — then all Dejain's minions went on a hunt."

"Half Bostian's, too," Leef said. "Wanted in on the fun."

David said, "We thought they were after Sveneric. They might have been. At first. But this morning they got Adam."

"Who got Adam?" MV demanded.

"Efael, by now. Though Yeres took him." David turned his head. "What happened, Erol?" His tone said, *Where did you ignore orders and fail?*

"Kitchen," Erol whispered. "W-went to bake bread at predawn w-watch. Dejain had a trap w-waiting. He called for us." Erol smacked his forehead. "By mind."

"Me and Erol got there at the same time," Leef muttered. "Saw Yeres. Magic net around Adam, glisten like a slug trail. Saw 'em vanish in transfer."

"Beyond?" David rapped out.

Leef looked uncertain, but Erol shook his head. "No. S-stink. World gate."

David blanched, and avoided looking MV's way. They understood what that meant, though as yet the others didn't.

Laban's expressive brow furrowed, and he gave the others a narrow-eyed glance. "Why Adam?"

"It might be related to Dejain's disappearance," David said heavily.

"It wasn't my fault," Noser exclaimed shrilly. "Not me! Not really!"

Everyone knew that tone. MV grabbed the smaller boy by the front of his shirt and slammed him up against a wall. "You said something. What?"

"I didn't! Not really! It was just stupid!"

MV began slamming him against the wall so that his head rocked, and Noser cried hysterically, "It was ages ago! I just said to that stupid old mage that Adam was Detlev's favorite because he *is*! He got to go *camping*, and we had to wand a thousand *stalls*—"

"Shit," MV said, and dropped Noser.

The boy fell to the floor, huddling in on himself. "I just said it mad, like, not serious. I didn't say anything else," he whined.

"You didn't have to, idiot," David snarled.

"But where's the shrimp?" MV asked.

Laban's head lifted wearily. "Found out from the outer perimeter sentry post he ran off—"

Detlev opened the door.

David began, "Noser was blabbing to Dejain—"

"She told me," Detlev said grimly. "Just now, before she died. I stayed long enough to break Yeres's blood-knife spell. I'll be back when I find Adam."

Detlev transferred.

MV glanced at David and muttered, "He never went after you and me."

David leaned his head against the wall, eyes shut, his face drawn with exhaustion. "With you and me, Efael's game was recruitment—a test—maybe the back of the hand to Detlev while he and Efael maneuvered for command." He opened his eyes. "This, with Adam, is going to be an interrogation. Efael will begin with anything that'll put him on Roy's trail."

"I hope he gets Roy." Noser looked left and right for approval, but no one gave it to him; most glanced at the door through which Detlev had vanished.

Laban repeated, "Begin?" Then remembered what MV had told them, that wintry day in Khanerenth.

Nobody spoke.

Thirty-three

ADAM FOUND HIMSELF IN a place of bleached-pale stone and white marble, the ground flagged in shades of gray. Square buildings supported by columns, slanted roofs edged with friezes breaking the severe lines. Everywhere carving curled coyly, twisted in agony, rioted in lustful arabesques, mocking the heroic statuary and mythology of an age long past, and to Adam utterly alien.

He sensed magic so heavy that it felt like a cage of glass around him, with nothing beyond. A lack of vigilance? No. In that early hour when he reported to the kitchen to help bake the day's bread, he had been tired, but vigilant. He was always vigilant, now. He had still walked into a magical trap.

After a wait impossible to judge, the magical net fell away from him, and he looked up into Efael's cruel face, and at the thin, lizard-quick dart of Efael's tongue over his lips in a fleering grin of expectation. Efael smelled of acrid sweat and blood; a drying rust grimed his fingernails. Both hands.

"Run," Efael said, turning one of those hands out toward what appeared to be a patterned path between columns carved into bound figures straining, sightless eyes raised toward the sky.

"No."

"No?" Efael repeated, and raised a hand to stop the

snigger of the three Black Knives waiting impatiently behind. He'd expected this one to beg from the outset.

"I know what you do to people," Adam said, his heartbeat so fast and frantic he felt it crowding his throat, making it difficult to breathe. But he clasped his trembling hands behind him, and forced himself to slow his breath. "If you're going to do it anyway, why all this pretense of running?"

"Because it's fun," Efael said. "Because I like it. Because if you bore me, then I'll entertain myself watching them take you, one by one. See how they're waiting?"

Adam forced himself not to look, but to keep his gaze steadily on Efael's dark eyes.

"If you give me a good fight, then they only get to watch." Efael whipped a hand up, cracking Adam across the face. "Run."

Adam ran. He was fast, because he'd had to be. He could hear their surprise, then the harsh crowing triumph of the chase.

Adam knew he'd lose, as he had no idea where he was going, except that he was imprisoned in this false environment whose general lineaments were almost familiar, but not familiar enough to signal bolt holes. The only clue he had was that he had gone through the world-gate. He had smelled this stale tinge of smoke before.

Stay alert! Two Black Knives rounded one of the buildings in front, teeth bared, eyes manic and angry, their auras fluorescing around them red-veined with lust-fueled rage. When he tried to jink to the side, there was a third waiting, hooting a signal.

What does he want . . . what does he want . . .

They closed. He evaded two hands, got in one solid hit before one grabbed his hair from the back and threw him over a stone bench hard enough to crack ribs, which seized in agony. The shock flashed his mind-shield away, so open that his flesh against the marble reverberated through countless layers of past pain and terror, a blurring of sensory horror that snagged on the familiar identity far below, only in child form: Siamis.

Adam flicked the shield closed, and around him the voices changed, mocking to hungry, triumph to intent. Boots crunched down on his outflung hands, taking the top of his skin off; he recognized the intent to spark fear — recognized the magnifying effect of anticipation — held on and fought for control.

The smell of the air . . . memory . . . once, Detlev had taken the boys to a world where the people had built spired buildings called cathedrals, completely indefensible, full of unfamiliar symbols grouped in familiar triads and fours and twelves. Vaulted ceilings in the Sartoran style and yet not, stained glass windows with symbolic figures that lit to glory in the golden light, and oh, the exquisite sound, so that a whisper, the scrape of a foot, resonated with gravitas until, from above, the high voices of children sang in counterpoint, their heart-piercing purity like the tap of silver on crystal.

And while those voices limned the light, Detlev explained how humans had given order and shape to mysteries — awe, inspiration, ineffable joy — then hardened them to law, from which they would escape, and reform, again and again.

As rough hands ripped his clothes from him, and another boot heel stamped on his tangled hair spilled on the stones, Adam thought, I am a cathedral. He closed himself inside the memory of light and sweet sound, and shut out the world of blood and pain. His mind, trammeled in the desperate clamor of the body, cut free.

I know what Efael wants, Adam thought on a ripple of inward laughter, and as a shock of agony far worse than the first yanked him back again, he obliged the crowding jackals with screams.

Adam understood the process, having seen animals at it — and he understood how some animals acted upon others in a cruel parody of procreation. This, too, Detlev had explained once: how humans in this, as in most things, had become expert, fashioning an instinct into a weapon.

But animals had limited choice. It was their natures driving them, and here there was clear choice, that the ugly thud-suck rhythm, counterpoint to the drum beat of blood through his head, made a mockery of what should have been sweet fire and joy.

How stupid I was to assume one type of power.

Pain shocked him back yet again as he was thrown flat to the ground, face down. His chin hit the stones as two booted feet planted themselves on the ground at either side of his head, which was jerked up by the hair.

"Let us see how sweetly you can beg."

He left his body to do what it must to survive, his mind fleeing into the cathedral of light and singing, thought winging from wall to wall striving to make meaning from meaninglessness, order from a maelstrom of pain.

Force is not one thing I see a difference between the force of fear and the force of pain though they go together but there is moral force and the force of habit and the force of guilt and of loyalty and the force of greed and ambition yeah no yeah still different from pain and fear and which are the stronger weapons?

The dross of the physical must either be borne, or forever lost. And so he reached down, and pulled on the sloppy, filthy, blood-slick and shivering weight of his body, and in seaming himself within it once again hit the despairing thought that Norsunder is not merely a place, it exists in all of human nature.

He choked, coughed, sagged.

"And now that I have your undivided attention, we will talk," Efael whispered, his breath hot against Adam's ear, his tongue slow and tender in licking sweat, blood, and tears.

Very long ago, Detlev discovered that Efael and Yeres's progenitors had been autarchs, long dead and forgotten before Svirle found the twins and brought them to Sartorias-deles nearly five thousand years ago, to take on the messy tasks he despised.

Yeres shrugged off the past, her primary goal eternal youth and enough power to do anything she wanted. Not true of Efael, whose passions we've seen.

Siamis had made it his first project as a mage to track down all Efael's many hideouts until he stumbled on the one central to all his own nightmares. Not a one of Efael's lairs was anything but horrifying. But on a world parallel to that of Efael's birth, he had recreated, in a zealous obsession with detail, the furniture of depravity that had formed his perception of the universe.

I found it, the young Siamis had said to Detlev. *It's all there: the temple, the altar, the steps, everything. Now I'm going to destroy it.*

No, Detlev had ordered, and in giving that order, wondered when the inevitable would occur, Siamis's first refusal. *No. Don't you see? The hidden citadel is now a weakness.*

So it had proved. It was not Efael's favorite. He did not use it often—as time was measured, once every few centuries, even longer. Detlev had to try the more frequent lairs first, regretting the time it took to test for, and get around, wards and traps.

Nothing. Nothing. Nothing.

Ah.

He prepared for the long transfer, knives at the ready, and used the Old Magic slide so that he emerged at a run. The expected vanguard was there, but Detlev ripped their intent from their minds, and disabled them in three strikes.

Two more Black Knives thought they were sneaking up, and that made five.

Efael looked up sharply, twice sated and exhausted after nearly two days of unrelenting activity within the flow of time. Though the crawling, craving hunger was never far away, a yawning void within, its center a pit of molten rage. Shock stilled him at the unexpected sight of Detlev, the fallen bodies of badly wounded Black Knives marking his approach. Shock, then a pulse of sweet, anger-fueled heat of anticipation.

Detlev stood before him, knife in hand. Breathing normally, not spent at all. And the outer guard lay incapacitated, not dead. All these were deliberate. A negotiation. Acknowledgment of impasse, here where Efael's magic was so strong the air withered the skin, but Detlev was fast enough to escape.

Yeres ought to have been here to back him up.

"You came for your favorite," Efael taunted, playing for time. Where was Yeres? He booted Adam, who flopped onto his face, blood pooling under him. Efael gathered strength for a spell—

"I don't have favorites. But I have a use for him." Detlev raised the knife, looking very ready for a fight to the death.

Efael backed off a step, remembering what Connanre had accomplished for him and Yeres, and laughed. There was always another game, and Detlev was finished in Norsunder. "Take him. I'm done."

Detlev and Adam vanished a heartbeat before Yeres appeared behind Efael. "You're late," he said in disgust.

"I couldn't get through the Beyond. It was . . ." She twirled her hand in the gesture that meant thick with intent, nearly impossible to navigate as it was reshaped around them by those with Dena Yeresbeth. Even now, she felt as if one of Them had entered on her heels, but Efael clearly saw no one, and she forced herself to ignore that sense of inimical eyes on the back of her neck.

She drew her mouth down in a moue as she looked around, and tried not to breathe in the stenches of extreme violence. "Disgusting. Why did you summon me?"

"To trap Detlev," Efael muttered, as the wounded Black Knives began to stir, painful sideways glances in his direction. He'd deal with them later.

Yeres crossed her arms, smirking. "I see that went well."

"Fuck you."

"When?" She gave a crack of laughter. "This afternoon?" She reached down to pat the front of his man-leather pants. "Seems to me you're done for the day." And when he made an obscene gesture, though without much force behind it, she indicated the blood that Adam had left behind, and then put her hand on her hip. "So what did you learn from this so-called favorite?"

"Nothing. He knew nothing more than any of them."

"I *told* you," she said, her voice smug with moral superiority. "Unlike you, *he* never makes the same mistake twice. You'll *never* get at him through his pets again, ever. That includes the crotch-droppings. Don't you see it? He collects them, plays at being master and teacher, then drops them."

"For what other purpose but to train his own commanders for the invasion?"

"That's ended," she said with satisfaction. "Connanre gave me Detlev's ships."

"It was too easy. There's something else. I can feel it." Efael wiped the hair off his forehead, his gaze contemplative on the congealing pools of Adam's blood.

Yeres rolled her eyes. For Efael, everything always had to be so *physical*. "I can assure you, breaking his wards was *not* easy. But I did it, while you've been playing." She looked around in disgust. Why was she here, wasting precious, aging time—time that not even spells could get back? "Leave Detlev until after the invasion, and Ilerian will give him to you as a reward. Why waste time until then?" She flicked dismissive fingers at the revolting mess surrounding them, and transferred back to the safety of the Garden.

Efael followed her, unaware that she had indeed come with a shadow.

Siamis—having exerted himself to deflect Yeres through the Beyond long enough to keep her away— stepped down from the temple where, four thousand seven hundred years ago, he had nearly bled out his life, and took from his sleeve the tokens he had bespelled.

Making a slow circle, he walked the perimeter and laid down tokens every nine paces, as memories rose like specters and faded away. He'd defanged them ages ago, leaving only the invisible scars that shaped one, cognizant or not. He was cognizant.

Without any particular emotion except a mild enjoyment, he raised his hands, clapped, and watched a quake ripple through the stone, rocking pillars and roofs, breaking the streets, upending benches and the monuments to human suffering. And when it had been reduced to rubble, he clapped his hands again, as a green fire swept through, slow at first, then circled faster and faster into a spiral that shot upward into the cluttered, thick air of the world, and after he transferred out it burned away to ash.

Thirty-four

ADAM LANDED ON THE floor in Detlev's warded office. David and MV, who were in their own room killing time in useless speculation, heard the thump and stampeded to the office. They stood side by side, taking in Adam's broken, blood-smeared body curled on its side, the knobs of his spine stark. The others crowded in behind them.

"Right," MV said on an exhaled breath. To Rolfin and Leef, "Door."

Rolfin glanced around, his gaze nicking David's sword propped in the corner. He received permission with a lift of David's chin. Rolfin used the hilt of the sword to knock the rusty old hinges off the pintle. He and Leef caught the door before it fell and laid it next to Adam.

"Keep that leg from moving," MV rapped out.

Willing hands carefully lifted Adam, as blood dripped off him, splat, splat, splat. They laid him on the door as Adam's breath hissed through broken teeth.

Then the four of them—Leef, Rolfin, David, MV—picked up the door and walked Adam through the cleaning frame, which snapped away filth, leaving component water and fresh-welling blood. They continued straight on to Adam's room, where Erol was in the process of tossing a scattering of art, chalks, a pen, and an ink bottle off the bed.

They laid the door on the edge of the now-empty bed, then carefully shifted Adam off the wood as Laban dashed to their private stash of first-aid gear. He tossed a dollop of green kinthus into a cup, poured in water, and carried it in.

David glanced up, his expression clearing when he saw what Laban held. David lifted Adam's shoulders. Laban steadied Adam's head with one hand, and carefully tipped the cup to Adam's ruined mouth. Adam slurped, choked, slurped. His quick, gasping breathing began to smooth to hitches and shudders, and then, at last, to slow indraws and exhales.

When the kinthus blanketed the pain, he opened his eyes, pawing the air with his broken fingers. "Why-ah," he croaked, and spat out a tooth, which landed on his palm. His bruised face distorted in a horrible travesty of a smile. "Aw why-ah."

MV bent down to take that bloody tooth, and with care, worked his finger past Adam's puffy, torn lower lip to fit it into its socket. David slid his fingers down to either side of Adam's jaw and held him in a vice-grip as MV grimly felt along the rest of the kicked-in teeth, straightening each, as tears of pain leaked from Adam's closed eyes and ran over David's hands. When the teeth were all reseated, MV began the spell that locks teeth into injured jaws.

Detlev appeared in the doorway. David laid Adam's head down and backed off. As MV kept up the lock spell, Detlev massaged the pieces of Adam's fractured leg bone back into place, then turned to his left shoulder.

The others hovered in the background. Noser looked wide eyed from Vana to Rolfin. "He's broke. They broke his mind."

David bent to pull clean clothes from Adam's trunk, then on second thought put them back and sent a glance at Curtas, who went to get clean bed linens. "He said 'lies, all lies.' He lied to Efael," David said, straightening up.

Laban was going to scoff, but he caught a fast glance between David and Detlev, as Noser hunched up, a snail into the shell of his bony back.

MV felt down Adam's other leg. "Bruised. Bad. But I don't feel anything broken. Want me to do his hands?"

"Yeah. We can finish here," David said to Detlev. "If you're going after Roy."

"I believe Roy is out of reach," Detlev said in a tone so

devoid of affect they all tightened into alert.

No one spoke as MV and Detlev straightened and magic-bound all the broken fingers then worked down Adam's body, holding closed the many knife slashes as they did binding spells.

At length they were done. Noser widened his eyes, then dug his elbow into Vana's side. "Guess I'll be going down to the stable," he said loudly, and ran off.

Glances ricocheted from Vana to Laban, to Rolfin, to Leef. Erol was already gone. Rolfin studied Adam, his expression difficult to interpret. Erol reappeared, slipping among them in his unobtrusive way, a brimming cup of water carried in both hands.

This he gave to David, who helped Adam drink half of it, leaving the remainder tinged rose. Adam closed his eyes. David snapped out the clean quilt that Curtas had brought and laid it over Adam, pulling it to his chin. Adam flicked a blood-shot glance at Curtas in silent question, and Curtas tugged the quilt up over Adam's face so only his tangled riot of damp curls was visible.

Detlev flicked his eyes toward the next room, and they walked into the office, where Detlev leaned against the desk, looking more tired than the last time they'd seen him. "About Roy. You don't appear to appreciate the gift," he said.

"What gift?" David protested. "Roy wasn't responsible for freeing Five. Yes, he took down the fortress wards three years ago, but MV or I could have done that, if you'd given us orders. Yes, he also walked off with the flute thing, but don't tell me he knew what to do with it."

"Somebody did," Detlev said. "And he got it to that some-body. Five is completely inaccessible, and Norsunder has lost its foothold on Geth. Roy seriously set back Efael. He and Yeres are deep in the Beyond. While Adam recovers enough to bear the transfer, you may all consider your next step."

Silence fell. Some went out, clinging to old habit rather than deal with the prospect of change, of really breaking up, instead of mere pretense.

David remained, staring at the wall beyond which Adam lay. "Why?"

Detlev said, "Bringing back to this world all the varieties of physical suffering through sexual dominance is Efael's pet project."

"It's how he was raised, am I right?" David asked.

"Yes."

"I thought everything was about the mind with the Host," MV said, his gut churning.

"It is. Mind-raid, mind-rip—you might, now that you know the word, say mind-rape—is the first step in what we call soul-eating," Detlev replied. "Svirle finds the physical equivalent petty. Tedious. He regards Yeres and Efael as tools, much as they assume otherwise. But once Efael was brought to handle the physical coercion aspect of the first war, he then endeared himself, you might say, to Ilerian by taking him off-world to sample all the physical delights the human body that Ilerian had taken was innocent of. Eventually he tired of the limits of the flesh, so though Efael's pet projects would be a matter of indifference to him now, he will not interfere."

Even if death was to be the result? David was going to ask—because they all knew of the ancient magic bound to acts of violent, non-consensual sex, even more disturbing because how could magic *know*? But it did know. Even Efael took his victims not just off the world, but altogether away from all the worlds around the sun Erhal, for his rape games.

Anyway, David didn't ask, because he knew Ilerian would be utterly indifferent, as long as there were plenty of souls left for him to rip free of living flesh and devour.

Detlev had gone to the inner room. David followed. "Do we hunt the shrimp down?"

"Leave him be."

David hesitated, wanting to question, but sensed it was all the answer he would get. He slipped out past Rolfin who remained where he was in the office, scowling at the floor. Detlev stepped through the cleaning frame, then stood patiently.

Rolfin took a deep breath. He had waited all this time, and the moment was here, but he didn't feel ready to deal with the answers. He asked anyway. "Was it random? My shooting Peitar Selenna."

"No."

"Why, then?"

Detlev flicked a glance in Adam's direction. Rolfin understood. What he didn't know couldn't be ripped out of him, fingernail by bloody fingernail, as Adam had just experienced.

Yet he waited for an answer.

Detlev's tone altered. "You accepted the order. And

carried it out."

Rolfin looked away, his bow-callused thumb fingering the outer seam of his trousers, then he said, "The bolt. Right over the heart. I knew if I refused, you'd put one of the others to it, and they might have been off a finger or two. It would have been worse."

"It would most definitely have been worse."

Rolfin's head nicked down, and with no pride whatsoever, merely stating a fact, he said, "I'm the best shot. But—" He paused, gaze straying again to Adam's door. "Was I wrong to kill him, when I felt it was wrong?"

"That you have a question," Detlev said, "ought to in some wise answer you. Continue to question, and to act with awareness of consequences."

"That's no answer. I know that every action causes a reaction, second and third order. You've repeated it enough times. But I thought the hand through the water meant we move and get out without leaving a trace."

"It does."

"But I thought it also meant not leaving a . . ." Rolfin doubled a fist and bumped it against his chest. "Reaction here."

"The magic on that bolt was transfer magic. If you'd been even slightly off, he would have suffered alone until he bled to death. Your clean shot enabled his identity, his . . . " Detlev spoke Ancient Sartoran words that Rolfin didn't remotely grasp, and he heard the imprecise term *spirit* ". . . to go elsewhere without a painful interval. Is that answer sufficient?"

Rolfin gazed at Detlev, his face lengthening in horror. "You didn't send his mind to *him*, did you? Ilerian?"

"No. I said enabled, not forced."

Detlev stopped there, and Rolfin stared at him, waiting for more, until the pause became a silence. And yet he sensed that there was more that he was not being told. "Enabled." That seemed to mean that Peitar wanted that unnamed destination. *That you have a question ought to in some wise answer you.* What was he to make of that?

Then he thought of Adam lying on the floor bleeding and broken, trying to say that he'd lied, all lies. Oh, yes, there was more, and it had to be too dangerous to know. Rolfin about-faced and ran downstairs, leaving Detlev to sink wearily into his chair and gaze sightlessly through the window at the bleak landscape beyond.

Thirty-five

Roth Drael

IT WOULD BE DIFFICULT to say who hated Detlev the most, out
of those who insisted they must be there at the meeting that
everyone felt was a historic occasion.

What sort of occasion remained to be determined.

There were certainly some among those who gathered in
the ruined city of Roth Drael during a winter storm who
hoped to see the worst villain of all time executed before their
eyes in a vastly overdue act of justice. Mearsieanne — who was
not even on Tsauderei's list of invitees, but heard second-hand
and insisted on being there — came hoping to see him lying
dead on the floor.

Tsauderei had not been able to turn her away by claiming
lack of space, as his old friend Mondros had refused to come,
saying that there seemed to be some kind of trouble in Chwahirsland, and the reclusive Igkai — hermit mages who looked
out for the world's unspeaking creatures — had (not surprisingly) also refused. Further, the Colendi regency council had
intercepted Tsauderei's letter to whoever represented mages
in Colend, requesting a report. Therefore, they had extra
space, and he knew she had badgered enough people to find
that out.

Finally (surprisingly) Siamis himself intervened, the only time he spoke an opinion during that long, exasperating night of exchanged letters, saying, why not let Mearsieanne be there since it seemed to mean so much to her. Tsauderei couldn't see why Siamis would bestir himself on behalf of someone of no importance, from a kingdom of no importance, much less a person who slandered him tirelessly, but Tsauderei gave in. It was easier.

So, she was there. And what she saw in that magically protected room broken by Detlev's allies thousands of years ago was the same hated man who'd taken her away from her own time, and stuck her under enchantment for three generations, all due to mere whim. She hoped with such a stomach-churning intensity that Senrid, or some other barbarian, would take steel to him that she tasted metal in her mouth. She sat as far from him as she could, while still in hearing.

In the place of honor—on one of the three actual chairs, all mismatched, heirlooms from different centuries—Atan sat, a formidable array of magical traps and tokens worked into her elaborate gown embroidered over with acanthus, wheat, and oak motifs in Sartoran purple and gold. Senrid and Mearsie-anne were the only other monarchs there. Outside of Liere, who was neither mage nor monarch (despite honorary titles, given her when just before she turned twelve years old), the rest were senior mages all.

Liere's presence startled Senrid. He hadn't seen her for a long stretch—the longest they had gone without getting together. She seemed subtly different, perhaps taller? Maybe it was that she'd managed to let her ragged hair grow out a little, and it was a healthier color, though she was as scrawny as ever. But her smile was the same as she made her way to his side.

Sitting down next to him on a low bench, she whispered, "They asked me to listen in the mental realm for trickery. I wanted to explain that I couldn't do anything, but Siamis told me not to. He promised nothing terrible would happen, but my presence might help."

Senrid gazed across the weird room with its cracked white walls to the man standing behind Detlev's chair. Siamis had even brought the sword named Truth. He leaned against the wall in a relaxed posture, as though prepared to endure a long wait.

Senrid's gaze returned to Detlev, who had agreed to
submit to a partial stone spell. He was, as usual, dressed
simply, wearing no visible weapons. But Senrid was certain
that even trussed up with ropes and chains he'd be dangerous,
and so he'd come armed with his throwing knives as well as
double-edged daggers in his boot tops.

Tsauderei sat at the apex of the triangle made by Detlev
and Atan, everyone else in a secondary, wider circle, on a
jumble of benches and cushions that Erai-Yanya and her mage
student Hibern had arranged.

Senrid's gaze snagged on black-haired, black-eyed Hibern,
another old friend — one initially from his own country. He
hadn't seen anything of her in recent years, though once she
had been the Young Allies' most dedicated advocate. Their
eyes met, and she turned over her palm in greeting.

Tsauderei said, "We're all here. Tell them what you told
me yesterday."

Detlev glanced his way, then out at the silent auditors.
"I've left Norsunder. My intent is to retire to the countryside,
where I have built a house."

"On my land," Atan said, though she knew well that those
western reaches were only part of Sartor in name.

Detlev flicked her a glance. "It's days of very hard travel
from your westernmost mountain border."

"Why there?" she asked, knowing that she was rude, but
she didn't care. It was he — or one of his assassins — who had
murdered her entire family. That she was alive at all was
partly accident, and partly due to Gehlei's courage.

"Because it's days of very hard travel from any sort of civilization, but close to the warmer currents of the Sartoran sea."

"Why now? After all these centuries? Why couldn't you
hide away and become someone else's problem years hence?"
Mearsieanne burst out bitterly.

"I don't intend to become your problem," he said.

"I don't believe a word you say."

"Then why are you here?"

"Because I had to hear your lies, to know what we have to
fight against," she retorted, her voice trembling with hatred
and anger.

Detlev said to Atan, "You have wards preventing me from
entering your capital. That is true of Bereth Ferian as well. You
can always ward me from here after this meeting. I don't

foresee having to visit any of these locations again."

Atan fingered her protections, and glanced at Tsauderei, off-balance and out of her depth in a way she hadn't experienced since she first walked into war-torn Sartor as a girl. All night she'd thought up increasingly hard questions, but in the light of day, she wasn't sure she wanted to hear the answers to many of them.

Except one.

She nodded briefly to Tsauderei, who said, "When you invaded Sartor more than a century ago. Then enchanted it. If there was any reason outside of unreasoning cruelty and a taste for random slaughter, I think there are several—if not most—here who would like to hear it."

"The random slaughter was on the secret orders of Jeniad, captain of the strike troops, who were supposed to put down the defense and then withdraw immediately upon surrender. You know that climate, magic, and bad land management has ruined the soil at Norsunder Base. The initial goal was to occupy Eidervaen and make it over into a forward base, the city itself to be kept intact. But Jeniad loosed his companies to loot and kill, setting fires after."

The older Sartoran mages stirred: that century-ago battle was a few years ago for them.

"The invasion was going to happen, whoever accompanied Jeniad as mage. I used the opportunity to test an enchantment. The specifics are a variation on what you call the Emras mirror ward. In dark magic, you can anchor on a death, which is not a spell available in light magic, except as relinquishment of a magic-extended life."

Senrid caught movement—Hibern, leaning forward intently. Mearsieanne stiffened as if slapped.

Detlev went on, "The limitations on the enchantment you know, one of which was how easily it broke under the right circumstances, when it was already fading. These sorts of enchantments must be exactly laid out. Rightly done, it can take a year or more. That one was accomplished too hastily, in less than a day."

Atan said, "Whose death did you use? My father's? My mother's?"

"They were already dead," Detlev said. "Against orders. I used Jeniad's."

Senrid watched that impact the listeners.

"Where did this Jeniad's companies go?" Atan asked, after a tense pause during which half of the listeners wondered how they could possibly corroborate Detlev's words. "We saw none of them when the spell vanished."

"That's another of the limitations," Detlev said in a tone devoid of any emotion. "No one knows."

The only sounds were rustling of clothing as some recoiled, and intakes of breath.

Then Tsauderei said, "Bringing us to the next question: you told me that Norsunder is going to invade. Again. Sooner than later."

"I expect so." Humor briefly narrowed Detlev's eyes. "My access to future plans, you must understand, has ended."

"Why? Why *now?*" Tsauderei thumped his fist on the arm of his chair.

Detlev turned his head. "But it isn't now. It would have been now, if Efael hadn't suffered profound defeat with the breaking of Aldau-Rayad's enchantment."

Tsauderei's white brows twitched together. "Those supply caches that Siamis gave us?" His gaze shifted between Siamis and Detlev.

"I was in charge of storing those," Detlev said. "Awaiting use, pending resolution of a struggle for command between Yeres's favorite Henerek, Bostian, and one other commander."

"You?" Mearsieanne accused.

"No. His name is Aldon. He's a prime candidate for leading an attack, though he recently surfaced up in Fhleria."

Atan, who knew her world map, only looked concerned, but Senrid breathed, "One of the military kingdoms. Old Venn colony."

Atan waved off Fhleria. They would be the Land of the Venn's problem. "But you could. You *have.*"

"I could," Detlev said. "And I have. On orders by people you do not know, in situations now buried in the detritus of history."

"Who assassinated Peitar Selenna?" Tsauderei asked. "It was someone young. What little evidence exists — including the fact that there is so little evidence — points to one of your teenage assassins."

At the name "Peitar Selenna" Detlev's brow furrowed. Was that a question? Tsauderei sighed inwardly, wondering if Detlev even remembered the name. They were talking to a man who'd been popping in and out of time for four, almost five millennia. There was a very great chance he had no idea who Peitar was—and no one had ever proved that his boys had shot Peitar.

MV had insisted he didn't know anything about that, and indeed, Tsauderei had found out through independent inquiries that the very day it happened, MV had been in Jaro Harbor signing purchase papers on a boat. Paid for with his earnings, after months of sailing with a privateer who had recently turned out to be a deposed Khanerenth prince. That, too, had been corroborated.

And while MV could have transferred in, done the deed, and transferred back to Jaro, the hired guide had insisted under kinthus that he'd been with the killer the entire day. And that the killer was husky and had black eyes. One could call MV's lean, muscular form husky at a stretch, but no one would mistake those light brown eyes with yellow flecks for black.

Then Detlev said, "I can sit here and field random questions as long as you have patience to ask, I can claim actions as my own or lay the blame on others, but how will you prove the truth, and what will you get by trying? And even if I enter into the details of my past, what will you really learn without the context? For example, imagine a summer's day nearly a thousand years ago, high on a mountain pass. If I told you that I'd taken control of a young man's broken mind in order to bolster his right arm during one of the world's worst slaughters, in order to circumvent an even greater one, what would you really comprehend?"

Tsauderei scowled. "But I'm not the one bringing up irrelevant—" He broke off when he thought of an infamous name from nearly a thousand years before. "Erkric the Blood Mage," he breathed. "Was it *that* battle, when Erkric was using blood magery?"

"Successfully, too," Detlev said. "He had control of the Venn emperor."

"Wait." Senrid shot to his feet. "That's *my* history. Erkric was going for control of our king, so he could launch my ancestors across the continent to Sartor." He was about to add caustically, *Isn't that what you Norsundrians wanted?* But his brain caught up with his mouth: context. And Norsunder not being a united entity. Senrid sank down again, mentally grappling with the reach of a duel, both magical and military, going on across centuries.

The one thing he was now sure of was that the mysterious Ramis of those days had to be one of Detlev's guises.

The rest of those present ignored Senrid and his blather about battles that had not happened, many ascribing it to typical Marloven bloody-mindedness. The name "Erkric" had their attention, some whispering, others frowning.

"Erkric's dead. Isn't he?" Tsauderei asked.

"Yes." Detlev's amusement showed in his voice. "Yeres reserved that pleasure to herself. I can assure you that the grimness of his end surpassed that of any of his victims."

The new head of the Sartoran mage guild looked across the room at Detlev. "We thought his influence gone, until some of his texts showed up in Chwahirsland."

Detlev answered the implied question. "Where they fell into the hands of Kessler Sonscarna, in spite of both Efael and Yeres holding the present king and trying to wrest his various secrets from him. If Efael has not already freed Wan-Edhe, he will very soon. This, too, you need to factor into your future plans."

He then addressed them all. "I've told you what you can expect, though none of us know exactly when, or how it'll be led."

Atan said slowly, "I realize I have no lawful influence over where this house of yours is. And yet you did me the courtesy of telling me. I'd like to request a further courtesy, or warning: is the 'house' a fortress full of warriors?"

"It's just a house," Detlev said. "You're welcome to come and inspect it. A single glance by anyone with military training would deem it indefensible. Its design reflects the Colendi style during the reign of Mathias the Great."

"Should I be preparing for any of your enemies in Norsunder to overrun us in order to get to it?" Atan crossed her arms.

"Few of them would be able to find it," Detlev answered. "Of those who might be able to find it, none are likely to attack a house that has no military, historic, or even sentimental importance."

His tone was reasonable, and he spoke readily. It even felt like truth—whatever that meant. And yet Senrid still sensed that some other meaning underlay every word, that this was, at last, the game he'd always known was there, that he and others had been made part of. And yet he was no closer to understanding its rules, much less its goal.

Tsauderei said, "According to you, there is no single Norsundrian target."

"Correct."

"So who, in your opinion, is the worst of them — the biggest threat?"

"Ilerian, the founder of Norsunder."

"What is his objective?"

"You all are aware that magic potential has been slowly seeping back into the world over the centuries since the battle you've been calling the Fall." Detlev waited for the little signs of agreement and assent. "Ilerian wants to use the magic potential of this world to branch out."

"Use it . . . how?" Erai-Yanya spoke up from where she stood at the back.

"Devour life. Worlds."

Some listened in affronted disbelief, others stared angrily, believing Detlev was trying to deflect them from his own crimes, he was trying to shift blame, he was trying to do anything but warn them of something so frightening that their minds refused to grasp the idea.

Atan rose. "I've heard enough. If you have any further communications, please send them to Tsauderei." She walked out.

Tsauderei grunted, and began rocking back and forth, preparatory to rising — waving off offers of help from both sides.

Mearsieanne got to her feet, sent Detlev a glare of hatred, and marched out as well.

Siamis's thought reached Detlev *:She will never know she was nearly the first. You think she'll take the bait?*

:I expect you to monitor that.

By then Tsauderei had heaved himself to his feet, and gestured to remove the partial stone spell.

Detlev promptly vanished.

Siamis turned to Liere and Senrid. "You both should really go see the house Curtas designed and constructed as his master builder project. I think you'd like it."

Senrid was going to say something derisive, then he remembered that Liere had been living in the same space with Siamis for the last three years. She was not only still alive, and in possession of her wits, but she looked less anxious.

Disgusting as the thought was, maybe they'd even become friends. Wasn't that what lighters wrote poetry about, making peace and spraying good will all around like a cosmic sneeze?

Senrid stood there poised between distrust and curiosity. He remembered, vividly, Siamis's last gesture with that damned sword of his, before they all left Geth-deles. "So that was an empty threat with the sword," he said, sarcasm making his voice come out thin. He hissed out a breath. "Or did the sudden hop to the other side happen after you murdered Derek Diamagan?"

Siamis glanced reflectively at the broken ceiling and the sky beyond, then back at Senrid. "Right now, I think the only thing you'll believe is my pointing out that Derek attacked first. I was faster."

Senrid's lips shaped a denial, but memory of that, too, was vivid. Siamis smiled faintly, as if he knew what was going through Senrid's head though Senrid had as tight a mind-shield as he'd ever made.

Siamis's tone was even, observant, as he added, "Your city is still warded against us."

"Us." That, too, was deliberate: Siamis and Detlev were a team again. Well, Senrid had never believed in their feud. *You will not see me coming.*

"And the ward will stay that way," Senrid said, tossing his transfer token on his palm.

"Your choice," Siamis said mildly.

"So. The sword." The words were wrung out of Senrid, though beneath the real question was that threat of Detlev's.

Siamis glanced skyward again, eyes narrowed consideringly. Then he said, "After. What did you do?"

Senrid flashed his toothy grin. "Did everything I could to work against you." *You.* It worked for both questions, the spoken and the hidden. Or what Senrid had thought was hidden.

Siamis said, "Exactly." He turned his head. "Liere? Ready to return?"

"Sure." She darted a brow-furrowed from one to the other. "I don't like to leave Lyren long." She smiled at Senrid. "Please come visit."

"Been busy," he said, knowing it was weak. "But you could come visit me."

"I will! After your summer games are over. I know how busy you are, and we're still in the middle of winter session at the school." Her face brightened in the old familiar way.

Siamis and then Liere vanished, leaving Senrid alone with Hibern. He flexed his hands, annoyed at how his heart was still thundering against his ribs, and he spoke as carelessly as he could to her black, observant gaze, "Where have you been?"

"Here." Her mouth turned sardonic. "Studying," she added. And more seriously, "Wards and lattices, from dark and light."

Senrid let out a breath, knowing how dangerous and difficult those studies were. "You left the alliance."

Hibern looked away. "When Karhin was killed . . . I know I'm not responsible. But I'd been so enthusiastic about bringing her and Thad in. I couldn't help the feeling that if I'd kept my mouth shut, they'd still be alive. I'm keeping myself here. Studying. Feels safer."

He couldn't argue. Regret was one of his oldest ghosts.

Hibern turned away as the voices from the next room rose. She walked in, and he followed more slowly. He didn't really intend to eavesdrop as he moved up to the archway leading to the next room, but stood well back. He wanted to avoid being seen by Mearsieanne, who always regarded him as if she expected him to cut her throat. The way Senrid had felt when he glared at Siamis, in fact.

Loathing the idea of being anything like Mearsieanne, he made a reckless decision: he'd go to Bereth Ferian to visit. Try to keep an open mind.

Then Tsauderei shuffled past him, leaning on a cane as he headed toward the Destination tiles. Atan broke off her low conversation with one of the guild mages. "Tsauderei, did you notice Detlev never answered your question about Peitar?"

"Oh, I noticed. But I wasn't certain I really wanted to hear the answer. Because I did believe him when he talked about the Host. The records all corroborate his words." Tsauderei leaned with both hands on his cane, a tall, gaunt figure, though the traces of his once magnificent build could be seen in the line of his shoulders, and his narrow flank under the robe. "Erkric the Blood Mage!"

A guild mage said, "Our records are specific that Erkric's teacher was Yeres."

Tsauderei grunted affirmation, then turned to Atan. "Anyway, leveling accusations is not going to bring Peitar back."

He sighed heavily. "I've got to get these old bones of mine home and write it up for Mondros while it's still fresh in my mind. Then I have to put it into suitable language for those Colendi nobles who have a stranglehold on the young king."

Atan dipped her head in a nod. She had never corresponded privately with Shontande Lirendi—the regency council saw to that—but her ambassador to the Colendi court made the situation clear. Shontande was in effect a prisoner in the most beautiful palace in the world, surrounded by luxury. He was smart, beautiful, popular—and powerless. She wondered what would happen when he came of age, what, next year? The year after?

Then Mearsieanne said venomously, "Do you know exactly where Detlev's house lies?"

"So you can provide a target for Norsunder?" Tsauderei's brows beetled upward. "Sometimes your hatred is indistinguishable from any of these Norsundrians, Mearsieanne. In fact, worse."

She pressed her hands to her laboring heart, noting the sideways, uncomfortable glances in the others. They did, they agreed!

"I would *never* consort with Norsunder," she said in the trembling voice of conviction. "I would give my *life* to fight them, to eradicate their evil. Not add to it!"

Tsauderei gestured tiredly. "We all know you hate Norsunder, yes, and suffered from them, in various ways. As has every single person in this room. My suggestion is, go back and do what you can to ready your kingdom's defense."

Mearsieanne bowed her head. "That," she said on a low note, "I shall." She vanished.

Atan stared at the floor where she had been, and then to Senrid's surprise, she turned her heavy-lidded eyes his way. "Senrid," she said. "You helped me once before. Might I ask your advice again?"

Senrid lifted a shoulder. "You can't want my army."

"No," she said, a corner of her mouth lifting in an almost smile. "An education, yes."

"Let me guess," he retorted. "In . . ."

"Strategy and tactics," she said. "If they're coming at us anyway, I have to understand. It's clear that wishing all would use good will only prevails where good will exists. Norsunder seems to have a shortage of that."

Senrid flashed a grin. "I'll talk about those things as much as you like. Though there's someone much closer to you who understands the terrain at your end of the continent, and the type of training to be found at your end of the continent."

"Oh?" Atan asked.

Senrid said, "Ever heard of Remalna?"

"Tiny country along the coast just above Mardgar," Atan said. "I believe there is a new king, much an improvement on the old. Do you know someone in that country who can help me?"

"The king himself. Vidanric Renselaeus — a distant relative of both me and Leander, by the way — trained at my academy. He had to put his training to practice not all that long ago, in order to get rid of that bad king."

"I see. If I can figure out a way to approach him without making it awkward —"

"Just tell Vidanric I sent you," Senrid said. "That should bustle you past the diplomatic shuffle."

Atan thanked him again, and Tsauderei swept his gaze around. "This is my suggestion. First, we all stay in contact. Anyone hear of anything to do with Detlev, report it to the others. If he sticks to his house and his word, fine. But the merest whiff of anything nefarious, I suggest we band together and not stop until we take him down —"

The flash and stirring air of transfer, and Lilith appeared. "Am I too late? Yes, I see that I am." She closed her eyes as Tsauderei gave a succinct, and highly idiomatic, summation of the interview.

At the end, Lilith opened her eyes, and Senrid wondered what she'd heard besides the spoken words. "Before the recent events," she said. "I encountered Detlev in company with Connanre and Yeres, at the Al-Athann cave on Aldau-Rayad. He contacted me on the mental plane and promised two things, if I ceased interfering with his movements. The first was the freeing of that world, which came to pass. I cannot see how that could possibly benefit him. The first wards they put up were against his reentry. The second . . ."

She looked upward, and to the astonishment and dismay of those watching, the liquid gleam of tears gathered along her eyelids. "Let me say this: I regard our future interactions as an armistice. I would encourage you to leave him be."

Then she transferred away.

Thirty-six

ADAM SLEPT, LOCKED WITHIN his cathedral mind-shield. When the kinthus wore off, replaced by a full spectrum of pain, for a time he lay as still as he could, reflecting on the colors of pain. In the places of broken bones and ripped flesh, white throbs as intense as lightning, pulsating with lurid agony. Beneath the bruises the red of embers. Bright summer-sun orange in his jaw, in the skin lacerations.

He knew the other boys only by their auras.

He'd sense a shift in the air currents, and there was midnight-sky-blue Ferret with more green kinthus, this time in steep. Ferret? When did he return? The fragrance of the steeped herb reached down into Adam's lungs, loosening a different kind of ache. He drank fast, gasping against the cataract of emotional reaction, and lay back to still the waters.

When he sensed another stir in the air, it was emerald-green Laban, with broth.

One by one over that day and those following they came by, offering little things. Golden Vana stacked his drawings and replaced the chalks in their wooden box. Red-and-gray streaked Noser sat at Adam's bedside, singing the songs they'd revamped as boys that he still found intensely humorous, and in triumph even produced one of his own: he'd changed the words from the famous ballad "Meritha the Ship-taker" and wrote a new song, "Efael the Fart-sniffer."

Adam listened to the good will behind the tuneless voice and silly words, then dreamed. When he woke from a nightmare, shivering and sweat-drenched, steel-bright David was there beside the bed, and began reading aloud from a Geth history they'd enjoyed as boys.

Adam drank whatever they gave him, gradually losing the sense of the words. They didn't matter. He listened to the rise and fall of David's voice, and sank down and down again, sensing the guardian spirit outside his mind-shield that made no attempt at contact. It was there, shielding his own shield, until he no longer needed to close himself into the cathedral of solitude, of imagined light and air.

In discrete increments, Adam widened his awareness of the world. Food, water, it was all there, with someone waiting whenever he woke; speech was beyond him, and somehow they knew that, and didn't speak either, except to read or to sing; the easy silence, the awkward but careful touches, the offerings were all he could bear.

Finally he could sleep through the night, and they sensed that, too.

Detlev entered the commanders' mess hall at the Base, after his last tour of the command center to glance at the map there: no markers whatsoever at Fhleria. Then Bostian did not know that Aldon was living under an assumed name up north. Or Bostian knew but was keeping the secret close.

Bostian himself was not around. Only underlings sat in the mess hall, waiting for orders they hoped for every day, if just to break the boredom of endless patrol and drill. It was rare enough for any of the real rankers to descend on this place, and a flicker of interest ran around, even among those who professed to look down on Detlev's brats who had no rank.

Detlev appeared to be unaware of the eyes watching him. He walked out again. None of the watchers felt the message that fled from mind to mind. One by one the others drifted out, usually just behind other people on their way to those at stable and practice court.

David jammed his hands into his pockets as he considered MV, who was now a full hand taller than he, with the roughened jawline of one who'd had to have recourse to the beard spell. "What is it?"

"Listened to 'em?" MV asked.

"I haven't had time to listen to my own thoughts," David said.

"Curtas's got plans, now that he's got his master builder certificate, duly svedded by the guild office in Mardgar. Laban's still hot to right all the wrongs in Everon."

"I know." David lifted a shoulder. "He won't listen."

MV flashed a grin. "I think you should meet Senrid. The old orders surely don't matter anymore."

David rubbed his eyes. "Did. Twice, both times in Chwahirsland."

"No, no, that doesn't count." MV snickered. "He's a fast little shit. Mouthy."

David shrugged again. He'd expected no different. "Out of all of us I expect Adam'll make it easiest."

MV tipped his head consideringly.

"You don't think so?" David asked, surprised.

"Residuals," MV said.

David gave a soft whistle. "There's that. Well. You?"

"Once I take a squint at this house of Curtas's, back to my boat. Hit a port for some fun—" MV paused, eyeing David, who didn't look a day older than he had when Detlev let them lift the Child Spell. After which David was sent to the Beyond. "Then maybe visit the old geezer again."

"What? You won't become someone's court decoration?"

MV snorted a laugh, and ran up the stairs ahead of David. David followed more slowly as MV vanished down the hall. The tallest of the bunch, and the oldest, MV was also the one who'd seemed to fit the Norsundrian life the best. That is, he didn't just like action and risk, he lived for it.

A couple of years ago, David would have thought that MV would be the one to refuse to hop the wall given the chance. But as he thought back along the years they'd known one another, he realized the anger-driven viciousness that had characterized MV after his Efael experience had taken a turn after that disastrous encounter with the Mearsiean girl. That defined the difference. Anyone else—Bostian, his captains and followers—would, and did, kill anyone in their way, weak or strong, innocent or intent. MV measured himself against the best and fastest and strongest opponents he could find.

Instead, it was Noser the follower and Laban the passionate who were causing the most problems.

They had gathered in the office—even Ferret was there—some carrying weapons and gear, others with nothing.

Detlev indicated the desk, which had a pile of transfer tokens on it.

"These are spelled to take you to my house," he said. "From there you can do what you wish. If any of you have another destination in mind, you've only to speak."

Adam had lain where he was as the others trooped past. When they were in the office, the door closed, he stood, and though the pain boiled up fresh, hot, and crimson as blood, it could be borne. With his fingertips wrapped in cotton to protect the raw nail beds, and the broken fingers splinted, he carefully palmed up his old travel pack and his journal, and used what stealth he could manage to get downstairs, one agonizing step at a time.

He made it to their private court. He'd not had time to use the belt magic to stash the journal when the watch bell rang that day, or the grubby paint-stained book would be gone, with the belt, to Efael's place of pain and desecration. Before running down to the kitchen he'd stashed it under his mattress.

Without looking at the carefully written, triple-coded journal, he used his palm heel to shove it into his pack with the drawings, and the chalks, and ignoring the agony in his hands, bent to light a fire with the boys' firestick. Despite the thin and bitter rain beginning to fall, the magic on the stick kept the flame burning steadily. He placed the pack on the fire, and leaned against the wall to watch it burn to ash. Then he killed the fire, braced his back against the wall, and used the side of the foot of his bad leg to smear the ash into the liquid murk of the ground, trusting the magic holding his shattered bones together not to fail. Chips of bone rubbed and ground together, but held.

Then, sweating heavily, he leaned back against the stone wall, letting the rain cool his face until the worst of the trembling began to ease.

When he opened his eyes to force that first step of his return, he found Detlev there, the acrid rain beading in his hair and on his face. "Adam."

That was all he said, but the sound of that voice, reaching back into early childhood when a worried family thought Adam insane, and he had thought himself insane — that voice had pulled him slowly into the world.

Before, he couldn't speak. Now he could not stop.

"It's not the violation." Adam's voice was hoarse, a whisper. It hurt to speak because of his teeth held in place only by MV's spell, but he forced himself to enunciate. "MV warned us. I knew what was coming, and escaped as much as I could, even tried to game Efael at first, giving him a show at horror and resistance, but when I saw that he would take and take, it became real enough, but I always knew where I was, until I perceived line, light, the detail . . . Art — that place." He choked up. "Art." His voice lifted, high and breathy. "As a *weapon*."

"Adam. You know that anything can be used as a weapon," Detlev said. "To the mind that only perceives the world in terms of force."

"But not art." Adam breathed on a strained note of betrayal. "Never art. I thought . . . art was . . ." *Innocent? Sublime?* Those were the wrong words, and the right words. "Pure." No, that was wrong, too.

"Experiment with *kerygma*, a word from Efael's own vocabulary, though he denies its existence," Detlev said.

But Adam was not yet ready — he did not know if he would ever be ready — for reaching outside the protection of his mind-shield to go worldview-wandering. He closed his eyes, then forced them open, because this was the promise he had made himself before coming downstairs. "That place was beautiful."

"No, it used the materials and the lineaments of beauty —"

"—to say there is no meaning. In anything. It's all illusion."

"That's what Efael wants you to believe. The strongest power he can have over you is to reduce your understanding to his meager standard. But you know what beauty is."

"I don't know anything anymore."

"You know your own experience. You have seen that beauty raises the spirits of the young, the old, the rich, the poor, the lost and dispossessed. Beauty is the open door through which the denied, the powerless, the bewildered can still walk. It has the power to move entire peoples. It is stronger than steel."

Adam clenched his teeth against a sob.

The quiet voice went on. "Beauty is mysterious and enduring. It lasts longer than political boundaries because it enspirits that part of us below and above words, the emotions that bind us and lift us out of human limitations. It celebrates tenderness and hope, grief and joy."

Adam leaned against the wall, tangled hair in his face, mitten-covered palms sliding over his eyes. "I thought. Art would keep me aloof from ugliness. And evil."

Detlev said, "You chose to abrogate awareness or responsibility, shielding yourself behind art. It sufficed for a time. Now you will choose differently." He held out a hand. "The others are gone. It's time to leave this place. You understand what to fight against. Now come and learn what to fight for."

Thirty-seven

Sartor, Shendoral Forest

IT WAS NEAR TO dawn several days later when Trieste walked tiredly into the woodland watched over by the indigenous Loi. The horse's sides were slick with sweat, head low. Sveneric sat straight-backed and wary, though his hands were cold and his eyes burned with exhaustion. He could see his breath as the sun topped the eastern horizon.

An hour later, the sunlight reached dark gold fingers between the thick-growing trees. The forest was silent, the scents of water, greenery, and autumn heavy as incense on the air. Sveneric breathed deeply, looking this way and that as he rode along a narrow trail.

Presently he became aware of living beings around him. Animals, and then humans, paced him silently just out of sight and hearing. He dropped his hands onto his thighs and Trieste slowed obligingly to a walk.

When they reached a wide clearing, two figures stepped from the brush at either side. Sveneric touched Trieste's neck, and the mount stopped, swinging his head down to scent for water. Sveneric studied the figures before him, waiting expectantly.

Two boys a few years older faced him, one white-haired

and slim-fingered. A morvende! His snowy hair was so different from Sveneric's one brief encounter with the only other morvende he had ever met. This boy had a merry face and a bright, clear mind. He wore a thin tunic embroidered over with silver and green leaves and did not seem to notice the cold air. The other boy was short and stocky, wearing well-worn clothes in forest green and brown. His dark eyes were direct, his grin a challenge.

"Who are you?" the morvende asked. "You are dressed like the Norsunder ones."

Sveneric gave his characteristic short nod. "I am Sveneric. You?"

"I'm Aurel. This is Kim. We live here in Shendoral. Why are you here?"

"I ran away from my people at the Base. My horse needs care."

"How old are you?" Kim asked curiously, and a little warily.

"Eight."

"We're twelve," Kim said, with a gesture of bravado. "What was your name again?"

"The whole of it is Sveneric Y Reverael Hindraeldrei. Though the last one doesn't have meaning anymore, I'm told."

"Y Rev—that's ancient," the morvende said, his eyes narrowing. "Are you—"

"Detlev's son," Sveneric said. He kept his hands away from his knife belt, and pretended not to notice Kim's fingers closing on something sheathed under the loose, tattered shirt. "I can see that now you don't trust me."

"No," Kim stated. "Why should we?"

Sveneric heard the years of bitter enmity in the youngster's voice. He'd known he'd have to face this reaction, probably sooner than later. Keeping his hands still, he said, "I promise you I don't intend any harm to anyone here. But my horse needs care."

Aurel and Kim exchanged looks, and then Aurel said, "Well, your dark magic can't do a thing in this forest, but still I think we'd better get Linet."

"Linet? That's Merewen Dei?"

Kim's brows snapped together. "Yes," he said flatly.

Aurel sighed. "It's not like knowing her name is a danger. Look, you wait here with him, and I'll go get her." He waited only for Kim to nod, then he disappeared into the underbrush without leaving a trace.

"May I dismount and care for the horse?" Sveneric said politely. "See, Trieste is thirsty and sweaty."

Kim gave a jerky nod, pulling out a short knife. Sveneric appeared not to see it, though he noted from the youngster's stance and grip on the knife that he was not as adept at fighting as he was at woodcraft. If necessary, he could easily disarm Kim. He just hoped it would not be necessary.

Kim moved back a step or two as Sveneric slid down off Trieste's back. His feet almost buckled under him, and he had to steady himself against the horse's sweat-slick sides. He took a deep breath, then two, bending finally down to pull some good, clean moss. The ground seemed farther away than he'd thought.

"How long you been traveling?" Kim asked.

"Five days," Sveneric said, rubbing the moss over Trieste's coat, plucking more, rubbing and rubbing until he cleaned away the cooling perspiration. At least Trieste had found things to eat. Sveneric had run out of food two days before. Two very long days.

Trieste stood still under Sveneric's ministrations and look-ed about, ears flicking. Sveneric touched the animal's mind and found thirst, but no stress. They walked toward a nearby stream, Kim pacing them warily. They stopped so that Trieste could drink, then nose about to crop the sweet grass on the bank.

"Do they—your, um, people—know that you left?" Kim asked after a time.

"By now they do."

Kim lifted his chin. "They can't come in here."

"No. The danger will be when I leave," said Sveneric. "And only to me."

Aurel and Linet stepped noiselessly from the forest. Sveneric studied the famous newcomer with interest. Linet wore the form of a short girl with long hair and blue-tinged skin. She had a friendly smile, and her gaze was clear and direct. He met her eyes and sensed sun warmth in mind and heart.

Sveneric could not hear her thoughts, nor did he feel any touch in the mental realm, nonetheless she turned to her companions and said, "He's all right. Welcome to Sartor's best forest, Sveneric! Come away to our camp."

"That would be great," Sveneric said.

Aurel laughed, looking relieved. Kim relaxed visibly, and stashed the knife back in his clothing.

Sveneric walked beside the tired horse, following the other three along a twisting path deeper into the forest. Presently they reached a wide clearing. Through the mighty branches of old trees, he glimpsed platforms and ropes.

"Stay here," Linet said. "I'll get a blanket to make your horse comfortable, and my friends will make you comfortable."

Trieste went willingly with Linet, which Sveneric found interesting. Usually the horse distrusted strangers and tolerated few of the humans it knew. Sveneric scarcely had time to watch them disappear, for youngsters came from above and around him, some of them carrying food. Of various ages and backgrounds, all wore forest clothing, their expressions curious.

He watched as the camp went about preparing a meal, which was then shared: mostly nuts in various forms, with tubers and fruit. He ate until he couldn't eat any more, then spent the day in a fog of tiredness and euphoria, which included sitting against a log and watching sunlight spangle the water in a stream and sift in golden haze through the tall trees above.

They prepared another meal at sunset, after which they sang songs, told stories, and one group acted out a skit. He could see by the sidled looks his way that a lot of this was for him. He didn't know any of the songs, though one reminded him of a song Laban used to sing at bedtime when Sveneric was small.

When they got ready to sleep, Aurel brought him a thick blanket. "You can sleep anywhere," he said. "Platforms in the trees, or on the grass here. You're safe."

"Thank you," Sveneric said. He shook out the blanket, rolled up in it under the whispering branches of a tree, and stared up at the winking stars through the gently moving tree branches.

He breathed slowly, and listened on the mental plane: silence. He contemplated that for a time. For once there was no malignant mind choosing to amuse itself by spying on him, but neither was there a contact from those he loved. He was alone. In leaving Norsunder, he had also left Detlev and David and Adam and the others. That tightness closed his throat again, the same tightness he'd felt when he walked away from David.

The truth was he missed them. Missed them terribly.

None of them had ever treated Sveneric with evil intent, but he could hear on the mental plane the ambitions and secret desires of Norsunder Base's warriors. And though the boys seemed different, except for Noser, whose mind was like a cracked mirror, only partially repaired, there was that terrible memory from Ian.

The rest of them, Sveneric could not read, so he did not know what their true intent was. Sometimes in Sveneric's dreams, David walked a cliff narrow as a knife blade, with falls to either side into spikes of black ice on one side and burning lava on the other.

Detlev had gone much into the Beyond, where he was as invisible as if he were dead, and Sveneric was alone here among these strangers who looked at him with fear or distrust, or the sort of wariness you give to an enemy. No. That was the way of self-pity. He could acknowledge the bad feelings, but with them he must acknowledge the sense of rightness in having chosen this path. Lonely it might be, but not forever. As for Detlev and the others, he could find them if they made their way across the knife edge. . .

At dawn Sveneric woke up, after the first good sleep he'd had since leaving.

He sat up, wishing he had a sword at hand so he could do Detlev's warm-up. But he did not, and anyway, he recognized the wish as an emotional need—*hand through the water*, mind and body serene and smooth—not as a physical need. He did the warm-up with his hands only, then contented himself with some concentrated stretches to take the kinks out of neck and back after his long day and longer ride. After that, when his blood flowed well and his muscles moved with the ease of warmth, it was full daylight and he looked around.

The camp was alive with activity. Youngsters repaired ropes, built things, and walked to and fro on errands, chattering more normally. People moved about on the tree platforms above, doing chores hidden by the thick foliage.

Sveneric had always known the lesson "don't trust looks only"—but among Norsundrians your life depended on applying that to other situations. Power, danger, evil, those were the things he'd been trained to consider, to avoid, to recognize and to shape and use. How to run, and to stay hidden. But this situation, the unfamiliar, even unappetizing-looking food. Who would have thought the lesson would apply to harmless things? He looked down at the plate, glad that the lighters also had things to teach as he savored the delightful tastes and textures. This kind of lesson he liked learning.

When he was done, a girl somewhat older than he approached. She wore forest brown and green. Her face was round, but her features were marked with the eyes and brows he knew from the files characterized the Landises, and to a lesser extent some of the Deis and the Delieths.

"Julian?" Sveneric stood up politely. "Jessan told me in my dream you might come."

Julian nodded, studying him with interest. "You must be Sveneric. Nice to meet you at last."

"And you."

She grinned. "You're so polite! They said the poopsies are polite. When they want to be. Well, you won't get any fake politeness here. Where are you heading?"

"Sarendan," Sveneric said. "To find Ian Selenna. After, I don't know."

"Depends on the search," Julian said, unsurprised. "As it happens, I can take you to Sarendan by ways your old pals will never find, in case you're worried that you're being hunted."

Morvende geliaths, Sveneric thought, with a thrill of anticipation—and a cold, terrifying memory of his brief encounter with Ilerian of the Host. He'd barely been able to shut himself away, and he still wasn't certain he'd been able to hide his identity.

"Thank you," he said.

Thirty-eight

THE NEW HOUSE HAD been built on a low hill, set at a very wide angle as though to cup the low northern light of winter, and the western breezes of summer. The southeast side was sheltered by mountains rising in escalating sets toward the snow-crowned peaks of Sartor's extreme western border, which would afford shade from the strong summer sun.

A waterfall cascaded down at one side, winding its way below a broad terrace toward a river snaking away toward the sea, which could be glimpsed from the upper story, a considerable ride distant. The beginnings of a road marked the ground beside the river, probably made by the builders hauling stone, scavenged wood, and the rest of the building materials.

David's first thought had been that yes, this place was not even remotely built for defense, and yet that northwest view over the gently rising land pretty much guaranteed that anyone approaching would be spotted a couple days before they saw the house. The formidable mountains protected the back side, silent sentinels that would daunt the hardiest army.

The style was plain, even severe, built of the light stone found plentifully in the region, the only decorative element the trefoil clerestory above the long, arched windows. Colend had elaborated on arched windows over the centuries, but David had studied the same sources that Curtas had, and he recognized a very old symbol in the simple yet compelling circular threes.

The terrace was a mosaic of light stone in subtly different shades, describing a series of interwoven loops and arcs. No one but Adam, leaning out from a second story window, noticed the Purad pattern. Most of the boys saw only that this terrace was big enough for sword fighting practice.

Curtas had spent the past few days supervising the finishing touches to the house. He stood in the center of the terrace, grinning proudly, but his gaze anxiously shifted between them all as they recovered from the transfer and approached. The only other decorative elements were the young silver-leafed argan trees at either end.

"What d'ya think?" he asked, then saw that everyone's attention had shifted to the doorway, set into a larger arch carved into the light stone, where a familiar fair-haired figure stood. Then trod down the shallow terrace steps at a leisurely pace.

"Siamis?" Laban exclaimed.

"The very same."

Gazes shifted back and forth between the boys and Siamis. Most turned to David for clues, and when he didn't react, tension eased. All right, obviously they'd been blindsided. But so had Norsunder, those who judged by such measures reasoned. They were glad to see him again.

Well, almost all. Laban's glower did not change.

"Come inside," Siamis said. "Detlev's upstairs, giving Adam new books. There's some furniture, but a lot is still empty."

"This is your place now, too? Is that it? Past is nothing, poof, it was all a joke?" Laban stood before Siamis, arms crossed, head thrown back at a dramatic angle. The only reason why no one decked him was because he couldn't help looking like a stage hero. He was utterly unselfconscious about his striking good looks, only becoming more spectacular as he lengthened from vivid-featured boy into extravagantly handsome adolescent. Not for him the gawky stage.

Siamis's smile turned rueful. "It was never a joke. And no, this is not my home. Though I might visit from time to time. You'll note there are plenty of rooms."

There it was, that agreeable singer's voice, remembered from early childhood: it was Siamis who'd taught Laban to sing. But Laban could never get his tone to hint at subtle meanings. When he tried, he sounded stupid.

Siamis has a home? The question telegraphed between the others in shrugs and rolled eyes, but he'd gone inside again, drawing them after.

He was right. Little furniture as yet in the airy rooms that had been cut at different levels: they could see that the summer side had higher ceilings, and the winter rooms were smalller. Most of the big rooms were dominated right now by potted trees, Curtas having brought in fruit and aromatic trees from various lands. They paused inside, tension still simmering.

Detlev came down the stairs. "Neutral territory here, boys," he said. "There's always Norsunder Base if you haven't had enough fighting."

"Until the Host show up," Laban cracked.

"They won't," Detlev said, unemotional as always. "Here."

"I know, I know, it's just a house," Laban drawled, rolling his eyes. And at Curtas's pained expression, he added hastily, trying to look appreciative, "though a fine one. But will Efael see that? The Host has their mysterious long plans, but we've all seen that Efael likes blood while he's waiting, and nothing is too petty."

Detlev smiled. "Efael has what he wanted, a clear field. If he spares me a thought, it will be to contemptuously dismiss any lair of mine as a retreat to lick my wounds."

"How's Adam?" Curtas asked, low-voiced.

"He knows he has to stay off that leg until it begins to heal." Which was *an* answer, but not *the* answer—but then he knew the real answer would be *Ask him.* Only Curtas was a little afraid to, that the Adam he had always known might be forever broken. But as the words faded, the tone sank in: reassurance. Curtas let out a breath he hadn't known he was holding, as Detlev turned to the rest of the newcomers.

Detlev gestured open-handed. "You're welcome to come and go as you will. There's the Destination pattern." He indicated the terrace outside. And, answering the unspoken question rising among the more reflective among them, "Everyone lives with the consequences of their actions. Most of them seldom realize it. They will never need to. That will not be true for any of you. You will have cause to regret every decision, every action, every light word. Welcome to the world of ethics."

"Piss," Laban muttered.

Since obviously no one was going to entertain him with a dust-up, Noser shoved past them all, uninterested in anything but bagging the biggest unclaimed room. Vana ran behind him.

At that moment, a head stuck out from the kitchen door, belonging to a scarred, tough-looking man they recognized as one of Detlev's agents back at the Den on Five, and Detlev followed him inside. It was apparent that he'd brought a trusted few out with him, and some were apparently going to act as staff.

MV said to Ferret, "Was that you, tracking Aldon?"

Ferret nicked his chin down. "Found him in Fhleria. False name."

"Representative government, right?" Curtas asked.

David said, "In Fhleria, only warriors can vote for chieftain, though guilds are run as usual. The elected chieftain has five years, then has to run again."

"Voting! What a stupid system," Laban said. "I mean, would you really want the likes of Zhenc, say, or that bullying Nath woman, or even worse, the totally insane like Kessler Sonscarna all voting?"

"You think inherited kingship is any better?" MV said derisively.

"At least they get trained," Laban retorted.

"At what? Spending money? Parading around looking tough? Have you already forgotten Glenn Delieth?"

"Every system that puts human beings in charge of others is suspect." Siamis's calm voice cooled the rising heat of conflict. "The mystery is, how anyone gets others to follow them, especially straight into disaster. Aldon, I'm certain, is lying through his teeth, saying whatever he thinks they want to hear, in hopes of winning himself an instant army."

"Or meeting a competitor's knife," Leef said.

"We can hope," MV said, looking around the circle.

Here they were, on the outside. Again. Some with new scars, most with new bruises, facing a future that promised more pain. But they had the now, and that was not so bad. Grab it while you can.

"I'm already bored," MV said, first two fingers propped on his skinny hips, elbows at an angle of challenge. "I'm going back to my boat and head for Jaro Harbor. I know some places along the dock where the beer is cheap, and the sailor girls aren't picky. Anyone want to go with me?"

David wasn't surprised that he'd guessed right: while he'd been suspended in the Beyond, most of the others had aged past him, crossing a certain threshold and discovering the world of sex. Another complexity of human interaction to deal with; though he could feel the lure like the summer sun still below the horizon, he'd seen enough of the emotional burn to be glad he was not there yet. Life was already full of sudden fires. He wandered off to see what kind of library Detlev was putting together.

Rolfin had leaned back so the warm sun shone on his face. "Any willing boys?"

MV eyed him. More had changed since he'd gone to sea than he'd assumed — it seemed the others were catching up. "You lean right?"

Rolfin spread his hands. "Yup."

MV swung around to eye Leef. "You?"

"Left." Leef jerked a thumb downward. "I've *got* a prick. No interest in anyone else's. You say the girls aren't picky? The ones back at Base wouldn't look at us. Except to laugh. Said we had nothing to offer."

"I know a place," Siamis interjected here, "you might enjoy. And gain some skills while you're at it."

The word *skills?* semaphored between them, then they turned the intensity of question back to Siamis.

"Oh, boys. You have so much to learn." He smiled provocatively.

The terrace was soon empty.

Thirty-nine

NO SUCH ATMOSPHERE CELEBRATORY or instructive had prevailed in Mearsies Heili.

After the historic confrontation with Detlev, Mearsieanne transferred home, where she let loose with a temper tantrum that drove the servants tiptoeing away to find work elsewhere in the palace, and sent the girls to the underground hideout in hasty retreat. Not that anyone felt unsafe. They knew that Mearsieanne would never hurt anyone. But hearing yet again her rant about Norsunder, Detlev, evil, what she wanted to be done to them, and how much she lost a century ago when she was forced into enchantment, left them with nothing to say.

Clair listened as long as she could because she felt it was duty— Mearsieanne seemed to need an audience. But when the heated rant got to Tsauderei, who (Mearsieanne said) had gone completely senile, *daring* to accuse her of . . .

That was when Clair stopped listening. Her own questions proliferated in her mind. Once Mearsieanne had talked herself out, which left her exhausted and stricken with headache, Clair had firmed a resolution.

A few days later, the questions were still there, and so was the resolution. Clair got one of the transfer tokens that she and Mearsieanne had made, and transferred to Bereth Ferian, which lay under the dark sky of winter.

Liere was the first one to find her. Clair's shoulders relaxed when Liere appeared in the doorway to the Destination chamber, shrouded in winter clothes. "Clair? I hope nothing is wrong."

"I need to talk to . . ." Clair couldn't quite get the name Siamis out, so she said, "Roy. Is he here? Do you think he would talk to me?"

"Of course! He and Arthur are in the magic library. Let me take you." They began walking, and Liere cast her a considering glance. "Was Mearsieanne still angry?"

Clair gave the only answer possible: "She has reason to be."

"Yes," Liere sighed. "Yes. So many say that." She looked blankly down the beautifully tiled hallway, rich with tapestries and statuary. "And will. It's so . . . so strange. The news. About Detlev."

"It was strange after Siamis left Norsunder, too," Clair said. "Do you think he talked Detlev into doing it?"

"I don't know. All he said was to accept it as real. Not a ruse." She lowered her voice. "There are some who insist this is a new ruse." Then she paused and glanced down the hall. No one was in sight, though somewhere in the distance echoed the laughter of kids. "Clair, others have said you don't want to talk about what happened to you when Detlev's gang took you prisoner, but if you can bear to speak about it, what was your experience with him?"

Clair *had* been unwilling to talk about it with most people, but Liere was different. She'd been a Norsundrian target far longer than Clair had. Her question would not come out of martial ardor, or a lurid thirst for details. "He was mostly gone. I only talked to him a couple times. I thought it was horrible. Both times. But it turned out my fears were worse than what actually happened." She paused, catching a subtle reaction in Liere, too quick to define.

Clair mentally shrugged. Since Liere seemed to be waiting, she wrinkled her nose. "Though the second interview was awful because it was all about hypocrisy, and unfair judgment, and people — on our side — talking about how superior they are to Norsunder. Which I believe," Clair added. "Oh, one thing that terrible year convinced me of, is, bad as some of us can act sometimes, we're way better than they are. But, well, what he said, we're kind of seeing it now."

Mearsieanne's name was not spoken, but it lay in the air between them. To get away from it, Clair ventured a question. "What was your experience? I know Siamis chased you all over, during the days of his enchantment. Did Detlev?"

"When I was a prisoner in Geth." Liere pressed her thin fingers together. "I thought that mental realm nightmare so horrifying. At the time I believed it was the worst they could do, but now I wonder if that was just noise. A little like when Arthur used to pretend to be a monster to Lyren and Mac, and roar, and wave his hands around, and make dreadful faces. And chase them around but never quite catch them. And they were scared, and acted scared, but they were never in any danger."

"You weren't in danger?"

"Oh, I was. But it could have been *so* much worse. Most of those frightful people could have broken my neck like a twig, and Detlev could've easily killed me in the mental realm without bothering to stir from his chair. I don't think I was worth the effort. I'm only just beginning to understand what coinherence really means, but I know enough to see that, oh, he hinted at the scary monster—maybe to amuse himself, I don't know—and my own fears made it worse. I managed to frighten *myself* half to death." Liere tipped her head. "He was after the dyr, not me, and when I told him I had no idea where it was—and he knew it was true—he said I was a decoy and couldn't get rid of me fast enough."

Clair nodded soberly; she could see that Liere believed she was beginning to penetrate the layers of Norsundrian deceit and intent, but Clair wondered if Liere was only seeing what they wanted her to.

The girls got out of the way of a servant carrying a stack of linens, and retreated to the library, where they found Arthur balancing on a stepladder, a stack of old paper in one arm, the other hand moving along age-shabby titles. Roy sat at a table, bent over a scroll, a glowglobe at either side so no shadow was cast by his hand as he wrote.

"Clair," Roy said in surprise. "I didn't know you were here."

Clair said, "Roy, I want to know what you think. Is it real? Detlev not being part of Norsunder anymore. I thought he *was* Norsunder."

Roy set his pen down with such care that it was apparent his mind was far away. As he had ever since his return from Geth, he remembered Detlev's promise that they would speak again. For a long time he'd brooded over that before he finally talked to Siamis and Arthur, at first slowly, then more and more as he reevaluated everything he'd ever learned. Thought. Believed. He and Arthur had spent most of the past week discussing this new twist.

He turned to Clair. "Siamis says it's true. I've come to trust what he says about events now, though we don't talk about the past. I think . . ." His expression shuttered, and he said, "Maybe we should go. Ask directly. Because I will say this. Though Detlev didn't always tell us everything—sometimes he wouldn't talk at all—I don't remember him ever lying out-right."

"Go. Get it over with." Arthur jumped down from the ladder. "Otherwise you'll keep gnawing on it. And the senior mages want all our attention on the blood mage text search." He waved at the stacks of papers on the far table, and said to Clair, "Now that Prince Kerendal is not just king in name, but of age, the Venn are talking to us. However, everything has to be translated from Old Venn." He lowered his voice to one of doom. "There are a *lot* of runes."

"Right. Right," Roy repeated under his breath, wondering if any of the boys were there at that house, and who would strike first.

As to that, he'd been sparring with Siamis for an appreciable time. He squared his shoulders, eyeing the sturdy girl with the odd pure-white hair that hid her face as she studied her hands. "Clair."

She looked up, her hazel gaze wary but not angry. He didn't niff any anger, or even resentment. Instead, he sensed the intensity of her question. It was almost a longing.

He said, "The truth is, maybe because of your experiences on Five—on Aldau-Rayad—but Siamis once said, if you ever showed up here with questions, I was to let him know, and he gave the Destination pattern. Do you want to go with me? It's a long transfer."

Clair dropped her gaze, as conflicted as she'd ever been in her life. That was exactly what she wanted, and yet equally strong was the impulse to retreat to the safety of her home. But she could imagine CJ's questions, and remembered all of

Mearsieanne's wild surmises. She was tired of guessing in circles. What she needed was the truth. Or if she couldn't get that, at least some words from those in question, rather than third-hand speculation.

She sent a questioning look at Liere and got a nod in return. "Okay," she said.

The transfer halfway around the world wrenched them one by one. Roy and the two girls appeared on the Destination tiles at Detlev's house.

Once she recovered, Clair expected another utilitarian Den within a fortress. The house and grounds looked to her like they belonged in the Colendi countryside. There was even a young garden. At the other end of the terrace, several of Detlev's boys watched as two fought with swords. Liere turned away, but Clair and Roy noted that the pair fighting — MV and Curtas — were both blindfolded, as Rolfin and David called out sword moves.

Liere said, indicating the hills behind the house, "This is just the sort of place Adam used to paint."

Roy watched David, who seemed to have stayed the same age, though everyone else in the terrace had gotten taller and filled out. He was also too thin for his size, and Roy wondered what he'd been doing instead of eating regular meals.

The swords clashed and clanged, then Curtas dropped his, cursing as the others laughed. He groped around for the sword as David turned Roy's way, smiling the old reflective smile. But it was different after all. Roy saw self-mockery in that smile, under the very real amusement. Roy remembered, and he knew David also remembered, that the last time they saw one another David had beaten Roy senseless.

"Life seems to have treated you well," David said.

"I'm alive." Roy kept his face and voice blank, and saw appreciative irony narrow David's eyes.

"Firejive," David said in a light voice — their silly code that they had thought so secret and so strong, when they were very young.

Roy spread his hands, reddening a little: he understood the welcome beneath the irony.

David gave a soft laugh. "If you've nothing else to do, come out and try a new game."

Roy knew it was not a game at all, but the first level in a new style of training, one that incorporated Dena Yeresbeth.

Siamis had been teaching him for half a year. So the boys were learning it too.

Roy said, "Maybe," and followed the girls to the door.

The house was cool inside. Detlev and Siamis were both there, the diffuse light limning Siamis's fair hair and outlining his slim, elegant form as he listened to an unfamiliar man demonstrating something with a couple of lengths of wood. Though Roy and Arthur had reached an understanding, he still could appreciate such sights, and laughed at himself. Life certainly took its unexpected twists and turns.

The three lifted their heads toward the new arrivals, then Detlev said, "We'll do it your way. Carry on." He made a well-remembered hand gesture, no more than a flick of the flingers. How odd that seeing it again hurt so much.

Roy's perspective had changed. He was nearly as tall as Detlev now, and the man's face did not seem as old as it had. For the first time in his life, Roy considered how relatively young Detlev had been when his world had pretty much ended. And Siamis had been a child.

There was the same direct hazel gaze. Roy's thoughts were masked, and Detlev did not probe, but Roy knew that his old leader could probably read him as well as if he'd not guarded his mind — or nearly as well. And now that he was here, all the questions that had kept him awake for countless nights dried right up.

Detlev's eyes crinkled with humor. "Why don't you go outside. Enjoy the summer day. Isn't it dead winter up north?"

Roy took that as permission to debrief with David, a far less daunting proposition, and perhaps get in some practice at the same time. As he retreated, Detlev and Siamis exchanged a glance and divided the two girls, one to each.

Liere looked around, and said with what she thought was polite interest, "Where is the little boy I've suddenly heard so much about?"

Detlev heard the resentment Liere struggled against that her daughter had kept such a secret for so long, and beneath that the familiar sense of failure that had shadowed her all her life.

"He's not here," Detlev said. "Siamis tells me that your two are doing well up north. Mac shows an interest in magic studies."

"They're doing well because of Siamis," Liere said with

false brightness. "He's a very good teacher."

"He learned on very difficult students." Detlev tipped his chin toward the bank of windows overlooking the terrace.

Liere glanced out, and spotted Roy with a couple of the boys the Mearsieans called poopsies, involved in some kind of martial arts drill as they talked back and forth. You'd think Roy had never left them. He mirrored the pattern perfectly, a smile on his long face.

"How are your magic studies?" Detlev asked.

Liere looked away, and back to the man who had figured in nightmares that she had given herself. An overwhelming sense of futility made her shut her eyes. "Better." She rallied. "Siamis taught me how to coinhere with magic, but oh, it is so slow and painstaking."

"Yes, because the method you were taught was designed for people without coinherence," he said. "Part of your slow advancement is that you are still learning basic discipline with coinherence, but the other part is that using the magic method you were taught is similar to trying to walk while hobbled with stones on every limb. Your excellent self-discipline and your skills on the mental plane would flourish with another method of study entirely."

"What method? Whose?" she asked, surprise stilling the awful feelings that she'd thought she'd gotten rid of. But no, they'd just gone dormant.

"On Geth-deles," he said. "The practitioners call themselves the Ones. It's not a discipline for all. Students leave identity and past at the door. Wealth, rank, social position, all are irrelevant. Their goal is service through trained skills, including magic, and advancement is between you and your tutor. You work with others, you don't compete with them."

Liere drew in a slow breath. "That sounds . . . "Blissful. ". . . impossible. Lyren hates magic studies."

"My suggestion," he said, "is that you go alone. As you yourself pointed out, Lyren is doing well where she is. She's surrounded by guardians, and safety."

"I couldn't possibly leave her," Liere exclaimed. "For how long?"

"Anywhere from seven to ten years to reach senior status. I expect you'd get there in six."

"Six . . . years!"

He said nothing. She thought miserably of her total lack of

control over those children once they'd gotten past the adoring toddler status. How she'd spent her days trying to chase them. How Lyren still argued with her about small things. Siamis kept repeating, *It's a phase,* and even *It will pass, if you don't make it a challenge.* All of which she knew was right, and which left her feeling as much of a failure as she had ever felt as the fake Girl Who Saved the World. Only worse, because it wasn't Sartora failing at the impossible, it was Liere Fer Eider failing these two children. And herself.

"I couldn't possibly," she said.

"I understand. You don't want to leave your daughter. Would you be interested in a tour of the house? Adam is upstairs, fighting boredom while he waits for a broken leg to heal. Would you like to entertain him for a bit?"

With a breath of profound relief, Liere walked toward the stairs.

While they'd been talking, Siamis gestured to Clair. "Interested in a tour of the house?"

Clair nodded, but when they got to the next room, she ignored the room and turned her serious gaze up to Siamis. "You've been teaching Liere, as well as Lyren and Mac, am I right?"

"Liere's talents are formidable," Siamis said. "I've merely given her some drills that were part of childhood when I was small—think of them as akin to learning the alphabet, and basic numbers. I could give you drills designed to help your own cohesion. Be happy to."

An inexplicable feeling unfurled inside Clair, as if a bright, feathered creature stretched its wings. Then she thought of Mearsieanne, and it shriveled to dust. "I couldn't," she said, the words dragged out of her. Mearsieanne would not just hate it, she would feel betrayed. And to sneak, or lie, would make Clair feel she'd betrayed herself.

Siamis didn't hide his regret, but all he said was, "The offer's there. If the day ever comes when you feel you can. It wouldn't take long. You'd do most of it on your own."

Clair ducked her head, letting her hair swing forward to hide the tightness in her throat, the spring of tears she couldn't fight. And when Siamis said, "It appears Liere's on her way to visit Adam. Want to say hello?" Clair grabbed at the chance and nodded again. "You'll find him at the top of the stairs, down at the far end, left."

While Clair ran to join Liere, Siamis said to Detlev, "She won't. Mearsieanne again."

Detlev shook his head. "I failed twice with her. The timing has been terrible."

Siamis's expression tightened into grimness—rare for him. "We're not going to have enough of them in time, are we?"

"Every year—every month—that passes tips the balance a fraction our way."

Neither had to say, *But not far enough*.

Halfway up the steps, Clair remembered the awful things she'd said to Adam the last time she'd seen him. She slipped behind Liere, hesitant when they reached Adam's open door.

The room was large and airy, books stacked everywhere. Adam sat on a bed that had been dragged to the window and was piled high with pillows, one leg stretched out as he gazed down at the terrace, his mittened hands working slowly and awkwardly with needles and yarn.

He looked gaunt, his bones sharply etched in his face, then he turned his head and smiled, and there was a glimpse of the old Adam in those shifting shadows, many of which were healing cuts and bruises, they saw.

"Well! A surprise," he said, and carefully set aside his knitting, moving his hands as though the yarn and needles were made of glass.

His easy tone was a relief, and yet Clair was aware of a pulse of guilt when she remembered her resentment. "What happened to you?"

"I was clumsy," he said ruefully.

Liere, questing on the mental plane, hit a stone wall.

"Tell me the news of the world," Adam invited.

Liere always had trouble with chat. She wondered what she could possibly know that he didn't, considering who he lived with, but Clair took over. "What are you knitting?" She pointed at the yarn. "I like that braided pattern."

"I'm trying to relearn." He wiggled three or four of his fingers, the others stiff and still. Splinted, Clair saw. She eyed the thickness of those mitts as Adam said, "My goal is to make a pile of scarfs against next winter."

"Puddlenose tried to show me how to knit once, but I kept losing track of the stitches. He says his hands learned the patterns so he didn't have to think about it much, but I never could. Who taught you?"

"I learned how to knit from a sailor. A lot of them do it to keep awake on night watches."

Clair pored over the yarn balls. "That's what Puddlenose said! I like this bright red. That would be cheery in winter. What did you use to make the dye?"

They chatted on about dyes, colors, sailing, and travel until Roy reappeared and they decided to leave, Roy and Liere going all the way north again in a tremendous wrench.

Clair had come to Bereth Ferian equipped with her transfer token, so she endured a much shorter jolt to Mearsies Heili. She took a walk by herself, as she counted up all the reasons why it would be a very bad idea to get those lessons Siamis had offered.

But what else was there to do?

She knew what she wanted to do. As she wandered under the dappled light in the summery forest, she was aware of a shimmery feeling inside. It was odd, how many dreams since her return from Five that she'd had with little children in them. She had tried to attribute them to missing Irenne, to hearing about Lyren and Mac, and the Delieth twins, and little Ian. When Adam told them that they were expecting Detlev's son to arrive from Sarendan, Clair's thoughts went immediately back to that little boy in the critter cave who had been so still and self-possessed.

Family. It was so important.

Furthermore, family was *exactly* what Mearsieanne needed. And deserved! Clair knew that Mearsieanne would never adopt an heir. She placed too much importance on blood. But Clair also knew that she herself would never be able to promise to rule the way Mearsieanne felt it should be done. But someone who grew up learning Mearsieanne's ways, and loving her?

She stood there on the grass, hugging her arms around herself. It was a perfect day, the air so sweet and soft, peace within and without. She still didn't know where her life was going, but that was all right.

As magic glimmered at the back of her mind, unmistakable in effect, wonder surged through her, and laughter, and joy. She ran back to the underground cave, happiness streaming inside her like the bubbles in Dhana's lake. When the girls gathered, and she said, "It's time to add to the family. Do you all want to be aunties?"

"Yes!" "Oh!" "Our own little one?" "Think of the pie fights we'll have!" were the most discernable reactions, but all were enthusiastic.

"The Birth Spell, did it come to you?" CJ asked. "How? Why?"

"It's something I've been thinking about," Clair said, aware of that giddy sense of freedom in admitting something she'd suppressed. "As for the Spell, I can *feel* it. I could ignore it, but it pushes against the inside of my head, kind of. Well, what do you think? Shall I tell Mearsieanne before, or surprise her? After all, that's how my grandfather was born. You've heard how she said that the Spell just came."

"I think so, but pick the name first," CJ said. "So your little girl doesn't get stuck with Mearsieanne Two. I mean, it's nice, but . . ."

"I agree," Diana said. "Since it's just us here. Mearsieanne picked her own name when she took over the throne. And 'Tesmer' for her son. Who wants to be saddled with a name only old kings used?" She looked at CJ, puzzled. "Only, how do you know it's a girl? It could be a boy, you know. It's not like shopping — you don't get to pick."

"I just thought of course it would be a girl." CJ looked blank. "I guess a boy would be okay. We could get used to that, except what if he wants to run off to sail the world with Puddlenose?"

"A girl could do that, too," Clair pointed out. "Everybody think of the nicest names for boys and girls you know."

Falinneh could not help but think of silly names, of course. With some brisk debate, they settled on CJ's suggestion of Aurori for a boy or Aurora for a girl, and Clair shut her eyes and gave in.

The room filled with light, and there was a wriggling infant — Aurora. As her friends expressed delight and wonder, Clair blinked away tears.

As for Siamis's offer, now she would be too busy.

Forty

Sarendan

"WE'RE NEARLY THERE," JULIAN observed, twisting in the saddle to glance back at him.

Sveneric breathed deeply, listening to the sighing echo as he gazed about the gem-traces in the morvende tunnel that threw back the torchlight in a multitude of colors. "How old is this one?"

Julian shrugged. "Old. They're all old. That's all I can tell you. But when you come back, I'll introduce you to Sinder and Hinder. They can tell you everything you want to know. Especially Sinder." She pointed toward a rocky doorway. "Ready?"

Sveneric looked back one more time, regret strong. I'll be back, he promised himself. This was not an ending. It was a beginning.

He followed Julian silently out into the dark mountain air, aware that it really was both. He'd wrestled silently all the days of his travel with what he knew was terrible home-sickness. Except it wasn't the home he missed—not at all. Every day he rejoiced to be away from the ugly barrenness of the Base, rejoiced until he felt dizzy with all the new sights, smells, sounds, tastes and touches he took in. It was the separation and the silence from his father that hurt so much. The changing beauty of Sartor's geliaths had filled his senses, but the emptiness in his heart seemed endless.

He'd known it would be bad. To ease the pain, he kept reviewing over and over the last time he had seen Detlev, eating in the office, going over a history file together. A few words of praise, an admonition not to forget looking at trade figures. . .

He couldn't give any hint of his thoughts, or he'd be hated as much as they hated Detlev. He stayed silent as Julian led him down the mountainside in the chilly night air, and when they paused so that she could check for landmarks, he flung back his head and gazed skyward. Even the stars seemed cold and distant. Somehow they had seemed more accessible seen from Shendoral. But beautiful, always beautiful.

The more he saw of the lighters and their land, the more he knew that those who made up what was called "Norsunder" were wrong. That included his father and the boys. Why could he not hate them? Why did he want to turn his steps and go back? He shut his eyes, fighting desolation. He'd long since given up being afraid that Detlev would angrily order MV to hunt him down and drag him back. It would almost be a relief to have them swoop down and collar him, except — except —

"Couple more hours, then sun's up and we can go faster," Julian said. "We should arrive just before sundown. Say, you all right? Cold?"

Sveneric shut his teeth hard and forced his breathing to even out. "I'm all right," he said.

Julian shrugged. "We could getcha a blanket somewhere. Or better clothes. It's going to be hard to get you in, wearin' that Norsundrian stuff."

"No."

Julian shrugged again, and turned her eyes to the trail down toward Miraleste.

Why did he not want to change his clothes? It was stupid, wearing the uniform that David and the others despised, but it was what his father wore. He did not want to change, as if wearing these hate clothes somehow prevented the connection from being completely severed. But what would the people in Sarendan think, to see him riding down the streets?

What would Ian Selenna think? He had to know if Ian would accept him as he was. He'd meant to surprise him, but looking down at his gray tunic coat, he was uncertain about everything.

Then came the familiar voice on the mental plane *:Shrimpy?*

:I'm here, in Sarendan, and I'm coming.

Ian's gladness flooded Sveneric's mind like bright sunshine, easing some of the terrible loneliness of separation. Leaning over to pat Trieste's neck, he muttered, "Not long now." Then he tipped his head back and smiled up at the stars.

They rode into Miraleste by a circuitous route. Many of the streets had lamps, and in their light Sveneric could see that a great deal of the city was new. Wide streets, parks and squares here and there, canals of clean water running round the perimeter of the hills. It was an airy city, designed to take advantage of light and air.

The palace was fortified, built high up above a lake. It could be defended, though the gates stood open, and no soldiers stood watch on those parapets. A fountain had been put in a big square, its pure water free for all to use, or to enjoy looking at. His heart lifted at the benign intent behind that.

"Here's my idea," Julian said. "I'll go in the front way, and Lilah and her uncle'll be surprised to see me. You can sneak in the back way and meet Ian."

Sveneric nodded. "Thank you."

"It was fun," Julian said. Born over a hundred years ago and then taken out of time for nearly a century, she had no Dena Yeresbeth, nor did she trouble with a mind-shield. What she said, she also thought, an integrity that Sveneric had learned early to appreciate, even to cherish, having lived so long in a community of violent, angry people who lied as a matter of course — even to themselves. "I promised Lyren and Mac and Jessan," she said.

Sveneric urged the tired Trieste around the side wing of the palace, into a back garden. He tried a send, got an immediate answer, and within a short time a boy shorter than Sveneric ran over the lawns toward him.

"Shrimpy!" Ian said in a low voice. "I can't believe you're

really here! Was it hard?"

"To get away? Not really." Sveneric lifted a shoulder. "Can we get Trieste taken care of without causing any problems?"

"I'll see to it," Ian promised. "Wait, how will I lead him? He doesn't have a bridle or anything."

Sveneric demonstrated with a touch of hand to neck and mind to mind, the latter open to Ian. It was strange to them both, after having for so very long communicated only within dreams to actually be in the same space.

Ian put out an experimental hand, and duplicated Sveneric's touch. Trieste's ears flicked, his tail swished, but he turned his head willingly at the familiar touch of this new herd leader. Off they went, horse and boy, Ian calling over his shoulder, "Go up to my room and wait." And he gave Sveneric a mental pathway to follow.

Two secret passageways brought him up to Ian's rooms

He was standing in the middle of Ian's workroom staring at the floor when Ian entered behind him. Sveneric turned around and beheld a thin boy almost his height, with a sharp chin, tilted eyes and eyebrows.

Ian gestured into the bedroom. "Want some food or anything?"

Sveneric shook his head.

Ian, who was barefoot, hopped onto his bed and sat cross-legged. "Like it here?" he asked, waving his hand.

Sveneric looked around the big, well-decorated room. The windows faced west and north, which would let in lots of light, the northern ones in winter. The bed was rumpled, and clothes, books, and papers sat in haphazard stacks on the surfaces of exquisitely carved and painted furniture. Used to utter austerity, Sveneric found it cluttered, but not displeasing. He sighed before he realized he had.

Ian said, "Do you miss them?"

"What will you think if I say yes?" Sveneric asked.

"That you miss them." Ian shrugged. "Sit down! I know what it is to miss people—I still miss my da." He smiled. "But now you have *us*, and I have so much to show you."

Time passed swiftly.

There came a day when summer's heat abated, following a monumental thunderstorm that left rain-washed breezes sweeping over the lake below the city.

Ian and Sveneric had joined the castle guard in their drill routine in the garrison courtyard, overseen by the Regent, Darian Irad.

Regent, not king. Though Peitar Selenna had decreed that his uncle would follow him if Peitar died first, Darian Irad made it plain from the outset that he and his family planned to return to Geth-deles when Ian was ready for kingship.

Under Peitar's reign, in previous years, the guard had drilled increasingly intermittently, giving it up altogether over the hot months of the southern summer. That was now changed. Under the Regent's dispassionate eye, apathetic going-through-the-motions had altered to red-faced, sweaty effort.

As always, the guards made room for their small king, who was very much a mascot. Ian put in mighty effort not because he was particularly martial-mined — he secretly shared his father's dislike of things military — but because he felt they expected it of him. Beside him, Sveneric mirrored his movements, never going beyond the limits of Ian's skill. Only the guard commander and the Regent noticed how effortlessly he moved, a contrast to Ian's jerky, grunting exertions, but neither man said anything.

The only things known about this polite, self-effacing young visitor were that he was the son of the infamous monster Detlev, but also that he was, unaccountably, the young king's close friend. How they'd met was anyone's guess.

As for the boys, once this duty was done, they ran off, Ian with a grin of relief lighting his foxy features. Sveneric, who had risen before Ian in order to get in his real practice, smiled as Ian suggested they ride down to the lakeshore an give their horses a good gallop now that it wasn't so hot.

Sveneric, always watchful, appreciated the expressions of genuine liking of Sarendan's people for Ian as they rode through the streets toward the city gate. Ian chatted happily about Delfina Valley, interrupting himself frequently to return greetings from passers-by, but otherwise he seemed to take for granted not just his popularity, but the ease with which he passed through the city. Sveneric, born to a hard school, reveled in this unconscious peace, people behaving as if there had never been, nor could ever be, any other way to live.

On their return from a good ride, Ian ran off dutifully to lessons, leaving Sveneric to his usual pursuits, which had been reading in the royal library. He mounted the steps toward the library, halting when he recognized Siamis on the landing above, contemplating a new mural in the process of being painted on the long wall that reached upward to the inter-leaved molding under the ceiling mosaic. Joy ignited inside Sveneric, but from long habit he betrayed no sign outside of an extra leap to his step, mounting three of the marble stairs instead of two, until he reached Siamis.

They gazed up at the partially complete mural depicting Peitar Selenna, three times larger than life, wearing an improbable fine robe and holding kingly symbols of peace. But the reflective expression on his face as he gazed over the viewer's head toward the library had been painted by someone who knew Peitar as man rather than as king.

"He would have hated this," Siamis said.

Sveneric said, "I know."

Siamis turned to look down into Sveneric's young face, noting the healthy color there. The boy's expression revealed little, the sensitive mouth a flat, noncommittal line. "Detlev and the rest left Norsunder," he said in ancient Sartoran.

"I know," Sveneric said again, in the same tongue. "Why didn't he come?" The slight emphasis on "he" meant Detlev. Before Siamis could answer, Sveneric turned his gaze up toward Peitar Selenna's eternally patient gaze, and said, "It's because he caused his death, isn't it?" He faced Siamis. "Why?"

"Necessity," Siamis said, his mind shut against Sveneric's unnervingly subtle touch.

He was forming careful words when Sveneric's gaze diffused for a heartbeat, then two. Siamis held his breath, waiting, until Sveneric blinked, revealing no more than a minute lift of chin, and widening of eyes, but the overall effect was as if a candle had been lit within. Father and son had again opened the door between them.

Off-balance, Siamis said, "Do you want to come see the house?"

"What about Trieste?" Sveneric asked cautiously.

"He's happy here, isn't he? I'm certain Ian won't mind, but

we can ask. And you can come back any time you like in order to fetch him. A ride across Sartor in autumn might be pleasant."

Sveneric's lips parted.

"Yes. Any time you like," Siamis said. "That's what freedom means."

It was half a month before Senrid could get away to visit Liere. He needed to ride out to watch the academy wargame on the plains, then came the Games, which meant a lot of jarls showing up to watch and then take their boys (and girls, for it was clear that the new rules were not going away) home again.

Many jarls used this time to ask for private interviews, and to air their thoughts on politics. Senrid spent some time with Jarend Ndarga, Jarl of Methden, visiting for an unrelated cause, and tried without success to get him to send his nearly ten-year-old daughter to the academy the next spring.

Ndarga refused.

"Marend is small," Ndarga stated. "She'll always be small. She'd never have the size or strength to uphold Methden's honor in the academy, much less on the field of battle." Before Senrid could point out that skill did not depend on size, Ndarga added, "My wife is from the south. She thinks us barbarians. Her plan for Marend is to teach her fashion and elegance, so she can marry well in Toth or Telyerhas or even Perideth." Ndarga's severe expression lightened. "But when my little Retren is old enough, I'll send him to you."

Defeated, Senrid saw Ndarga off, and returned to his empty study. Every time he thought he'd won a change for the better, it was like he was pushed back again. He looked down at his hands, his shirt stuffed into trousers he'd worn for the last year. Boots that still fit. The very day he'd heard about Detlev leaving Norsunder, he'd rid himself of the Child Spell. He knew how it worked, but somehow he'd expected more of a dramatic change—either that, or the spell had ruined his bones, and he'd forever look like a fifteen-year-old runt.

He threw back his head, laughing in self-mockery. Had Ndarga been covertly throwing Senrid's own size in his teeth?

No. Ndarga was too straightforward for innuendo. If he hated your guts, he told you outright. Senrid rubbed his jaw, though the imprint of Ndarga's knuckles had long since worn away.

Nevertheless, the jarlan had had her say. Senrid hoped that ten-year-old Marend liked fashions and elegance. As for size, Detlev was now in the world. No longer could Senrid fool the Ancient Sartoran by seeming unchanged. If he ever had.

With an air of challenge, he removed the wards preventing Siamis, and the boys, from entering his capital. Detlev was a different matter. That ward was far older, deeper-laid by others long ago. And Senrid was in no hurry to reverse it.

Two days later, he had a window of free time, but no sooner had he cleared his desk when the outer perimeter patrol sent a runner, who came to Senrid as he moved between the guild interview chamber and Keriam's tower: "There's an outland visitor. He says his name is David, no family name or jarlate, but you will know who that means."

Forty-one

ON A FREE AFTERNOON, Senrid transferred to Bereth Ferian.

The north had entered that dreary, drippy part of winter, the snow dirty and slushy, the barren trees and low gray skies depressing.

The mage school had used magic to freeze over a bend in the river, and all the youth were skating. Senrid found everyone out there, eight-year-old Lyren drawing the eye as she gracefully twirled and leaped as if she'd been born on the thin wedge of metal bonded by magic to the bottom of her sturdy shoe. Mac raced with the magic students in a fast circle. Yanli kept trying to totter out onto the ice, raising skinny arms.

Senrid watched Yanli until Siamis scooped the child up and handed her off to a couple older students, who took her hands and skated out with her between them. She shrieked in pleasure.

Siamis turned Senrid's way.

"Where's Liere?" Senrid said.

"Her class is in charge of bringing the picnic food," Siamis said.

Senrid remembered his promise to himself and tested the waters with a question. "You know who Shontande Lirendi is, right?"

Siamis's eyes crinkled. "King of Colend. Or, king in name, presently."

"Well, during the alliance days . . ." Senrid briefly outlined everything, then finished, "Tsauderei told me that the lighters have control of the notecase magic, and I'm looking for trouble when nothing is there, and hoola loola loo. Do you agree?"

"I can see Tsauderei's point of view," Siamis said in that even, mild voice Senrid remembered from the bad old days. "Mages cannot interfere in governmental matters. The balance of tension between the two most powerful guilds in the world — mages and scribes — and governments takes work to maintain. And most people find it difficult to imagine a system that has been in place their entire lives, gradually built over centuries . . ." He clapped his hands together. "Disappearing."

Senrid stared at him, wary, intense. "But?"

"But what would you be doing, if you were planning a war?"

"Work out where to invade, and how to either compromise or take out communications, and secure supply lines," Senrid said, eyeing him intently. "Tsauderei thinks it impossible to bring down the scribe net."

"But you and I both know that anything can be compromised," Siamis said, speaking Senrid's thought. Then added, "Second question. How much do you really know about espionage?"

Senrid's lips parted, his mind moving rapidly. Siamis was obviously telling him something without telling him. He said, "What we need is a secondary communication method if the scribe net is compromised or destroyed."

Siamis ticked points off on his fingers. "We need something protected against tampering by Norsunder. We need something portable, easy to use. Finally, we need something in place that cannot be leaked beforehand." He dropped his hands, turning his head.

"Here we are!" a voice interrupted from behind.

"Anyone hungry?" Liere added. She and a tall red-haired boy appeared, carrying a basket between them, two more students following, similarly laden.

Senrid spun around at the sound of her voice, then turned back. "Damn. Of course. If someone is captured — broken — turned —"

"Any system is only as good as the weakest person in it," Siamis said. "Excuse me. I'd better go help corral the starvelings until the food is ready."

He walked off toward Mac, Lyren, and little Yanli as Liere approached from the picnic area, cheeks and nose ruddy. "Senrid!"

"You did invite me," he said, making a tremendous effort to wrench his thoughts away from what he'd just heard. Had Siamis really hinted that he, or someone, was going to take down the entire scribe network before Norsunder could get to it? And that he had some kind of substitute waiting somewhere, just in case? Heat and cold gripped the back of his neck as he said, "I had the Games to get through first."

"I remember. Are you hungry?"

He waved that off.

"You and Siamis were talking," she observed.

"About communications," he said, and recognized from her blank expression that whatever Siamis had been doing — or not doing — in the world's scribe network, Liere did not know about it. But then she wouldn't want to. She hated talk of impending war.

Senrid had been left with more questions than he'd begun with, though these were different questions. Because he discovered he was not quite ready to broach the big changes in his own life, he approached obliquely. "Did you know that Clair of the Mearsieans had a child?"

Liere grinned. "Aurora of the thousand doting aunties. Speaking of children, I met Sveneric. It seems that Detlev let him run away from home, all on his own, and he went to little Ian in Sarendan. As usual, Lyren and her group didn't tell anyone until it was done. Siamis brought him up here to meet Mac and Lyren in person."

"What's he like?"

"In some ways like a small Detlev," Liere said, then she paused, reaching for words. "And in some ways . . . different. Not different from Detlev, at least I can't say if he is or not, as I don't really know Detlev, I'm beginning to realize. All I know is his villain face."

"We all know that real well," Senrid said grimly.

"How well?" Liere countered. "When you think about it, how much damage did he really do to any of us?"

Senrid's gut tightened when he recollected that terrible

day on his border, and Detlev saying — after he'd ripped apart Senrid's wards and protections — *When I find the time to undertake your education, you will not see me coming.* Was that really a goad to learn more, to resist Norsunder harder? That was the problem, wasn't it — anything Detlev said could be true, a half-truth, or an outright lie, and Senrid wouldn't know the difference.

To get away from the worries that churned his mind late at night he said carelessly, "Anyone who thinks his damage was light or easy should talk Karhin Keperi. And Glenn of Everon. Oh wait. They're dead. Along with half of Everon, not to mention Sartor still catching up. Just to list a few, leaving out his games in my own country."

"Wasn't most of the killing in Everon all Kessler's idea?"

"That was Henerek's invasion."

Liere said, "Karhin's death was terrible, and I do hold that against those boys in particular, and Detlev for training them. But Glenn . . . he sometimes seemed a promising recruit for a silver tongue from Norsunder. And most of the Everoneth eyewitnesses admit that Glenn was partly responsible for that duel."

"I'm sure Glenn didn't expect to die. But he did expect to win." Senrid flicked his hand open. "Your point is, Detlev is our pet now, everything forgiven and forgotten?"

"Never forgotten," Liere whispered. "*Never.* As for forgiving . . ." Liere shook her head. "I don't really know, exactly. But maybe it was Detlev's having had a child. So rare, for Norsundrians, isn't it? Anyway, I'm beginning to wonder if it was Sveneric's coming into the world that made him start to switch sides."

Senrid shrugged. "If it's true, it should have happened a few thousand years ago. What's this brat like, besides odd? Which doesn't really tell me anything."

Liere looked down at her hands — her hands with nicely trimmed nails rather than bitten to the quick, her cuticles healed. The way they'd been when she returned from that off-world trip with Siamis and Tahra Delieth. "Lyren, who has been really smug, says that Sveneric was secretly on our side from when he was two or three years old. If you can believe a three-year-old knows anything about sides."

"Or secrets," Senrid said skeptically. "Someone was protecting them, obviously."

"It might even have been Siamis. Anyway, part of that group is the Delieth twins, and Ian Selenna and Dirk Sonscarna. Did you even *know* that Kessler had a son?"

"No," Senrid said. He wasn't surprised that the strange, mad Kessler Sonscarna kept that a secret.

"I didn't either," Liere said. "But the thought of it makes me . . ." She looked away, her expression pained, then looked back. "Anyway, they all managed to find one another, somehow, in the mental realm. They have some sort of secret space there. Which I comfort myself with when I think about little Dirk Sonscarna."

"I may know nothing about Dena Yeresbeth," Senrid said sardonically, "but there's definitely someone protecting them. A secret fort in the mental realm? Has to be Siamis. Maybe he's training his own army." Senrid snorted a laugh, but Liere didn't smile.

"Siamis has been giving me lessons," she said earnestly, as always, fighting against her own shortcomings. "Call it elementary dyranarya lessons. No, call it rudimentary lessons, before you can even get to elementary. It's helped me a lot."

Senrid got up, casting his gaze along the row of birch trees, and tapped his fingers on the back of the bench in an old Marloven drum tattoo. He'd come with a purpose. He'd hinted around long enough with the inane questions about Detlev's brat. All right, another hint. "Kind of fun to watch the new youngsters making their own plans."

Liere gripped her hands together, aware once again with a sharp inward pain of her own failure. That secret of Lyren's was the latest reminder of Liere's failure with Lyren—every single day, every single argument that she could never win lest her own daughter look at her with the same hatred Liere had felt toward her own father.

But as she was thinking that, Senrid watched those tightly gripped hands, and recognized the old, anxious Liere. He wondered if she was blaming herself for some mess Lyren and Mac had made, something typical of youngsters that age. One thing he had learned in reading his mother's letters was that physical age and emotional age were not the same thing: Senrid's aunt, a grown woman, had been every bit as bad a parent as Senrid's uncle. Liere was ten times better than *they* had been.

Then Liere broke his thoughts with a sudden outburst.

"Someday — ten or twenty years from now — if you ever decide to have a child, remind me to tell you what not to do."

Senrid turned around and leaned on the railing. "What if I did it now?" At the horrified look on Liere's face he backed up a step. Horror? Really? Unsettled, he tried to laugh it off. "The Mearsieans are after me to try the Birth Spell so that Clair's Aurora will have a playmate."

"Don't do it," Liere stated, her voice sharpened by the intensity of her unrelenting sense of personal failure. She couldn't bear to admit that in desperation she even secretly ended the Child Spell the year before, thinking that it would make a difference, that it would make her into a wiser, more authoritative figure for Lyren. She may as well not have bothered. She had no authority with Lyren, any more than she'd had with her younger sister Marga, who Lyren was like more than she was like Liere. In fact, she had less. If it wasn't for Siamis . . .

Liere shook her head. "Just don't." She looked into her own memories, not seeing Senrid's tightened shoulders, his fingers flexing once before he shoved his fists into his pockets.

That unsettled feeling sharpened, and Senrid had to know. "You think I'd be bad at it? Or is it us Marlovens? I don't always stab first and ask questions later. You should know that," he said, striving for a light tone.

Deep in her emotional stew, Liere misunderstood his joking tone. "Of course I do," she said. "It's just that . . ." She turned away, trying to figure out which objection to voice first.

He stared, trying not to laugh at the irony that here he'd been about to ask her to stand as witness. In case war was coming, he wanted to promise Marloven Hess some kind of continuity. And Liere was his first and longest lasting friend. But he couldn't get past that flash of horror widening her eyes.

Thoroughly rattled, he said, "If people still think that about me, I can imagine how it's going to go for Detlev's boys." He'd also come with the intention of talking over his unexpected interview with David of Detlev's gang the day before. But the words dried up, and he discovered that he didn't want to talk about it after all. In fact, everything he'd brought to discuss had blown up in his face.

Liere turned his way, frowning as she scrutinized him. What had just happened? "Why bring *them* up?"

Senrid shrugged again, wearing the old shuttered

expression, the bland smile that had been his armor ever since she'd known him.

Liere sighed, relieved to get away from the child discussion. "Well, it seems whether we want them or not, and Mearsieanne doesn't, we've got them. Some of them here — Roy and Arthur are as tight as they were before. But I can't think of any of them as allies."

"Enemy-allies?" Senrid's mouth twisted.

Upset far more by the wall that had suddenly appeared between them, Liere tried to breach it, but the subject was Detlev's boys, so her tone stayed stiff. "I guess it's better to have them on our side than against us, if what Detlev says about a coming war is true. They proved over and over how much more effective they were at being nasty than we."

Senrid said nothing. Liere watched him gazing at the single skater swooping and twirling out on the ice, and decided that this whole conversation was ended. "Well, I'm in charge of the food, so I should get back to it. Thank you for the visit."

Senrid lifted his hand. "Later," he said. And transferred away.

Liere heard Lyren's shrill, "Look at me! Look at me! I can do a spin!"

Liere forced a smile, then saw that Lyren was trying to get Siamis's attention. Not hers. Because Lyren always had her attention, whether she wanted it or not. But his mattered.

Liere shut her eyes, thrown back to that first day when she, Siamis, Tahra, Lyren, and Mac reached Geth. Another world, a place where no one had ever heard of "Sartora" — a new place to explore, without crashing into others' expectations. Siamis had given her that much, and she'd learned things. But not enough. It wasn't *long* enough.

She opened her eyes, forced herself to collect empty plates, repack the basket, and finally, finally, to follow everybody back inside. But she didn't hear any of the chatter. She closed her eyes again, and reached mentally.

And Detlev was there.

:How would I find that school on Geth?

:I will have a transfer token for you whenever you are ready.

Forty-two

SENRID WAS METHODICAL ABOUT planning, while carrying on the fiercest internal argument of his life. So very much had changed out in the world. He never would have believed he'd be corresponding with the Queen of Sartor about military organization, for example.

Then there were the changes right here at home. Beginning with learning that his father's overhauling the military regulations with an eye to insisting that no one was above the law had been a carefully contemplated first step in getting rid of the standing army entirely, in favor of a militia system: everyone, from high to low serving two to ten years, then choosing work other than war. And reporting to duty only in need.

How soon would he sprout a knife in his back if he even mentioned it? Maybe it was something best left to his successor. Who he probably ought to get, and start training.

Senrid readied a room, and ordered what he'd need. He even had names picked out — traditional, of course, Indevan or Ingrid — but he was aware at each step that he could go back, and no one would know. He could even lie about the baby supplies, saying they were a gift. He could always find someone who needed them.

The toughest argument was against his own *what ifs*,

culminating in a nightmare so vivid he woke suddenly, drenched in sweat and staring about his quiet, dark room uncomprehendingly until the thunder of his heartbeat began to diminish. He scowled at his shaking hands, mentally picking apart the nightmare so that he could diminish its power.

The source was obvious.

He'd always avoided the question of an heir because of his conviction that Detlev might try to hold the child hostage against the kingdom. Senrid wasn't often gripped by nightmares, but when they came most of them invariably centered on his three encounters with Detlev, all three having been what he considered the worst moments of his life.

The first and third happened on a cliff overlooking Marloven Hess's southern border. The second occurred while Senrid was a prisoner at Norsunder Base; the threats Detlev had uttered during each had steel-etched themselves in memory.

This nightmare distorted the incident at Norsunder Base. Senrid lay once again on the ground where he'd been flung after his unsuccessful escape attempt. Rough-hewn stone gritted under his cheekbone, and scraped the palm of one outflung hand.

Then the rap of heels on the stone stilled everyone. Nightmare expanded the actual corridor into a cavernous hall, so large the walls were lost in darkness. Once again Detlev loomed, one foot stepping between Senrid's nose and that outflung hand. *I shall have time for this one presently* . . . The words echoed from memory to nightmare.

"But he didn't have time," Senrid muttered, disgusted at his own fears. All those threats, now empty, yet here he was, his mind tying his psyche into knots. Over what?

He looked down at his hand, pale in the moonlight shining in his open windows. For some reason, it was almost always that Norsunder Base near-escape that formed the basis for the nightmares, though both incidents before and after had been far worse: the third, the most recent, had occurred after Detlev swept away in one contemptuous gesture the webwork of protections Senrid had worked on for most of a year. Then he'd said, *When I do find the time to undertake your education, you will not see me coming.*

There it was again, that reference to time. But that time had never happened. If Detlev had truly left Norsunder and was now neutral, it wasn't going to happen. An empty threat.

Pompous, in retrospect. The bombast of a villain — much like Senrid's uncle, the unmourned regent.

Senrid flexed his fingers, wondering why Detlev didn't step on that hand. Grind his iron-shod heel into it, bursting the skin and snapping every small bone. That would have been a more realistic threat than any words, sinister as they'd sounded. Violence was an easy tool, effective in that people would do a lot to avoid pain. It was the kind of violence that Efael gloried in, from all accounts, as well as half a dozen other Norsundrian head snakes. It was ridiculous to say that Detlev was above it, not with that long list of bloody destruction attached to his name.

Why the empty threats, all air and no action? Was it merely a game then, to scare the shit out of him and then forget about him in the next breath? As a person, Senrid didn't believe himself worth any more than anyone else. But as a king, he would be very much in the way of anyone with big plans for conquest, at least in the western end of the continent. You could hate and despise the Marlovens, but you couldn't ignore them. So . . . why, in all these years, hadn't Detlev managed to find, say, half an hour to lure Senrid out to get a start on the road to evil?

Mere hot air, one might say. Everyone said that Detlev didn't do or say anything without a purpose. Ten purposes, some of them for plans a century down the road. All that threat couldn't possibly be a mere front.

For the space of a breath, Senrid contemplated the scope of such a fraud, perpetrated on both the lighters and Norsunder. At the very least, it would mean looking at Detlev's emergences into the world, even his losses, from a very different perspective . . .

He snorted and flopped back on the pillow. Absolutely useless, trying to figure out what Detlev meant or didn't mean. He had no facts, only conjecture, which was an utter waste of time.

Meanwhile, he should look at the facts he had. For example, his decisions based on threats that no longer existed. Like the fact that among all the many vile, bloody events in Marloven history, no one had actually ever sneaked into the gigantic fortress inside the equally fortified city, guarded by hundreds of very alert sentries, to hold a baby hostage against the king.

Late one night a few days later, as summer thunder rolled across the sky, the duty Runner appeared at his study door, rain dripping off him. "Found the Chwahir at the Destination. They're bringing him in. Looks pretty bad," the Runner added.

"Jilo?" Senrid exclaimed. "Tell the steward to ready his room, and order the usual. Including hot chocolate."

A short time later there was Jilo, looking unchanged, including the gray tones to his pale skin. His light brown eyes were stark as he croaked, "He's back."

"Who's back?"

"Wan-Edhe. I broke the second level of the mirror lattice, too, and destroyed the spy eyes . . . he almost got me. But I had this on me at all times." A thin hand with gray nail beds opened, fingers trembling, disclosing a grimy token. Then Jilo collapsed into a chair. His head dropped back, his mouth a thin white line, his eyes shut, his body so rigid Senrid took half a step toward him, thinking he had to be wounded.

But the wound was not visible. As Senrid hesitated, from beneath Jilo's tightly shut eyes light shimmered, gathered, and before the first tears could fall, Jilo crumpled as a deep, harsh sob ripped through him. Senrid stilled as Jilo wept, unsure what to do. He didn't want to stand there. He wanted to run, but it somehow seemed cowardly to abandon such desolate grief.

Jilo wept until he was breathless, then shakily wiped his face on his sleeve. "Everything," he said hoarsely. "Undone. He'll not stop until it's all undone."

Senrid ventured a tentative, "But you knew that. It's almost the first thing you told me."

"I know. I know! I lived every day dreading his return. But expecting it. So did . . ." He shut his eyes again and fought down another sob. "So did the people," he said finally, his voice raw. "But they wanted me to run. To safety. The guards. The kitchen people, even. Those in the street, they all said *run*."

Senrid knew where he was now. "Because you gave them hope. Because what you did, it can be done again."

Jilo sighed, sagging in the chair, then wiped his grimy hair back. "It took me a couple weeks to get to the border. Mondros helped me. I asked him to send me here." He looked up, his face filled with the same desperate hope that Senrid imagined the Chwahir felt when they looked at Jilo. "Senrid, you got your kingdom back once. Tell me how you did it."

"But it's not the same," Senrid started, then shook his head. "Look, first get in some rest. Eat. We'll talk it out." Senrid opened a drawer to dig for his notecase. Tsauderei. Mondros. Arthur. Siamis? Why not? The relative comfort of kids against big bad adults was long gone, if it had ever really existed.

The young allies had become a real alliance, one he knew was necessary if they were to survive Norsunder arriving in force.

Next month, he promised Indevan/Ingrid. He could feel the Birth Spell there, like the sun before dawn. *Maybe next week, maybe next month, you'll come into this crazy world, and probably hate me forever for it.*

He laughed inside as he uncapped his inkwell.

AFTERMATH

ON A SPECTACULAR AUTUMN morning, after two long trips away, David was organizing the books on his desk into Must Read, Want to Read, and Should Read. That was the last finishing touch, not that the room was full of furniture—bed under one window, trunk for clothes. Desk. He'd played around with where to put them, because he could.

"Not bad."

David glanced at MV—recently returned from a summer on his boat—leaning lazily in the doorway. He pushed off and entered, indicating a pile of moldering tomes in the Must-Read stack. "You really going to slog through those?"

"I'm going to translate them."

"I'm already asleep." MV waved a dismissive hand, then frowned out the open window adjacent to the desk.

David joined him, and spotted Laban's dark head. The tight set to his shoulders and his defiant stance indicated he'd probably been arguing again with someone.

"Mouthing off, trying to pick a fight. Leef, then Curtas," MV said. "Can't believe he's letting Noser goad him. Think I should let some of his hot air out?"

David stared down at Laban, anger kindling. He wanted to smack Laban's sneer from his face. But then a memory flared: his fist striking Roy, knocking him across his room. And then the look in Roy's eyes before he passed out.

"He's still angry over Tahra ordering him out of Everon. Leave them both for Detlev," David said.

MV shifted his weight to glance behind him. "Shrimp," he said, white teeth flashing in a brief grin.

Sveneric appeared from behind MV, his eyes lifting from one face to the other. His shaggy brown hair was sun-streaked; he'd proclaimed that he was never getting a haircut again, or wearing gray, ever.

David laughed. "Back from your exploration already?"

"I'm going to climb up much, *much* higher, and camp outside." Sveneric pushed hair out of his eyes and pointed toward the southeastern heights. "There's a stream over that way, feeding into the river."

"Is there?"

Sveneric smiled, his intense gaze easing with a kind of tentative happiness. "There's fish in it. Come see."

David hid the urge to laugh at this evidence of Sveneric's almost-nine-year-old tastes. It was rare enough that he demonstrated such. Three were occasions when he scared them all by not even seeming human.

MV shoved away from the doorjamb. "Maybe later," he said. His fingers tapped restlessly, then he said, "I just got back from Tsauderei's lair."

"And?"

"The old geezer told me to return after I put in two years of study with the Healer mages. If he's still alive, he'll hand me the keys to the kingdom."

David could hear anticipation under the mockery. Even pleasure, the emotion complicated by a caustic awareness of how trustworthy anticipation could be.

Then MV jerked his chin at the window, and the terrace beyond. They could hear Laban's voice clearly, edgy with sarcasm, Noser's shrill voice taunting. "What do you think he'll do with the Nose?"

David already knew, because he'd seen Noser's memories, and now he understood some of them. Noser — Edde — was the only one of them from beyond a world-gate, with a past very much like Efael's. Detlev had said once if left alone he was likely to have become far worse, one of those mass-murderers who stained human history for centuries after they were gone.

"Noser talks big, but he'll keep the Child Spell," David

said. "He feels safer. And he's good around animals."

"Weird, that. Horses actually like him. Dogs, too."

Not weird, when you considered that, much as Noser could love anything, he loved horses and dogs, whose loyalty was unconditional. That loyalty and the group had been his only hold on sanity, tenuous as it was.

Another taunt from below, and MV lifted his head. "Think I'll stroll out and sniff the air."

Whoever Laban was arguing with couldn't be heard, but a fight was probably imminent, unless MV could halt things by his presence.

"Let's go," David said to Sveneric.

David still did not comprehend why it had been necessary for Detlev to have permitted Sveneric to make his break with Norsunder on his own. It reflected some of Detlev's other patterns with the boy. He certainly didn't spoil him—if anything, he seemed to be harder on him in some ways. Sveneric studied longer hours, and he'd started training at a much younger age. Toward the end, there, those last months before Sveneric made his break, Detlev had chosen to absent himself completely, leaving teaching solely to Adam and David. Sveneric had accepted this distance with that eerie stillness of his.

But then again, when father and son went into rapport, the exchange was so swift it was not necessary for them to block anyone else. That kind of nearly wordless exchange suggested an understanding of an almost preternatural kind.

David and Sveneric exited a side door, circumventing the terrace entirely, crossed behind the kitchen garden, and reached the stream that fed it. Sveneric, as if to give David's observations the lie, ran ahead with a yell of pleasure, splashing into the water up to his armpits, heedless of his clothes. He dove down, and emerged sputtering.

"There really are fish here!" he piped. "Come see."

"They won't be around long if you attack 'em like that," David said, dropping onto a grassy bank alongside the stream.

"Oh." Sveneric looked thoughtful. "Then I'll try to swim silently."

"Hand through the water, eh?" David asked.

"Yah!" Sveneric laughed, then shucked his clothes to dry on the bank, and slid quietly into the water.

David lay back, his eyes on the sky. A shadow crossed his vision, then Detlev came into view, his steps soundless on the grass. Sveneric emerged from the stream, grinned at his father, then sank again.

"Done furniture shopping?" David asked.

"For now." Detlev lowered himself to the grass. He picked up a smooth stone and tossed it in his hand. Detlev no longer wore Norsunder gray, but one could hardly call his manner of dress, which ran to tunics and long trousers of various neutral or undyed shades, ostentatious — or even interesting.

With Sveneric safely under water, David asked, "Why did you let the shrimp go like that, all alone? Was there a purpose?"

"Yes. Two." Detlev tossed the stone gently on his palm. "He defined his own life, and in doing so learned that he can survive whatever comes next, even if I don't."

The back of David's neck prickled at this casual acknowledgment of Detlev's possible death.

"Second. He learned of our having hopped the fence from his own group, which drew them tighter."

David wondered how long Detlev had known about Sveneric's secret group — no, that wasn't even a question. He'd probably been the one to set it up, and as usual, let Siamis take over guidance. Always acting as if he might not survive until tomorrow. David was just beginning to comprehend what it must have been like to exist so very long under the threat of sudden extermination.

"The next step in training," Detlev said, "is the truth behind the hand through the water. Not everyone is ready for it. You are. He is. Adam has been practicing it without knowing what it was."

"What truth? What does that really mean? It's a fighting style, a game, using as few moves as possible to win. Infiltration without being noticed. Old lessons."

"That was the beginning. Think of the next step as influencing third and fourth order consequences, and beyond, again without leaving a trace." Detlev turned his wrist and sent the stone skipping five, six, seven times over the water, to sink on the other side of the stream.

Sveneric shot to the surface, spitting water like a fountain — the fish had swum away. "I saw that," he crowed. "I can do better. Watch." He splashed down again and re-emerged with stones in his hands. Then, standing in the middle of the stream, he started shying them over the water.

"Six," Detlev said, smiling. "Hah. Six . . . seven!"

"Eight," David put in, counting the latest. "Not bad."

"I retire." Detlev held up his hand in the fender's salute.

Sveneric snorted a laugh, then dove back into the water.

Detlev selected another stone, tossing it lightly from hand to hand. "Among your recent journeys, did you make a visit to Senrid?"

"He was the first. The only thing I learned from him is that he doesn't trust any of us."

"There are very few people he trusts. I'd like you to become one of them, if you can. He's very disciplined, except on the mental plane. His talent is much too formidable to ignore. That's going to get him into trouble unless he learns some control."

David said, "It'll probably take years to get him to trust me."

"Do what you can."

David sighed. "What about Laban? He did not like having to be rescued from Tahra's form of summary justice."

"It's a big world. A big universe." Detlev shied his stone across the stream, and watched it disappear into the underbrush. "And this is a big house."

"Then our freedom *is* relative."

Detlev sent the stone skipping over the water, nine, ten, eleven times before it sank.

David said in a fierce undertone, "Before you pulled me out, I saw that ocean you made in the Beyond. A fleet—maybe fleets—of pirate ships. And now Yeres and Efael have them. How bad a loss was that?"

"Bad enough. It could have been much worse."

"Then they don't have them all?"

"Correct. Only the worst of them, the ones that will give them more trouble than they're worth." Detlev's smile was wintry. "It's a small enough triumph. Events moved too swiftly these past hundred years—even faster, the past ten—forcing me to use every deflection I had prepared for centuries. The best I could win was a few years. I don't know if it's enough."

"For what? What events do you mean? Does this have anything to do with Peitar Selenna's assassination?"

Detlev turned his head, lifting his chin toward the far end of the terrace, where Adam—still mittened, and leaning on a cane—was moving through the sword drill. "You know the risk."

David said, "If I'm right and it's all connected — the loss of Five, vagabond magic, Selenna — and I'm still expected to carry out some orders in Norsunder Beyond, I think should know how. Why."

"Some orders," Detlev repeated, humor narrowing his eyes briefly. "Siamis calls it the treasure hunt. Either of you would carry that out only if the Host comes out into the world, and I am unable to."

"Unable to" — ah. Like, if he was captured, or dead. Chill pooled in David's gut at this second reminder that Detlev was not certain he would survive whatever was coming next. "Oh."

Detlev turned his head toward the east, squinting against the bright morning sun rimming the Sartoran border mountains. "Come with me," he said, and what David discovered — and what subsequently happened — is recorded elsewhere.

But this record is drawing to an end.

Lives resemble rivers. Sometimes whitewater dashes over dangerous stones, other times wide and slow with deep currents beneath. But books and scrolls cannot flow indefinitely, so their makers tend to group life events in themes when they can. So it is with these few years of what I have called the Rise of the Alliance.

There remains one last journey to relate.

A village in Shingara

High in the mountains above the forestland and the many rivers with their floating riverboat towns, an ancient inn perches on the side of a mountain.

Autumn leaves had passed their brilliance and had begun dancing down the hillsides to fall into the rivers when a lone figure, leaning lightly on a walking stick, appeared in the doorway.

It's said that everyone in Shingara — which long ago, before the coming of the Marlovans, was known as Lower Olara — knows everybody, but no one knew this wide-eyed, smiling young man with the cloud of curly brown hair framing his face. And yet they knew the general shape of that face —

"He looks like Willam," an old woman declared loudly, as the world of late had begun to whisper, but she refused to go to the Healer to have her ears checked.

"I'm Adam," he said. "Is this the Olir family? I was told I came from here—"

"It's our Adam!" a woman cried, and rushed forward to fling her arms around him. The entire room erupted into sound, everyone talking at once.

"It is! He looks just like his grandda!"

"He's back!"

Adam unlimbered his pack, and brought out woollen scarves of red, gold, green, blue. "I came bearing gifts. I made them myself!"

"My dear, dear boy," the woman wept as she gabbled. "I'm your ma—that man up and took you away, ever so many years ago, you were so strange, you cried if anyone cried, you wouldn't eat. We were afraid you would fade away."

"I know, he told me," Adam said.

"Where you *been* all this time?" the old woman demanded.

A cousin—Willam—set aside his tiranthe, and with broad potter's hands, thumped Adam on the back. "We thought you gone for good."

"Where have I been? I've traveled, and learned."

"Were you alone?" his mother asked, hugging him to her again. She had browner skin then his, and her cloud of hair was much curlier, but she had the same wide-set brown eyes. "Everybody needs a family. But that man, he said he could help you. And we couldn't."

"I have a bunch of brothers, you might say," Adam replied, seeing he had the attention of all. Smiling, he counted on his gloved fingers. "An honorary uncle who teaches up at one of the mage schools. One brother is a builder, another trains horses. One's a musician. Another sings. The rest travel, looking for what they might want to do with their lives."

"And you?" An uncle asked.

Adam dug into his pack, and pulled out a tablet of paper, and a bag of new chalks. "I'm an artist. Shall I do your portraits while I'm here, and we get to know one another?"

About the Author

Sherwood Smith writes fantasy, science fiction, and historical fiction. Her full bibliography can be found on her website at https://www.sherwoodsmith.net

About Book View Cafe

Book View Café is an author-owned cooperative of professional writers, publishing in a variety of genres including fantasy, science fiction, romance, mystery, and more.

Its authors include New York Times and USA Today bestsellers as well as winners and nominees of many prestigious awards such as the Agatha Award, Hugo Award, Lambda Literary Award, Locus Award, Nebula Award, RITA Award, Philip K. Dick Award, World Fantasy Award, and many others.

Since its debut in 2008, Book View Café has gained a reputation for producing high quality books in both print and electronic form. BVC's e-books are DRM-free and distributed around the world.

Book View Café's monthly newsletter includes new releases, specials, author news, and event announcements. To sign up, visit https://www.bookviewcafe.com/bookstore/newsletter/

Made in the USA
Las Vegas, NV
21 February 2022

44350846R00425